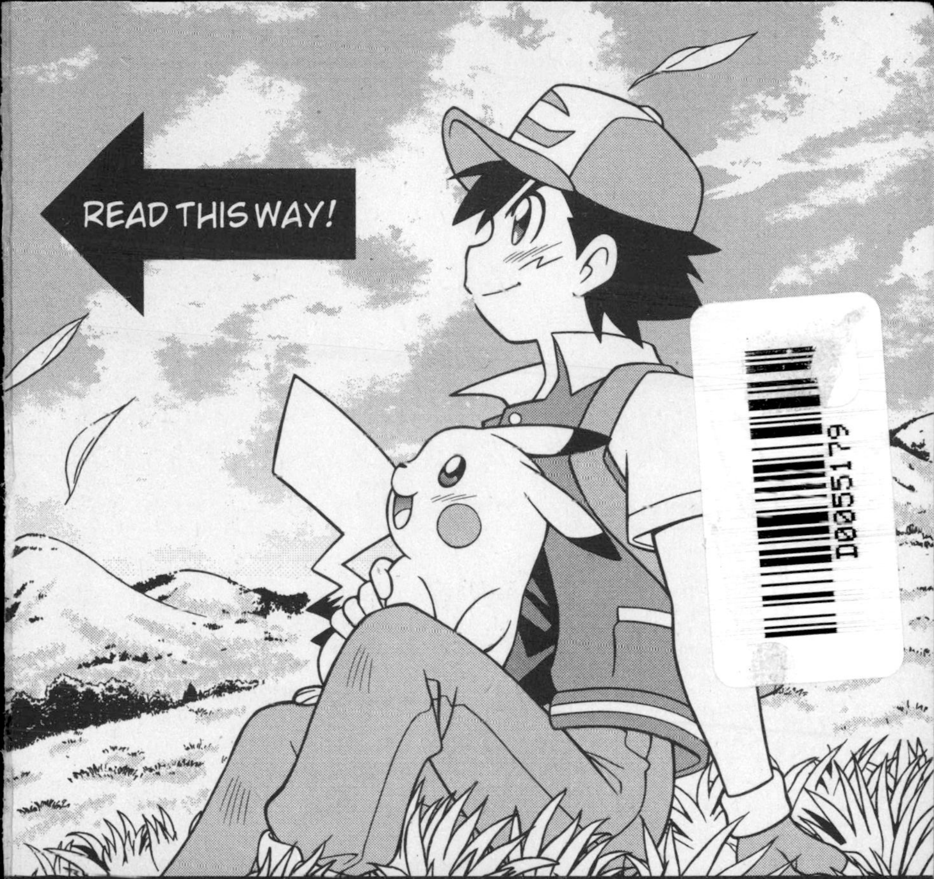
READ THIS WAY!

To properly enjoy this VIZ Media graphic novel, please turn it around and begin reading from right to left.

This book has been printed in the original Japanese format in order to keep the placement of the original artwork.

Have fun with it!

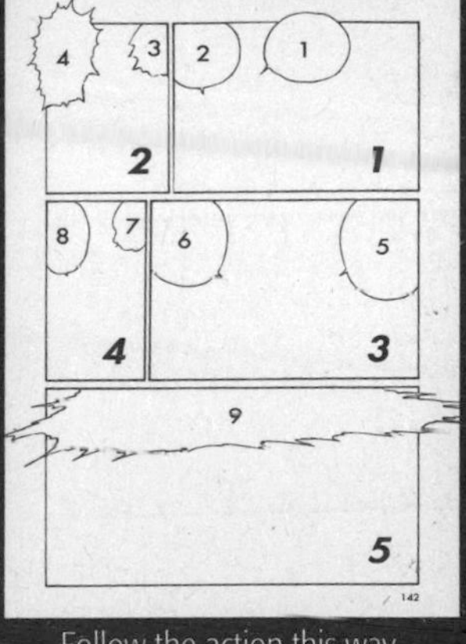
1
2
3
4
5
6
7
8
9
1
2
3
4
5
Follow the action this way.

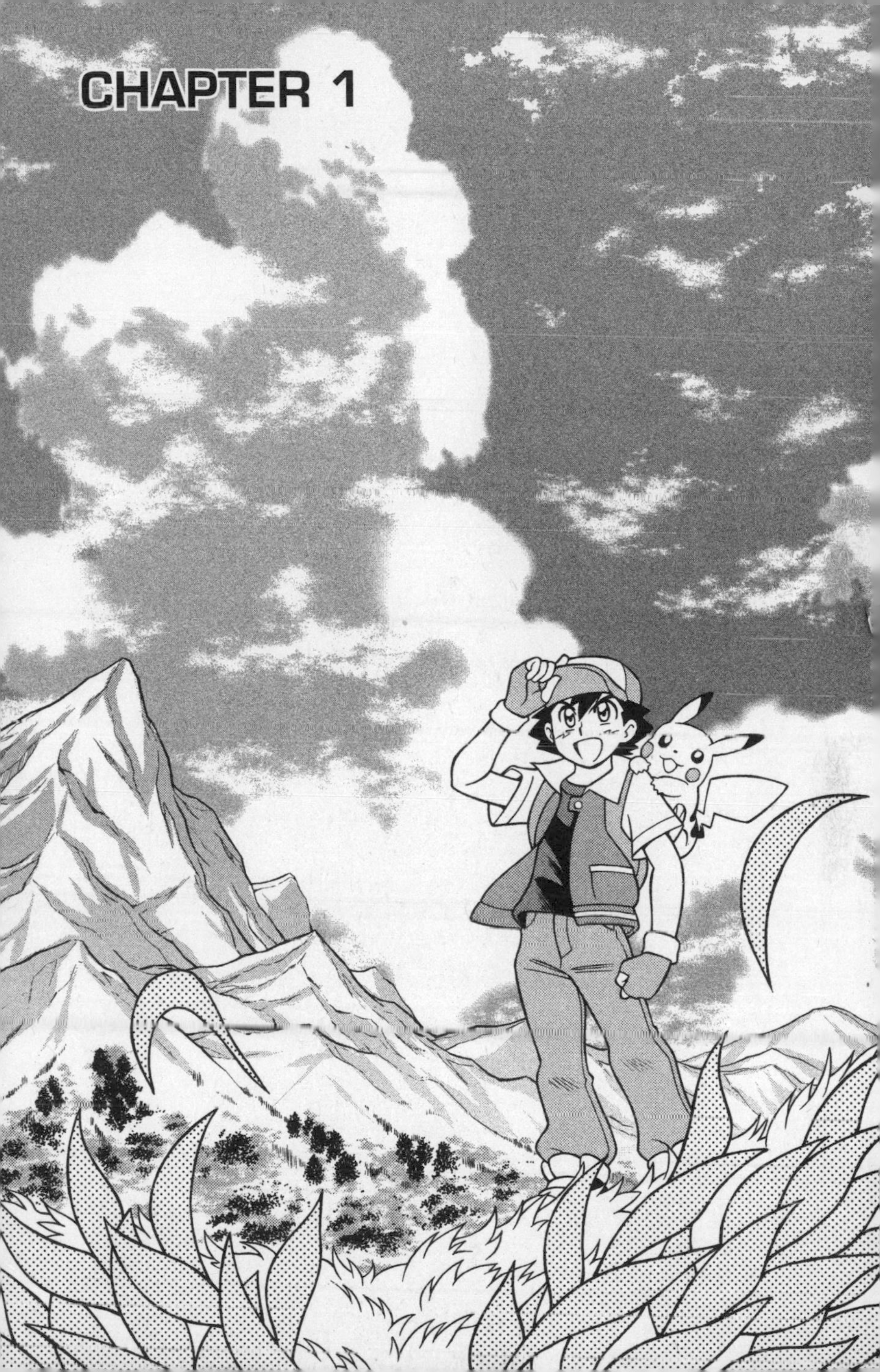
CHAPTER 1

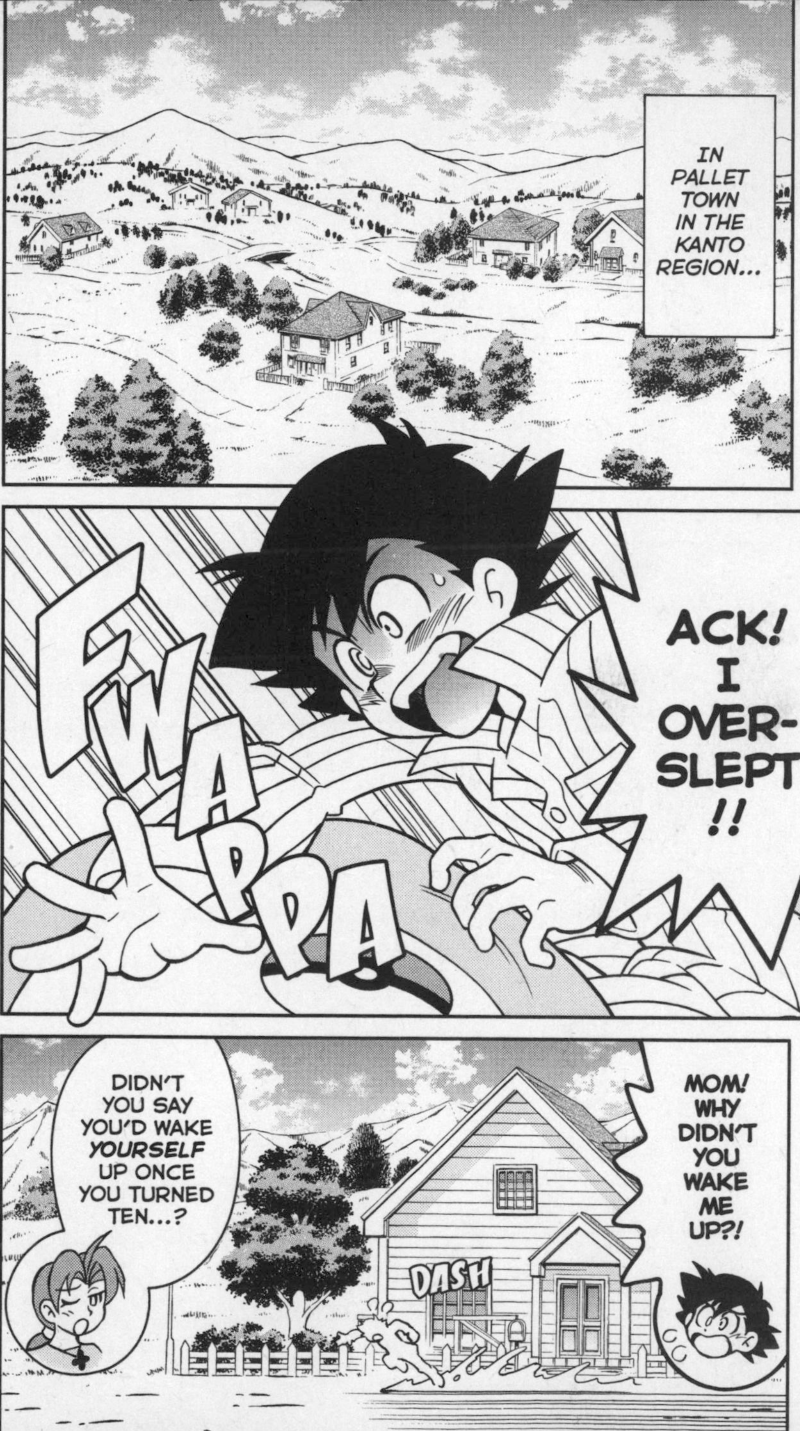
IN PALLET TOWN IN THE KANTO REGION...
FWAPPA
ACK! I OVER-SLEPT!!
MOM! WHY DIDN'T YOU WAKE ME UP?!
DASH
DIDN'T YOU SAY YOU'D WAKE *YOURSELF* UP ONCE YOU TURNED TEN...?

RYO
TAKAMISAKI

Hurray! The 20th Pokémon movie is out!
A lot of time has passed since I first met Ash
and Pikachu when I was just a fan myself.

All right! Time to put everything I've got
into drawing you all grown-up, Ash!

But wait…

What?! This is a story about the beginning?!
Ash isn't grown-up here?!

POKÉMON™

POKÉMON THE MOVIE

I Choose You!

Part 2

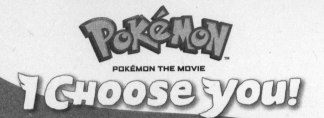

POKÉMON THE MOVIE

I Choose You!

Part 1

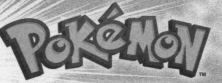

POKéMON™

POKÉMON THE MOVIE

I Choose You!

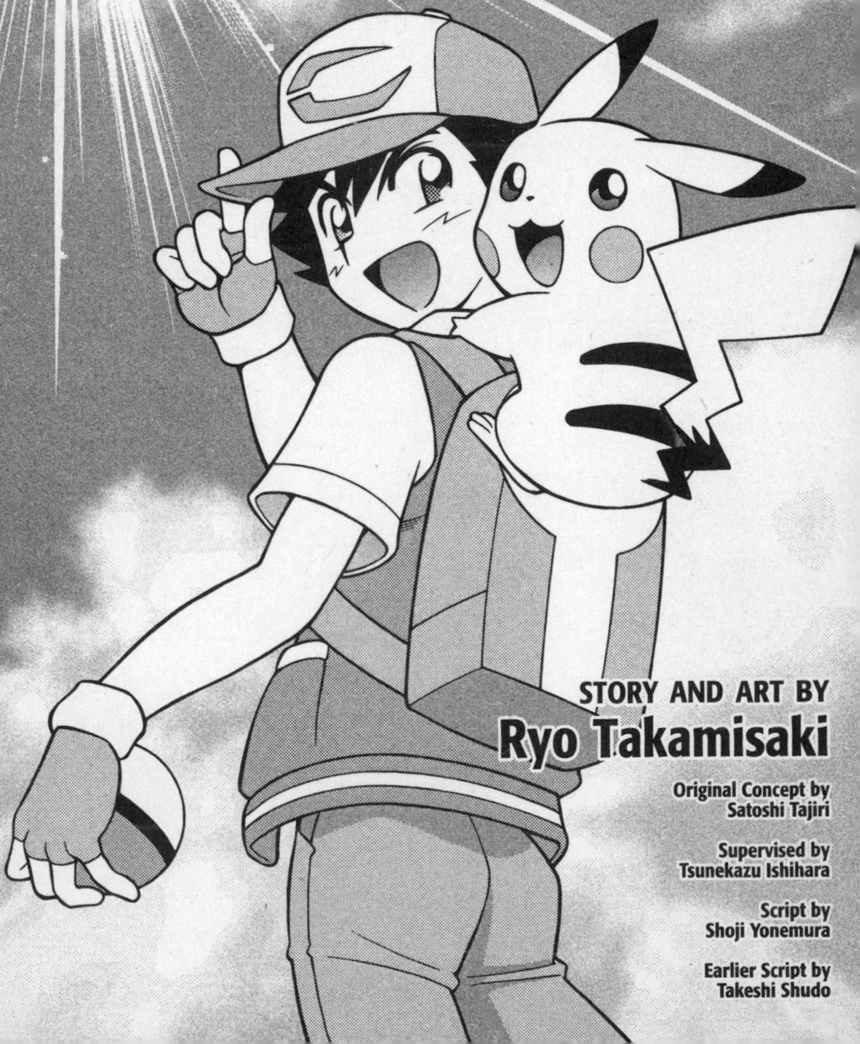

STORY AND ART BY

Ryo Takamisaki

Original Concept by
Satoshi Tajiri

Supervised by
Tsunekazu Ishihara

Script by
Shoji Yonemura

Earlier Script by
Takeshi Shudo

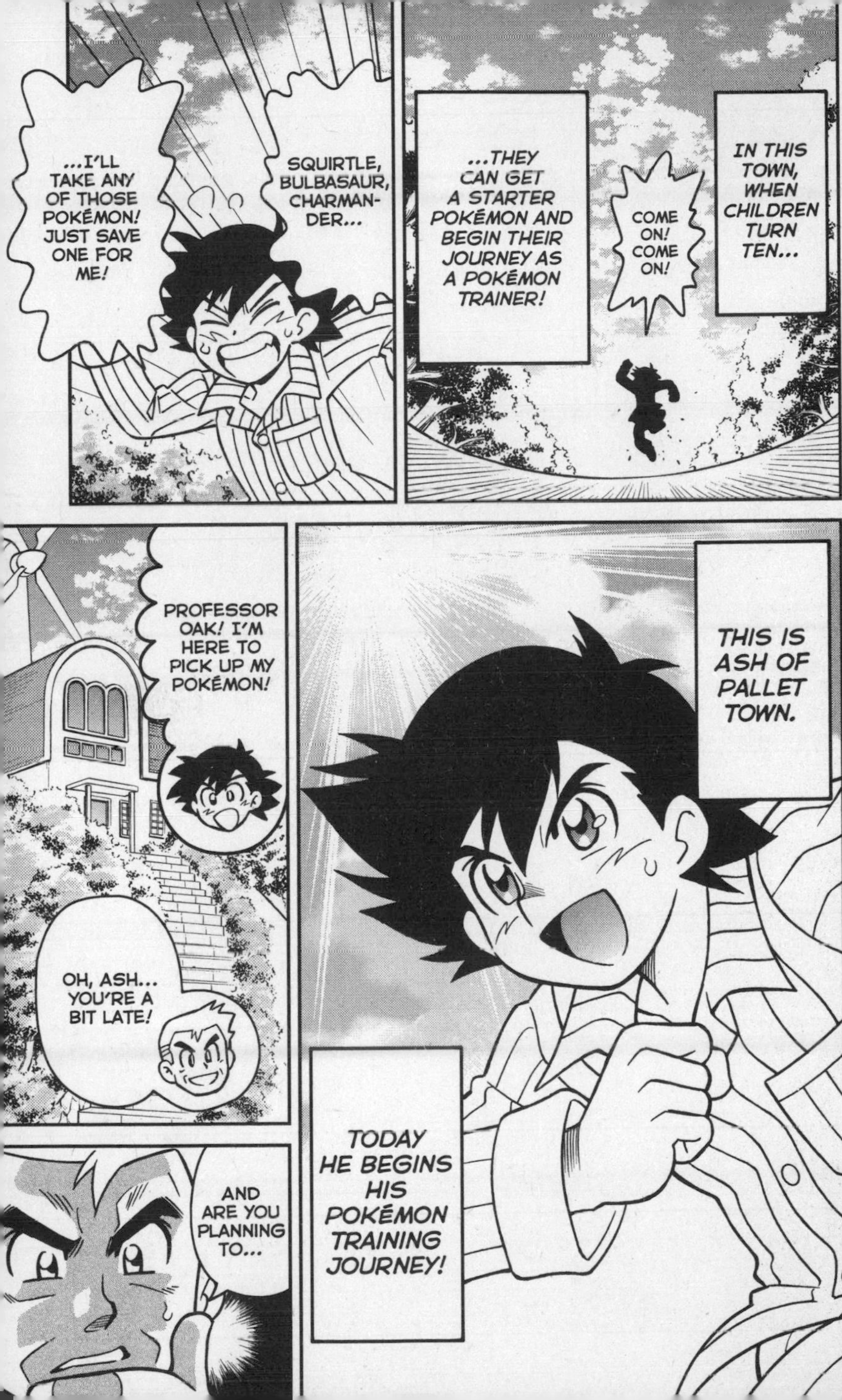
IN THIS TOWN, WHEN CHILDREN TURN TEN...
COME ON! COME ON!
...THEY CAN GET A STARTER POKÉMON AND BEGIN THEIR JOURNEY AS A POKÉMON TRAINER!
SQUIRTLE, BULBASAUR, CHARMANDER...
...I'LL TAKE ANY OF THOSE POKÉMON! JUST SAVE ONE FOR ME!
THIS IS ASH OF PALLET TOWN.
TODAY HE BEGINS HIS POKÉMON TRAINING JOURNEY!
PROFESSOR OAK! I'M HERE TO PICK UP MY POKÉMON!
OH, ASH... YOU'RE A BIT LATE!
AND ARE YOU PLANNING TO...

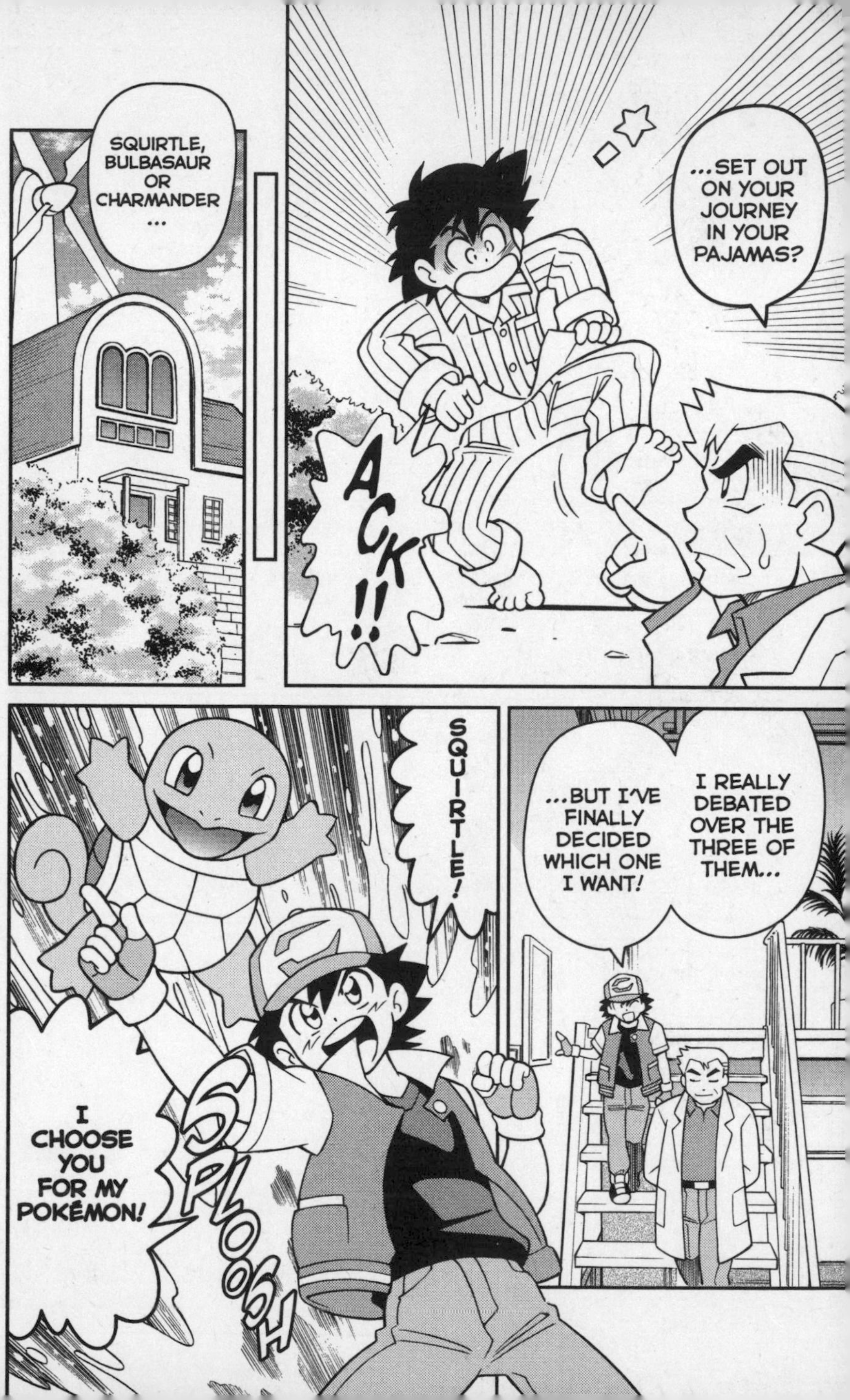
...SET OUT ON YOUR JOURNEY IN YOUR PAJAMAS?
ACK!!
SQUIRTLE, BULBASAUR OR CHARMANDER ...
I REALLY DEBATED OVER THE THREE OF THEM...
...BUT I'VE FINALLY DECIDED WHICH ONE I WANT!
SQUIRTLE!
I CHOOSE YOU FOR MY POKÉMON!
SPLOOSH

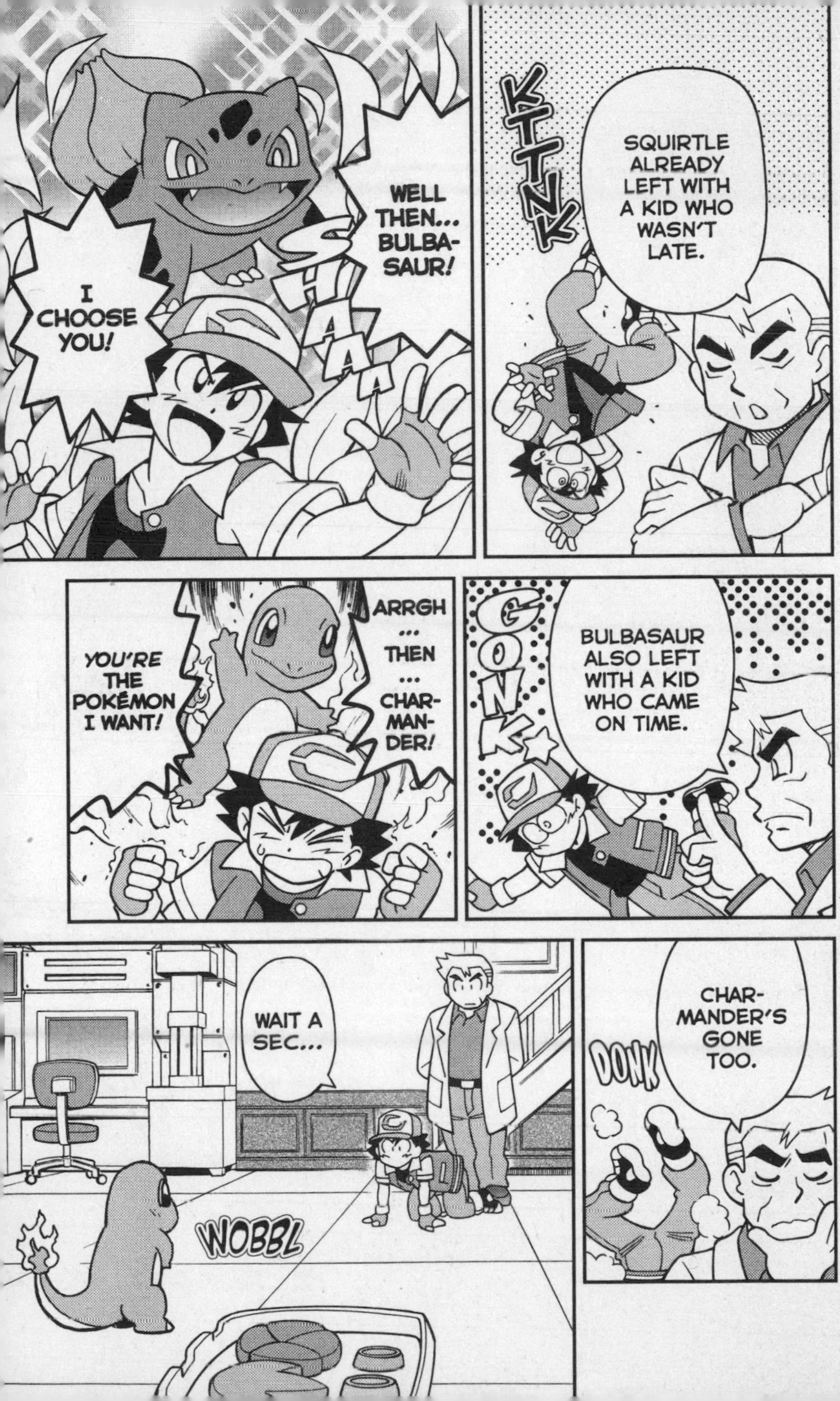
SQUIRTLE ALREADY LEFT WITH A KID WHO WASN'T LATE.
KTINK
WELL THEN... BULBA-SAUR!
SHAAAA
I CHOOSE YOU!
BULBASAUR ALSO LEFT WITH A KID WHO CAME ON TIME.
GONK
ARRGH... THEN... CHAR-MANDER!
YOU'RE THE POKÉMON I WANT!
CHAR-MANDER'S GONE TOO.
DONK
WAIT A SEC...
WOBBL

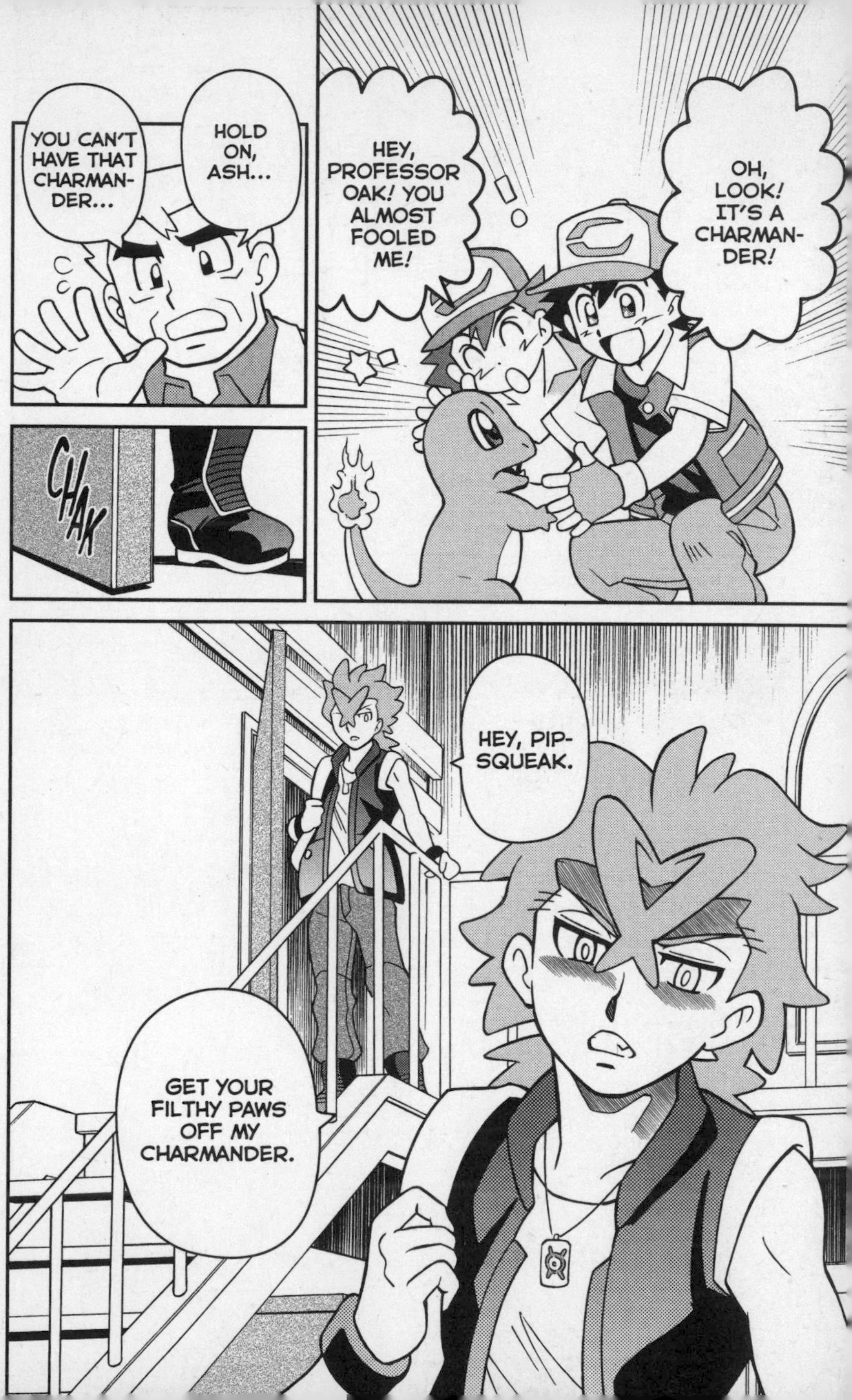
OH, LOOK! IT'S A CHARMANDER!
HEY, PROFESSOR OAK! YOU ALMOST FOOLED ME!
HOLD ON, ASH...
YOU CAN'T HAVE THAT CHARMANDER...
CHAK
HEY, PIP-SQUEAK.
GET YOUR FILTHY PAWS OFF MY CHARMANDER.

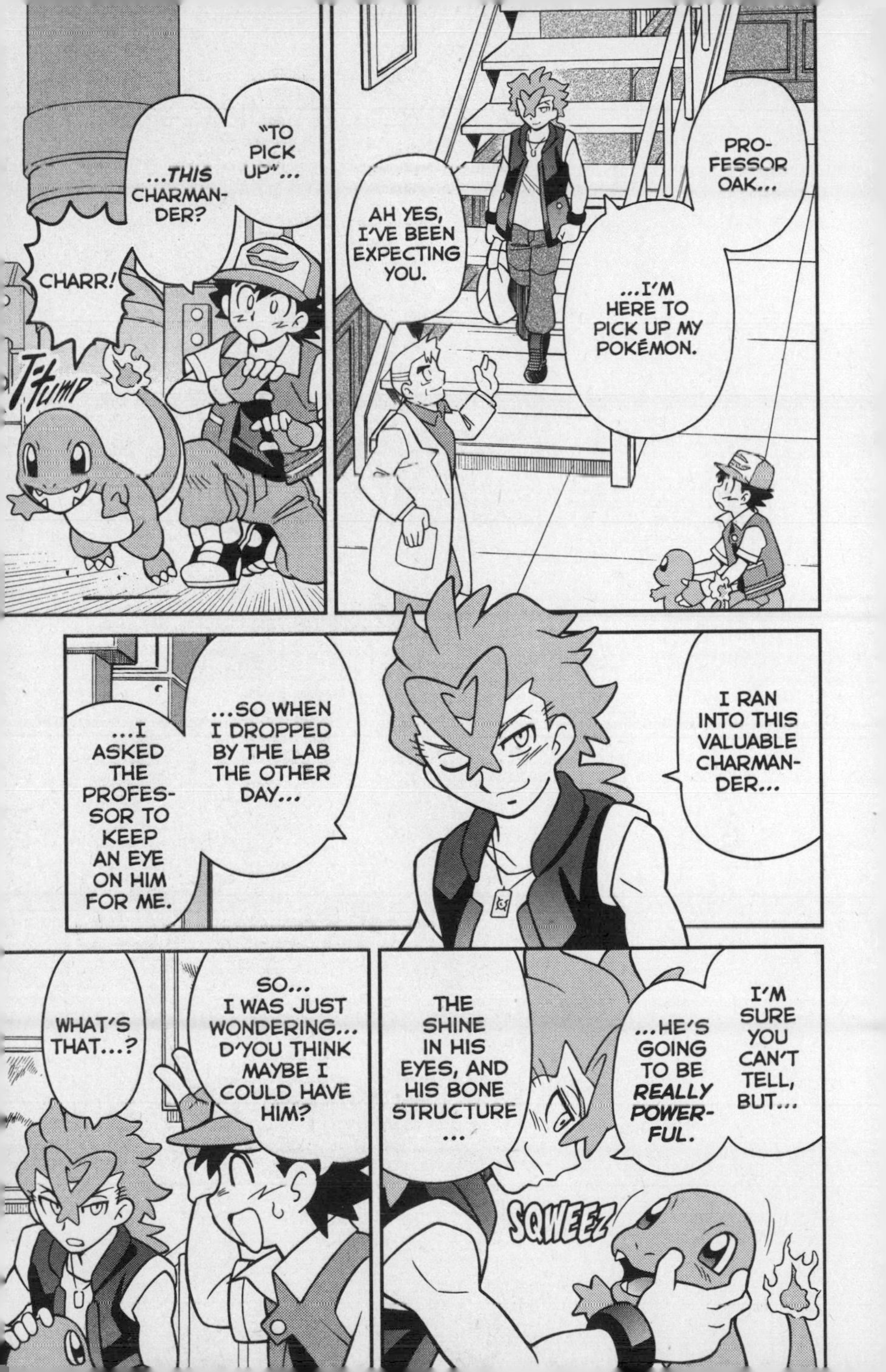
PROFESSOR OAK...
...I'M HERE TO PICK UP MY POKÉMON.
AH YES, I'VE BEEN EXPECTING YOU.
"TO PICK UP"...
...*THIS* CHARMANDER?
CHARR!
T-TUMP
I RAN INTO THIS VALUABLE CHARMANDER...
...SO WHEN I DROPPED BY THE LAB THE OTHER DAY...
...I ASKED THE PROFESSOR TO KEEP AN EYE ON HIM FOR ME.
I'M SURE YOU CAN'T TELL, BUT...
...HE'S GOING TO BE *REALLY POWERFUL*.
THE SHINE IN HIS EYES, AND HIS BONE STRUCTURE...
SQWEEZ
SO... I WAS JUST WONDERING... D'YOU THINK MAYBE I COULD HAVE HIM?
WHAT'S THAT...?

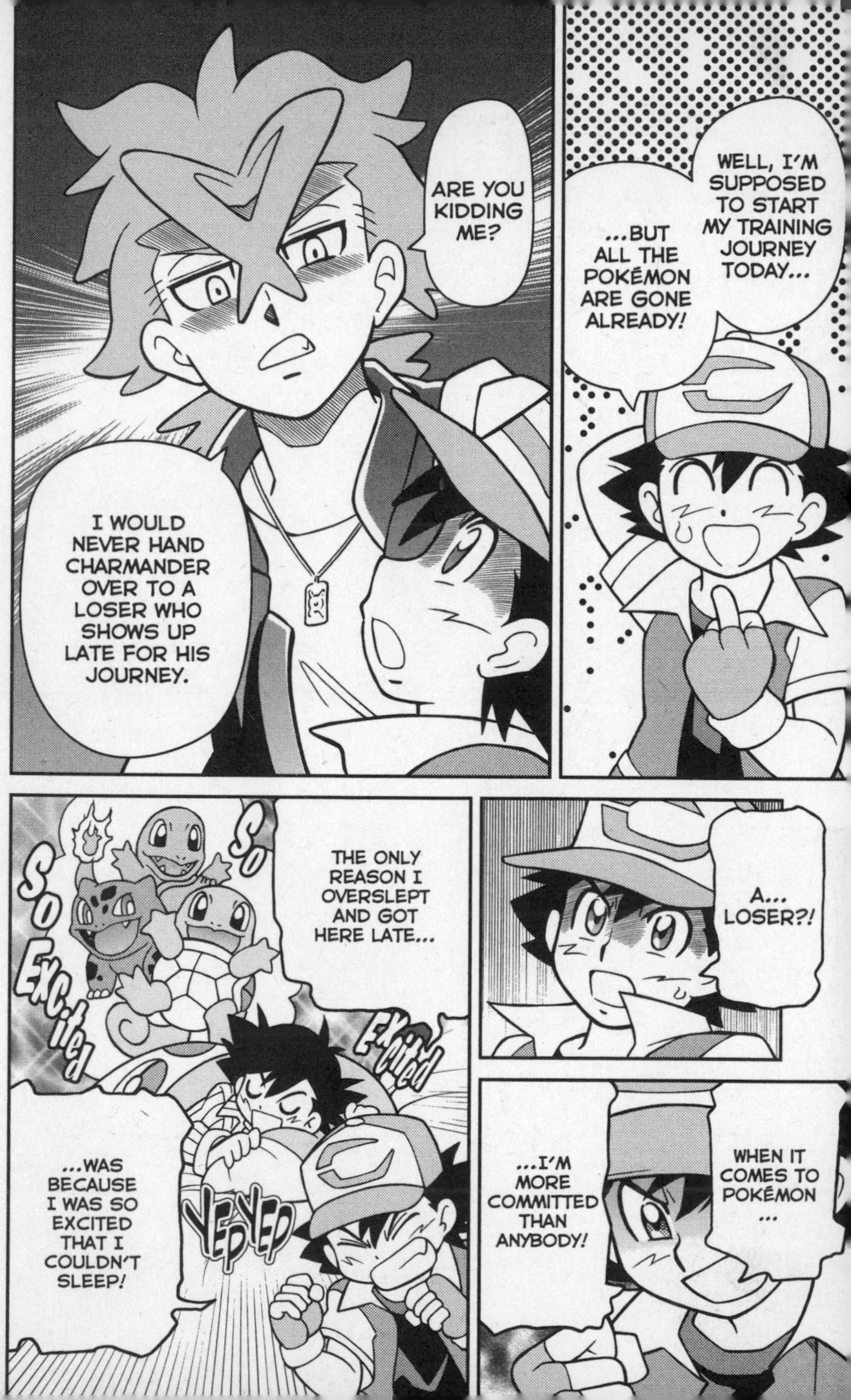
WELL, I'M SUPPOSED TO START MY TRAINING JOURNEY TODAY...
...BUT ALL THE POKÉMON ARE GONE ALREADY!
ARE YOU KIDDING ME?
I WOULD NEVER HAND CHARMANDER OVER TO A LOSER WHO SHOWS UP LATE FOR HIS JOURNEY.
A... LOSER?!
WHEN IT COMES TO POKÉMON...
...I'M MORE COMMITTED THAN ANYBODY!
THE ONLY REASON I OVERSLEPT AND GOT HERE LATE...
SO SO EXCITED
EXCITED
...WAS BECAUSE I WAS SO EXCITED THAT I COULDN'T SLEEP!
YEP YEP

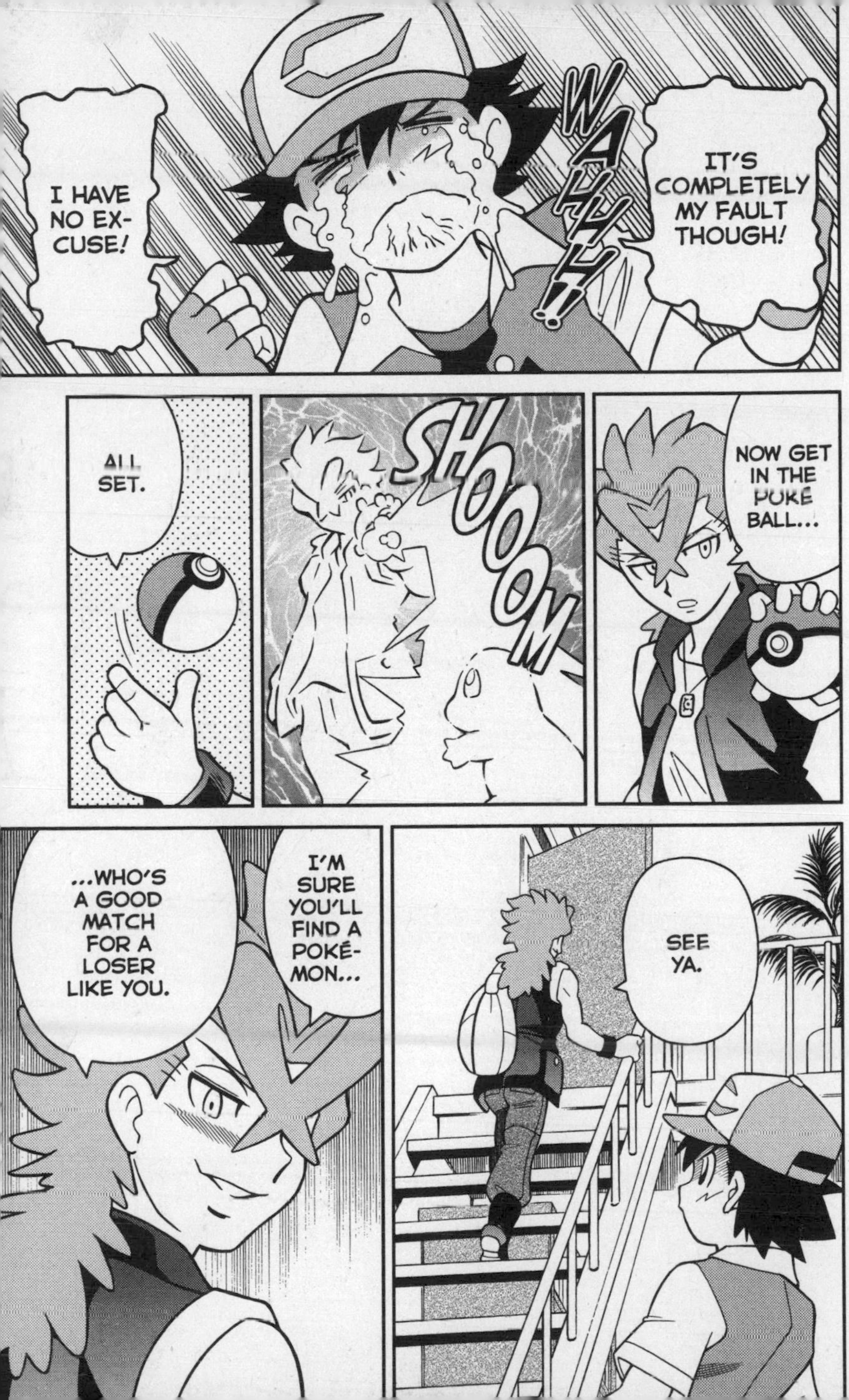
IT'S COMPLETELY MY FAULT THOUGH!
WAHHH!!
I HAVE NO EX-CUSE!
NOW GET IN THE POKé BALL...
SHOOOOM
...ALL SET.
SEE YA.
I'M SURE YOU'LL FIND A POKÉ-MON...
...WHO'S A GOOD MATCH FOR A LOSER LIKE YOU.

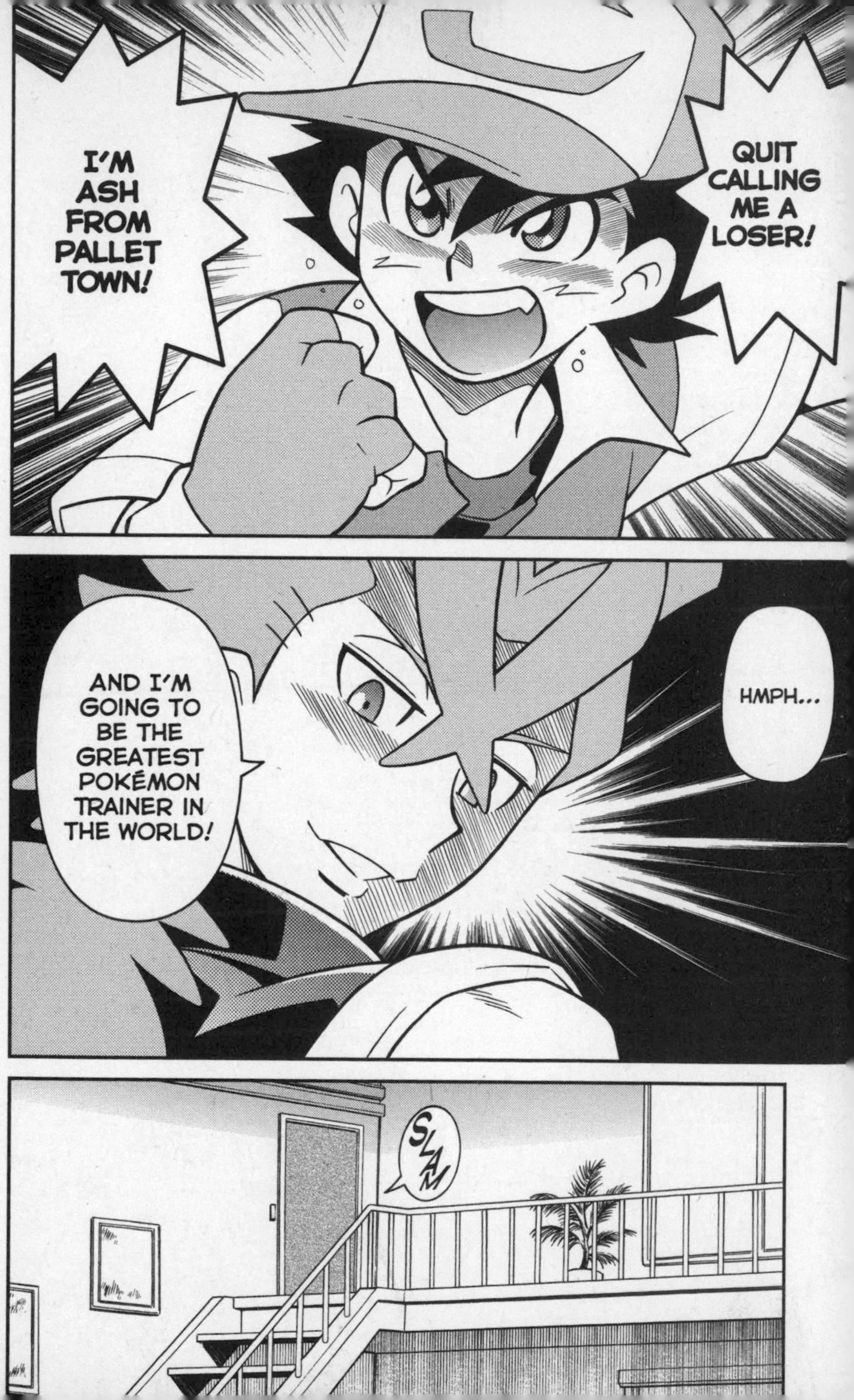
QUIT CALLING ME A LOSER!
I'M ASH FROM PALLET TOWN!
HMPH...
AND I'M GOING TO BE THE GREATEST POKÉMON TRAINER IN THE WORLD!
SLAM

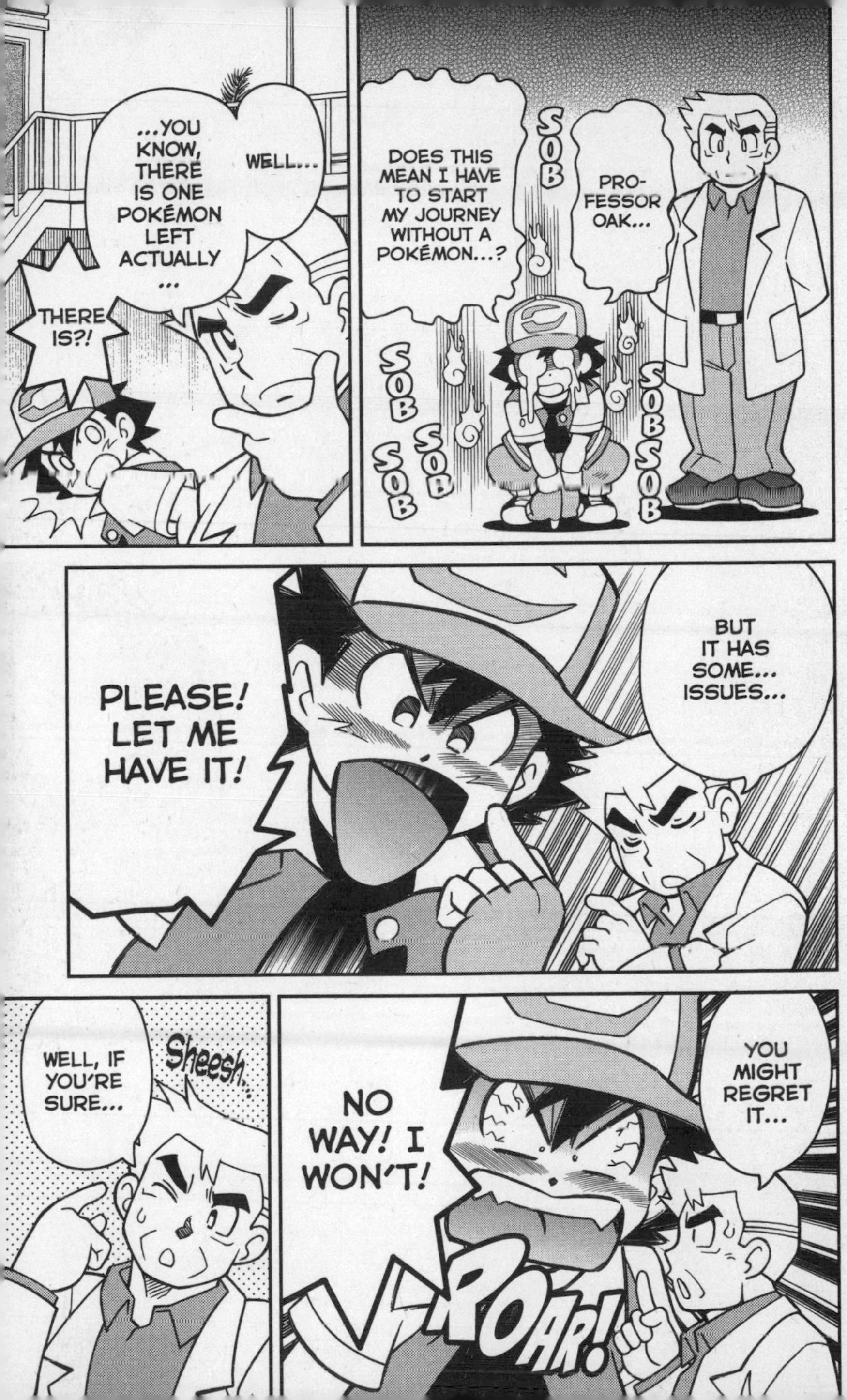
PRO-FESSOR OAK...
SOB
DOES THIS MEAN I HAVE TO START MY JOURNEY WITHOUT A POKÉMON...?
SOBSOB
SOB
SOB
SOB
WELL...
...YOU KNOW, THERE IS ONE POKÉMON LEFT ACTUALLY ...
THERE IS?!
BUT IT HAS SOME... ISSUES...
PLEASE! LET ME HAVE IT!
YOU MIGHT REGRET IT...
NO WAY! I WON'T!
ROAR!
Sheesh...
WELL, IF YOU'RE SURE...

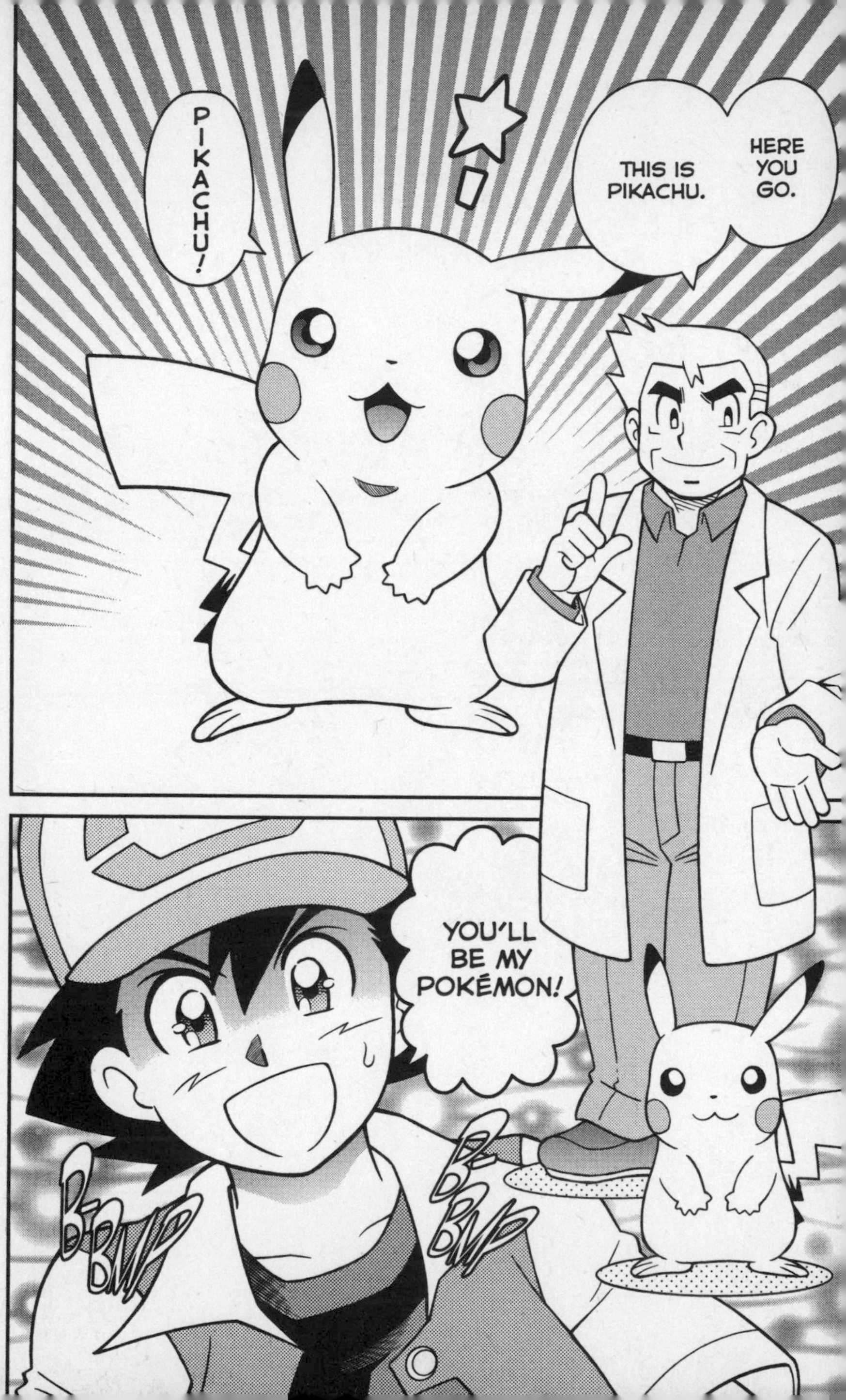
HERE YOU GO.
THIS IS PIKACHU.
PIKACHU!
YOU'LL BE MY POKÉMON!
B-BMP

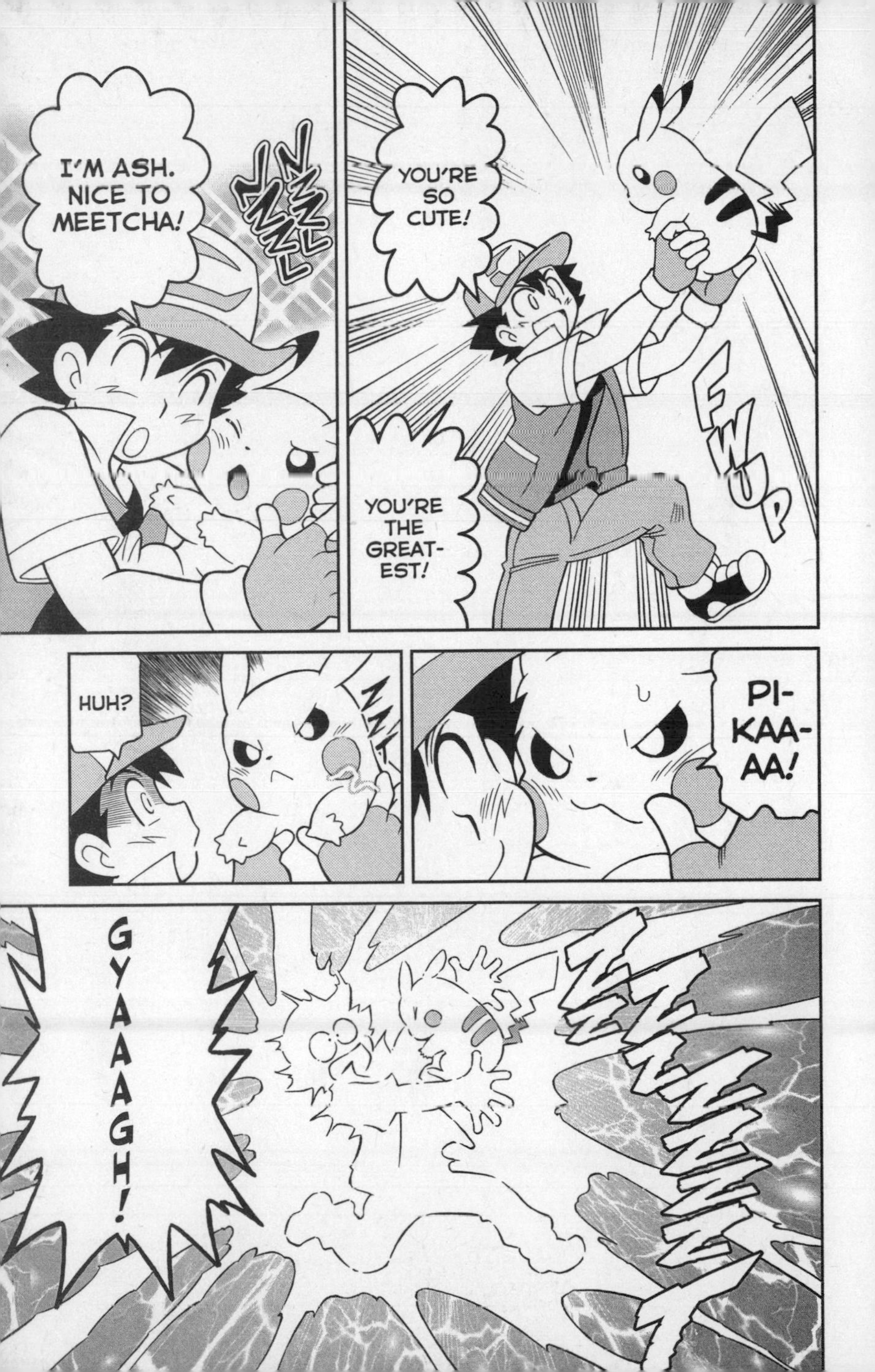
YOU'RE SO CUTE!
FWUP
YOU'RE THE GREAT-EST!
I'M ASH. NICE TO MEETCHA!
PI-KAAA-AA!
HUH?
GYAAAAGH!

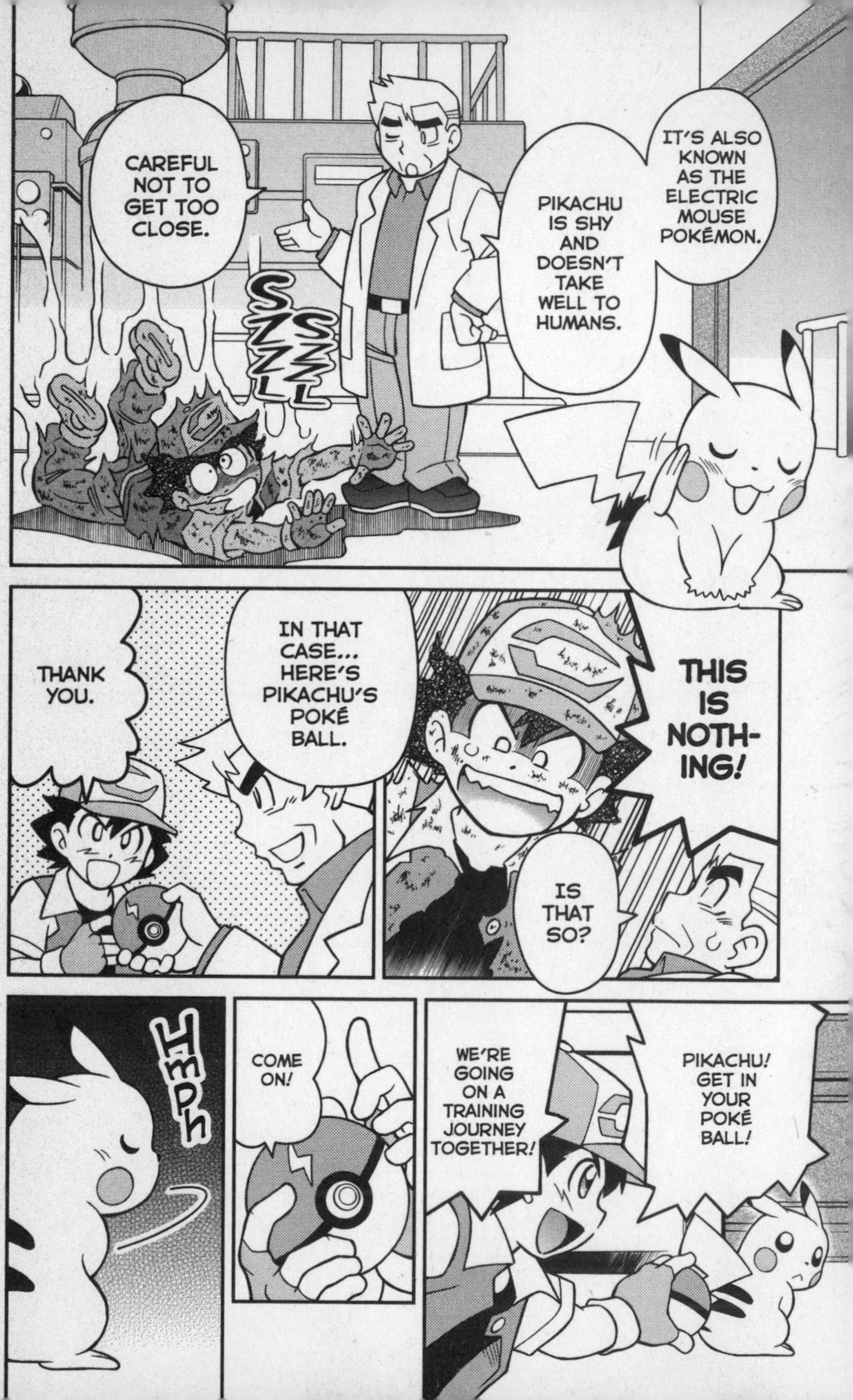
IT'S ALSO KNOWN AS THE ELECTRIC MOUSE POKÉMON.
PIKACHU IS SHY AND DOESN'T TAKE WELL TO HUMANS.
CAREFUL NOT TO GET TOO CLOSE.
SSZZZLL
THIS IS NOTH-ING!
IS THAT SO?
IN THAT CASE... HERE'S PIKACHU'S POKÉ BALL.
THANK YOU.
PIKACHU! GET IN YOUR POKÉ BALL!
WE'RE GOING ON A TRAINING JOURNEY TOGETHER!
COME ON!
Hmph

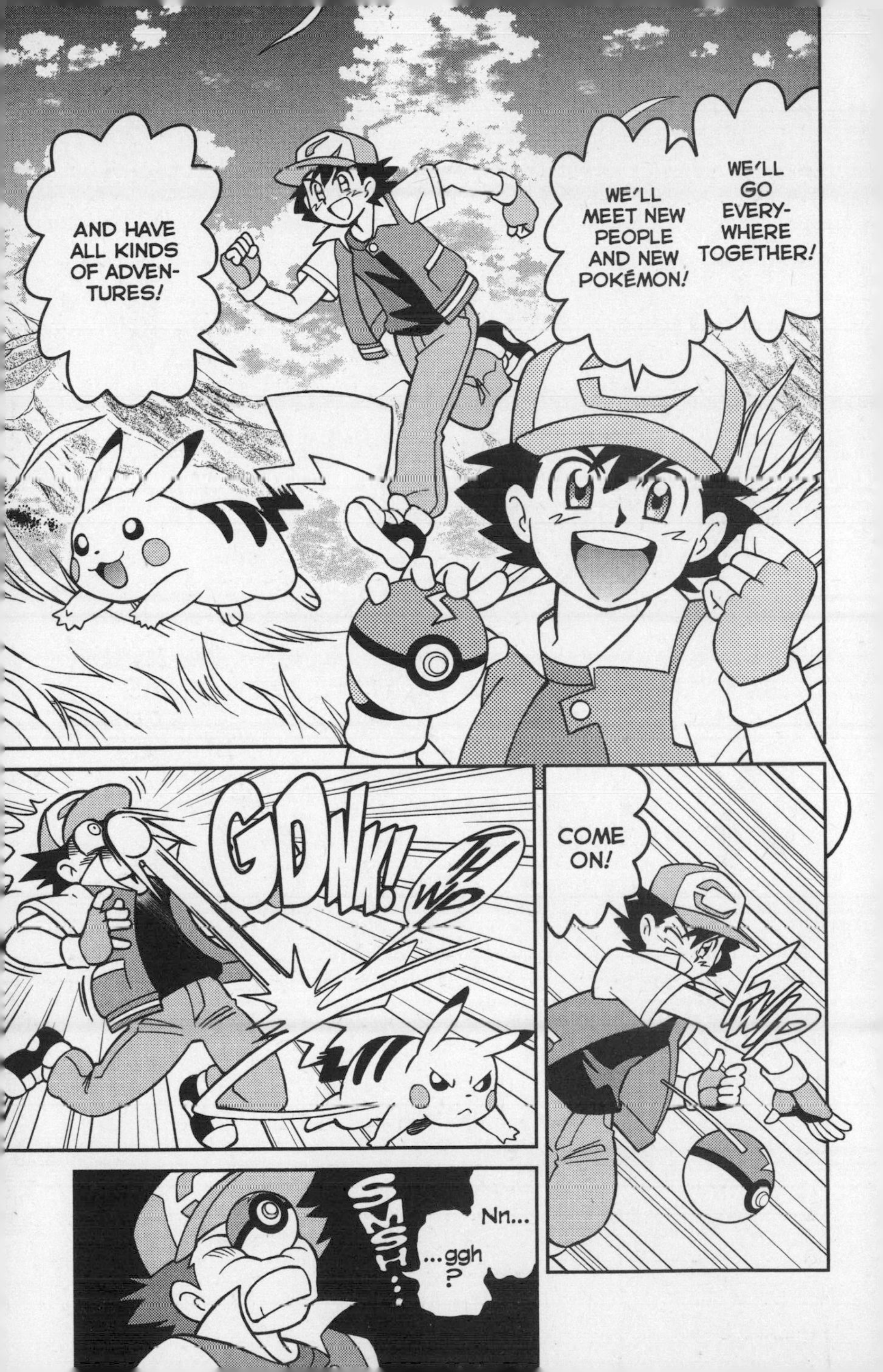
WE'LL GO EVERY-WHERE TOGETHER!
WE'LL MEET NEW PEOPLE AND NEW POKÉMON!
AND HAVE ALL KINDS OF ADVENTURES!
COME ON!
FWIP
GONK!
SMSH...
Nn...
...ggh?

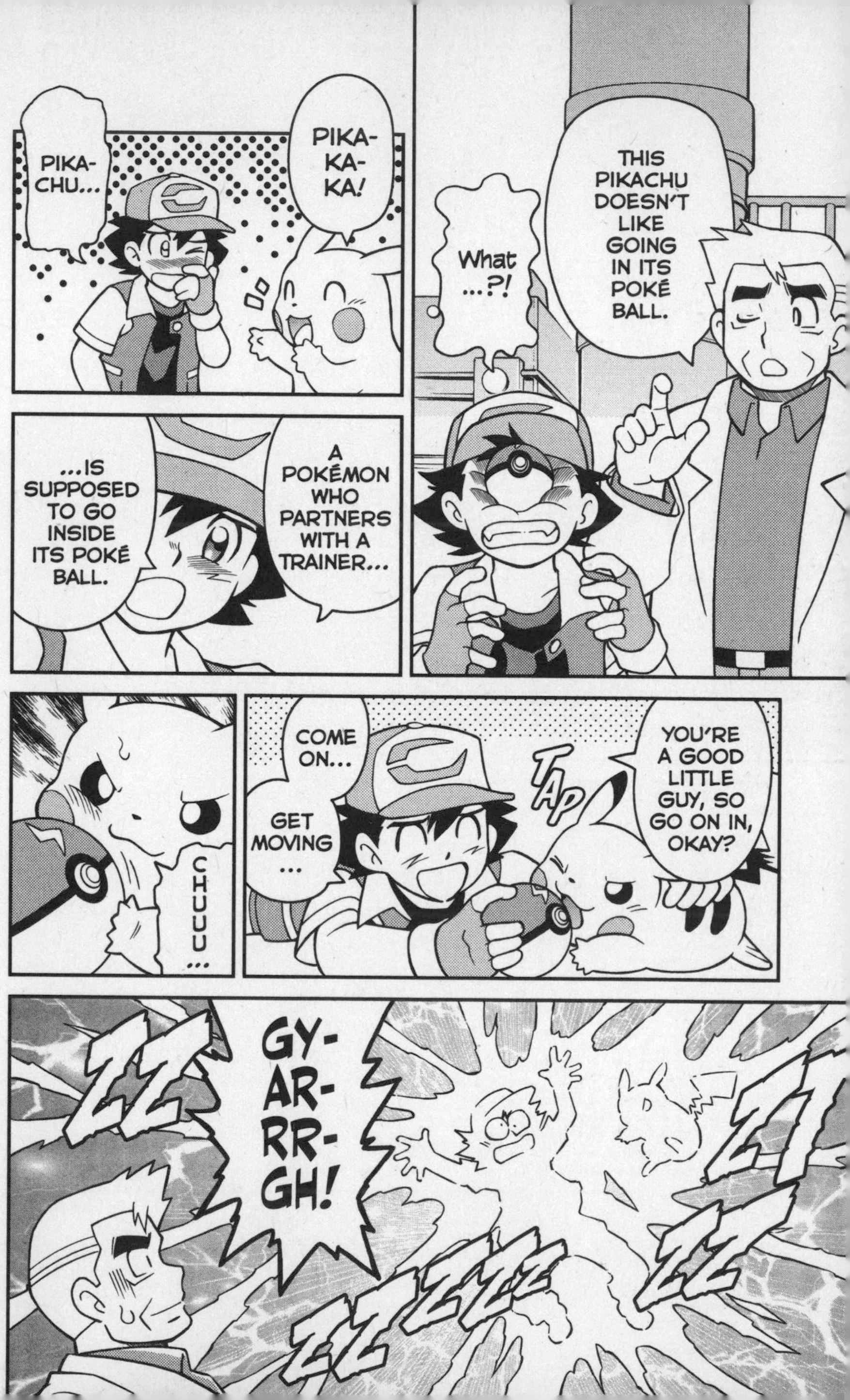
THIS PIKACHU DOESN'T LIKE GOING IN ITS POKÉ BALL.
What ...?!
PIKA-KA-KA!
PIKA-CHU...
A POKÉMON WHO PARTNERS WITH A TRAINER...
...IS SUPPOSED TO GO INSIDE ITS POKÉ BALL.
YOU'RE A GOOD LITTLE GUY, SO GO ON IN, OKAY?
TAP
COME ON...
GET MOVING ...
CHUUU...
GY-AR-RR-GH!

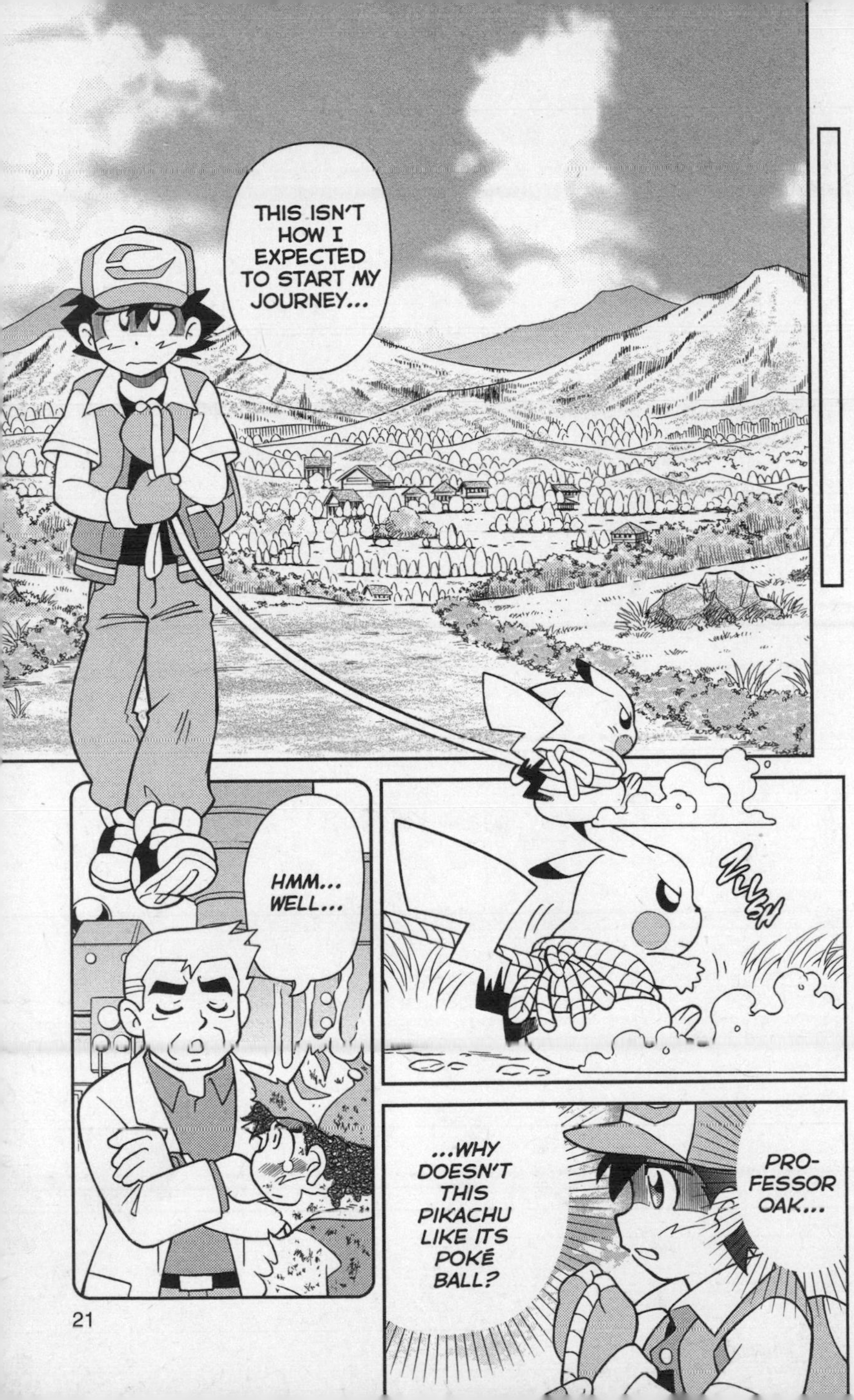
THIS ISN'T HOW I EXPECTED TO START MY JOURNEY...
PRO-FESSOR OAK...
...WHY DOESN'T THIS PIKACHU LIKE ITS POKÉ BALL?
HMM... WELL...

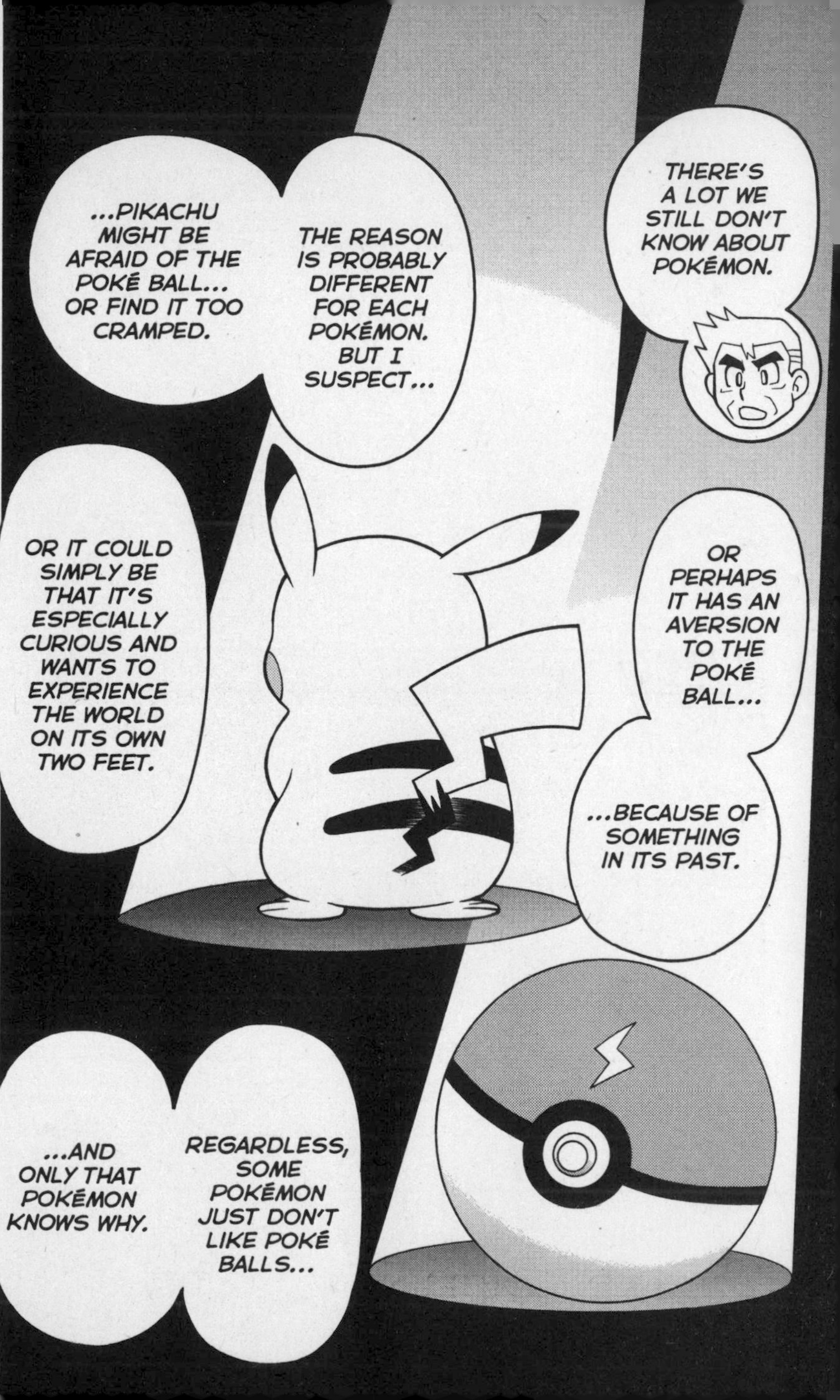
THERE'S A LOT WE STILL DON'T KNOW ABOUT POKÉMON.
THE REASON IS PROBABLY DIFFERENT FOR EACH POKÉMON. BUT I SUSPECT...
...PIKACHU MIGHT BE AFRAID OF THE POKÉ BALL... OR FIND IT TOO CRAMPED.
OR PERHAPS IT HAS AN AVERSION TO THE POKÉ BALL...
...BECAUSE OF SOMETHING IN ITS PAST.
OR IT COULD SIMPLY BE THAT IT'S ESPECIALLY CURIOUS AND WANTS TO EXPERIENCE THE WORLD ON ITS OWN TWO FEET.
REGARDLESS, SOME POKÉMON JUST DON'T LIKE POKÉ BALLS...
...AND ONLY THAT POKÉMON KNOWS WHY.

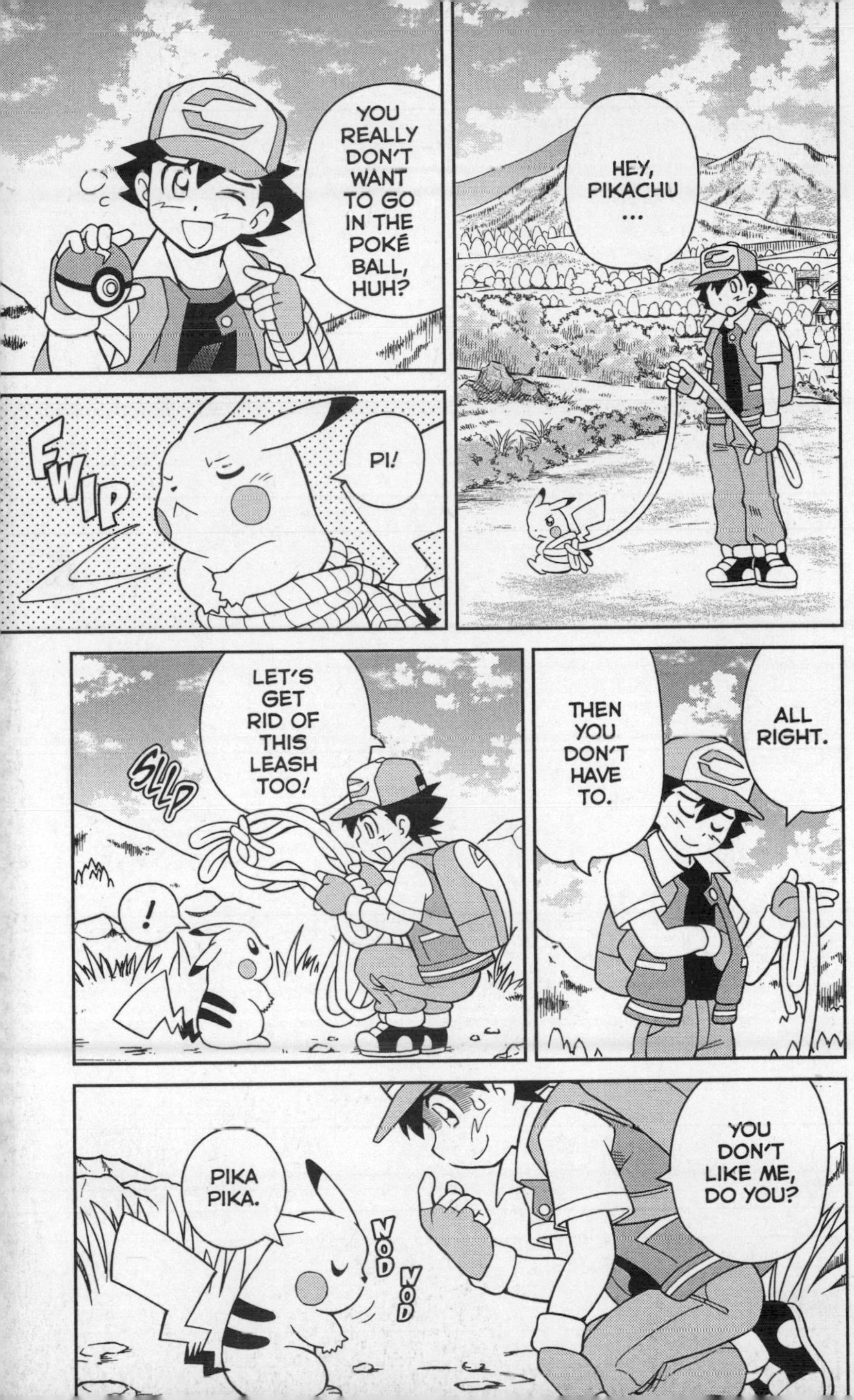
HEY, PIKACHU ...
YOU REALLY DON'T WANT TO GO IN THE POKÉ BALL, HUH?
PI!
FWIP
ALL RIGHT.
THEN YOU DON'T HAVE TO.
LET'S GET RID OF THIS LEASH TOO!
SLLP
!
YOU DON'T LIKE ME, DO YOU?
NOD
NOD
PIKA PIKA.

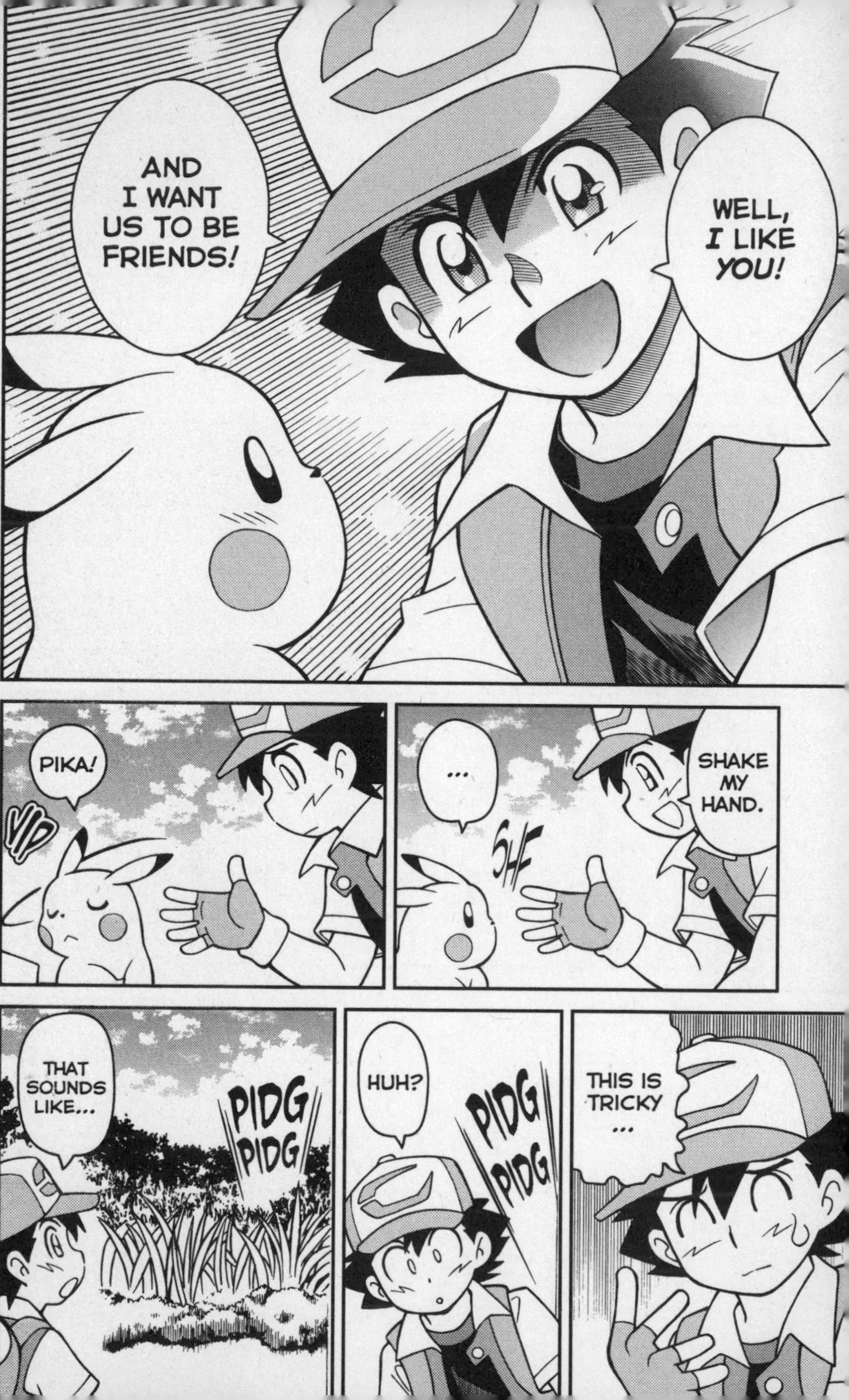
WELL, I LIKE YOU!
AND I WANT US TO BE FRIENDS!
SHAKE MY HAND.
...
SHF
PIKA!
VIP
THIS IS TRICKY ...
HUH?
PIDG PIDG
THAT SOUNDS LIKE...
PIDG PIDG

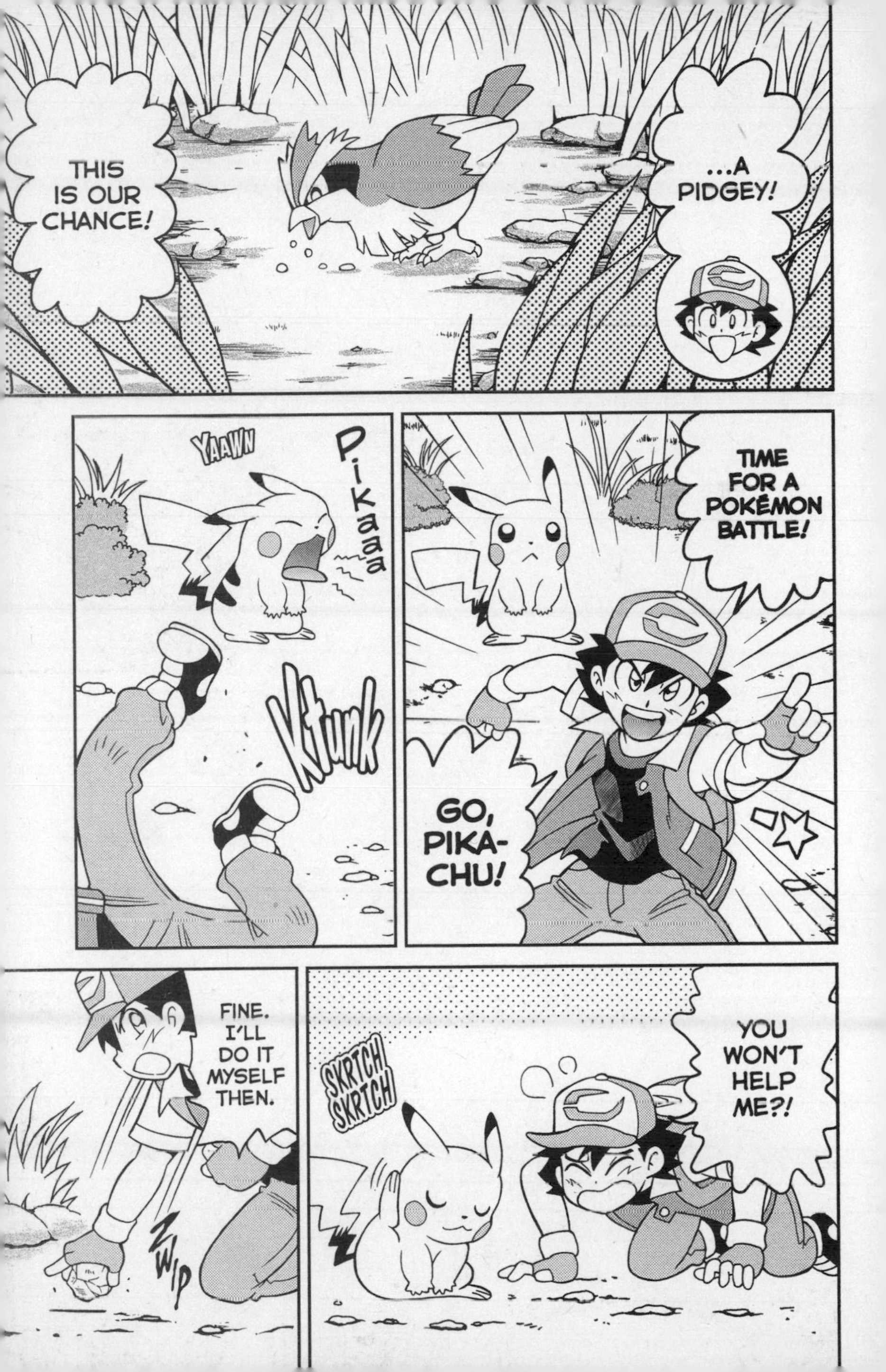
...A PIDGEY!
THIS IS OUR CHANCE!
TIME FOR A POKÉMON BATTLE!
GO, PIKA-CHU!
Pikaaaa
YAAWN
Ktunk
YOU WON'T HELP ME?!
SKRTCH SKRTCH
FINE. I'LL DO IT MYSELF THEN.
ZWIP

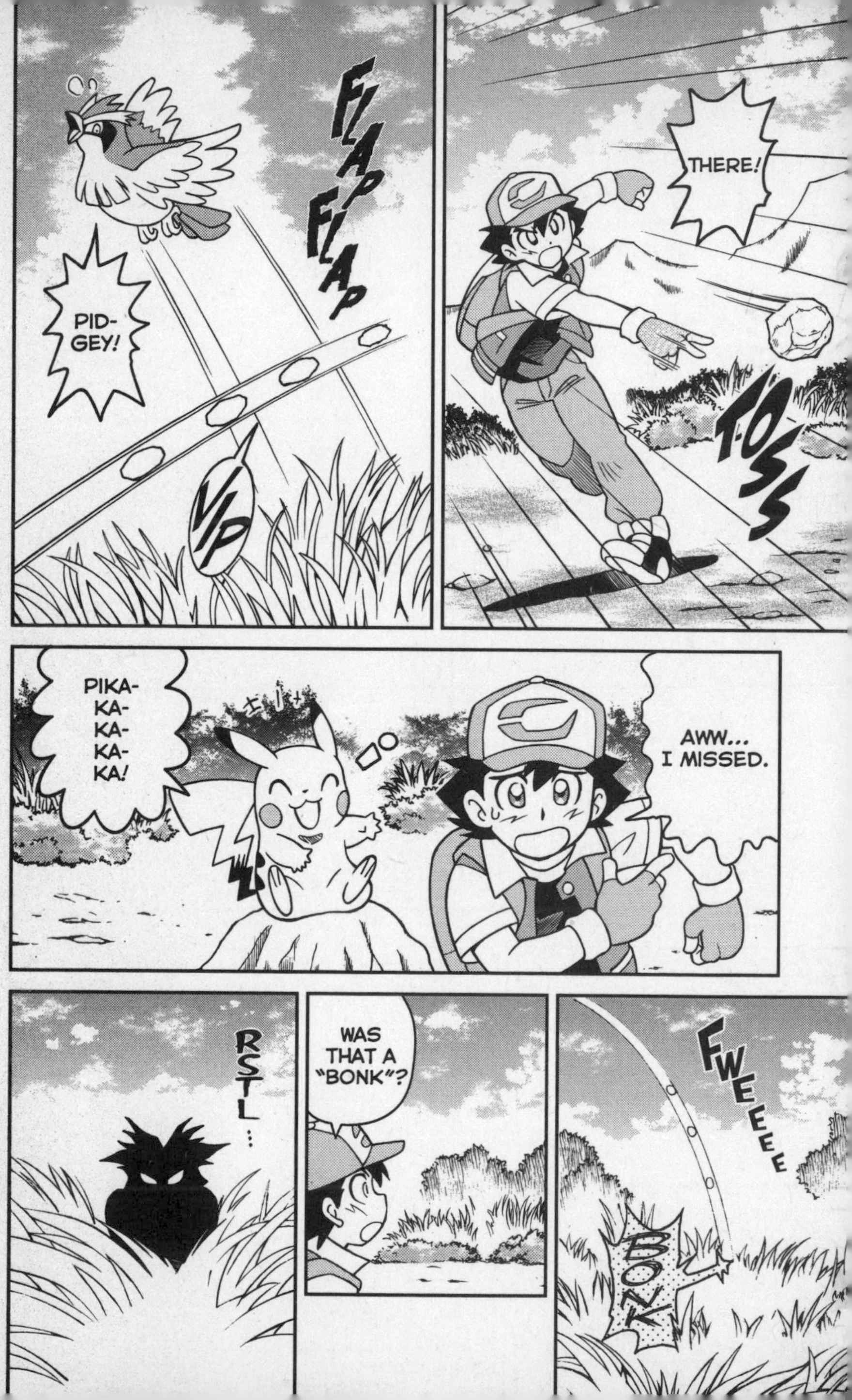
THERE!
TOSS
FLAP FLAP
PIDGEY!
VIP
AWW... I MISSED.
PIKA-KA-KA-KA-KA!
FWEEEE
BONK
WAS THAT A "BONK"?
RSTL...

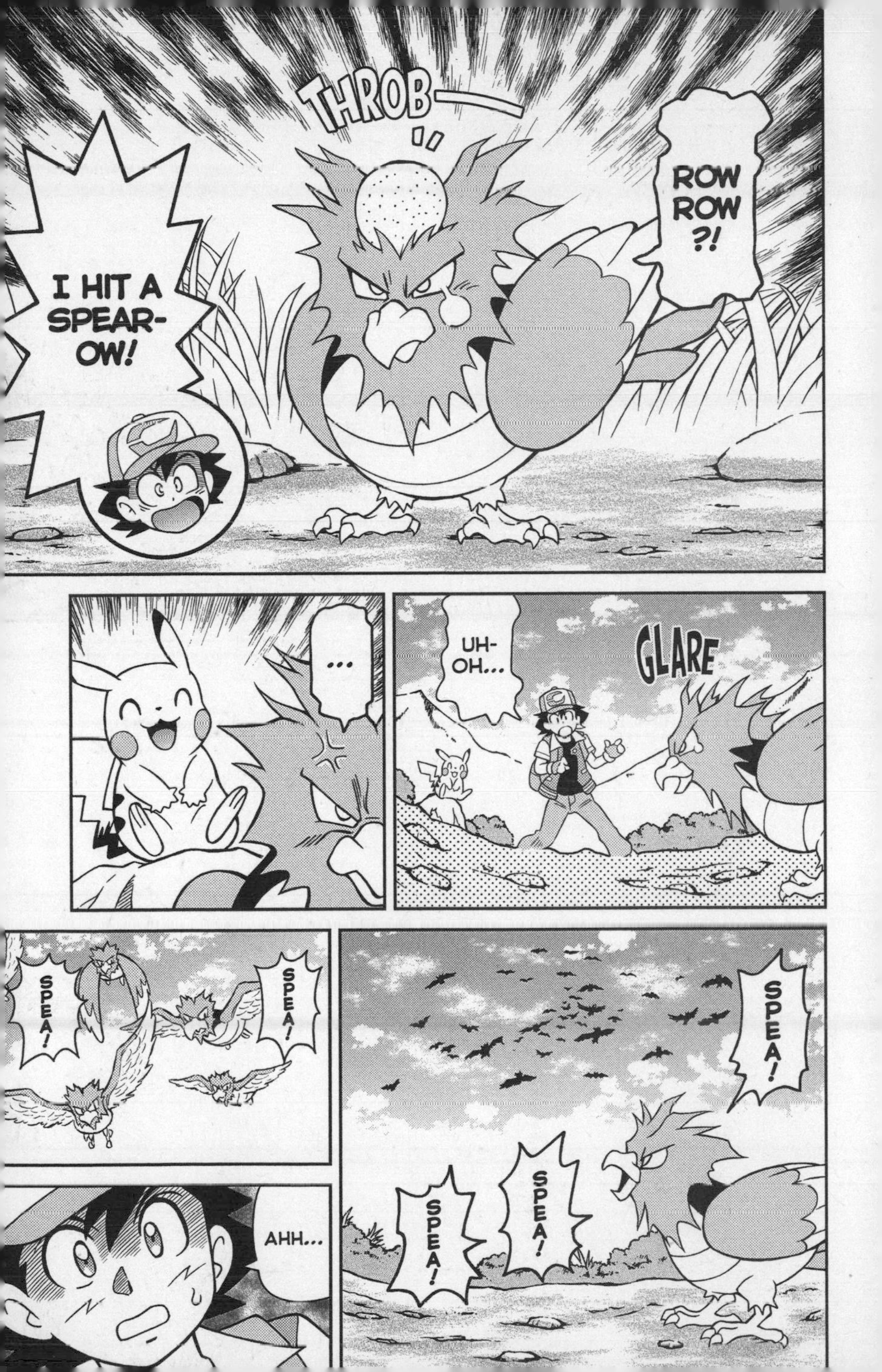
THROB—
ROW ROW ?!
I HIT A SPEAR-OW!
GLARE
UH-OH...
...
SPEA!
SPEA!
SPEA!
SPEA!
SPEA!
AHH...

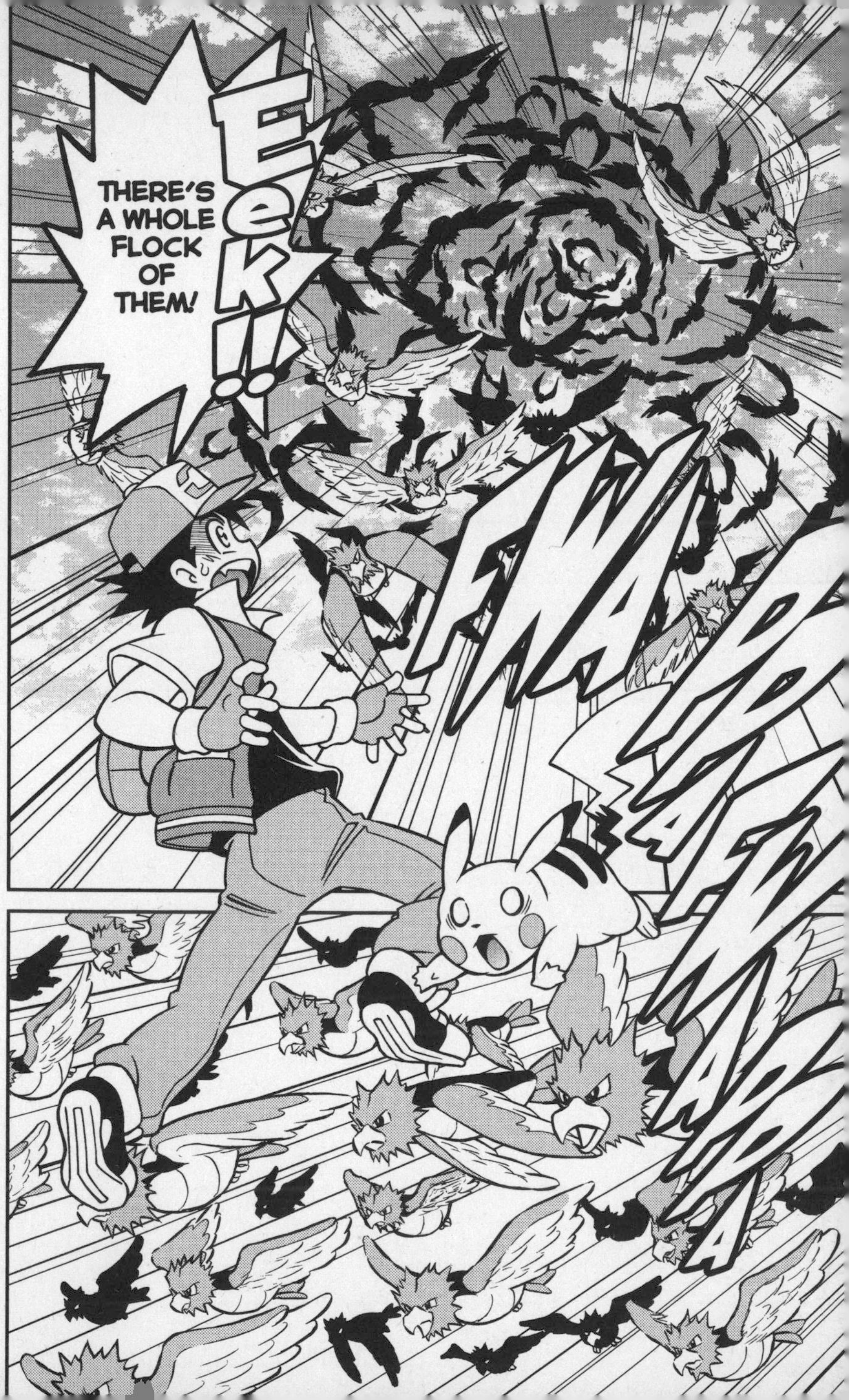
Eek!!
THERE'S A WHOLE FLOCK OF THEM!

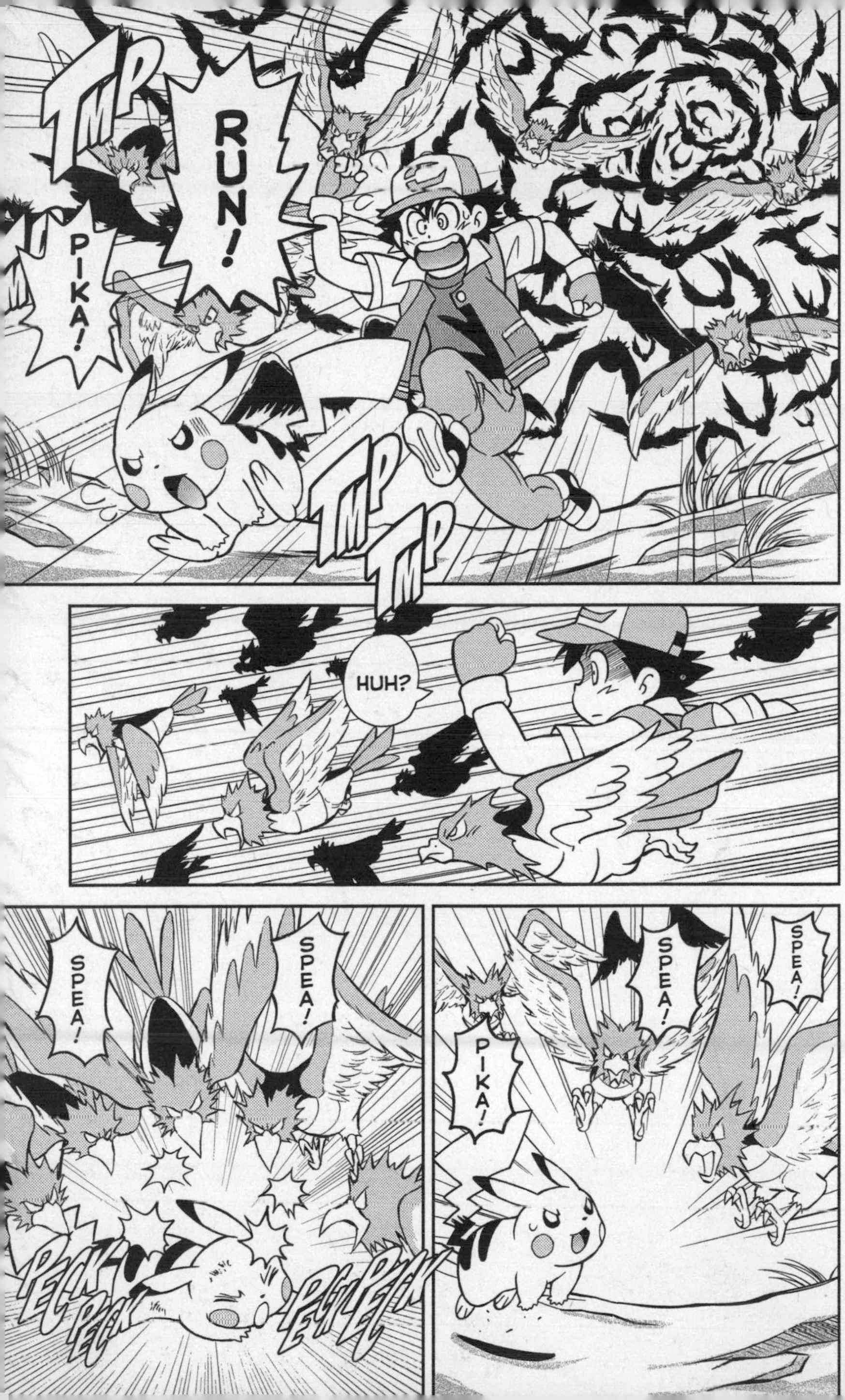
RUN!
TMP
PIKA!
TMP
TMP
HUH?
SPEA!
SPEA!
PIKA!
SPEA!
SPEA!
PECK PECK
PECK PECK

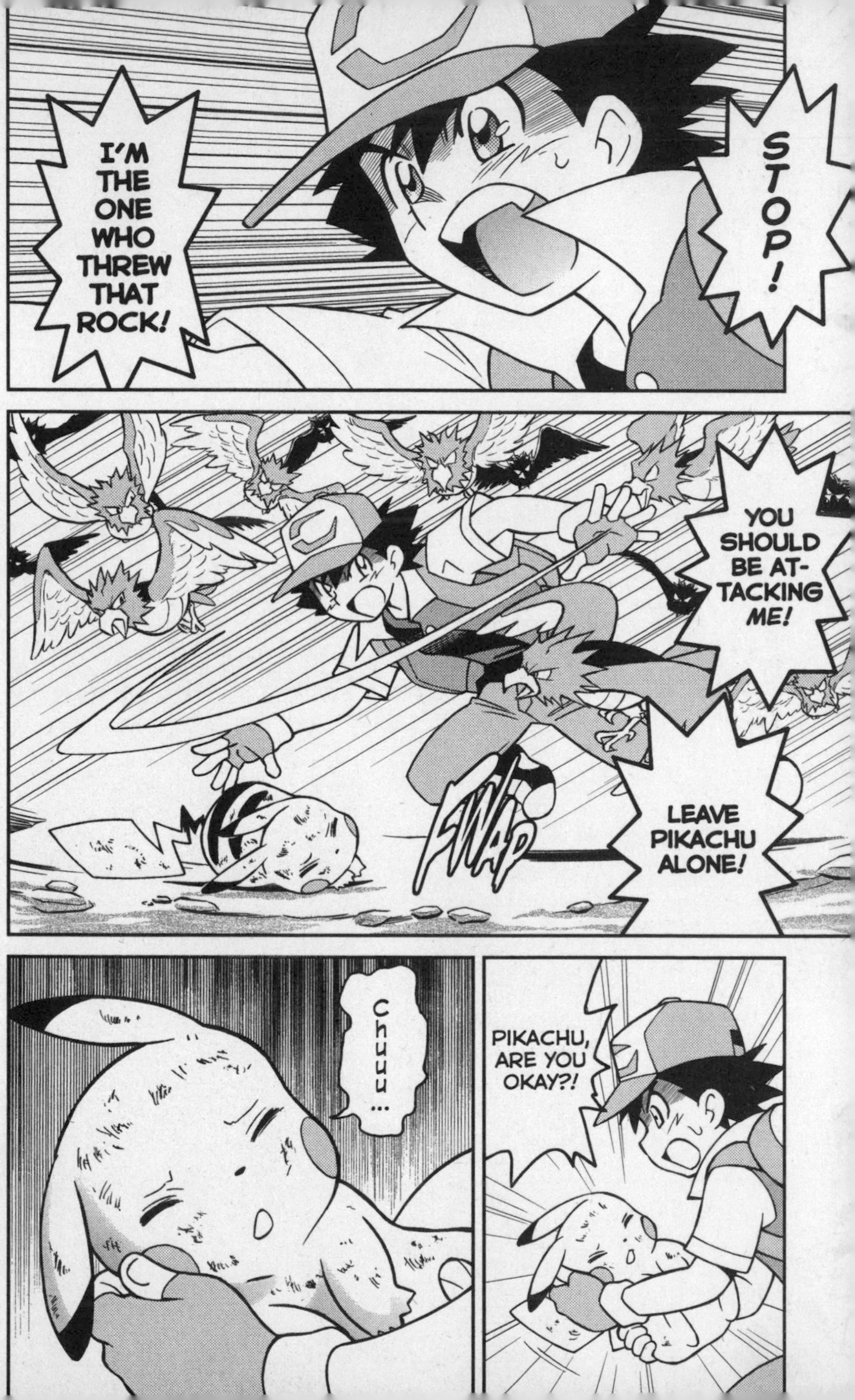
STOP!
I'M THE ONE WHO THREW THAT ROCK!
YOU SHOULD BE AT-TACKING ME!
LEAVE PIKACHU ALONE!
FWAP
PIKACHU, ARE YOU OKAY?!
Chuuu...

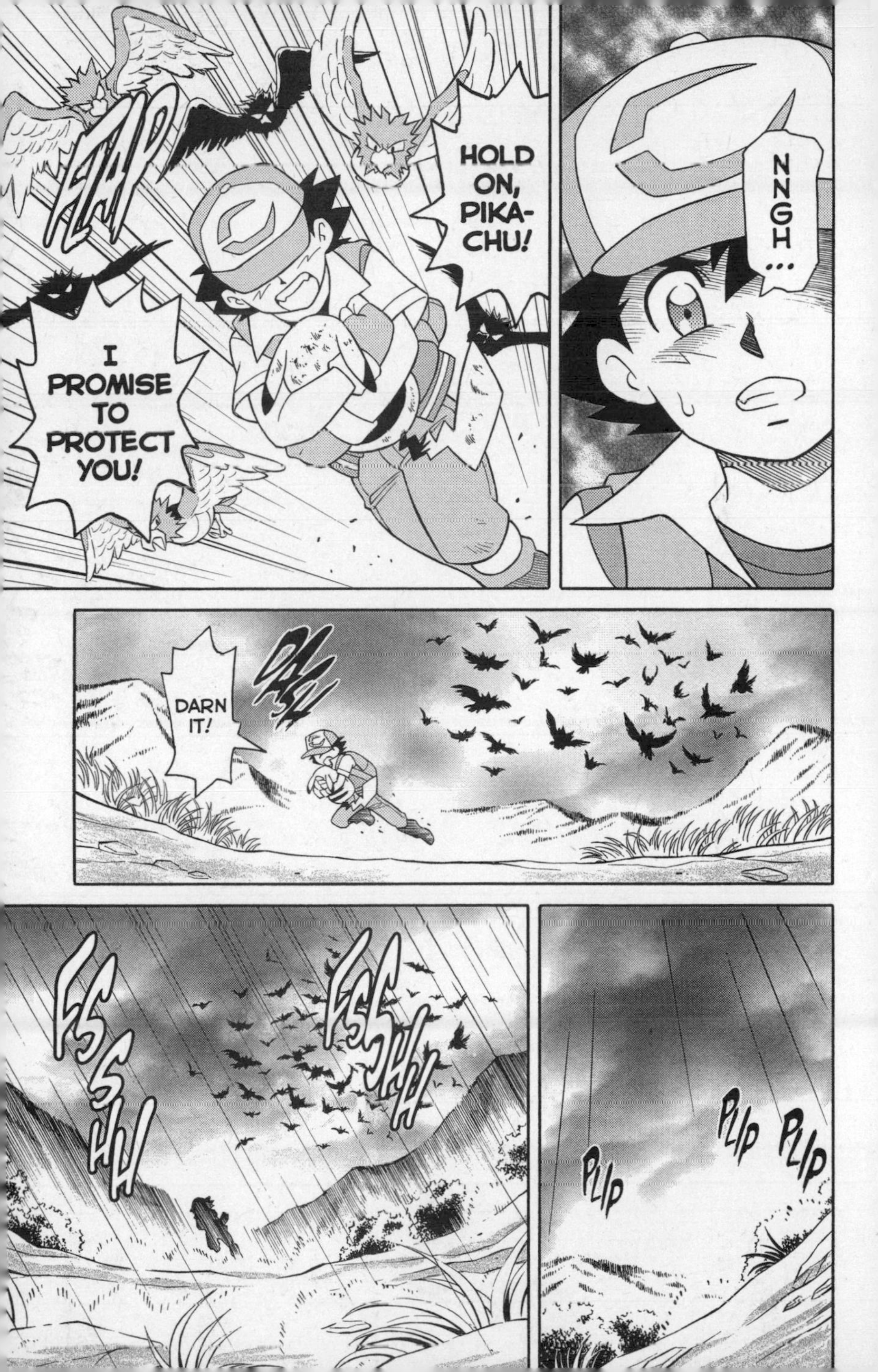
NNGH...
HOLD ON, PIKA-CHU!
FLAP
I PROMISE TO PROTECT YOU!
DASH
DARN IT!
PLIP
PLIP
PLIP
FSSHH
FSSHH

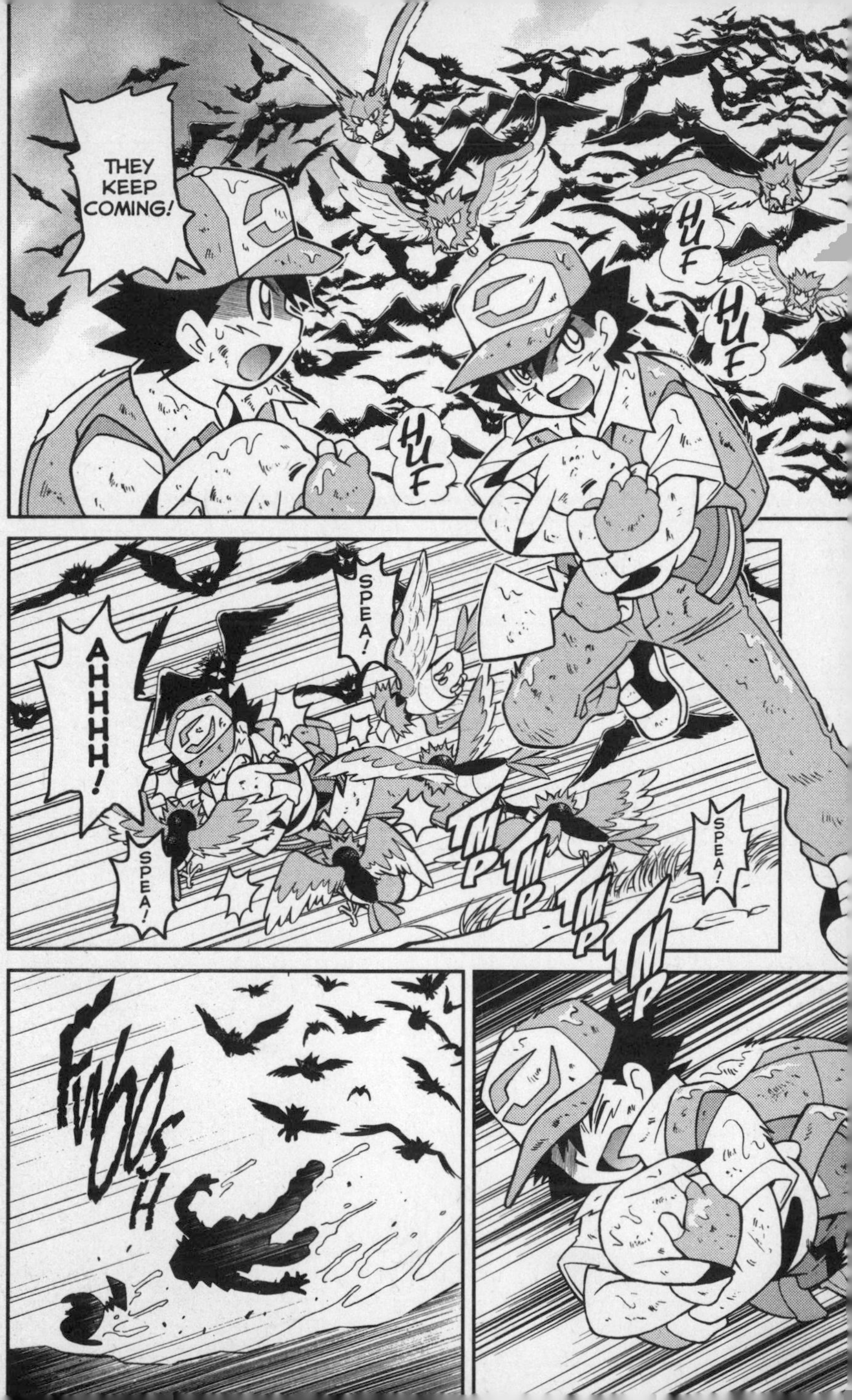

HUF
HUF
HUF
THEY KEEP COMING!
SPEA!
SPEA!
TMP TMP TMP TMP
AHHHH!
SPEA!
FWOOSH

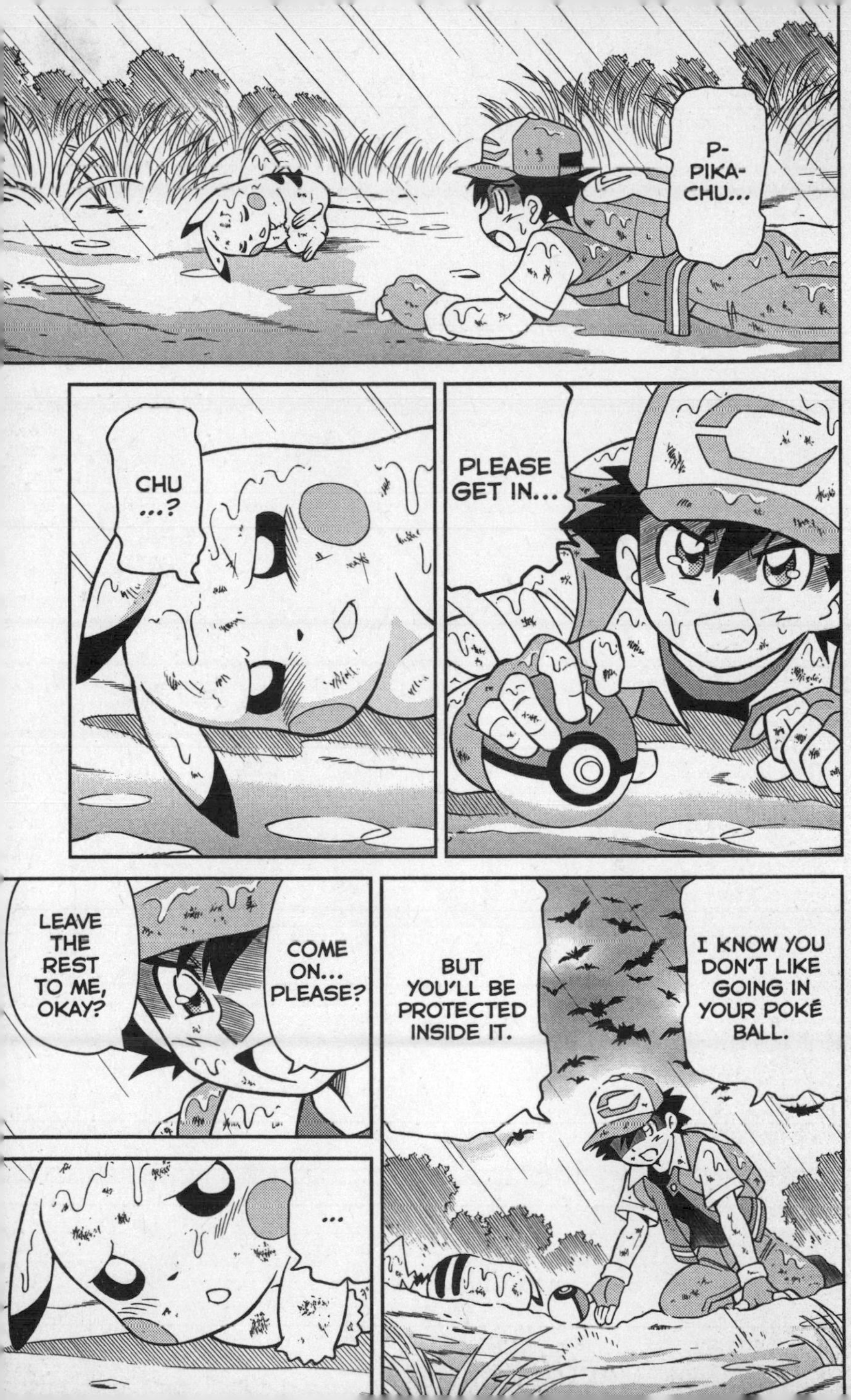
P-PIKA-CHU...
PLEASE GET IN...
CHU ...?
I KNOW YOU DON'T LIKE GOING IN YOUR POKÉ BALL.
BUT YOU'LL BE PROTECTED INSIDE IT.
COME ON... PLEASE?
LEAVE THE REST TO ME, OKAY?
...

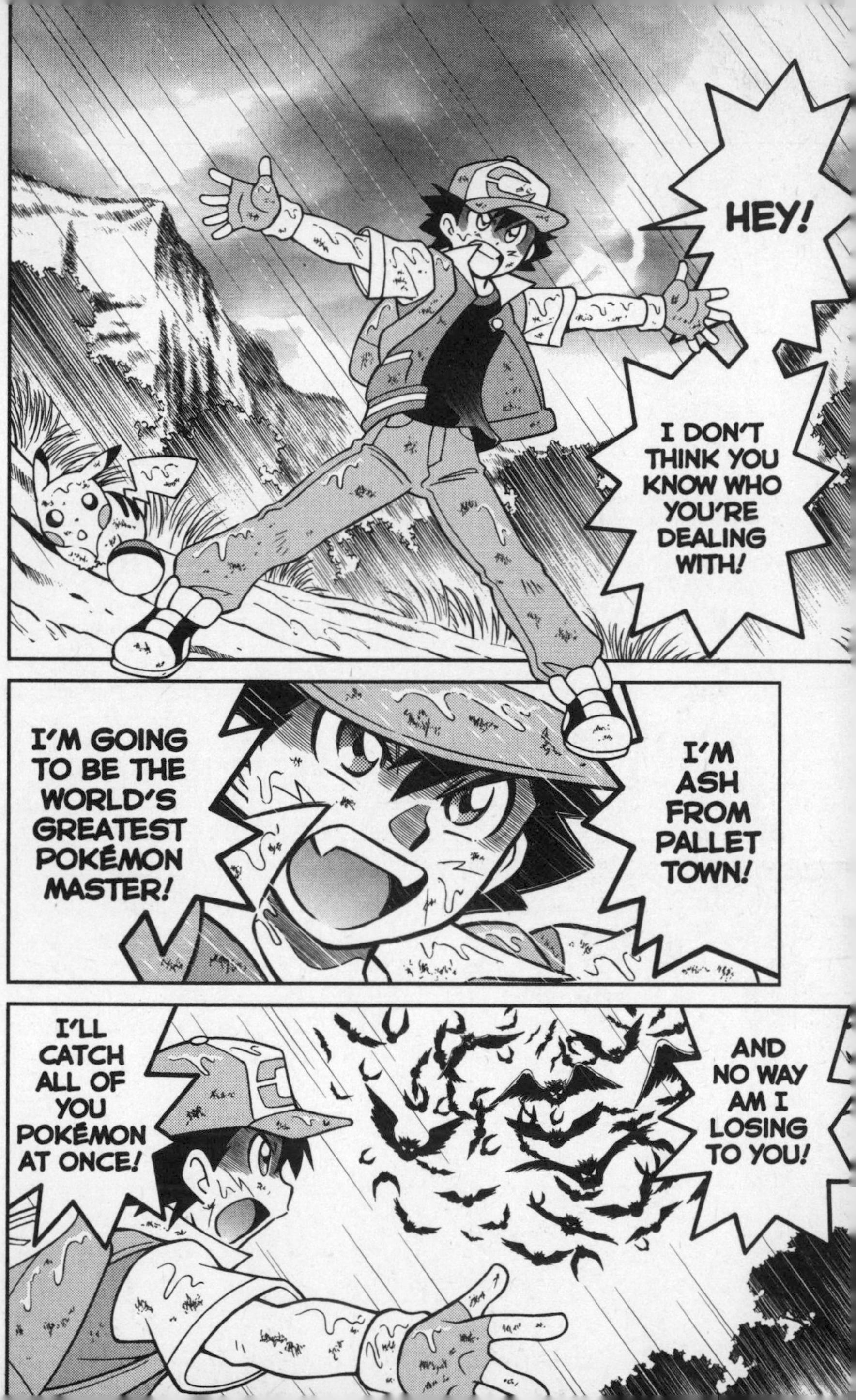
HEY!
I DON'T THINK YOU KNOW WHO YOU'RE DEALING WITH!
I'M ASH FROM PALLET TOWN!
I'M GOING TO BE THE WORLD'S GREATEST POKÉMON MASTER!
AND NO WAY AM I LOSING TO YOU!
I'LL CATCH ALL OF YOU POKÉMON AT ONCE!

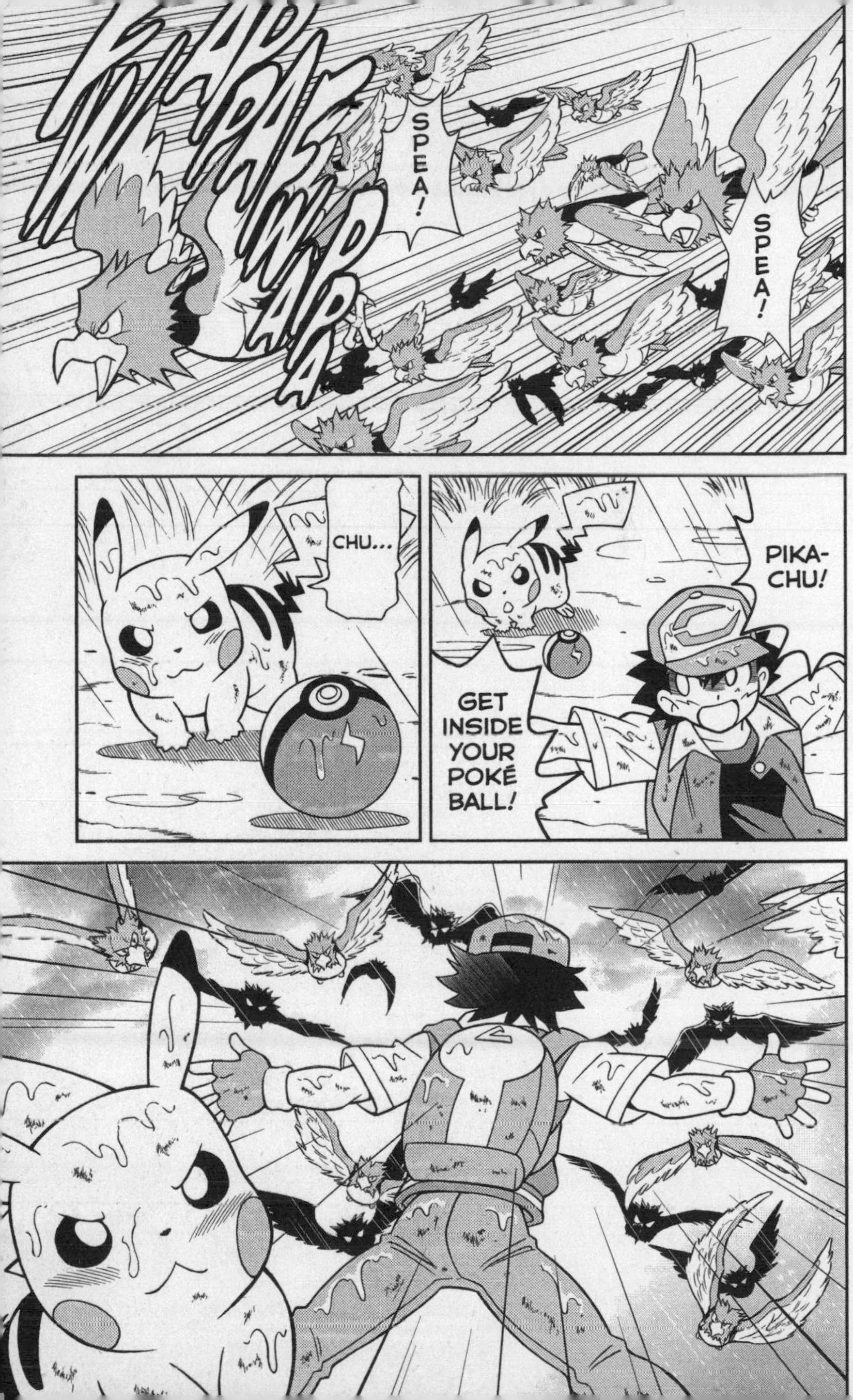

SPEA!
SPEA!
PIKA-CHU!
GET INSIDE YOUR POKÉ BALL!
CHU...

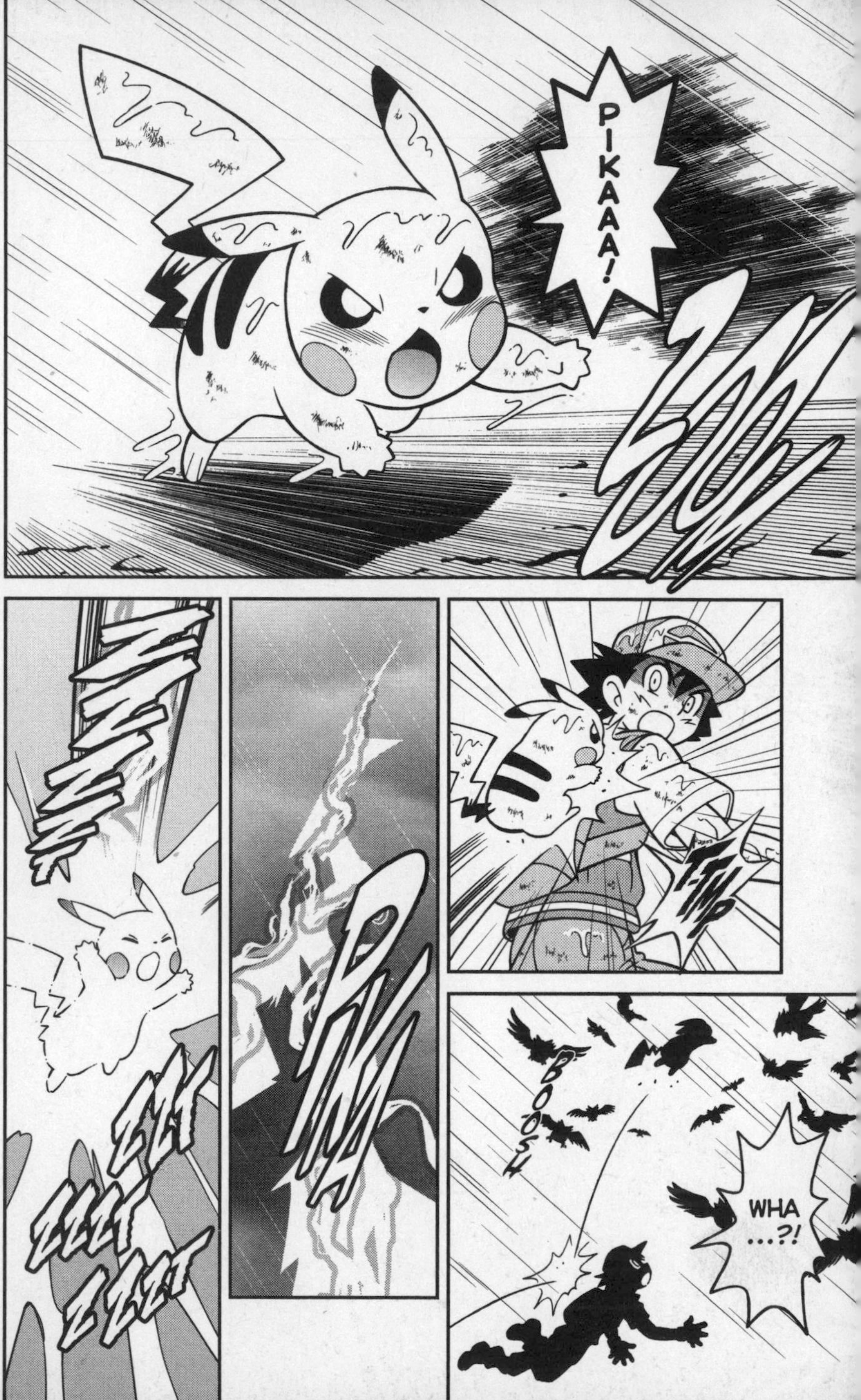
PIKAAA!
BOOOSH
WHA ...?!

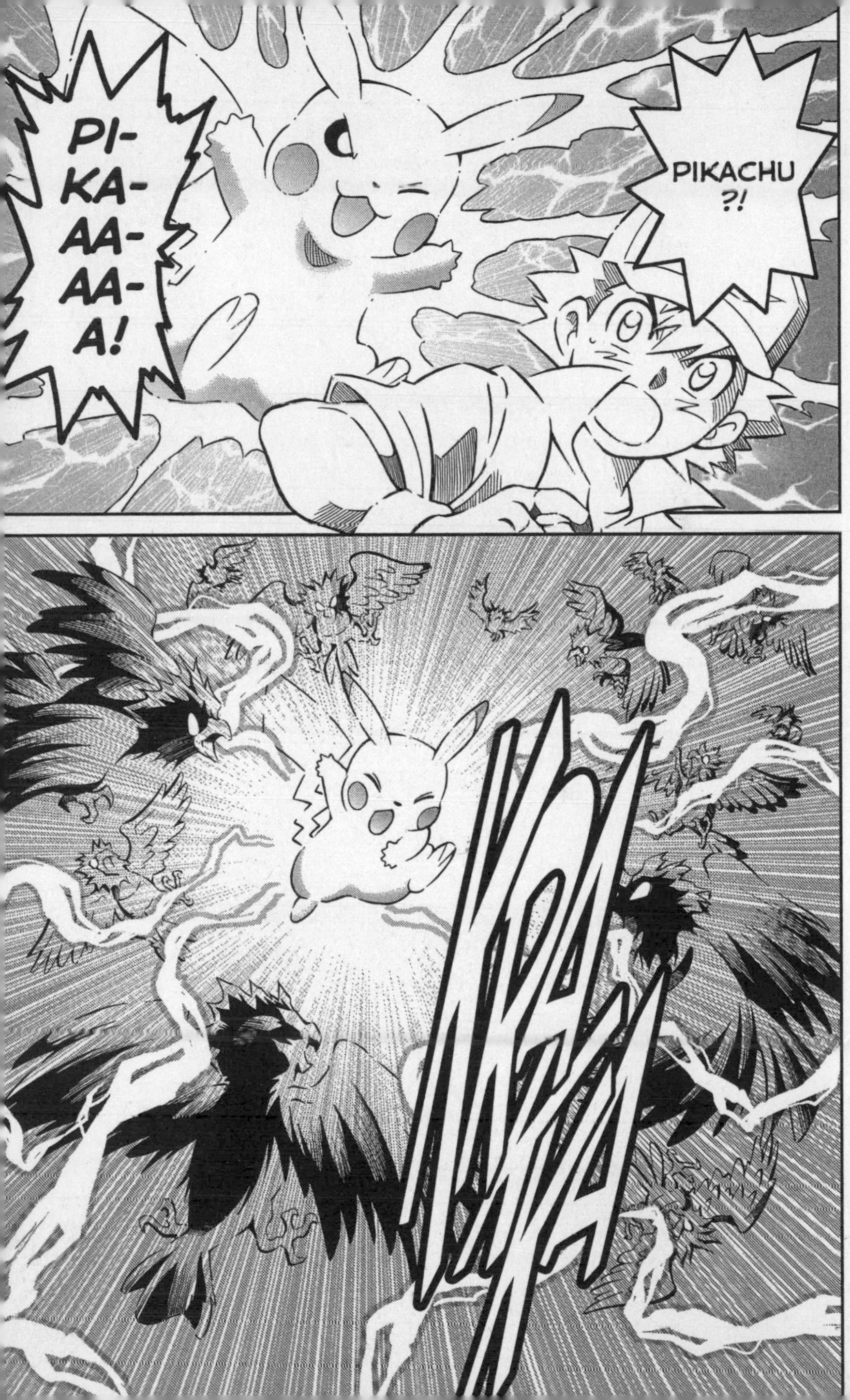
PIKACHU ?!
PI-KA-AA-AA-A!

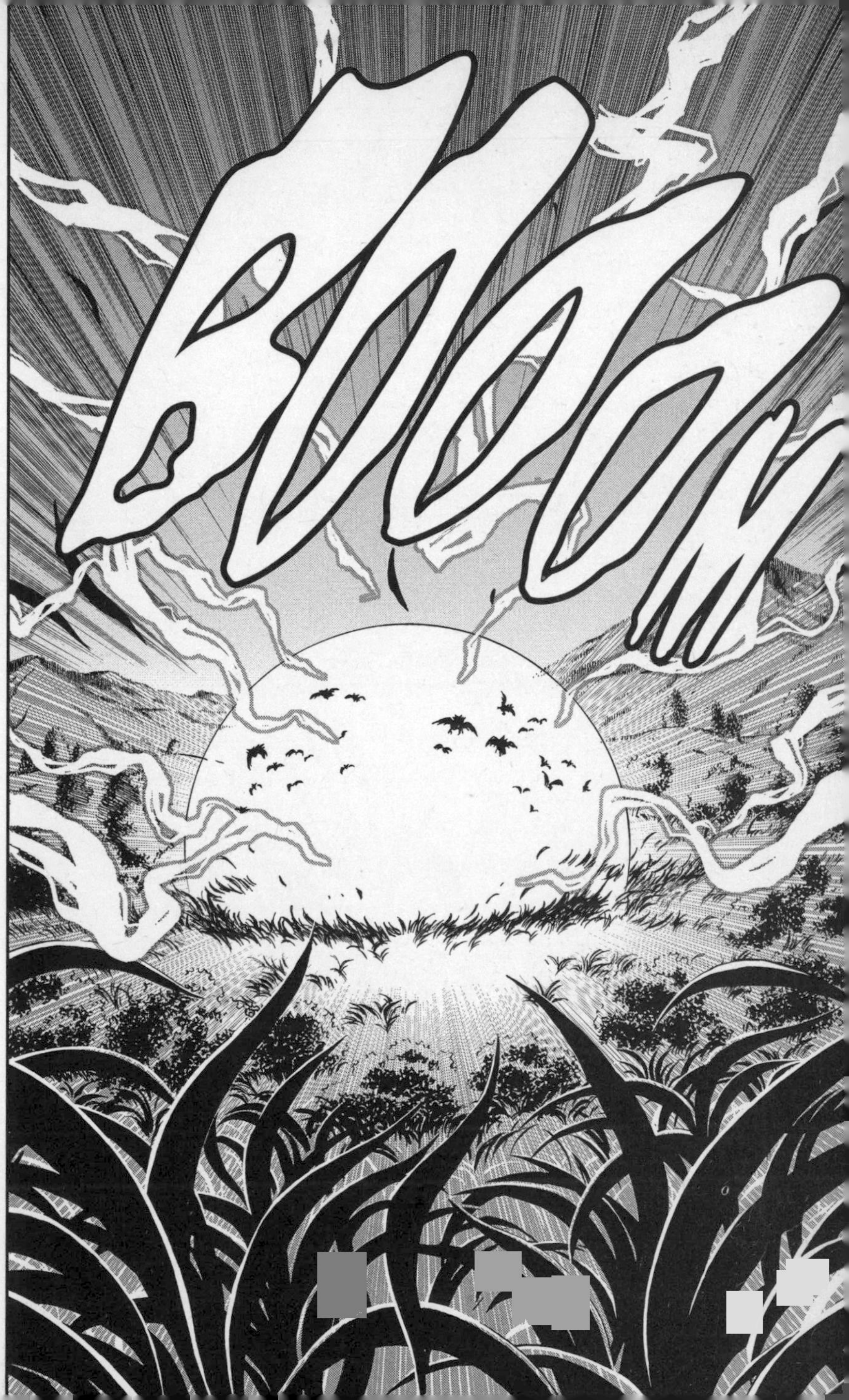

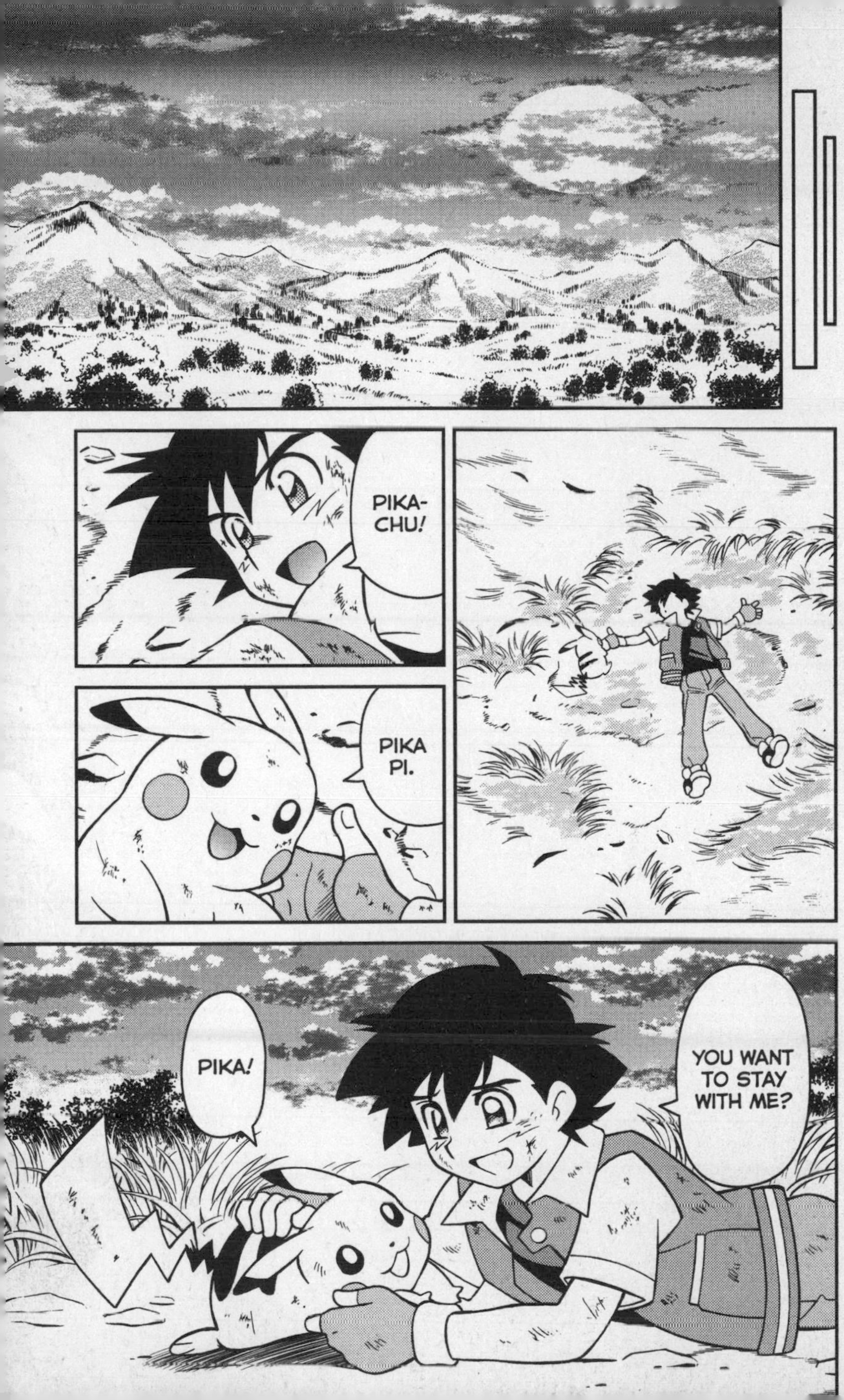
PIKA-CHU!
PIKA PI.
YOU WANT TO STAY WITH ME?
PIKA!

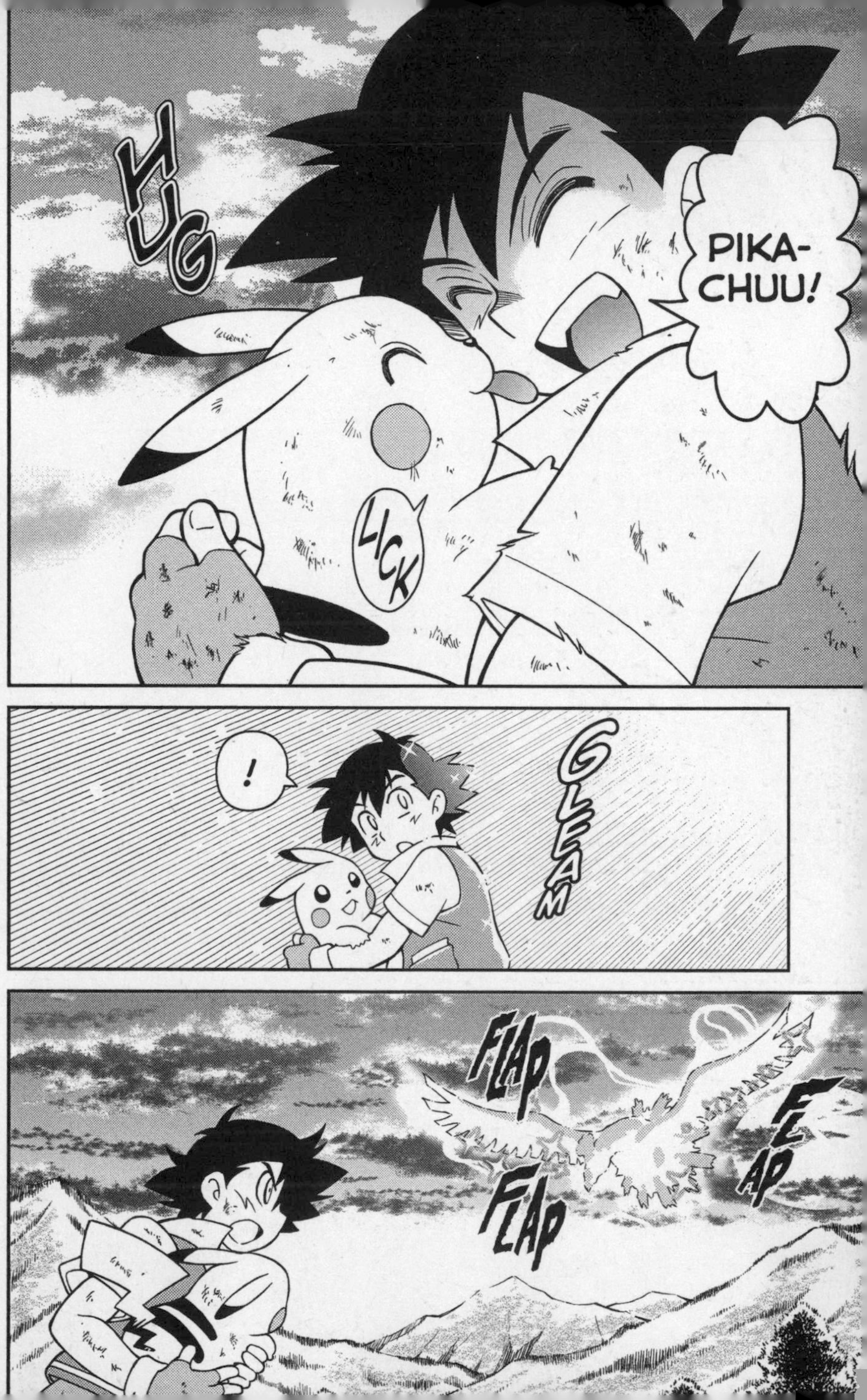
PIKA-
CHUU!
HUG
LICK
GLEAM
!
FLAP
FLAP
FLAP

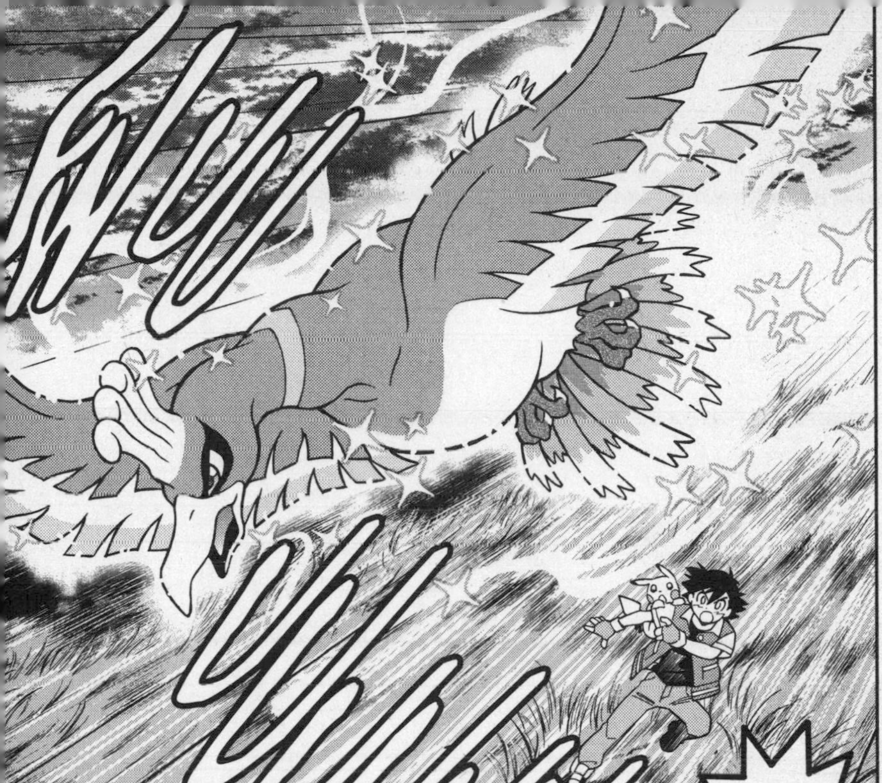
!!
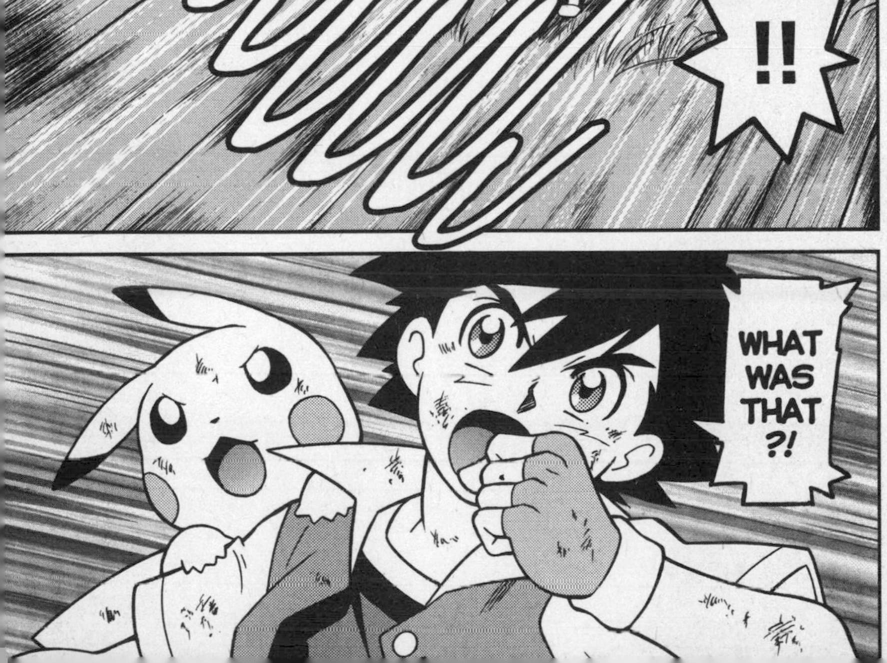
WHAT WAS THAT ?!

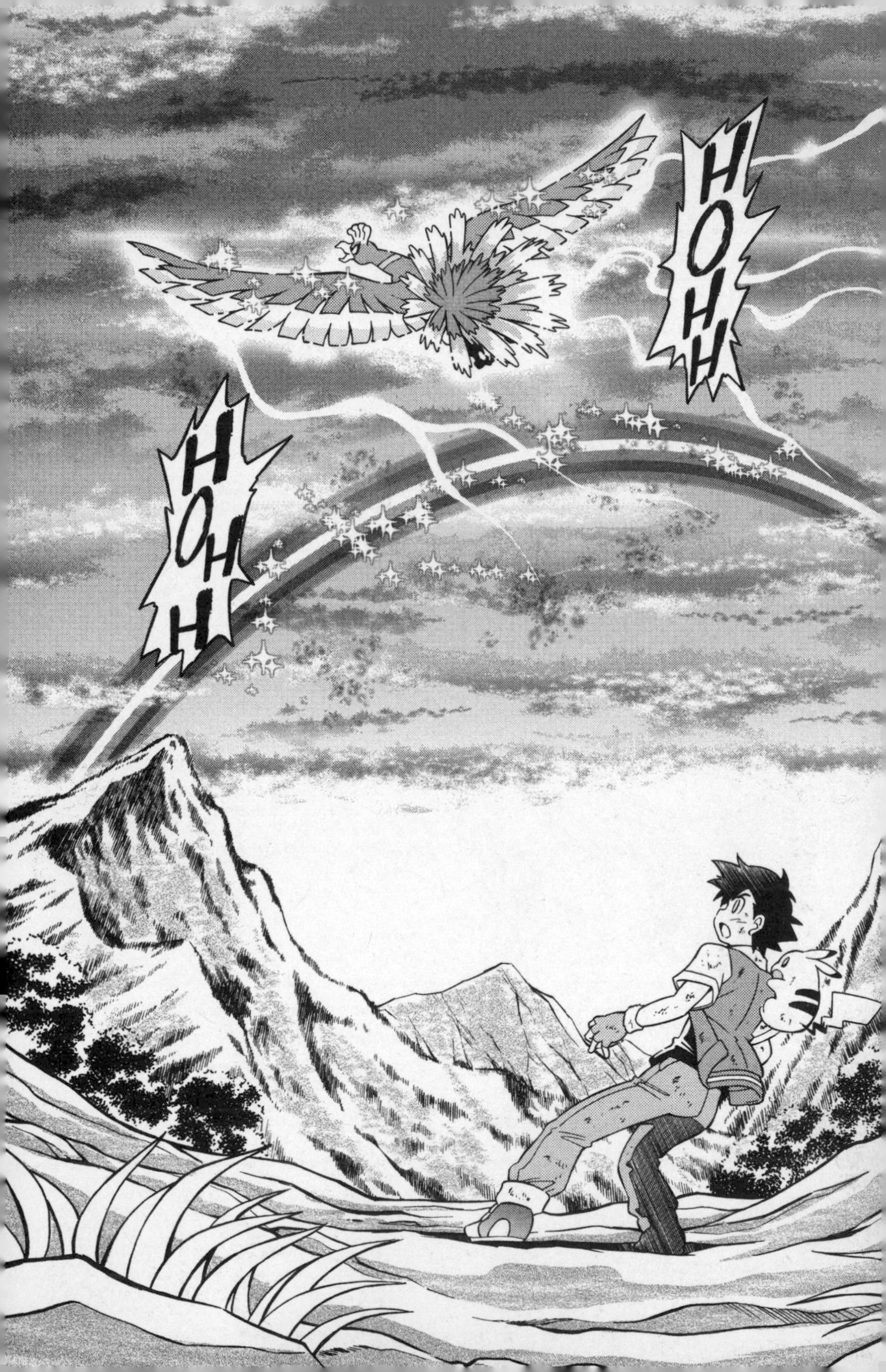
HO-OH
HO-OH

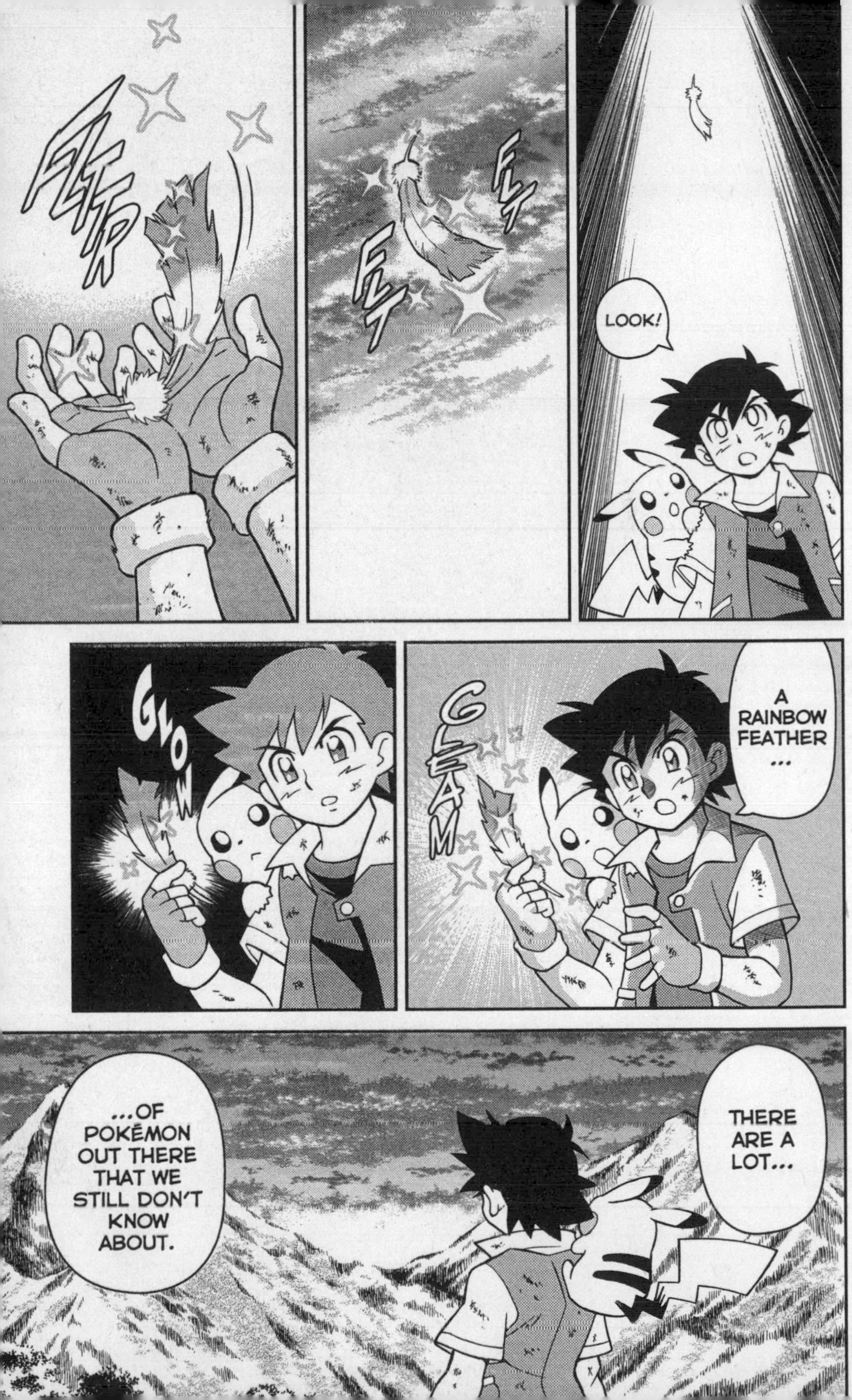

LOOK!
FLIT
FLIT
FLTTR
A RAINBOW FEATHER...
GLEAM
GLOW
THERE ARE A LOT...
...OF POKÉMON OUT THERE THAT WE STILL DON'T KNOW ABOUT.

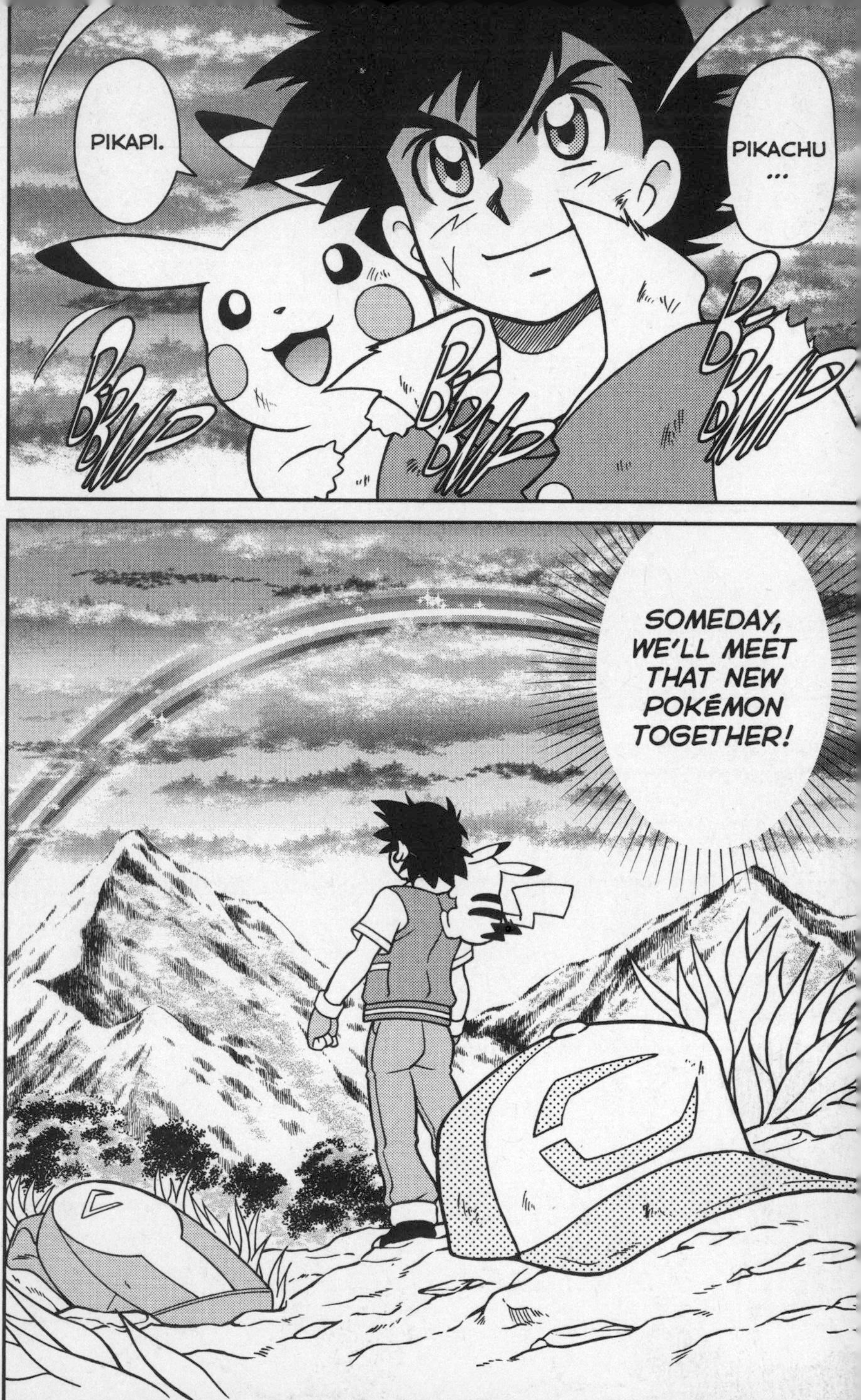
PIKACHU ...
PIKAPI.
SOMEDAY, WE'LL MEET THAT NEW POKÉMON TOGETHER!

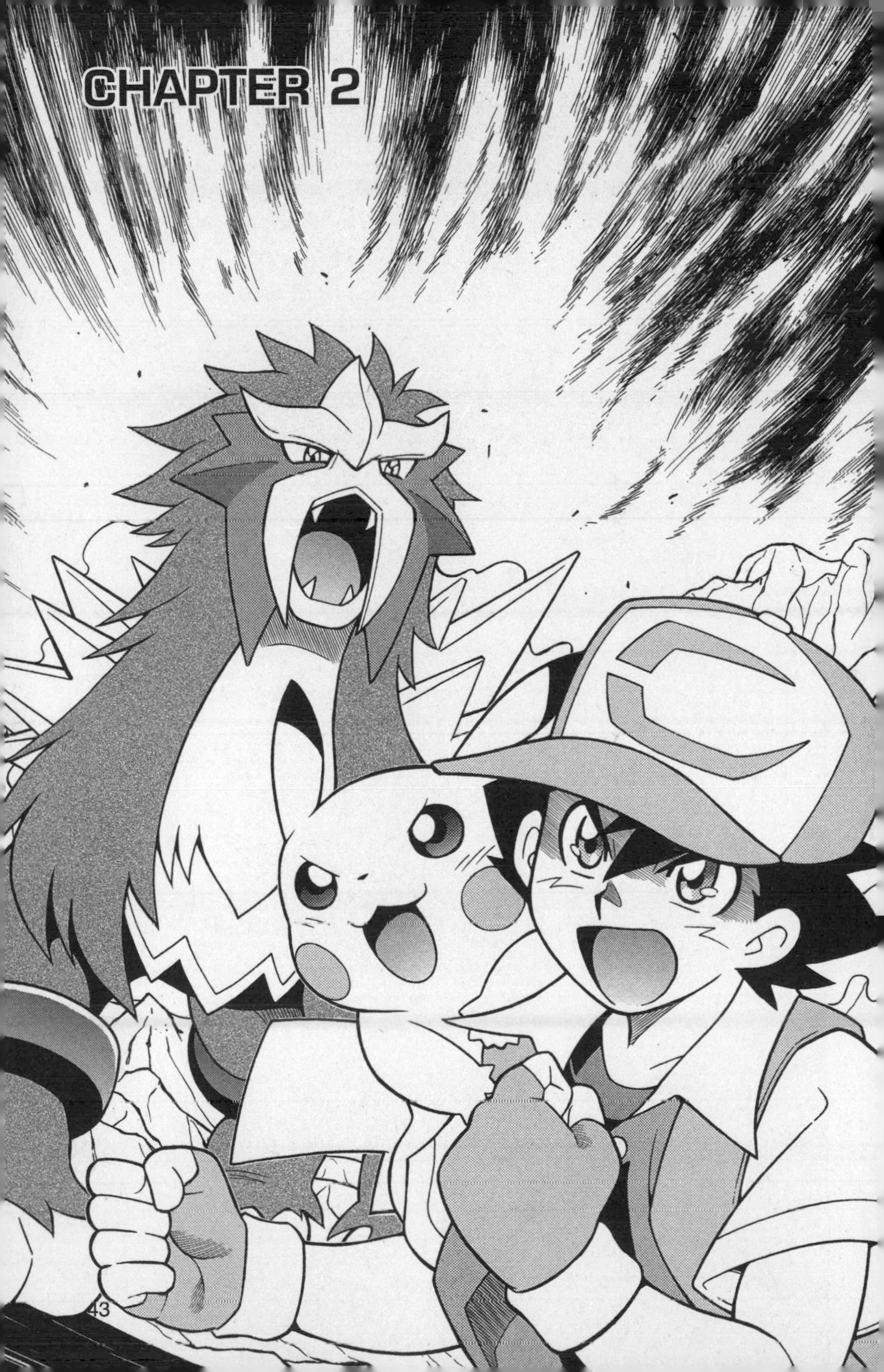
CHAPTER 2

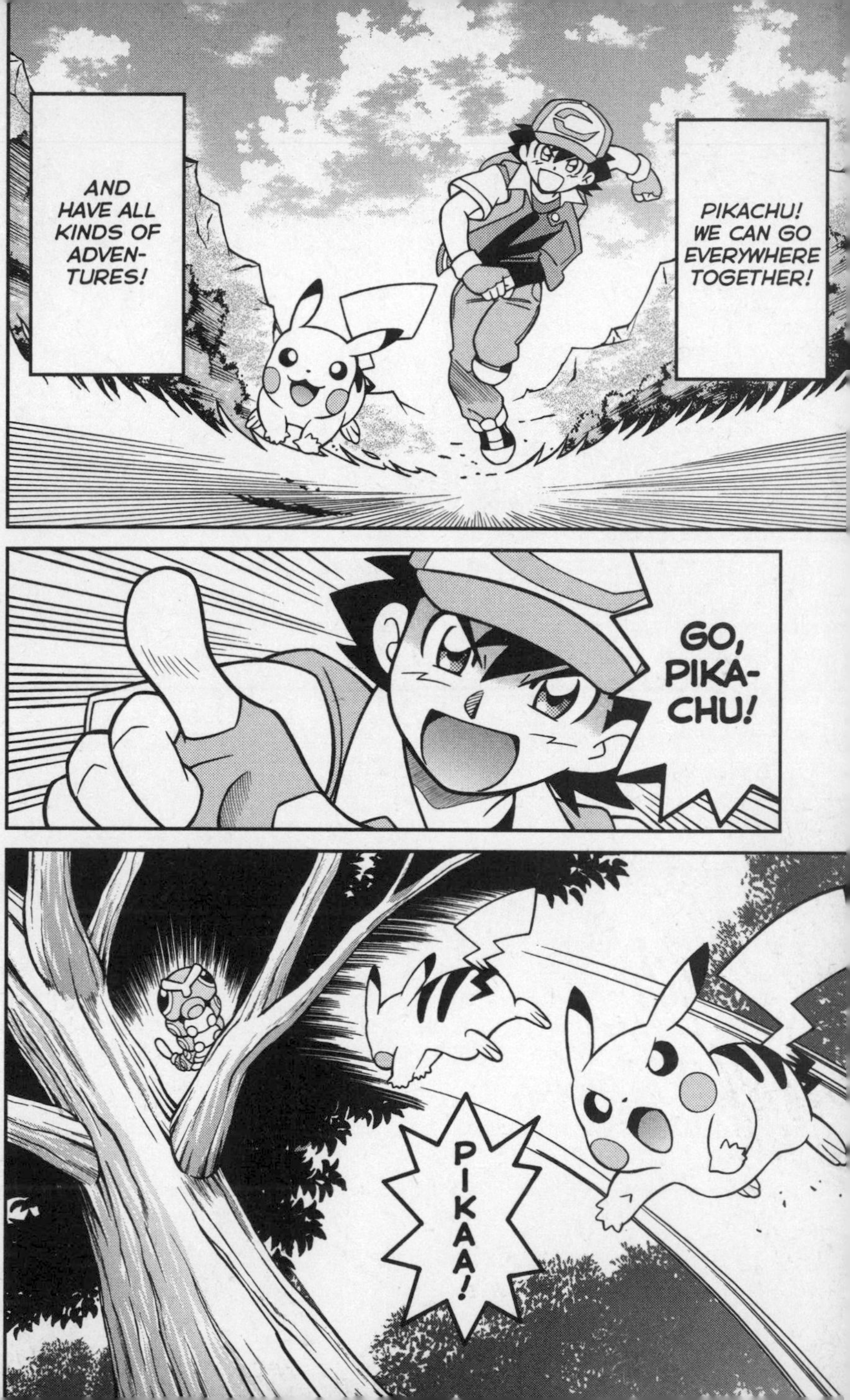
PIKACHU! WE CAN GO EVERYWHERE TOGETHER!
AND HAVE ALL KINDS OF ADVEN-TURES!
GO, PIKA-CHU!
PIKAA!

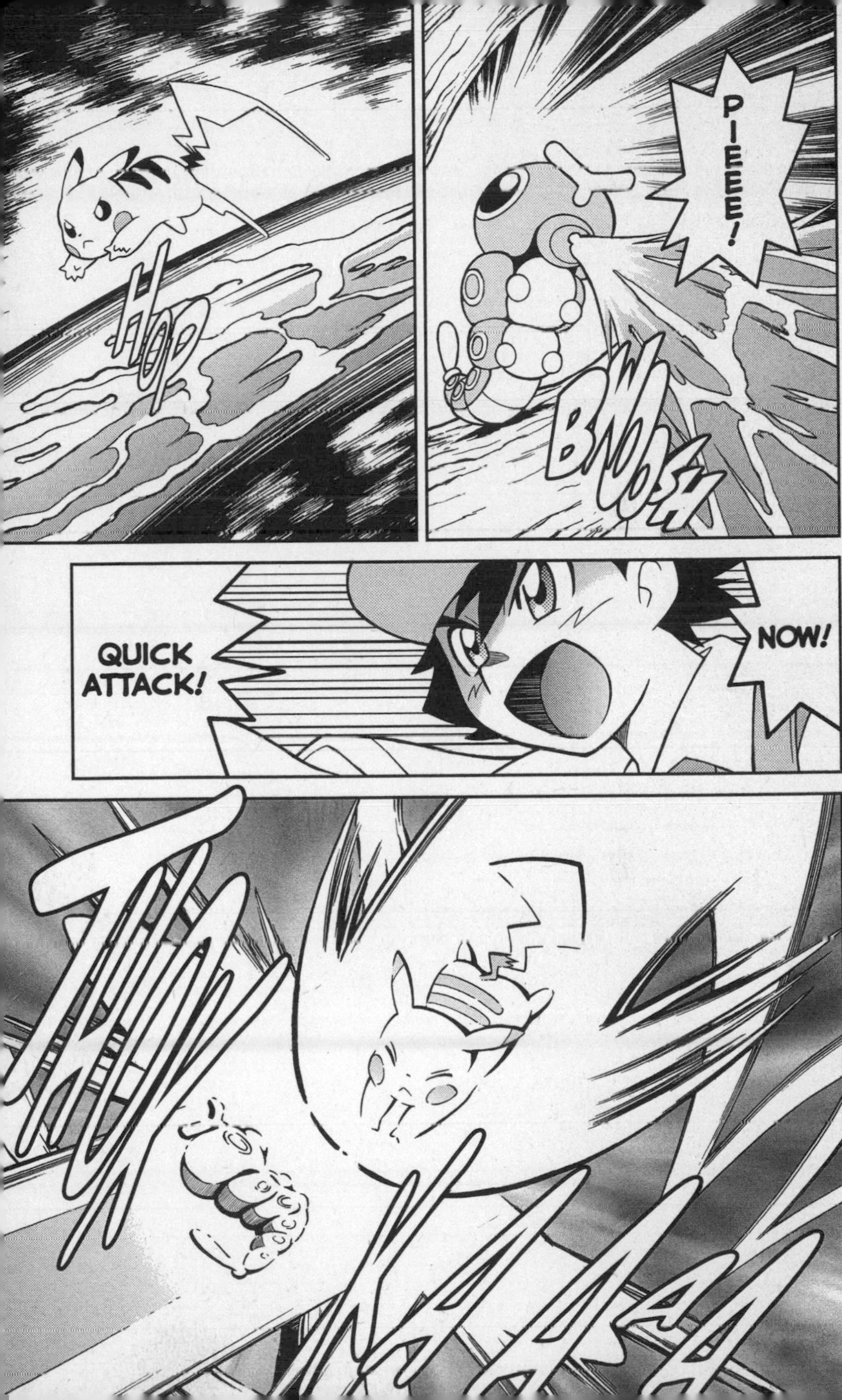
PIEEE!
BWOOSH
HOP
NOW!
QUICK ATTACK!

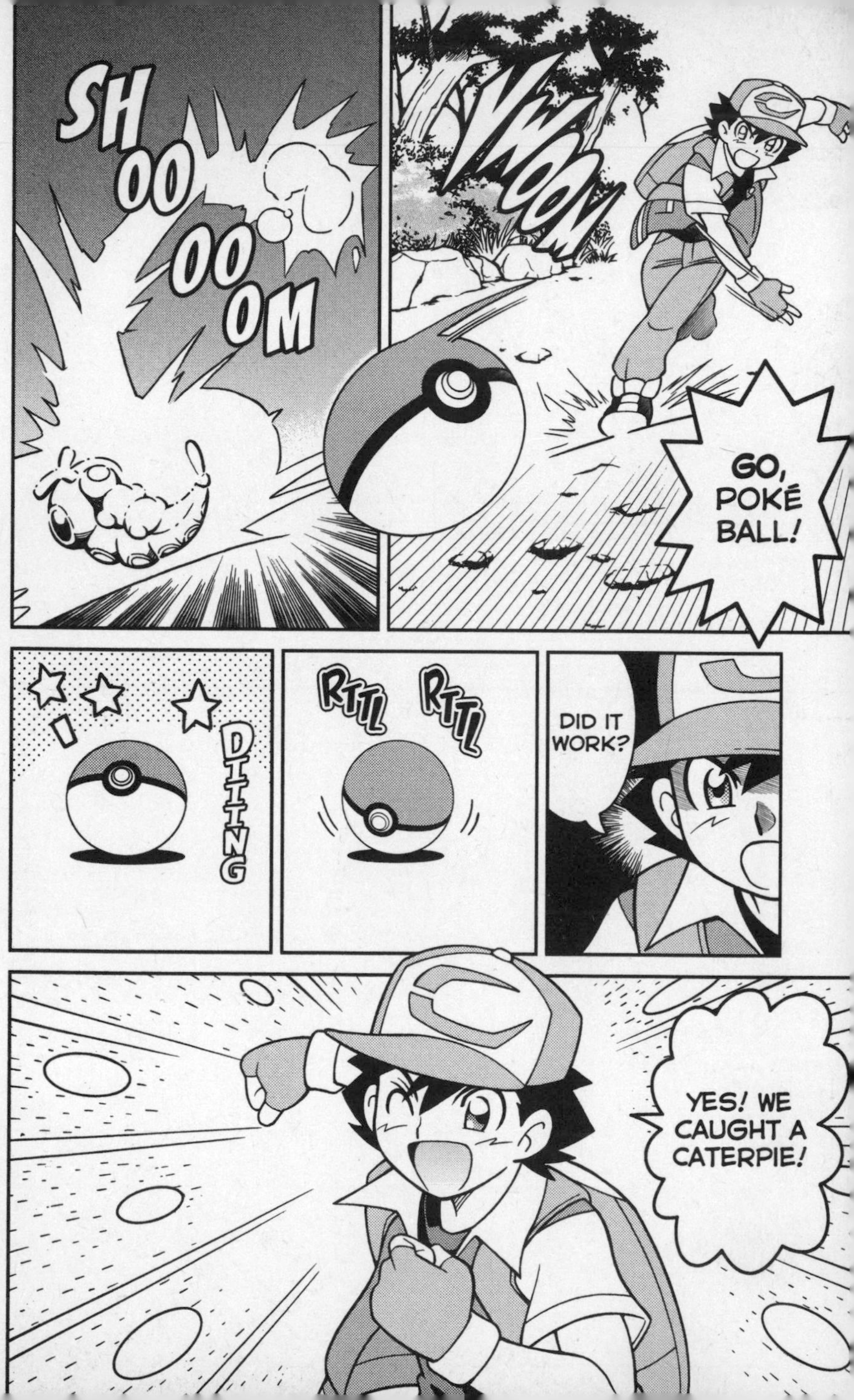
VWOOM
GO, POKÉ BALL!
SHOOOOOOM
DID IT WORK?
RTTL RTTL
DIIING
YES! WE CAUGHT A CATERPIE!

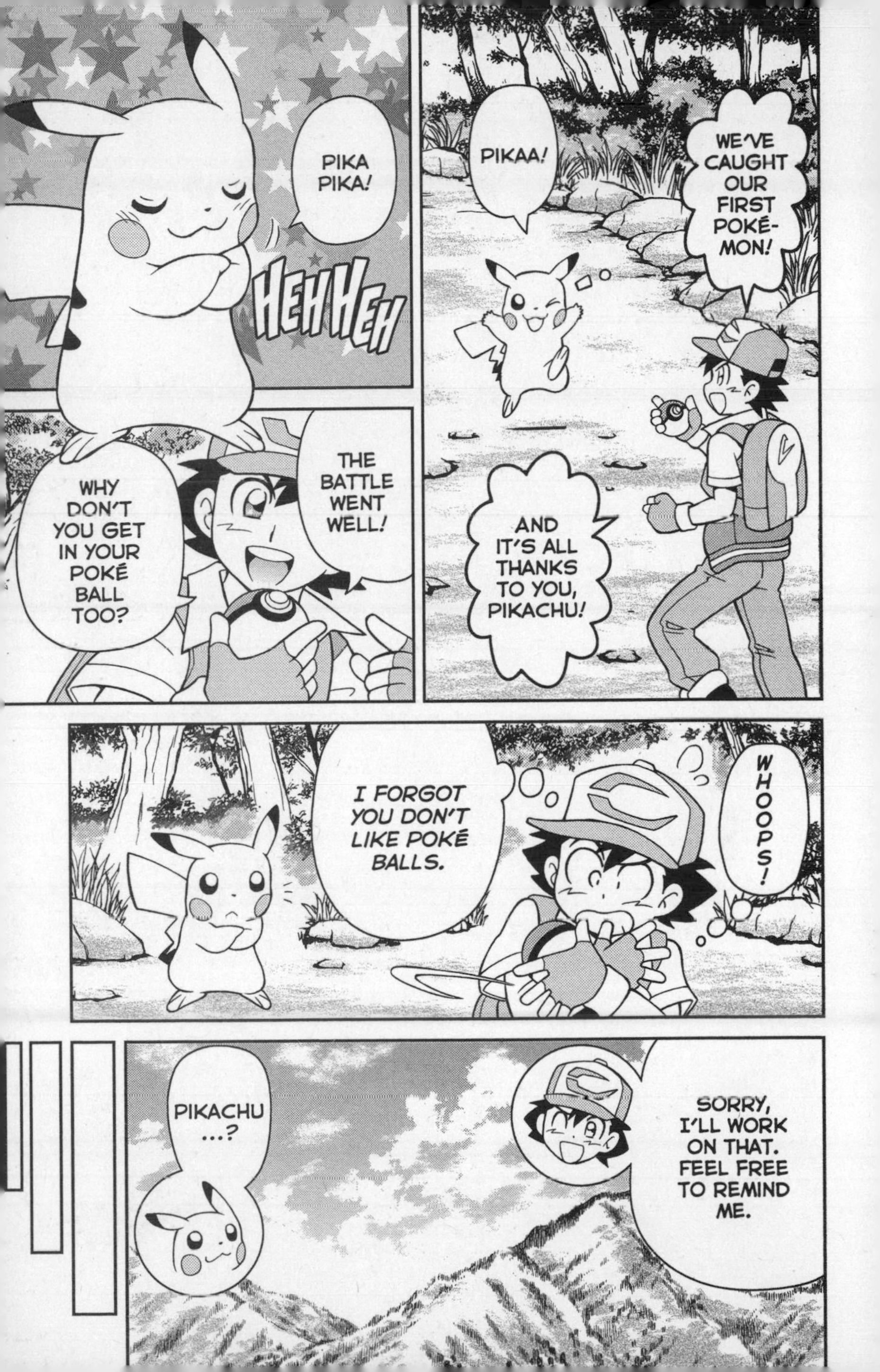
WE'VE CAUGHT OUR FIRST POKÉMON!
PIKAA!
AND IT'S ALL THANKS TO YOU, PIKACHU!
PIKA PIKA!
HEH HEH
THE BATTLE WENT WELL!
WHY DON'T YOU GET IN YOUR POKÉ BALL TOO?
WHOOPS!
I FORGOT YOU DON'T LIKE POKÉ BALLS.
SORRY, I'LL WORK ON THAT. FEEL FREE TO REMIND ME.
PIKACHU ...?

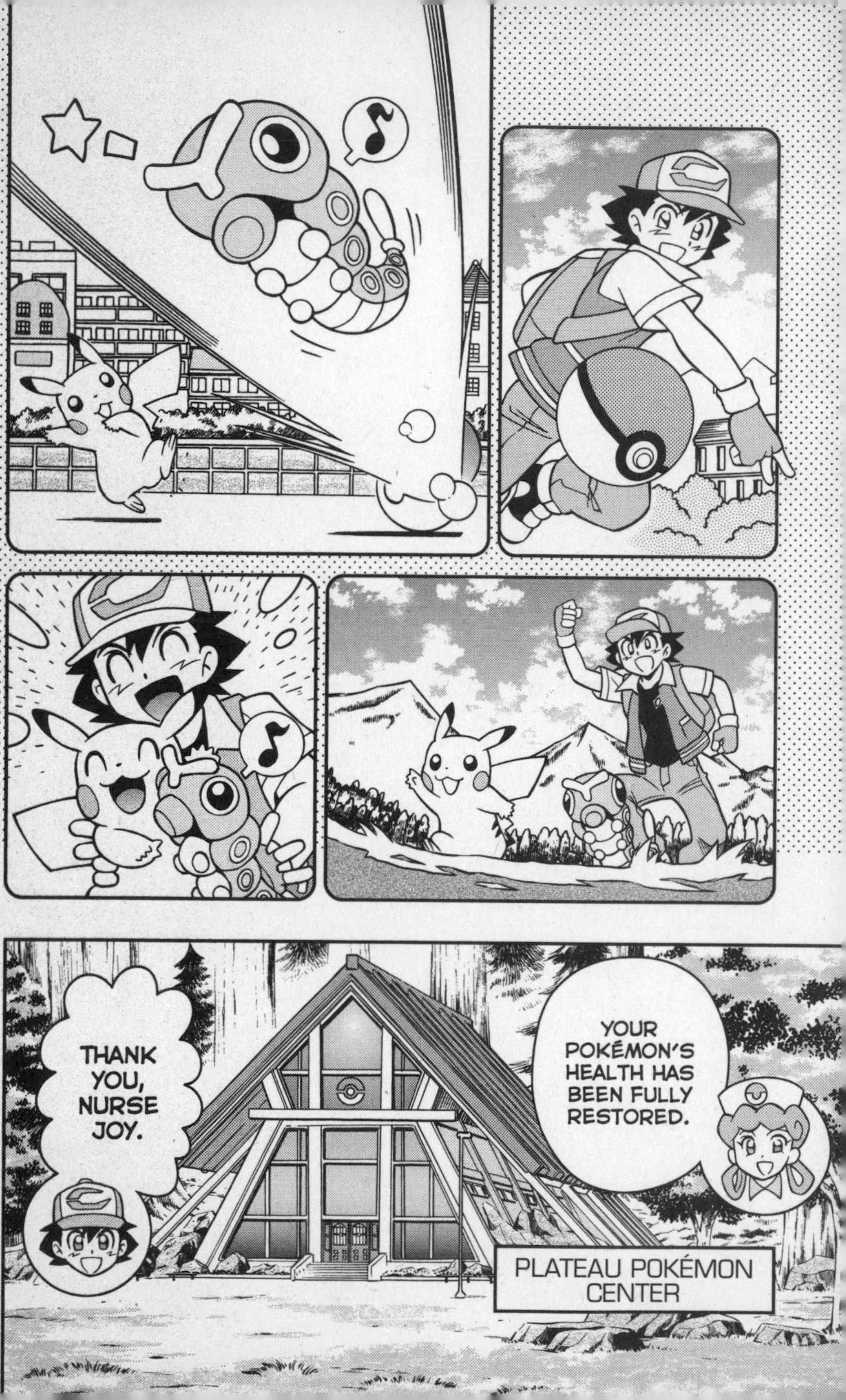
YOUR POKÉMON'S HEALTH HAS BEEN FULLY RESTORED.
THANK YOU, NURSE JOY.
PLATEAU POKÉMON CENTER

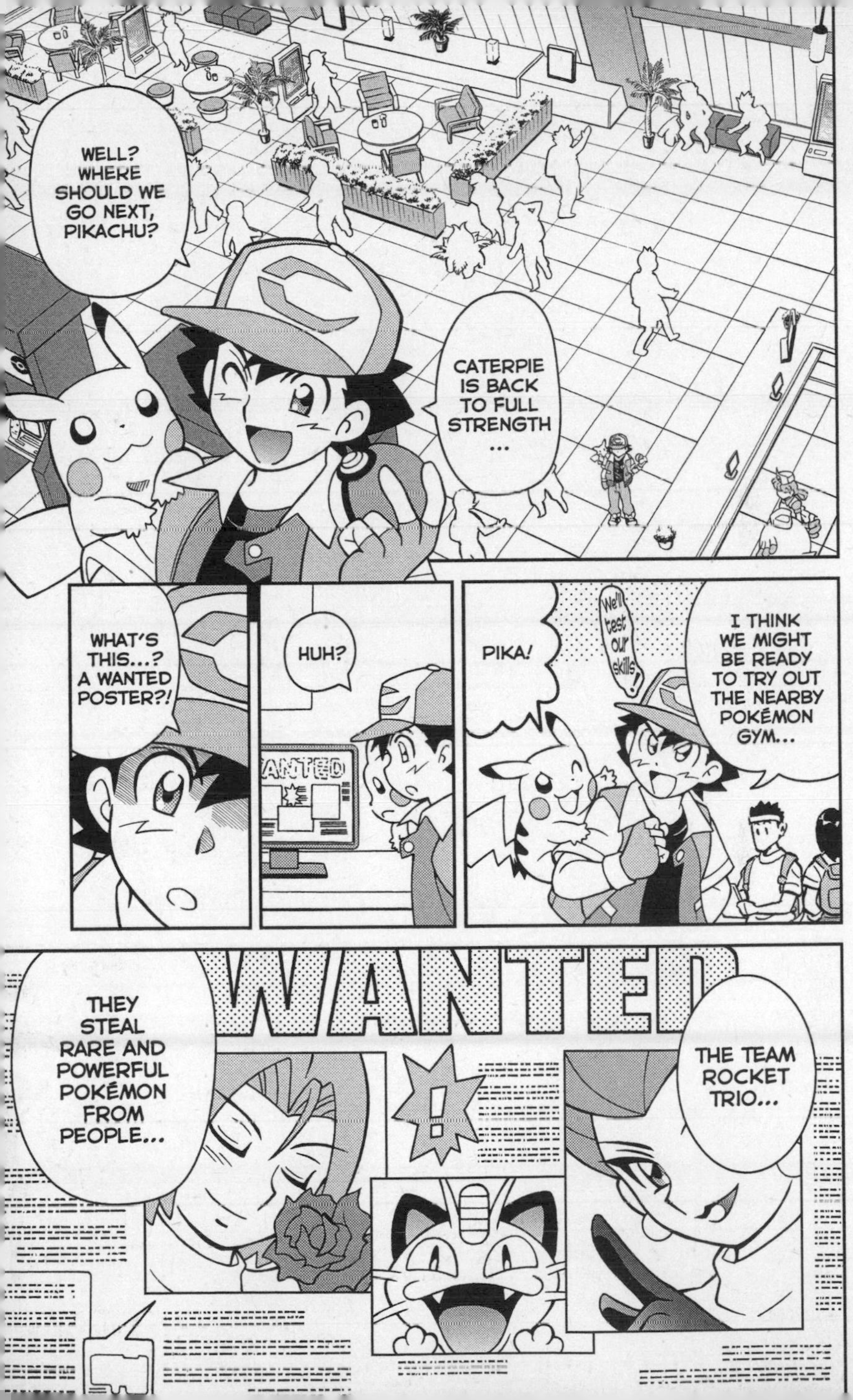
WELL? WHERE SHOULD WE GO NEXT, PIKACHU?
CATERPIE IS BACK TO FULL STRENGTH ...
I THINK WE MIGHT BE READY TO TRY OUT THE NEARBY POKÉMON GYM...
PIKA!
We'll test our skills!
HUH?
WANTED
WHAT'S THIS...? A WANTED POSTER?!
WANTED
THE TEAM ROCKET TRIO...
!
THEY STEAL RARE AND POWERFUL POKÉMON FROM PEOPLE...

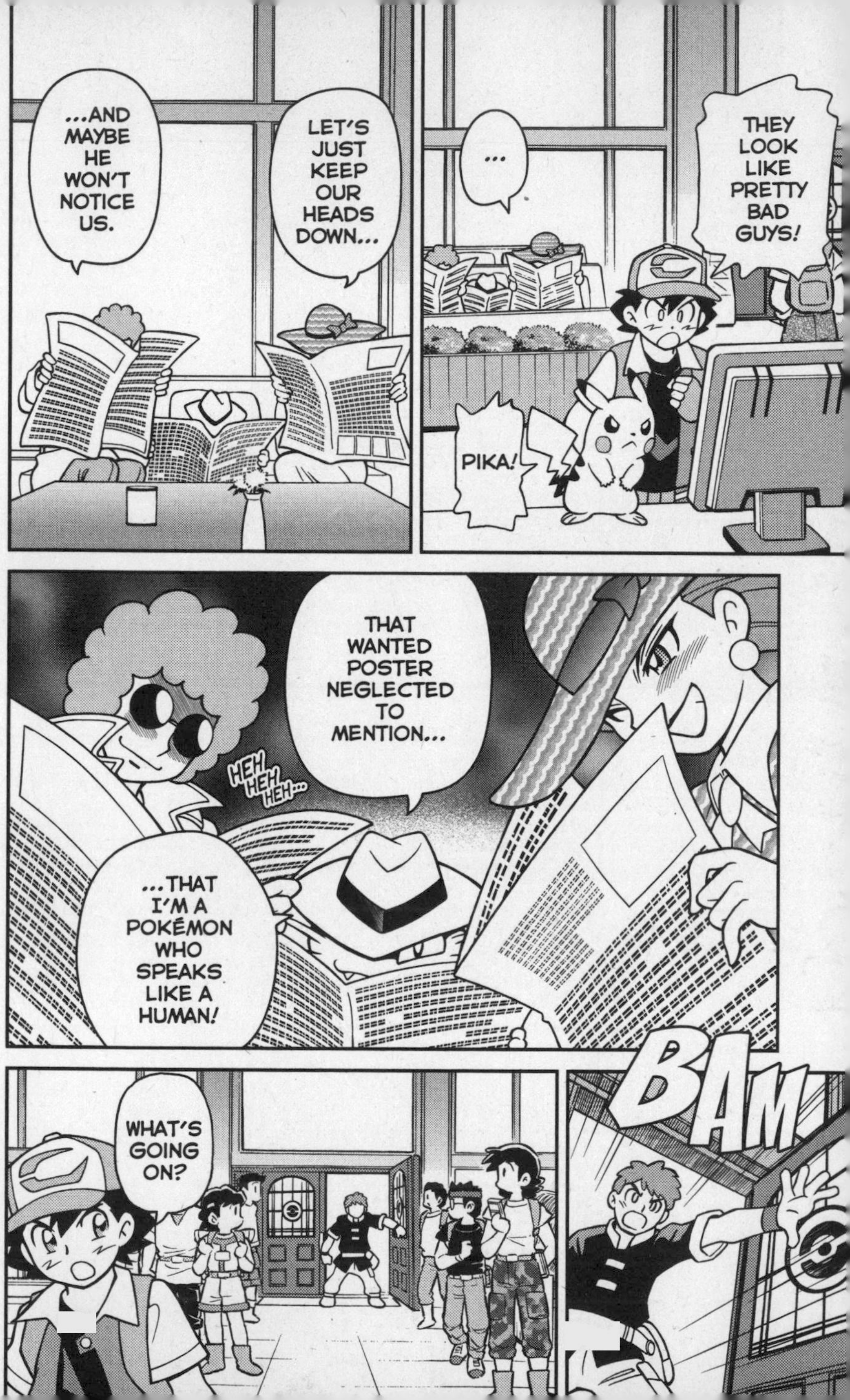
THEY LOOK LIKE PRETTY BAD GUYS!
...
PIKA!
LET'S JUST KEEP OUR HEADS DOWN...
...AND MAYBE HE WON'T NOTICE US.
THAT WANTED POSTER NEGLECTED TO MENTION...
HEH HEH HEH...
...THAT I'M A POKÉMON WHO SPEAKS LIKE A HUMAN!
BAM
WHAT'S GOING ON?

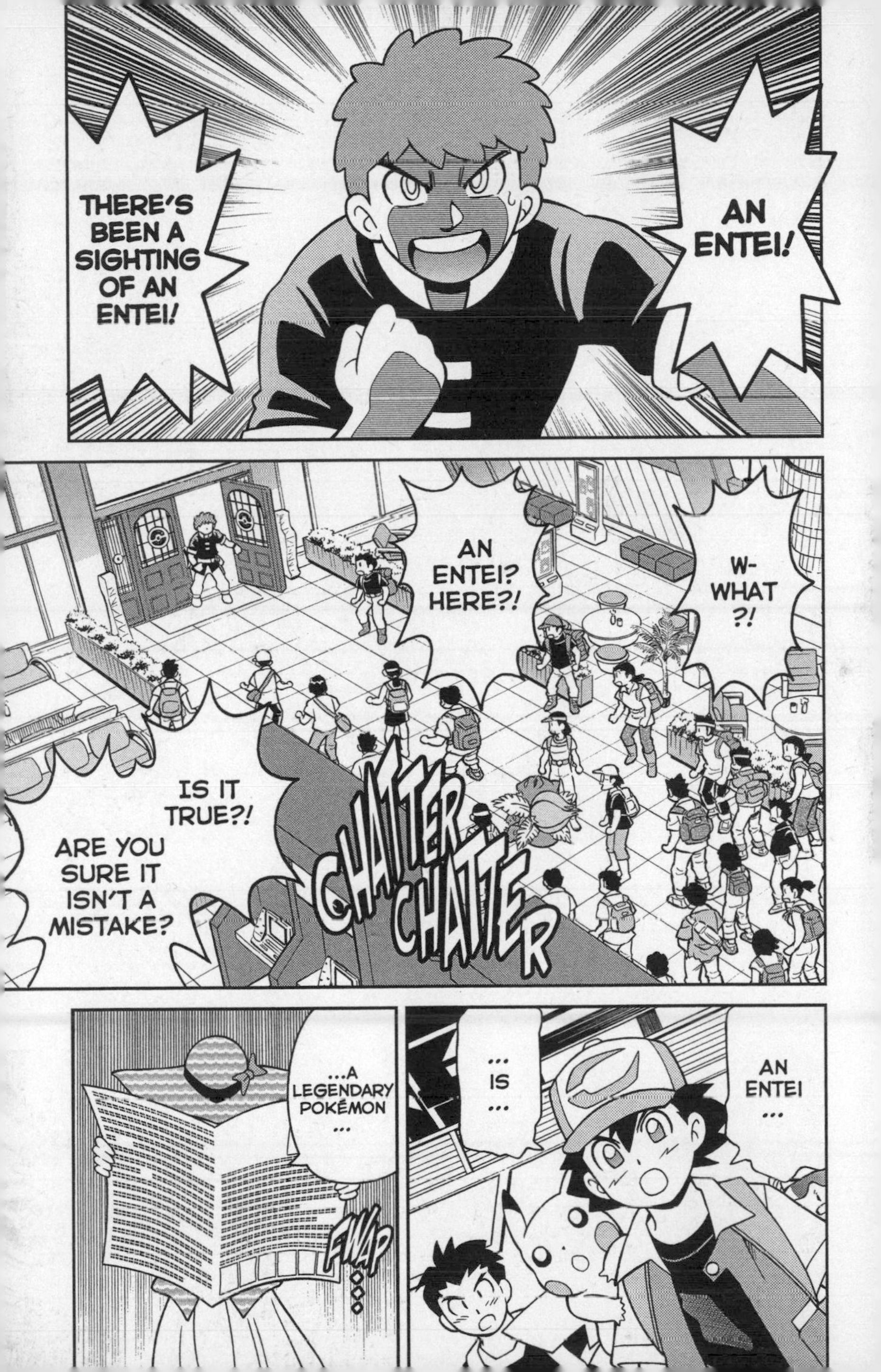
AN ENTEI!
THERE'S BEEN A SIGHTING OF AN ENTEI!
W-WHAT?!
AN ENTEI? HERE?!
IS IT TRUE?!
ARE YOU SURE IT ISN'T A MISTAKE?
CHATTER CHATTER
AN ENTEI ...
... IS ...
...A LEGENDARY POKÉMON ...
FWAP

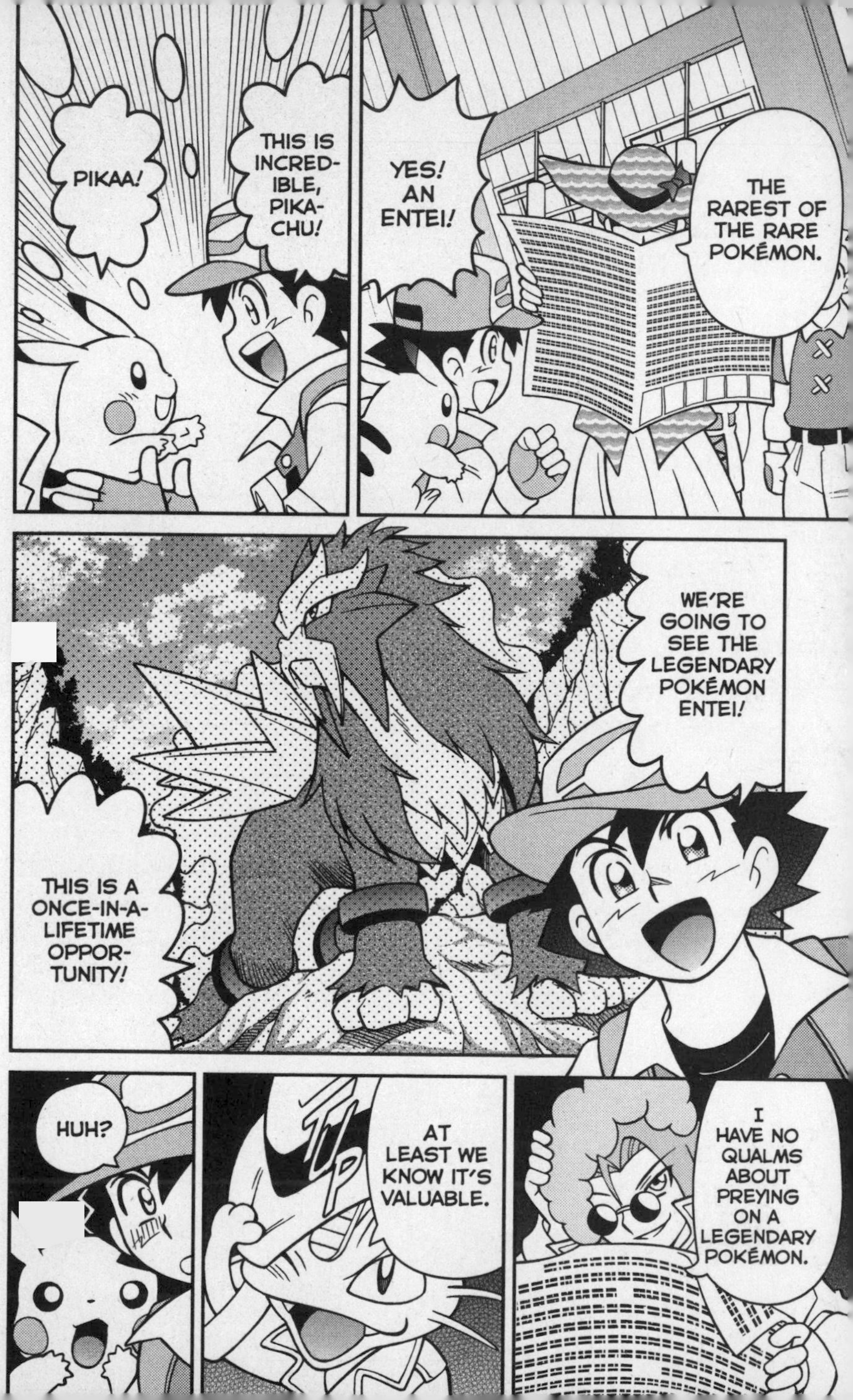
THE RAREST OF THE RARE POKÉMON.
YES! AN ENTEI!
THIS IS INCRED-IBLE, PIKA-CHU!
PIKAA!
WE'RE GOING TO SEE THE LEGENDARY POKÉMON ENTEI!
THIS IS A ONCE-IN-A-LIFETIME OPPOR-TUNITY!
I HAVE NO QUALMS ABOUT PREYING ON A LEGENDARY POKÉMON.
AT LEAST WE KNOW IT'S VALUABLE.
HUH?

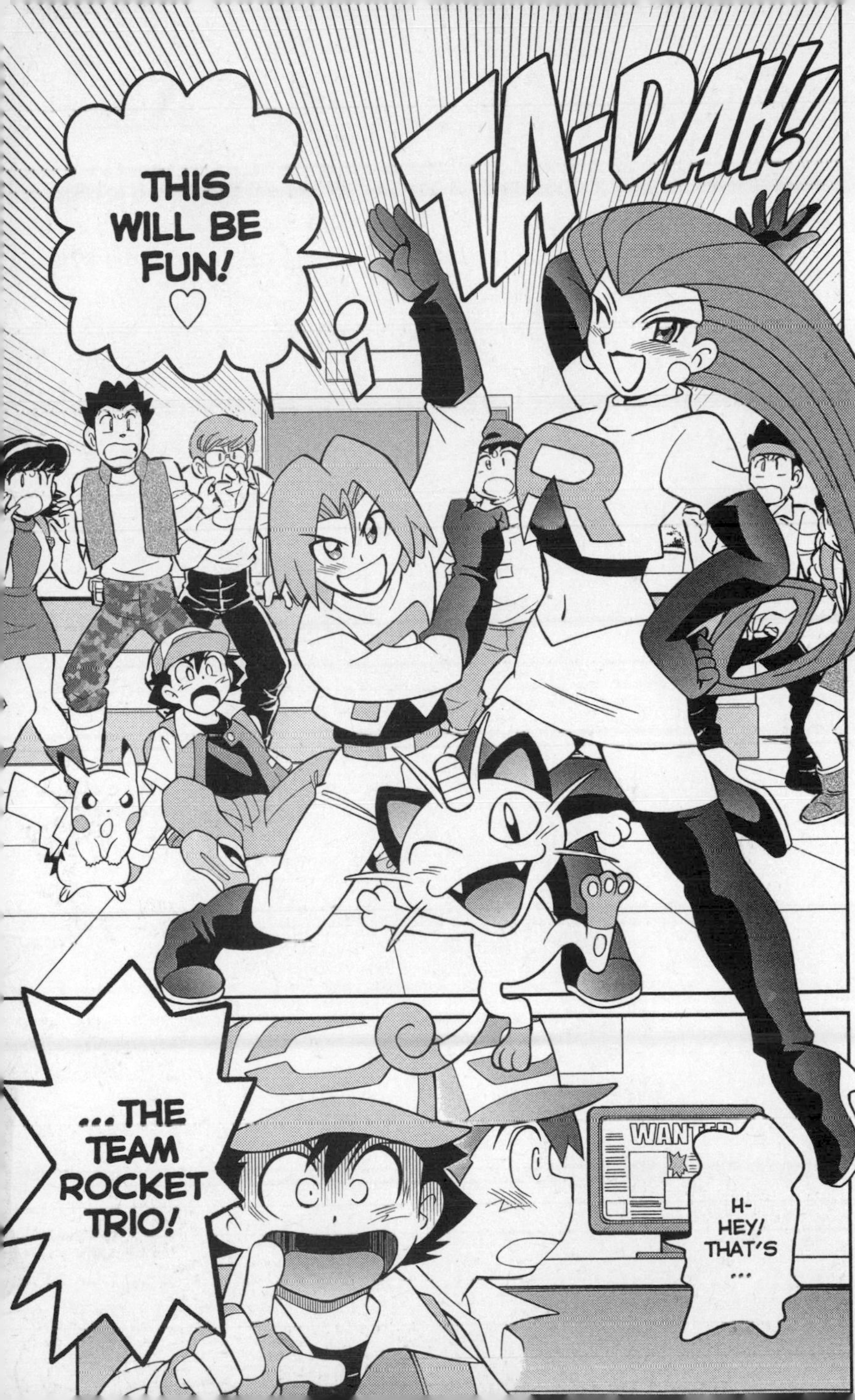
TA-DAH!
THIS WILL BE FUN! ♥
H-HEY! THAT'S...
...THE TEAM ROCKET TRIO!

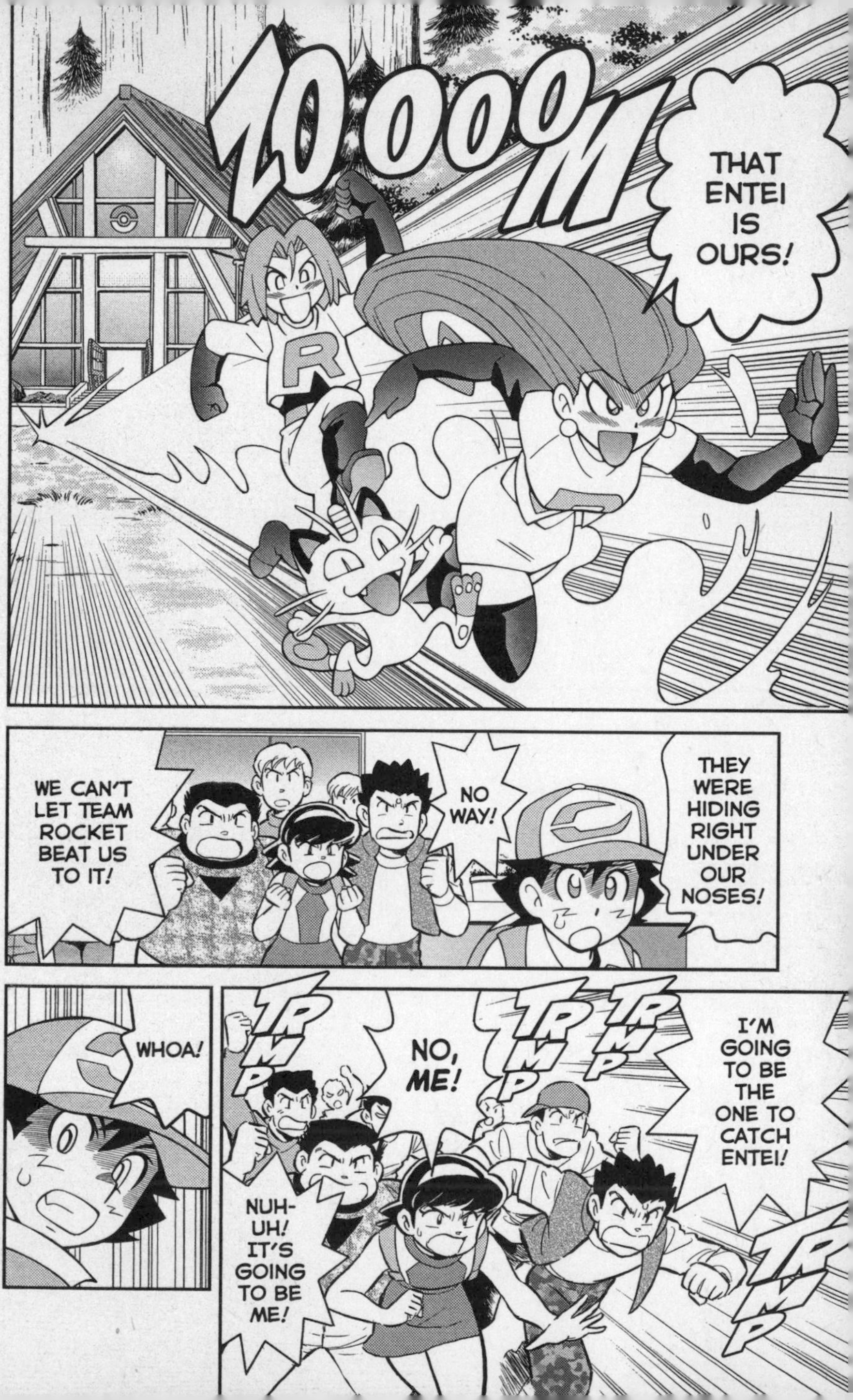
ZOOOOM
THAT ENTEI IS OURS!
THEY WERE HIDING RIGHT UNDER OUR NOSES!
NO WAY!
WE CAN'T LET TEAM ROCKET BEAT US TO IT!
I'M GOING TO BE THE ONE TO CATCH ENTEI!
TRMP TRMP
NO, ME!
TRMP
NUH-UH! IT'S GOING TO BE ME!
TRMP
WHOA!

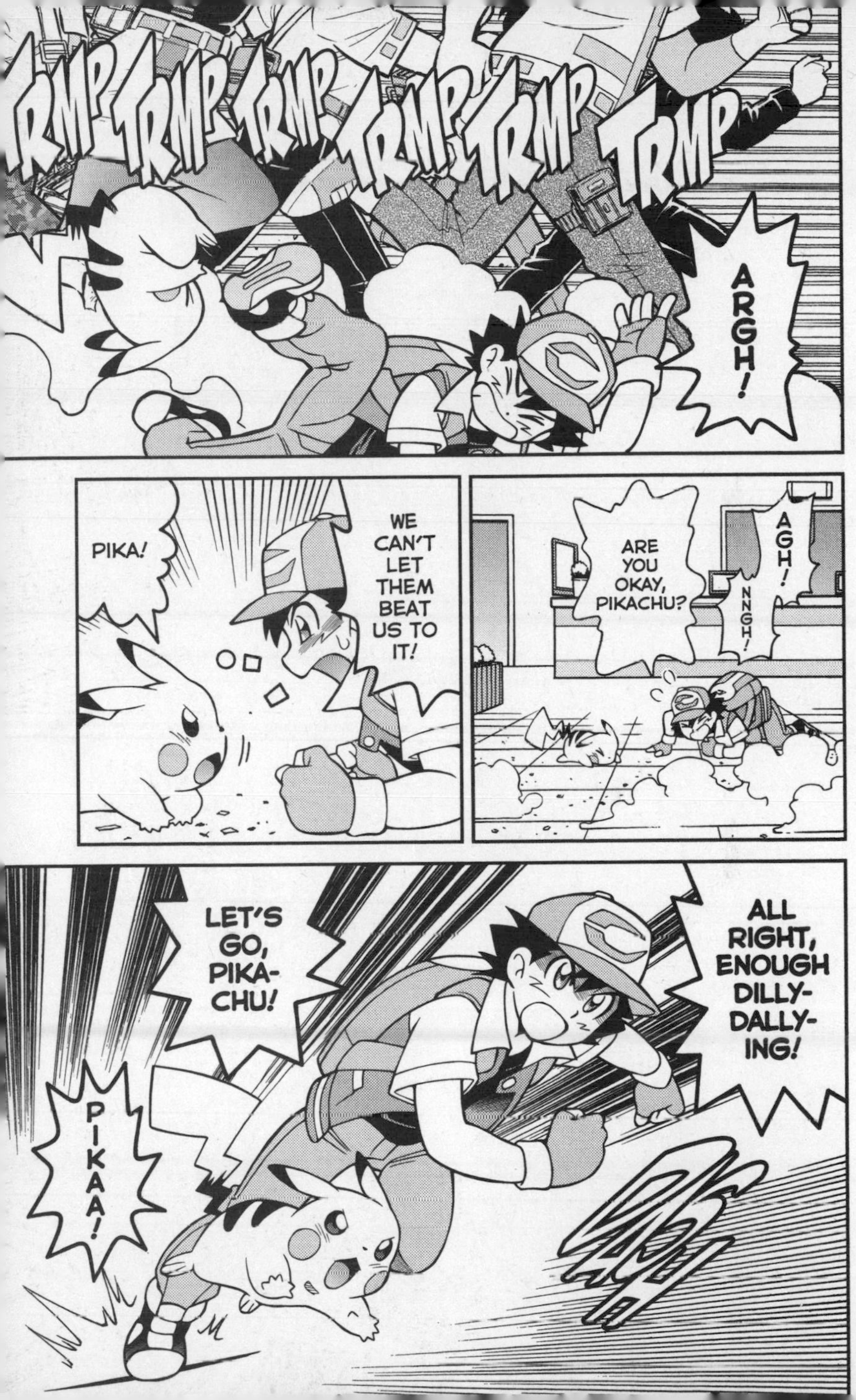
TRMP TRMP TRMP TRMP TRMP TRMP TRMP
ARGH!
ARE YOU OKAY, PIKACHU?
AGH!
NNGH!
WE CAN'T LET THEM BEAT US TO IT!
PIKA!
ALL RIGHT, ENOUGH DILLY-DALLYING!
LET'S GO, PIKA-CHU!
PIKAA!

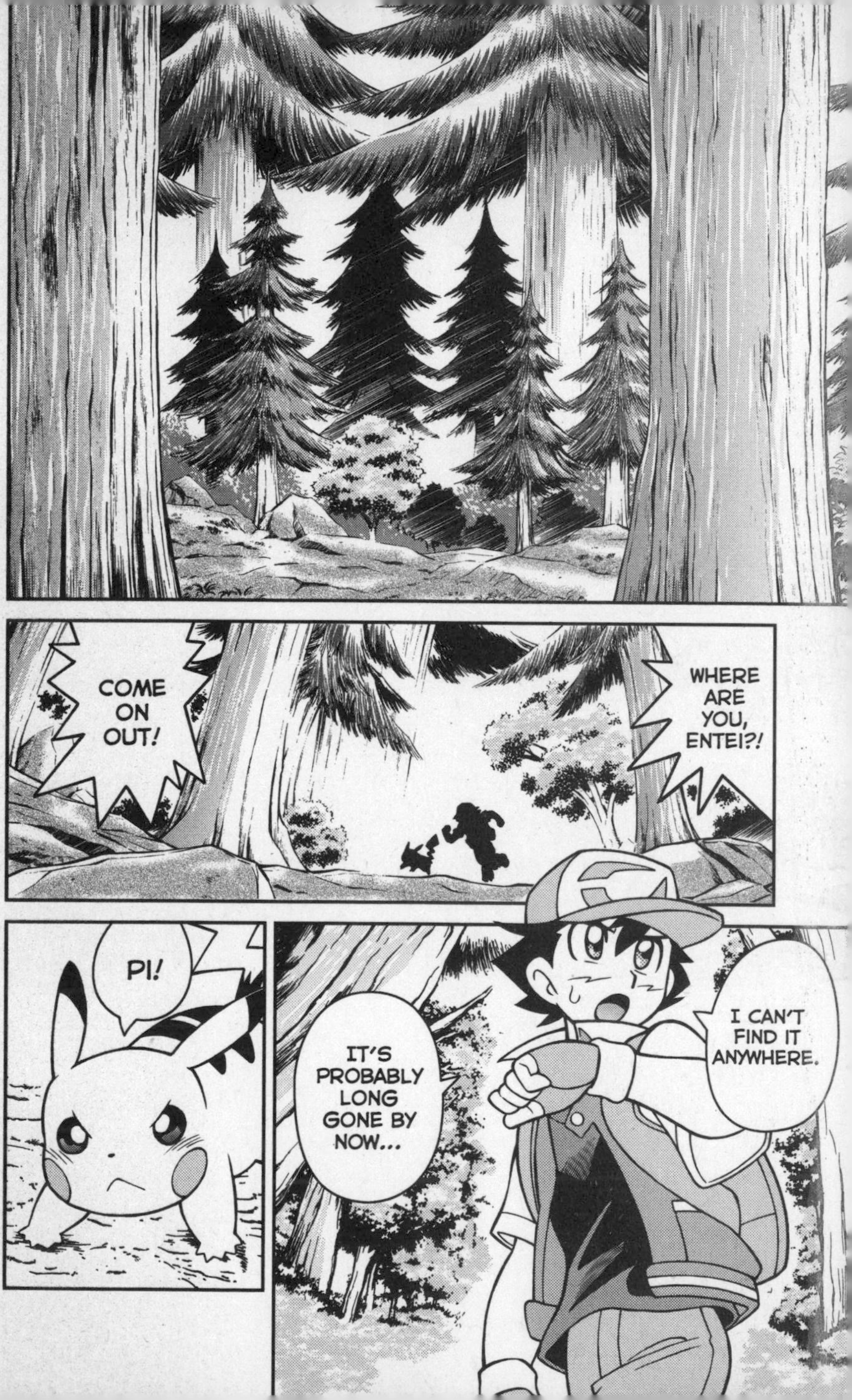
WHERE ARE YOU, ENTEI?!
COME ON OUT!
I CAN'T FIND IT ANYWHERE.
IT'S PROBABLY LONG GONE BY NOW...
PI!

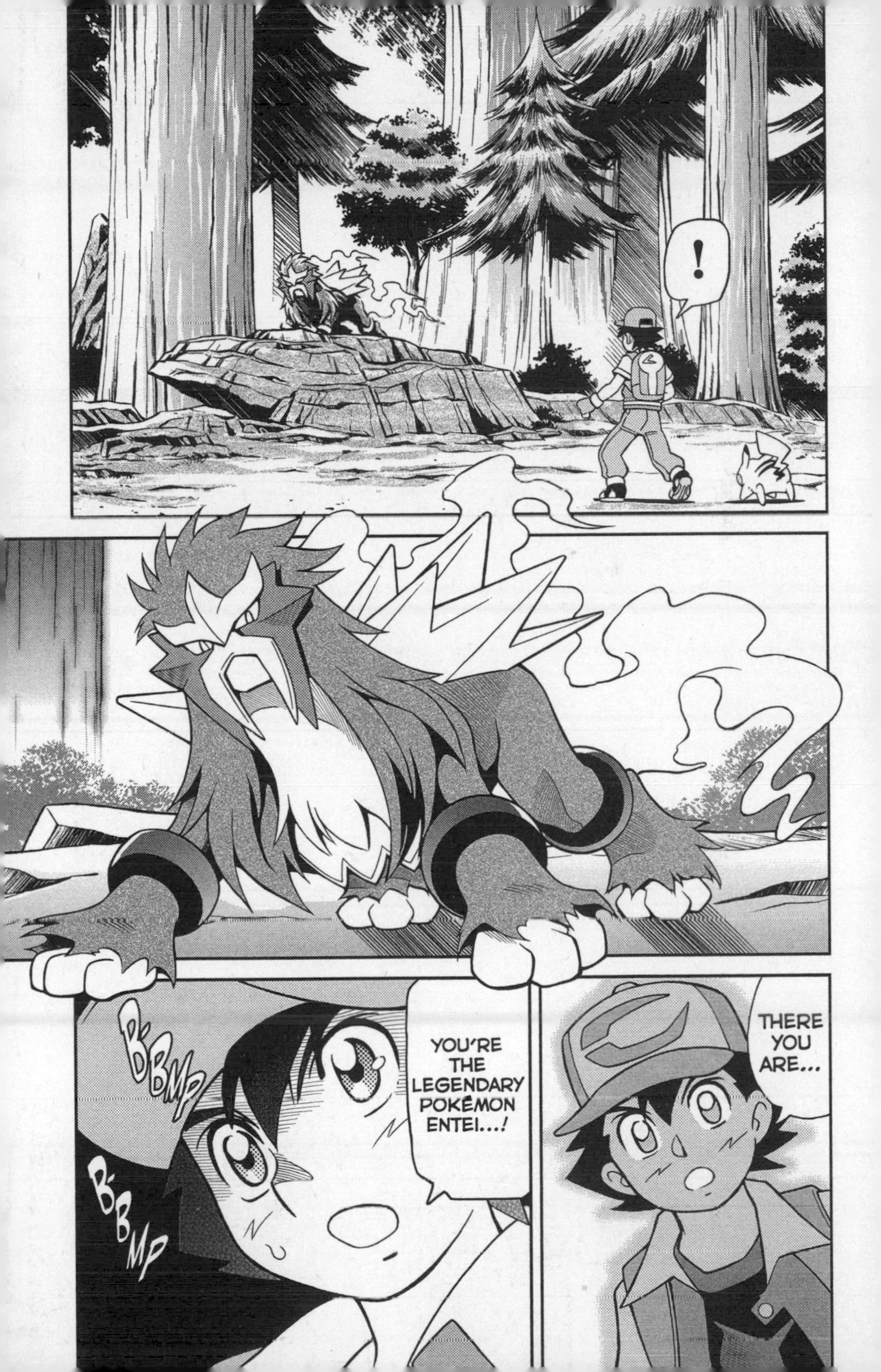
!
THERE YOU ARE...
YOU'RE THE LEGENDARY POKÉMON ENTEI...!
B'BMP
B'BMP

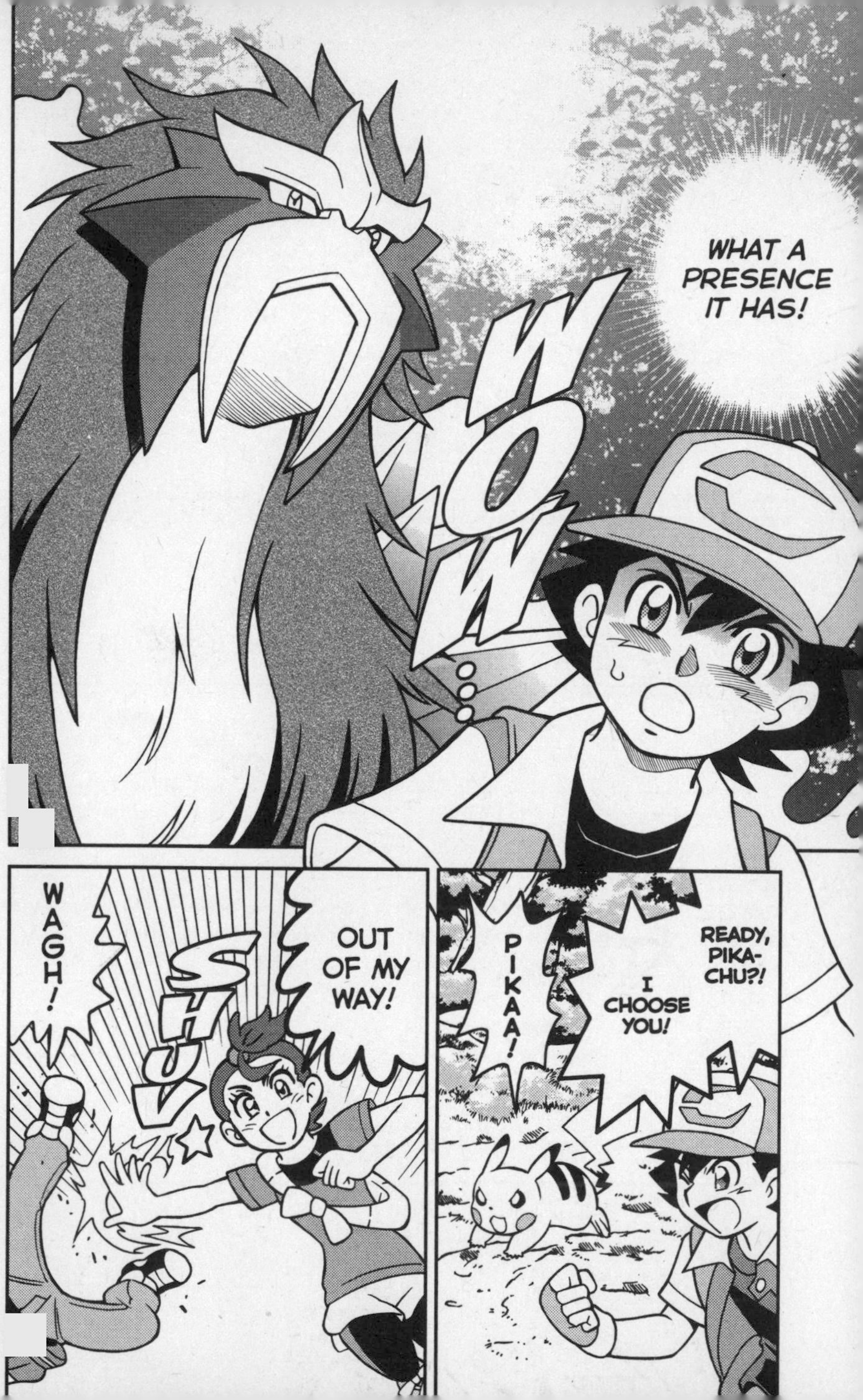
WHAT A PRESENCE IT HAS!
WOW
READY, PIKA-CHU?!
I CHOOSE YOU!
PIKAA!
OUT OF MY WAY!
SHUV
WAGH!

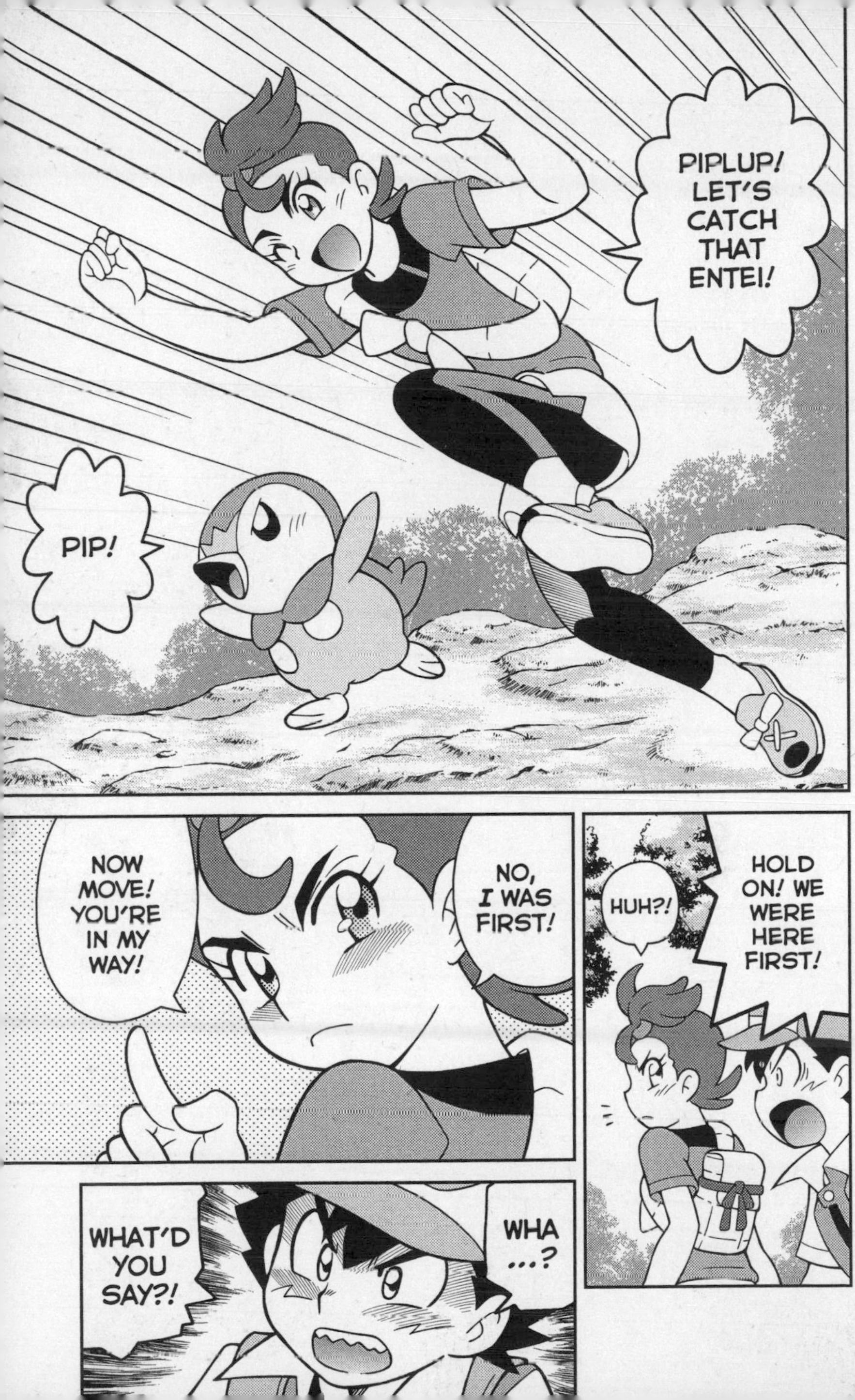
PIPLUP! LET'S CATCH THAT ENTEI!
PIP!
HOLD ON! WE WERE HERE FIRST!
HUH?!
NO, I WAS FIRST!
NOW MOVE! YOU'RE IN MY WAY!
WHA ...?
WHAT'D YOU SAY?!

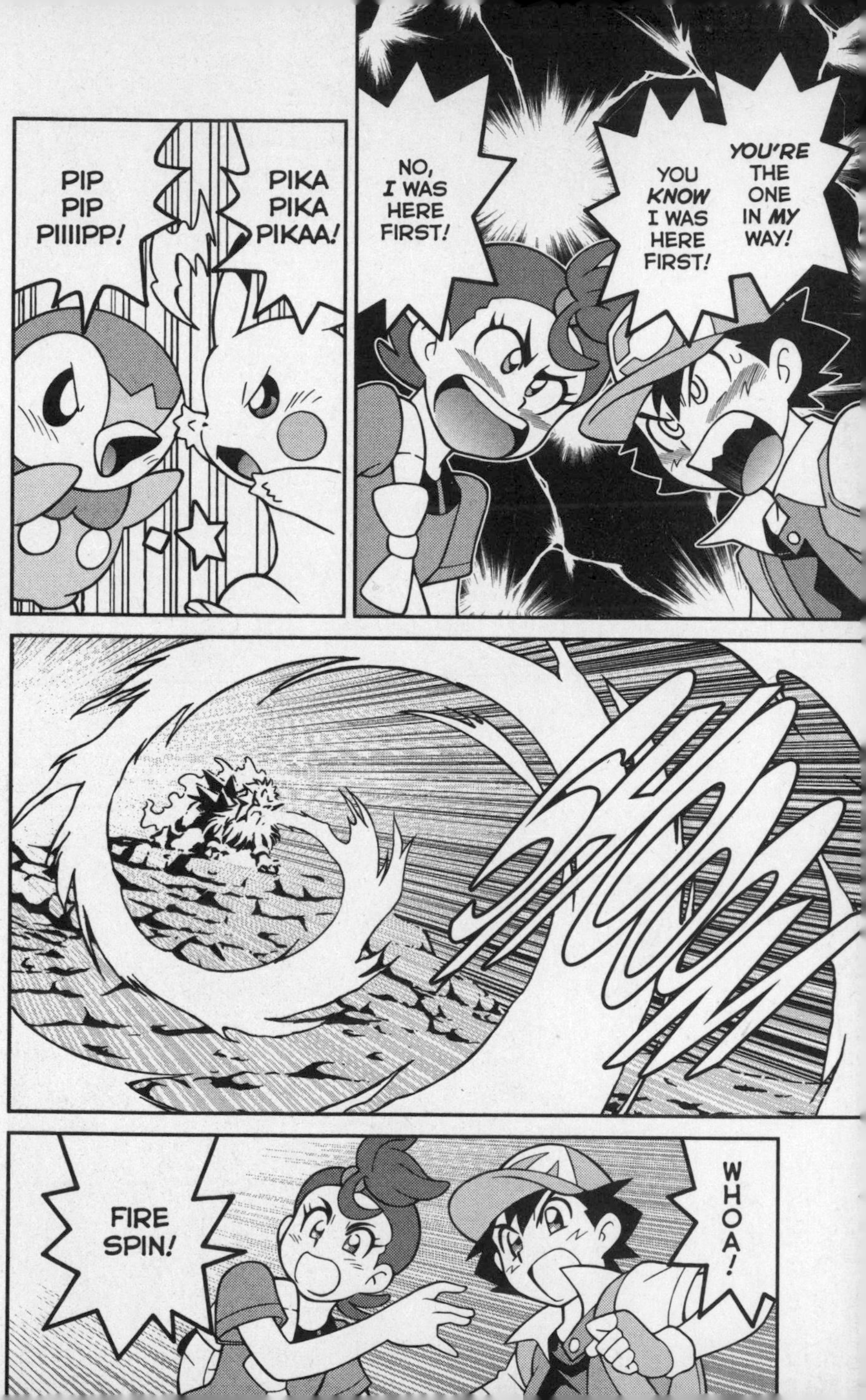
YOU'RE THE ONE IN MY WAY!
YOU KNOW I WAS HERE FIRST!
NO, I WAS HERE FIRST!
PIKA PIKA PIKAA!
PIP PIP PIIIIPP!
WHOA!
FIRE SPIN!

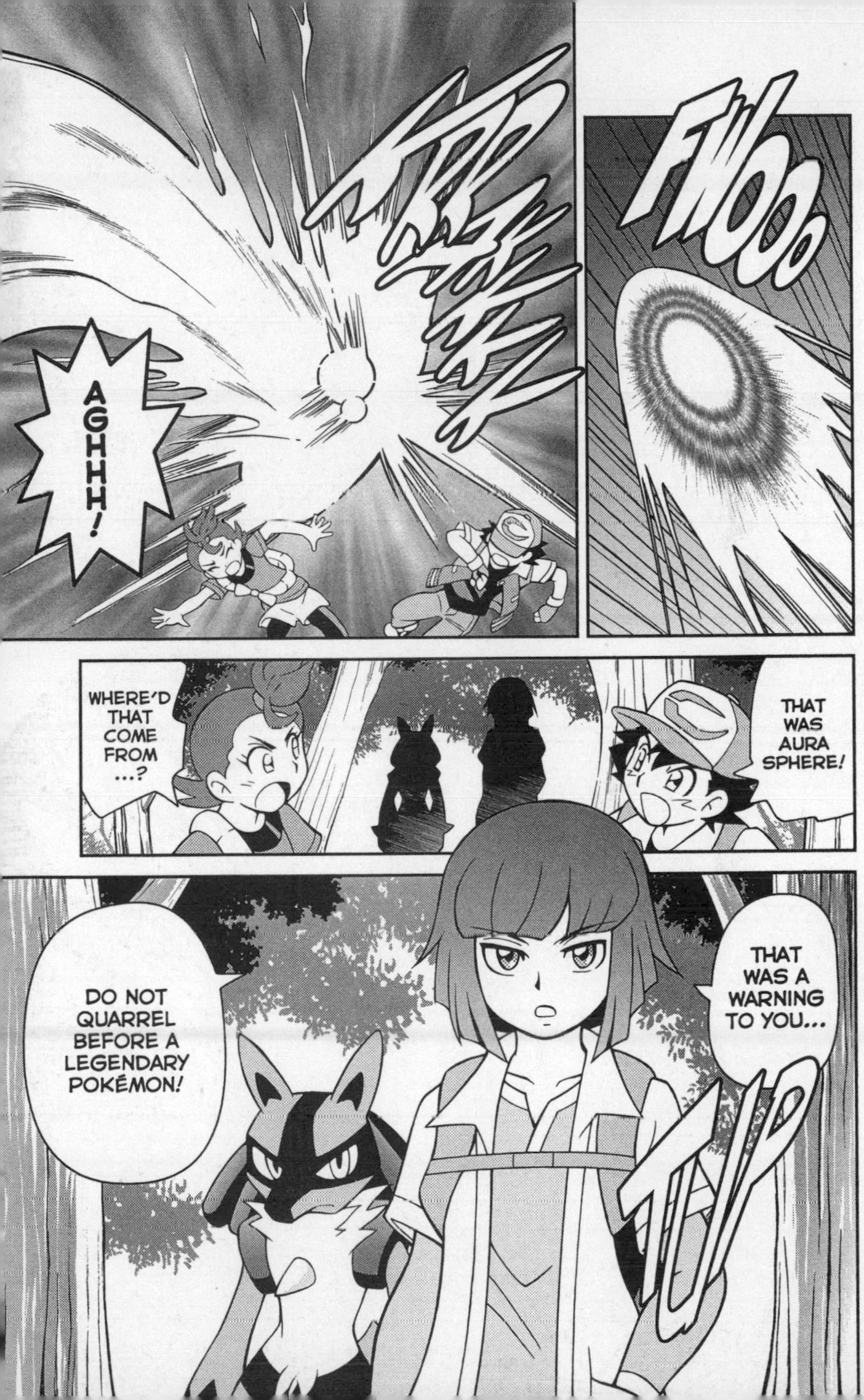
AGHHH!
THAT WAS AURA SPHERE!
WHERE'D THAT COME FROM ...?
THAT WAS A WARNING TO YOU...
DO NOT QUARREL BEFORE A LEGENDARY POKÉMON!

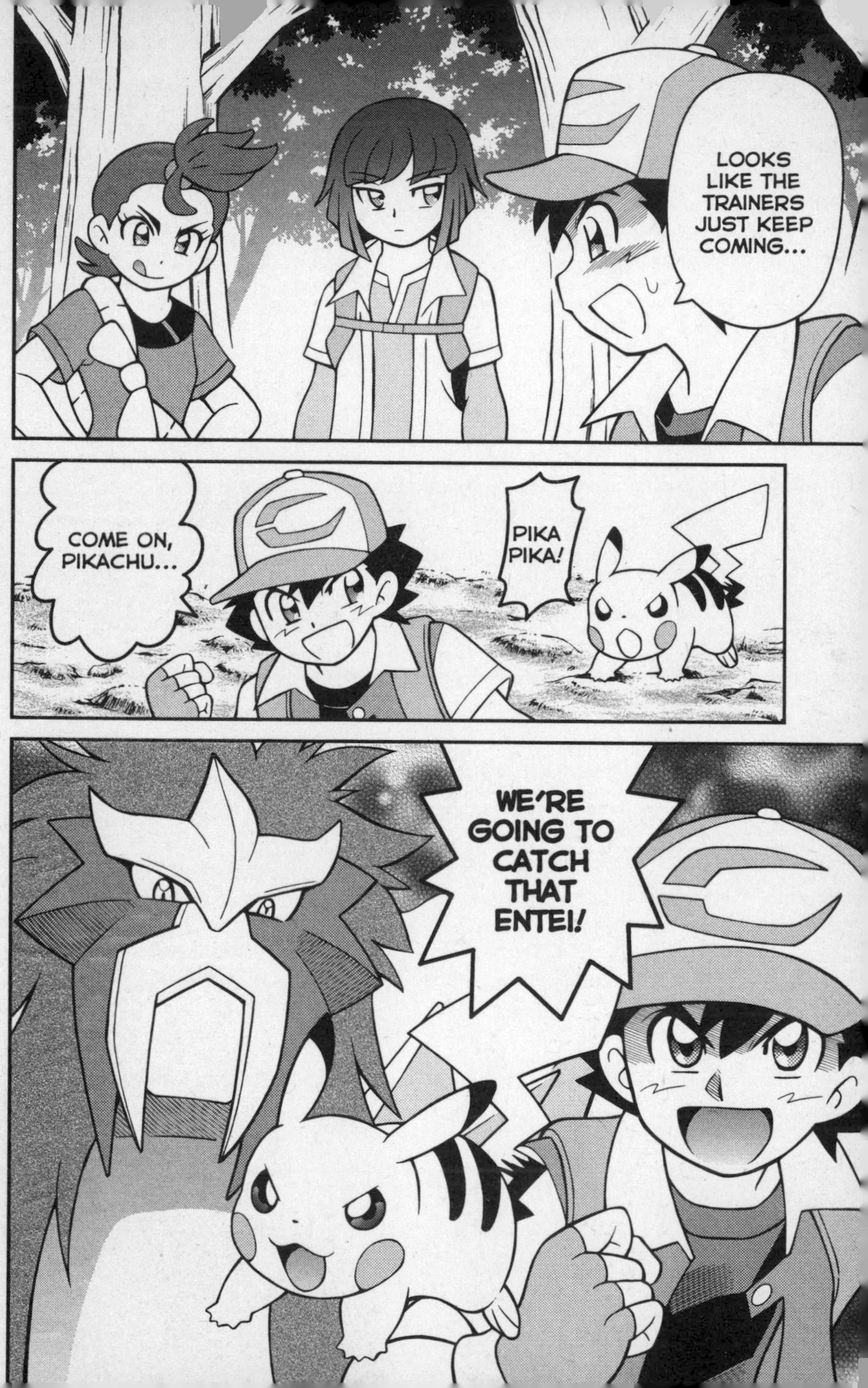
LOOKS LIKE THE TRAINERS JUST KEEP COMING...
PIKA PIKA!
COME ON, PIKACHU...
WE'RE GOING TO CATCH THAT ENTEI!

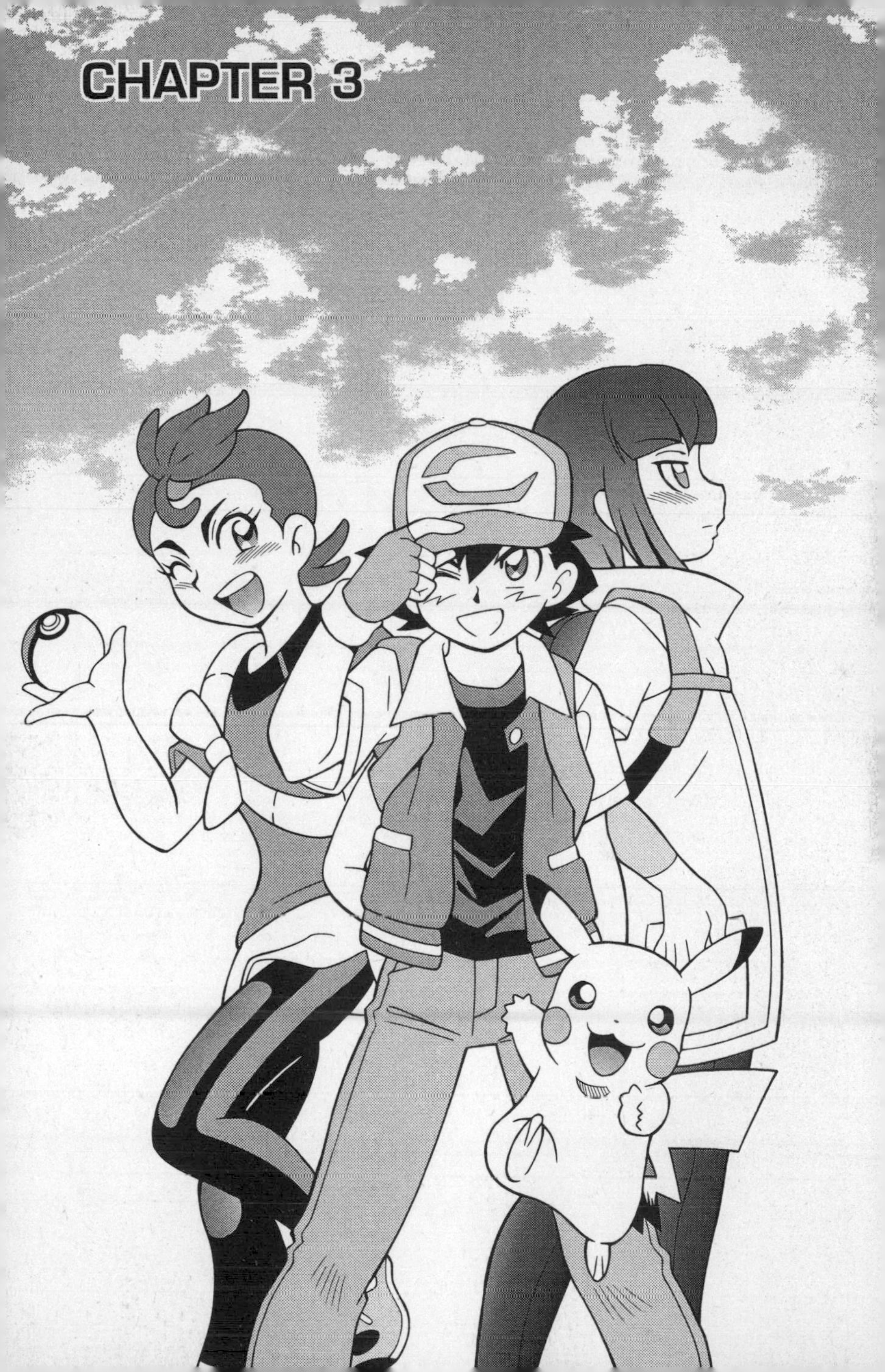
CHAPTER 3

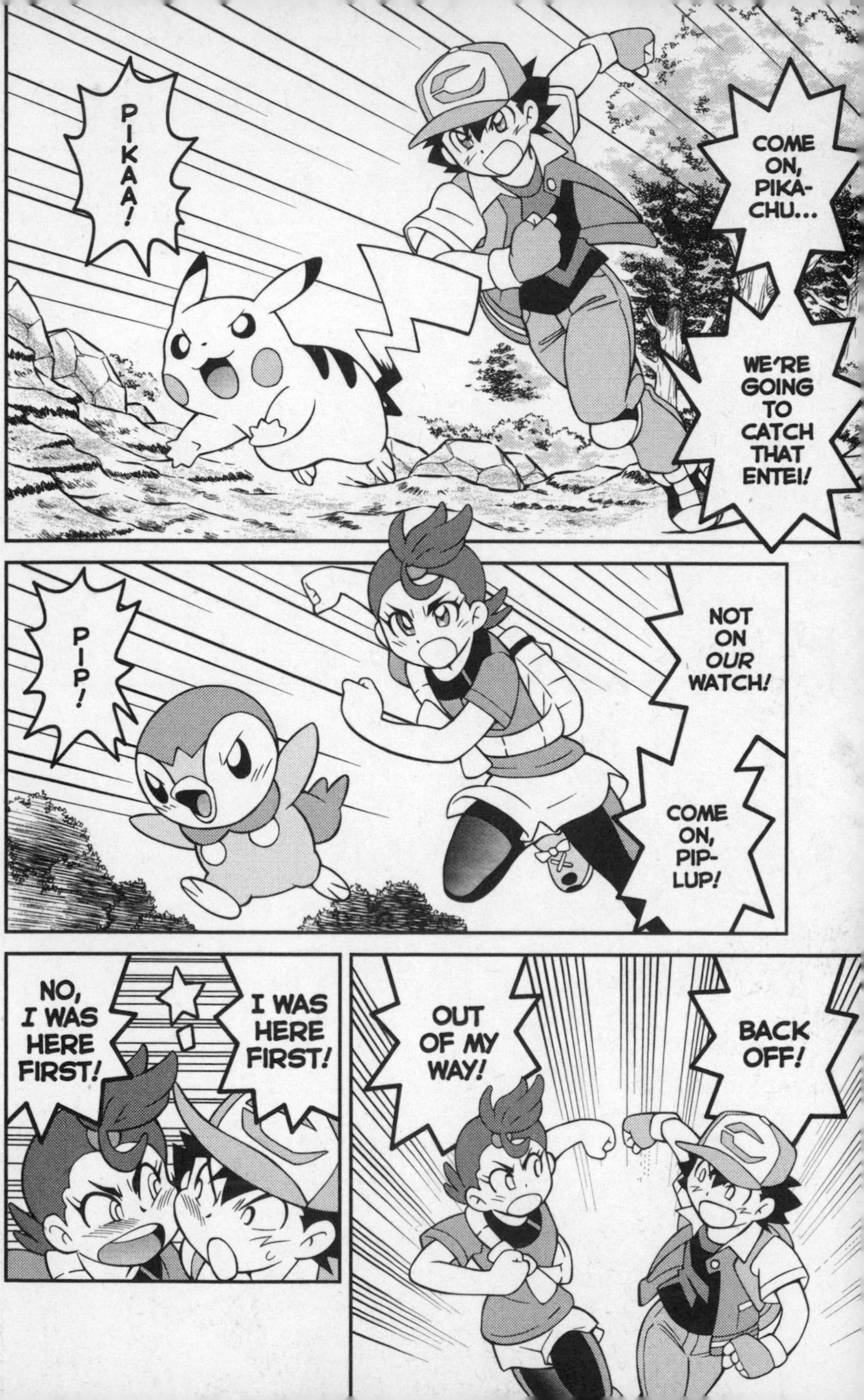
COME ON, PIKA-CHU...
WE'RE GOING TO CATCH THAT ENTEI!
PIKAA!
NOT ON OUR WATCH!
COME ON, PIP-LUP!
PIP!
BACK OFF!
OUT OF MY WAY!
I WAS HERE FIRST!
NO, I WAS HERE FIRST!

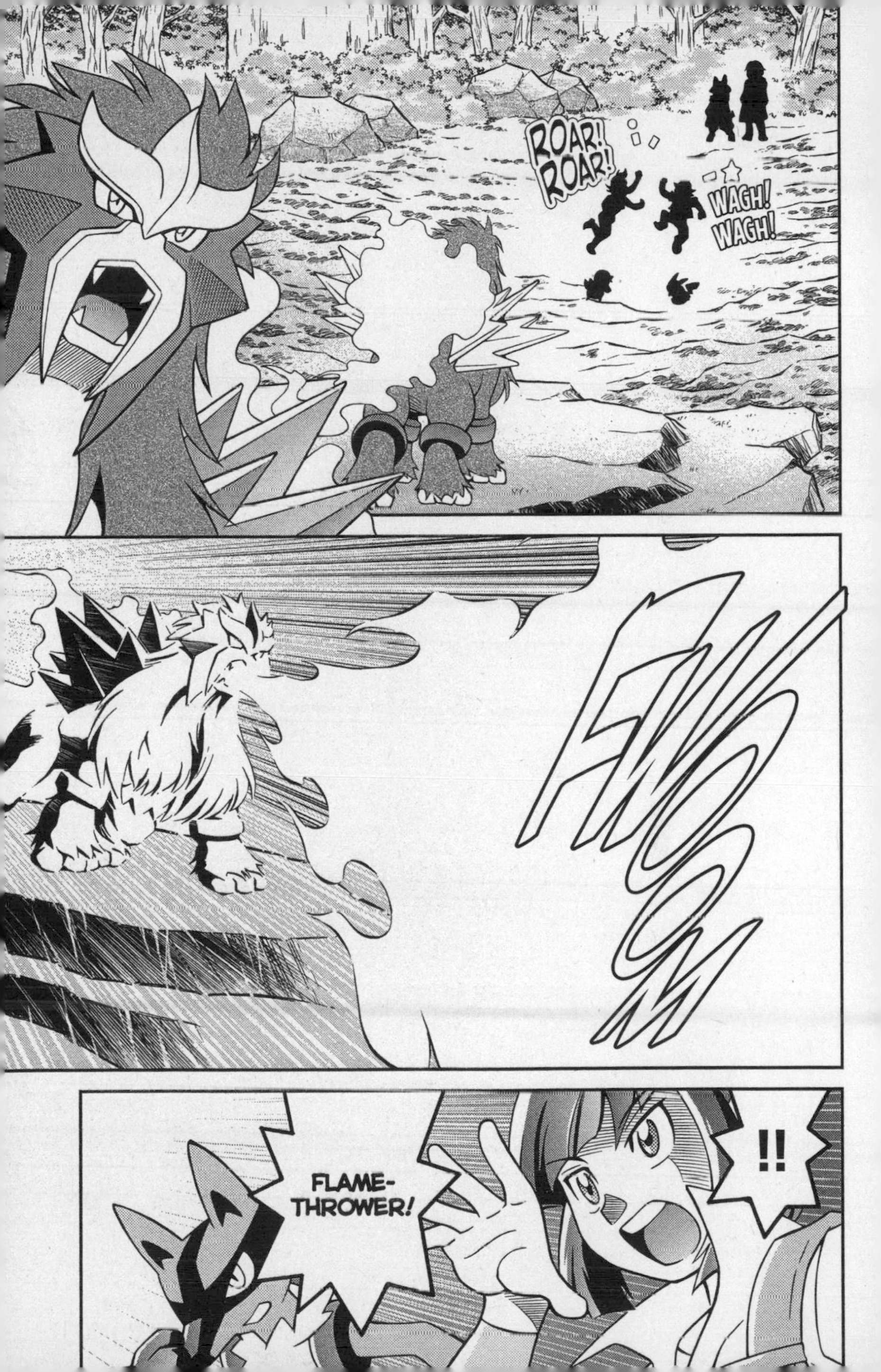
ROAR! ROAR!
WAGH! WAGH!
FWOOM
!!
FLAME-THROWER!

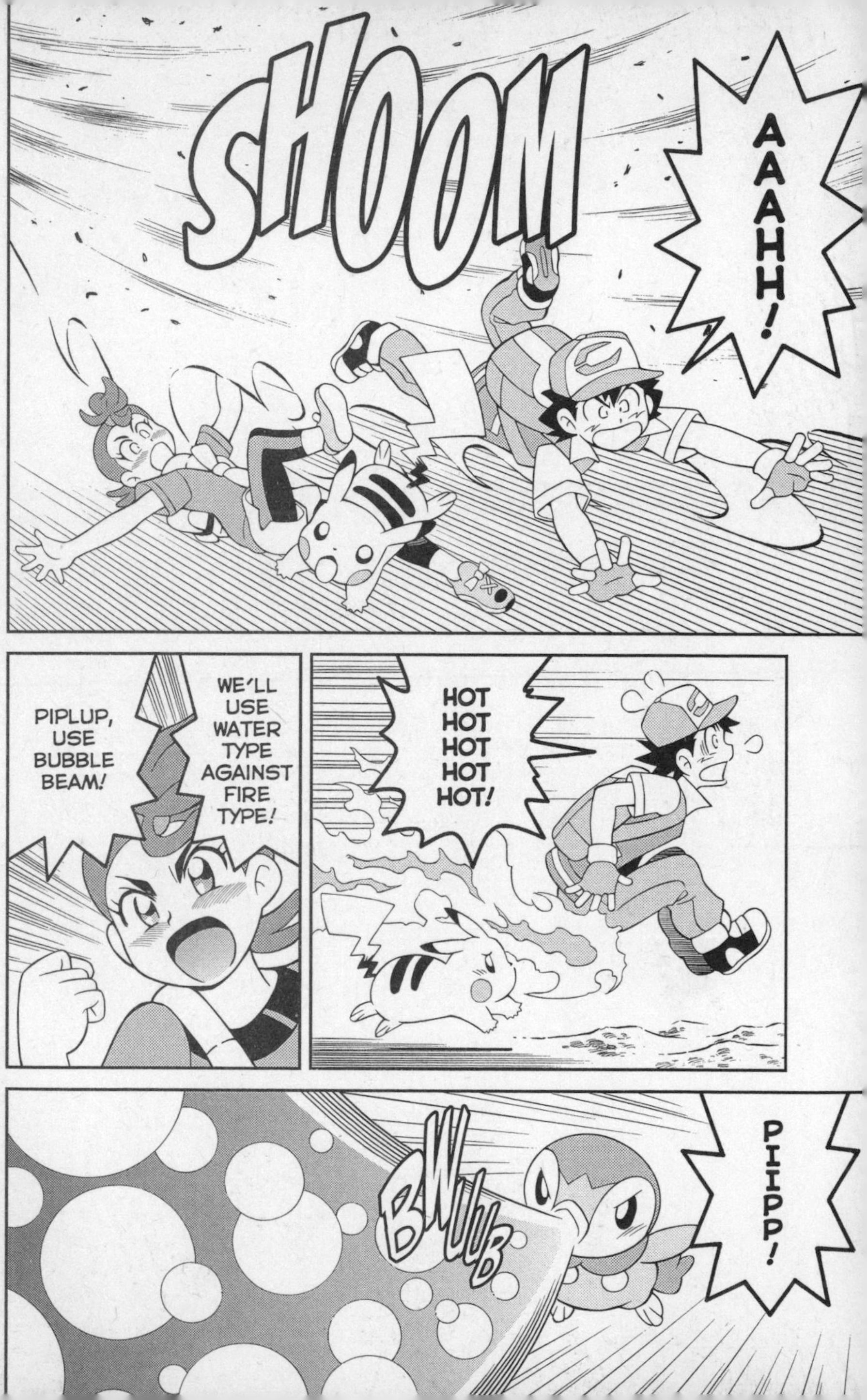
AAAHH!
SHOOM
HOT HOT HOT HOT HOT!
WE'LL USE WATER TYPE AGAINST FIRE TYPE!
PIPLUP, USE BUBBLE BEAM!
PIIPP!
BWUUB

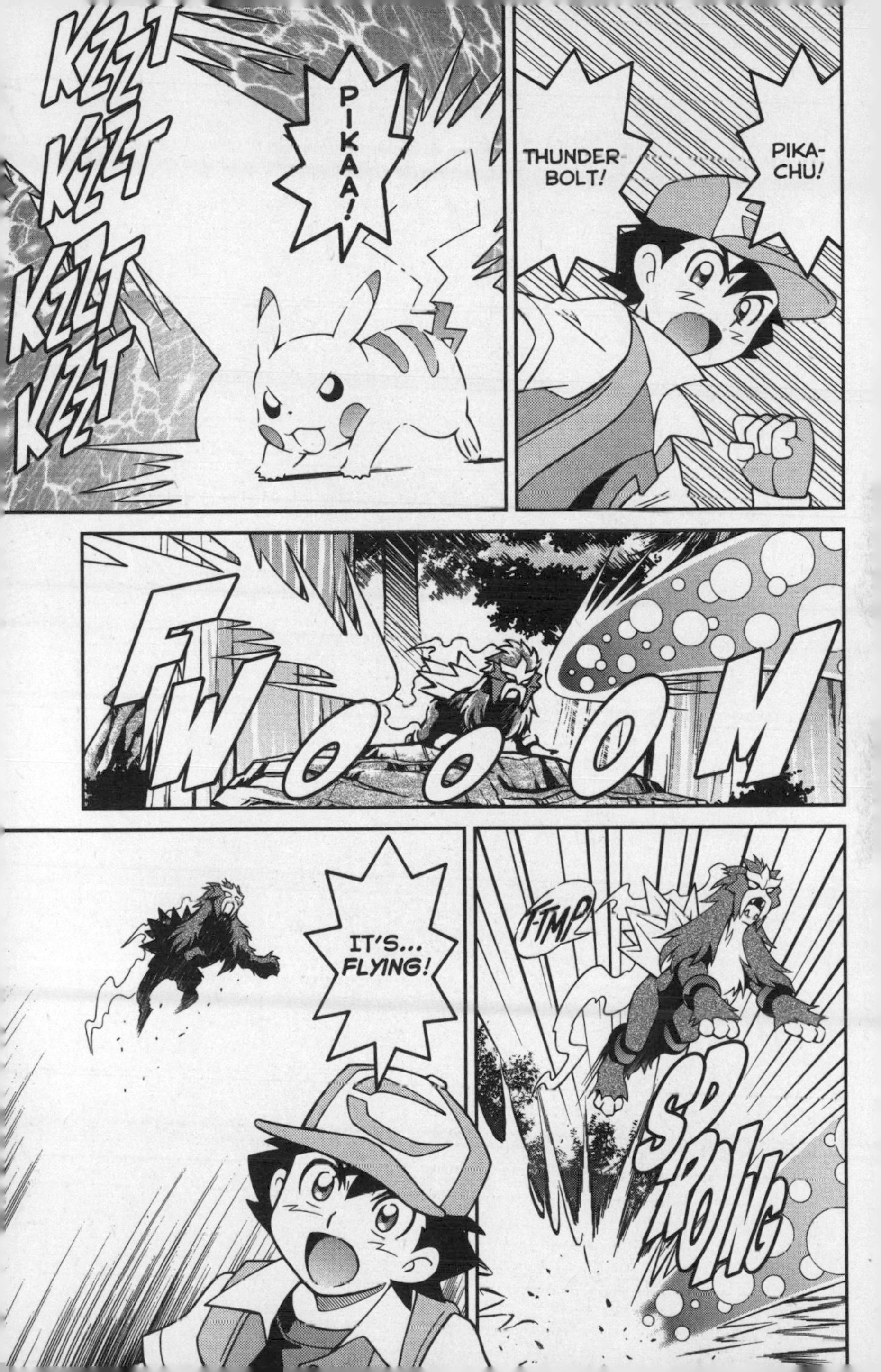
PIKA-CHU!
THUNDER-BOLT!
PIKAAA!
KZZT
KZZT
KZZT
KZZT
FWOOOM
T-TMP
SPROING
IT'S... FLYING!

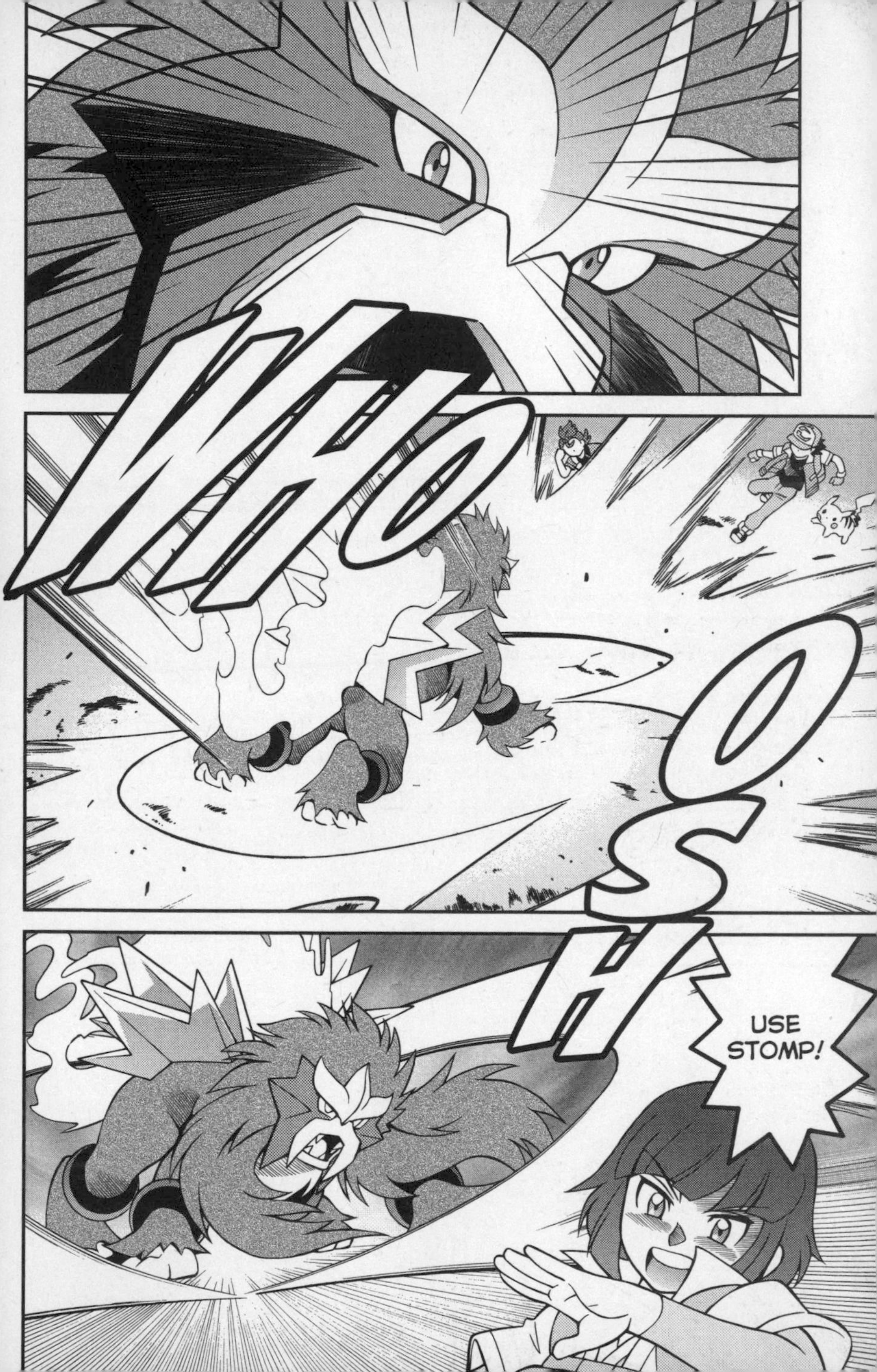
WHOOSH
USE STOMP!

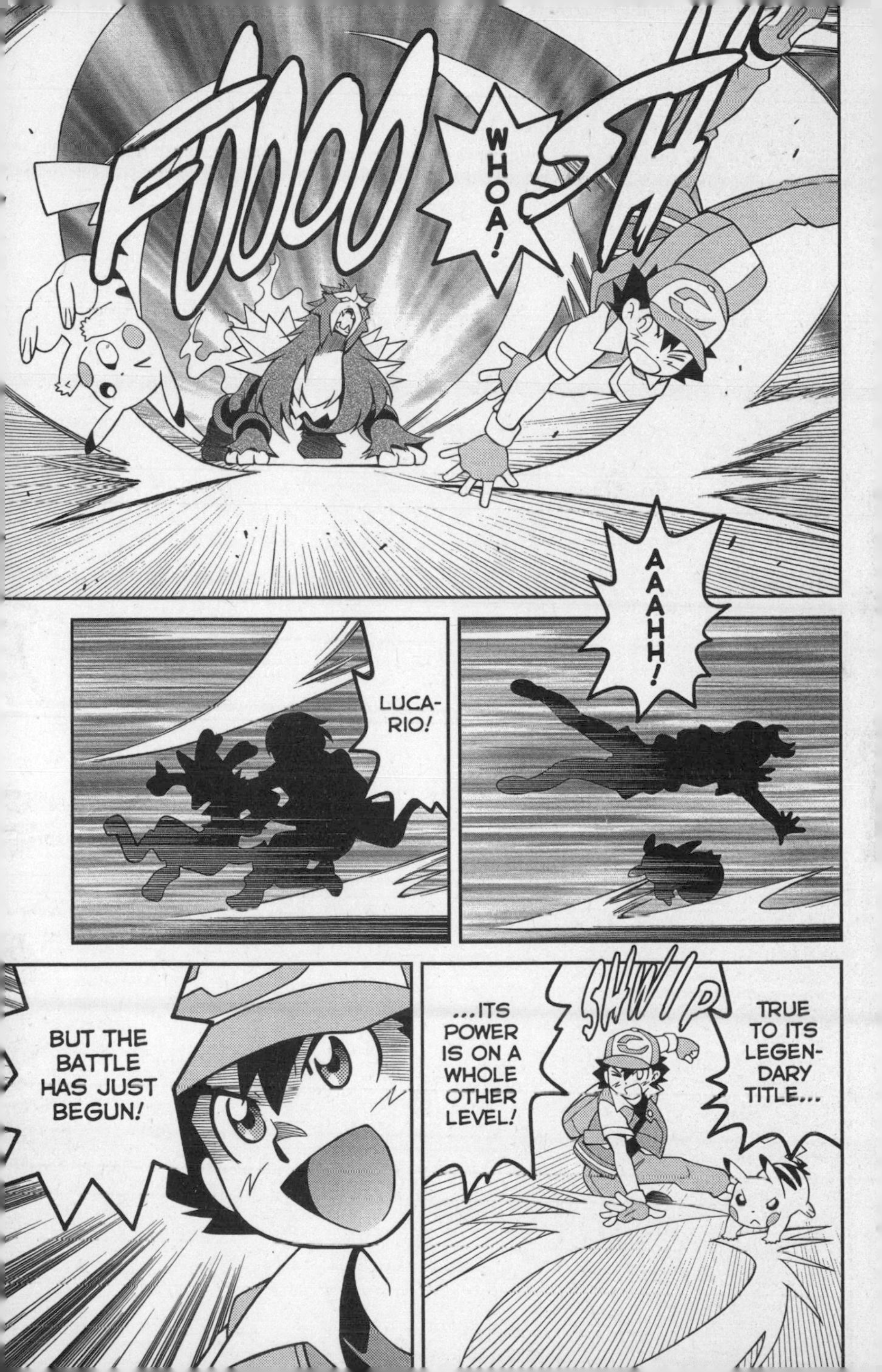
FWOOOSH
WHOA!
AAAHH!
LUCA-RIO!
SHWIP
TRUE TO ITS LEGEN-DARY TITLE...
...ITS POWER IS ON A WHOLE OTHER LEVEL!
BUT THE BATTLE HAS JUST BEGUN!

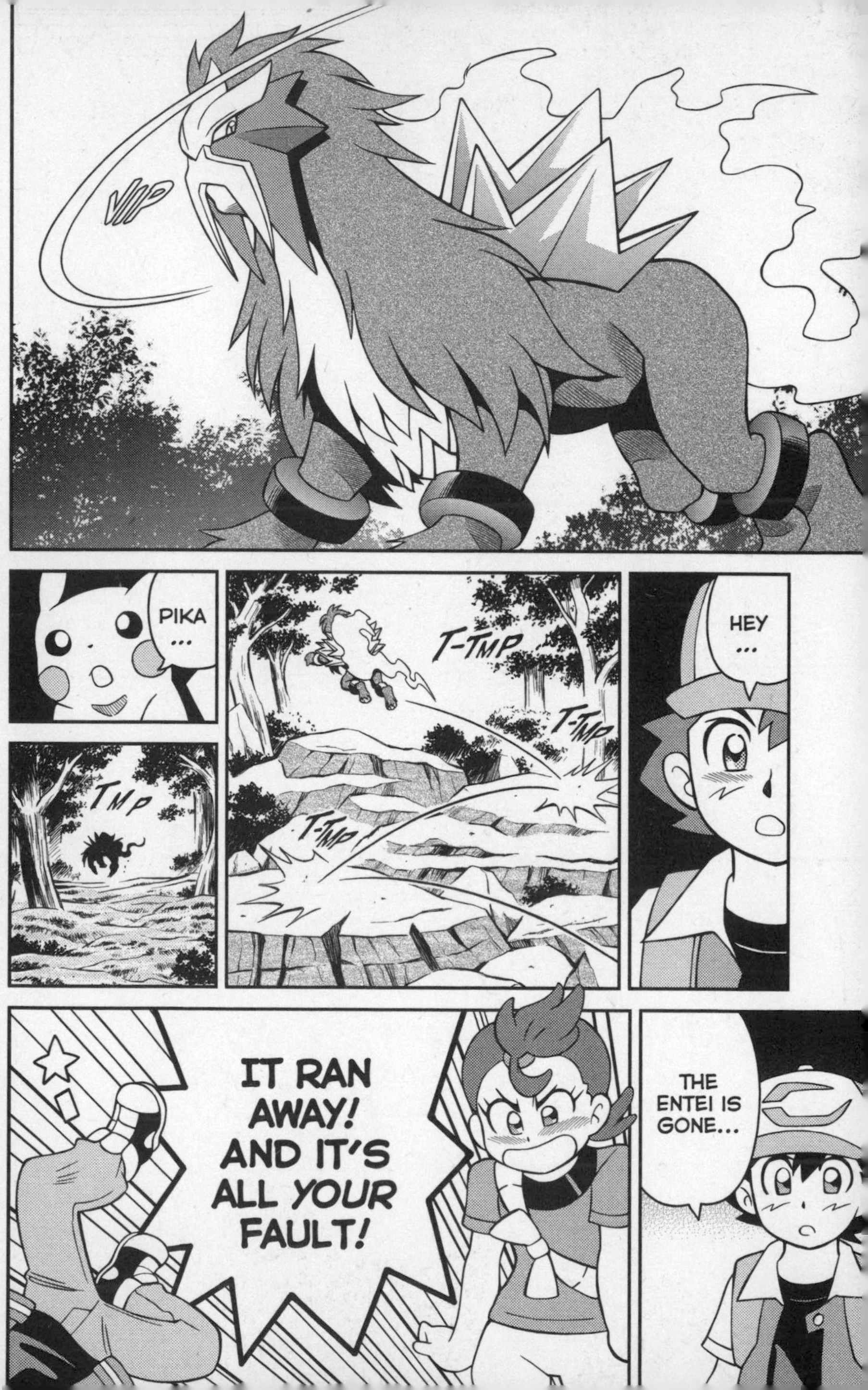
VIIP
HEY ...
T-TMP
T-TMP
T-TMP
PIKA ...
TMP
THE ENTEI IS GONE...
IT RAN AWAY! AND IT'S ALL YOUR FAULT!

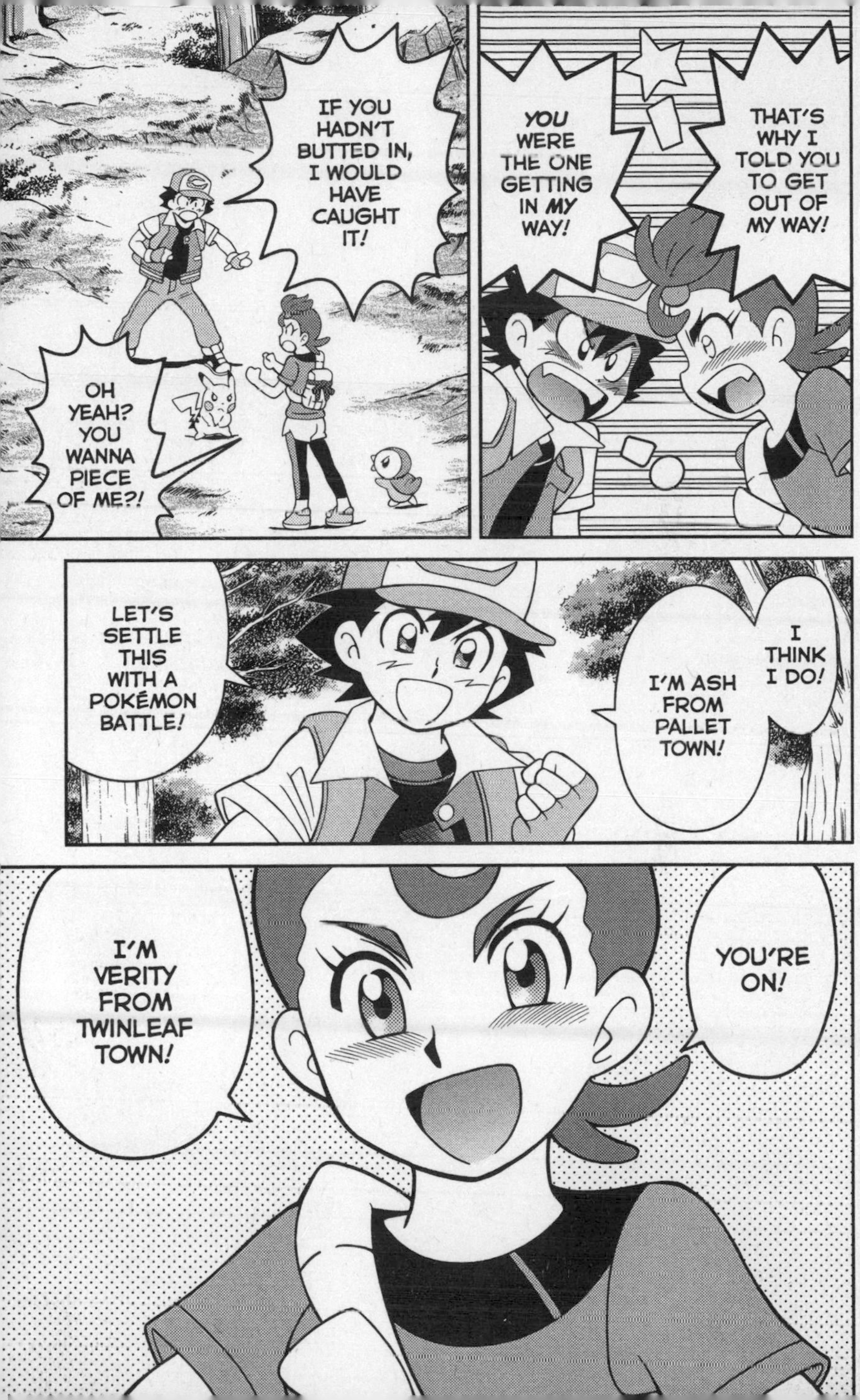
THAT'S WHY I TOLD YOU TO GET OUT OF MY WAY!
YOU WERE THE ONE GETTING IN *MY* WAY!
IF YOU HADN'T BUTTED IN, I WOULD HAVE CAUGHT IT!
OH YEAH? YOU WANNA PIECE OF ME?!
I THINK I DO!
I'M ASH FROM PALLET TOWN!
LET'S SETTLE THIS WITH A POKÉMON BATTLE!
YOU'RE ON!
I'M VERITY FROM TWINLEAF TOWN!

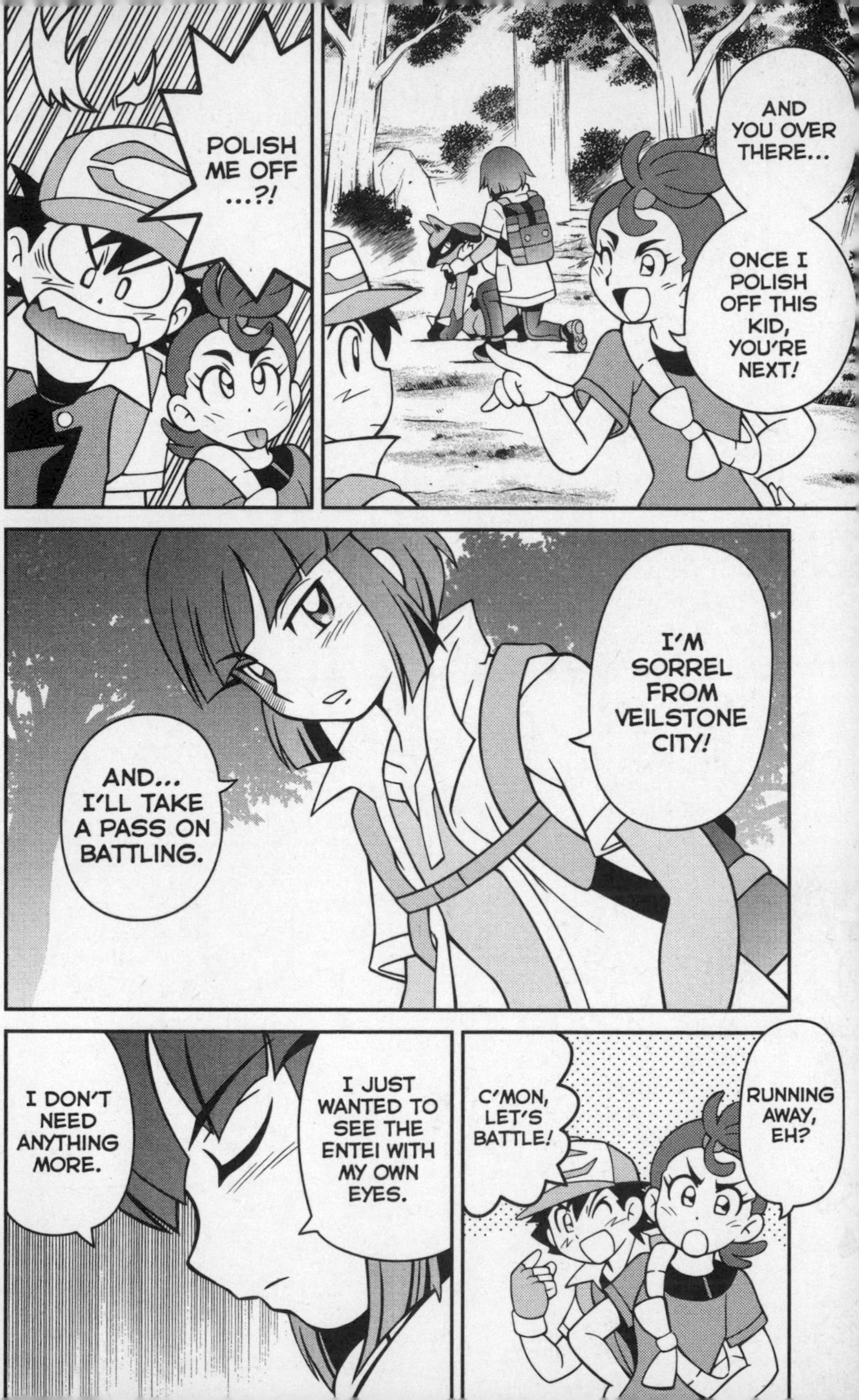
AND YOU OVER THERE...
ONCE I POLISH OFF THIS KID, YOU'RE NEXT!
POLISH ME OFF ...?!
I'M SORREL FROM VEILSTONE CITY!
AND... I'LL TAKE A PASS ON BATTLING.
RUNNING AWAY, EH?
C'MON, LET'S BATTLE!
I JUST WANTED TO SEE THE ENTEI WITH MY OWN EYES.
I DON'T NEED ANYTHING MORE.

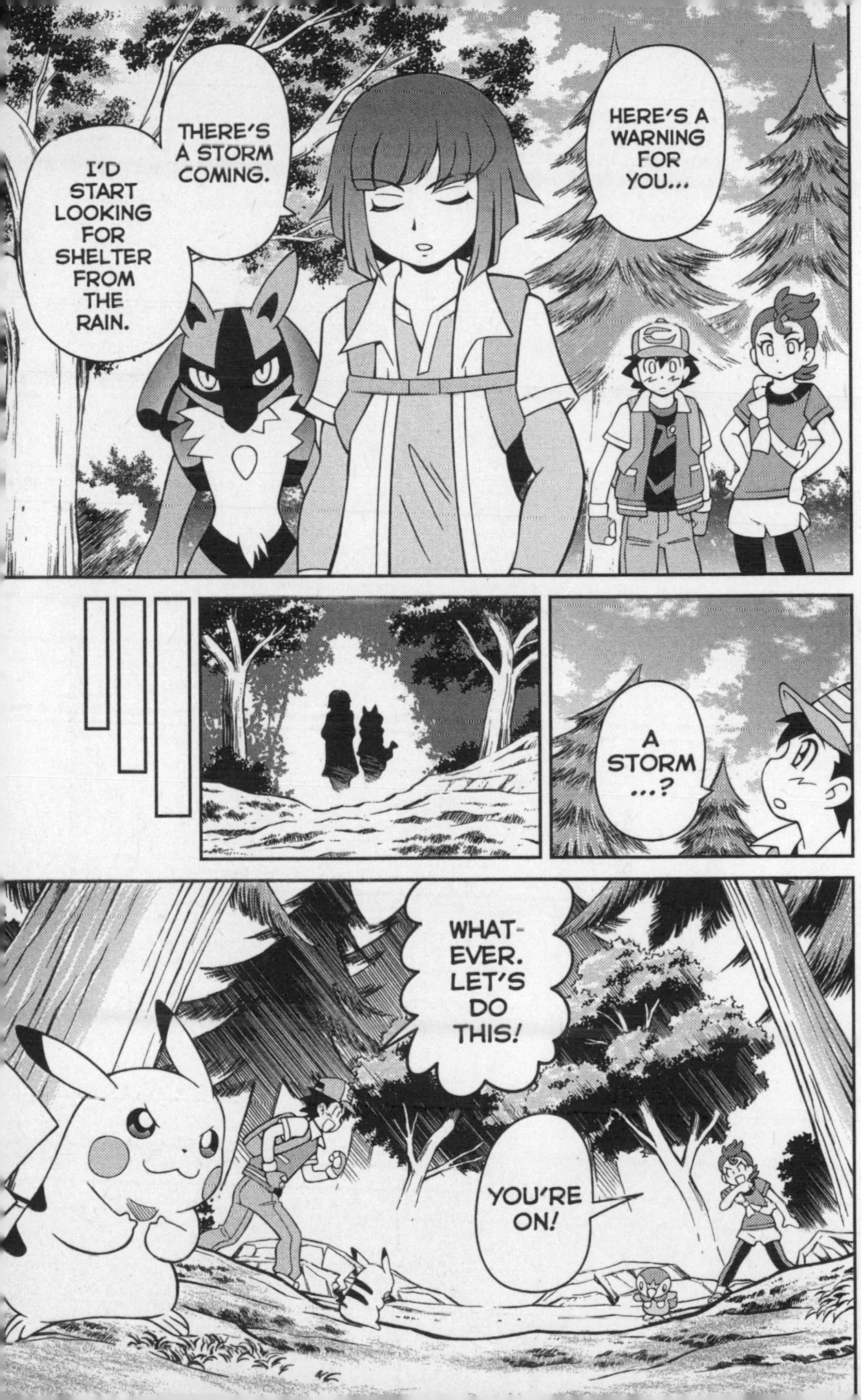
HERE'S A WARNING FOR YOU...
THERE'S A STORM COMING.
I'D START LOOKING FOR SHELTER FROM THE RAIN.
A STORM ...?
WHATEVER. LET'S DO THIS!
YOU'RE ON!

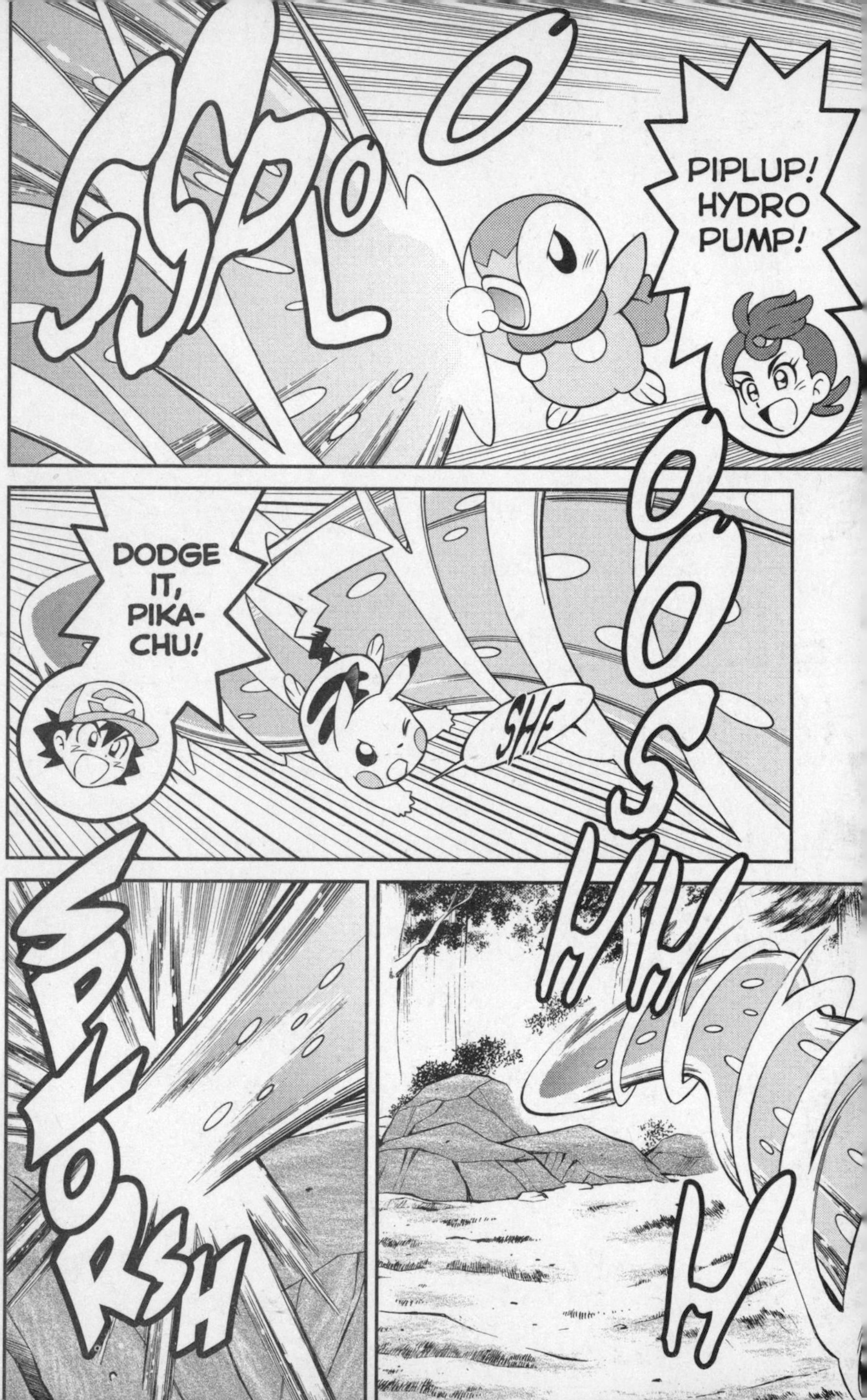
PIPLUP! HYDRO PUMP!
SSPLOOOOOOSHHHH
DODGE IT, PIKA-CHU!
SHF
SPLORSH

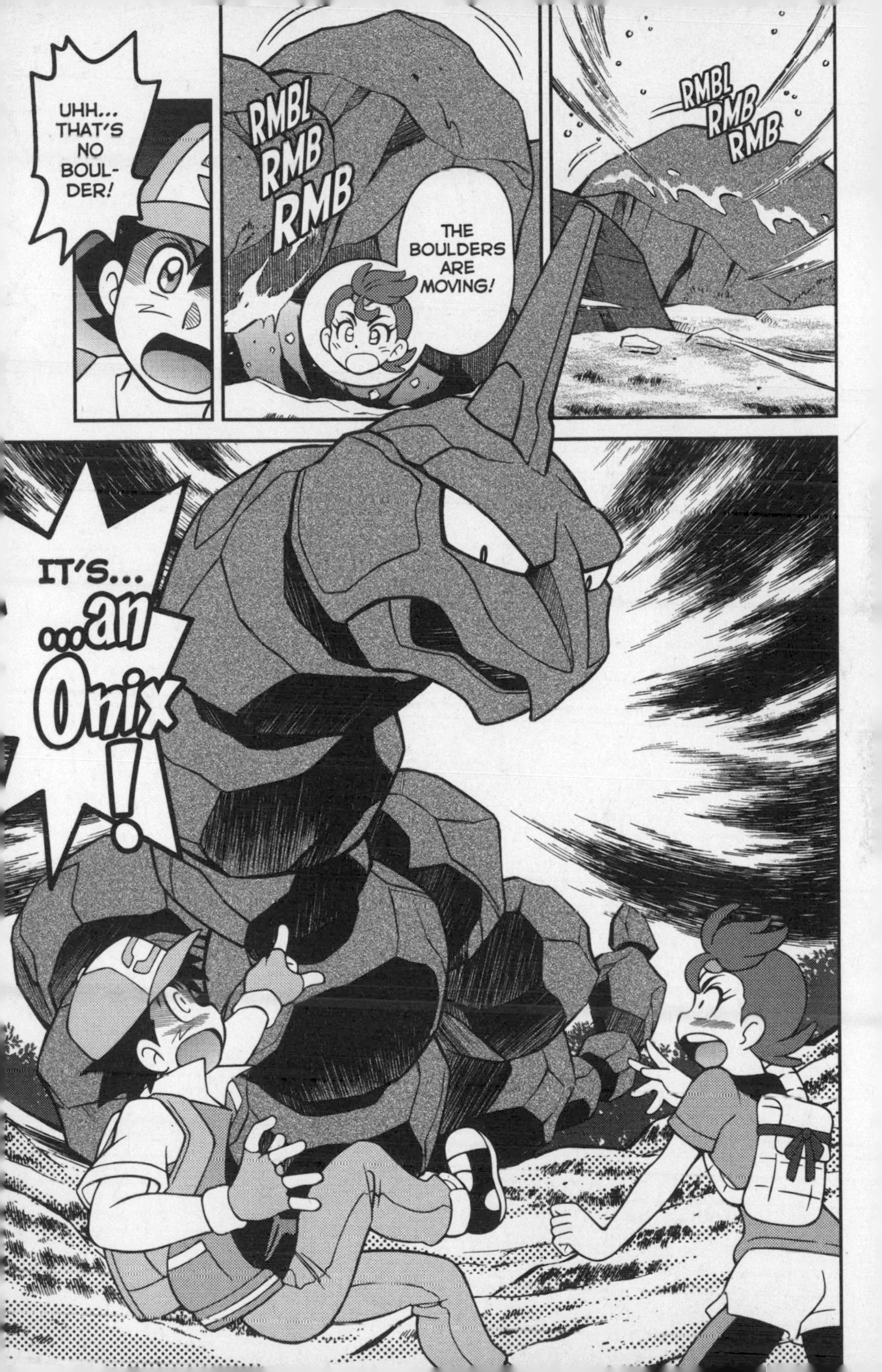
RMBL RMB RMB
RMBL RMB RMB
THE BOULDERS ARE MOVING!
UHH... THAT'S NO BOUL-DER!
IT'S... ...an Onix!

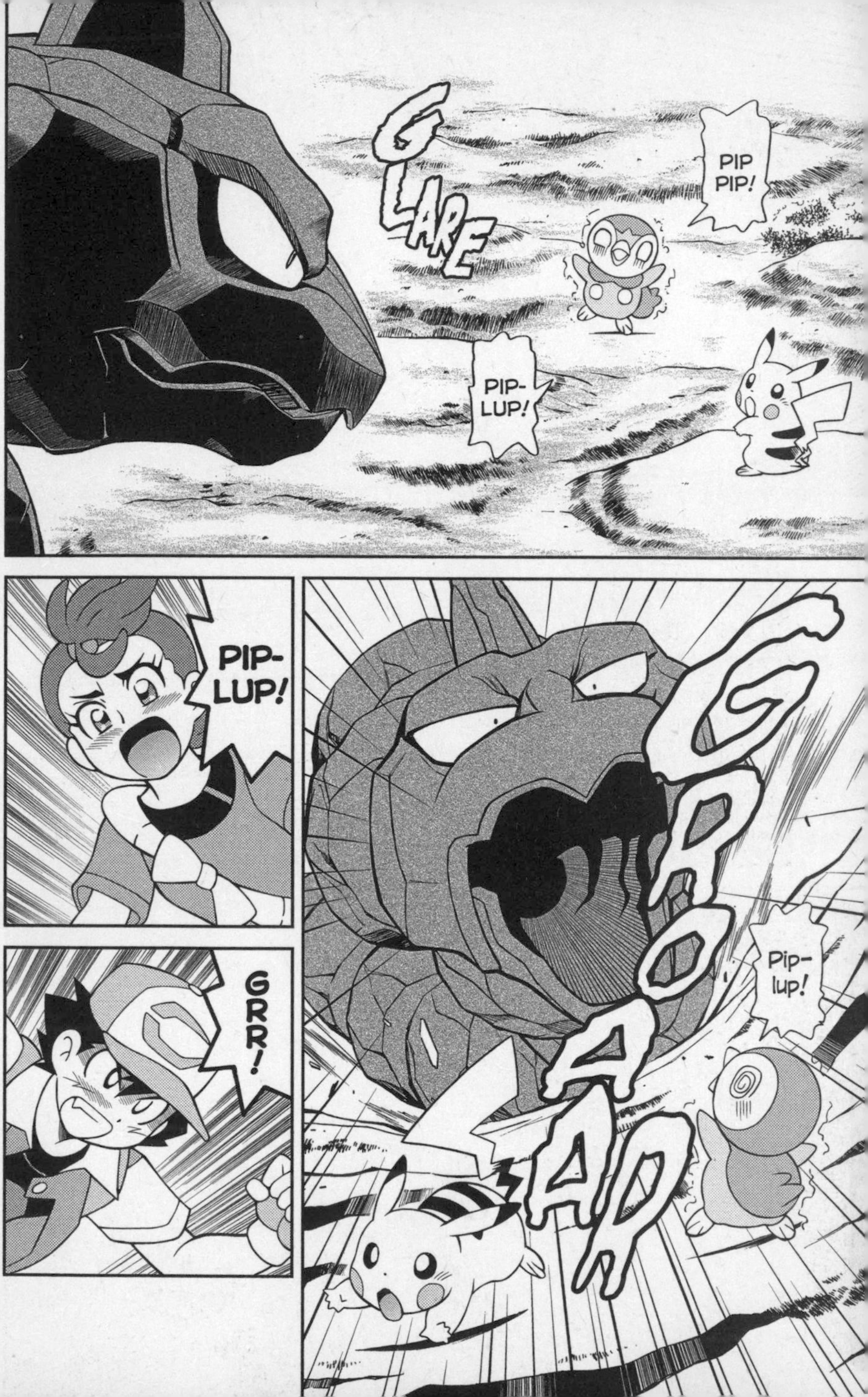
PIP PIP!
GLARE
PIP-LUP!
GROAAP
Pip-lup!
PIP-LUP!
GRR!

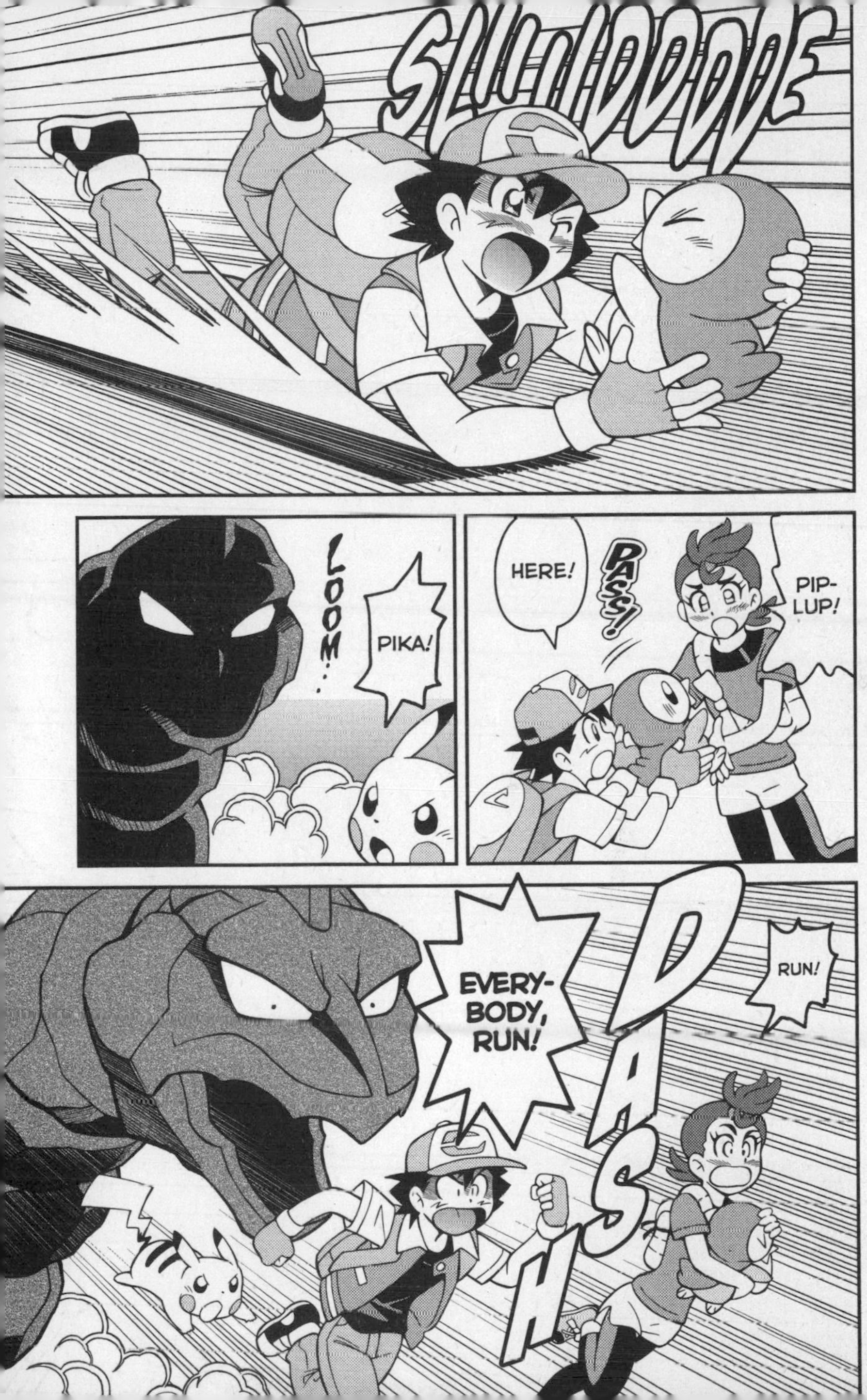
SLIIIDDDDE
HERE!
PASS!
PIP-LUP!
LOOM...
PIKA!
RUN!
DASH
EVERY-BODY, RUN!

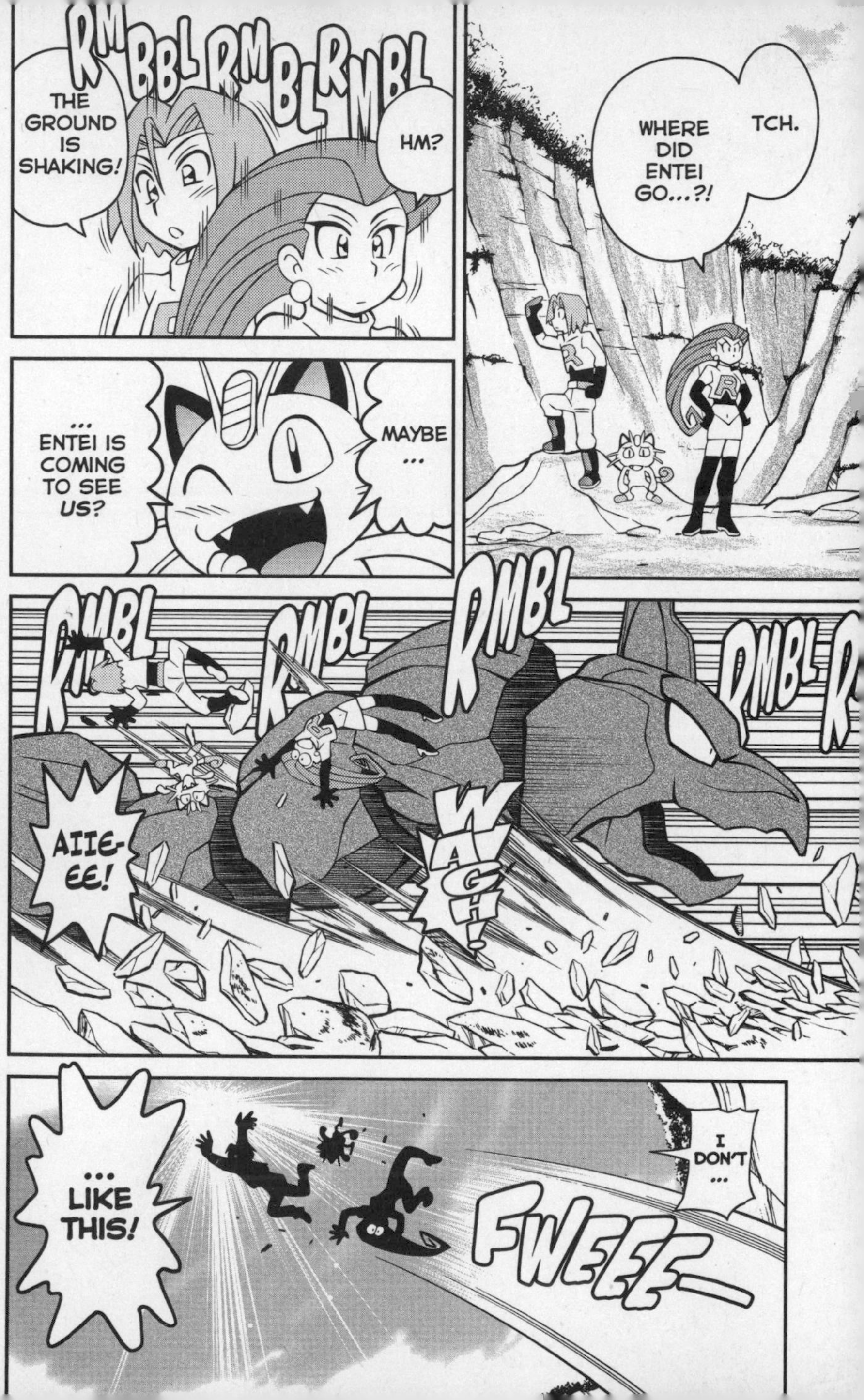
TCH.
WHERE DID ENTEI GO...?!
RMBBL RMBL RMBL
HM?
THE GROUND IS SHAKING!
MAYBE ...
... ENTEI IS COMING TO SEE US?
RMBL
RMBL
RMBL
RMBL
WAGH!
AIIE-EE!
I DON'T ...
FWEEE—
... LIKE THIS!

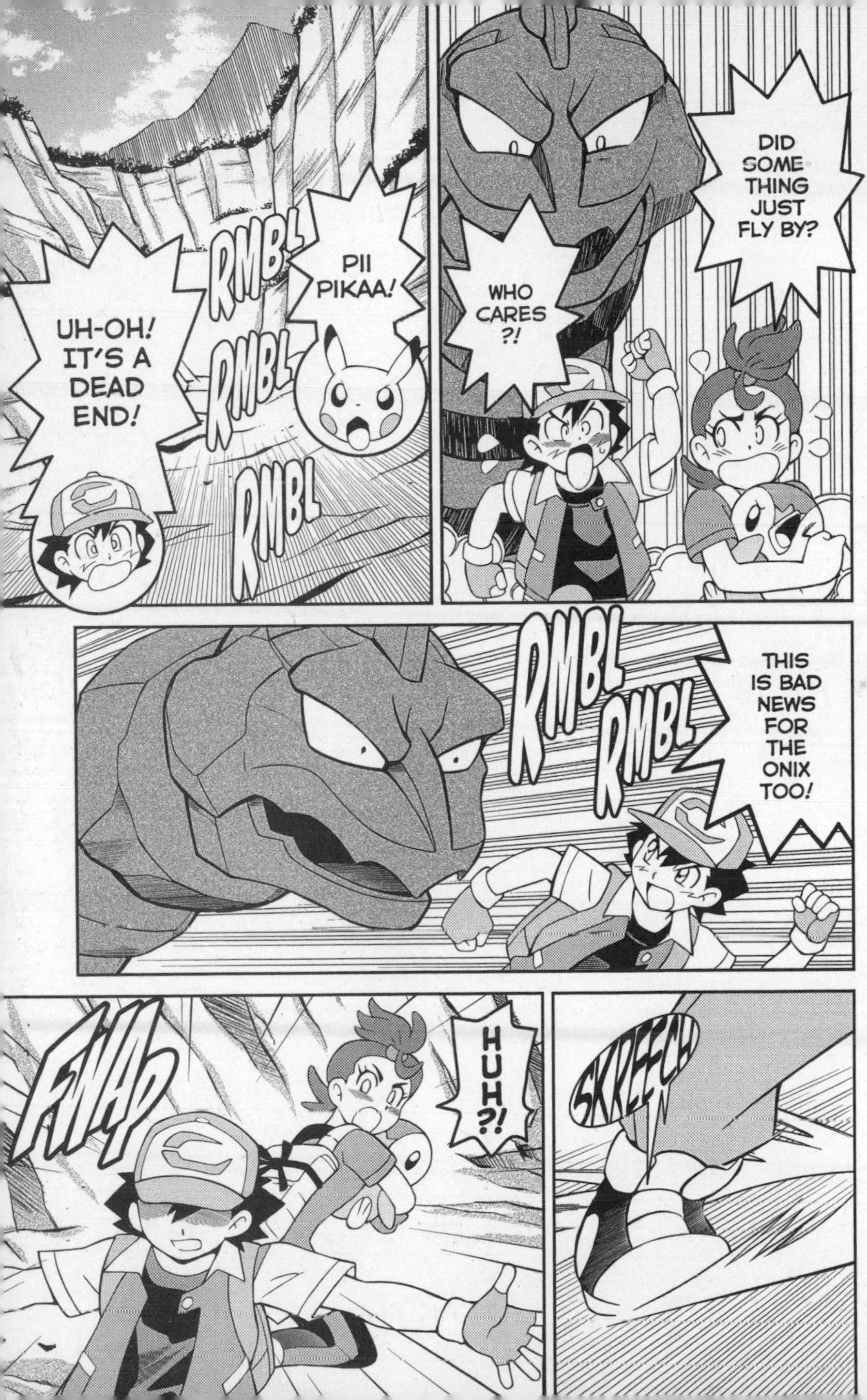
DID SOMETHING JUST FLY BY?
WHO CARES ?!
PII PIKAA!
RMBL
UH-OH! IT'S A DEAD END!
RMBL
RMBL
THIS IS BAD NEWS FOR THE ONIX TOO!
RMBL
RMBL
SKREECH
HUH ?!
FWAP

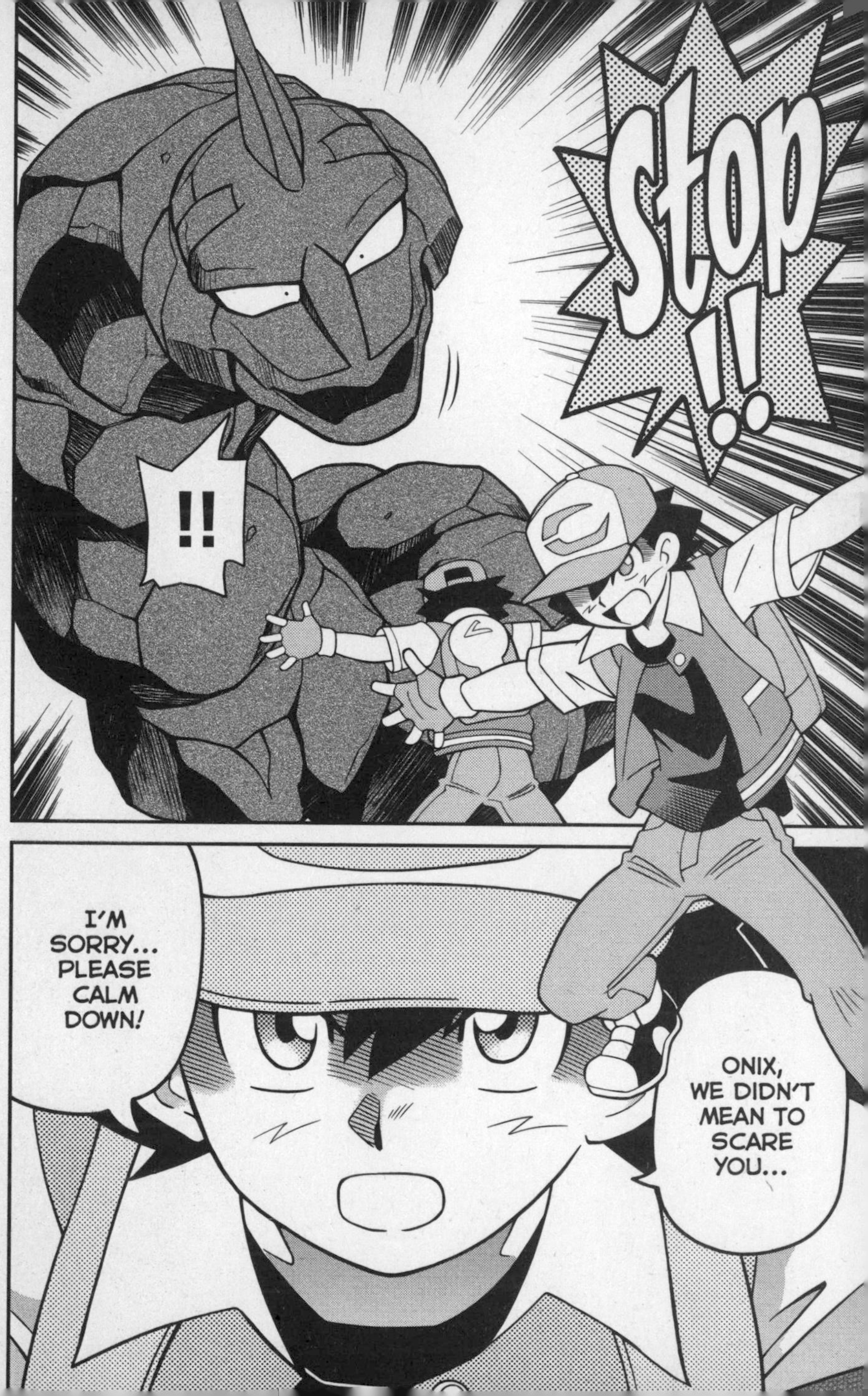
STOP!!
!!
ONIX, WE DIDN'T MEAN TO SCARE YOU...
I'M SORRY... PLEASE CALM DOWN!

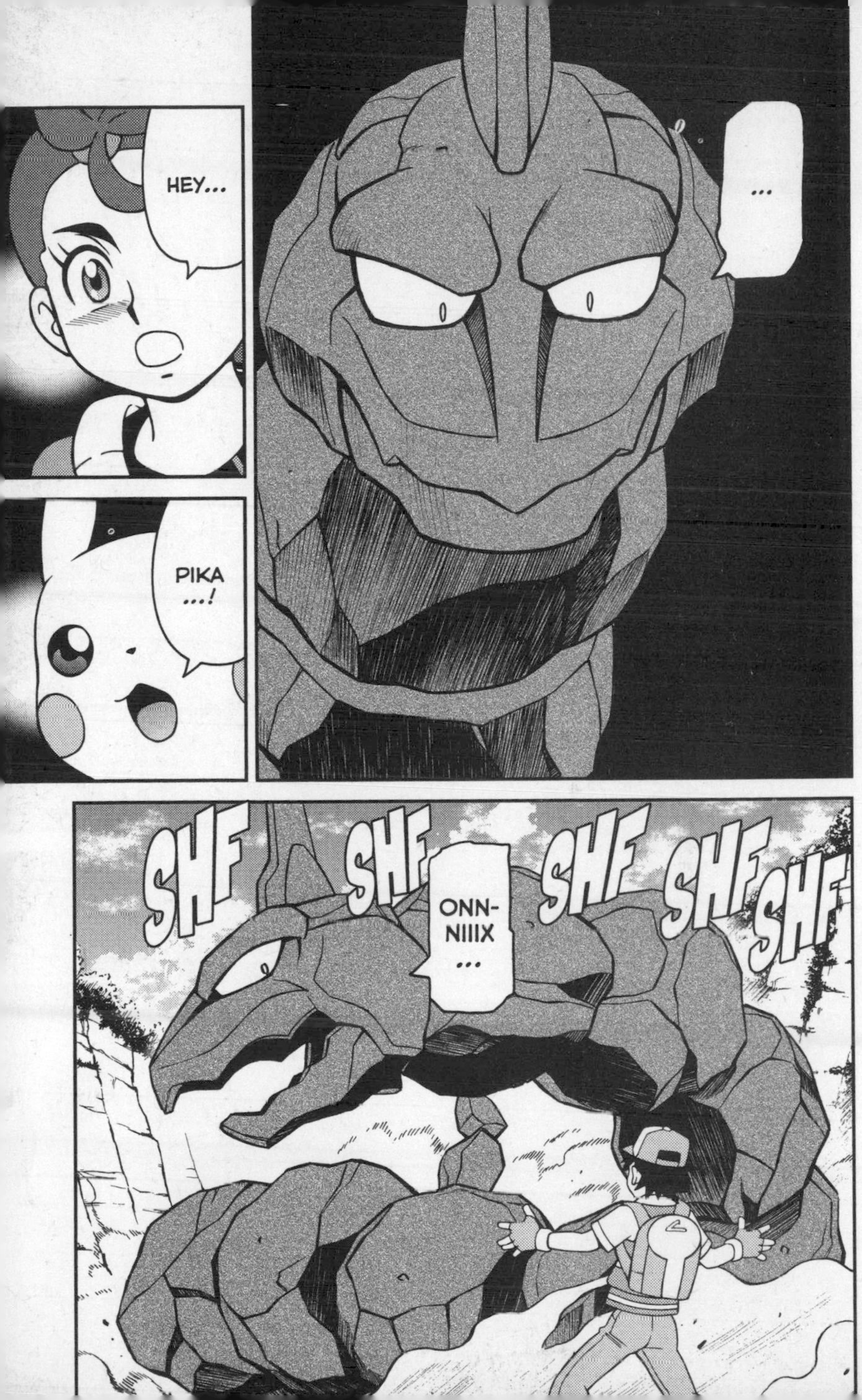
...
HEY...
PIKA ...!
SHF SHF SHF
ONN-NIIIX ...
SHF SHF

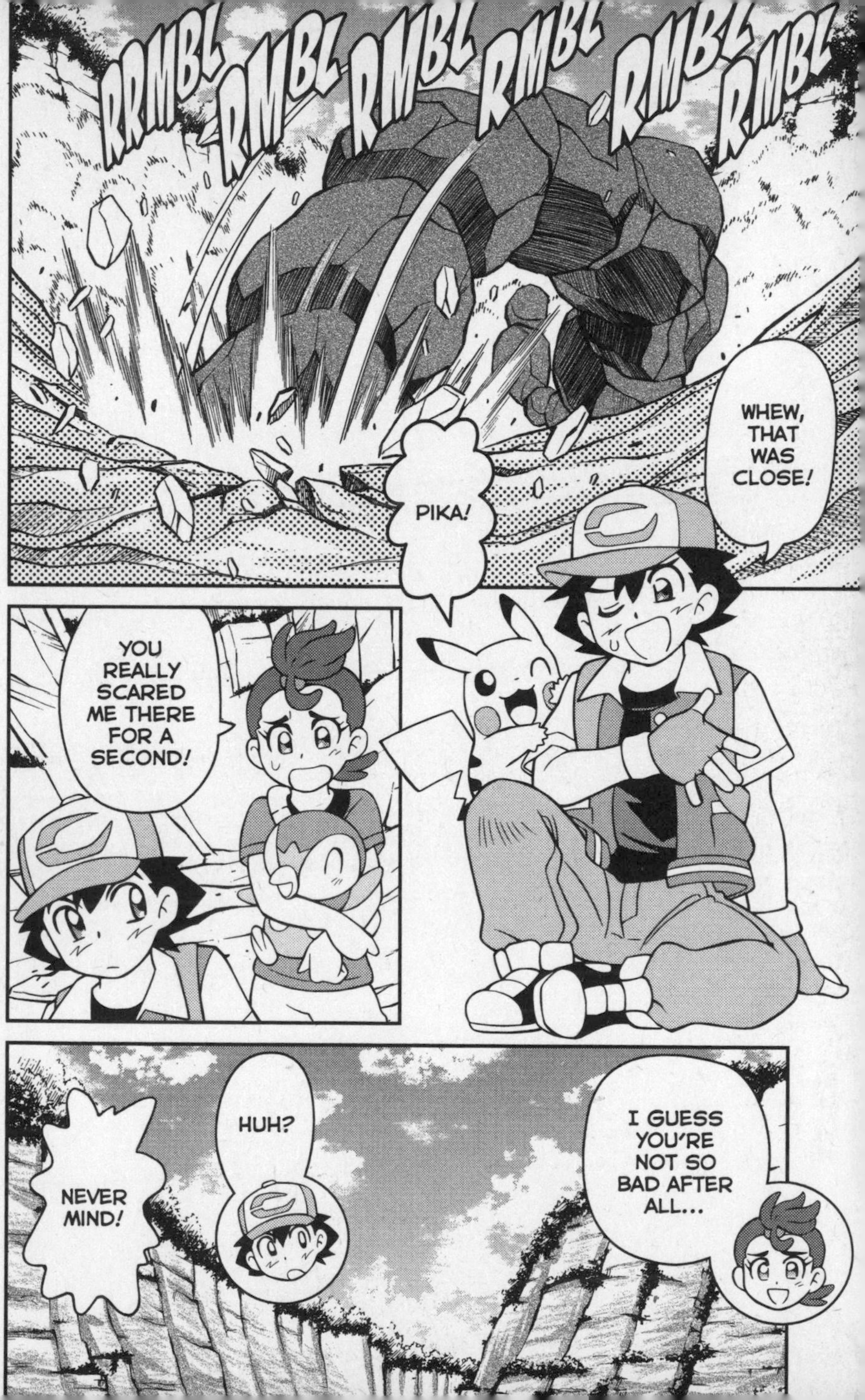
RRMBL RMBL RMBL RMBL RMBL RMBL
WHEW, THAT WAS CLOSE!
PIKA!
YOU REALLY SCARED ME THERE FOR A SECOND!
I GUESS YOU'RE NOT SO BAD AFTER ALL...
HUH?
NEVER MIND!

CHAPTER 4

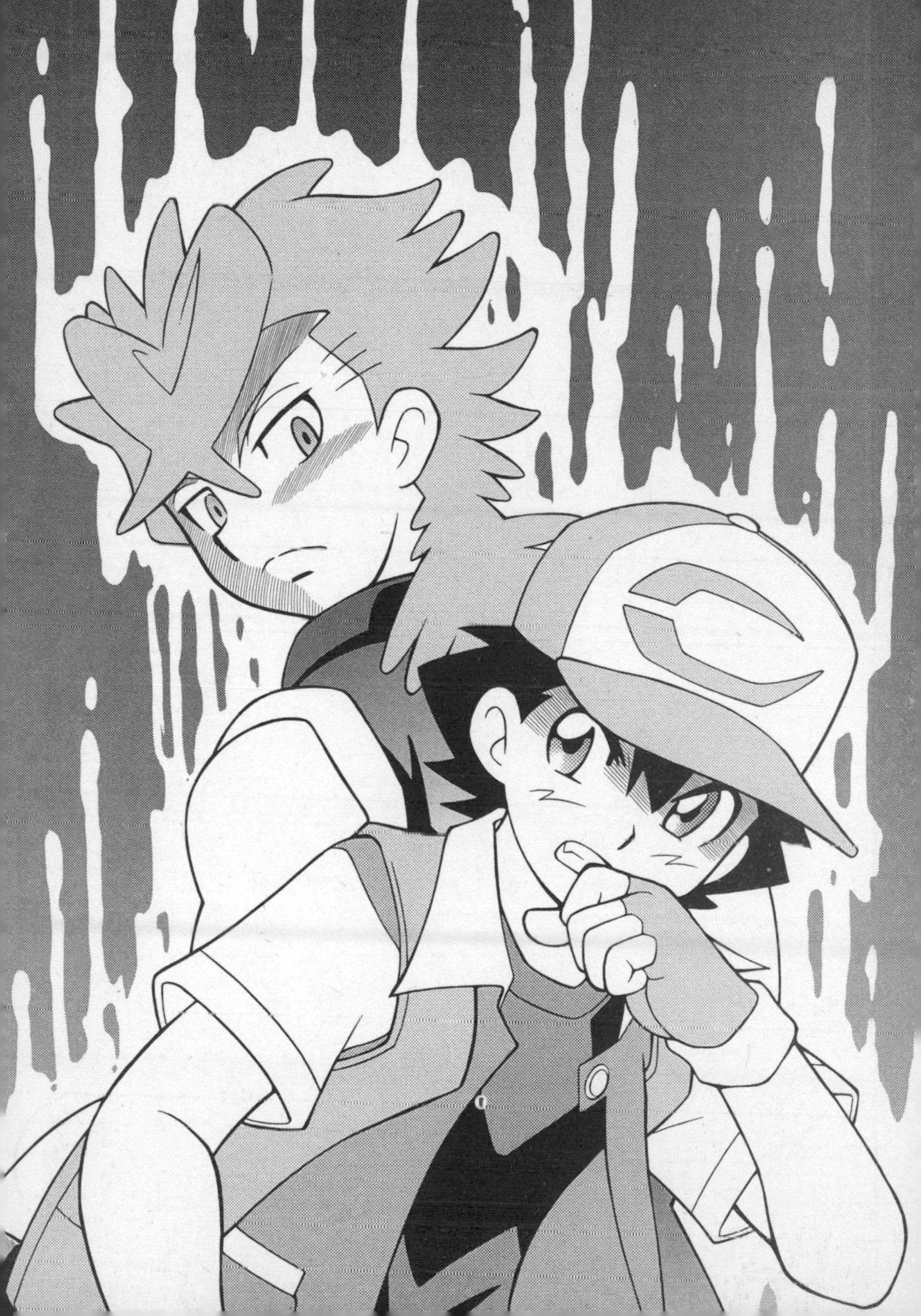

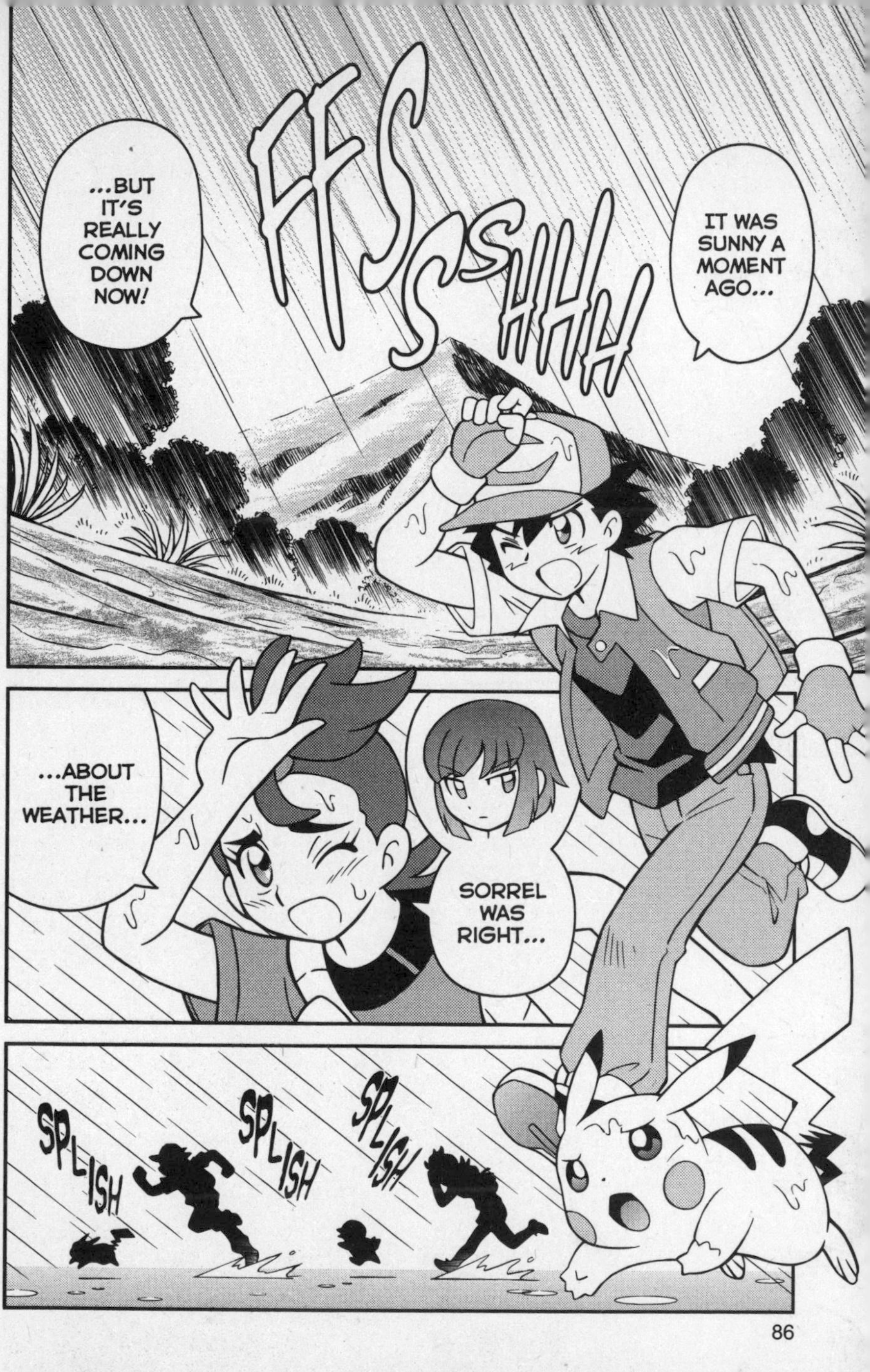
IT WAS SUNNY A MOMENT AGO...
FFSSSHHHH
...BUT IT'S REALLY COMING DOWN NOW!
SORREL WAS RIGHT...
...ABOUT THE WEATHER...
SPLISH
SPLISH
SPLISH

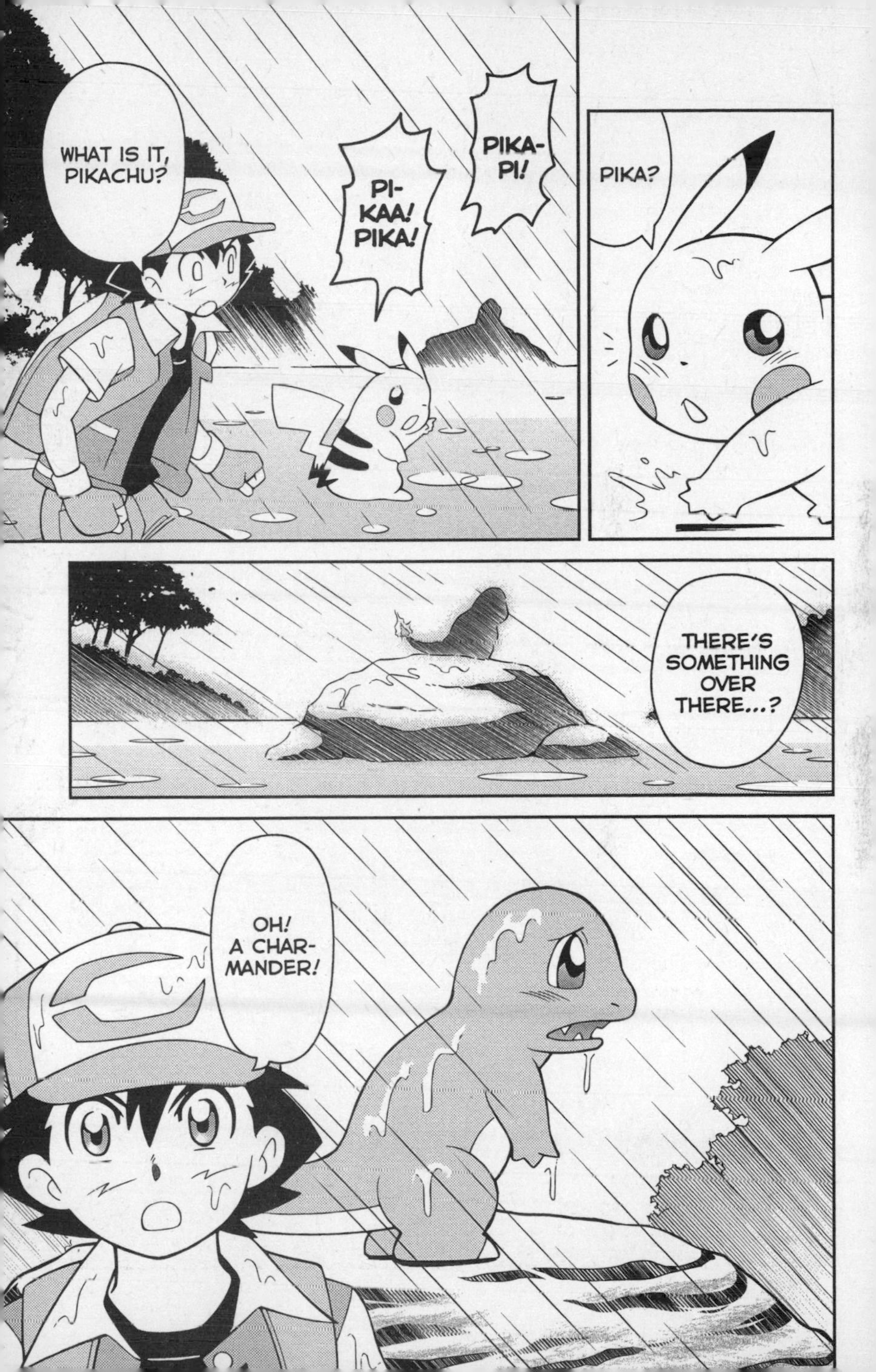
PIKA?
PIKA-PI!
PI-KAA! PIKA!
WHAT IS IT, PIKACHU?
THERE'S SOMETHING OVER THERE...?
OH! A CHAR-MANDER!

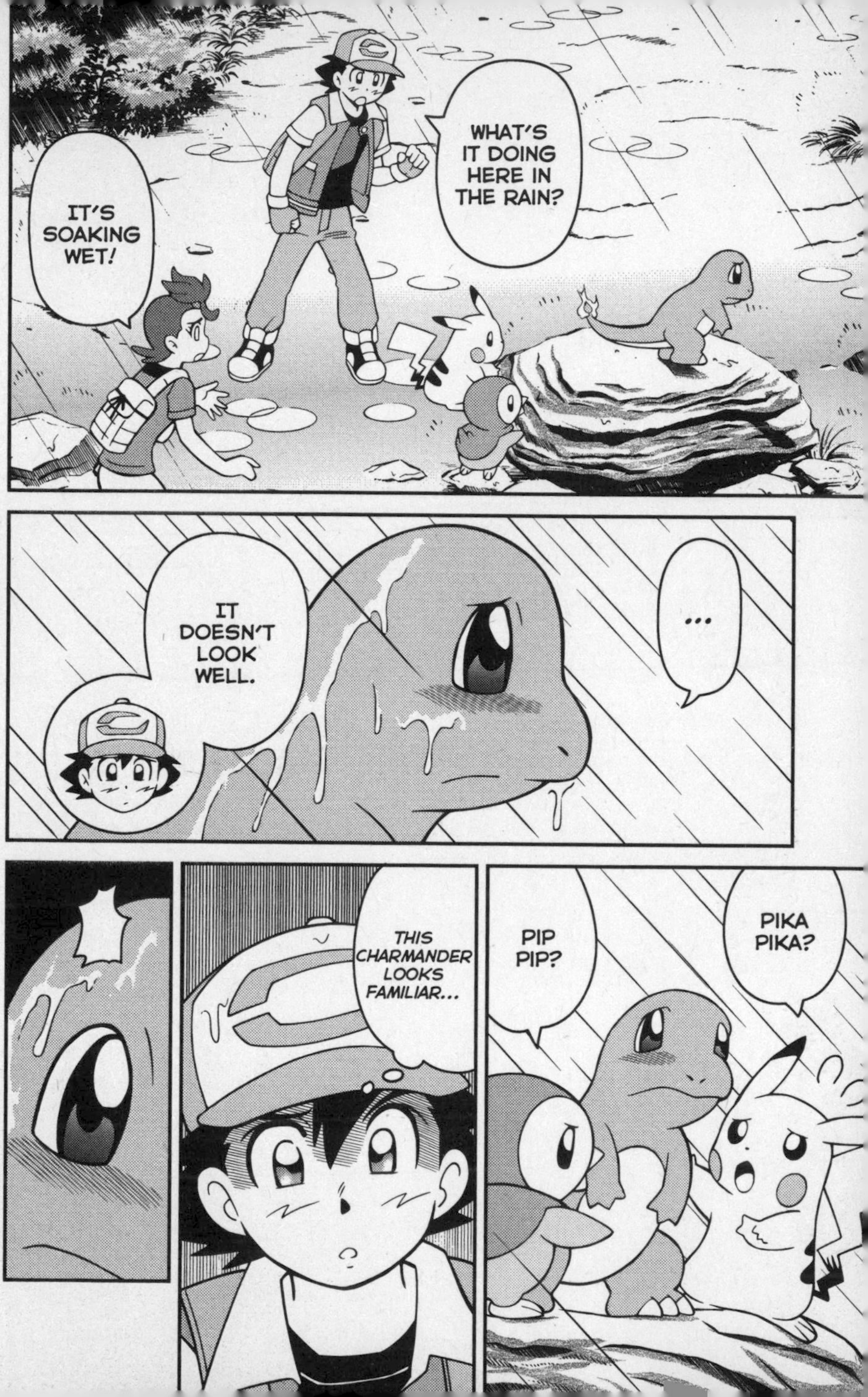
WHAT'S IT DOING HERE IN THE RAIN?
IT'S SOAKING WET!
...
IT DOESN'T LOOK WELL.
PIKA PIKA?
PIP PIP?
THIS CHARMANDER LOOKS FAMILIAR...

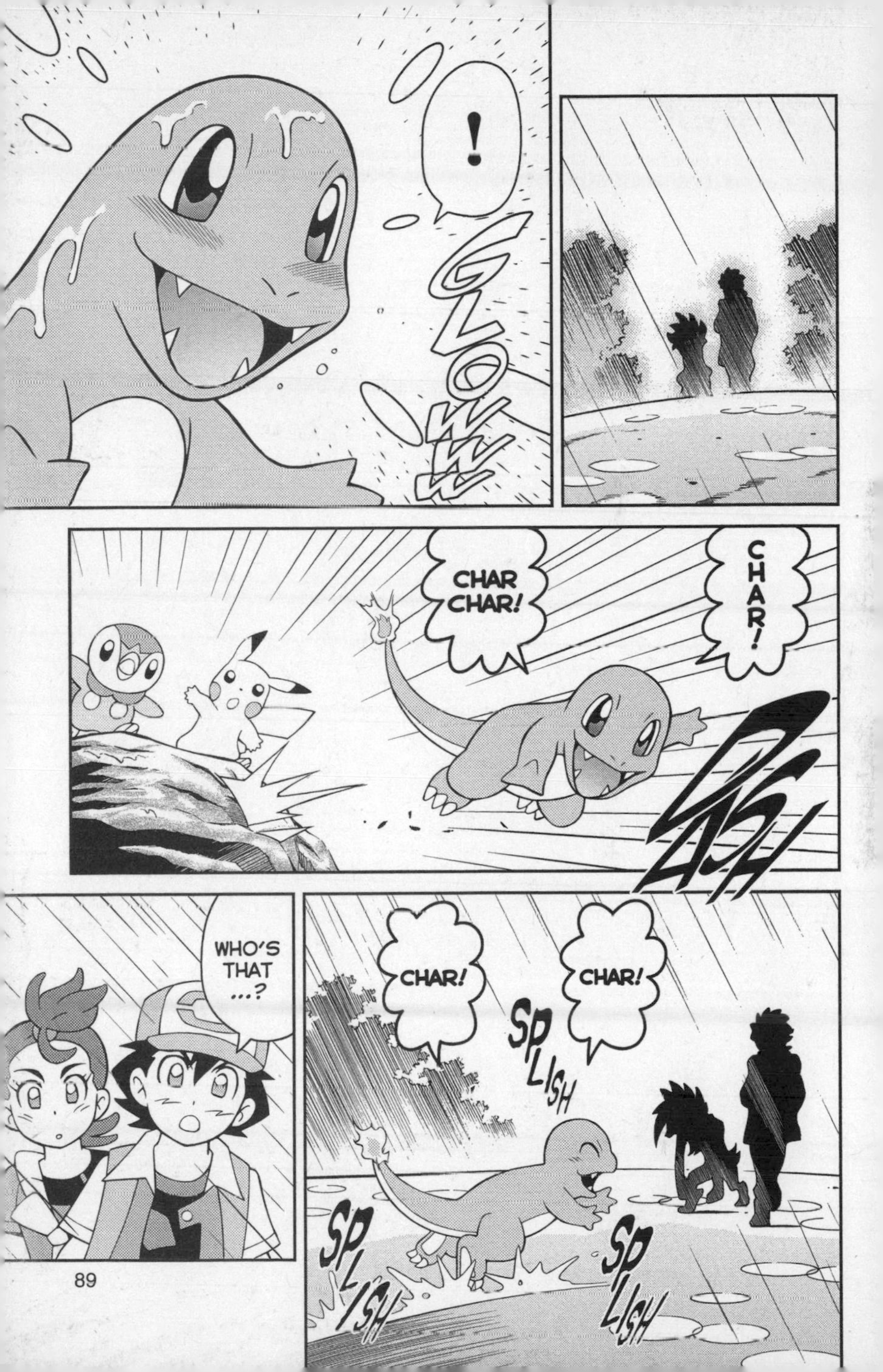
!
GLOWW
CHAR!
CHAR CHAR!
DASH
CHAR!
CHAR!
SPLISH
SPLISH
SPLISH
WHO'S THAT ...?

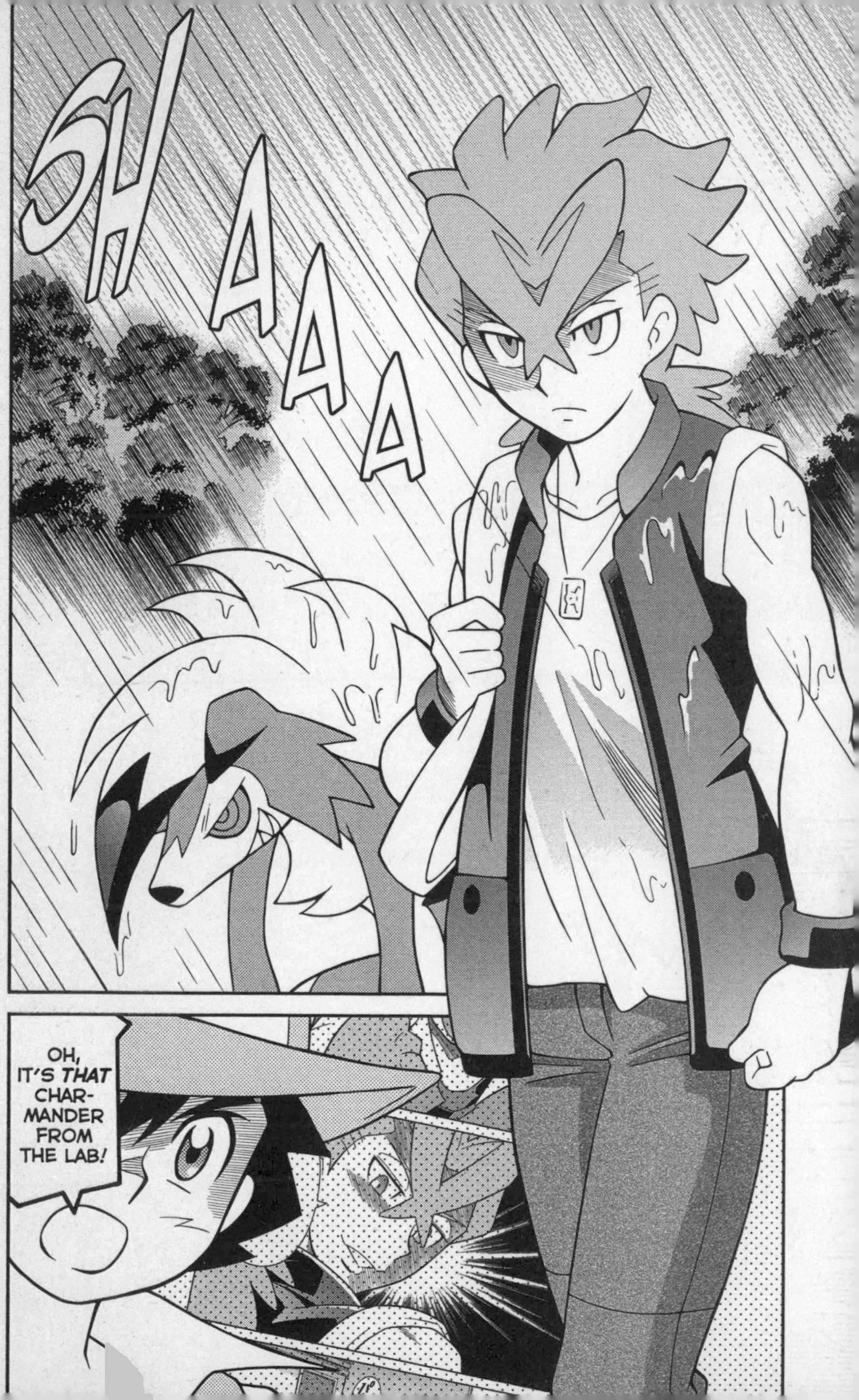
SHAAAA
OH, IT'S *THAT* CHARMANDER FROM THE LAB!

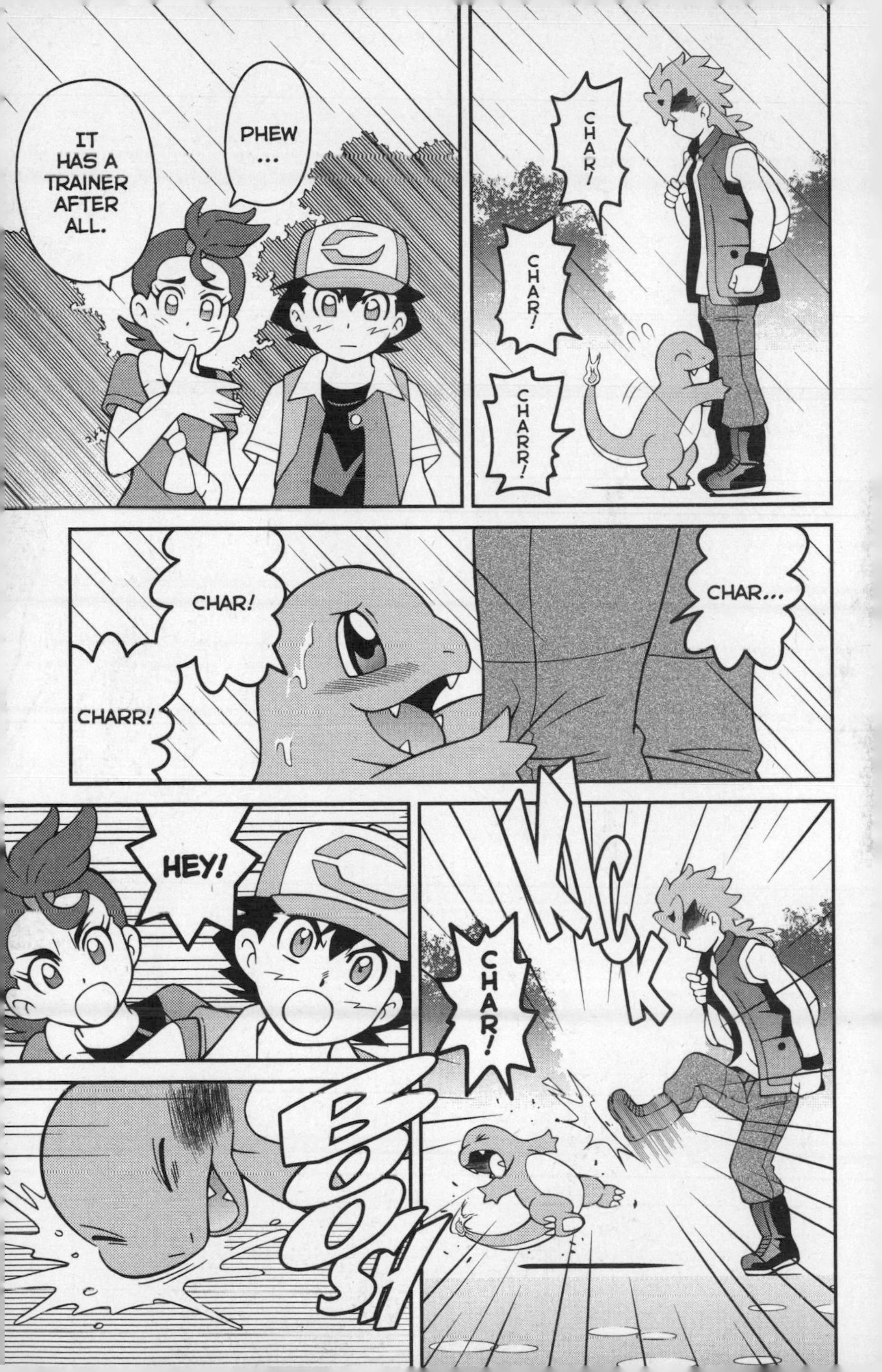
CHAR!
CHAR!
CHARR!
PHEW...
IT HAS A TRAINER AFTER ALL.
CHAR...
CHAR!
CHARR!
KICK
CHAR!
HEY!
BOOSH

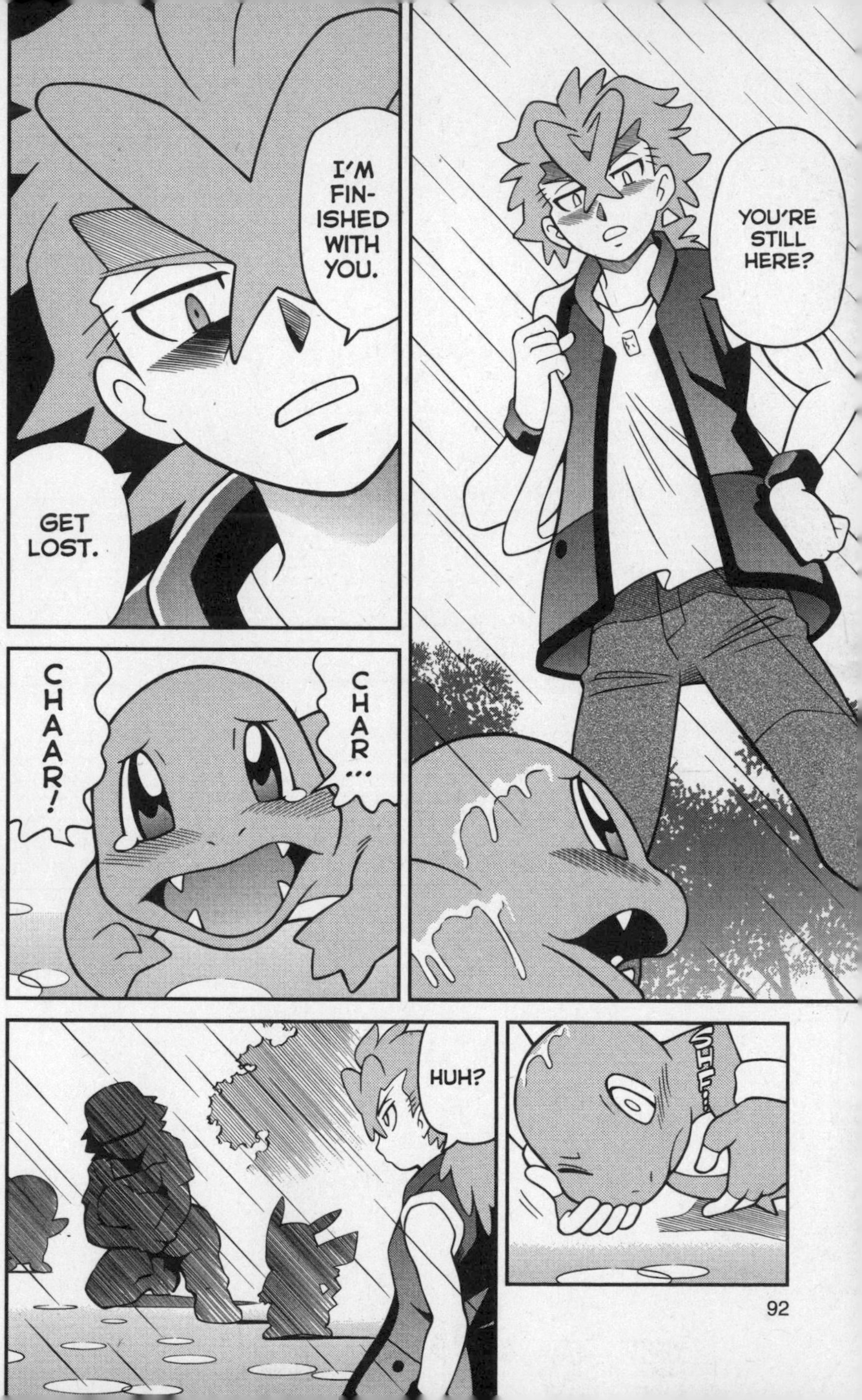
YOU'RE STILL HERE?
I'M FIN-ISHED WITH YOU.
GET LOST.
CHAR...
CHAAR!
SHF...
HUH?

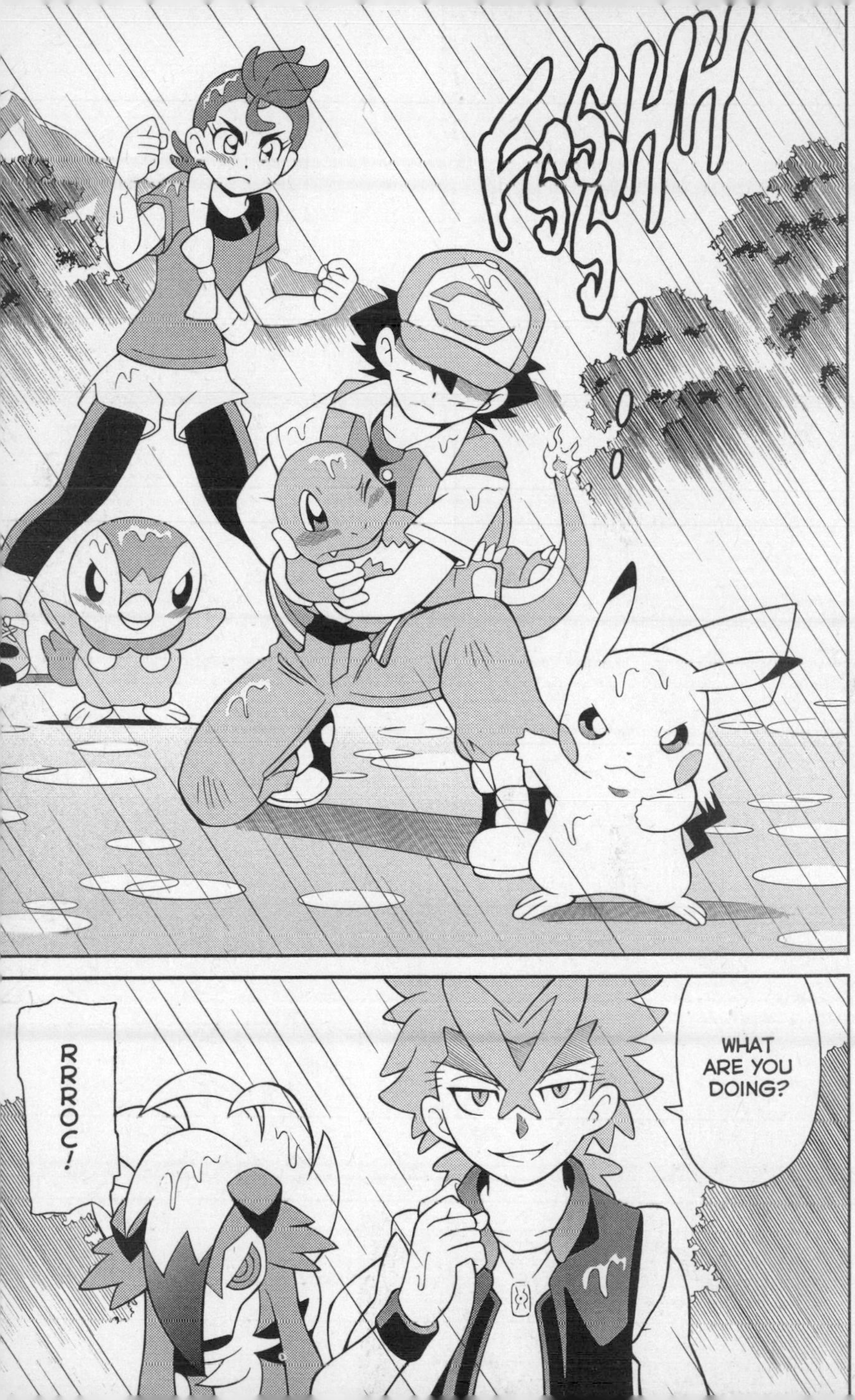
FSSSHH!
WHAT ARE YOU DOING?
RRROC!

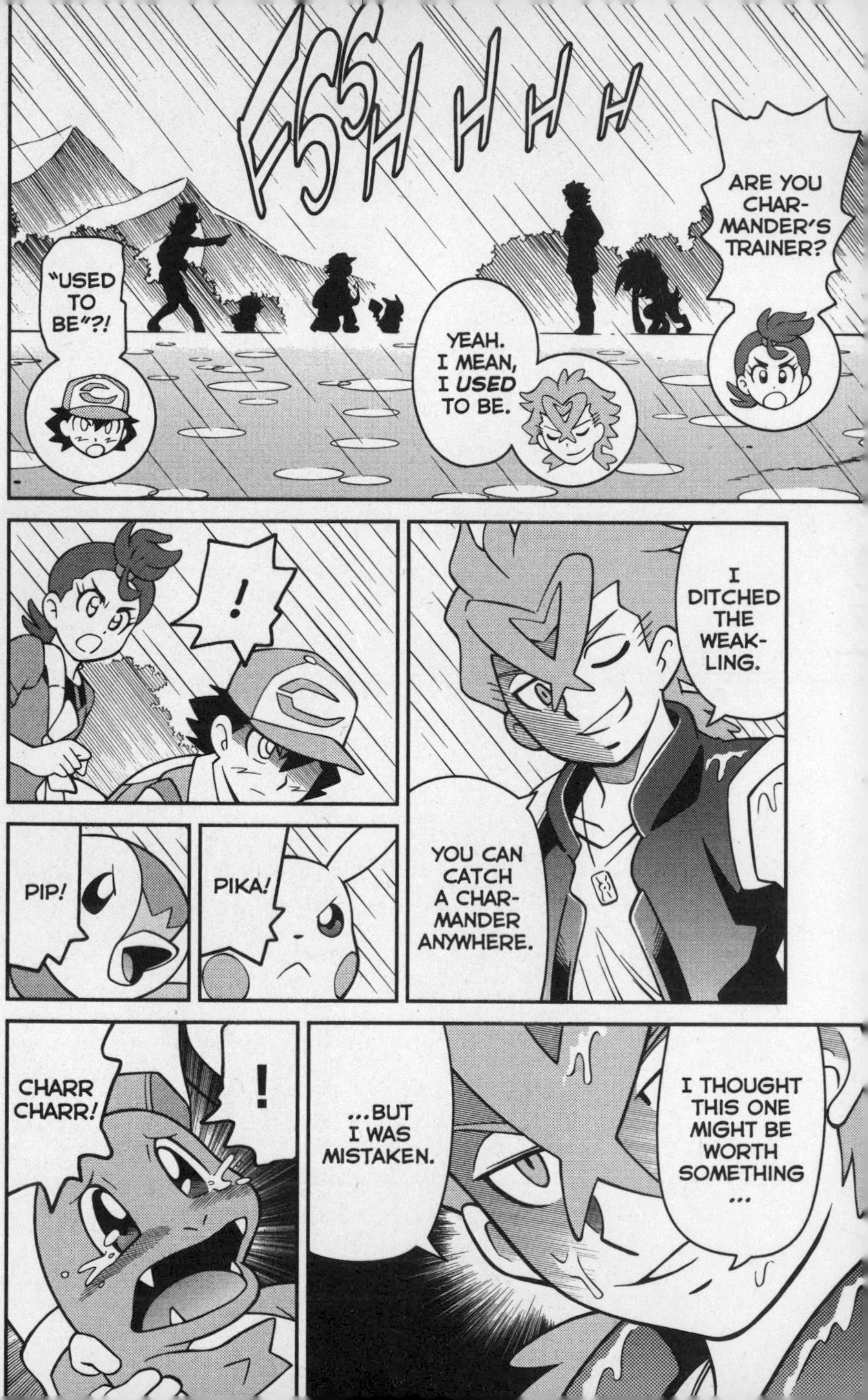SSHHHHH
ARE YOU CHAR-MANDER'S TRAINER?
YEAH. I MEAN, I *USED* TO BE.
"USED TO BE"?!
I DITCHED THE WEAK-LING.
YOU CAN CATCH A CHAR-MANDER ANYWHERE.
!
PIKA!
PIP!
I THOUGHT THIS ONE MIGHT BE WORTH SOMETHING ...
...BUT I WAS MISTAKEN.
!
CHARR CHARR!

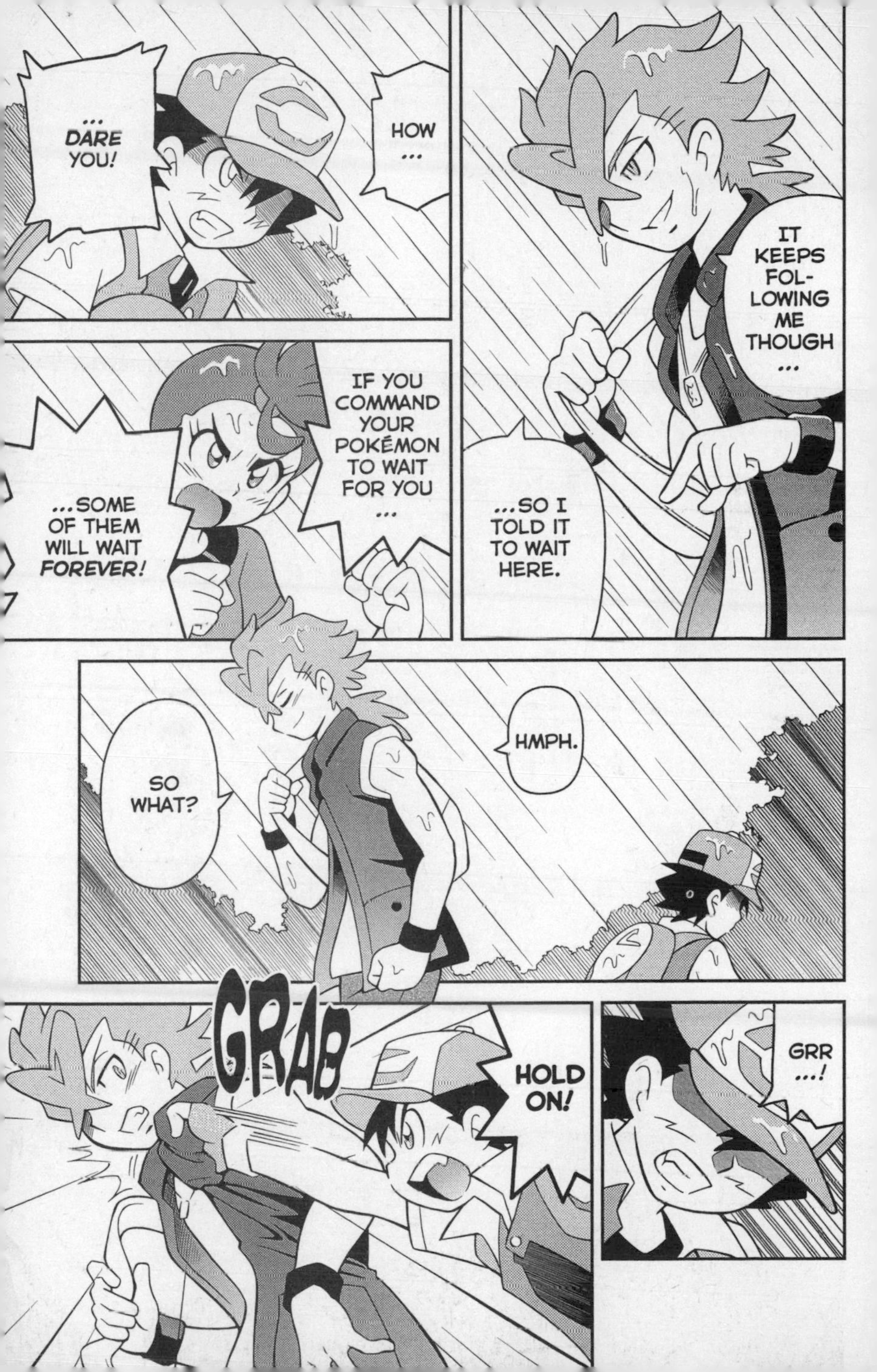
IT KEEPS FOL-LOWING ME THOUGH ...
...SO I TOLD IT TO WAIT HERE.
HOW ...
... DARE YOU!
IF YOU COMMAND YOUR POKÉMON TO WAIT FOR YOU ...
...SOME OF THEM WILL WAIT FOREVER!
HMPH.
SO WHAT?
GRR ...!
HOLD ON!
GRAB

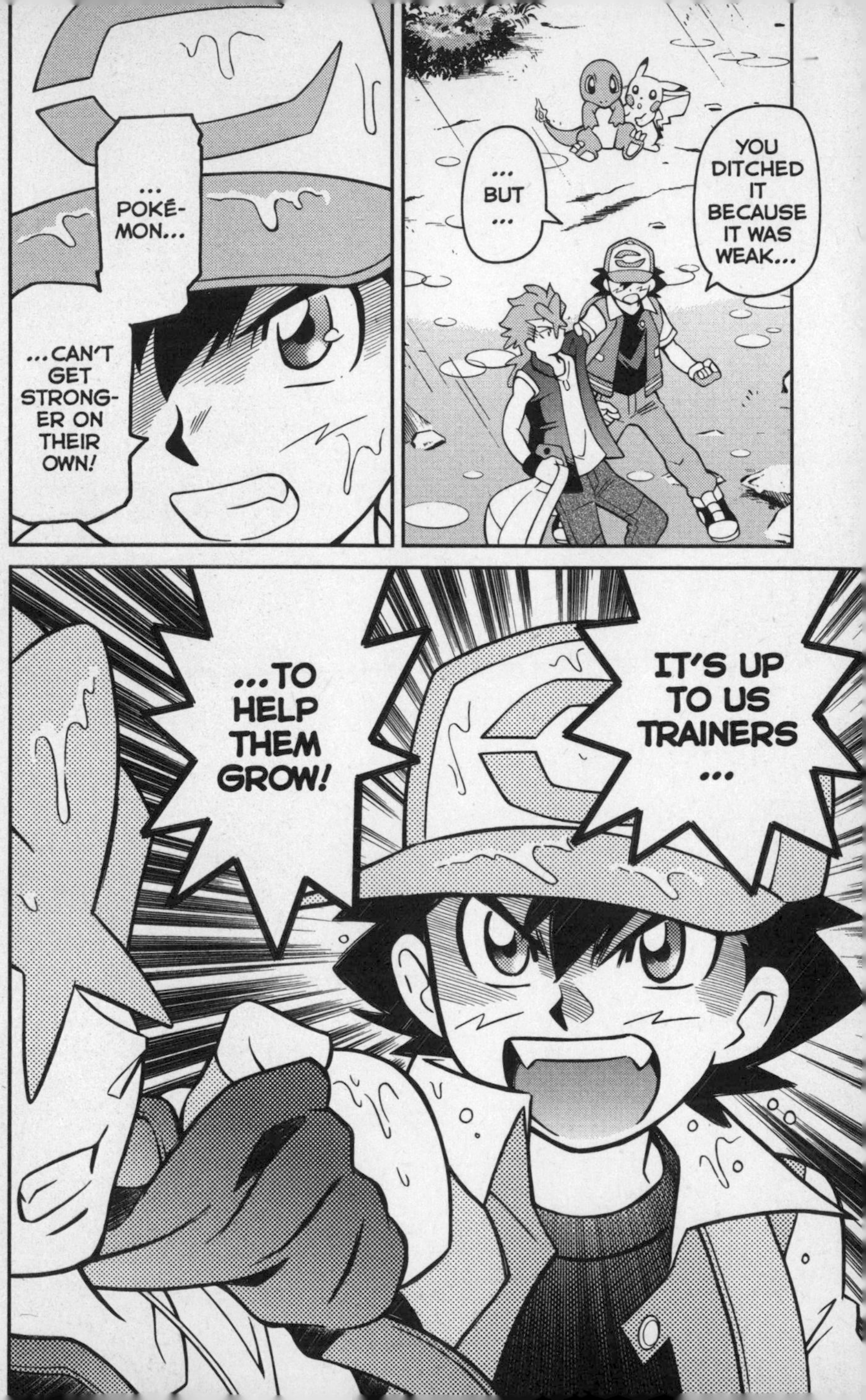
YOU DITCHED IT BECAUSE IT WAS WEAK...
... BUT ...
... POKÉMON...
...CAN'T GET STRONGER ON THEIR OWN!
IT'S UP TO US TRAINERS ...
...TO HELP THEM GROW!

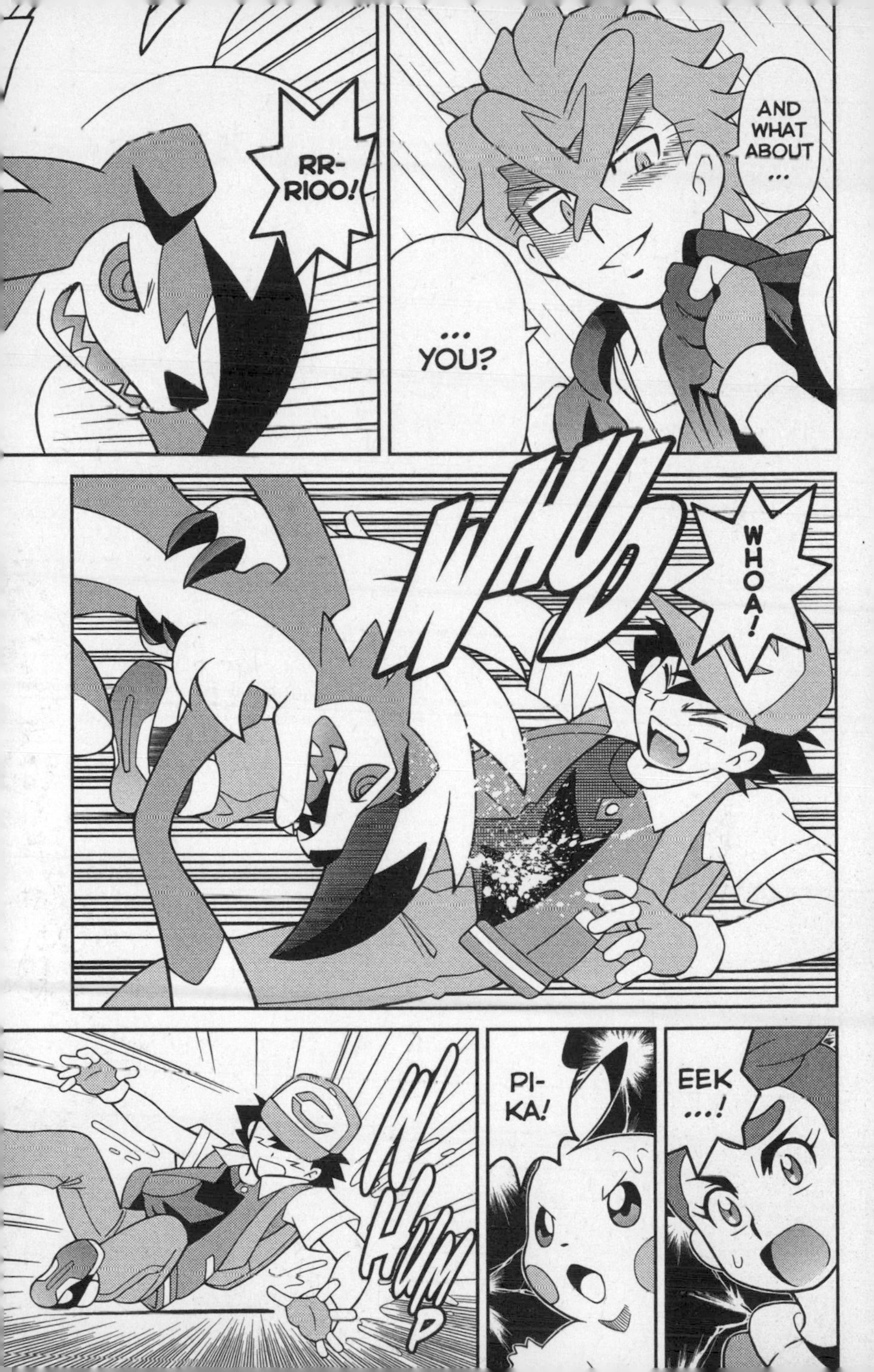
AND WHAT ABOUT ...
... YOU?
RR-RIOO!
WHOA!
WHUD
EEK ...!
PI-KA!
WHUMP

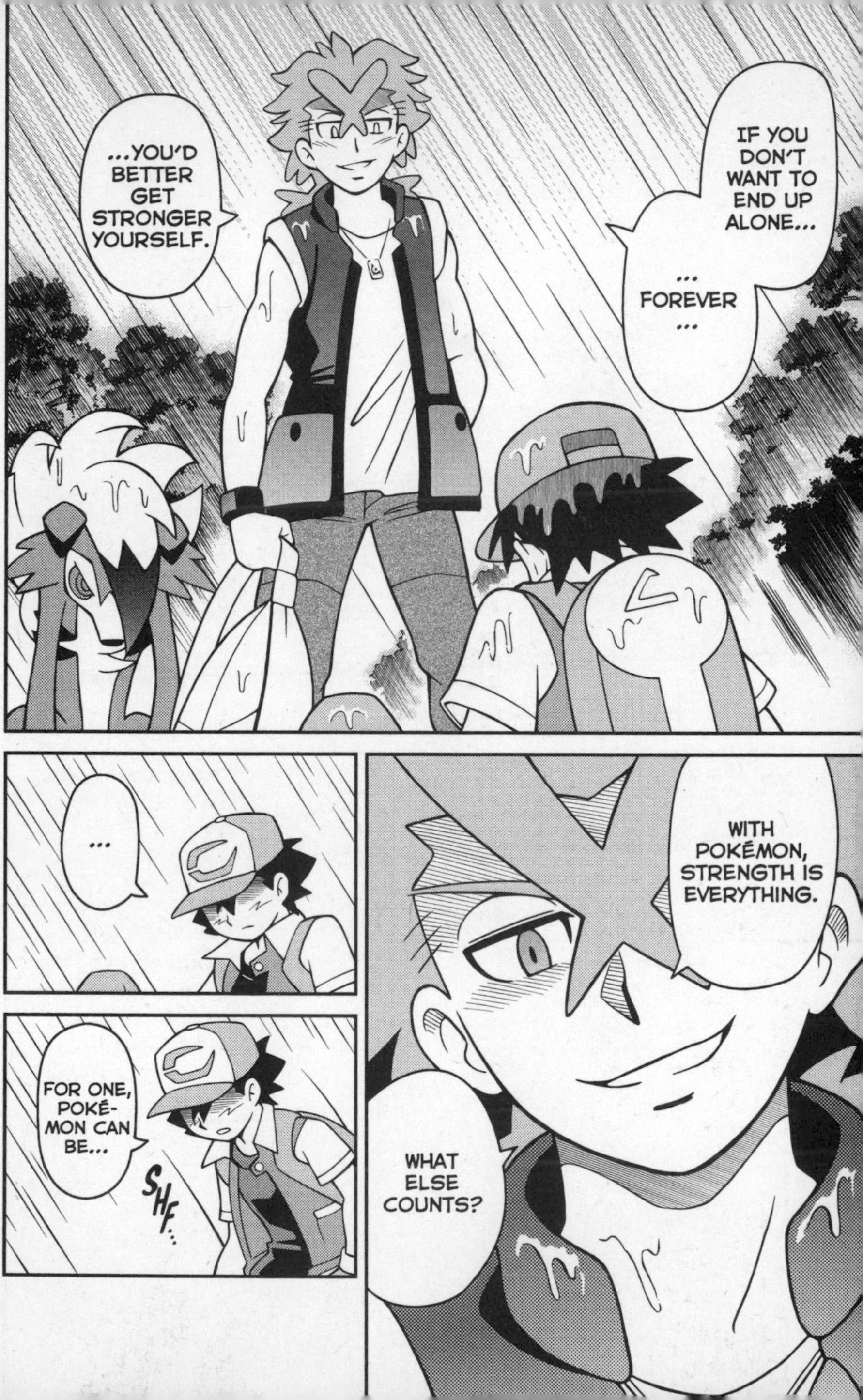
IF YOU DON'T WANT TO END UP ALONE...
...FOREVER...
...YOU'D BETTER GET STRONGER YOURSELF.
WITH POKÉMON, STRENGTH IS EVERYTHING.
WHAT ELSE COUNTS?
...
FOR ONE, POKÉ-MON CAN BE...
SHF...

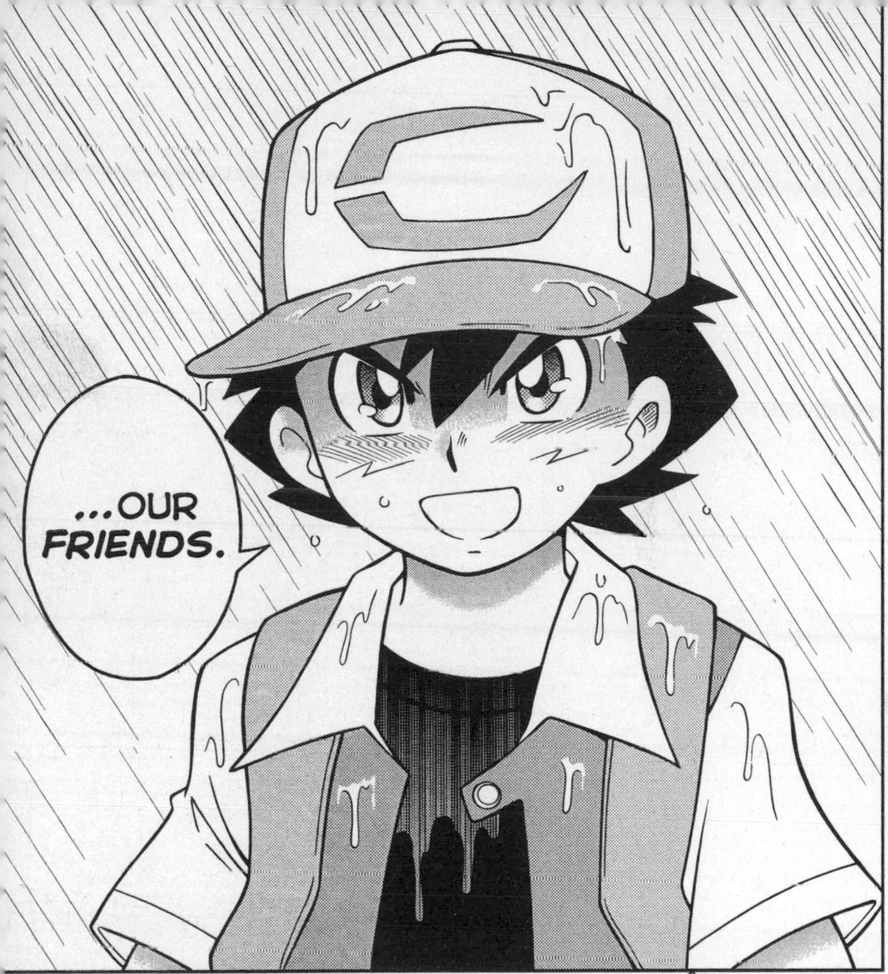
...OUR FRIENDS.

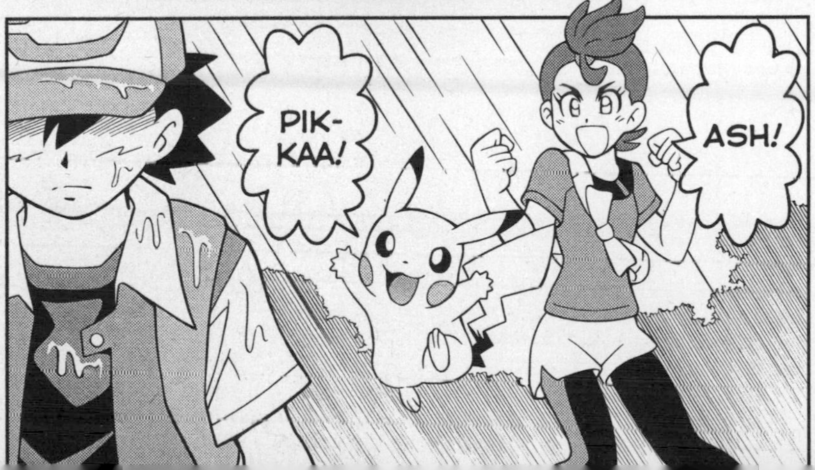
ASH!
PIK-KAA!

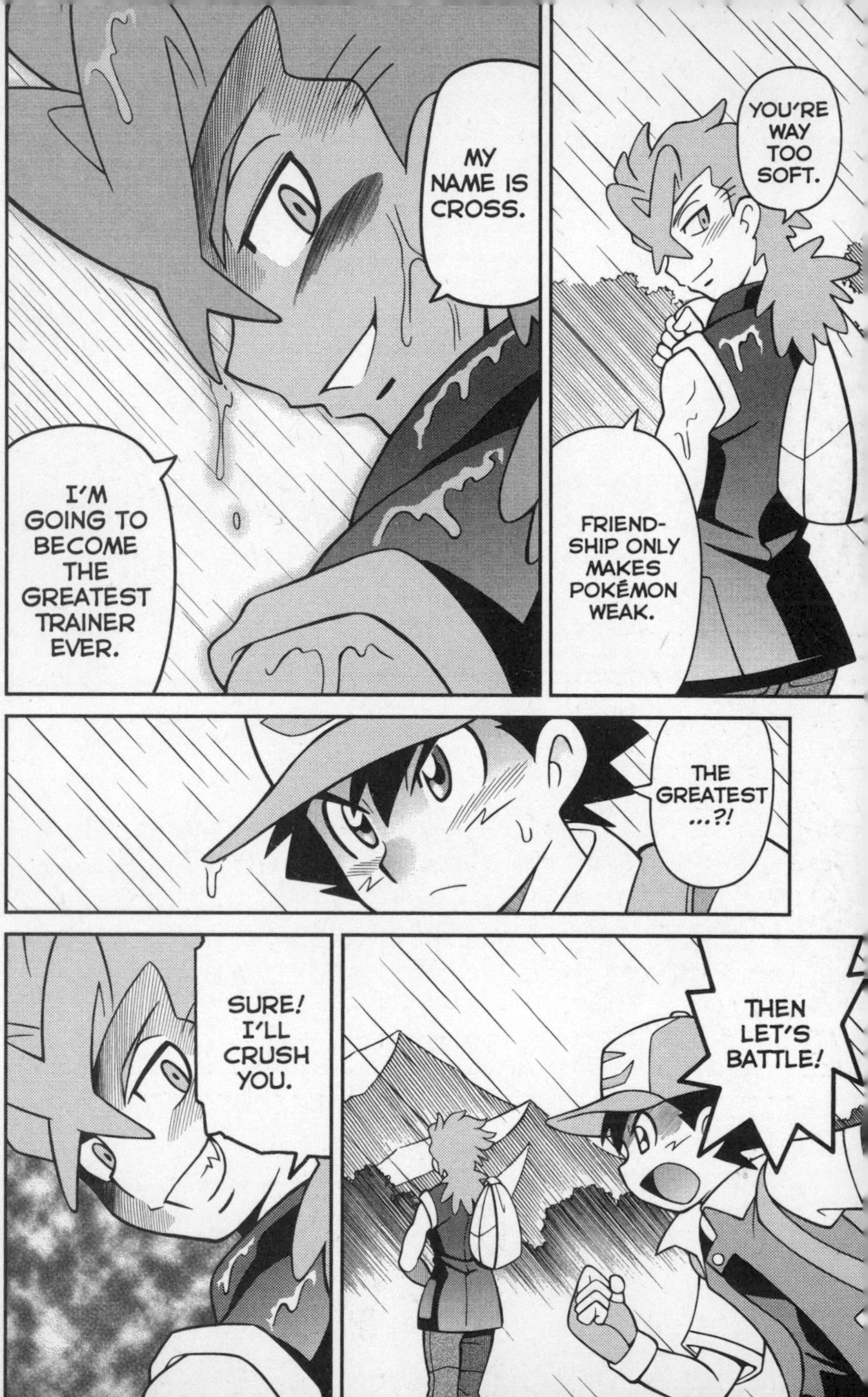

YOU'RE WAY TOO SOFT.
FRIEND-SHIP ONLY MAKES POKÉMON WEAK.
MY NAME IS CROSS.
I'M GOING TO BECOME THE GREATEST TRAINER EVER.
THE GREATEST ...?!
THEN LET'S BATTLE!
SURE! I'LL CRUSH YOU.

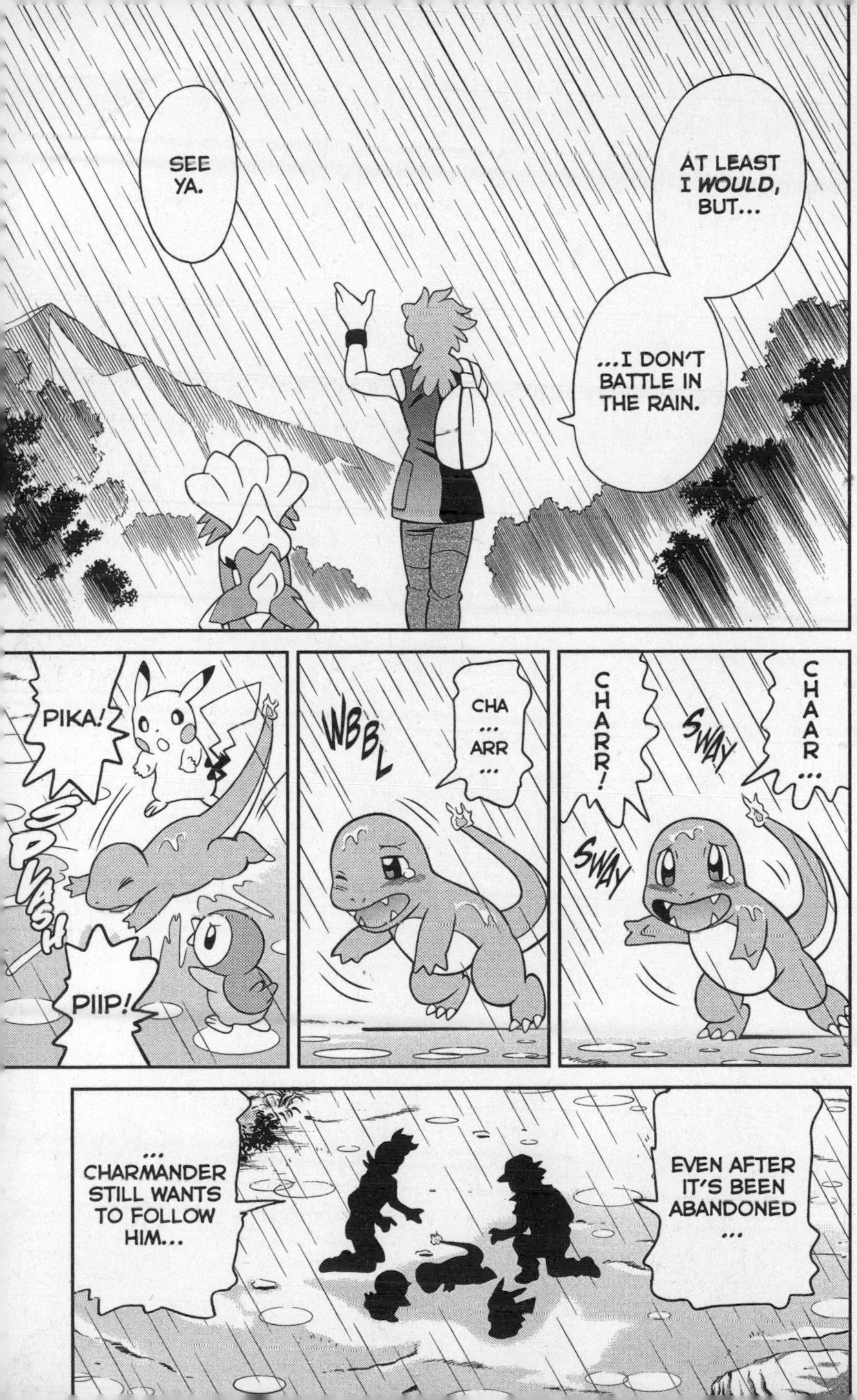
AT LEAST I *WOULD*, BUT...
...I DON'T BATTLE IN THE RAIN.
SEE YA.
CHAAR...
SWAY
CHARR!
SWAY
CHA... ARR...
WBBL
PIKA!
SPLASH
PIIP!
EVEN AFTER IT'S BEEN ABANDONED...
...CHARMANDER STILL WANTS TO FOLLOW HIM...

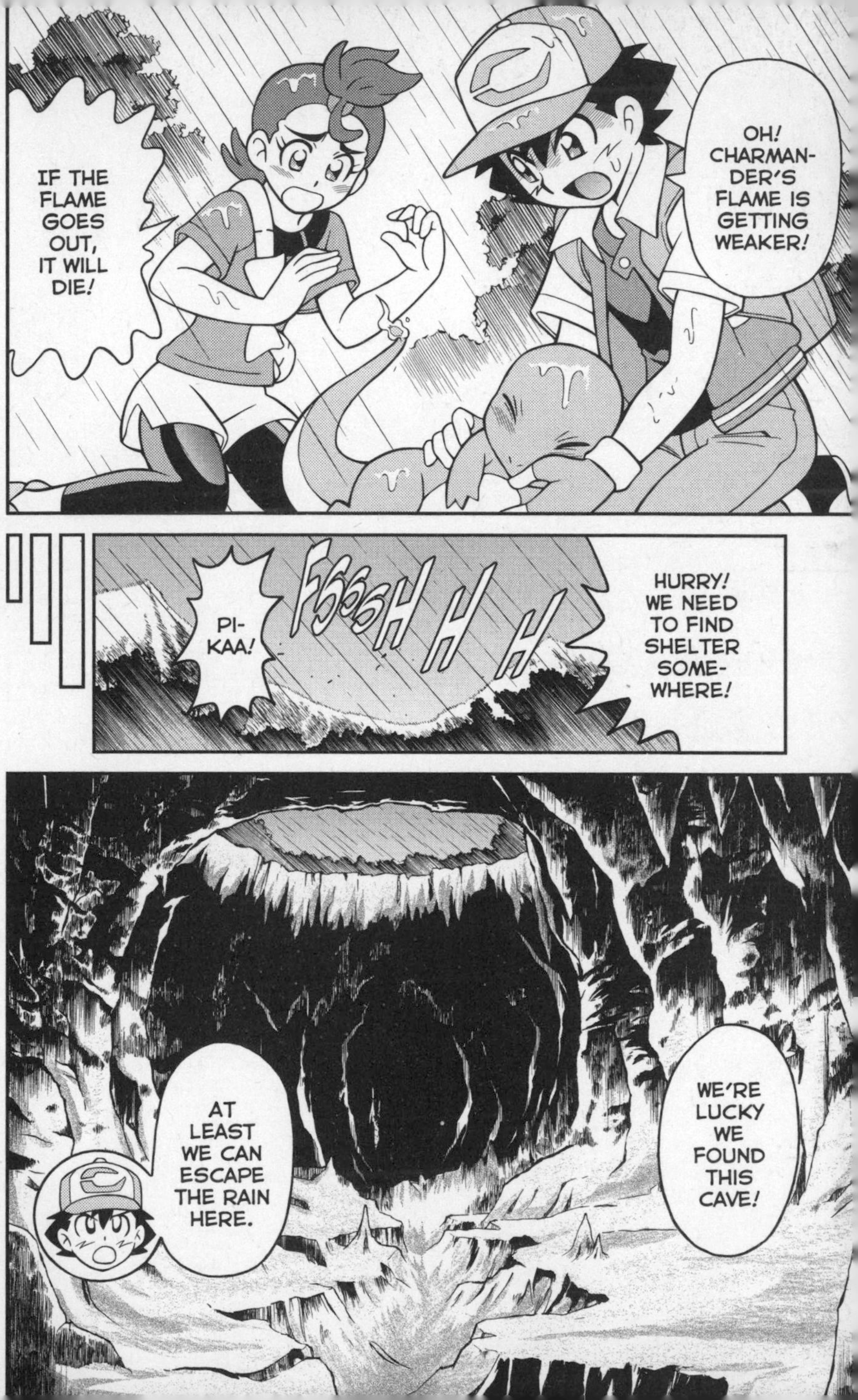
OH! CHARMAN-DER'S FLAME IS GETTING WEAKER!
IF THE FLAME GOES OUT, IT WILL DIE!
HURRY! WE NEED TO FIND SHELTER SOME-WHERE!
FSSSHH H H
PI-KAA!
WE'RE LUCKY WE FOUND THIS CAVE!
AT LEAST WE CAN ESCAPE THE RAIN HERE.

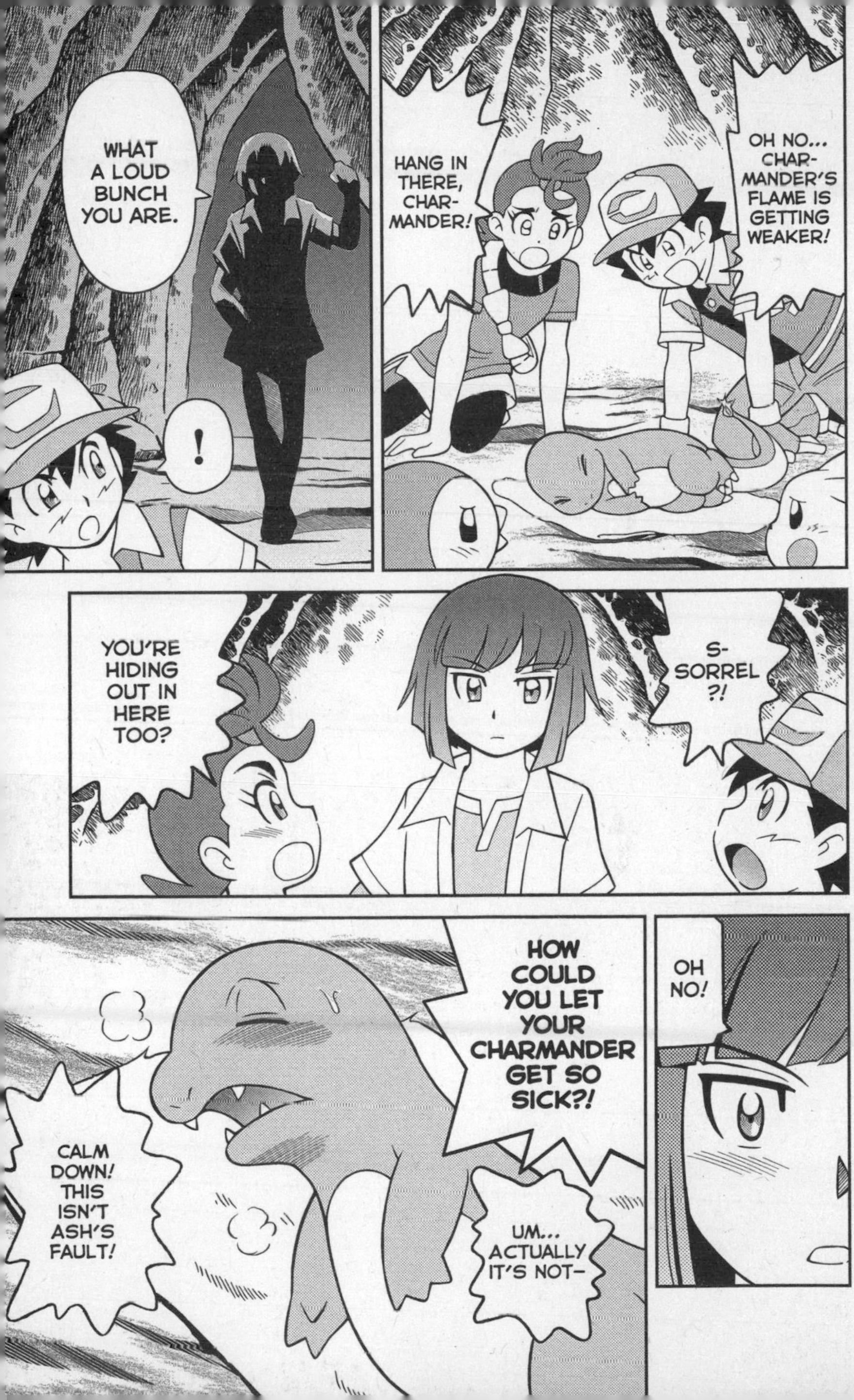
OH NO... CHAR-MANDER'S FLAME IS GETTING WEAKER!
HANG IN THERE, CHAR-MANDER!
WHAT A LOUD BUNCH YOU ARE.
!
S-SORREL?!
YOU'RE HIDING OUT IN HERE TOO?
OH NO!
HOW COULD YOU LET YOUR CHARMANDER GET SO SICK?!
UM... ACTUALLY IT'S NOT–
CALM DOWN! THIS ISN'T ASH'S FAULT!

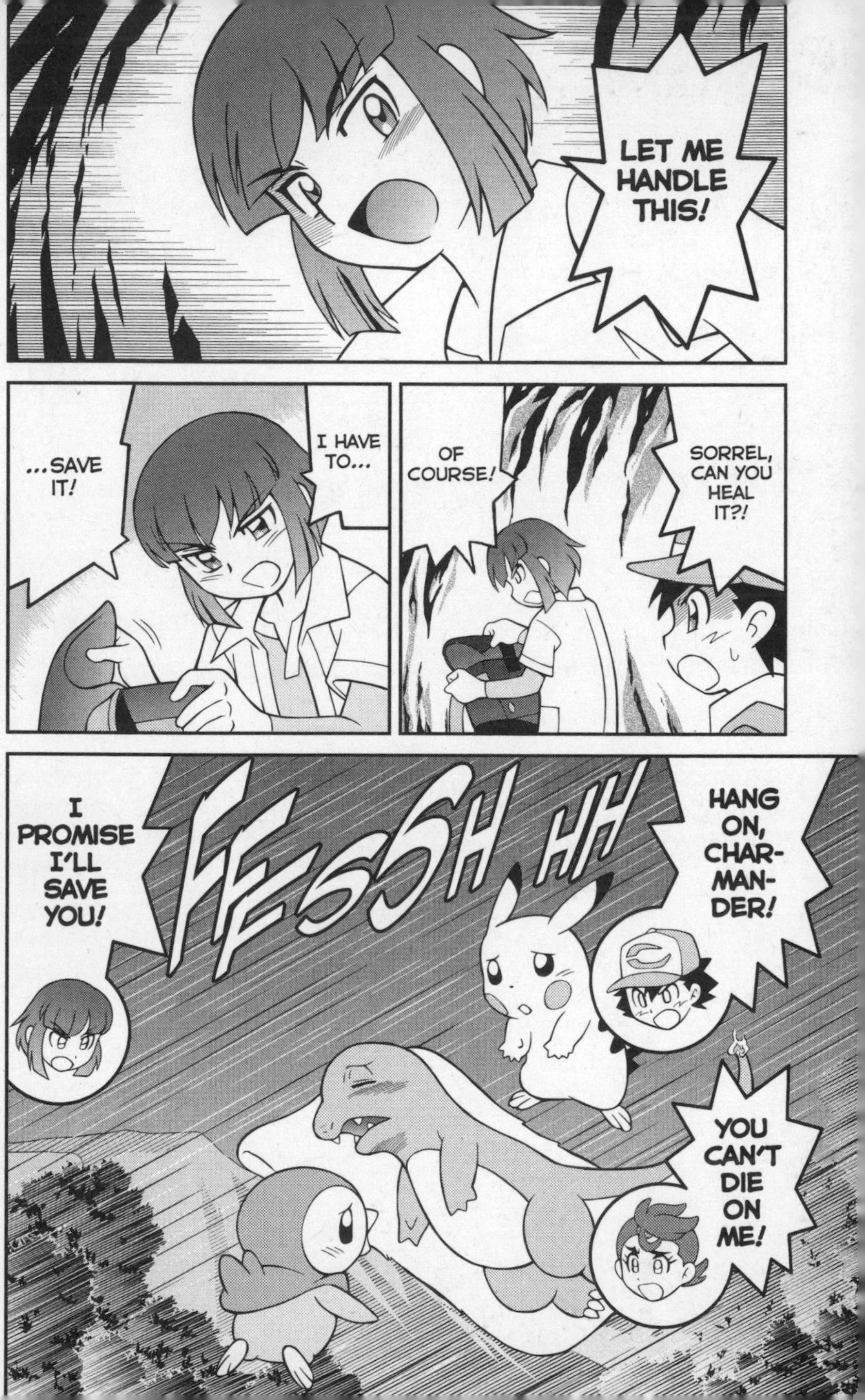
LET ME HANDLE THIS!
SORREL, CAN YOU HEAL IT?!
OF COURSE!
I HAVE TO...
...SAVE IT!
HANG ON, CHAR-MAN-DER!
FESSHHH
I PROMISE I'LL SAVE YOU!
YOU CAN'T DIE ON ME!

CHAPTER 5

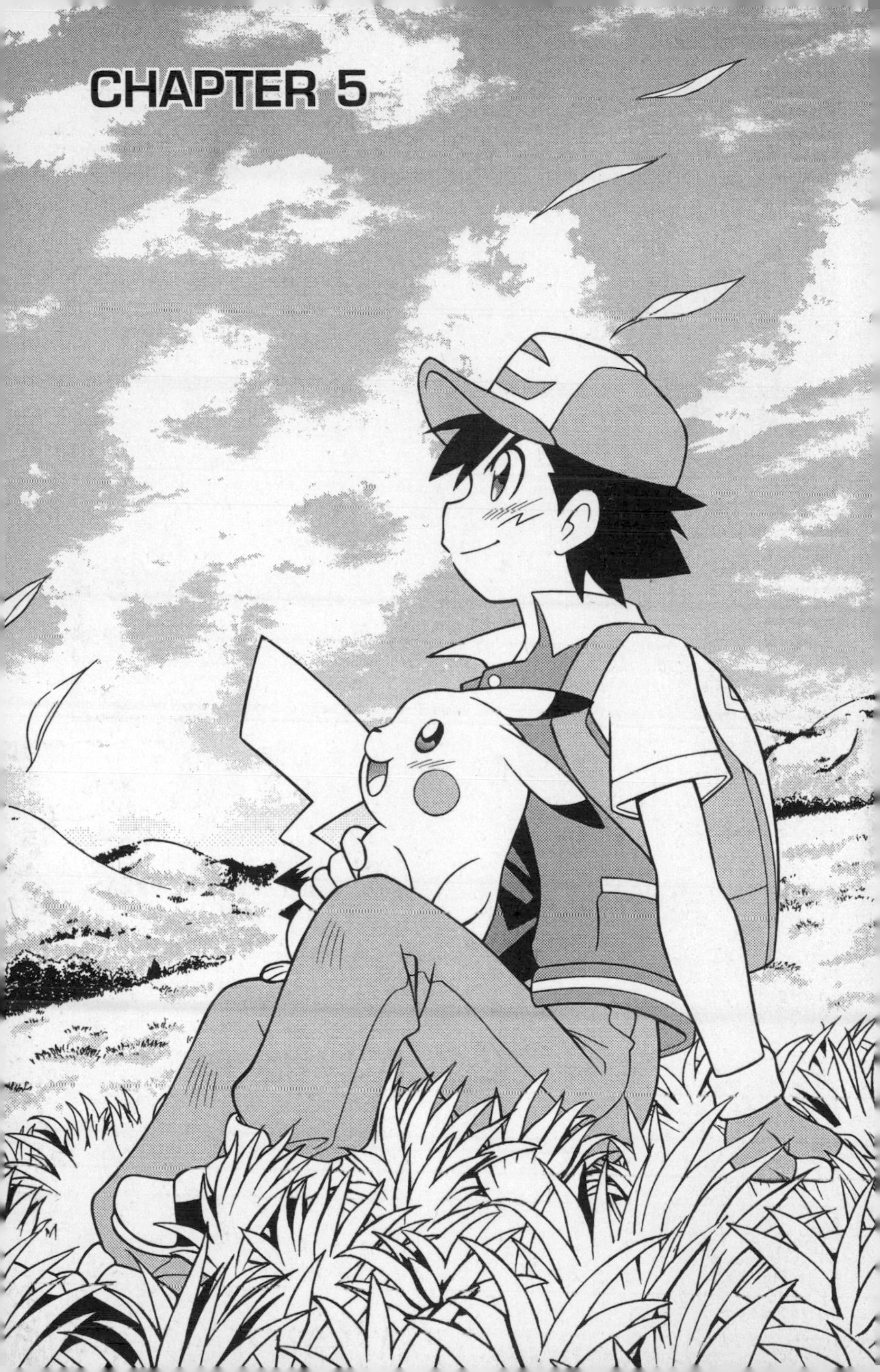

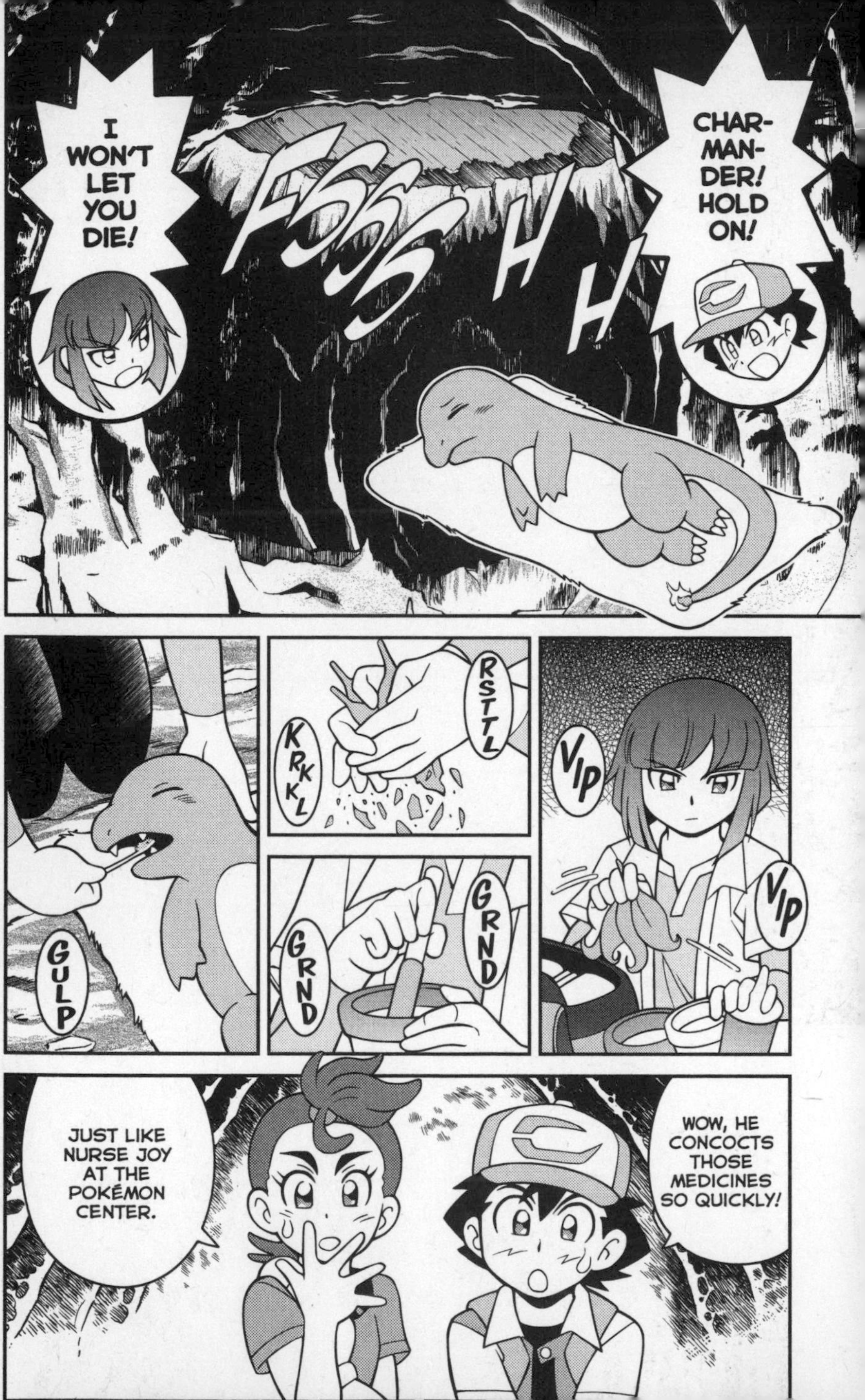
CHAR-MAN-DER! HOLD ON!
FSSSHHH
I WON'T LET YOU DIE!
VIP
VIP
RSTTL
KRKKL
GRND
GRND
GULP
WOW, HE CONCOCTS THOSE MEDICINES SO QUICKLY!
JUST LIKE NURSE JOY AT THE POKÉMON CENTER.

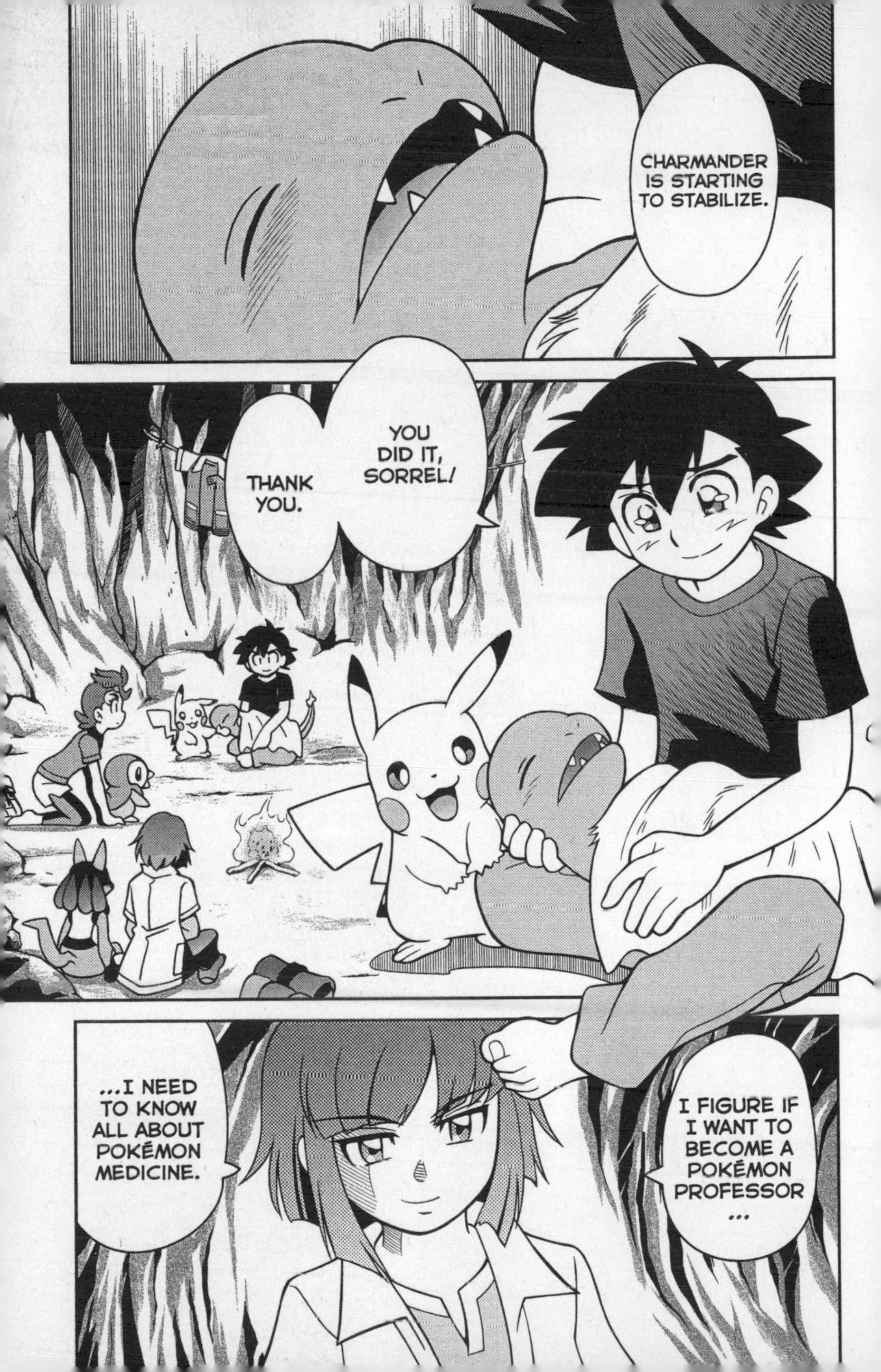
CHARMANDER IS STARTING TO STABILIZE.
YOU DID IT, SORREL!
THANK YOU.
I FIGURE IF I WANT TO BECOME A POKÉMON PROFESSOR ...
...I NEED TO KNOW ALL ABOUT POKÉMON MEDICINE.

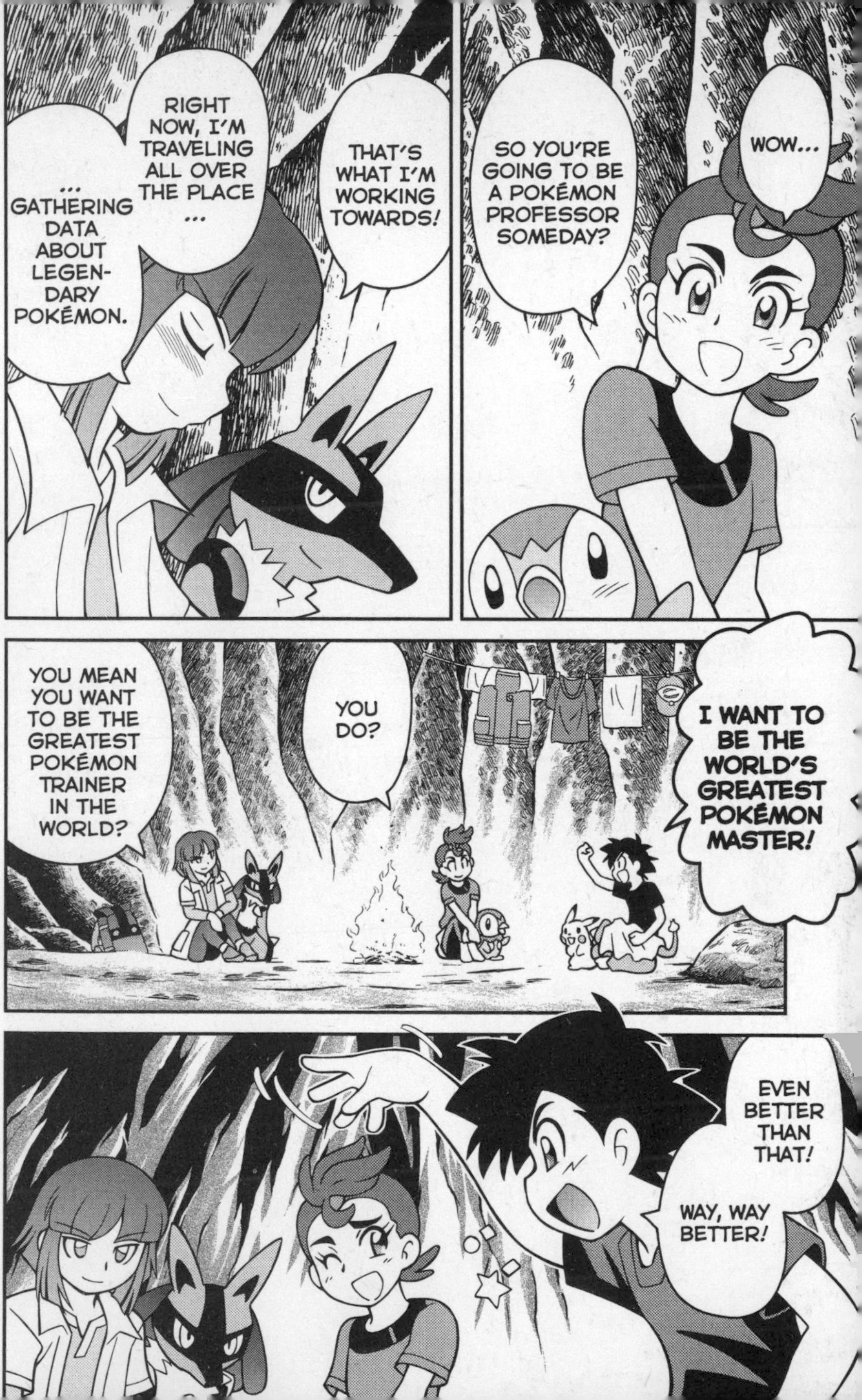
WOW...
SO YOU'RE GOING TO BE A POKÉMON PROFESSOR SOMEDAY?
THAT'S WHAT I'M WORKING TOWARDS!
RIGHT NOW, I'M TRAVELING ALL OVER THE PLACE...
...GATHERING DATA ABOUT LEGEN-DARY POKÉMON.
I WANT TO BE THE WORLD'S GREATEST POKÉMON MASTER!
YOU DO?
YOU MEAN YOU WANT TO BE THE GREATEST POKÉMON TRAINER IN THE WORLD?
EVEN BETTER THAN THAT!
WAY, WAY BETTER!

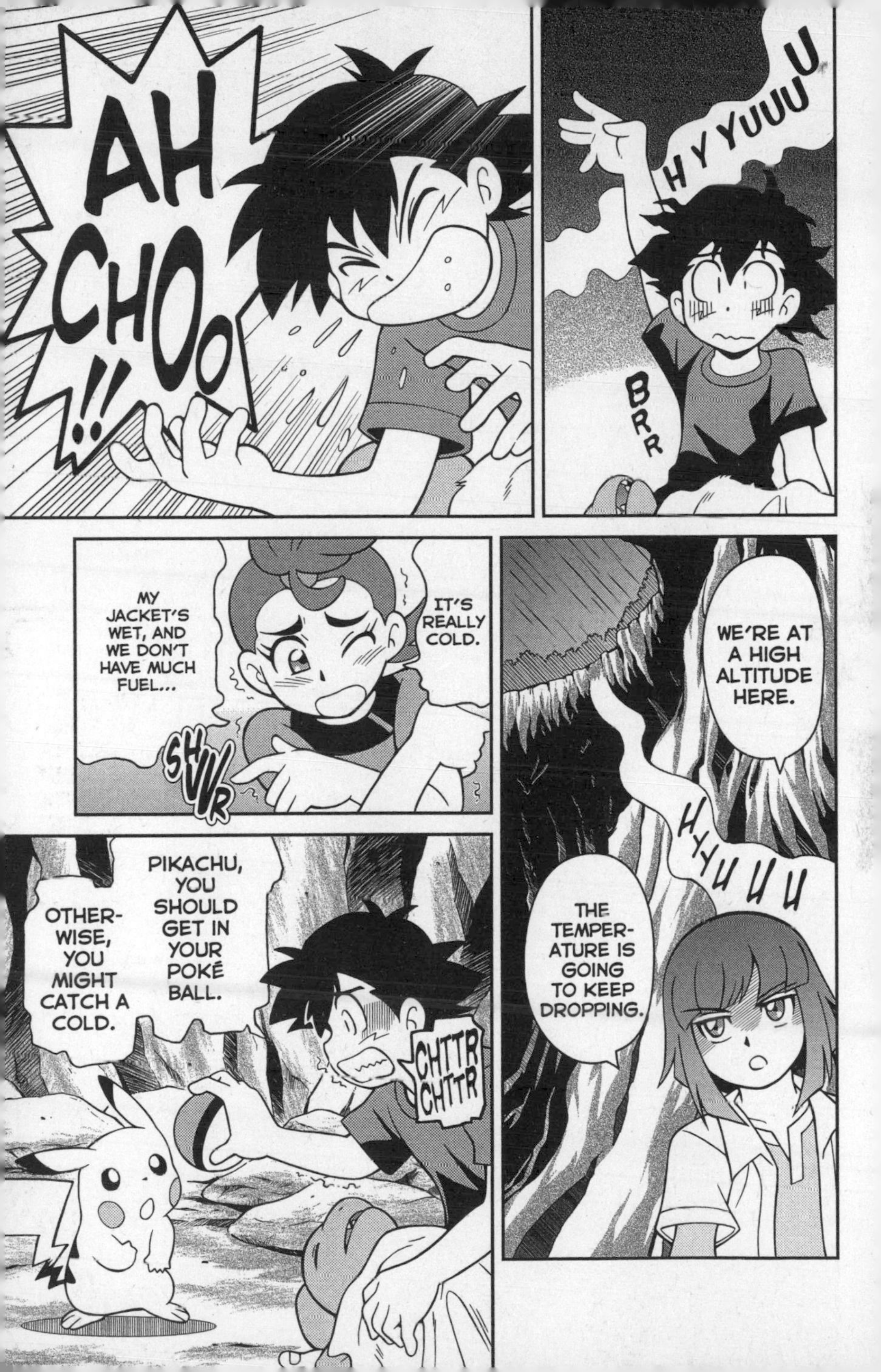
HYUUUU
BRR
AH CHOO!!
WE'RE AT A HIGH ALTITUDE HERE.
HHYUUUU
THE TEMPERATURE IS GOING TO KEEP DROPPING.
IT'S REALLY COLD.
MY JACKET'S WET, AND WE DON'T HAVE MUCH FUEL...
SHVVR
PIKACHU, YOU SHOULD GET IN YOUR POKÉ BALL.
OTHERWISE, YOU MIGHT CATCH A COLD.
CHTTR CHTTR

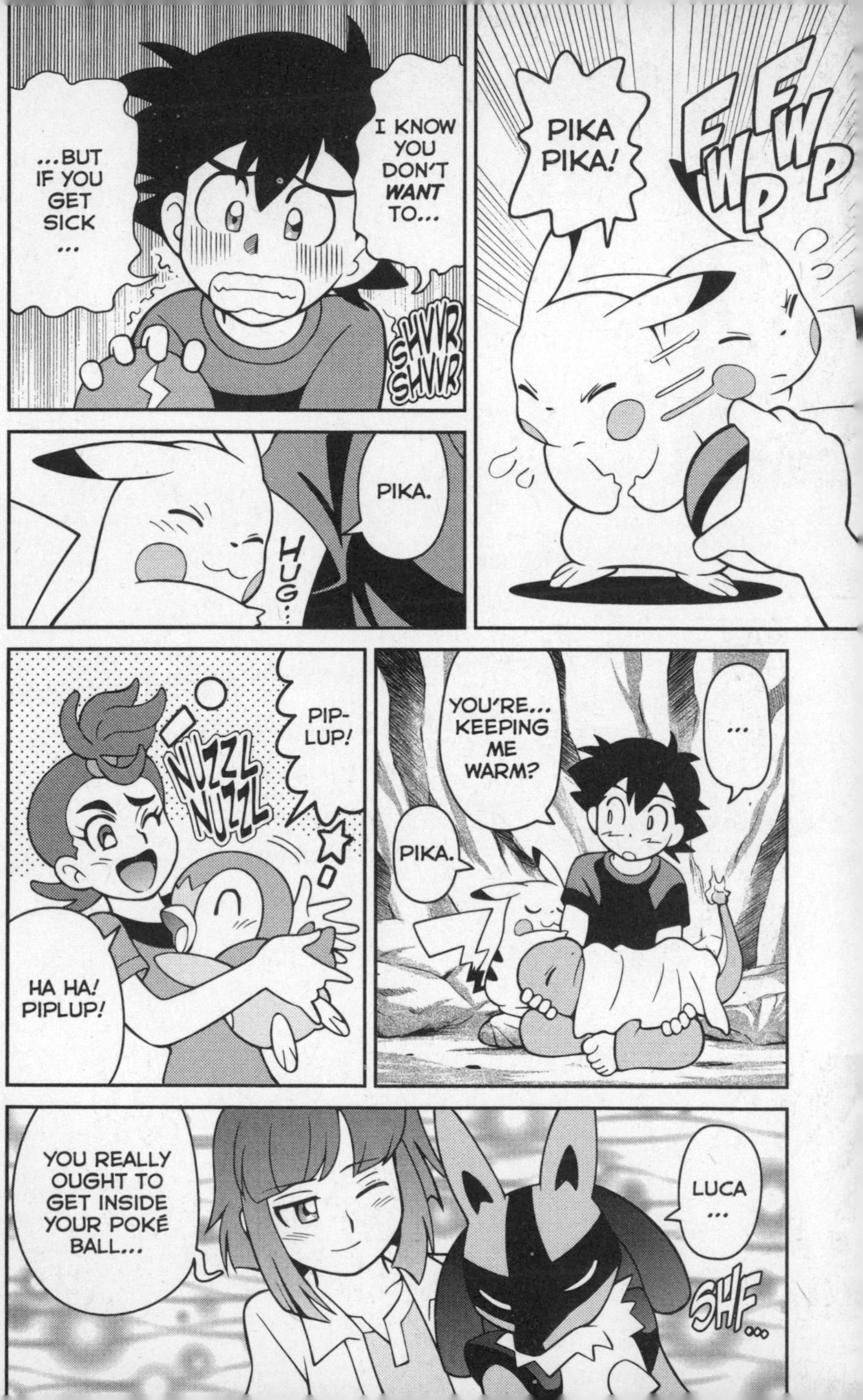
FWP FWP FWP
PIKA PIKA!
I KNOW YOU DON'T *WANT* TO...
...BUT IF YOU GET SICK...
SHVVR SHVVR
PIKA.
HUG...
...
YOU'RE... KEEPING ME WARM?
PIKA.
PIP-LUP!
NUZZL NUZZL
HA HA! PIPLUP!
LUCA...
SHF...
YOU REALLY OUGHT TO GET INSIDE YOUR POKÉ BALL...

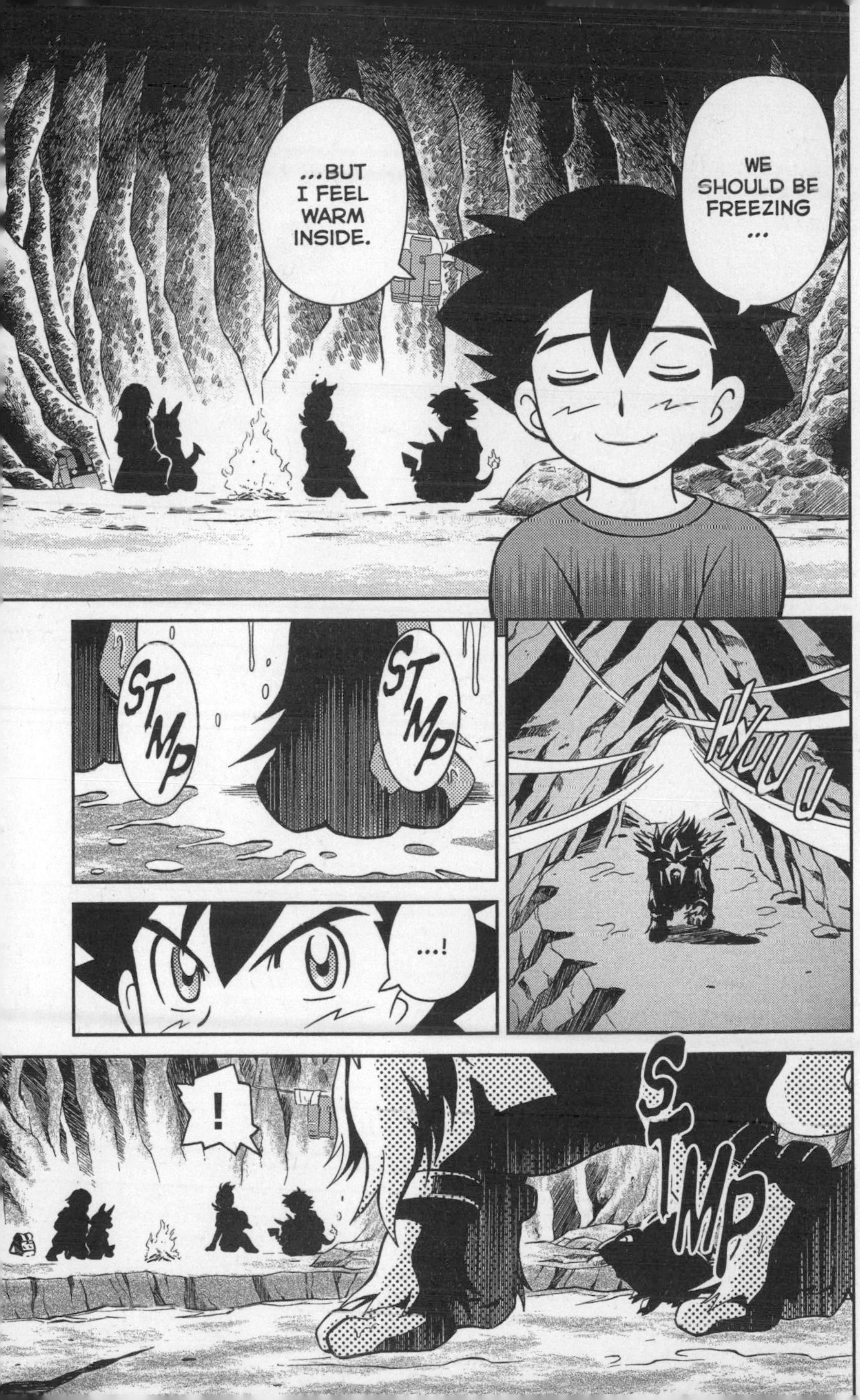
WE SHOULD BE FREEZING ...
...BUT I FEEL WARM INSIDE.
HYUUU
STMP
STMP
...!
STMP
!

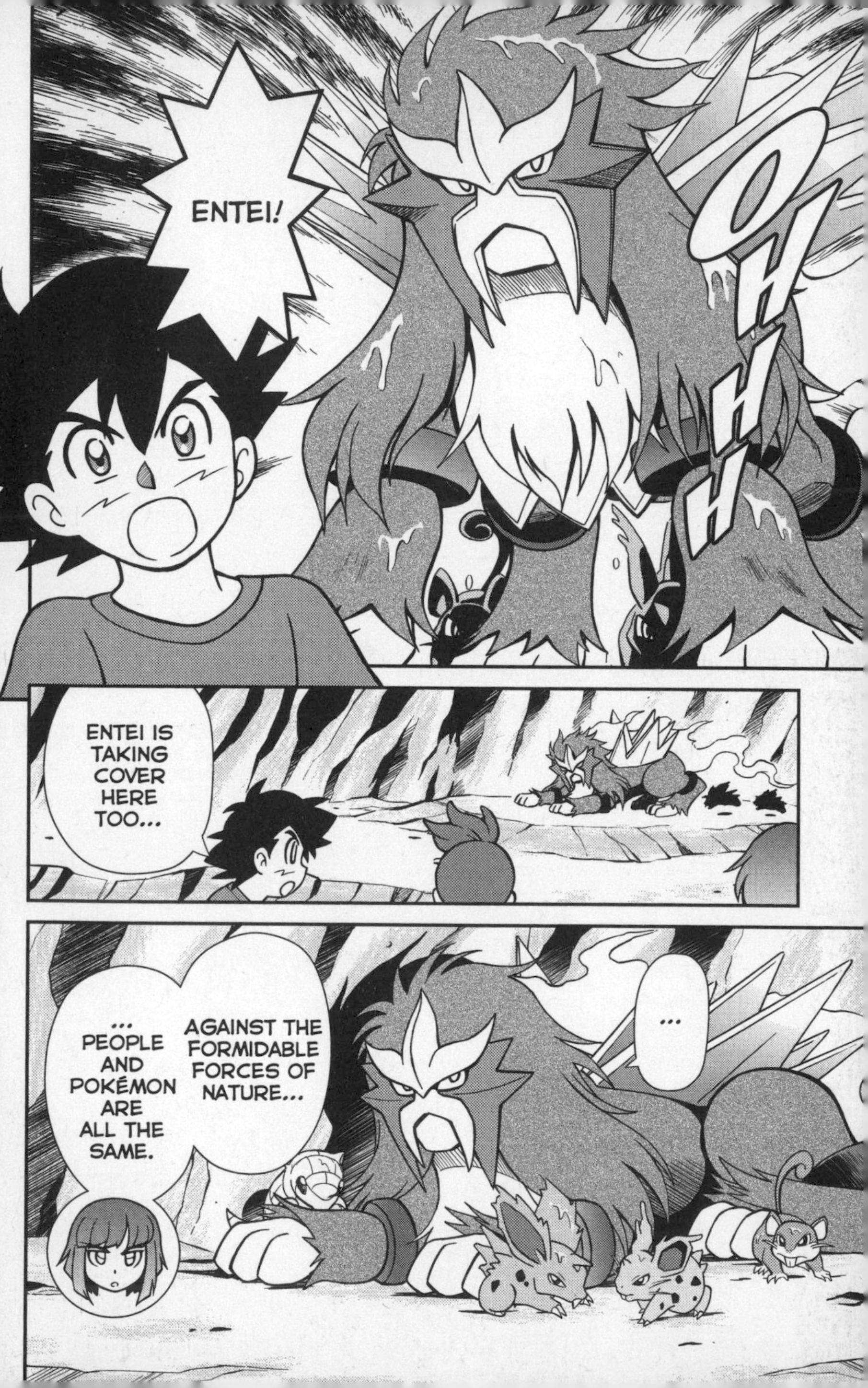
ENTEI!
OHHHH
ENTEI IS TAKING COVER HERE TOO...
...
AGAINST THE FORMIDABLE FORCES OF NATURE...
... PEOPLE AND POKÉMON ARE ALL THE SAME.

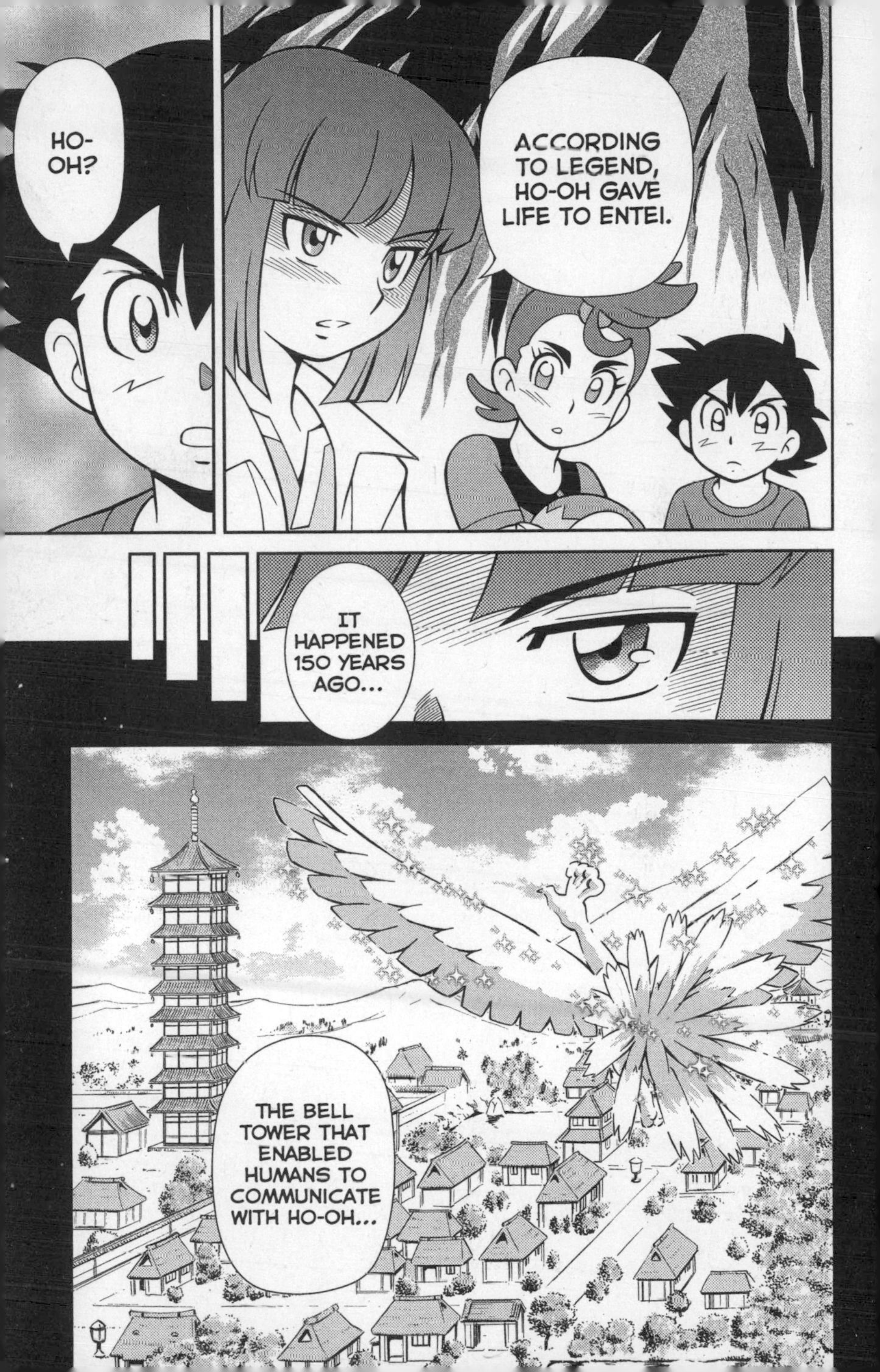
ACCORDING TO LEGEND, HO-OH GAVE LIFE TO ENTEI.
HO-OH?
IT HAPPENED 150 YEARS AGO...
THE BELL TOWER THAT ENABLED HUMANS TO COMMUNICATE WITH HO-OH...

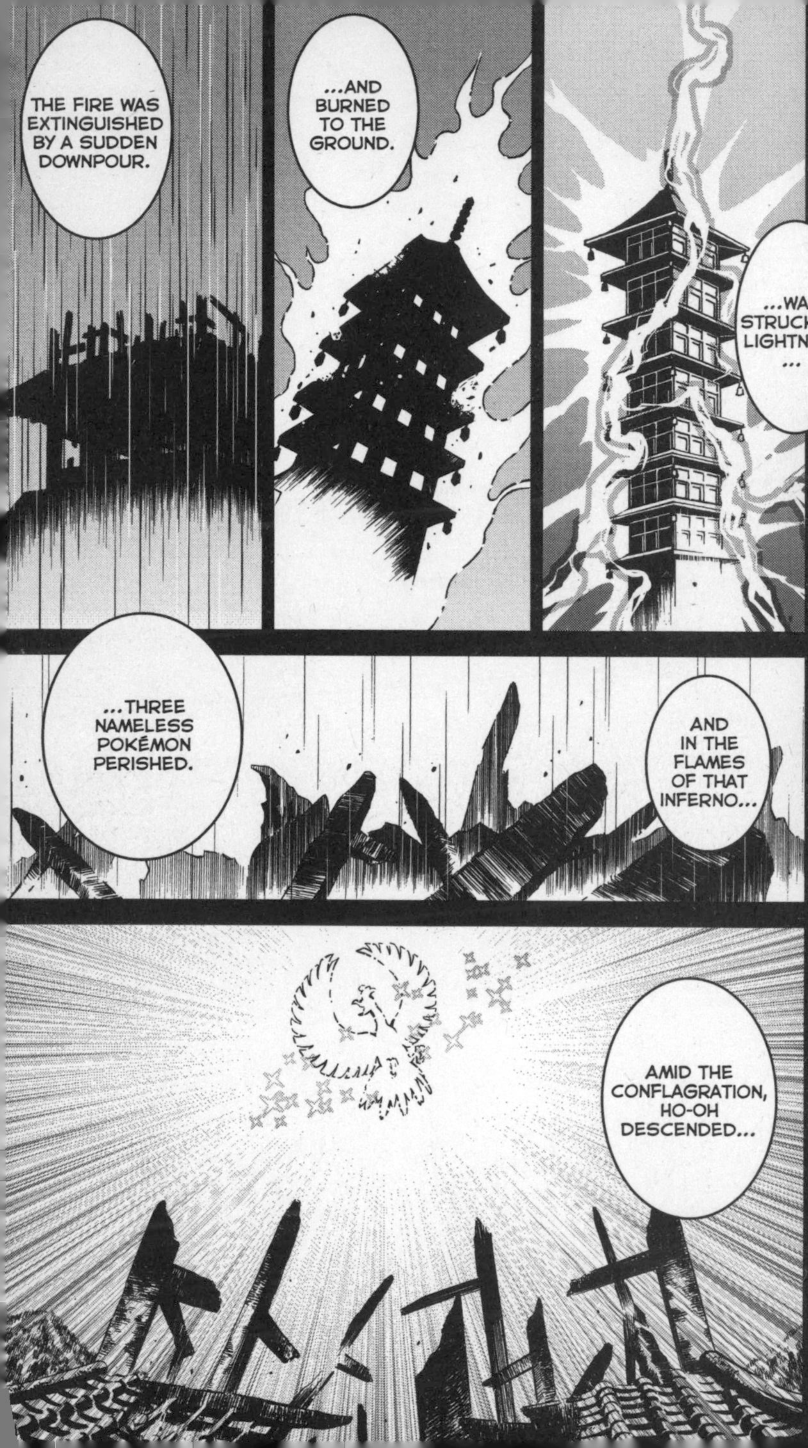
...WAS STRUCK BY LIGHTNING ...
...AND BURNED TO THE GROUND.
THE FIRE WAS EXTINGUISHED BY A SUDDEN DOWNPOUR.
AND IN THE FLAMES OF THAT INFERNO...
...THREE NAMELESS POKÉMON PERISHED.
AMID THE CONFLAGRATION, HO-OH DESCENDED...

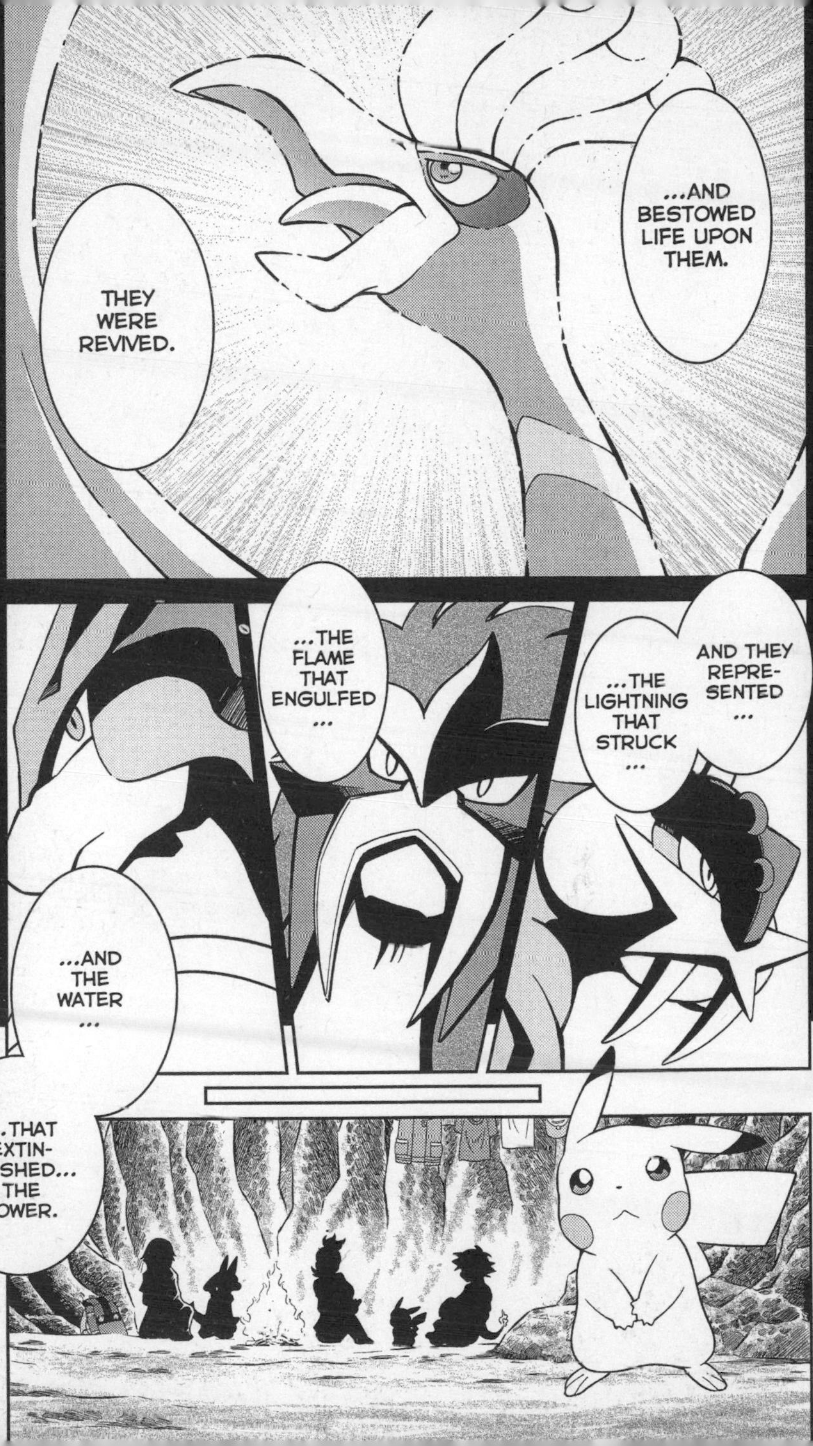
...AND BESTOWED LIFE UPON THEM.
THEY WERE REVIVED.
AND THEY REPRE-SENTED ...
...THE LIGHTNING THAT STRUCK ...
...THE FLAME THAT ENGULFED ...
...AND THE WATER ...
...THAT EXTIN-GUISHED... THE TOWER.

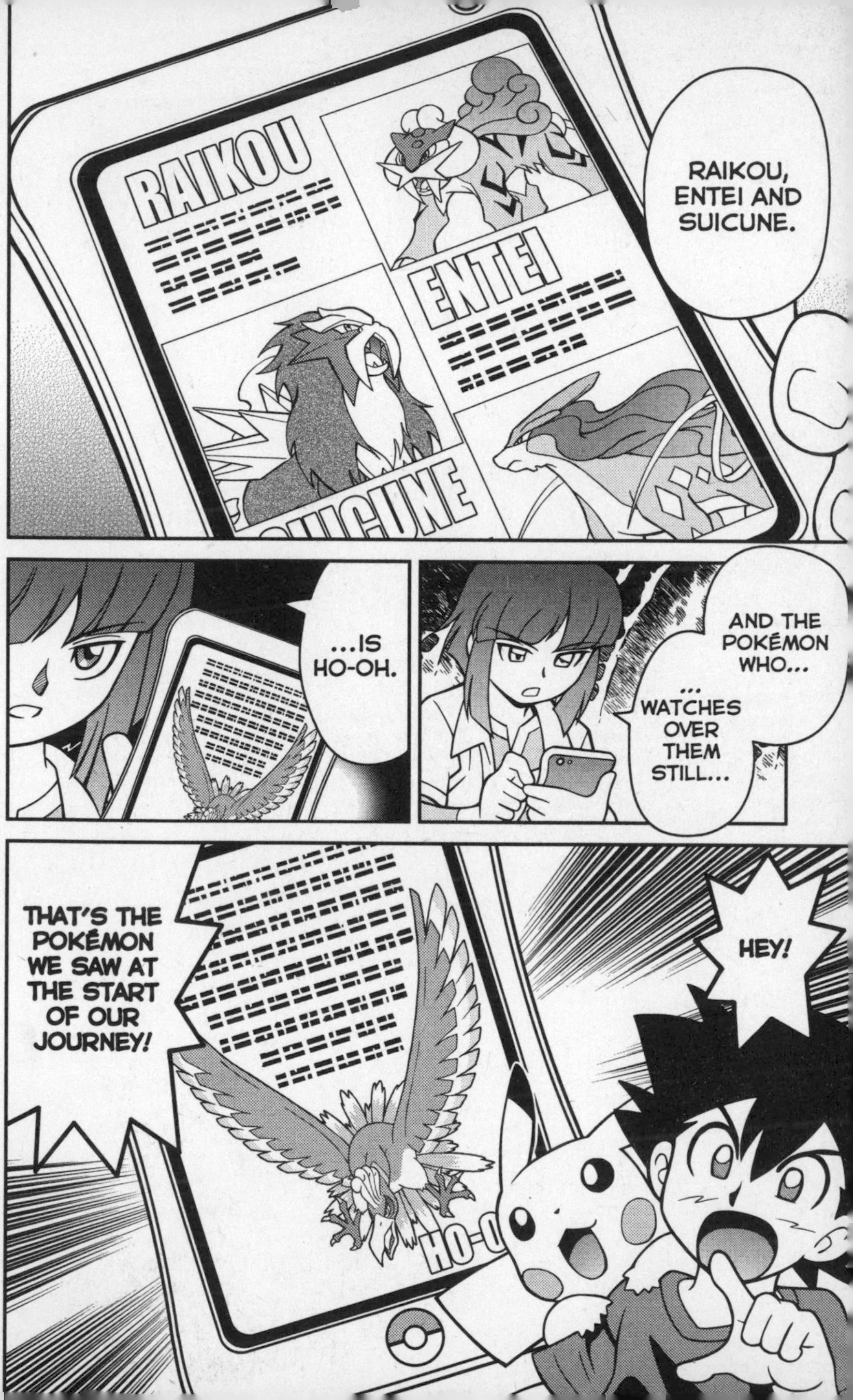
RAIKOU, ENTEI AND SUICUNE.
RAIKOU
ENTEI
AND THE POKÉMON WHO...
...WATCHES OVER THEM STILL...
...IS HO-OH.
HEY!
THAT'S THE POKÉMON WE SAW AT THE START OF OUR JOURNEY!

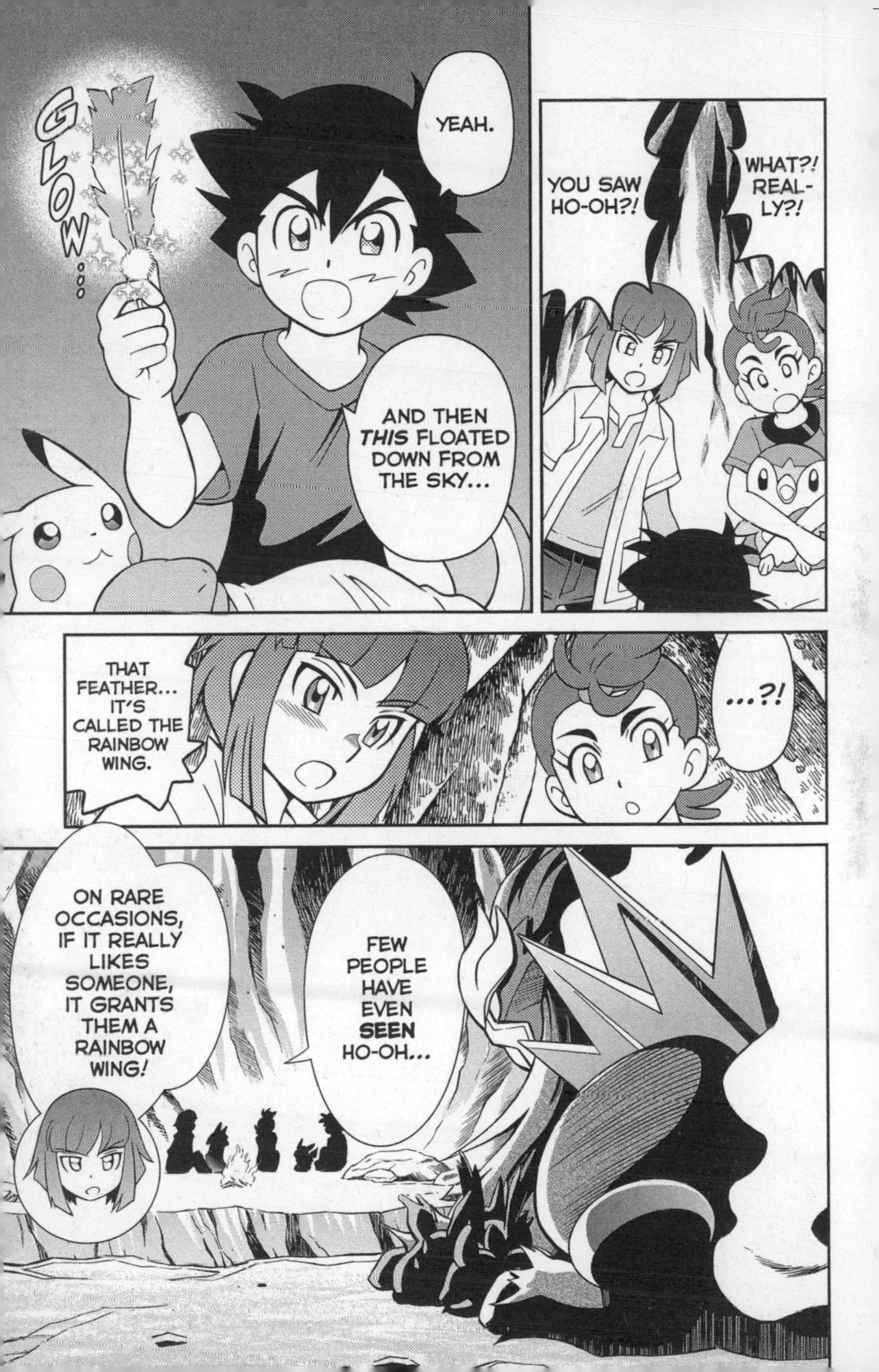
WHAT?! REAL-LY?!
YOU SAW HO-OH?!
YEAH.
GLOW...
AND THEN *THIS* FLOATED DOWN FROM THE SKY...
...?!
THAT FEATHER... IT'S CALLED THE RAINBOW WING.
FEW PEOPLE HAVE EVEN **SEEN** HO-OH...
ON RARE OCCASIONS, IF IT REALLY LIKES SOMEONE, IT GRANTS THEM A RAINBOW WING!

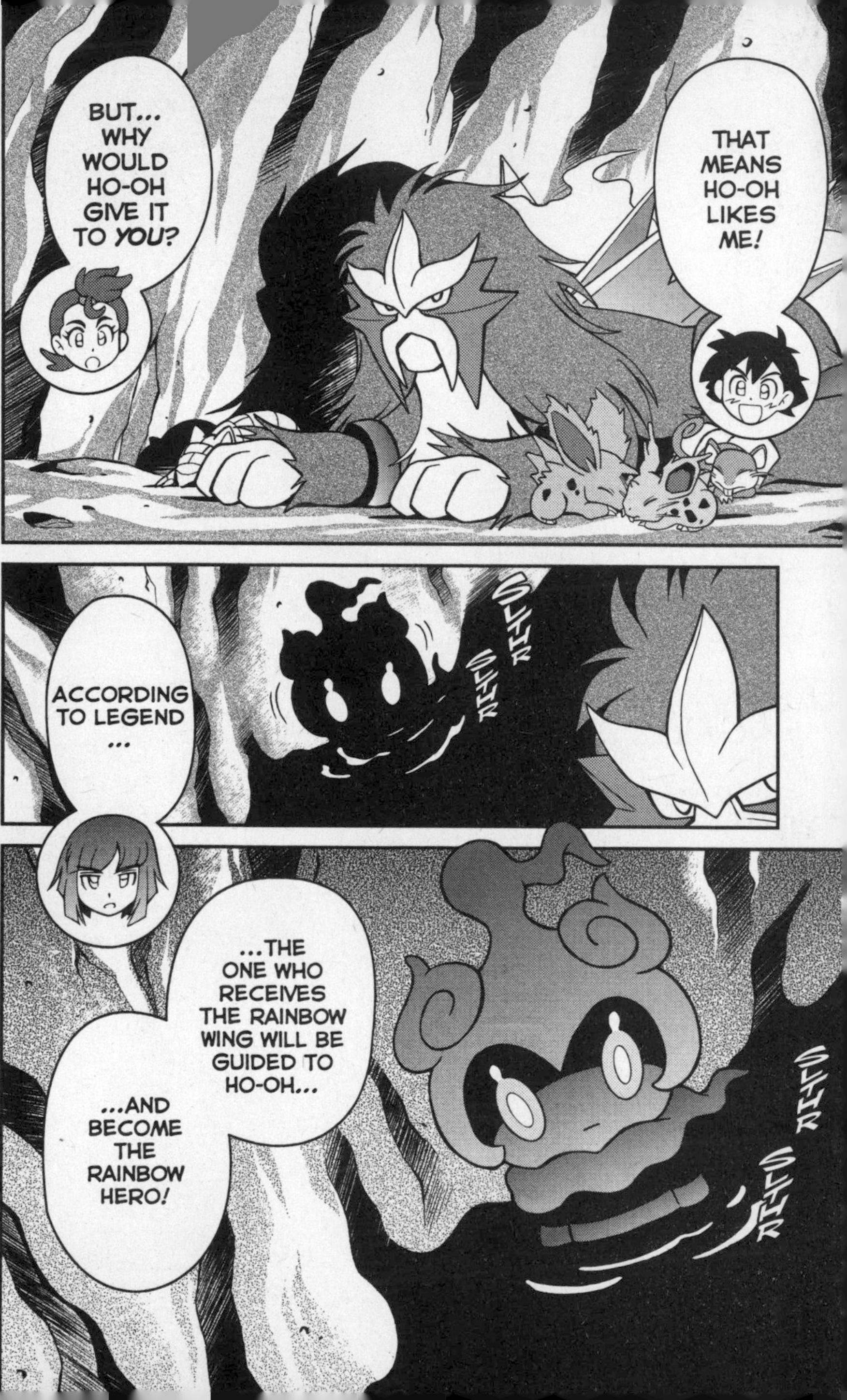
THAT MEANS HO-OH LIKES ME!
BUT... WHY WOULD HO-OH GIVE IT TO YOU?
SLITHR SLITHR
ACCORDING TO LEGEND...
...THE ONE WHO RECEIVES THE RAINBOW WING WILL BE GUIDED TO HO-OH...
...AND BECOME THE RAINBOW HERO!
SLITHR SLITHR

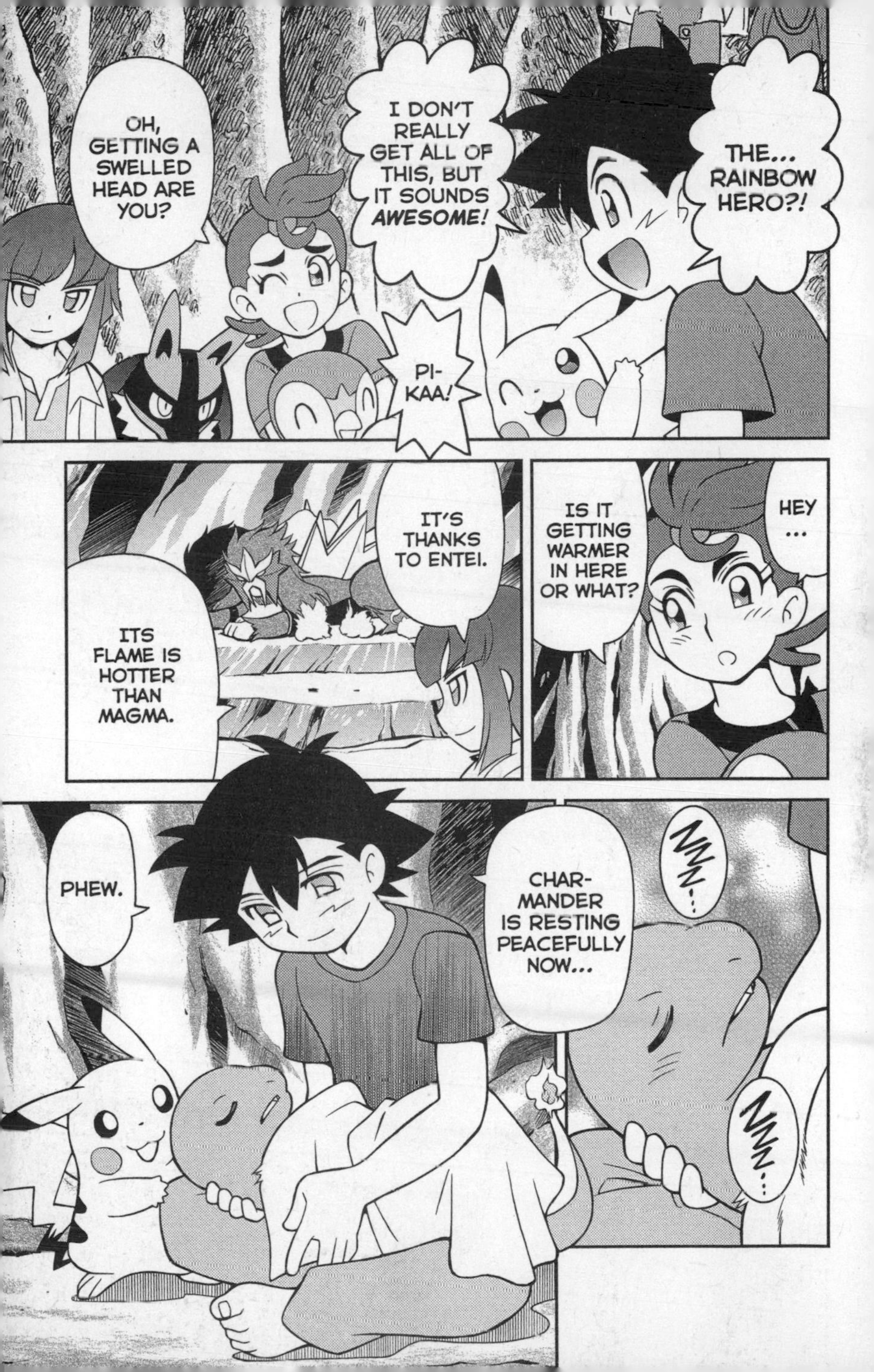
THE... RAINBOW HERO?!
I DON'T REALLY GET ALL OF THIS, BUT IT SOUNDS AWESOME!
PI-KAA!
OH, GETTING A SWELLED HEAD ARE YOU?
HEY...
IS IT GETTING WARMER IN HERE OR WHAT?
IT'S THANKS TO ENTEI.
ITS FLAME IS HOTTER THAN MAGMA.
ZZZ...
CHAR-MANDER IS RESTING PEACEFULLY NOW...
ZZZ...
PHEW.

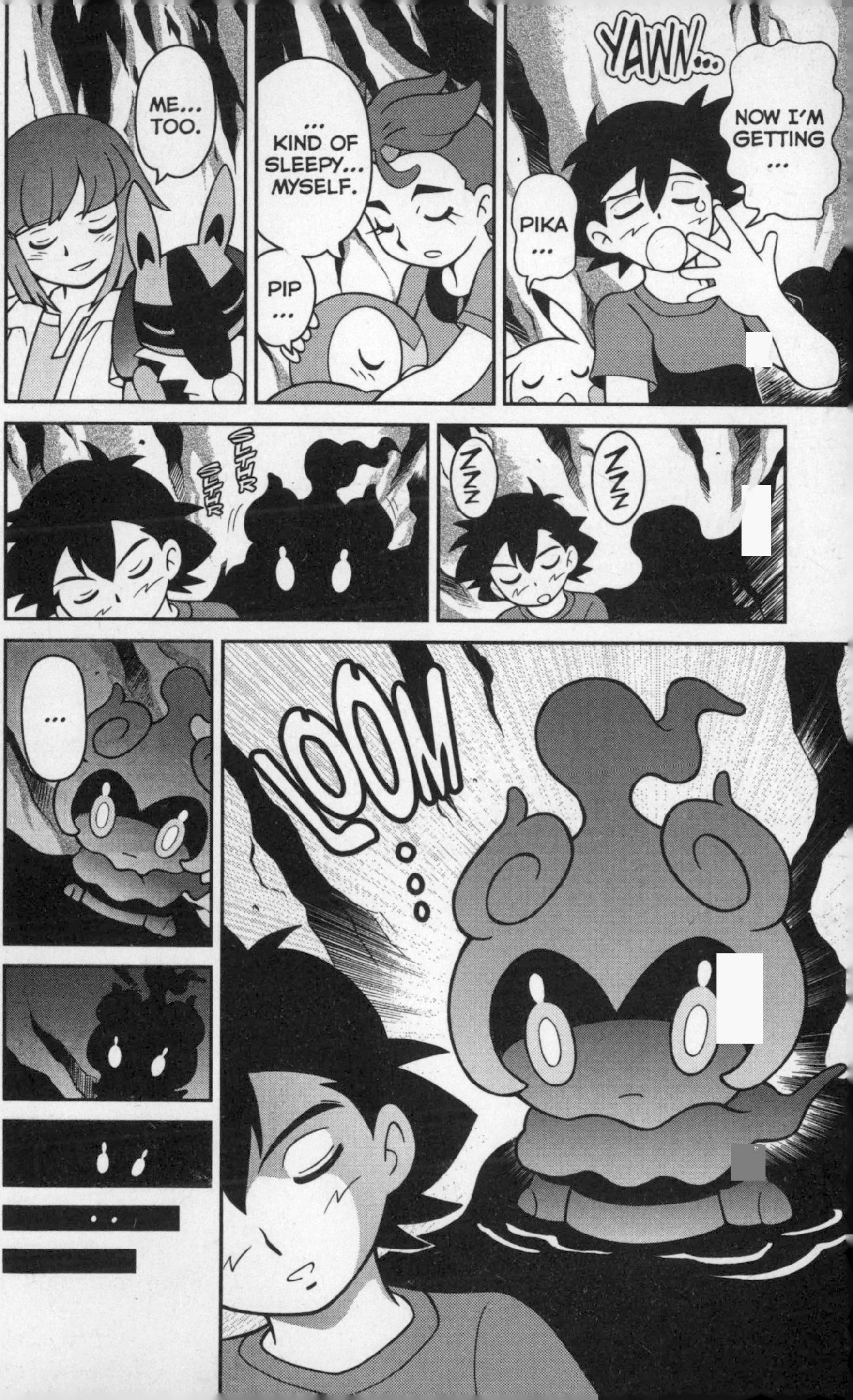
YAWN...
NOW I'M GETTING ...
PIKA ...
... KIND OF SLEEPY... MYSELF.
PIP ...
ME... TOO.
ZZZ
ZZZ
SLITHR
SLITHR
LOOM
...

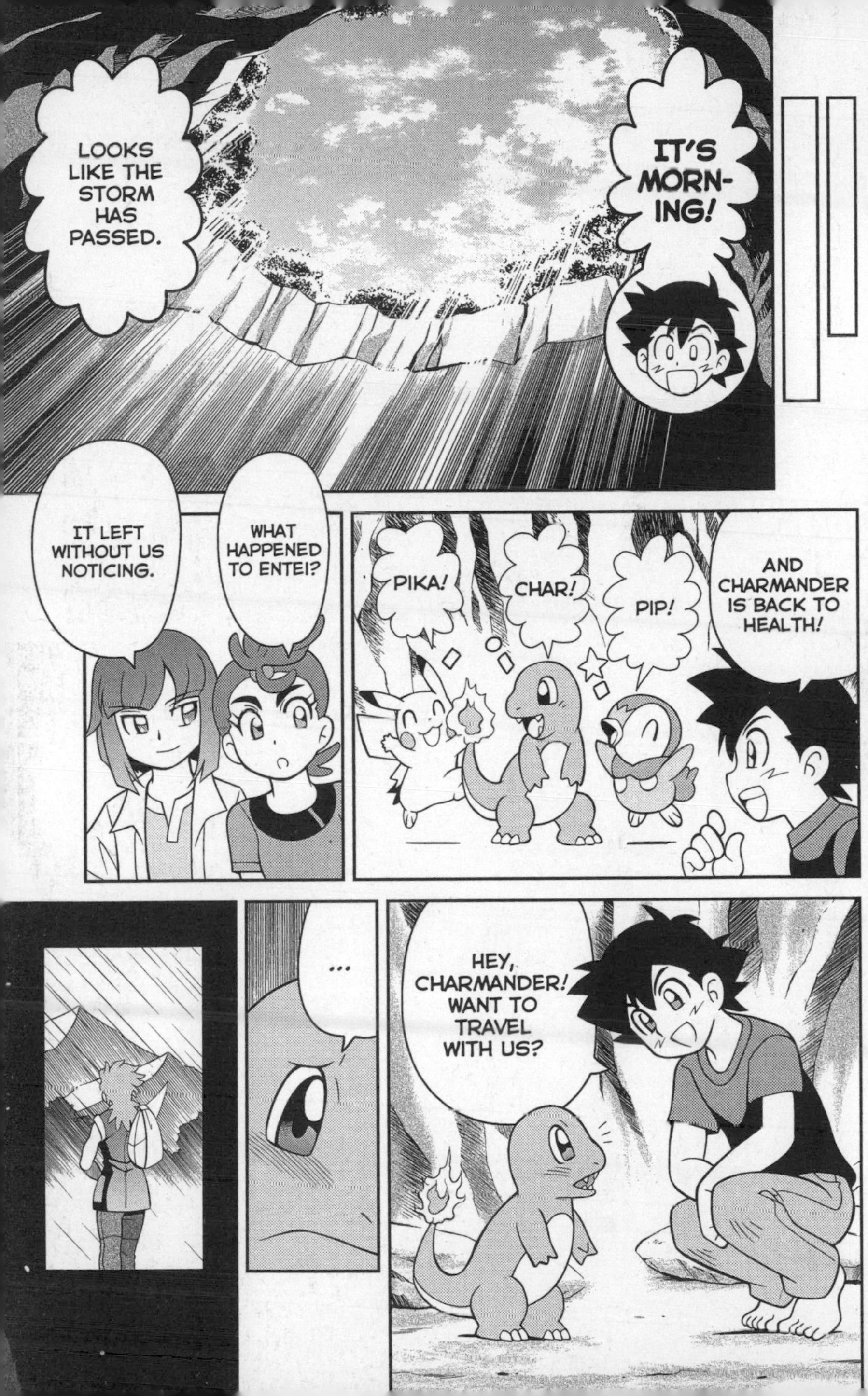
IT'S MORN-ING!
LOOKS LIKE THE STORM HAS PASSED.
AND CHARMANDER IS BACK TO HEALTH!
PIP!
CHAR!
PIKA!
WHAT HAPPENED TO ENTEI?
IT LEFT WITHOUT US NOTICING.
HEY, CHARMANDER! WANT TO TRAVEL WITH US?
...

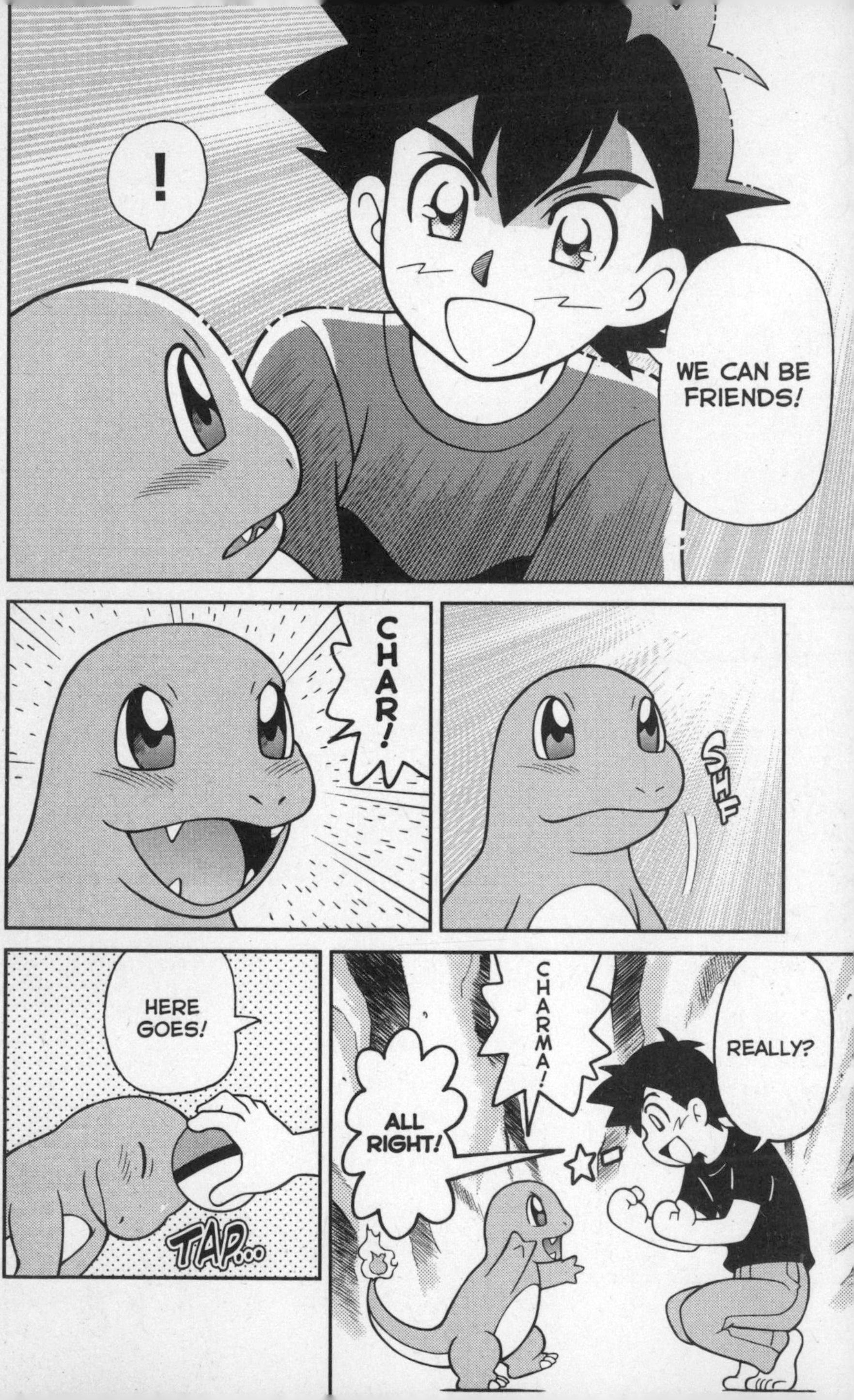
WE CAN BE FRIENDS!
!
SHF
CHAR!
REALLY?
CHARMA!
ALL RIGHT!
HERE GOES!
TAP...

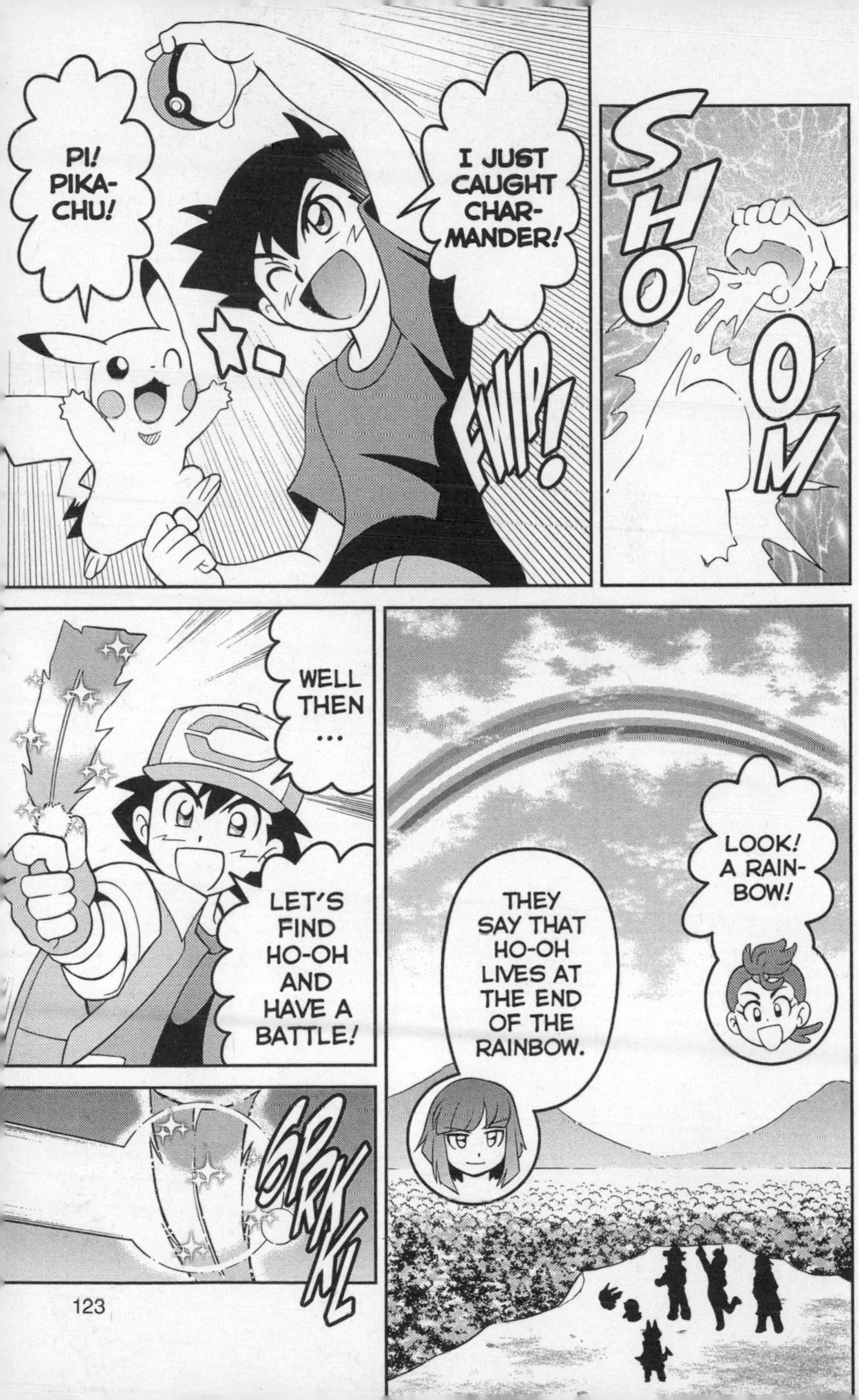
SHOOOM
I JUST CAUGHT CHARMANDER!
PI! PIKACHU!
FWIP!
LOOK! A RAINBOW!
THEY SAY THAT HO-OH LIVES AT THE END OF THE RAINBOW.
WELL THEN ...
LET'S FIND HO-OH AND HAVE A BATTLE!
SPRKKL

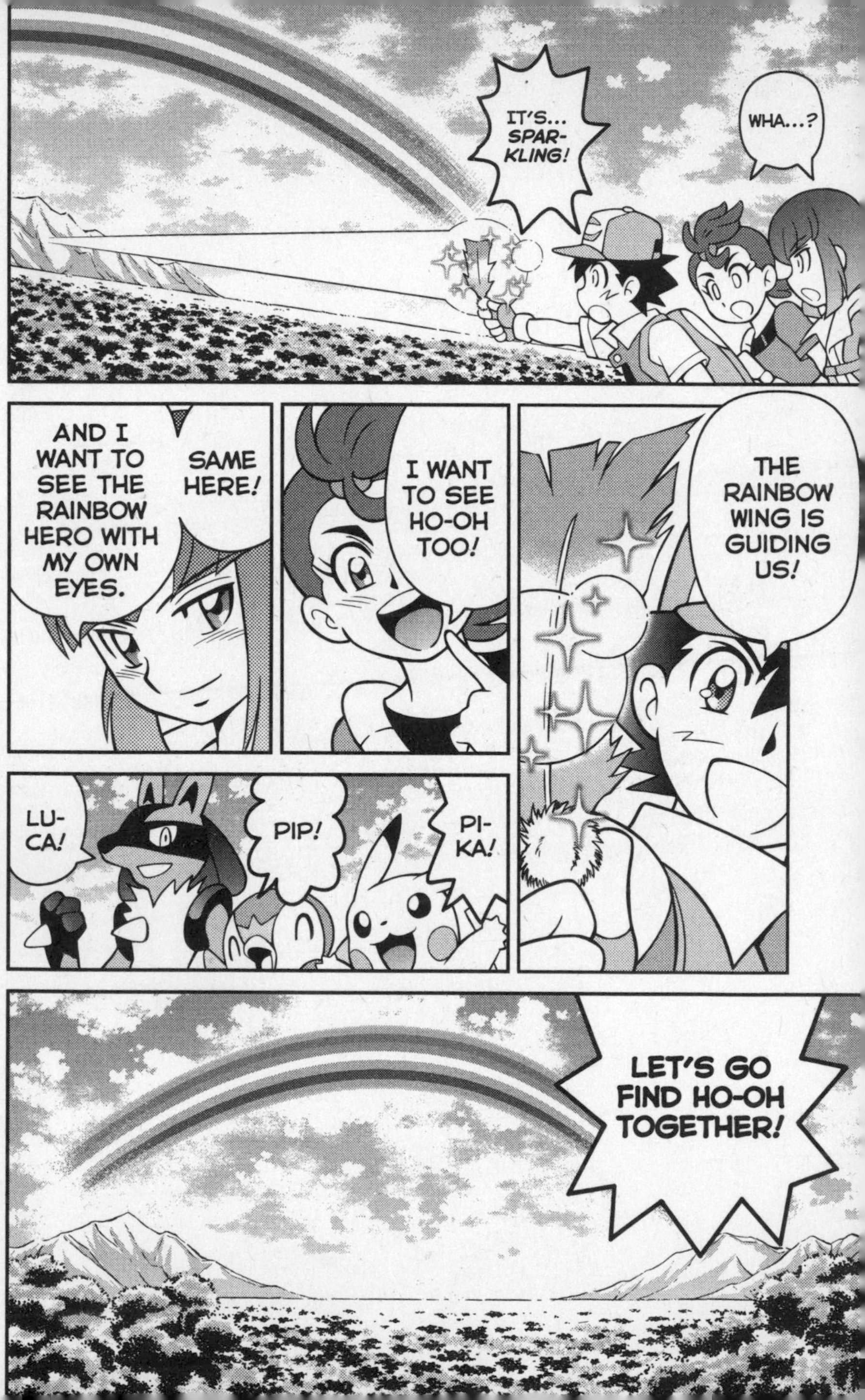
WHA...?
IT'S... SPAR-KLING!
THE RAINBOW WING IS GUIDING US!
I WANT TO SEE HO-OH TOO!
SAME HERE!
AND I WANT TO SEE THE RAINBOW HERO WITH MY OWN EYES.
PI-KA!
PIP!
LU-CA!
LET'S GO FIND HO-OH TOGETHER!

CHAPTER 6

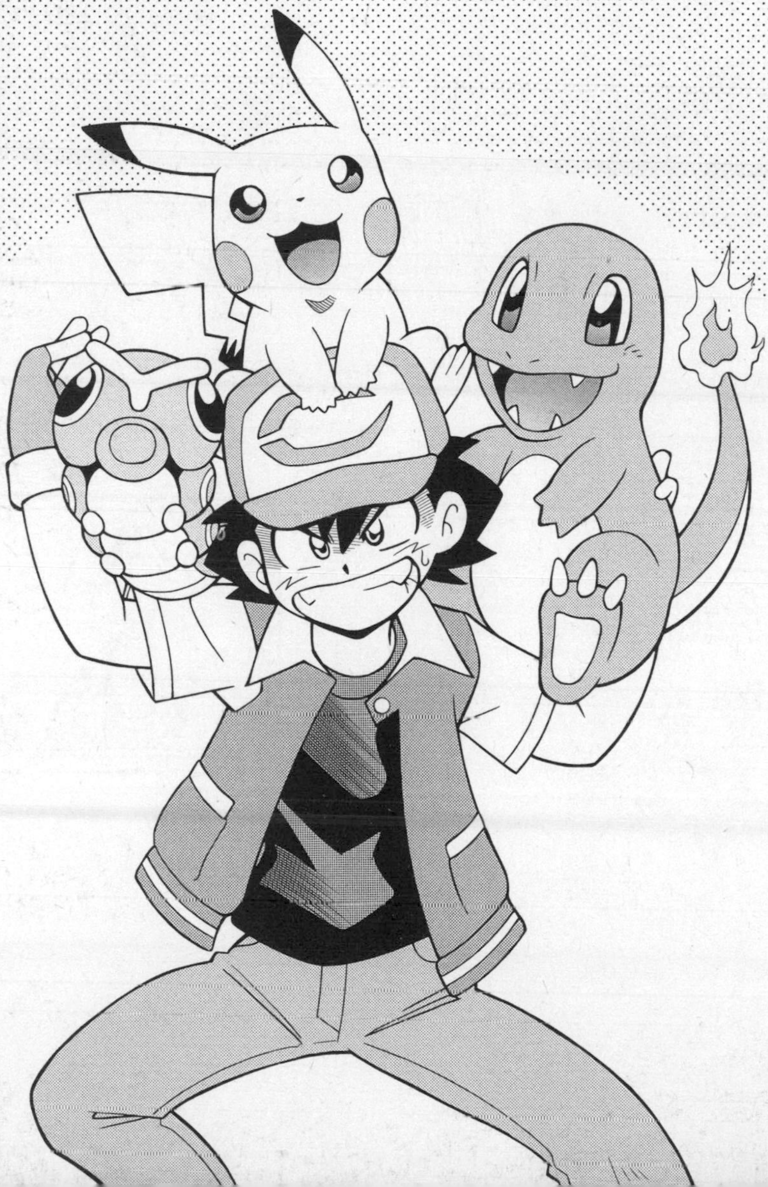

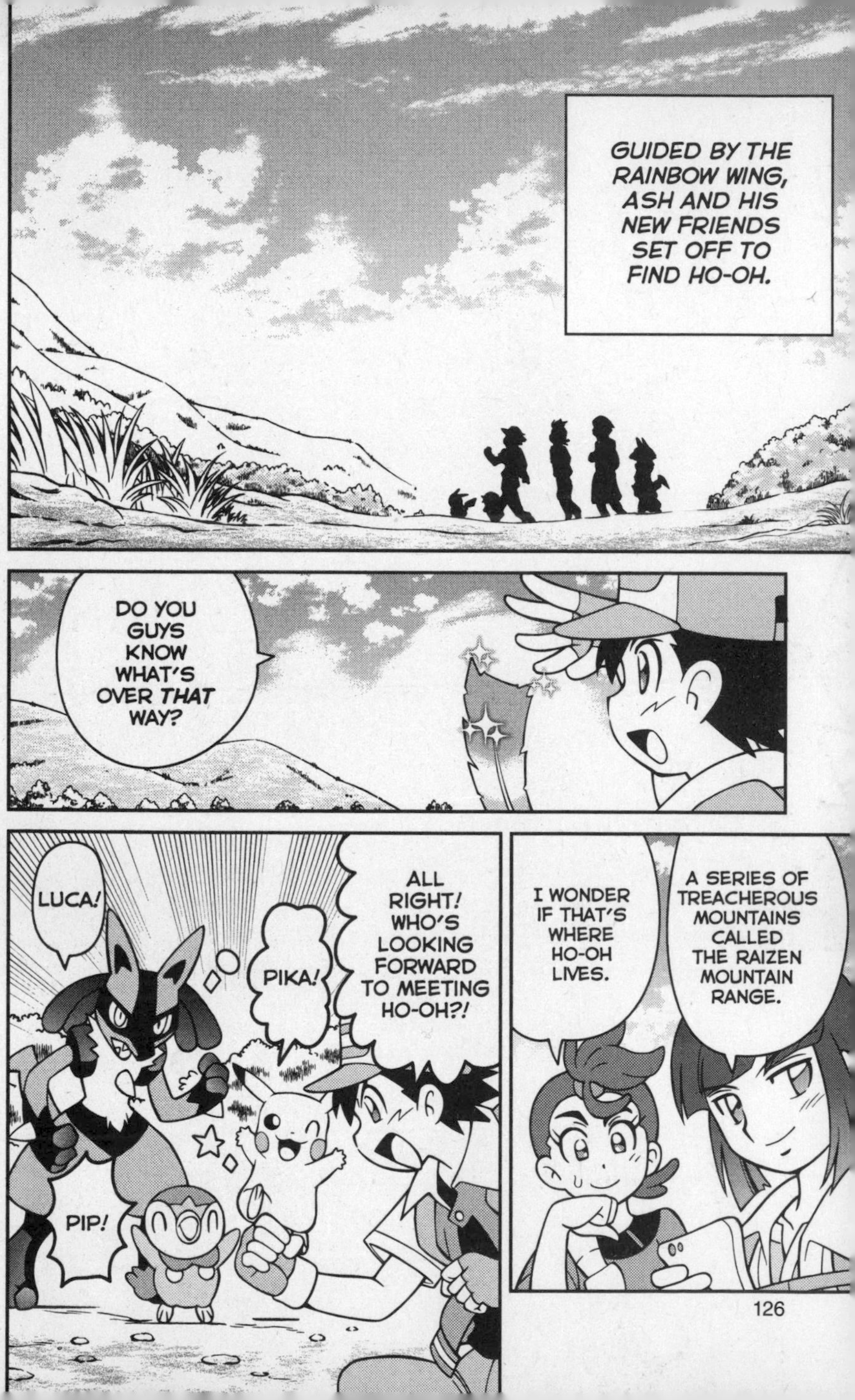
GUIDED BY THE RAINBOW WING, ASH AND HIS NEW FRIENDS SET OFF TO FIND HO-OH.
DO YOU GUYS KNOW WHAT'S OVER *THAT* WAY?
A SERIES OF TREACHEROUS MOUNTAINS CALLED THE RAIZEN MOUNTAIN RANGE.
I WONDER IF THAT'S WHERE HO-OH LIVES.
ALL RIGHT! WHO'S LOOKING FORWARD TO MEETING HO-OH?!
PIKA!
LUCA!
PIP!

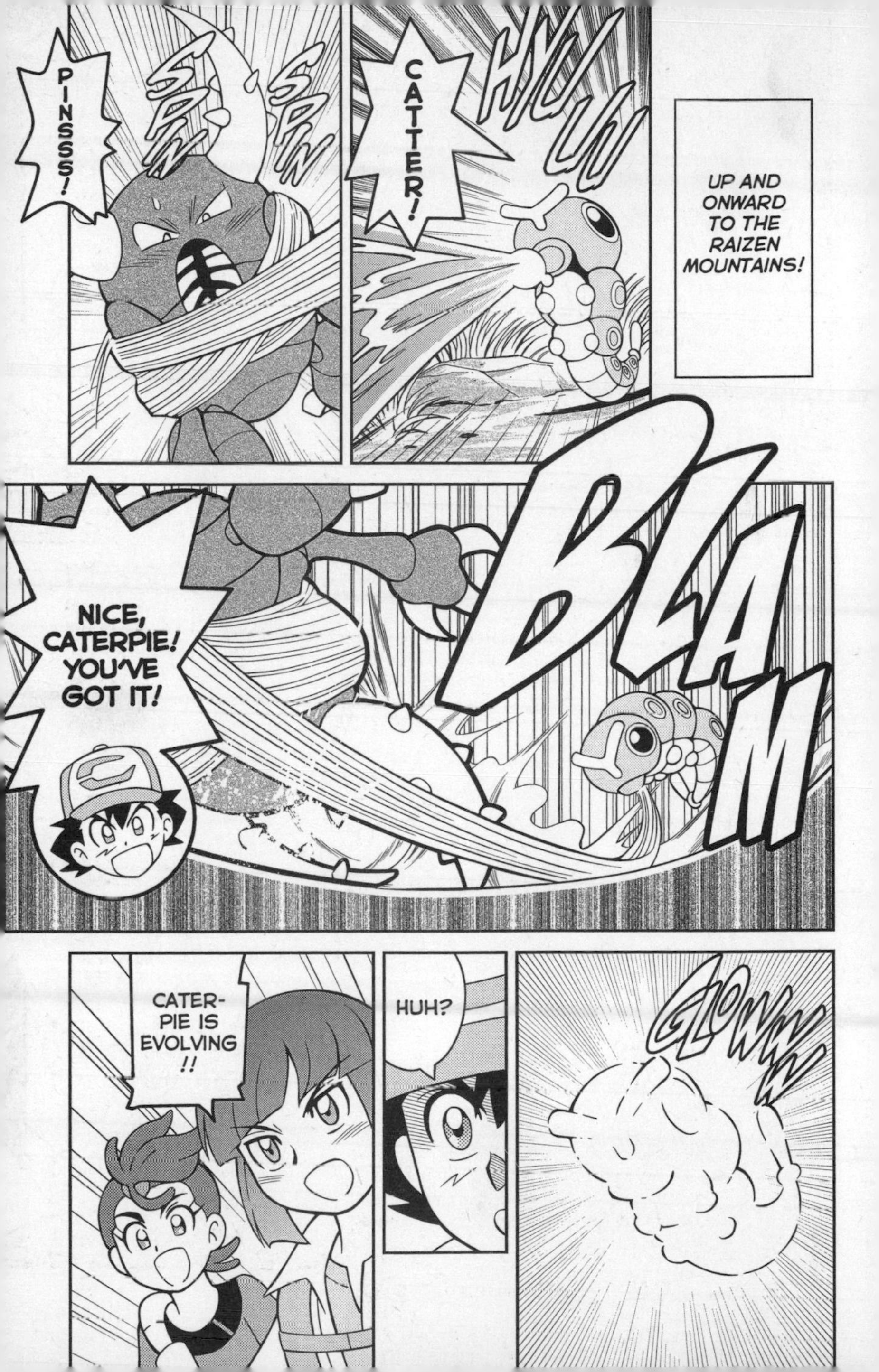
UP AND ONWARD TO THE RAIZEN MOUNTAINS!
HYUUU
CATTER!
SPIN SPIN
PINSSS!
BLAM
NICE, CATERPIE! YOU'VE GOT IT!
GLOWW
HUH?
CATER-PIE IS EVOLVING!!

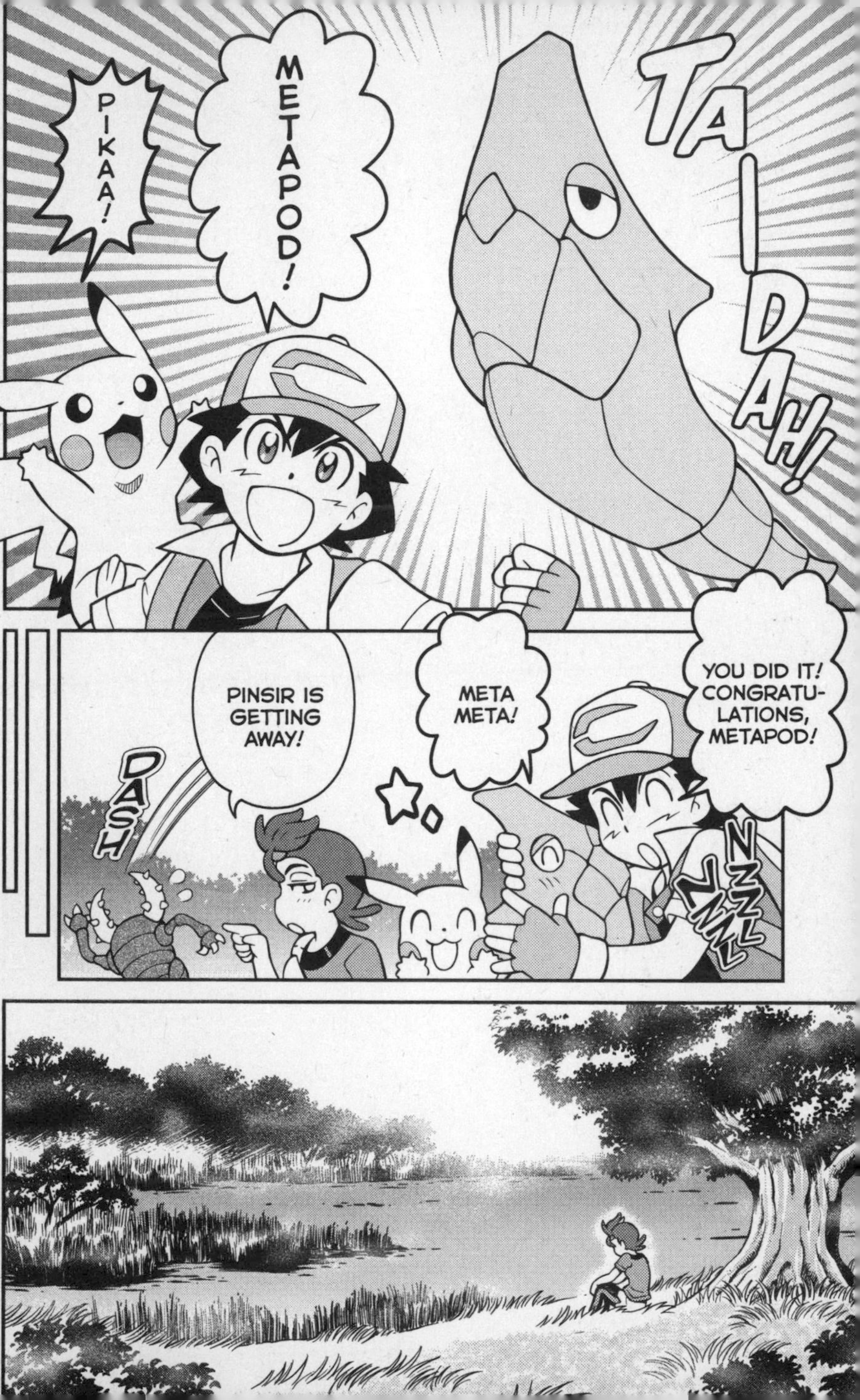
TA-DAH!
METAPOD!
PIKAA!
YOU DID IT! CONGRATU-LATIONS, METAPOD!
META META!
PINSIR IS GETTING AWAY!
DASH

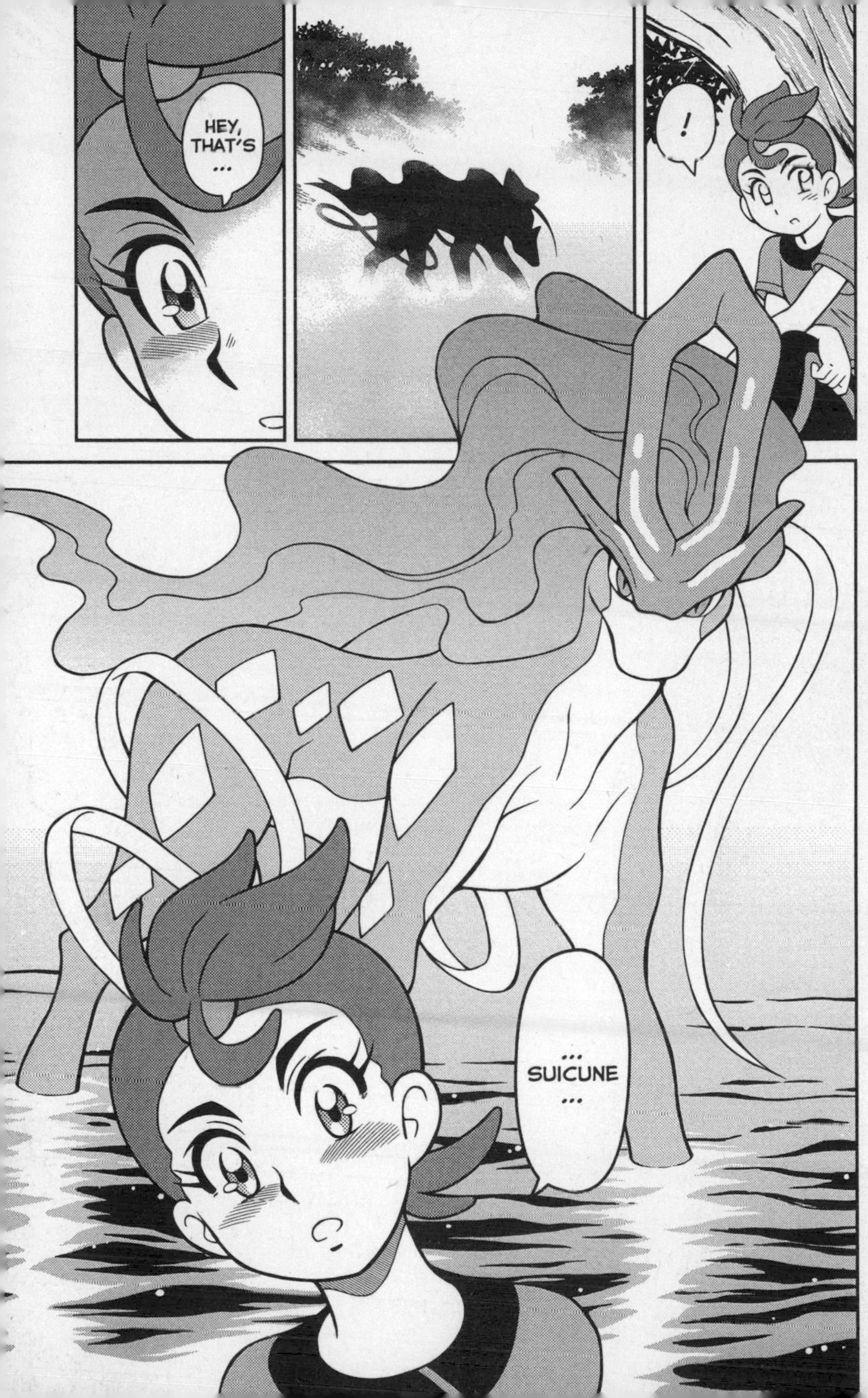
!
HEY, THAT'S ...
... SUICUNE ...

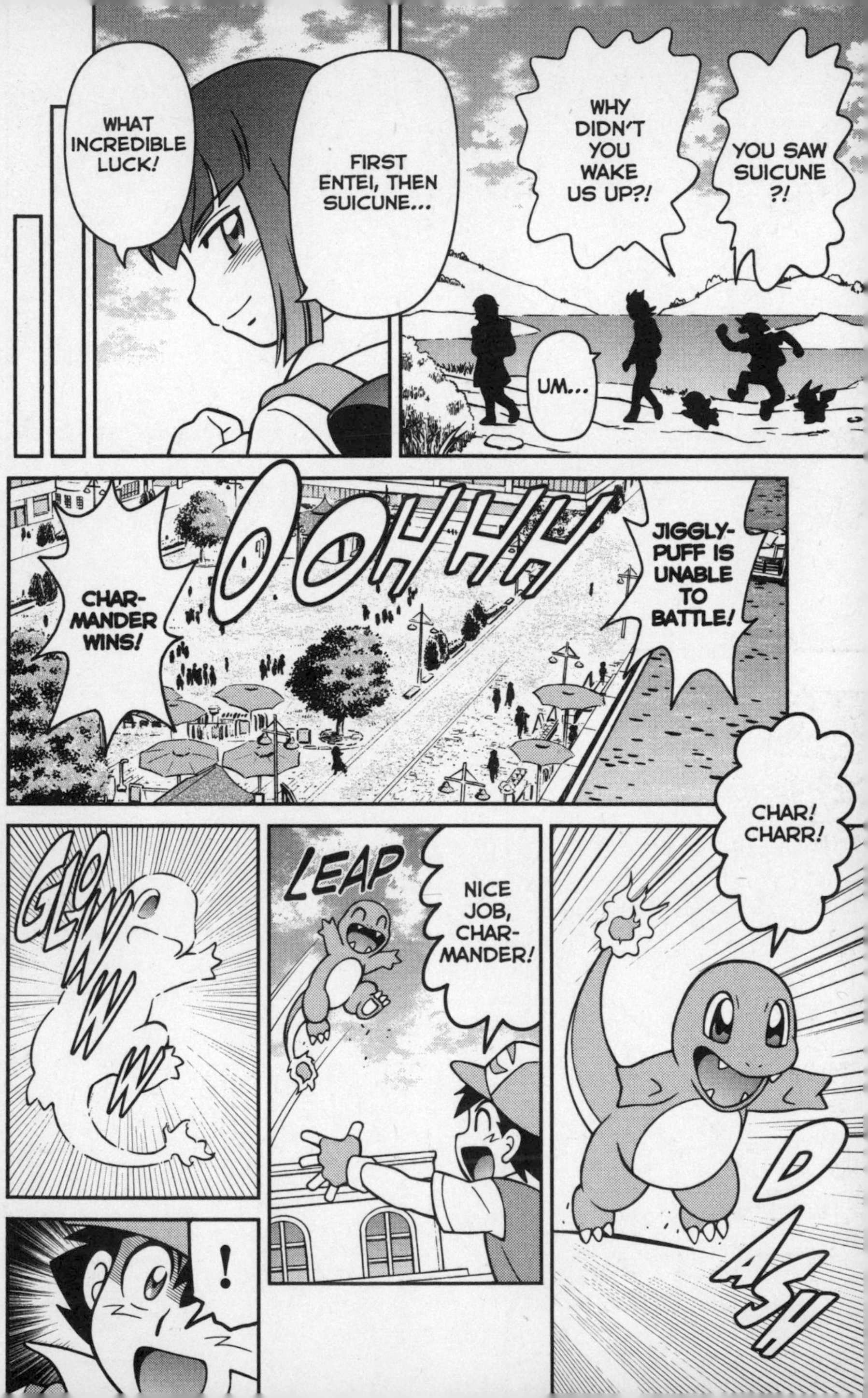
YOU SAW SUICUNE ?!
WHY DIDN'T YOU WAKE US UP?!
UM...
FIRST ENTEI, THEN SUICUNE...
WHAT INCREDIBLE LUCK!
JIGGLYPUFF IS UNABLE TO BATTLE!
OOHHH
CHARMANDER WINS!
CHAR! CHARR!
DASH
NICE JOB, CHARMANDER!
LEAP
GLOWW
!

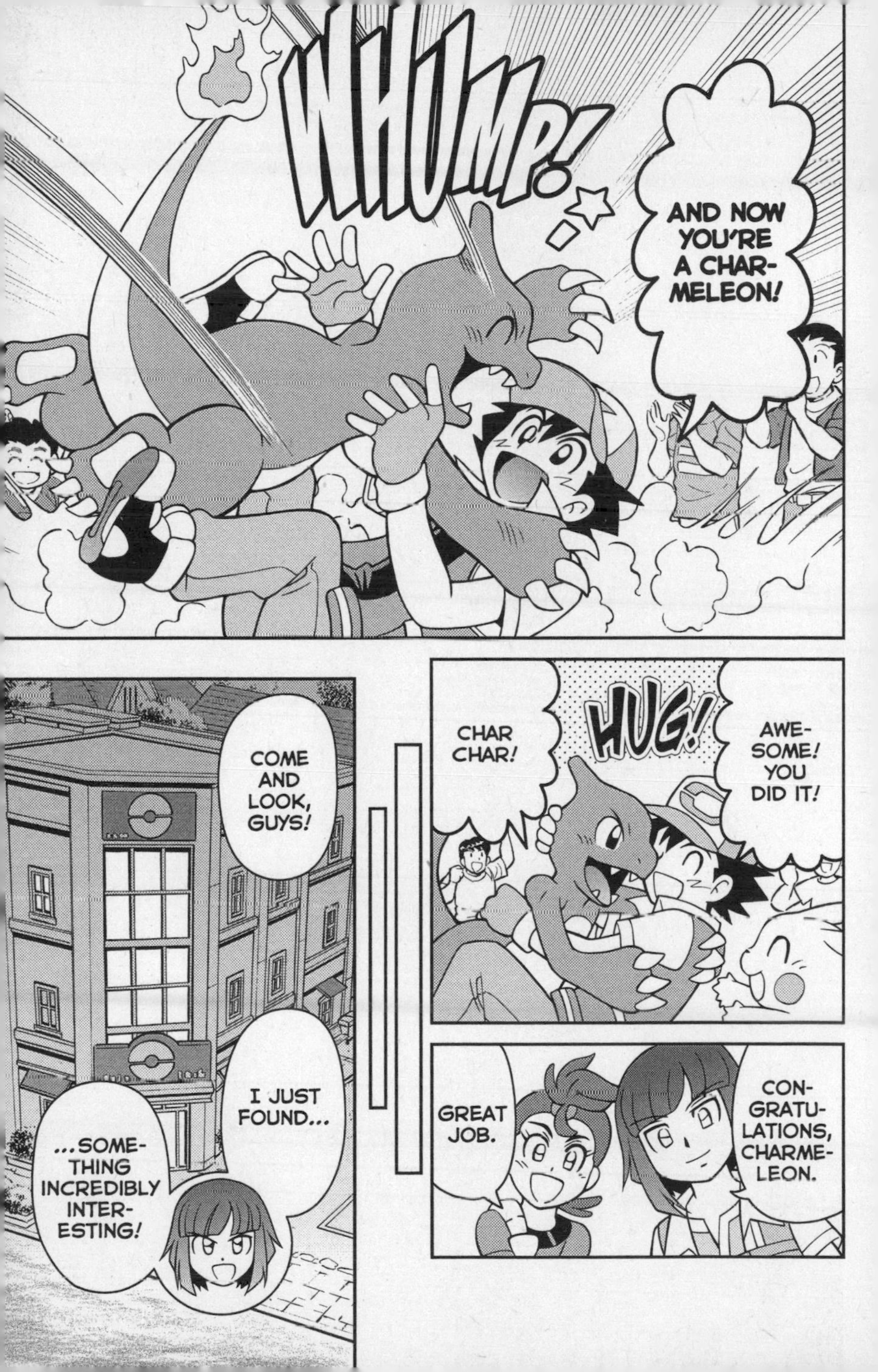
WHUMP!
AND NOW YOU'RE A CHAR-MELEON!
AWE-SOME! YOU DID IT!
HUG!
CHAR CHAR!
CON-GRATU-LATIONS, CHARME-LEON.
GREAT JOB.
COME AND LOOK, GUYS!
I JUST FOUND...
...SOME-THING INCREDIBLY INTER-ESTING!

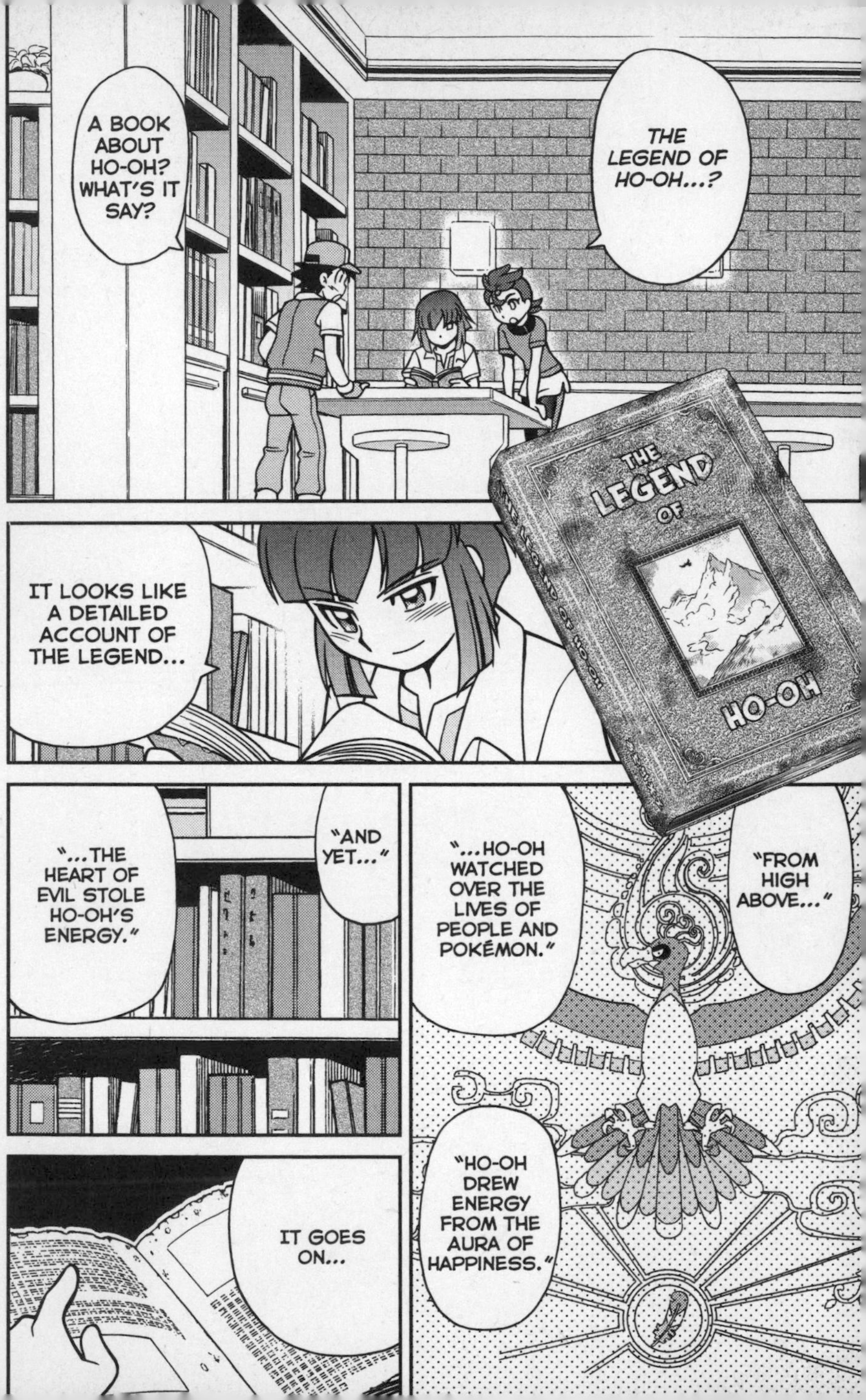
THE LEGEND OF HO-OH...?
A BOOK ABOUT HO-OH? WHAT'S IT SAY?
THE LEGEND OF HO-OH
THE LEGEND OF HO-OH
IT LOOKS LIKE A DETAILED ACCOUNT OF THE LEGEND...
"FROM HIGH ABOVE..."
"...HO-OH WATCHED OVER THE LIVES OF PEOPLE AND POKÉMON."
"HO-OH DREW ENERGY FROM THE AURA OF HAPPINESS."
"AND YET..."
"...THE HEART OF EVIL STOLE HO-OH'S ENERGY."
IT GOES ON...

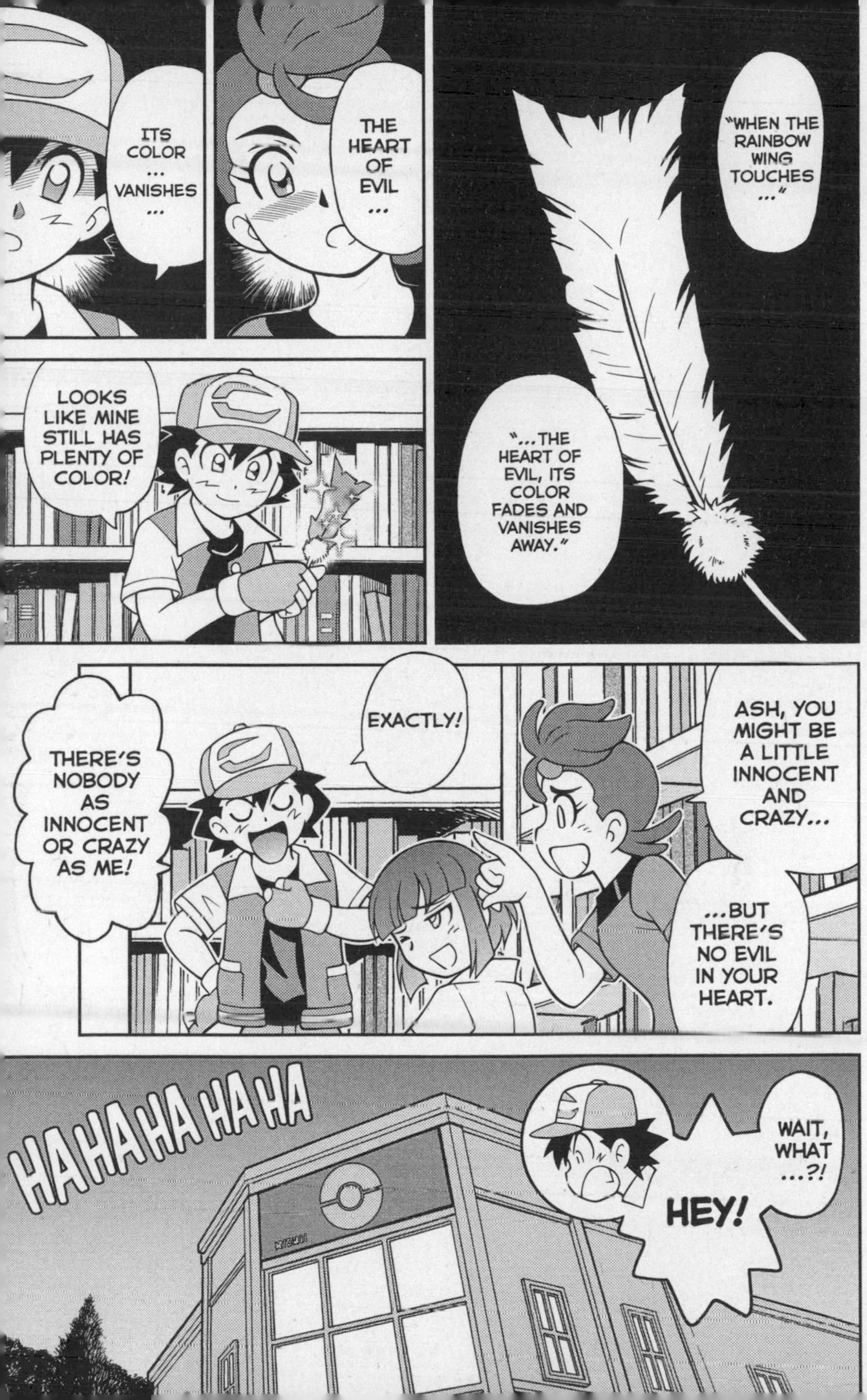
"WHEN THE RAINBOW WING TOUCHES..."
"...THE HEART OF EVIL, ITS COLOR FADES AND VANISHES AWAY."
THE HEART OF EVIL...
ITS COLOR... VANISHES...
LOOKS LIKE MINE STILL HAS PLENTY OF COLOR!
ASH, YOU MIGHT BE A LITTLE INNOCENT AND CRAZY...
...BUT THERE'S NO EVIL IN YOUR HEART.
EXACTLY!
THERE'S NOBODY AS INNOCENT OR CRAZY AS ME!
WAIT, WHAT...?!
HEY!
HAHAHA HA HA

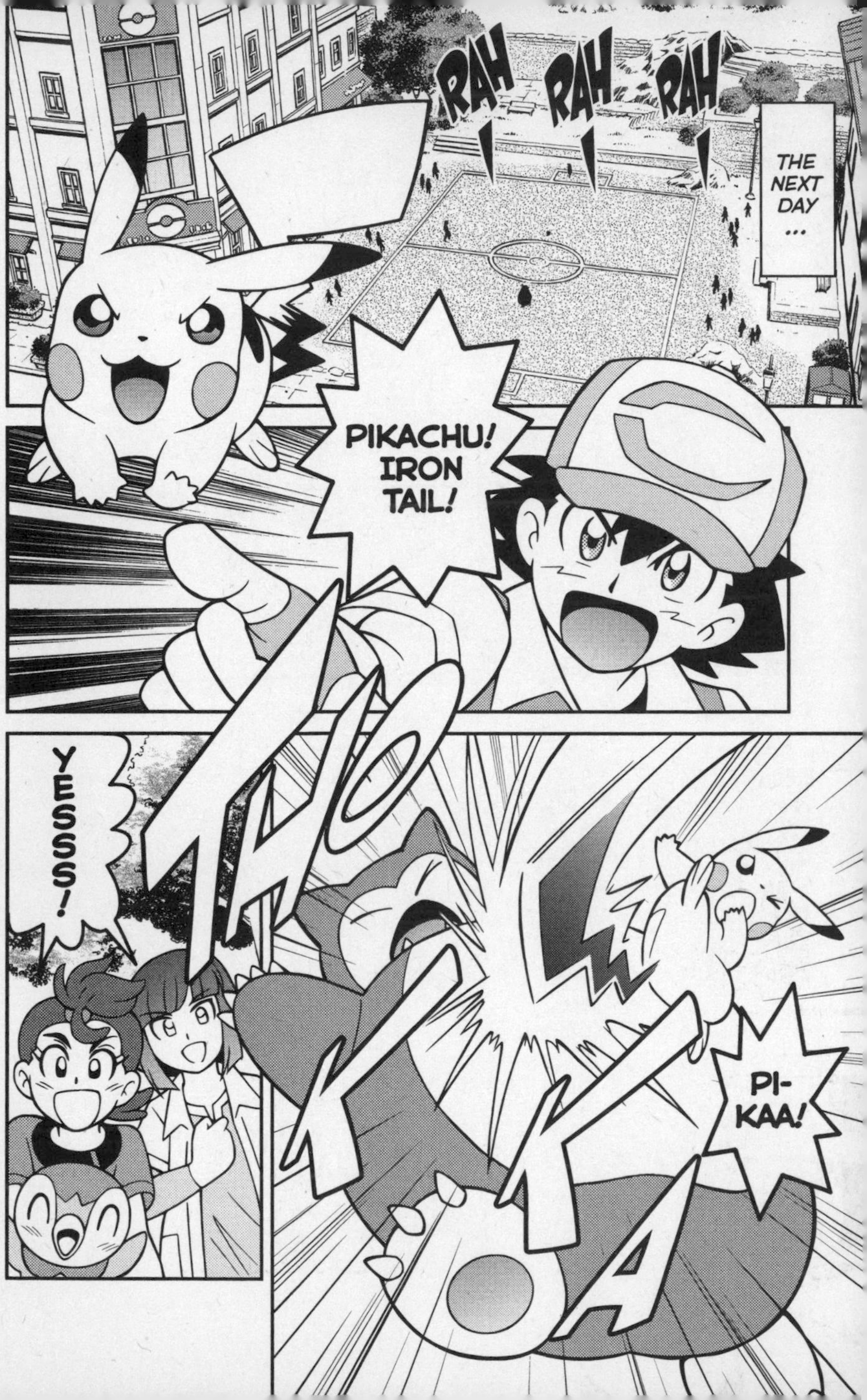
THE NEXT DAY ...
RAH!
RAH!
RAH!
PIKACHU! IRON TAIL!
PI-KAA!
YESSS!

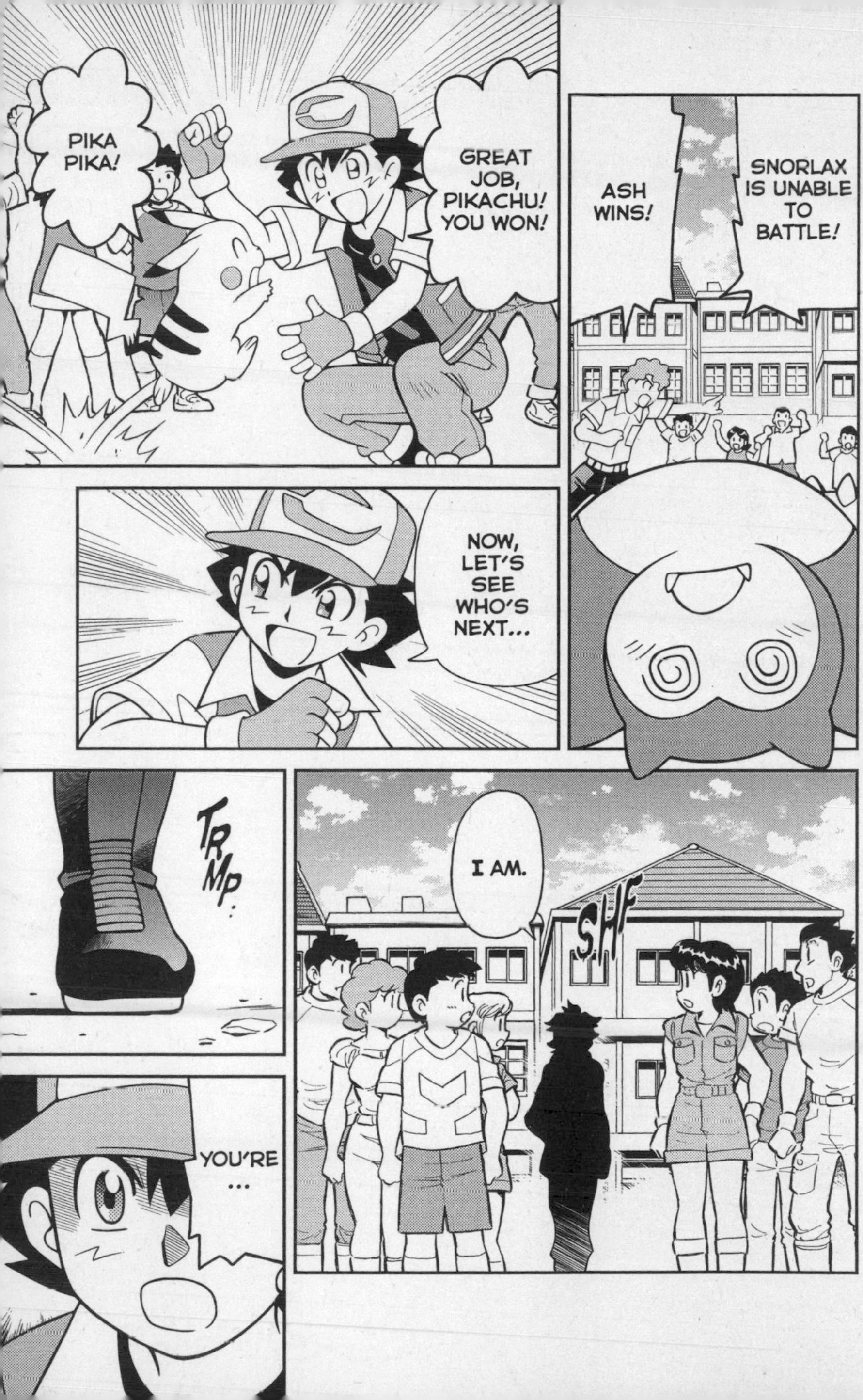
SNORLAX IS UNABLE TO BATTLE!
ASH WINS!
GREAT JOB, PIKACHU! YOU WON!
PIKA PIKA!
NOW, LET'S SEE WHO'S NEXT...
I AM.
SHF
TRMP
YOU'RE ...

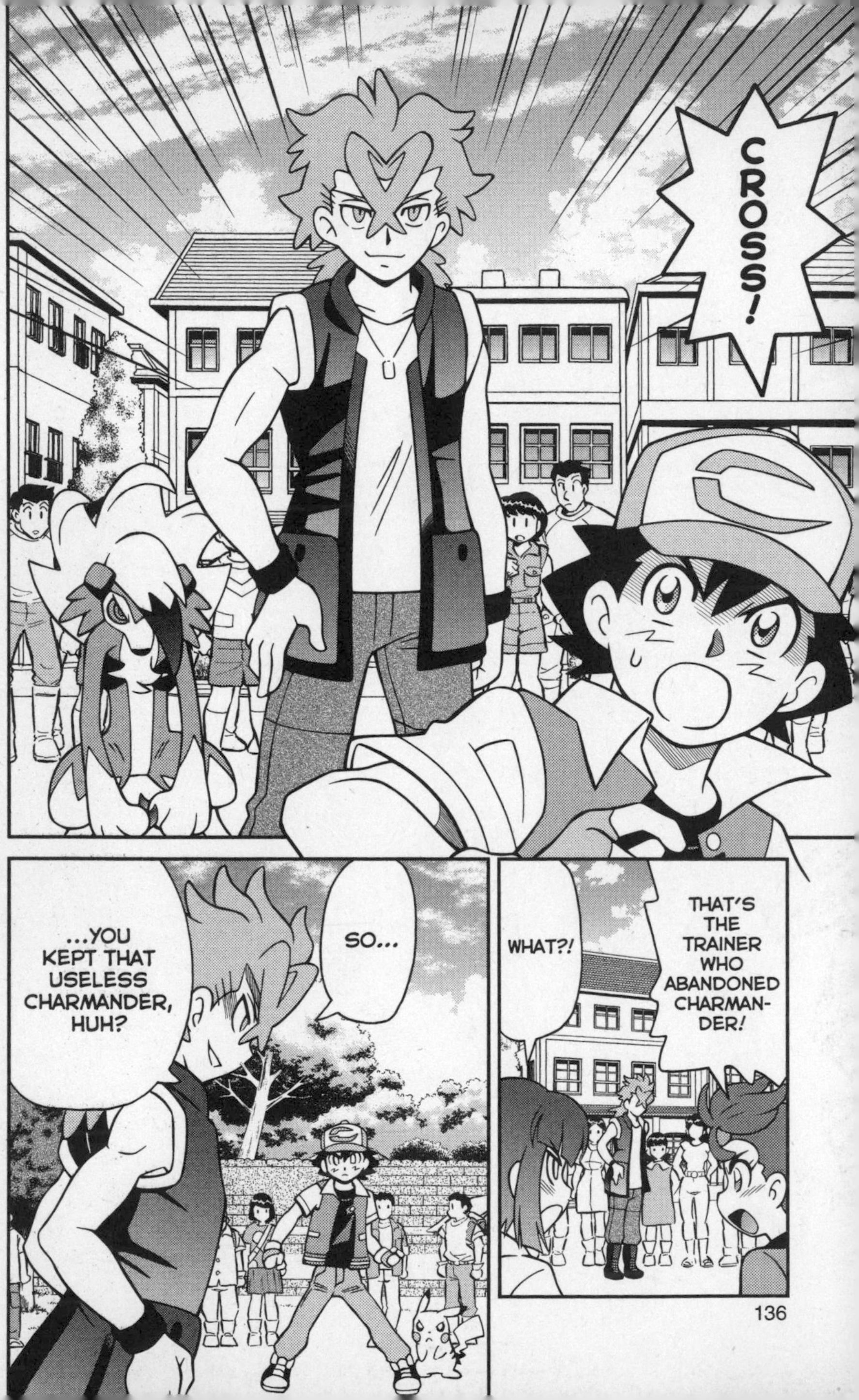
CROSS!
THAT'S THE TRAINER WHO ABANDONED CHARMAN-DER!
WHAT?!
SO...
...YOU KEPT THAT USELESS CHARMANDER, HUH?

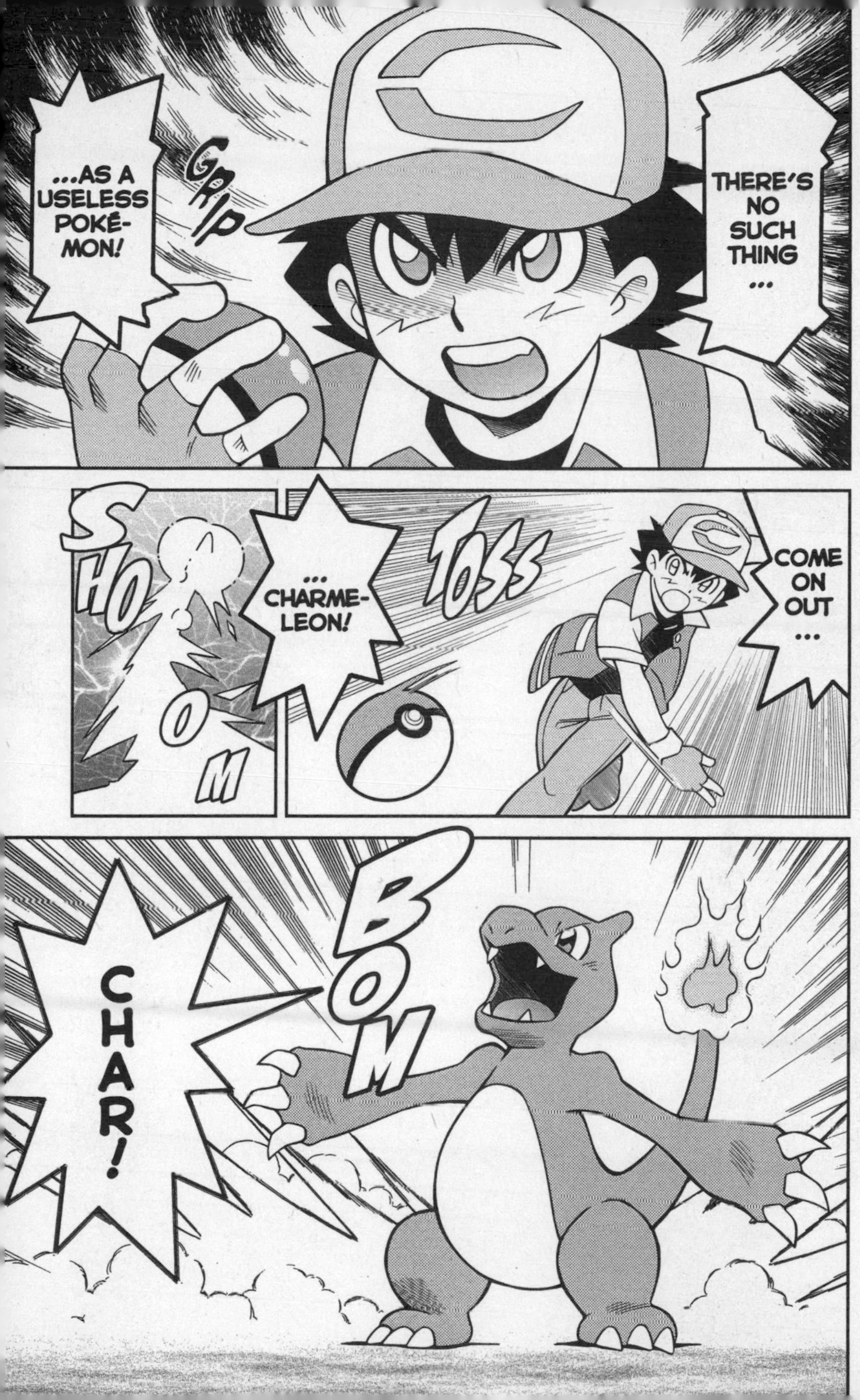
THERE'S NO SUCH THING ...
GRIP
...AS A USELESS POKÉ-MON!
COME ON OUT ...
TOSS
... CHARME-LEON!
SHOOM
BOM
CHAR!

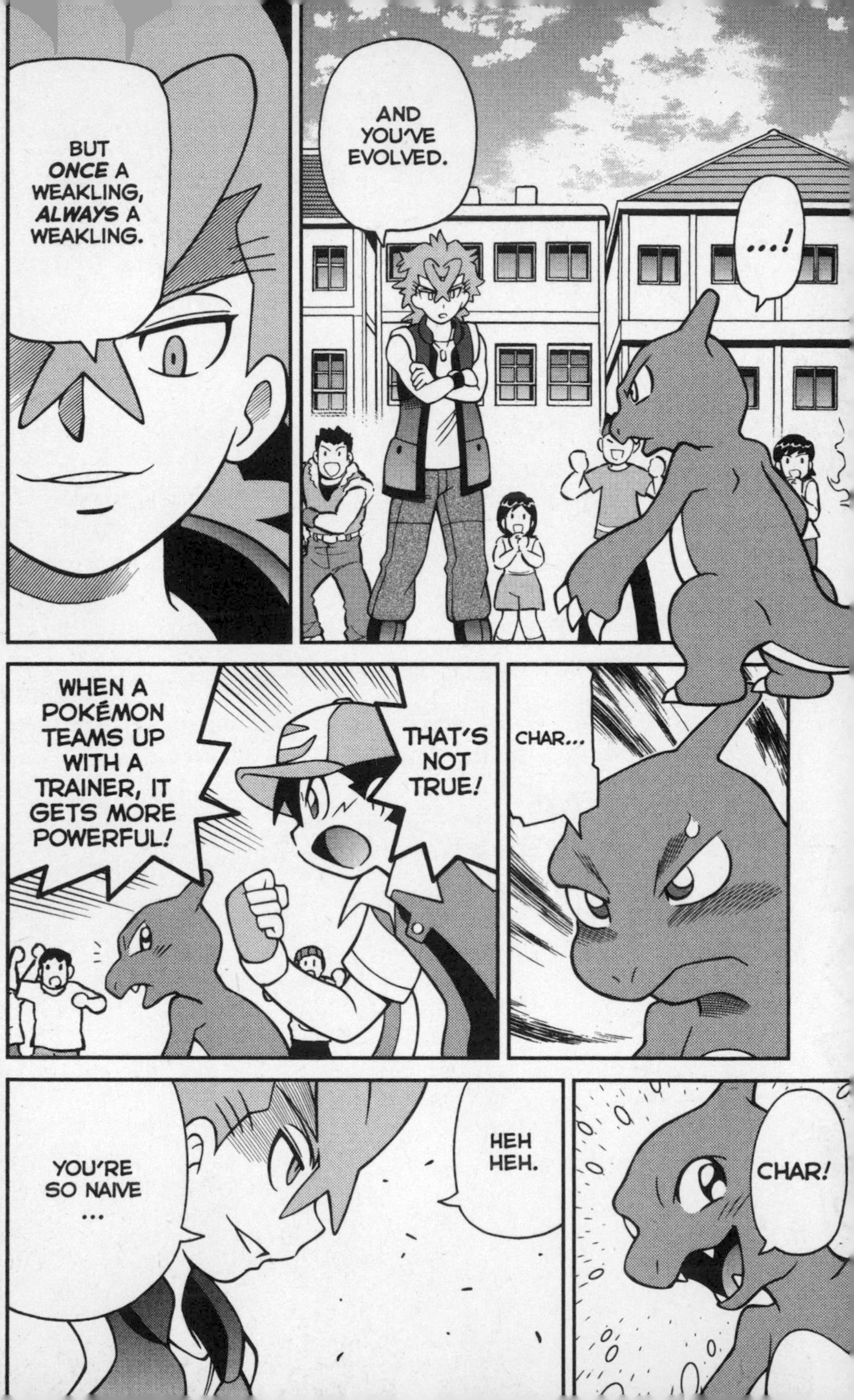
AND YOU'VE EVOLVED.
...!
BUT ONCE A WEAKLING, ALWAYS A WEAKLING.
CHAR...
THAT'S NOT TRUE!
WHEN A POKÉMON TEAMS UP WITH A TRAINER, IT GETS MORE POWERFUL!
CHAR!
HEH HEH.
YOU'RE SO NAIVE ...

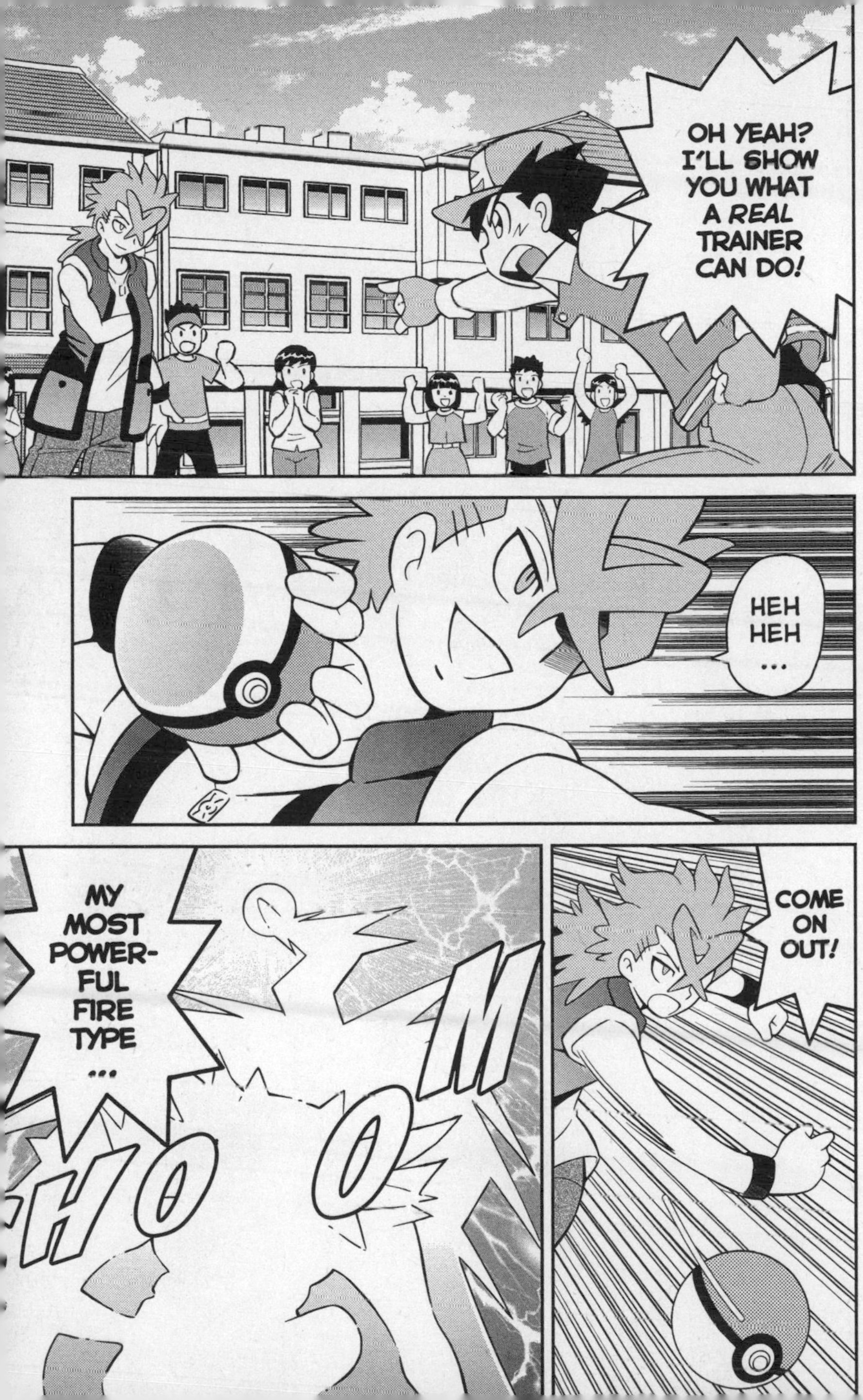
OH YEAH? I'LL SHOW YOU WHAT A REAL TRAINER CAN DO!
HEH HEH ...
COME ON OUT!
MY MOST POWER-FUL FIRE TYPE ...
HOOM

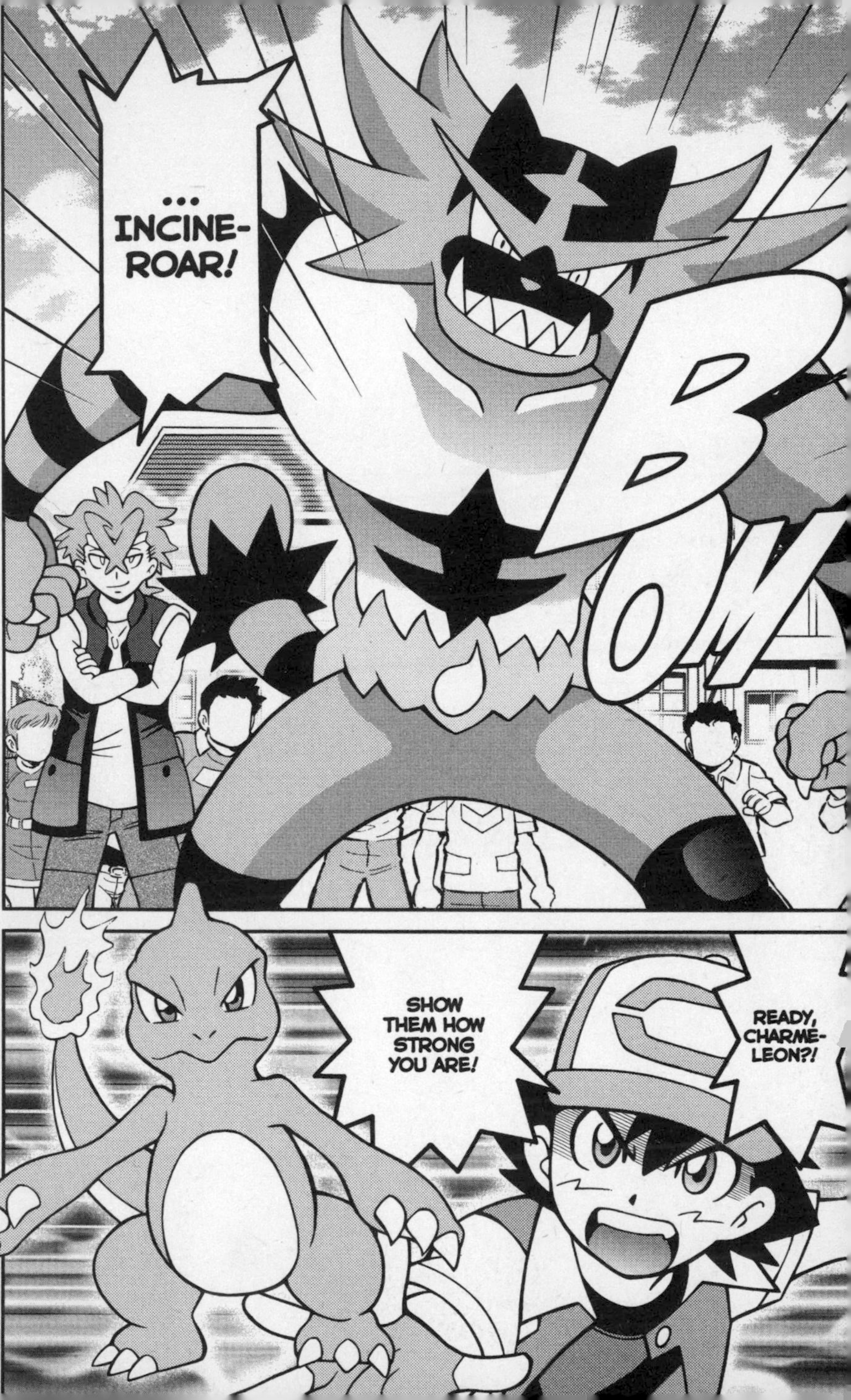
...INCINE-ROAR!
BOOM
READY, CHARME-LEON?!
SHOW THEM HOW STRONG YOU ARE!

CHAPTER 7

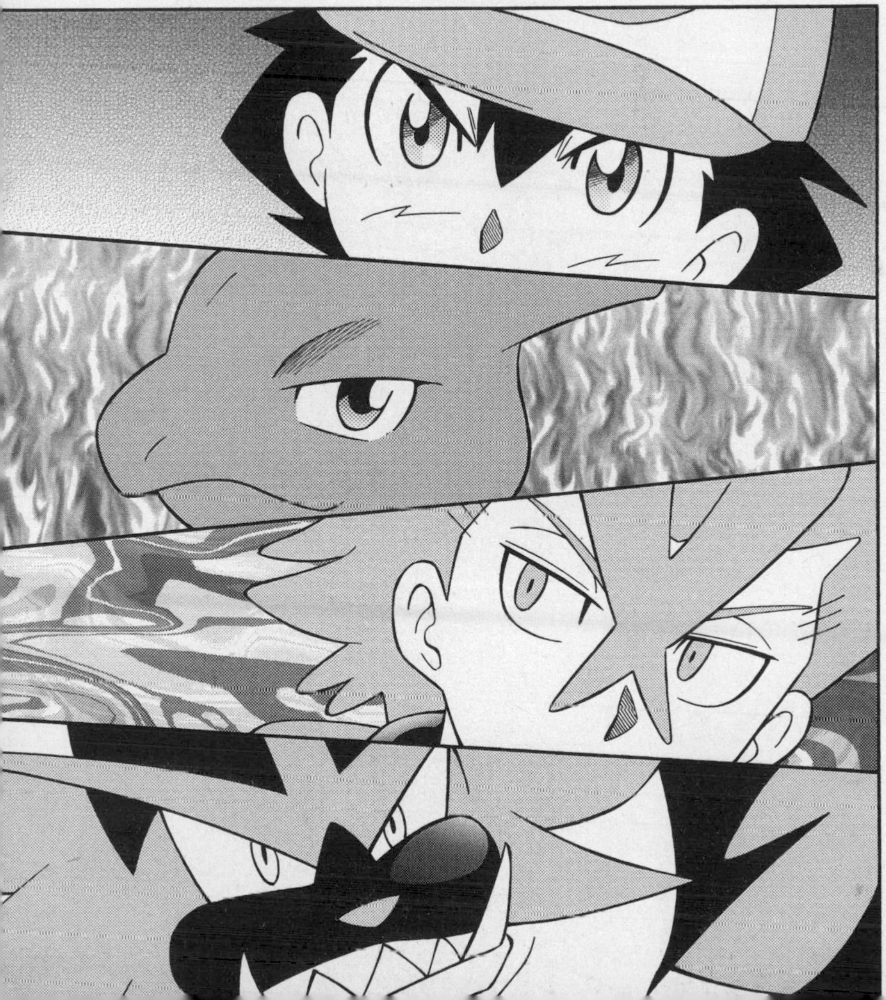

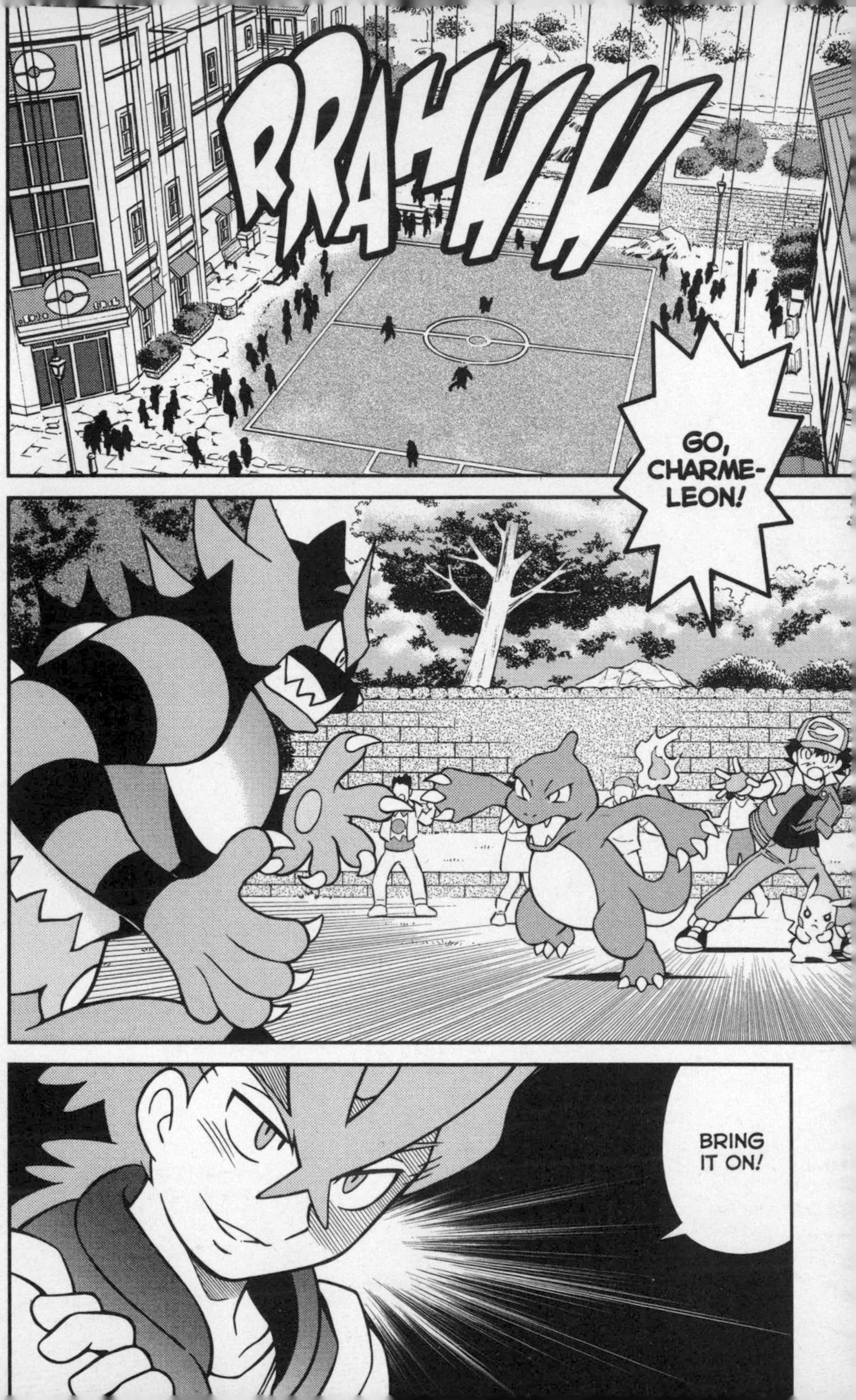
RRAHHH
GO, CHARME-LEON!
BRING IT ON!

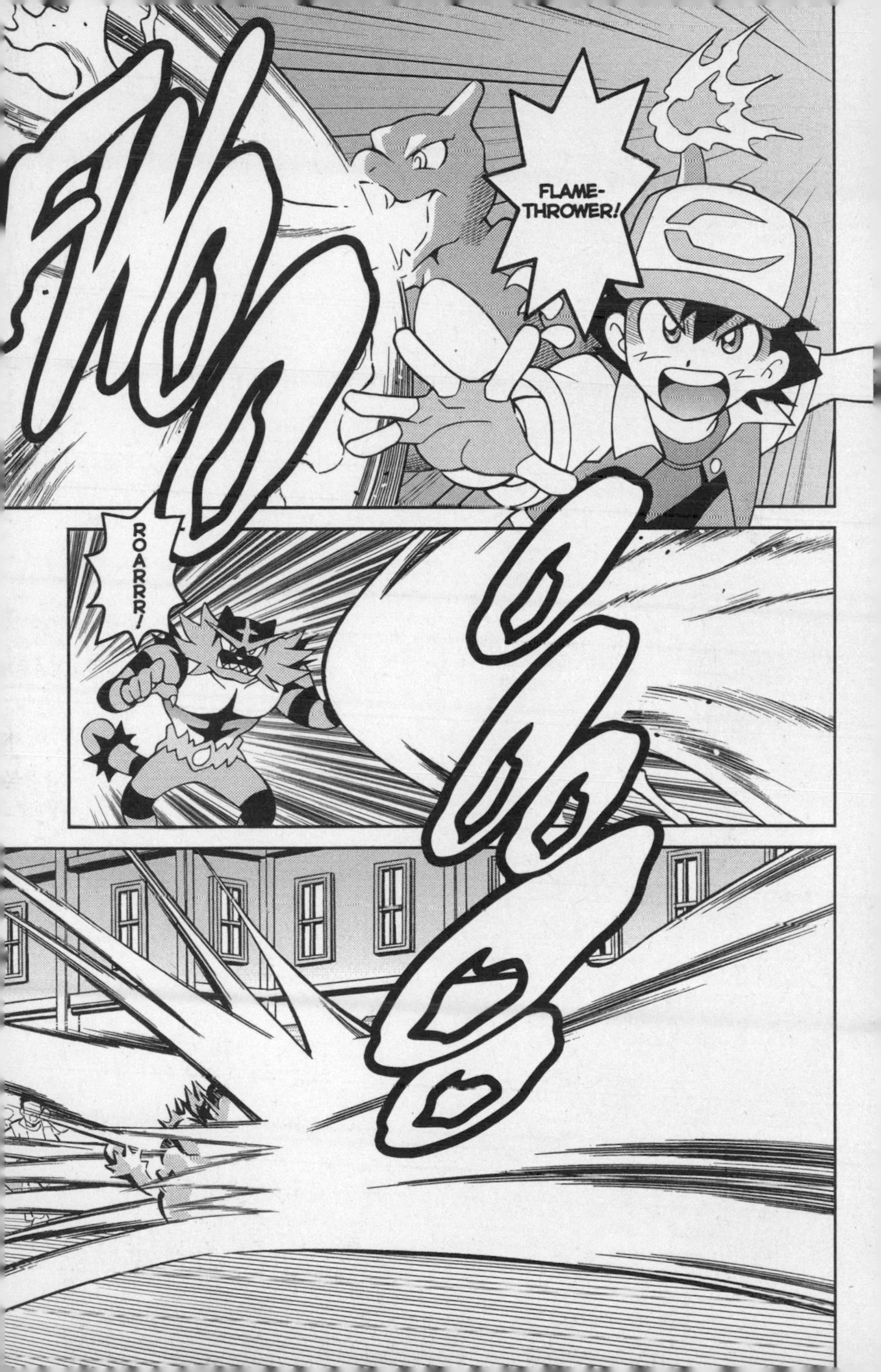
FLAME-THROWER!
ROARRR!

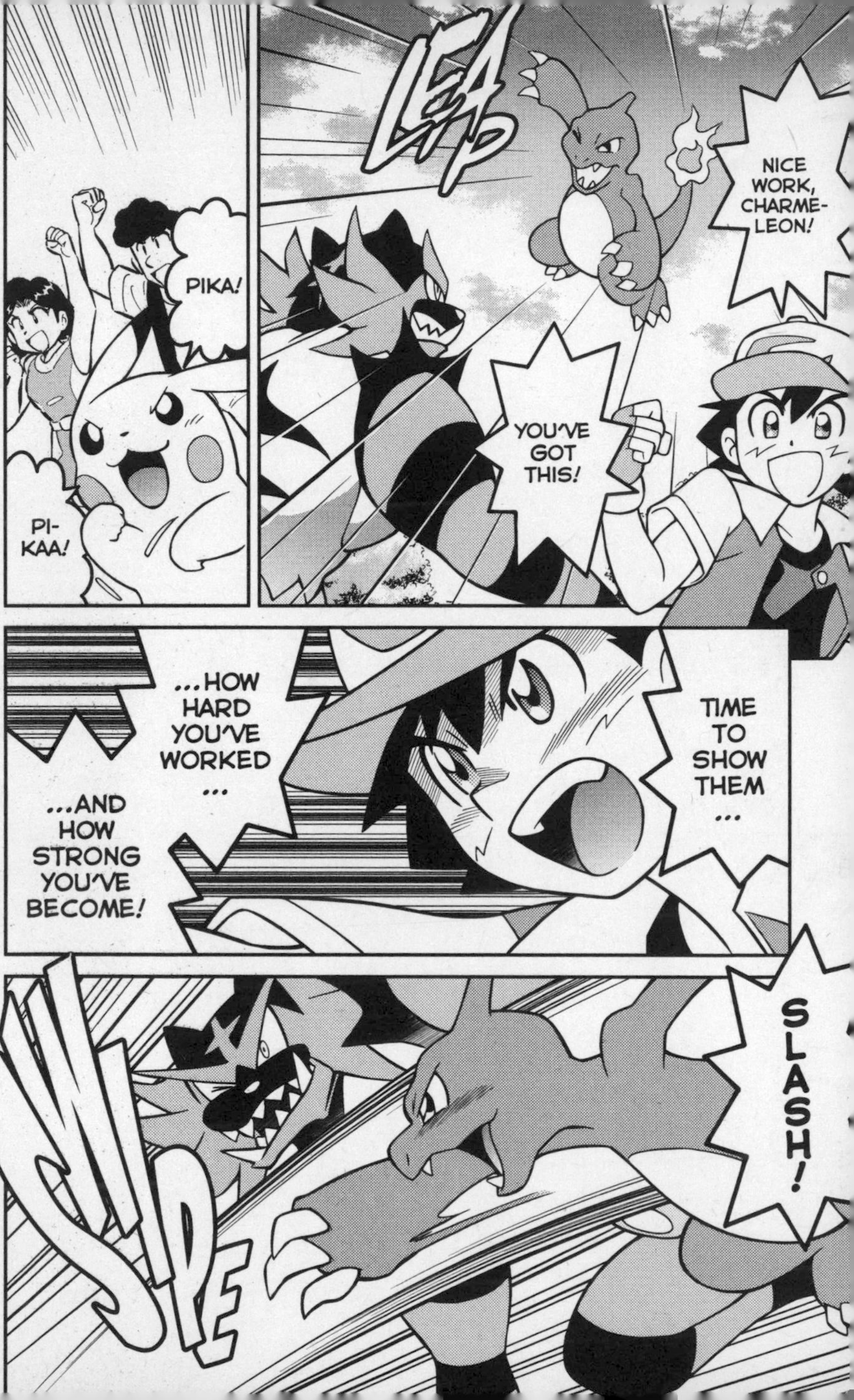
NICE WORK, CHARMELEON!
LEAP
YOU'VE GOT THIS!
PIKA!
PI-KAA!
TIME TO SHOW THEM...
...HOW HARD YOU'VE WORKED...
...AND HOW STRONG YOU'VE BECOME!
SLASH!
SWIPE

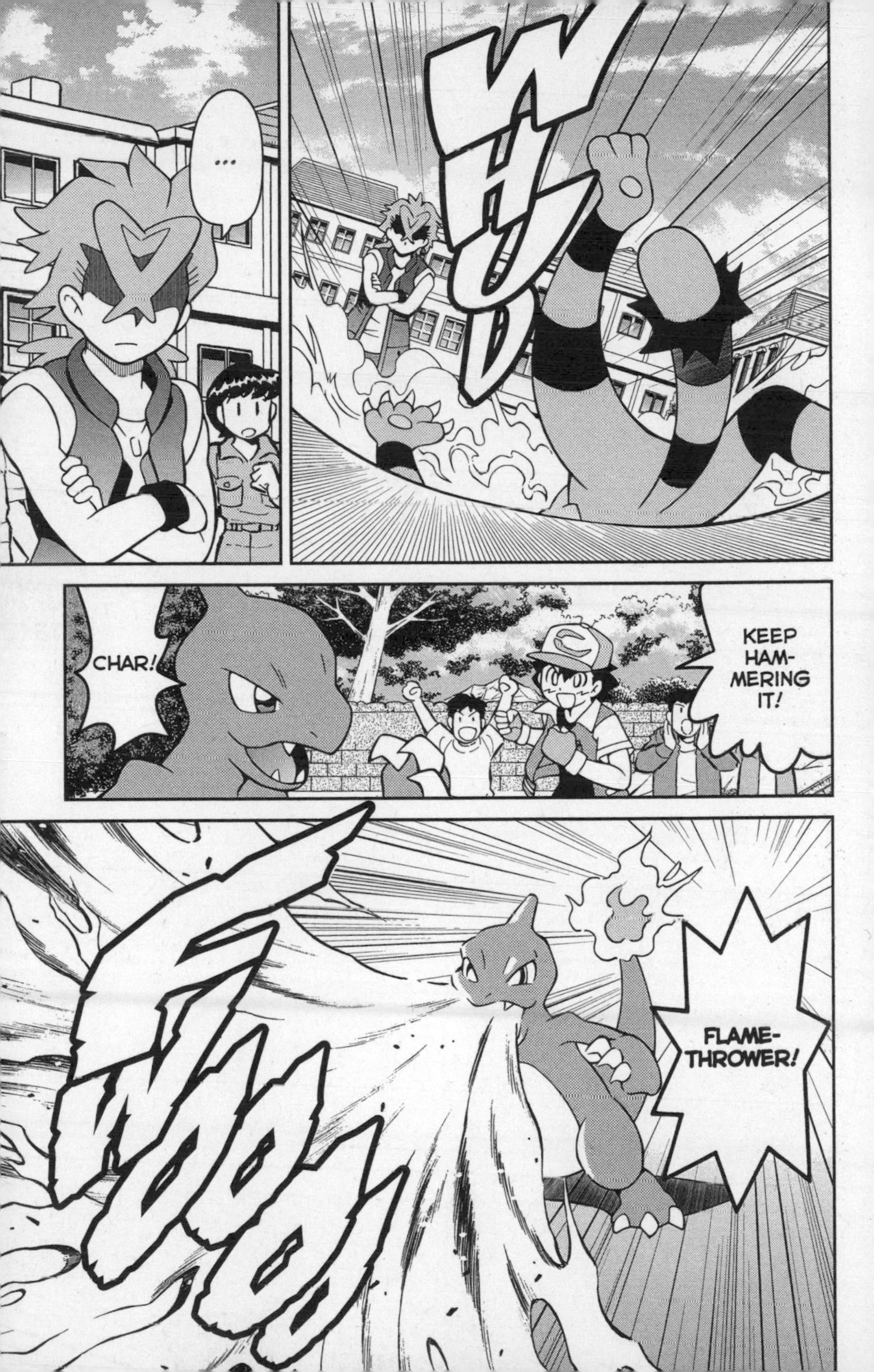
WHUD
...
KEEP HAM-MERING IT!
CHAR!
FLAME-THROWER!

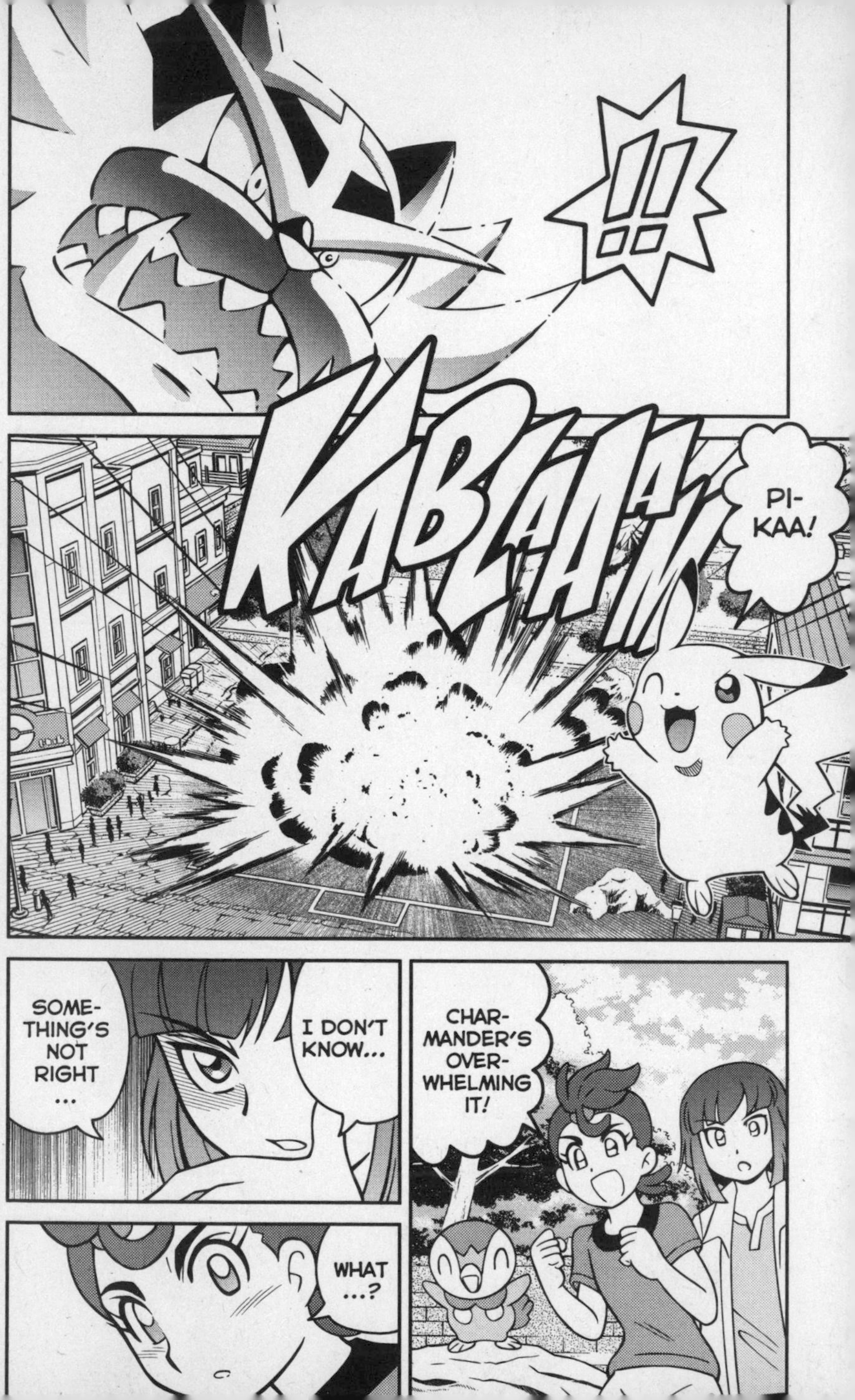
!!
KABLAAM
PI-KAA!
CHAR-MANDER'S OVER-WHELMING IT!
I DON'T KNOW...
SOME-THING'S NOT RIGHT...
WHAT...?

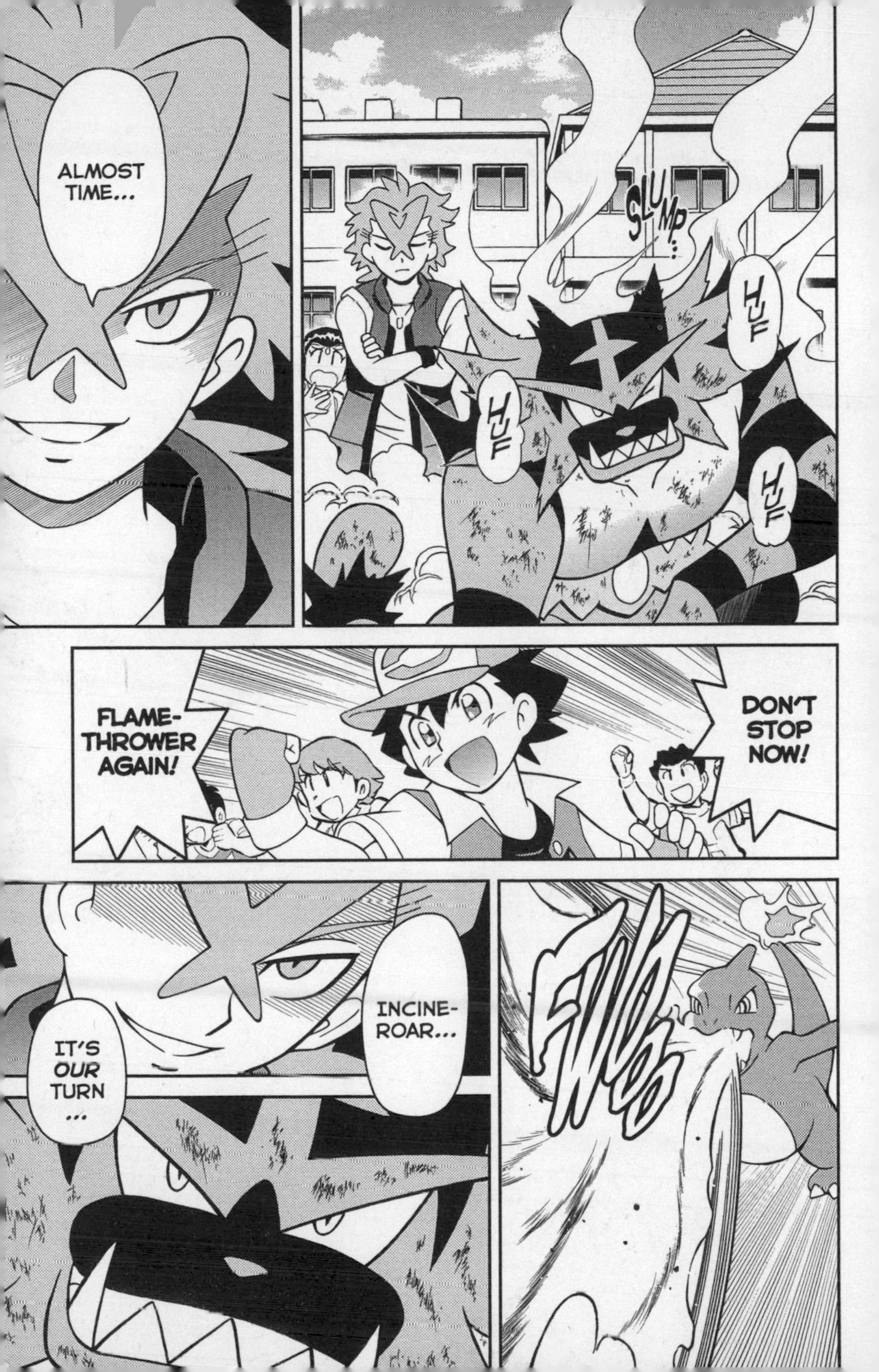
SLUMP
HUF
HUF
HUF
ALMOST TIME...
DON'T STOP NOW!
FLAME-THROWER AGAIN!
INCINE-ROAR...
IT'S *OUR* TURN...

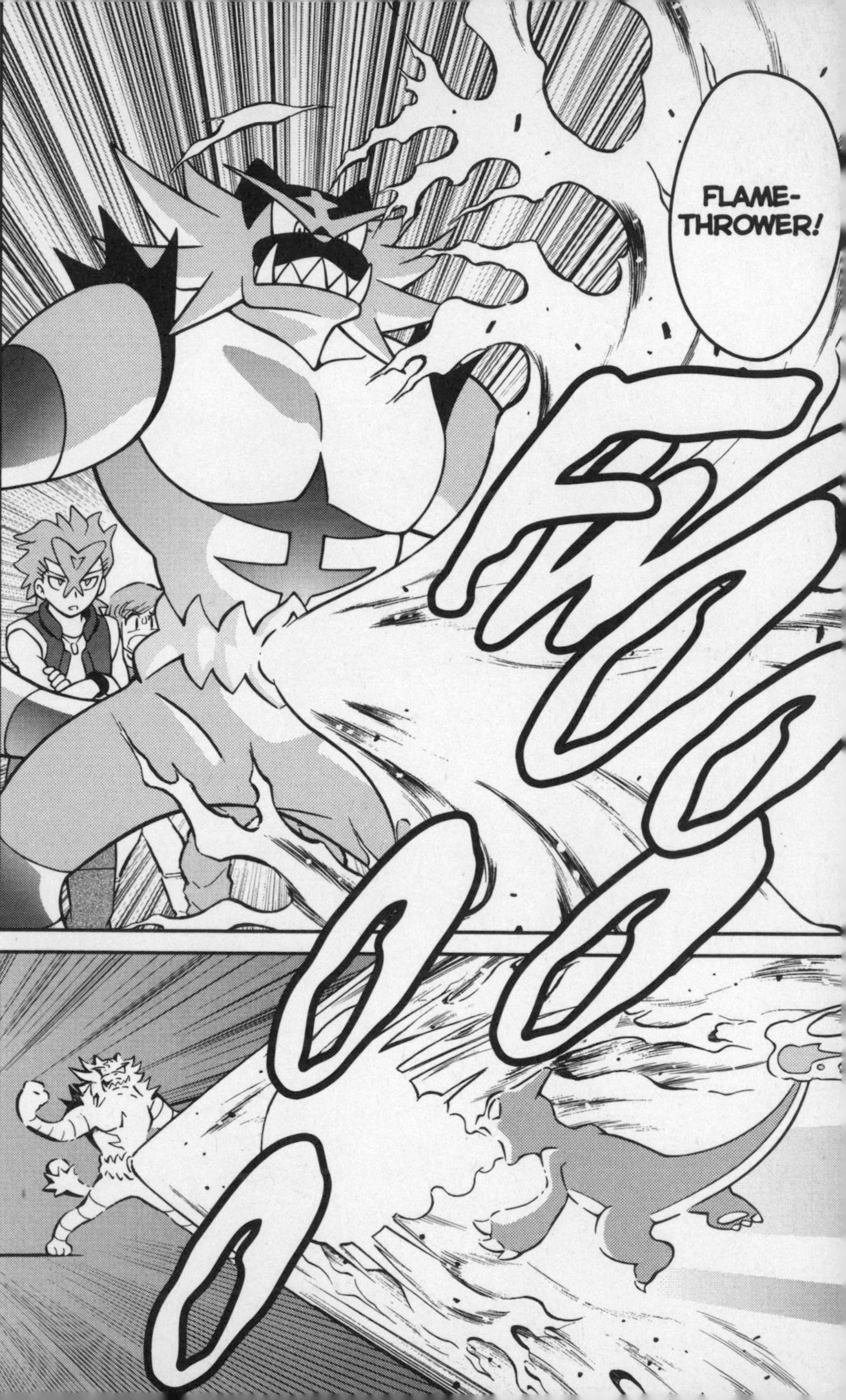
FLAME-THROWER!

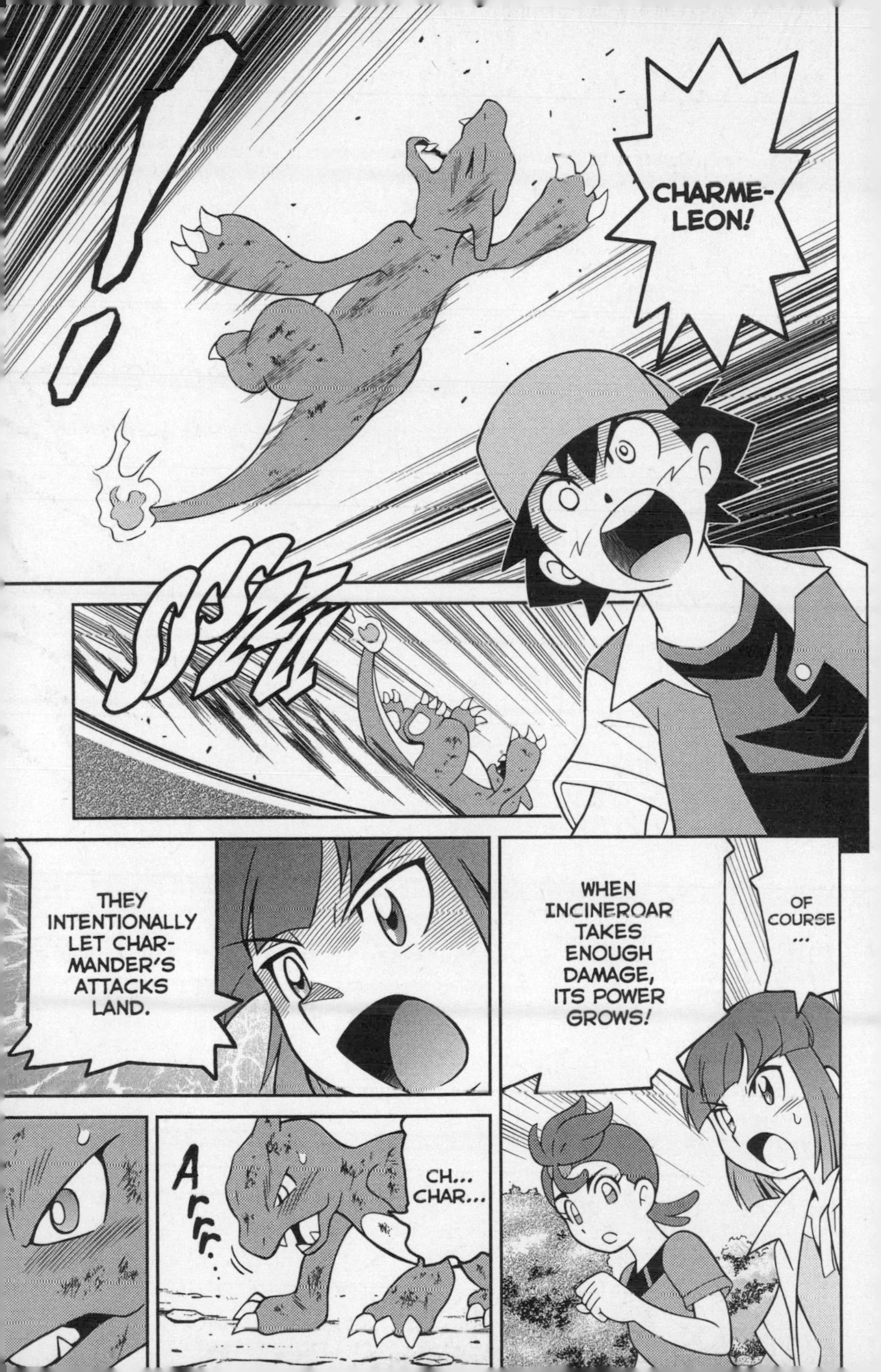
CHARME-LEON!
OF COURSE...
WHEN INCINEROAR TAKES ENOUGH DAMAGE, ITS POWER GROWS!
THEY INTENTIONALLY LET CHAR-MANDER'S ATTACKS LAND.
CH... CHAR...
Arrr...

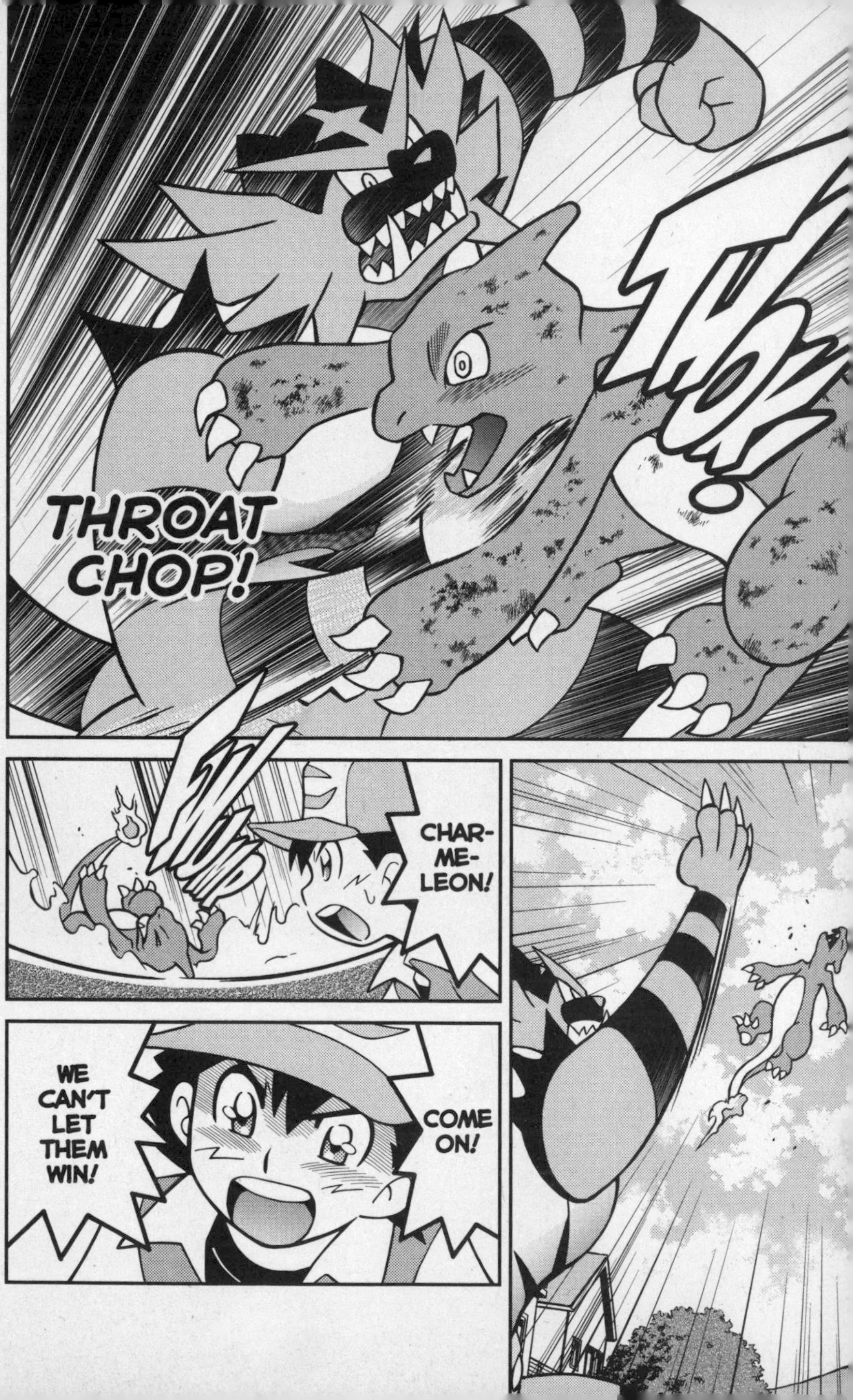
THOK!
THROAT CHOP!
CHAR-ME-LEON!
COME ON!
WE CAN'T LET THEM WIN!

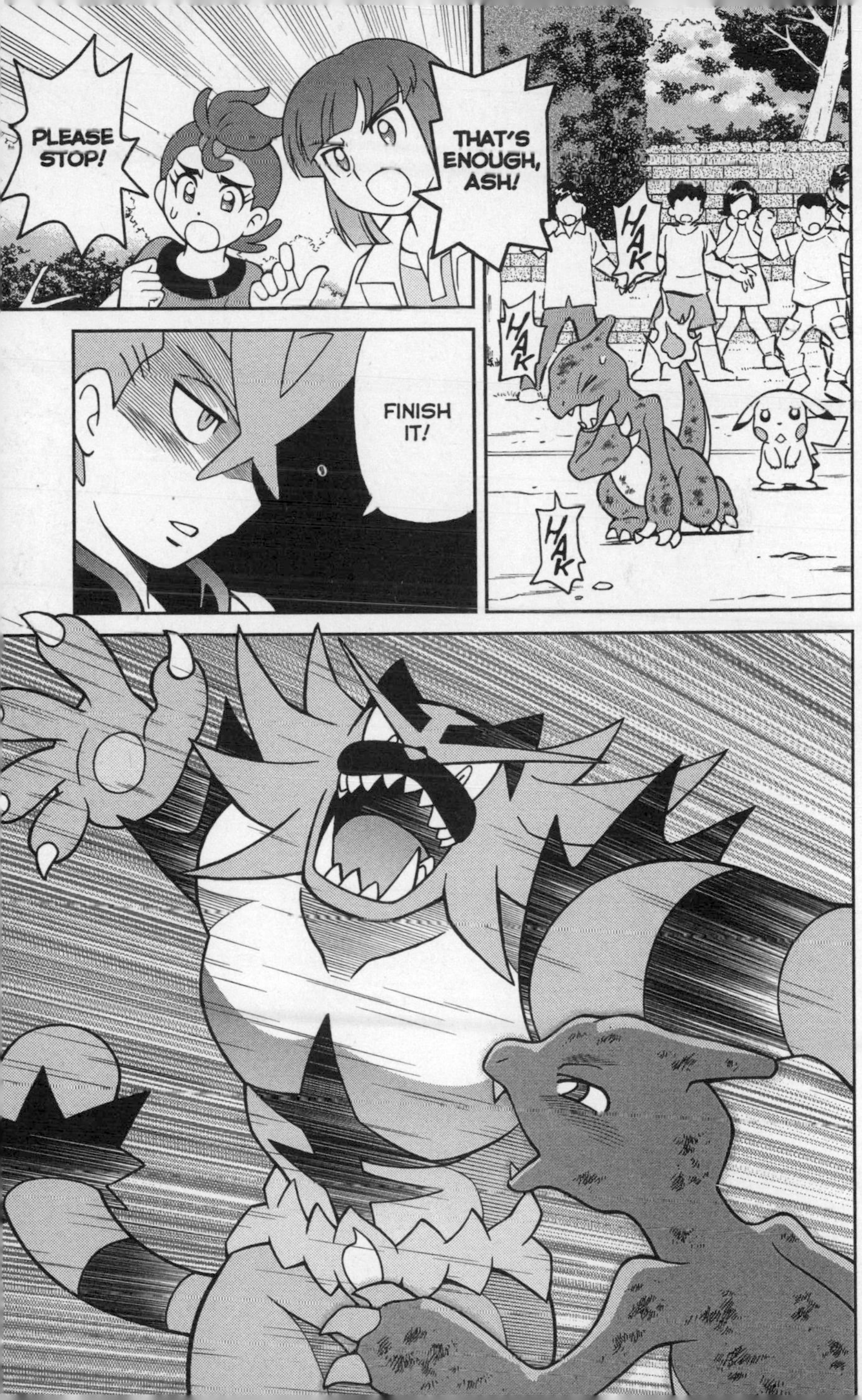
HAK
HAK
HAK
THAT'S ENOUGH, ASH!
PLEASE STOP!
FINISH IT!

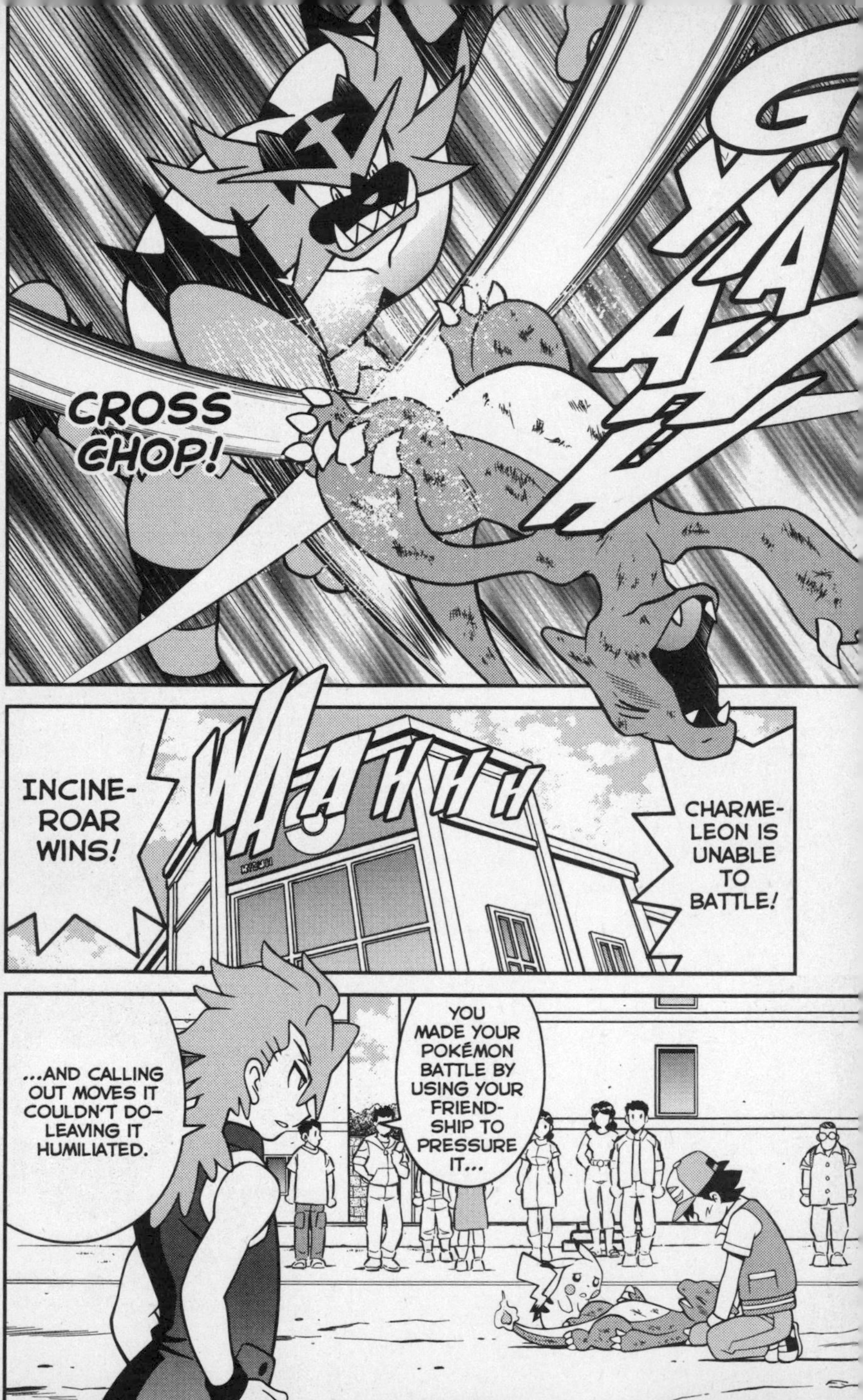
CROSS CHOP!
CHARME-
LEON IS
UNABLE
TO
BATTLE!
WAAHHHH
INCINE-
ROAR
WINS!
YOU MADE YOUR POKÉMON BATTLE BY USING YOUR FRIEND-SHIP TO PRESSURE IT...
...AND CALLING OUT MOVES IT COULDN'T DO—LEAVING IT HUMILIATED.

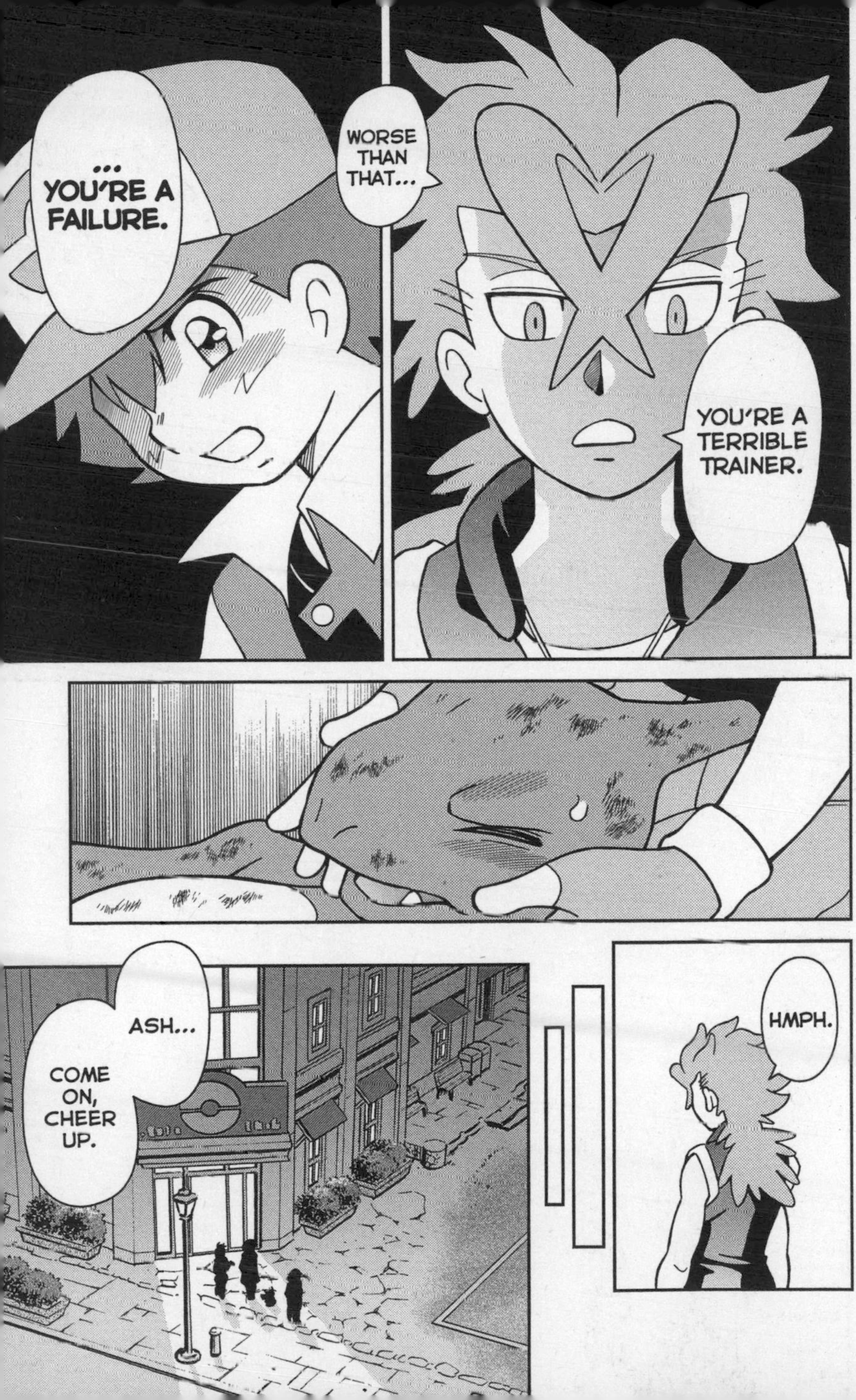
WORSE THAN THAT...
YOU'RE A TERRIBLE TRAINER.
... YOU'RE A FAILURE.
HMPH.
ASH...
COME ON, CHEER UP.

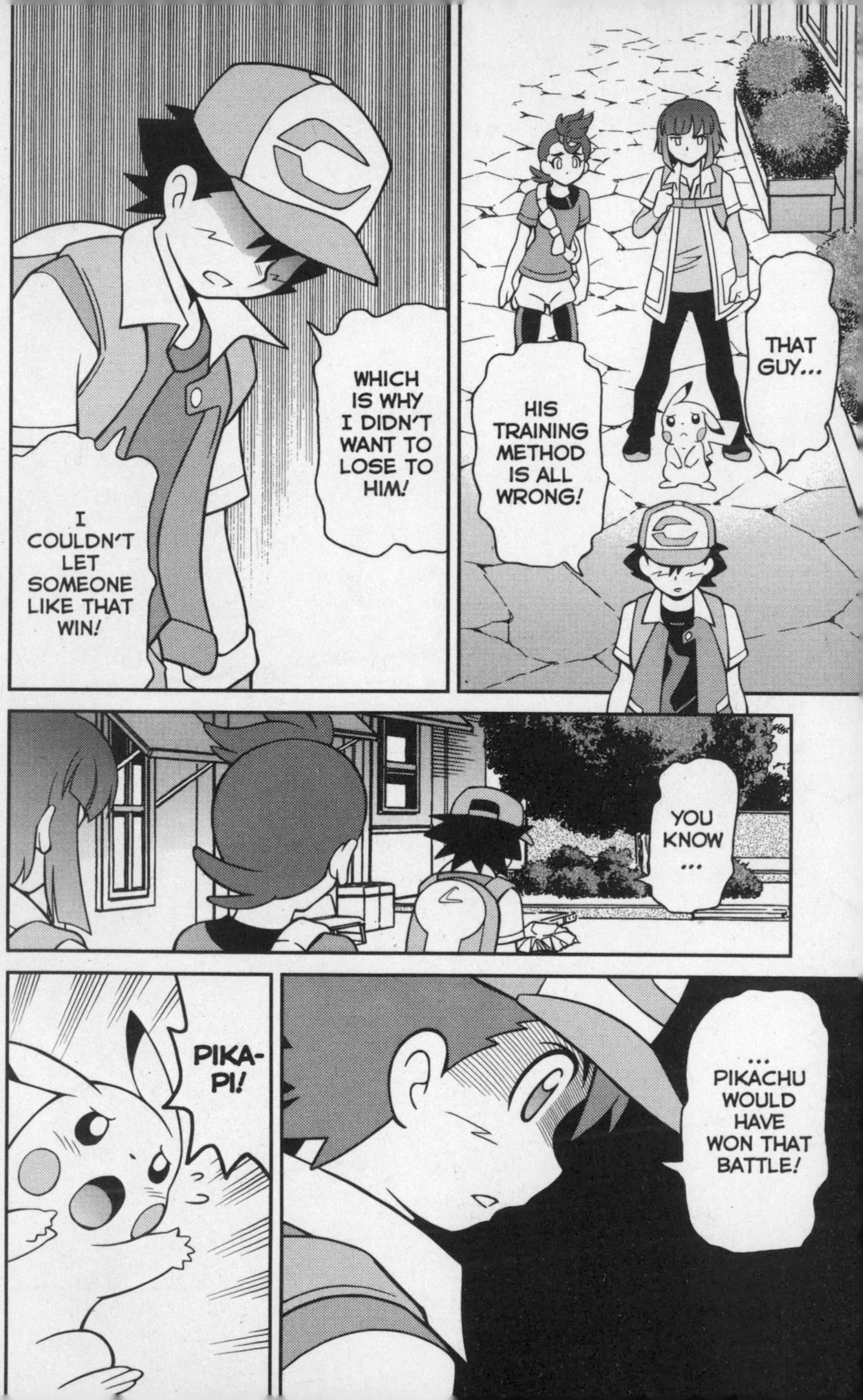
THAT GUY...
HIS TRAINING METHOD IS ALL WRONG!
WHICH IS WHY I DIDN'T WANT TO LOSE TO HIM!
I COULDN'T LET SOMEONE LIKE THAT WIN!
YOU KNOW ...
... PIKACHU WOULD HAVE WON THAT BATTLE!
PIKA-PI!

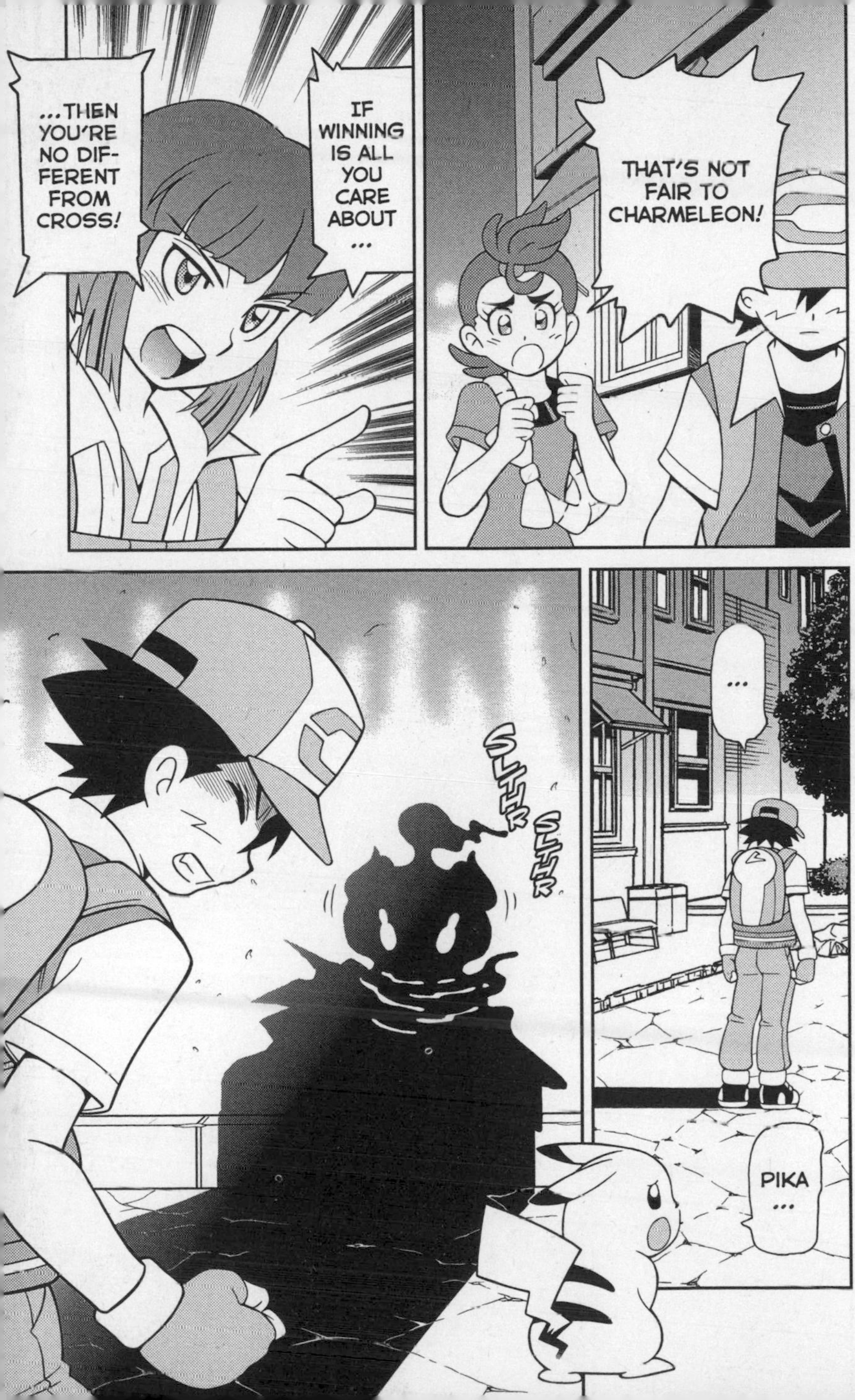
THAT'S NOT FAIR TO CHARMELEON!
IF WINNING IS ALL YOU CARE ABOUT ...
...THEN YOU'RE NO DIF-FERENT FROM CROSS!
...
PIKA ...
SLTHR
SLTHR

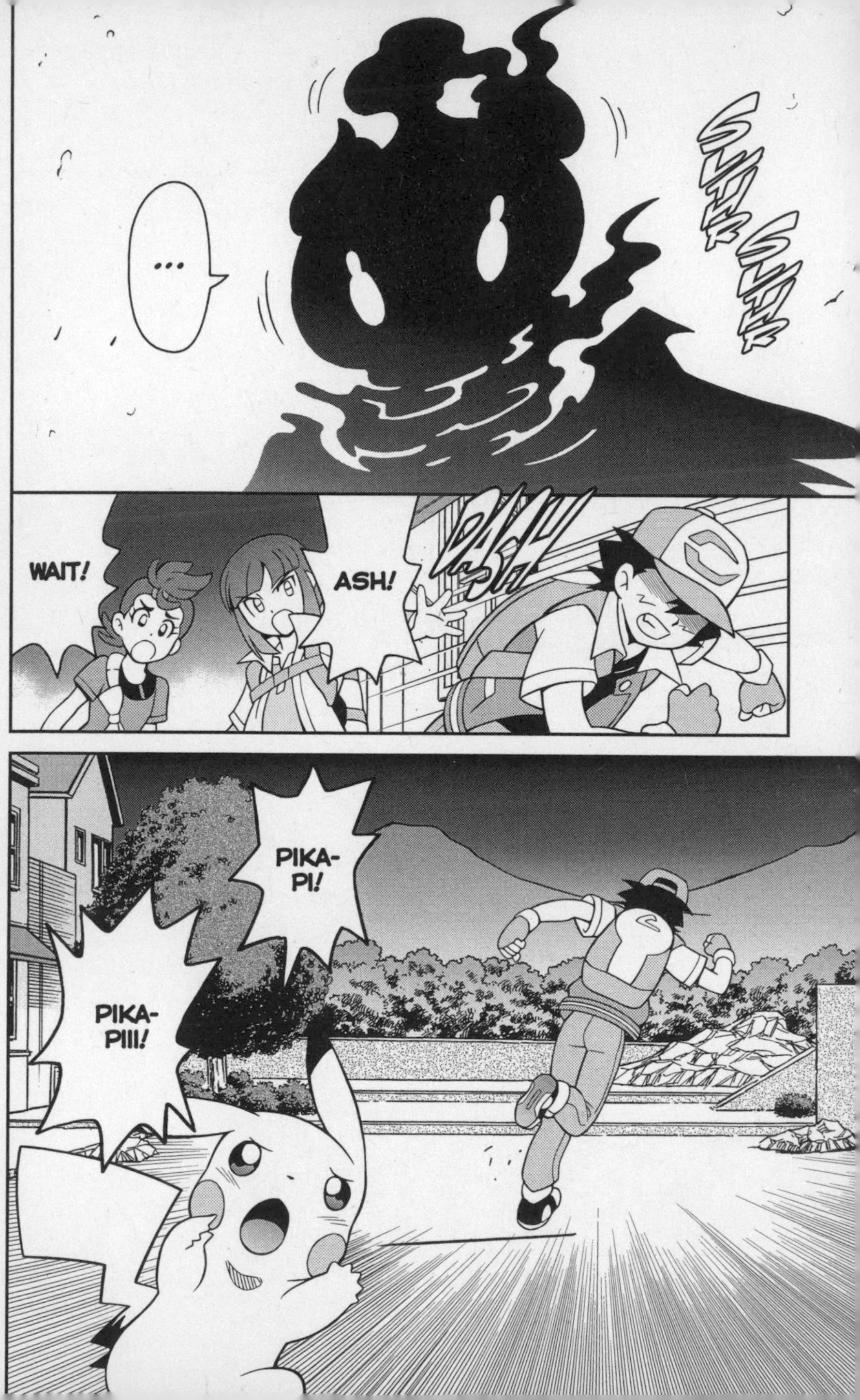
...
DASH
ASH!
WAIT!
PIKA-PI!
PIKA-PIII!

This is my second Pokémon manga.
The first was *Pokémon the Movie: The Rise of Darkrai*.

Back then, all my effort went into telling the Darkrai story, and I didn't get a chance to dig deeply into the characters of Ash and his friends. It's something I've always regretted.

Getting to create the graphic novel version of the movie *I Choose You!* has been a ten-year dream come true—my dream to tell the origin story of Ash and Pikachu!

As I draw, I imagine I'm participating in Ash and Pikachu's adventure. I hope that some of you share that excitement too as you read the story.

Now, without further ado, on to part two! I hope you enjoy it!

P.S. Incineroar is really fun to draw!

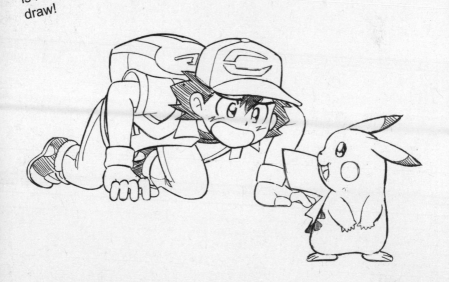

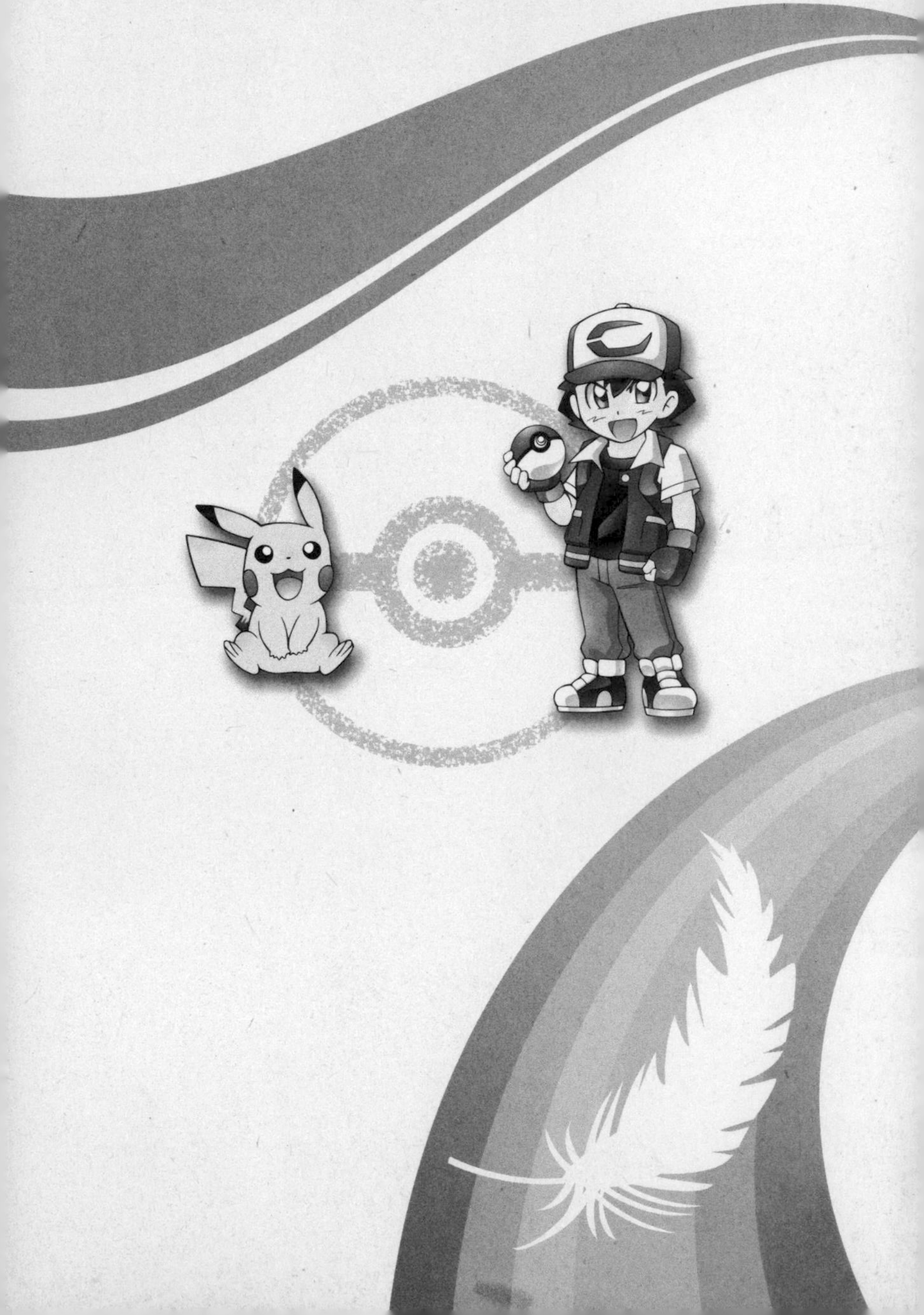

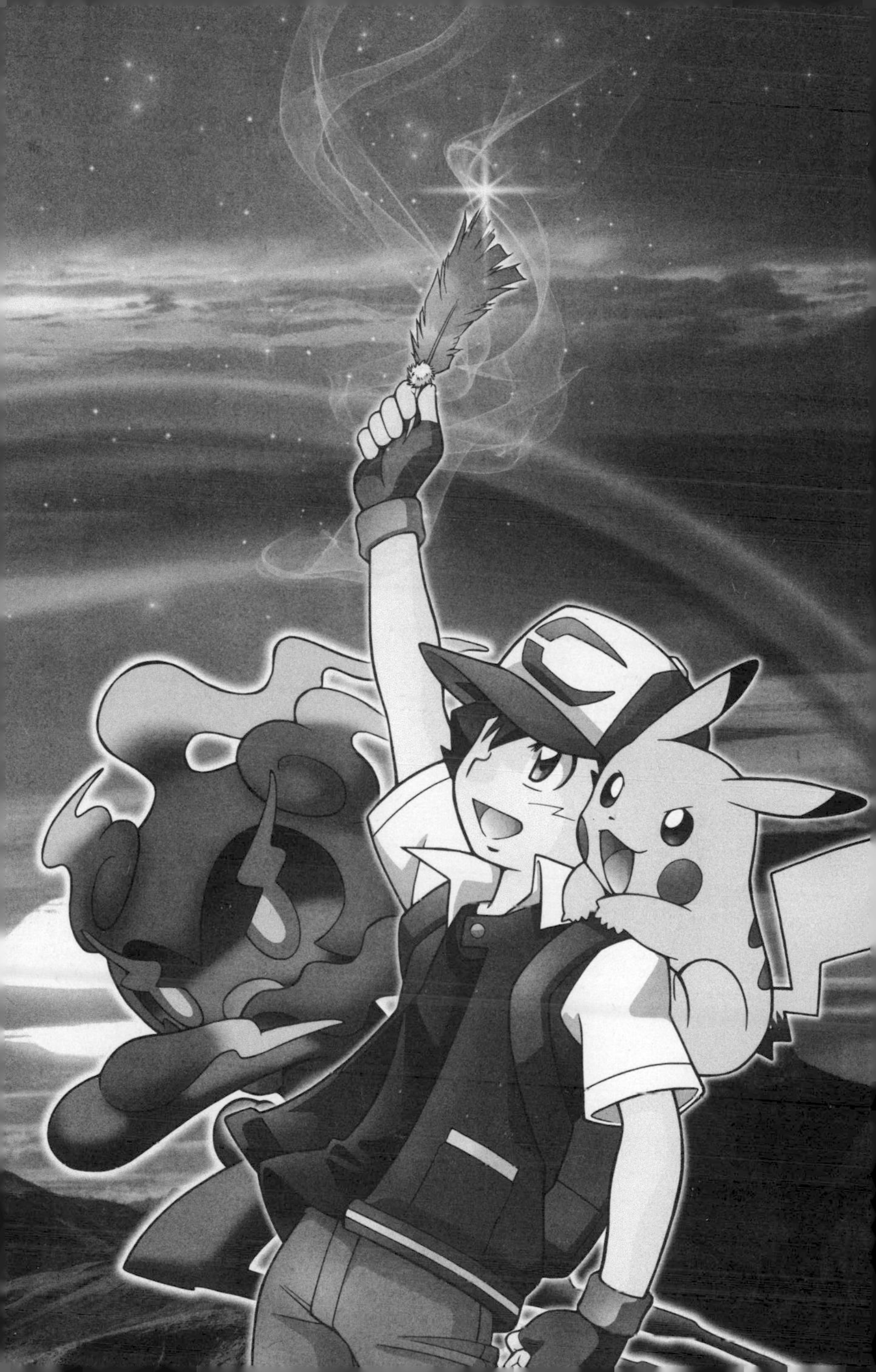

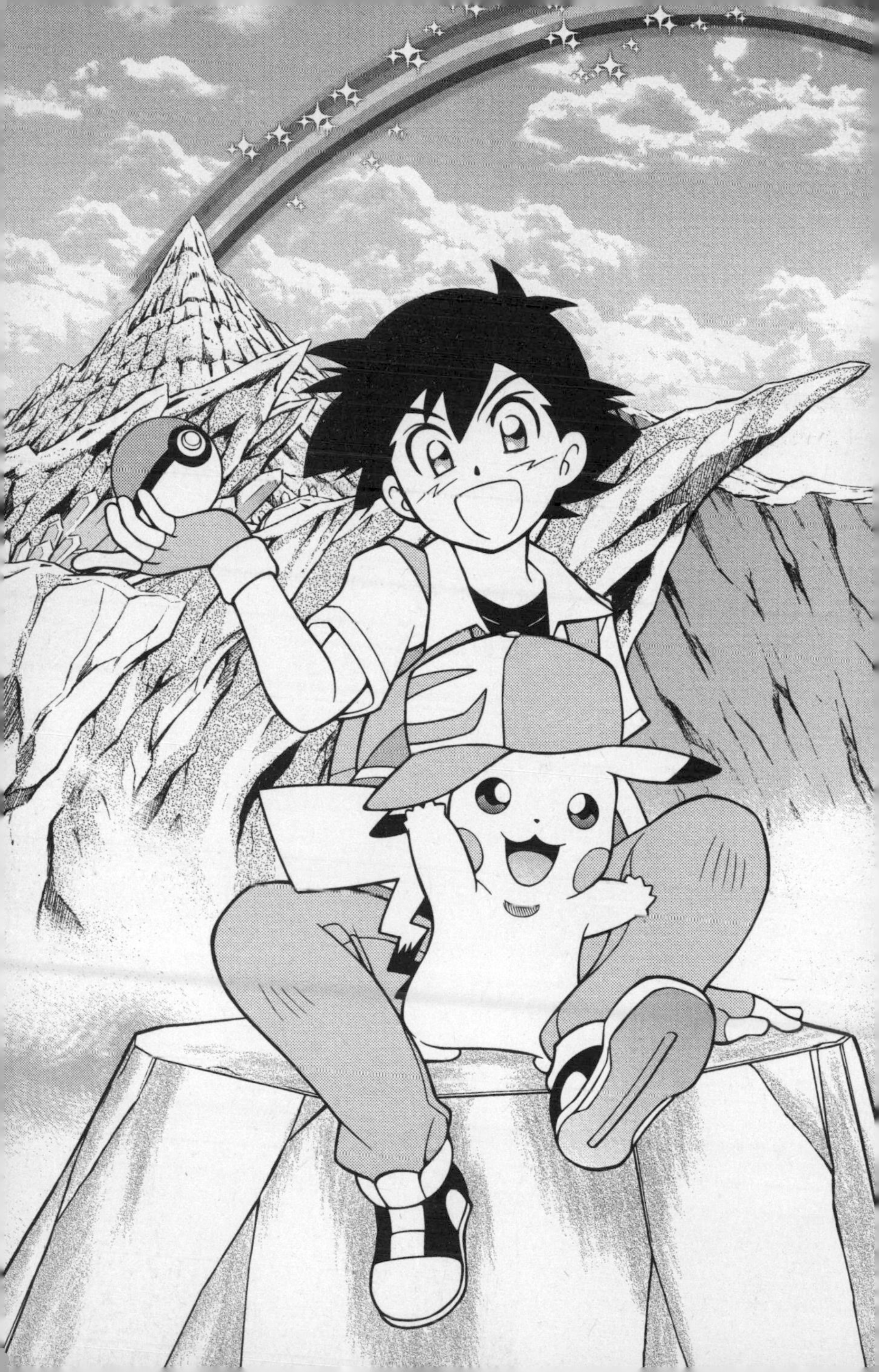

RYO TAKAMISAKI

While I was excited to draw Ash and Pikachu again, I was especially happy to get to draw Charmander and Butterfree. (That famous scene with them brought back memories!)

And Cross is still a favorite. (I like his bad attitude.)

I'm overcome with emotion thinking about what adventures Verity, Sorrel and the rest of the gang must be having now!

CHAPTER 8

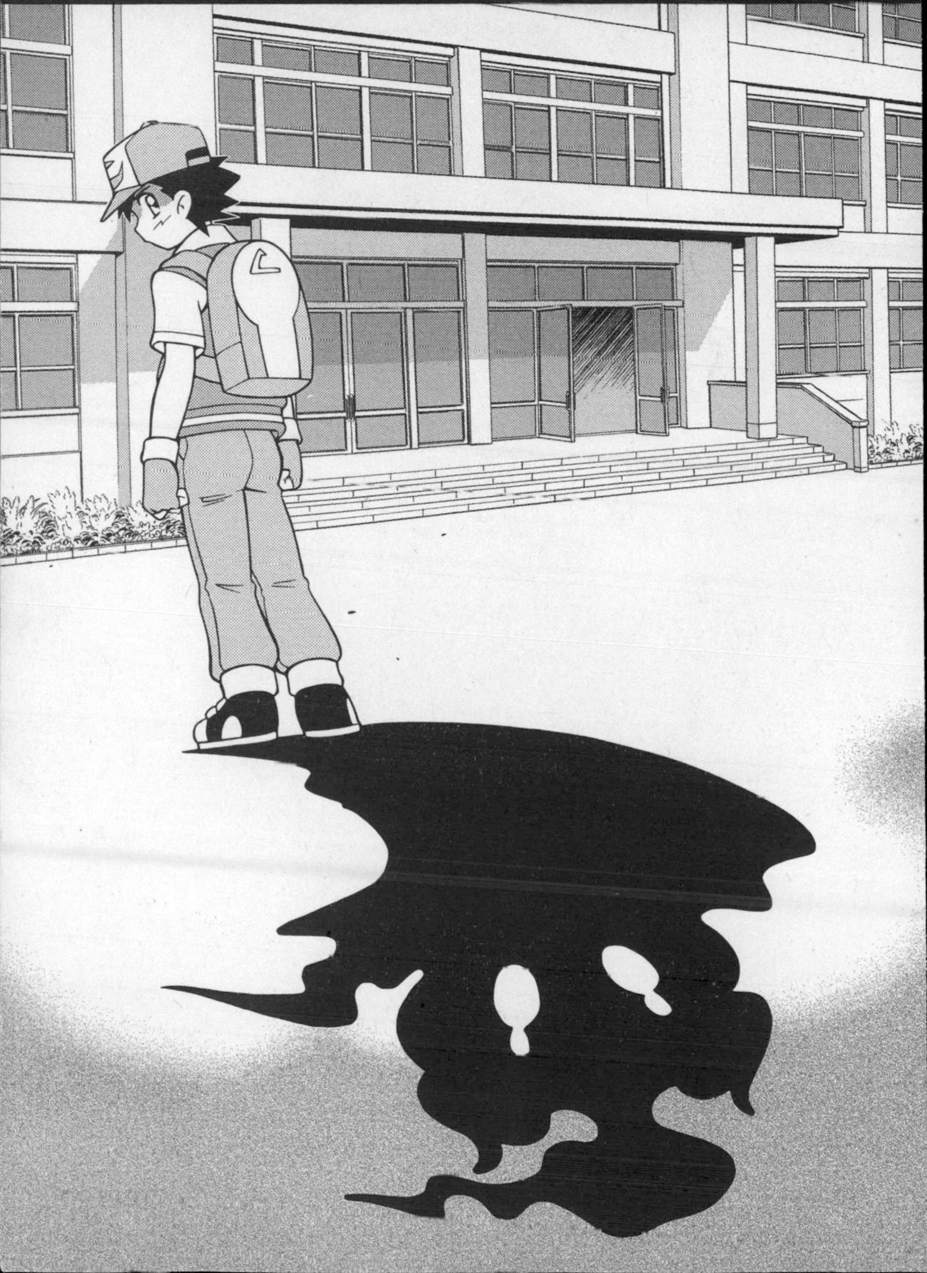

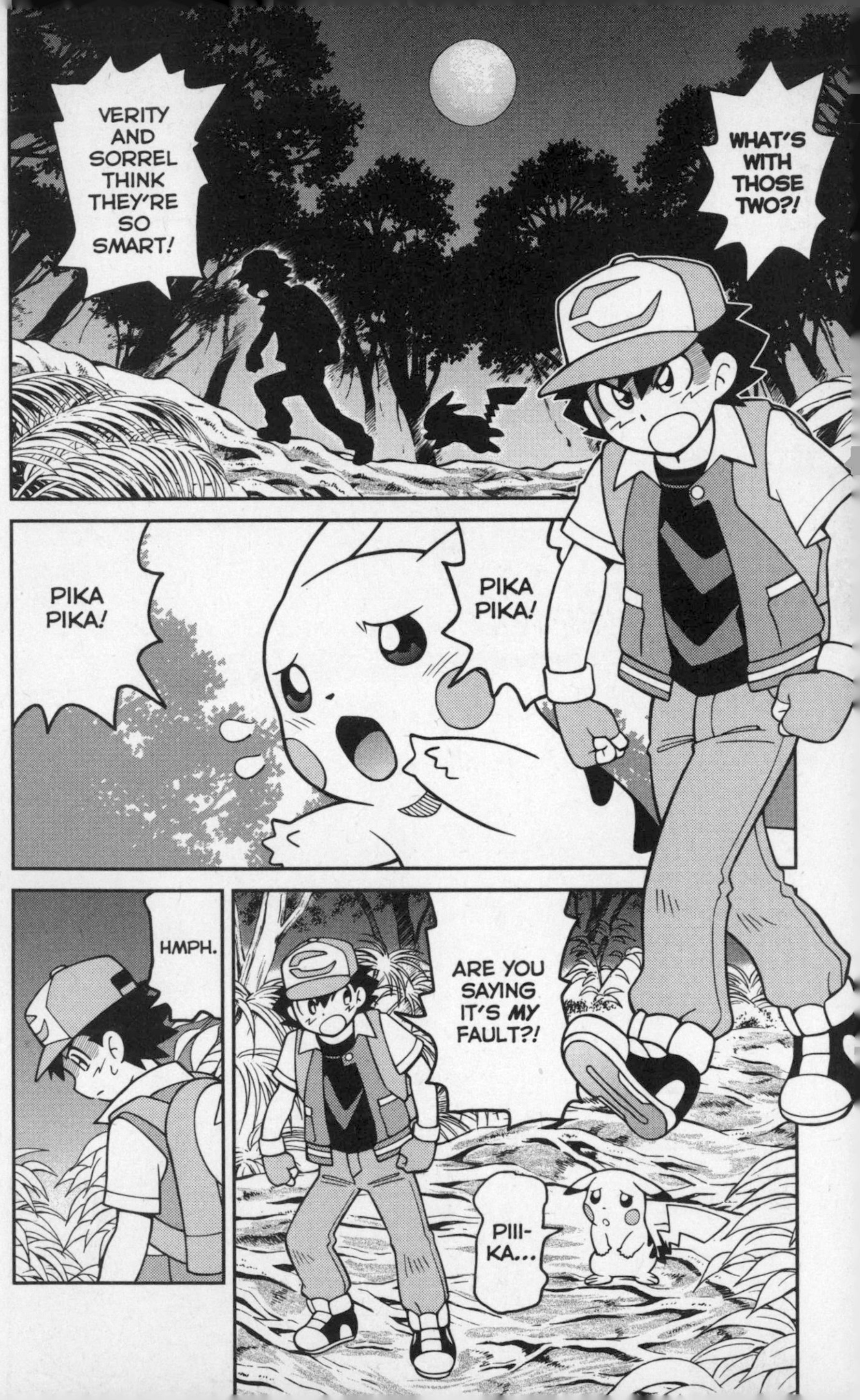
WHAT'S WITH THOSE TWO?!
VERITY AND SORREL THINK THEY'RE SO SMART!
PIKA PIKA!
PIKA PIKA!
ARE YOU SAYING IT'S *MY* FAULT?!
PIII-KA...
HMPH.

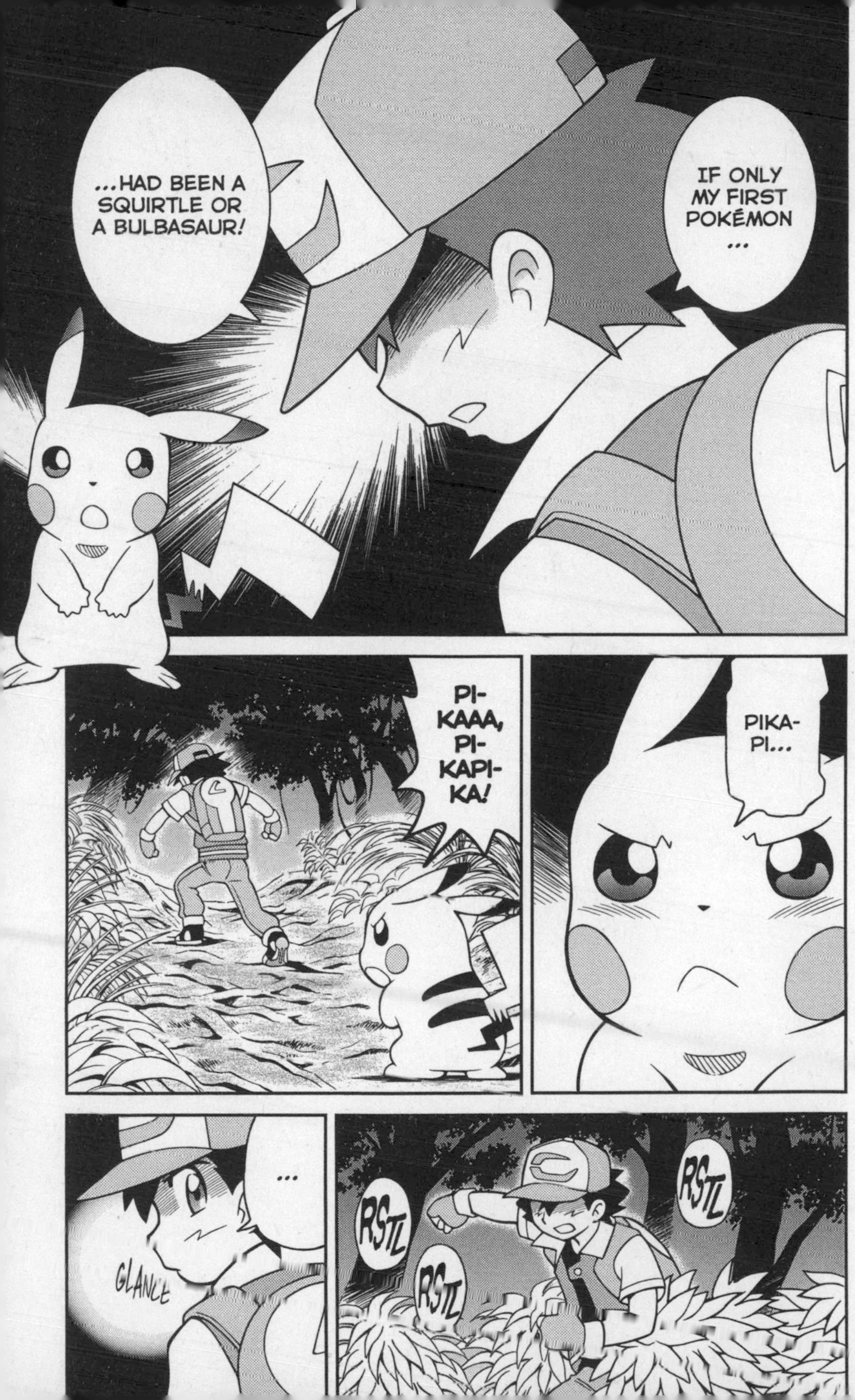
IF ONLY MY FIRST POKÉMON ...
...HAD BEEN A SQUIRTLE OR A BULBASAUR!
PIKA-PI...
PI-KAAA, PI-KAPI-KA!
RSTL
RSTL
RSTL
...
GLANCE

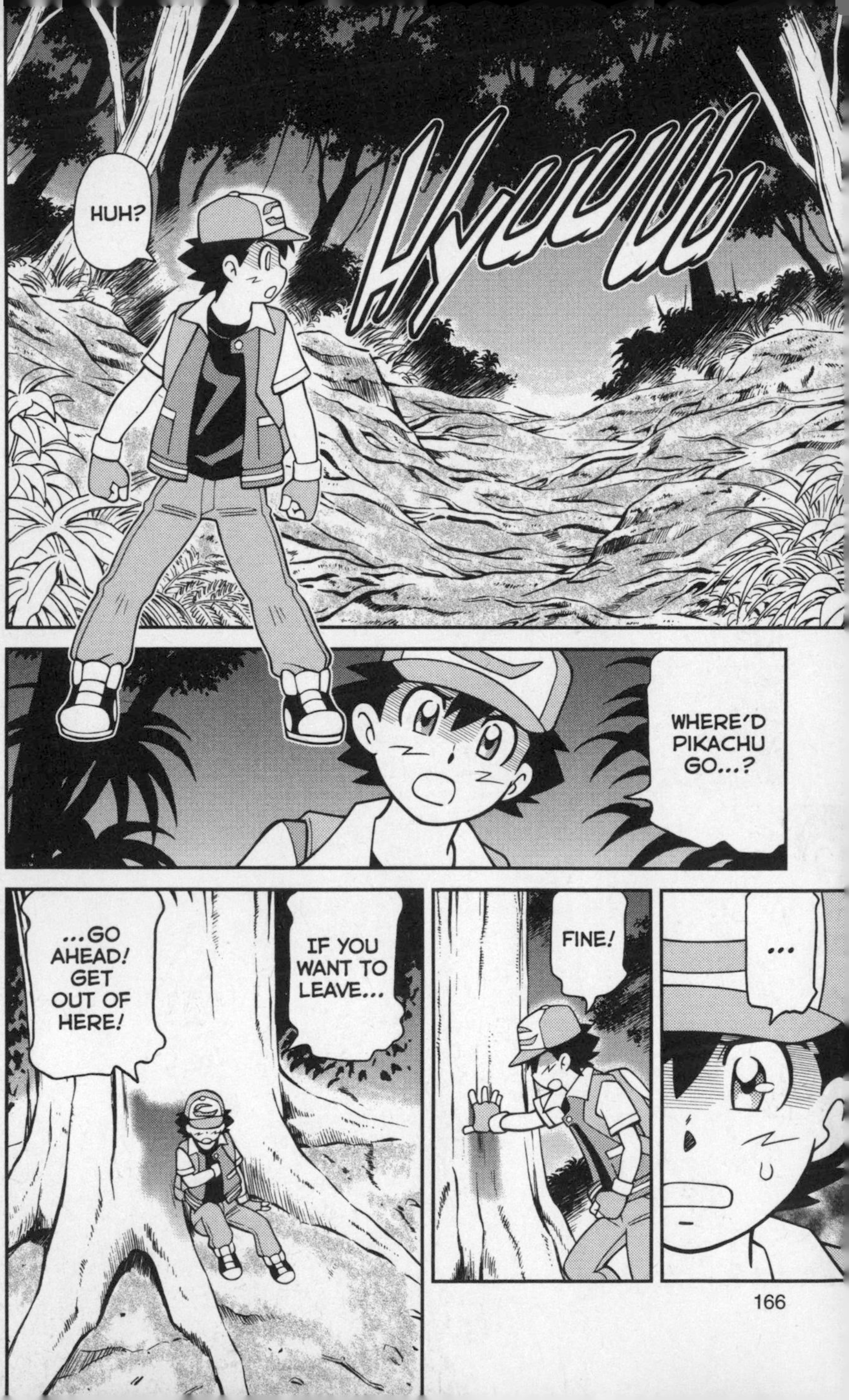
HUH?
WHERE'D PIKACHU GO...?
...
FINE!
IF YOU WANT TO LEAVE...
...GO AHEAD! GET OUT OF HERE!

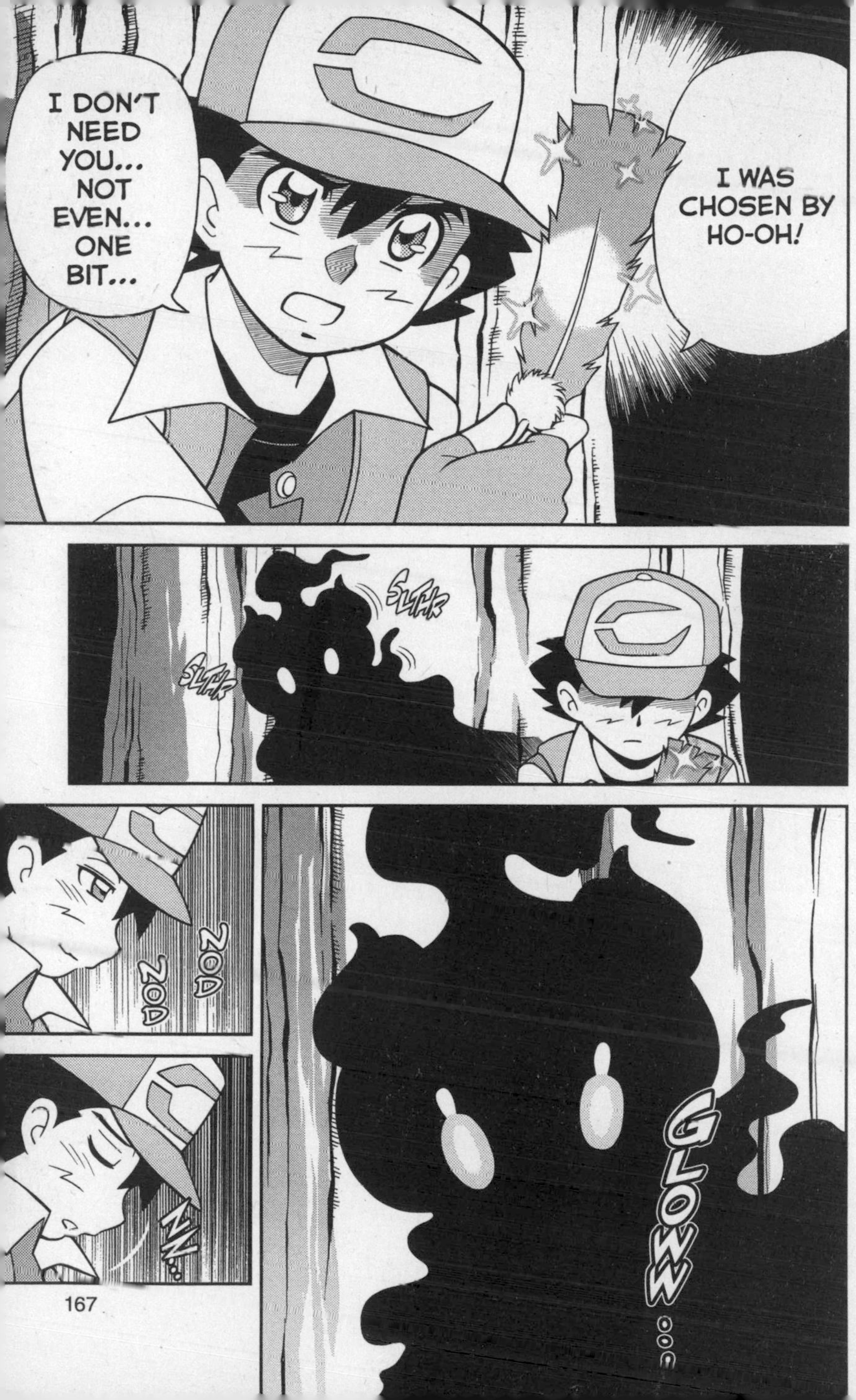
I WAS CHOSEN BY HO-OH!
I DON'T NEED YOU... NOT EVEN... ONE BIT...
SLTHK
SLTHK
GLOW...
NOD NOD
NN...

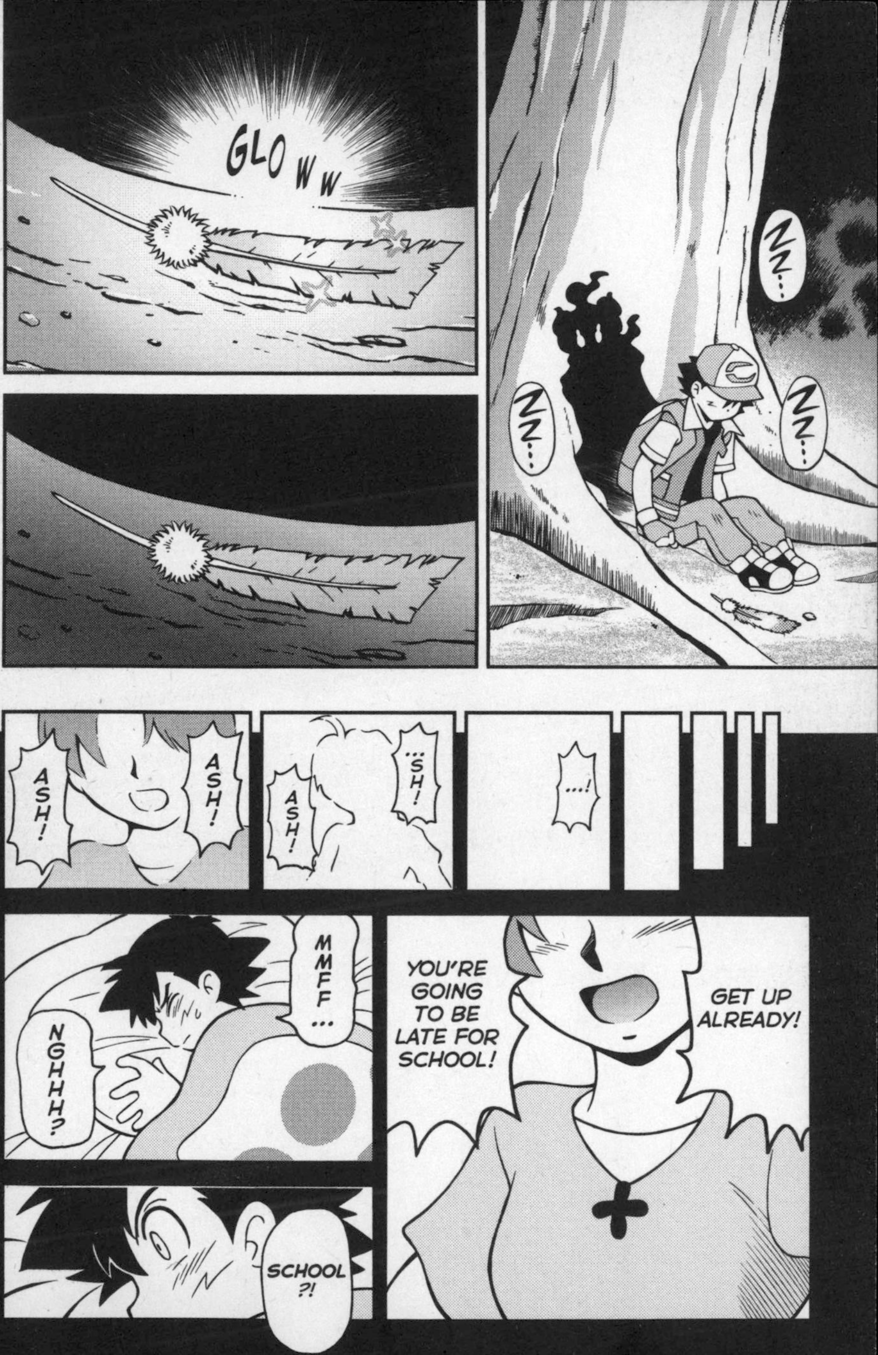
ZZZ…
ZZZ…
ZZZ…
GLOWW
…!
…SH!
ASH!
ASH!
ASH!
GET UP ALREADY!
YOU'RE GOING TO BE LATE FOR SCHOOL!
MMFF…
NGHHHH?
SCHOOL?!

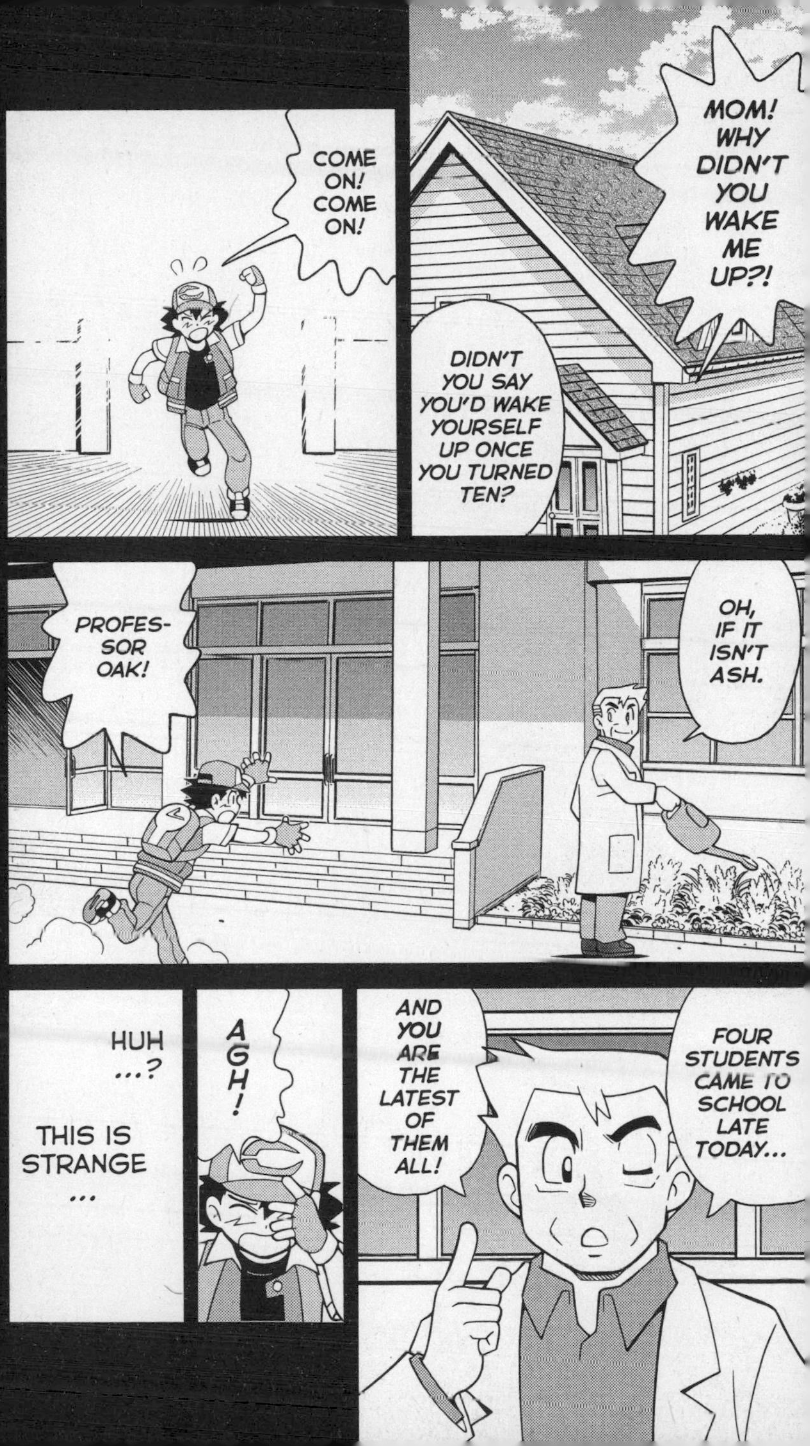
MOM! WHY DIDN'T YOU WAKE ME UP?!
DIDN'T YOU SAY YOU'D WAKE YOURSELF UP ONCE YOU TURNED TEN?
COME ON! COME ON!
OH, IF IT ISN'T ASH.
PROFES-SOR OAK!
FOUR STUDENTS CAME TO SCHOOL LATE TODAY...
AND YOU ARE THE LATEST OF THEM ALL!
AGH!
HUH ...?
THIS IS STRANGE ...

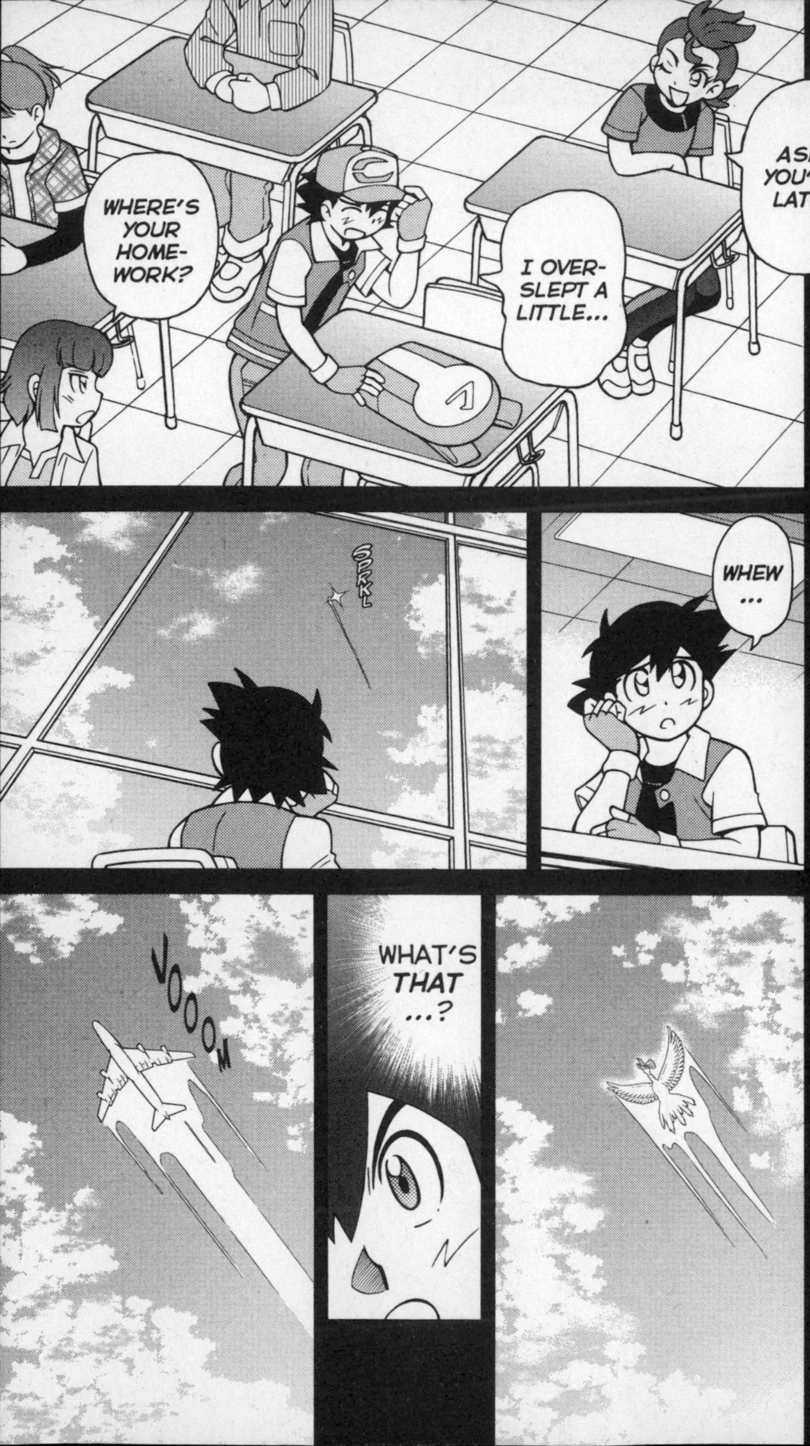
ASH, YOU'RE LATE!
I OVER-SLEPT A LITTLE...
WHERE'S YOUR HOME-WORK?
WHEW ...
SPRKL
WHAT'S THAT ...?
VOOOM

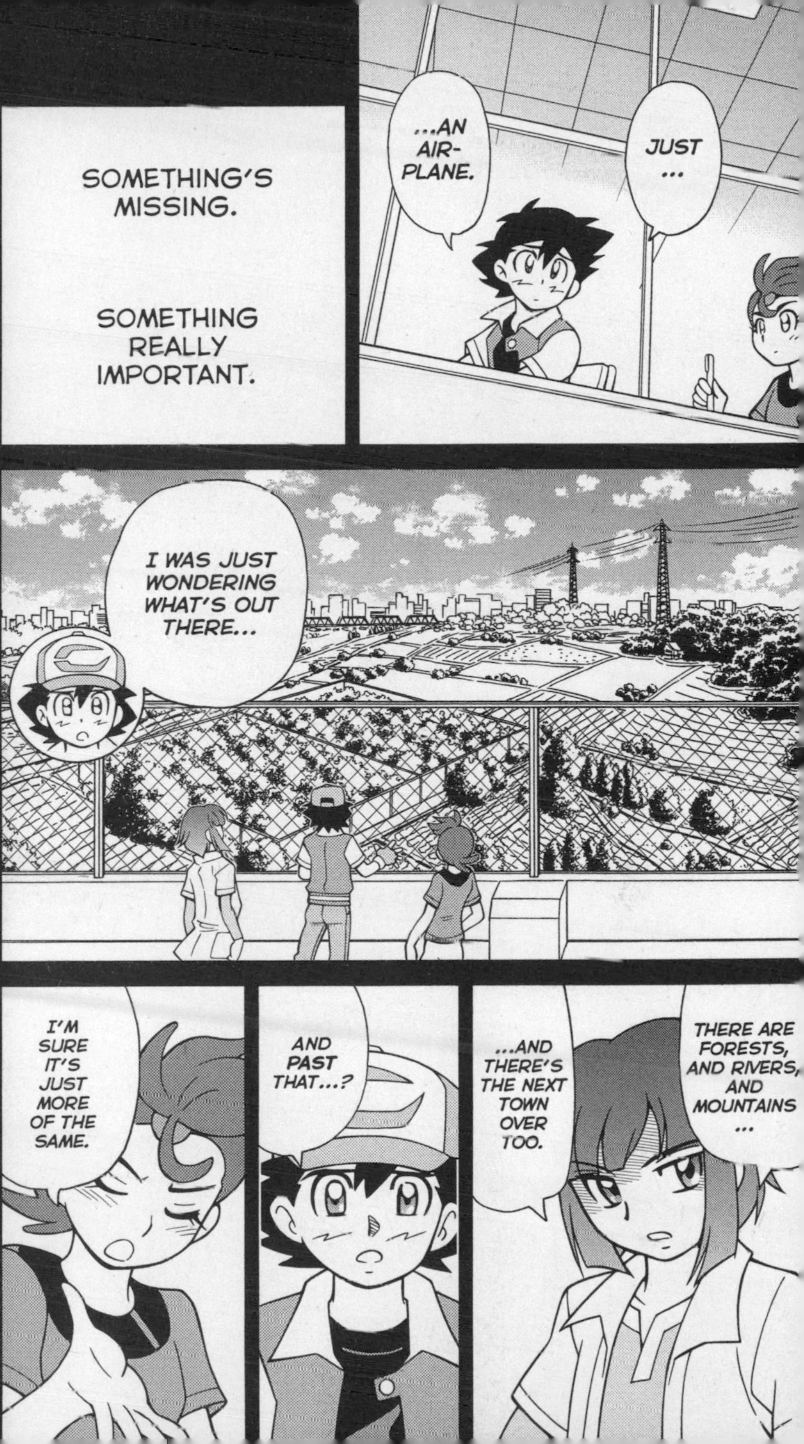
JUST ...
...AN AIR-PLANE.
SOMETHING'S MISSING.
SOMETHING REALLY IMPORTANT.
I WAS JUST WONDERING WHAT'S OUT THERE...
THERE ARE FORESTS, AND RIVERS, AND MOUNTAINS ...
...AND THERE'S THE NEXT TOWN OVER TOO.
AND PAST THAT...?
I'M SURE IT'S JUST MORE OF THE SAME.

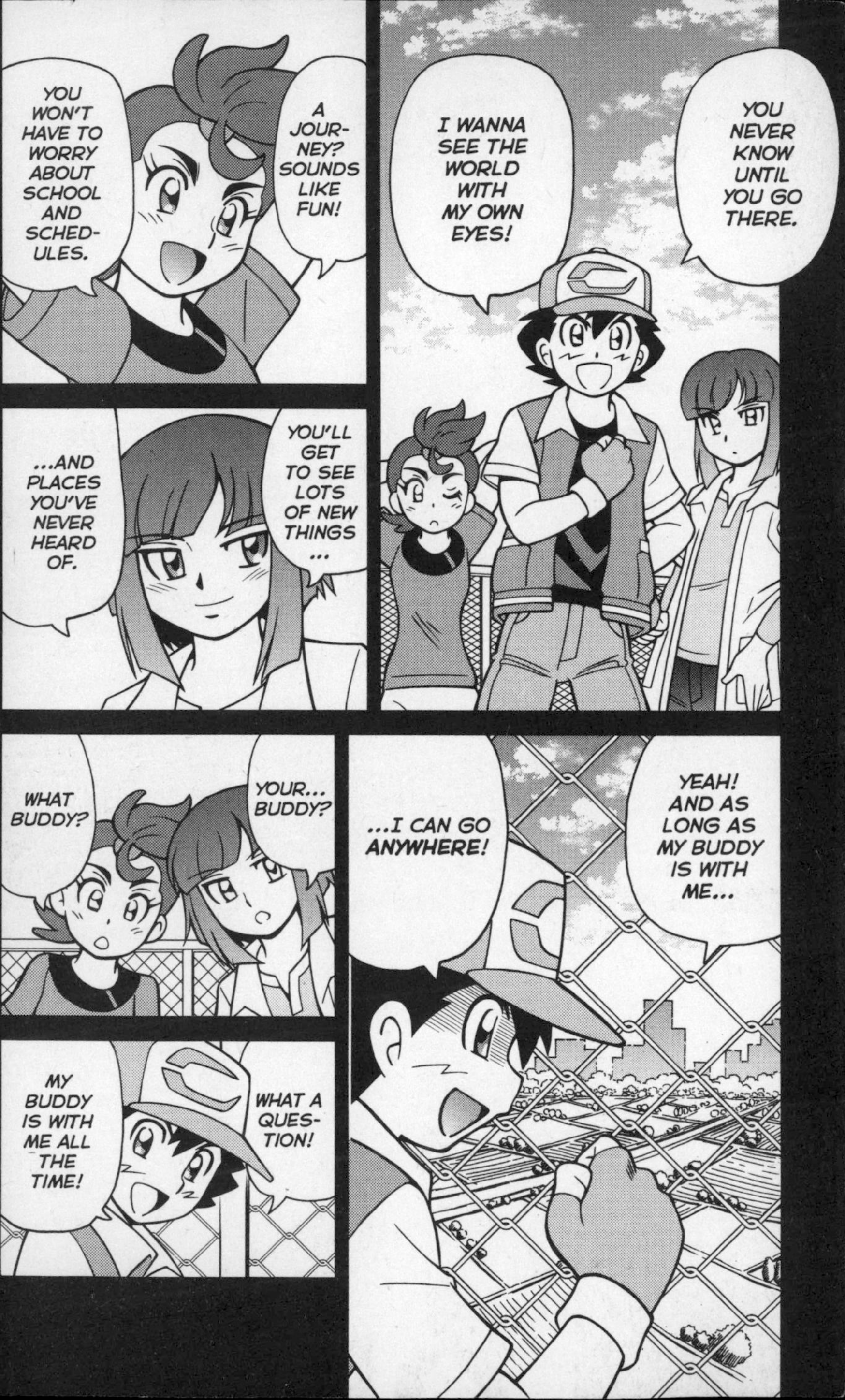
YOU NEVER KNOW UNTIL YOU GO THERE.
I WANNA SEE THE WORLD WITH MY OWN EYES!
A JOURNEY? SOUNDS LIKE FUN!
YOU WON'T HAVE TO WORRY ABOUT SCHOOL AND SCHEDULES.
YOU'LL GET TO SEE LOTS OF NEW THINGS...
...AND PLACES YOU'VE NEVER HEARD OF.
YEAH! AND AS LONG AS MY BUDDY IS WITH ME...
...I CAN GO ANYWHERE!
YOUR... BUDDY?
WHAT BUDDY?
WHAT A QUESTION!
MY BUDDY IS WITH ME ALL THE TIME!

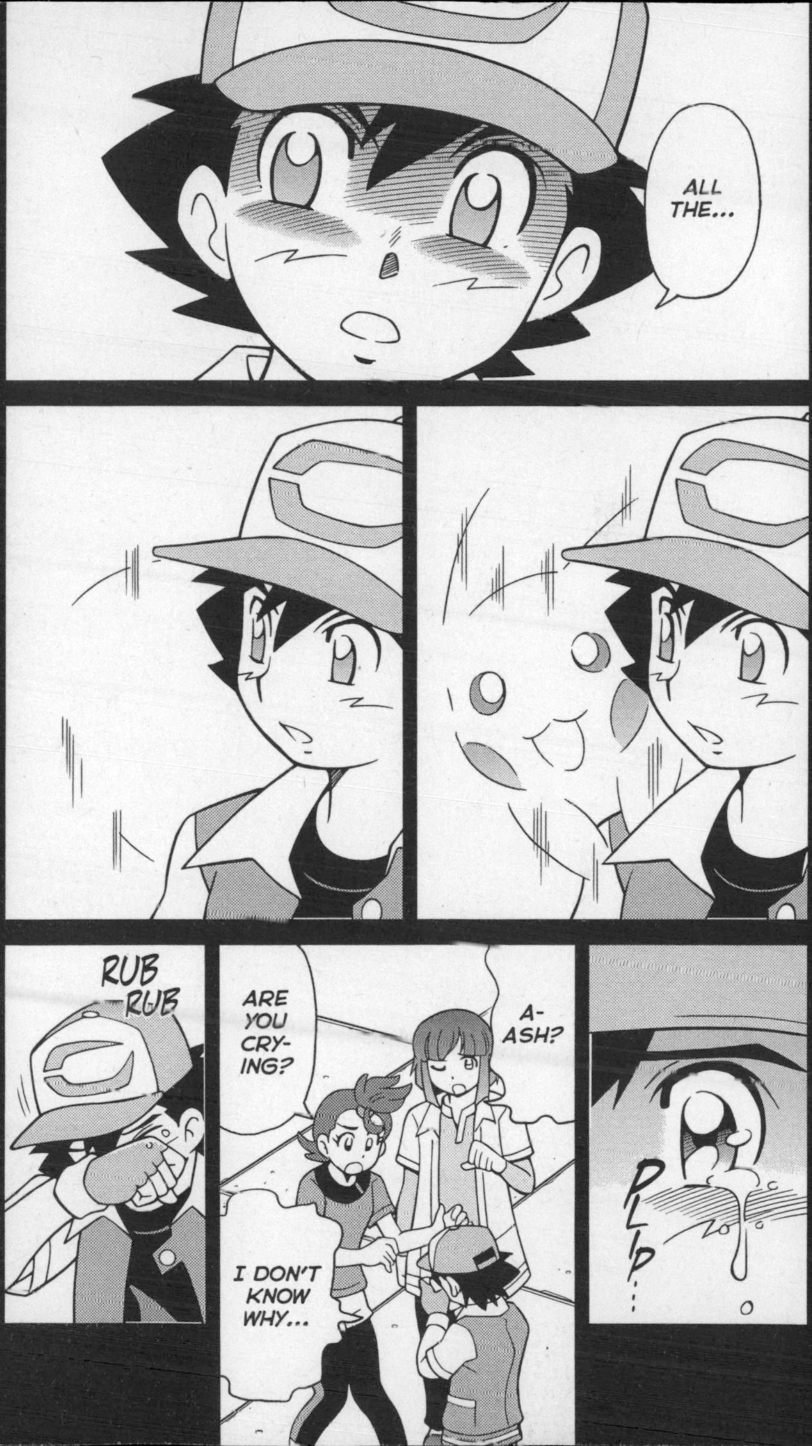
ALL THE...
PLIP...
A-ASH?
ARE YOU CRY-ING?
I DON'T KNOW WHY...
RUB RUB

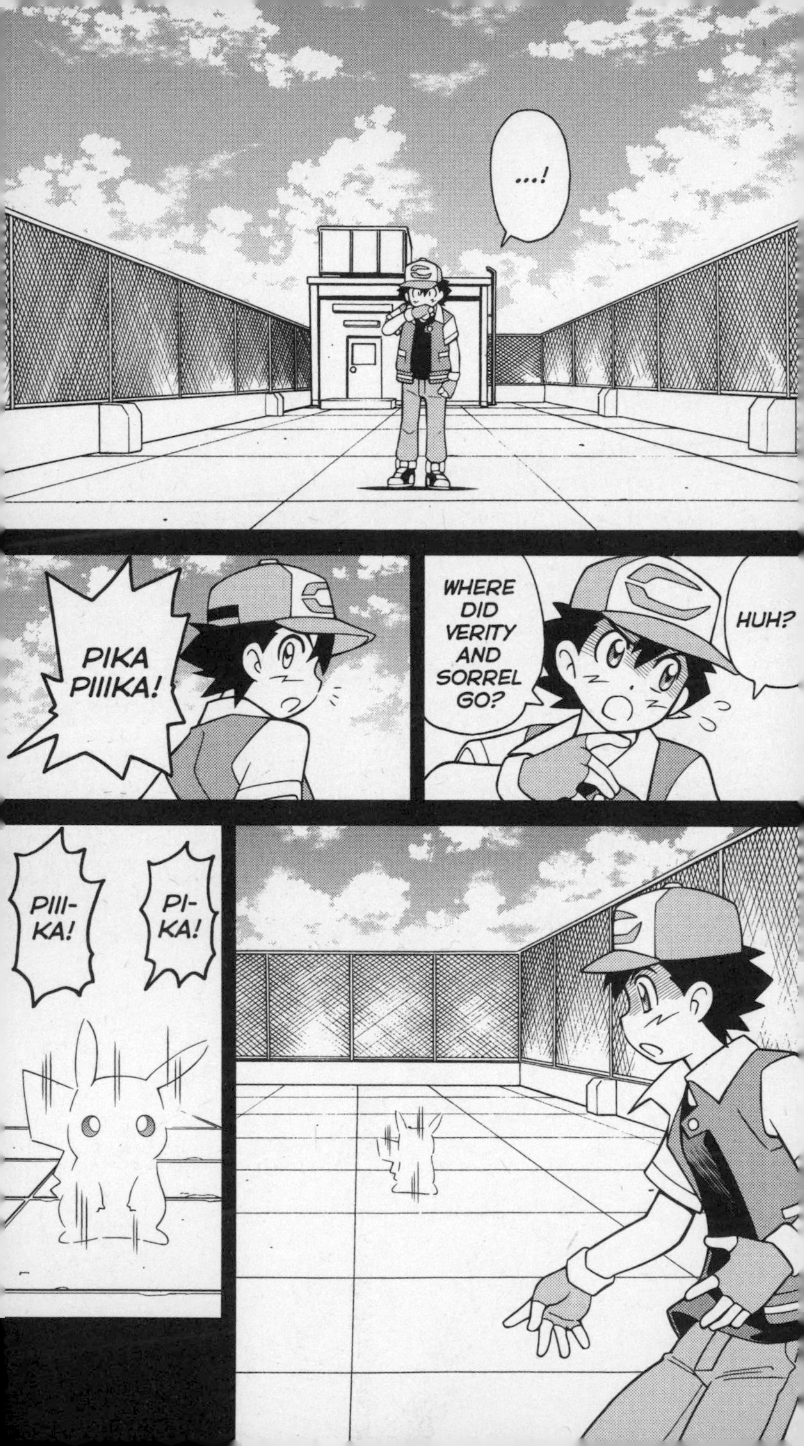
...!
HUH?
WHERE DID VERITY AND SORREL GO?
PIKA PIIIKA!
PI-KA!
PIII-KA!

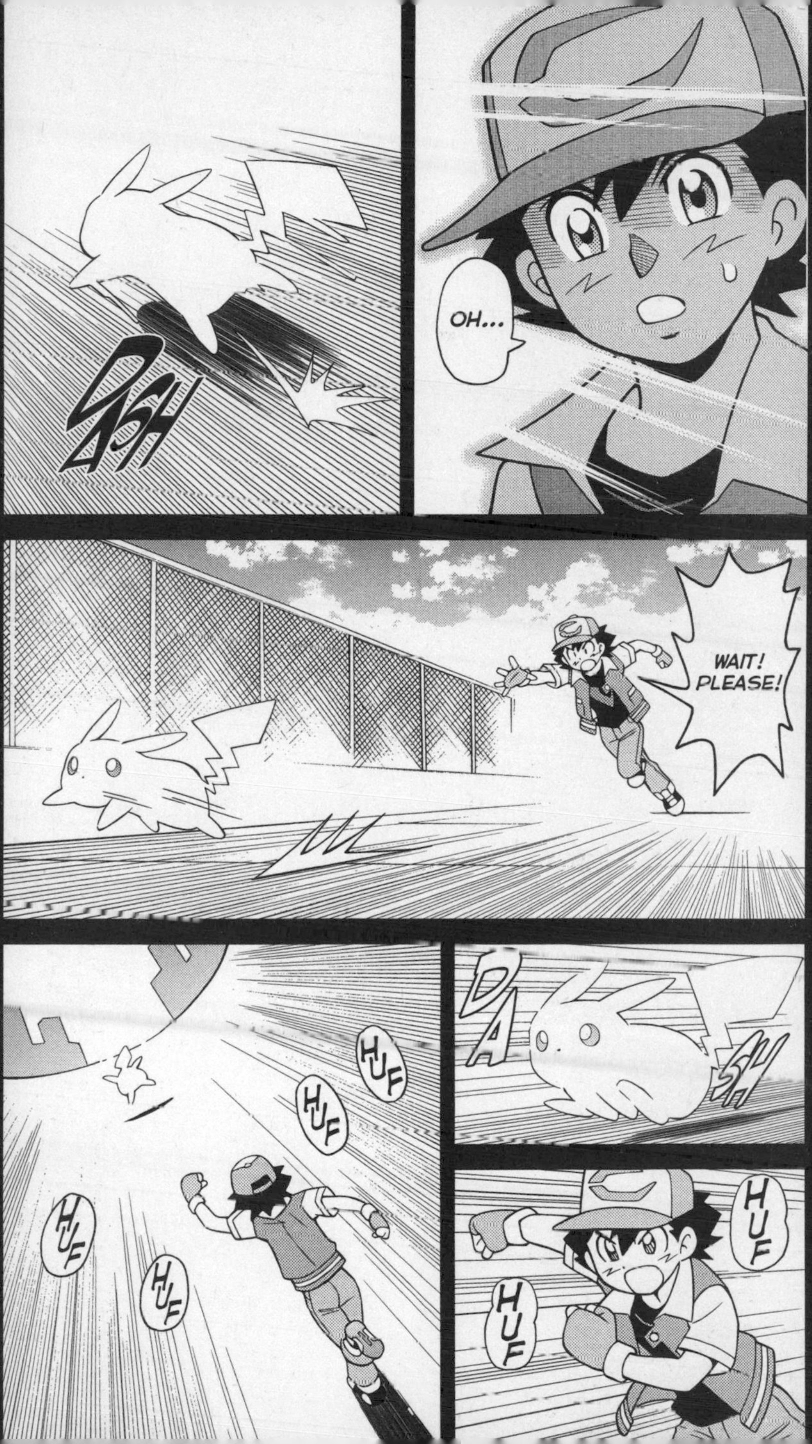
OH...
DASH
WAIT! PLEASE!
DASH
HUF
HUF
HUF
HUF
HUF
HUF

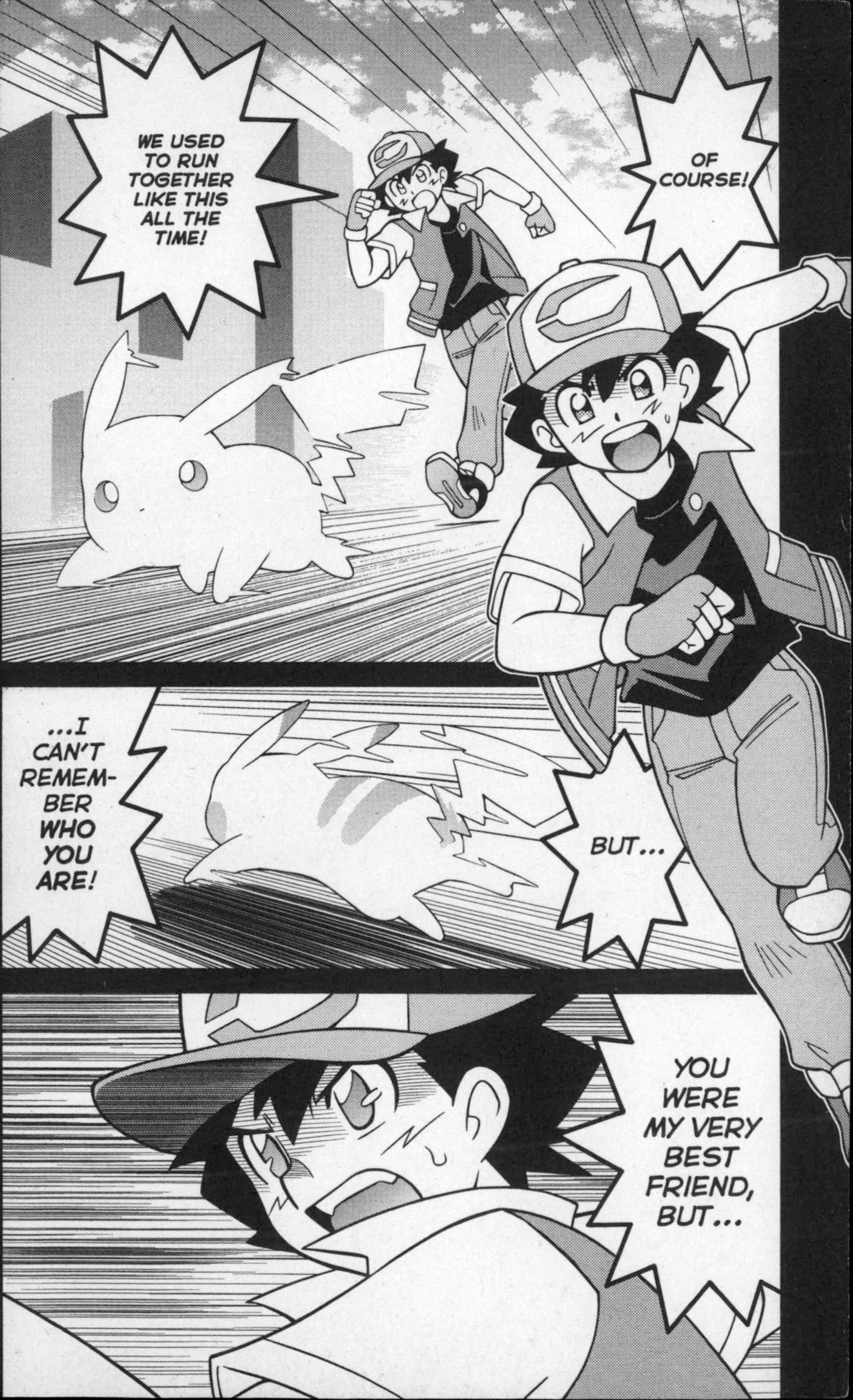
OF COURSE!
WE USED TO RUN TOGETHER LIKE THIS ALL THE TIME!
BUT...
...I CAN'T REMEMBER WHO YOU ARE!
YOU WERE MY VERY BEST FRIEND, BUT...

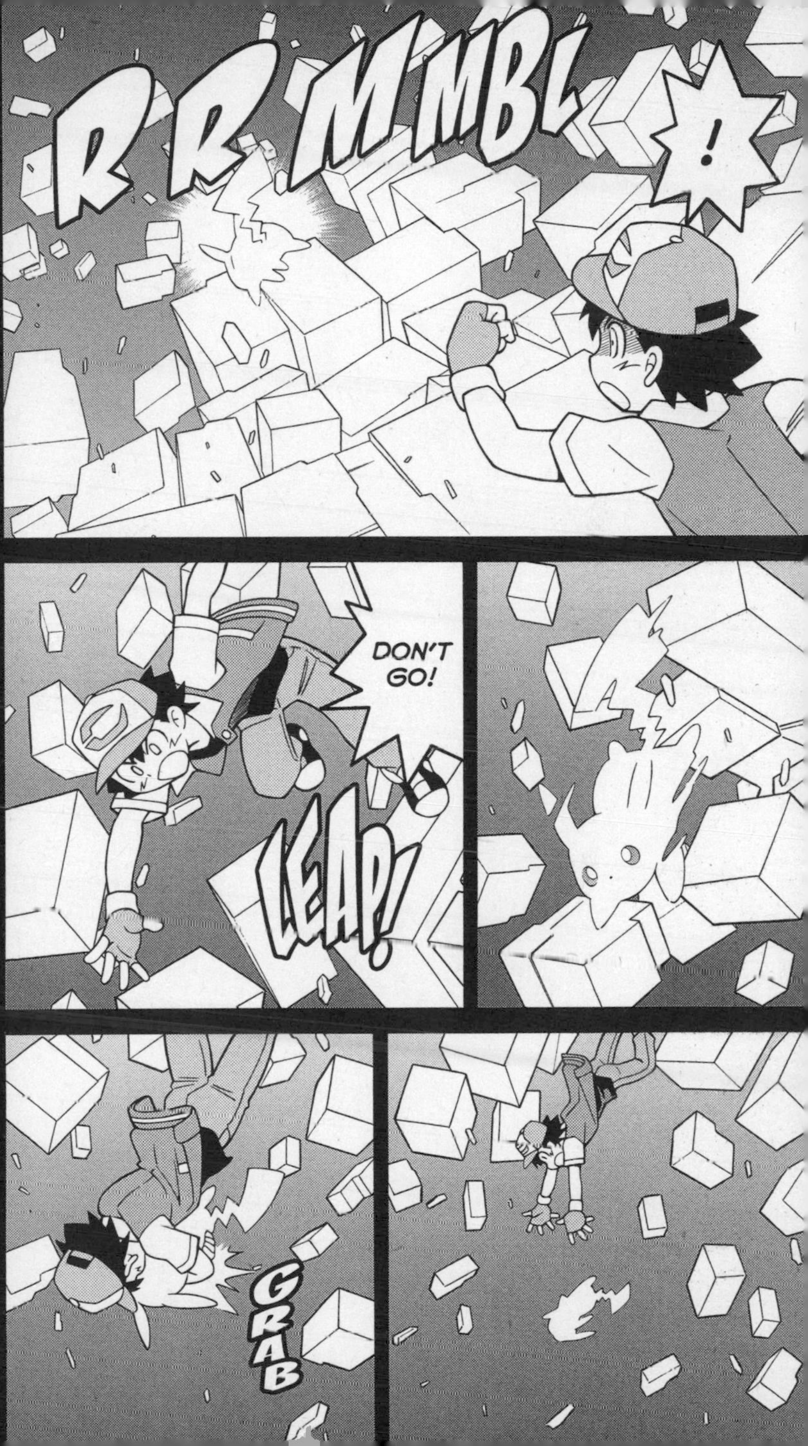
RRMMBL
!
DON'T GO!
LEAP!
GRAB

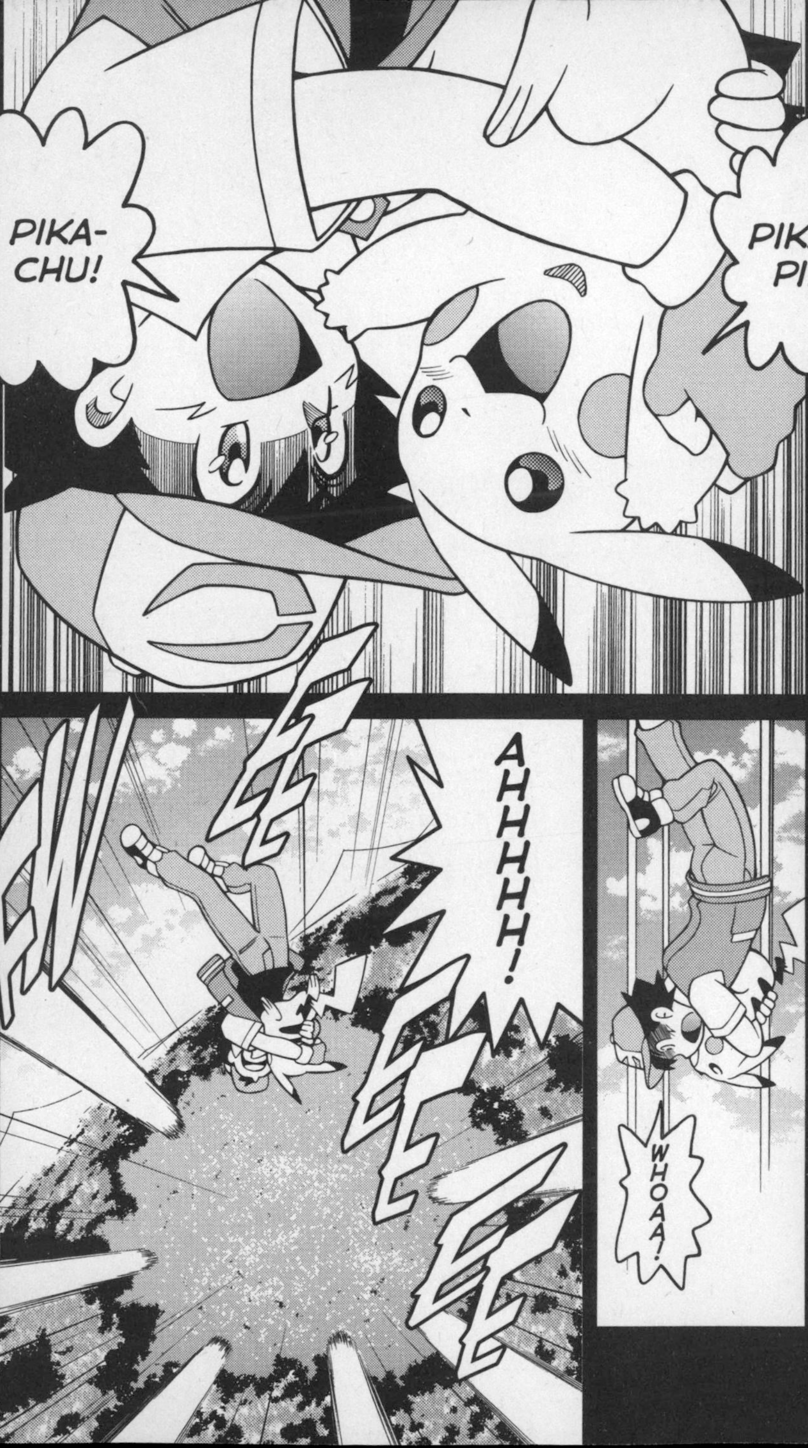
PIKA-PI!
PIKA-CHU!
WHOAA!
AHHHHHH!

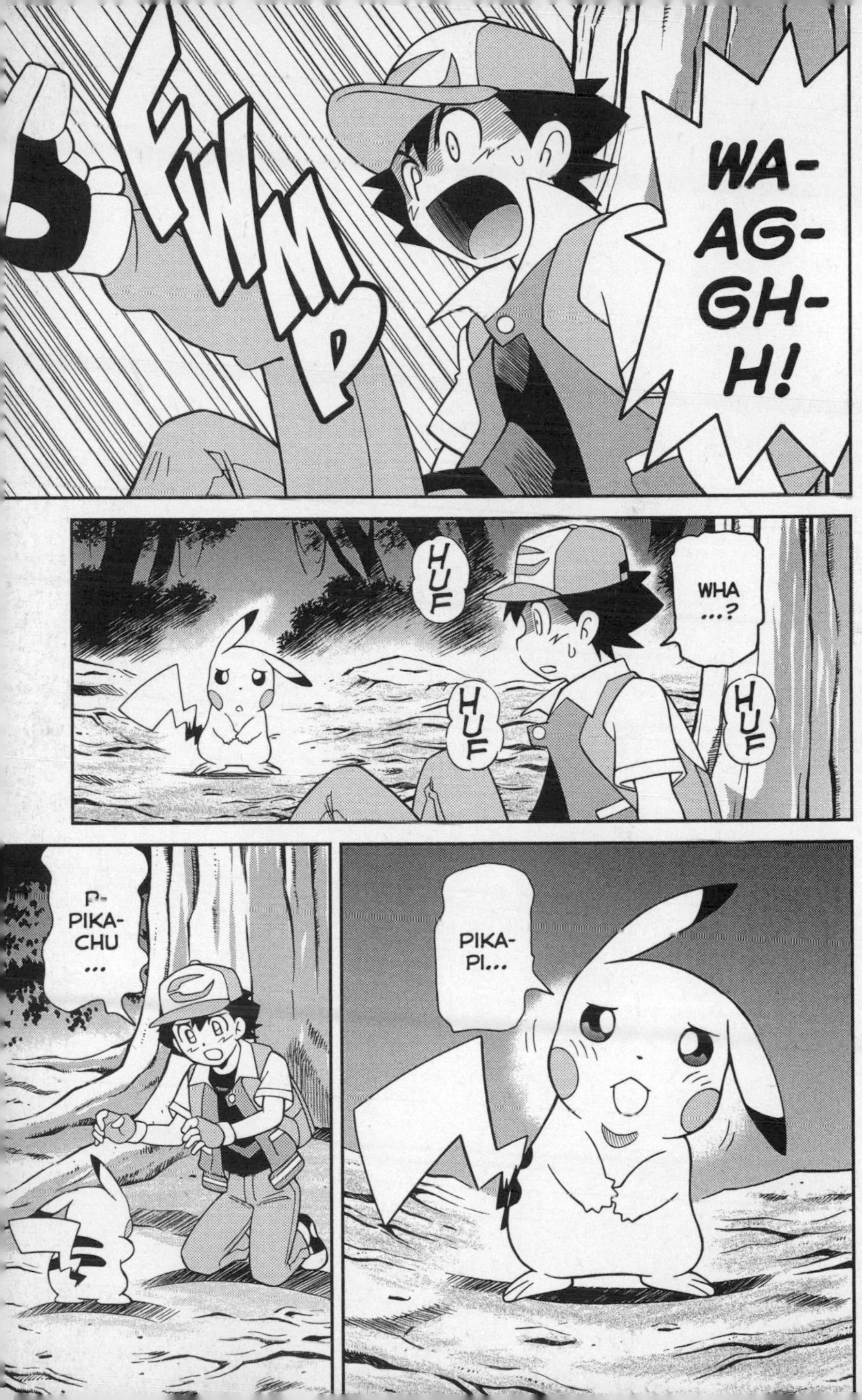
WA-AG-GH-H!
WHA ...?
HUF
HUF
HUF
PIKA-PI...
P-PIKA-CHU ...

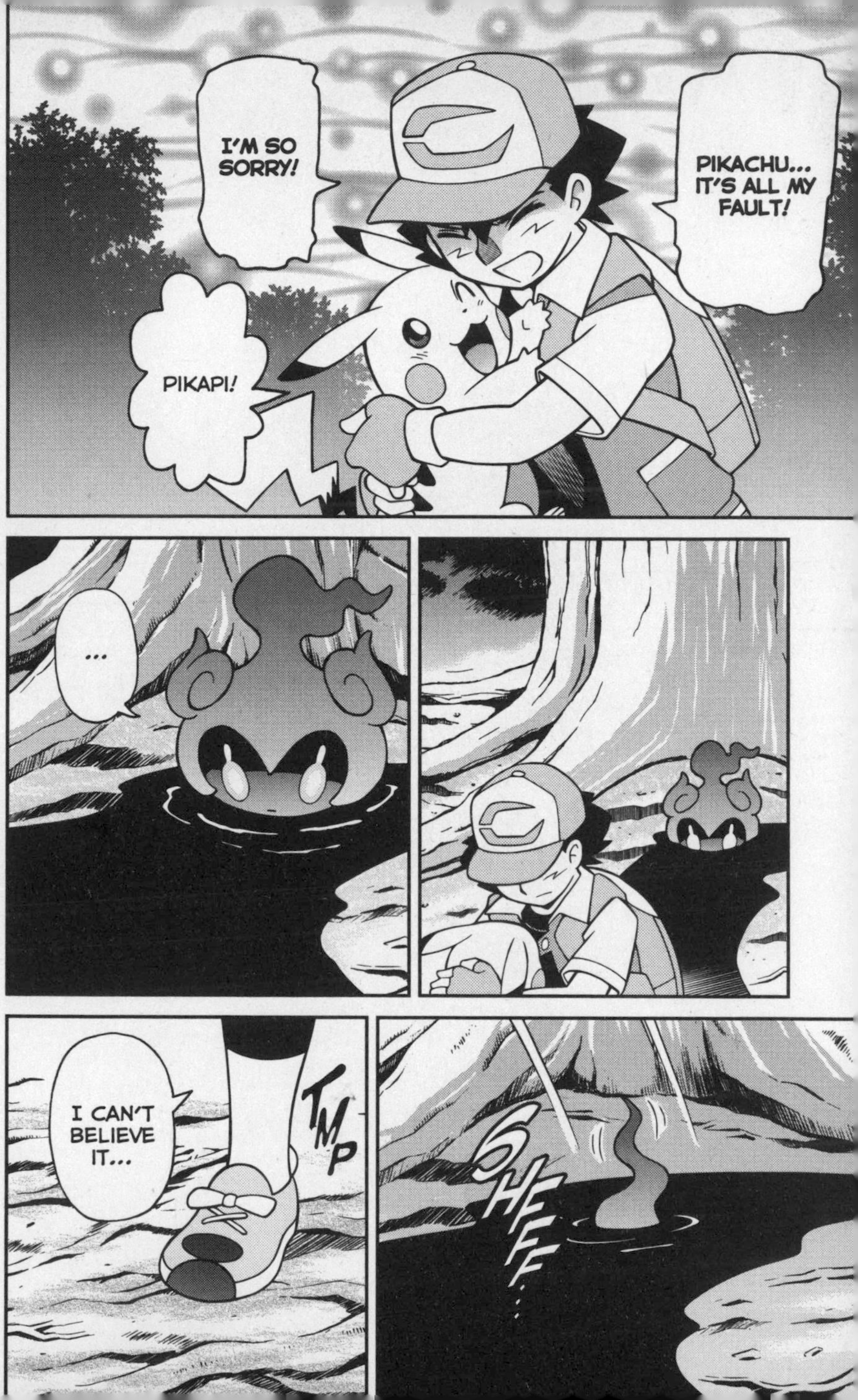
PIKACHU... IT'S ALL MY FAULT!
I'M SO SORRY!
PIKAPI!
...
SHFFF...
TMP
I CAN'T BELIEVE IT...

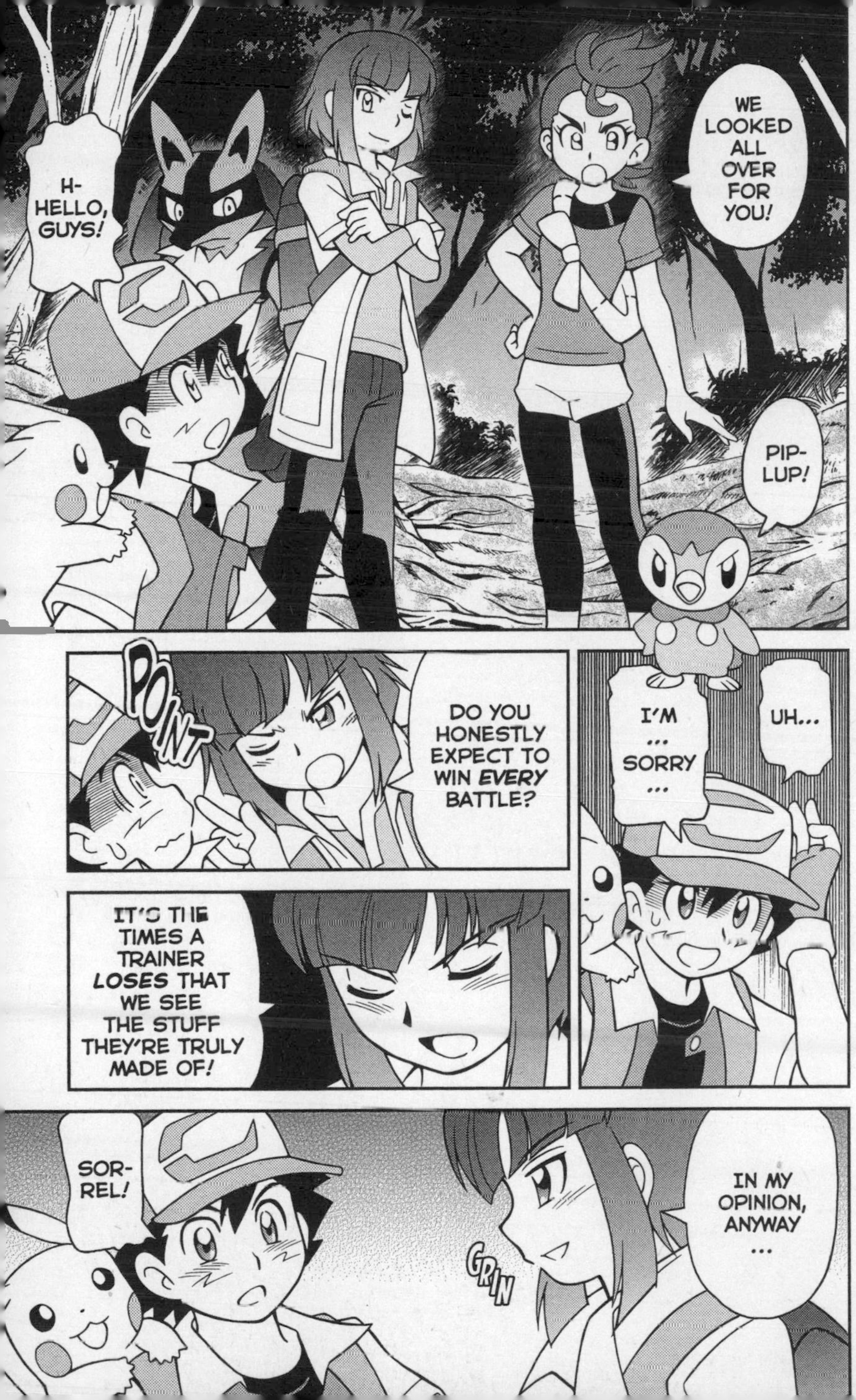
WE LOOKED ALL OVER FOR YOU!
H-HELLO, GUYS!
PIP-LUP!
UH...
I'M ... SORRY ...
POINT
DO YOU HONESTLY EXPECT TO WIN *EVERY* BATTLE?
IT'S THE TIMES A TRAINER ***LOSES*** THAT WE SEE THE STUFF THEY'RE TRULY MADE OF!
IN MY OPINION, ANYWAY ...
GRIN
SOR-REL!

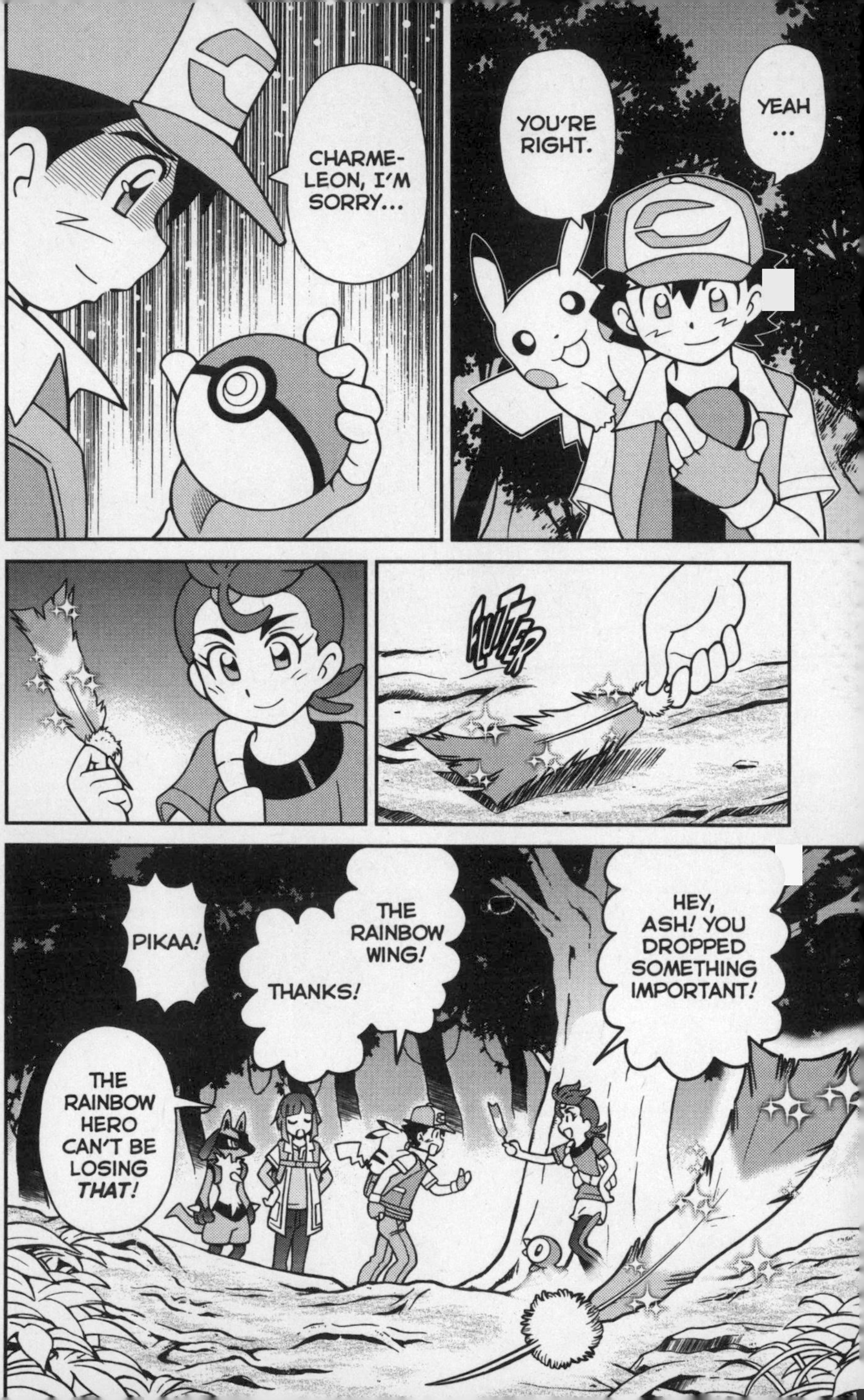
YEAH...
YOU'RE RIGHT.
CHARME-LEON, I'M SORRY...
FLUTTER
HEY, ASH! YOU DROPPED SOMETHING IMPORTANT!
THE RAINBOW WING!
THANKS!
PIKAA!
THE RAINBOW HERO CAN'T BE LOSING *THAT!*

CHAPTER 9

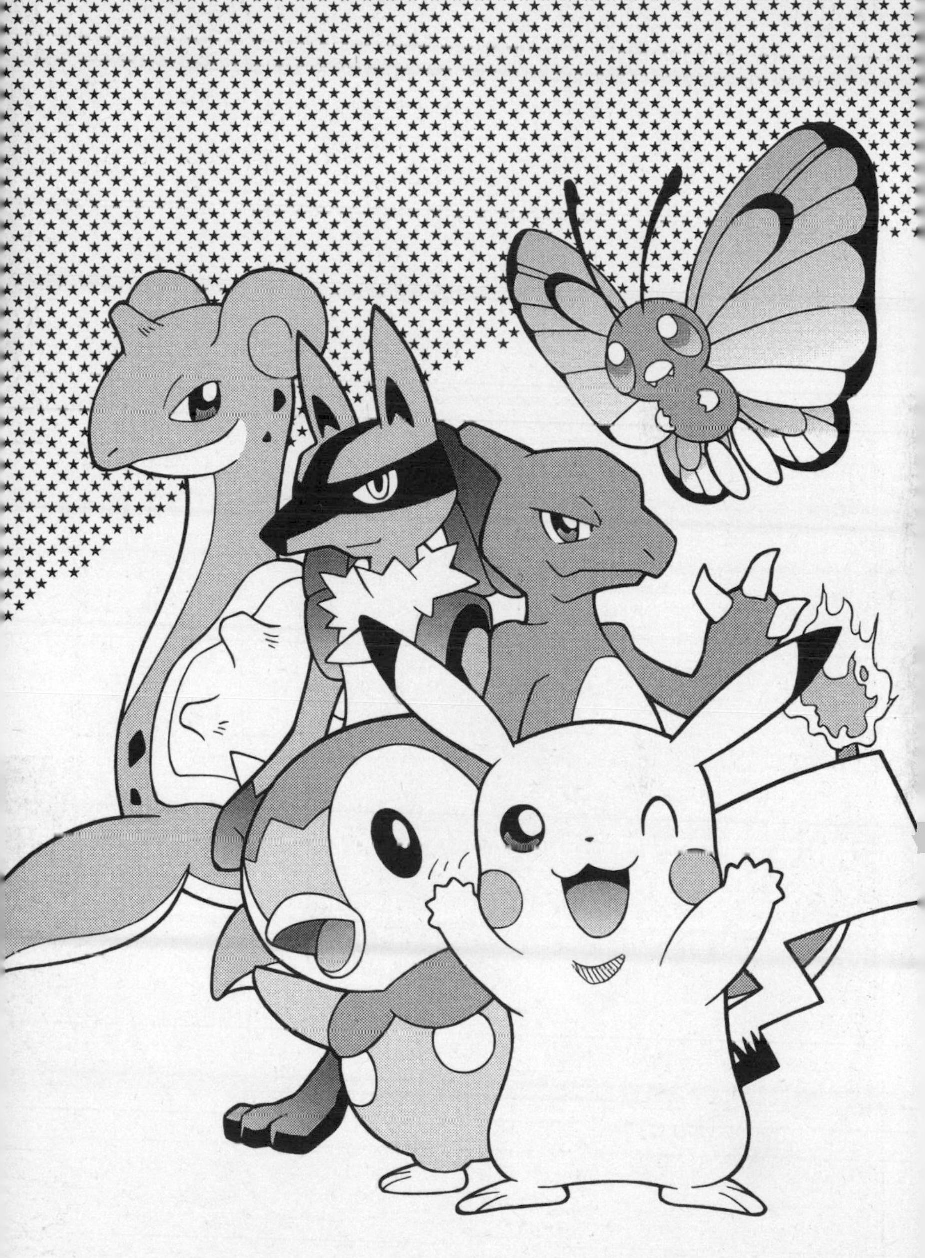

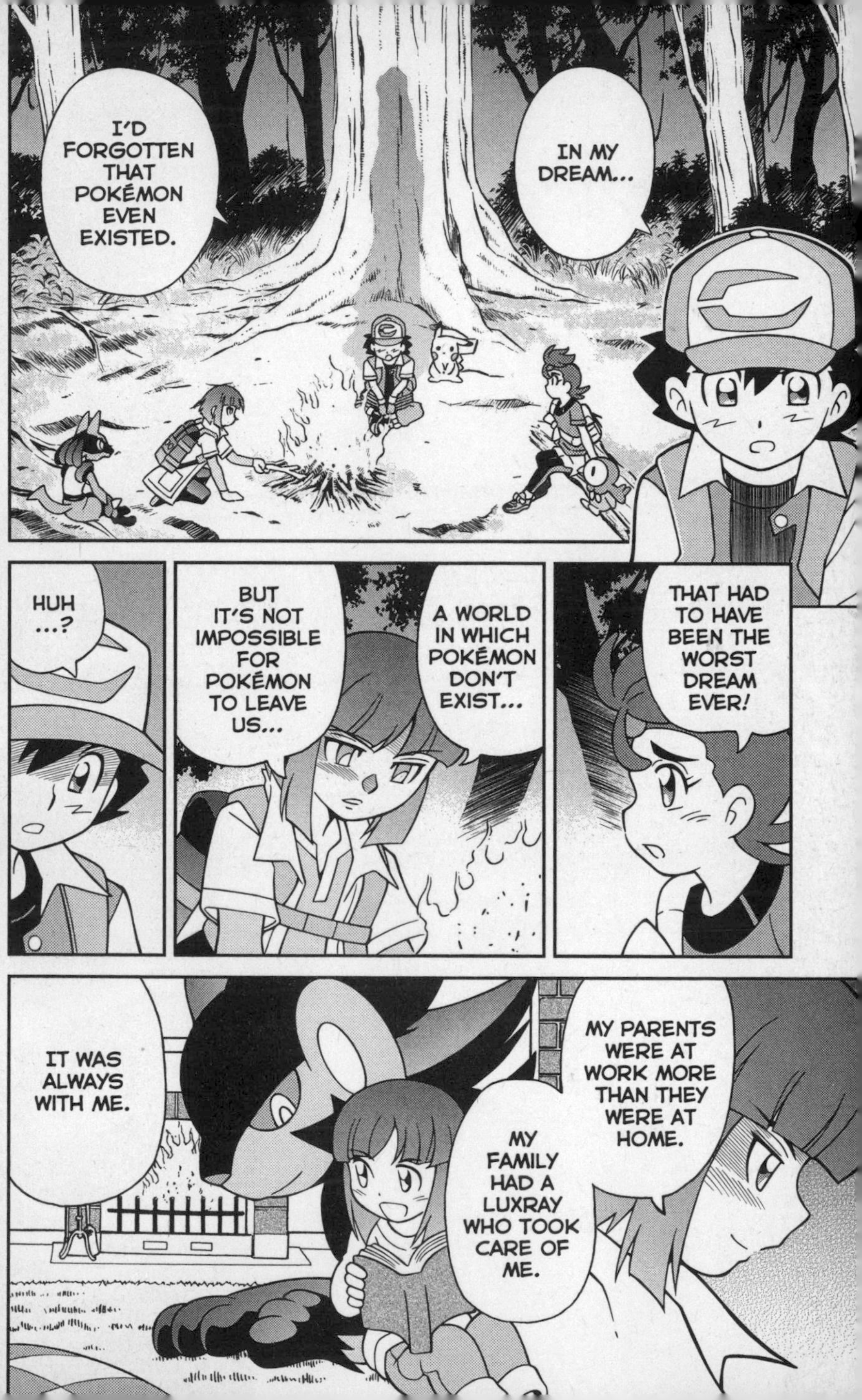
IN MY DREAM...
I'D FORGOTTEN THAT POKÉMON EVEN EXISTED.
THAT HAD TO HAVE BEEN THE WORST DREAM EVER!
A WORLD IN WHICH POKÉMON DON'T EXIST...
BUT IT'S NOT IMPOSSIBLE FOR POKÉMON TO LEAVE US...
HUH...?
MY PARENTS WERE AT WORK MORE THAN THEY WERE AT HOME.
MY FAMILY HAD A LUXRAY WHO TOOK CARE OF ME.
IT WAS ALWAYS WITH ME.

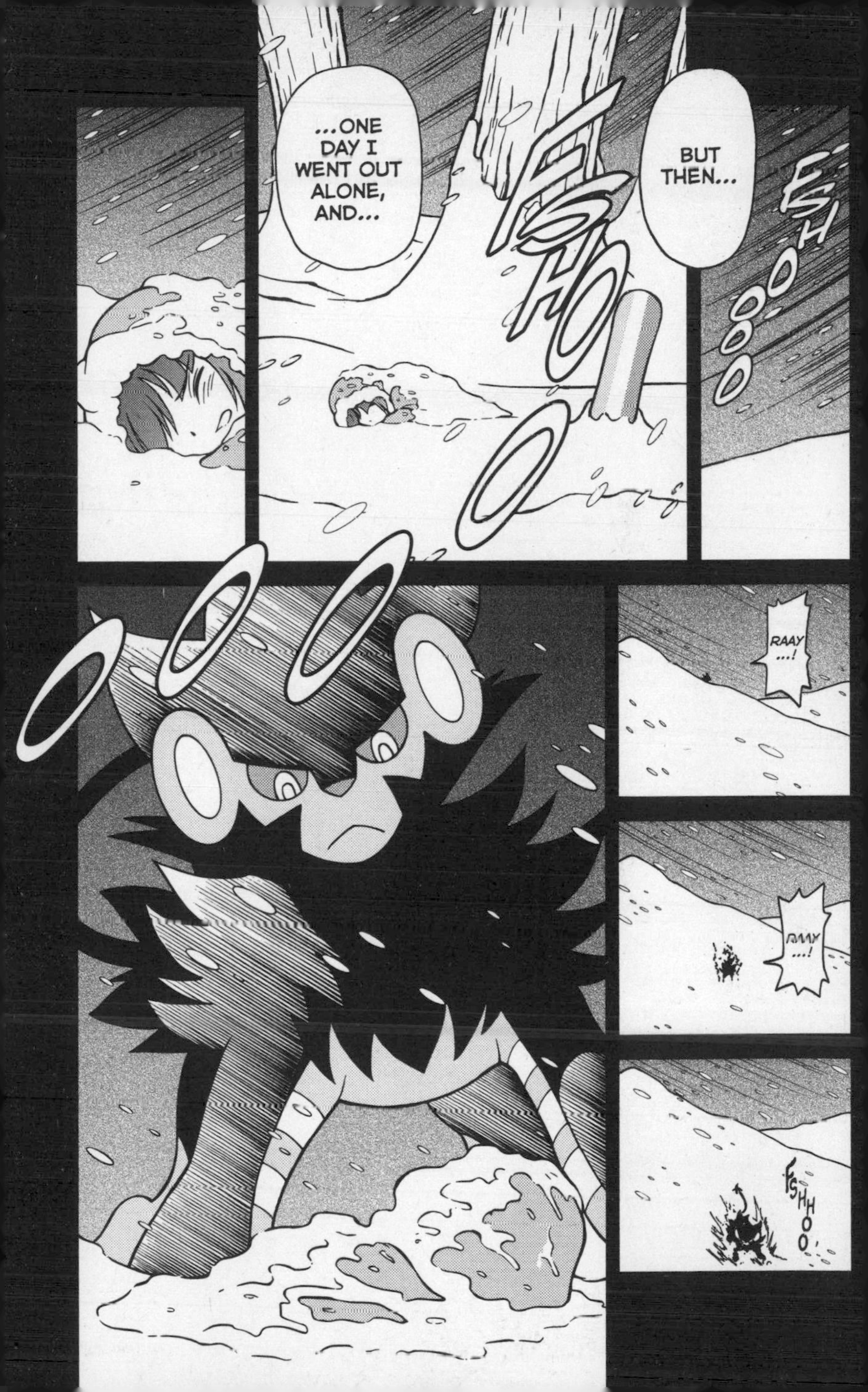
FSHOOOOO
BUT THEN...
...ONE DAY I WENT OUT ALONE, AND...
FSHOOOO
RAAY...!
RAAY...!
FSHHOO!

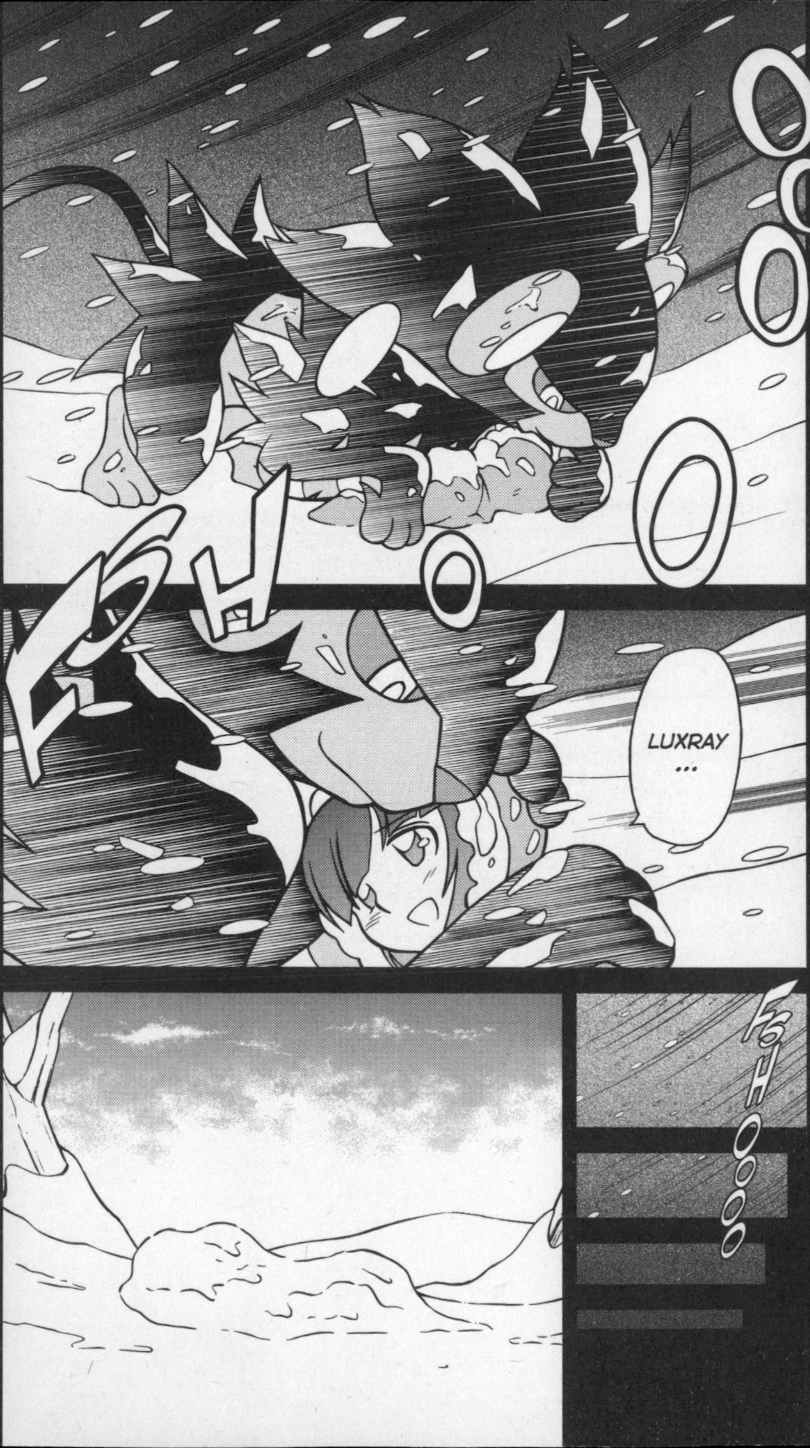
FSHOOOOOOO
LUXRAY ...
FSHOOOO

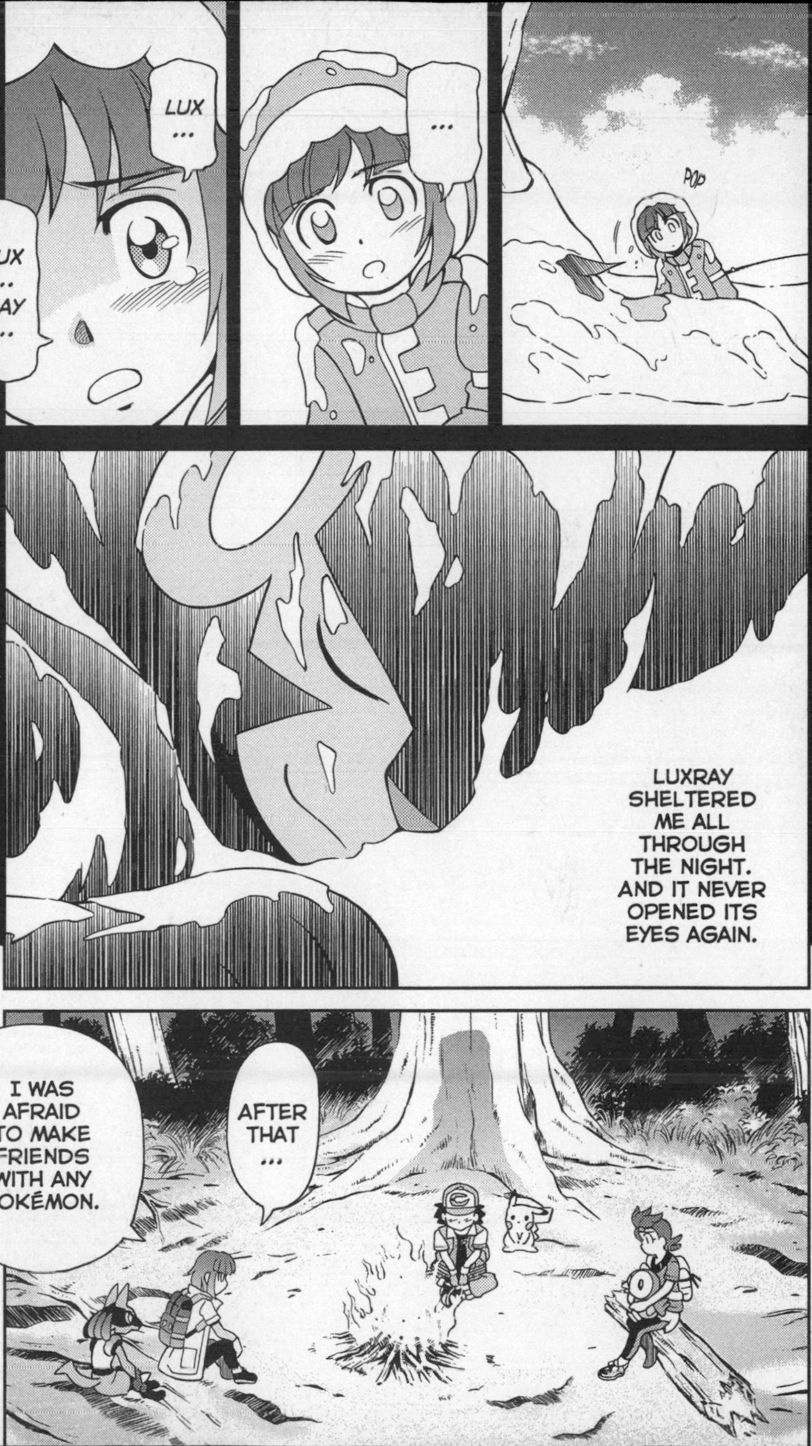
POP
...
LUX ...
LUX ... RAY ...
LUXRAY SHELTERED ME ALL THROUGH THE NIGHT. AND IT NEVER OPENED ITS EYES AGAIN.
AFTER THAT ...
I WAS AFRAID TO MAKE FRIENDS WITH ANY POKÉMON.

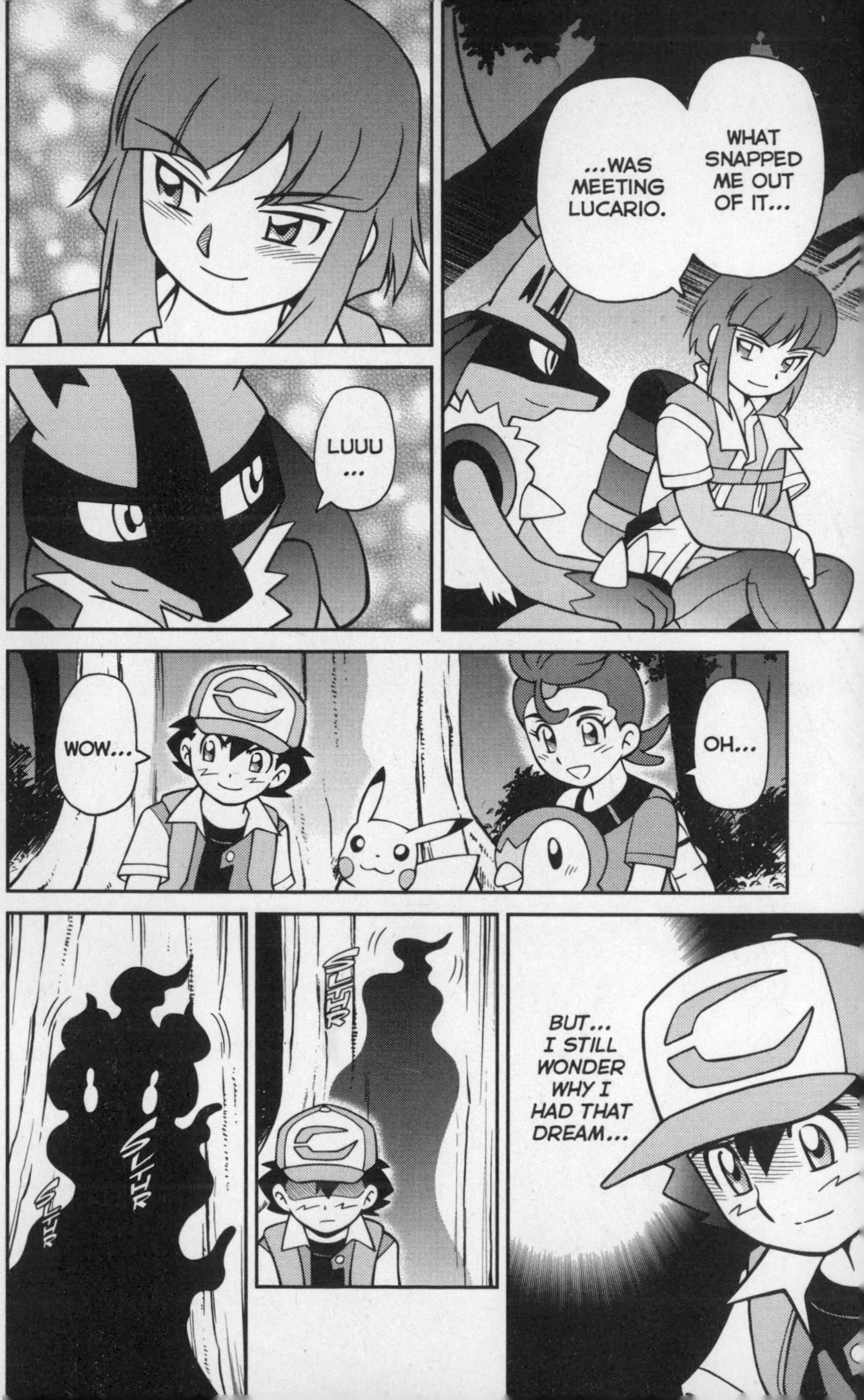
WHAT SNAPPED ME OUT OF IT...
...WAS MEETING LUCARIO.
LUUU ...
OH...
WOW...
BUT... I STILL WONDER WHY I HAD THAT DREAM...
SLITHR
SLITHR
SLITHR

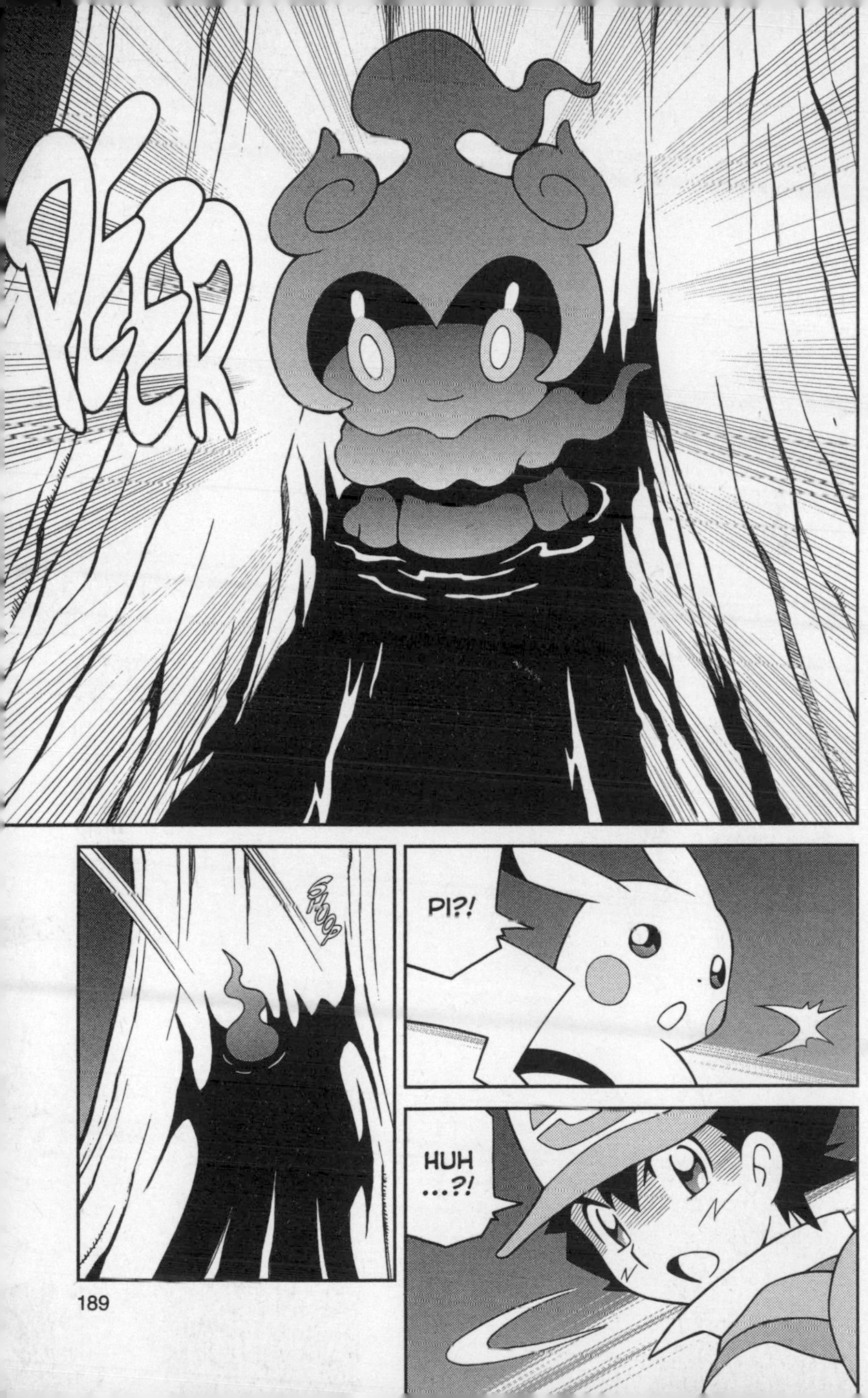
PEER
PI?!
HUH ...?!
SHOOP

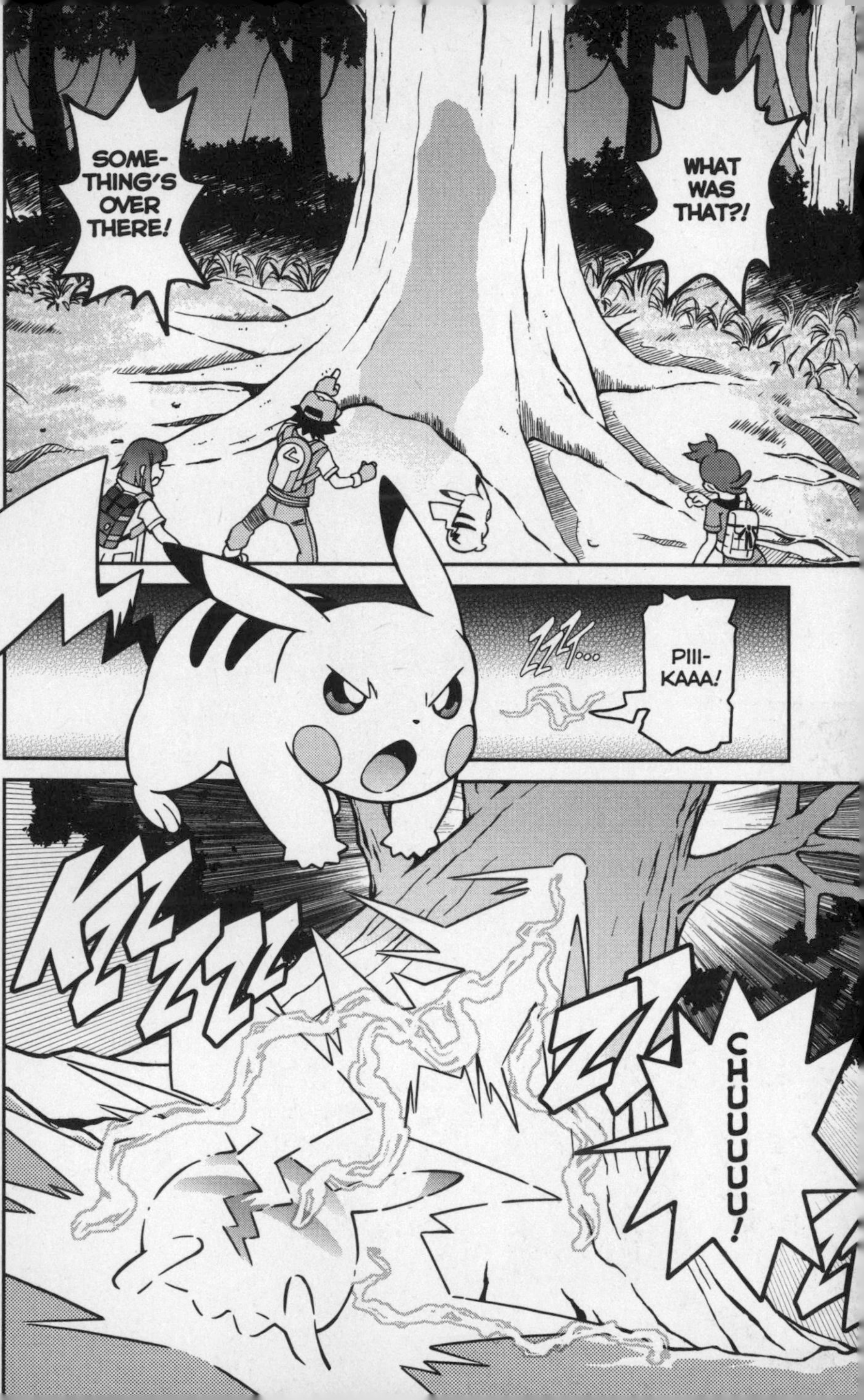
WHAT WAS THAT?!
SOME-THING'S OVER THERE!
PIII-KAAA!
CHUUUUU!

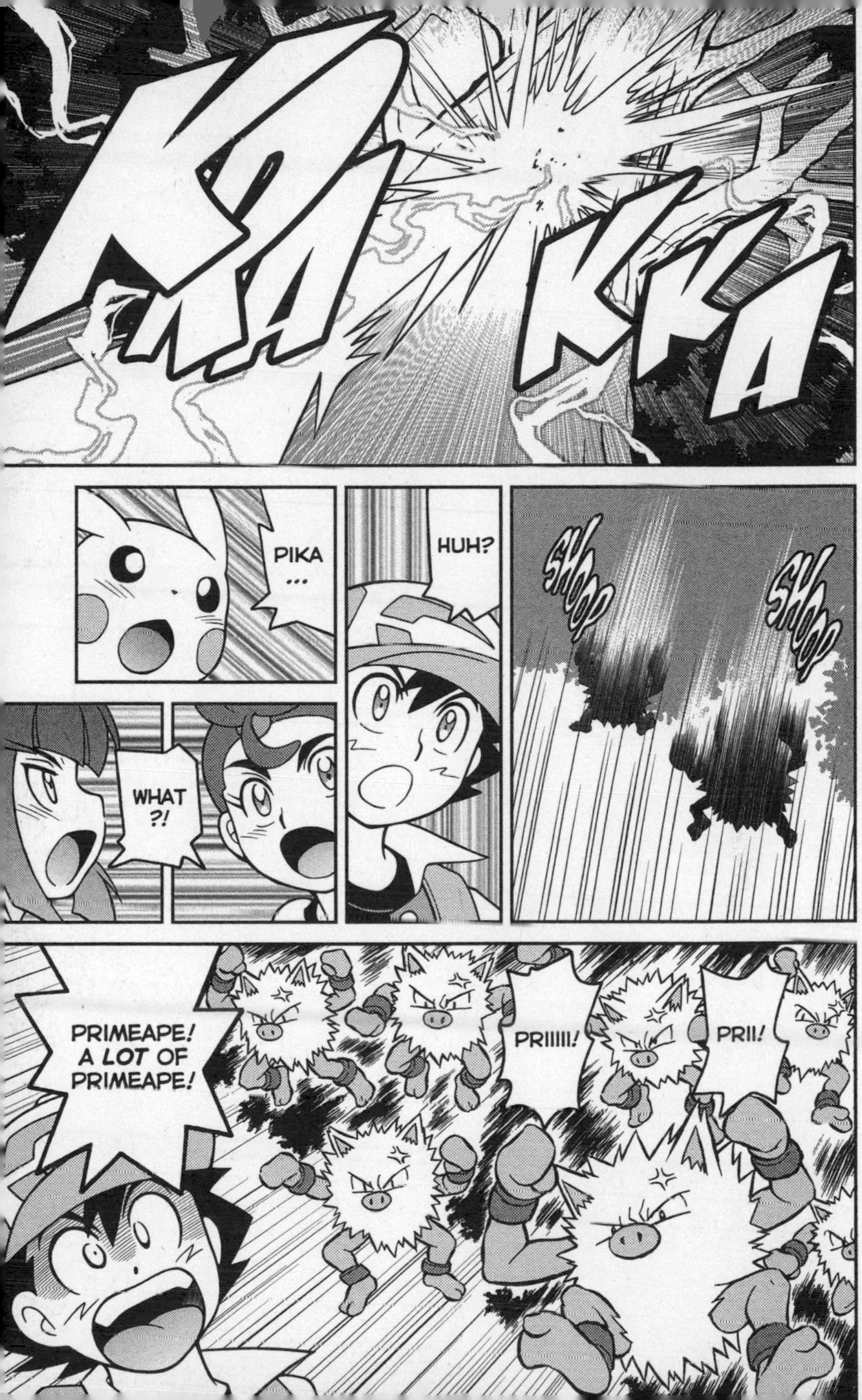
KA KKA
SHOOP
SHOOP
HUH?
PIKA ...
WHAT ?!
PRII!
PRIIIII!
PRIMEAPE! A *LOT* OF PRIMEAPE!

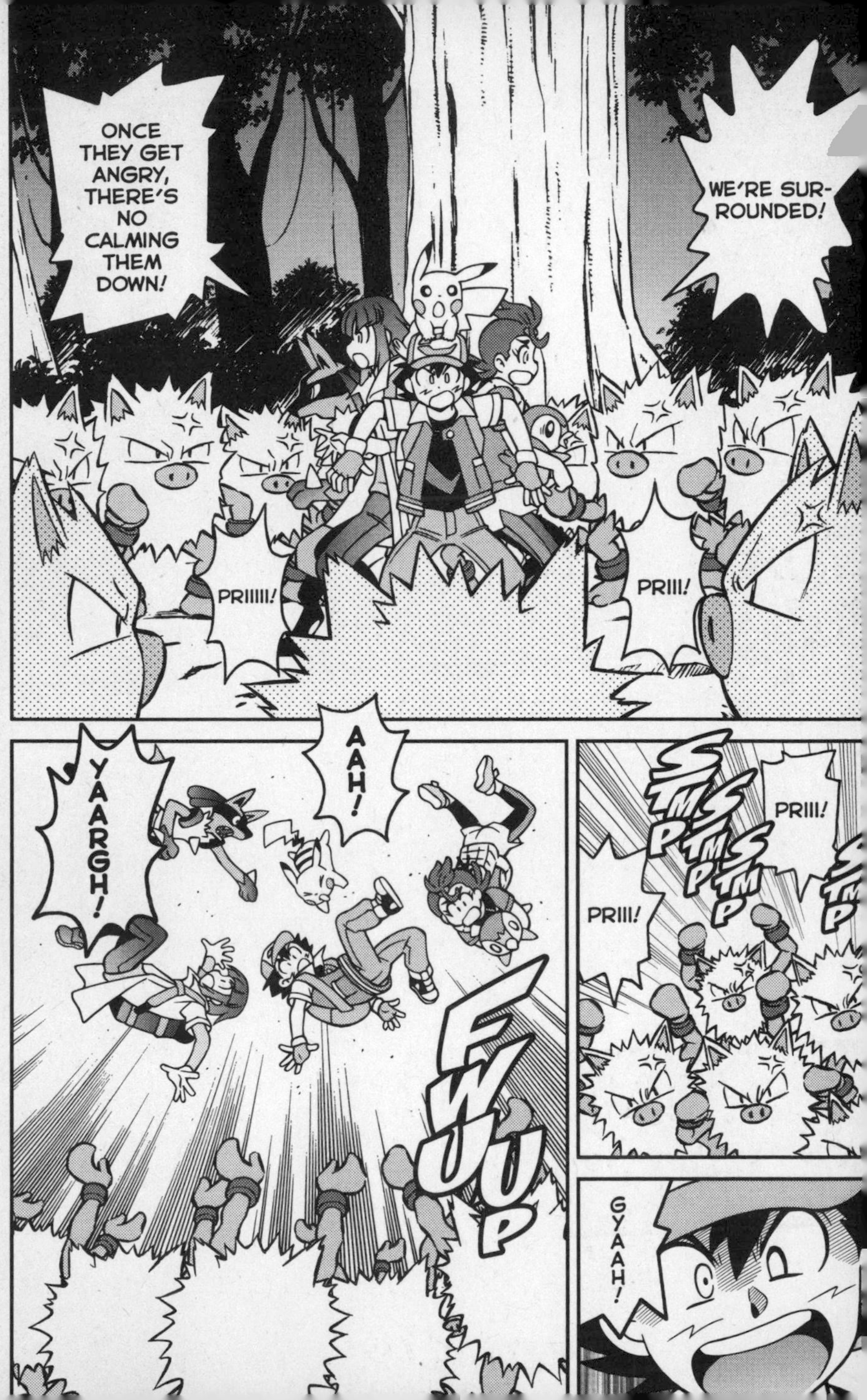
WE'RE SUR-ROUNDED!
ONCE THEY GET ANGRY, THERE'S NO CALMING THEM DOWN!
PRIII!
PRIIIII!
STMP
PRIII!
STMP
STMP
STMP
PRIII!
GYAAH!
AAH!
YAARGH!
FWUUP

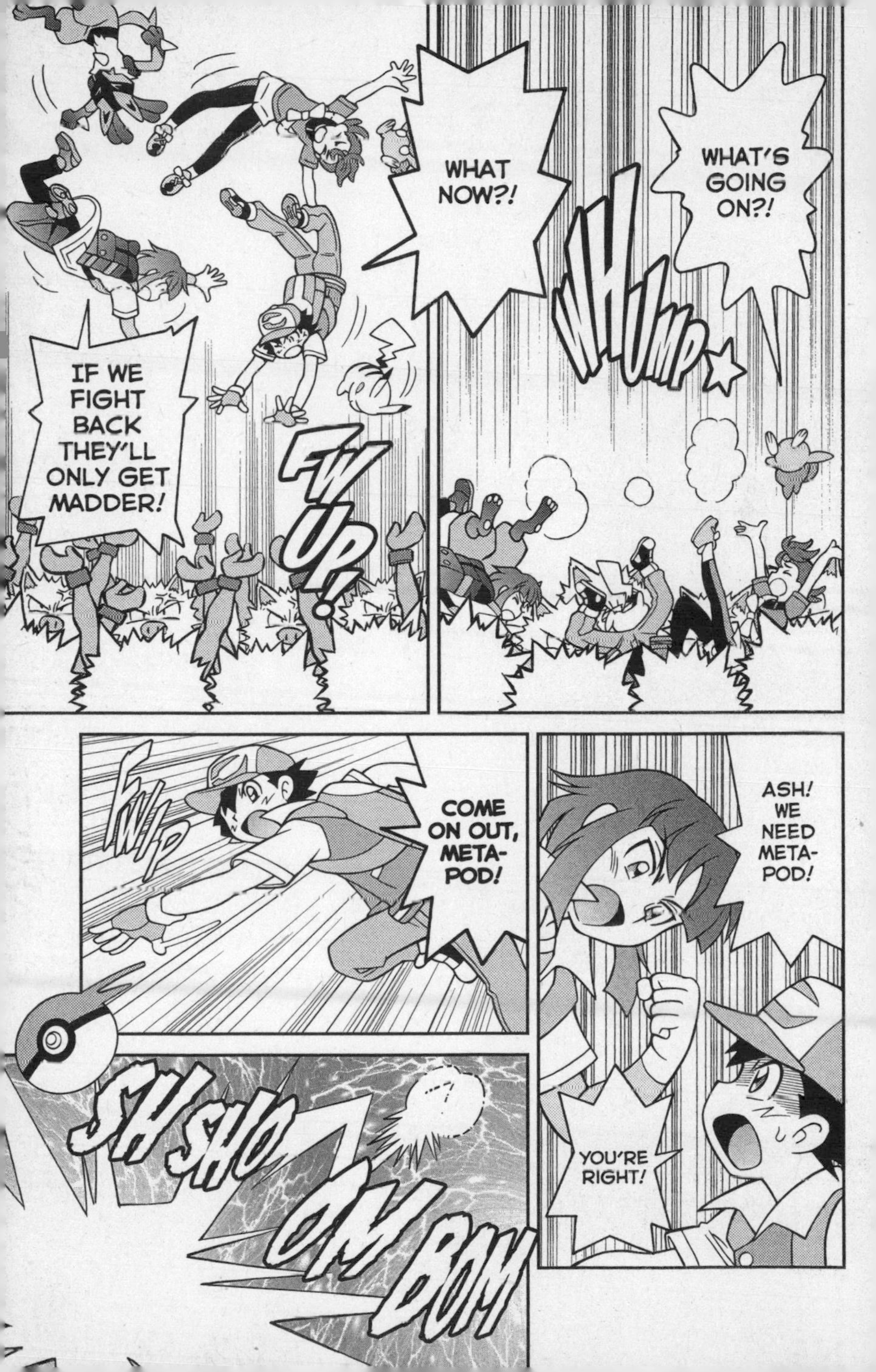
WHAT'S GOING ON?!
WHAT NOW?!
WHUMP
IF WE FIGHT BACK THEY'LL ONLY GET MADDER!
FWUP!
ASH! WE NEED METAPOD!
YOU'RE RIGHT!
COME ON OUT, METAPOD!
FWIP
...?
SHSHOOM BOM

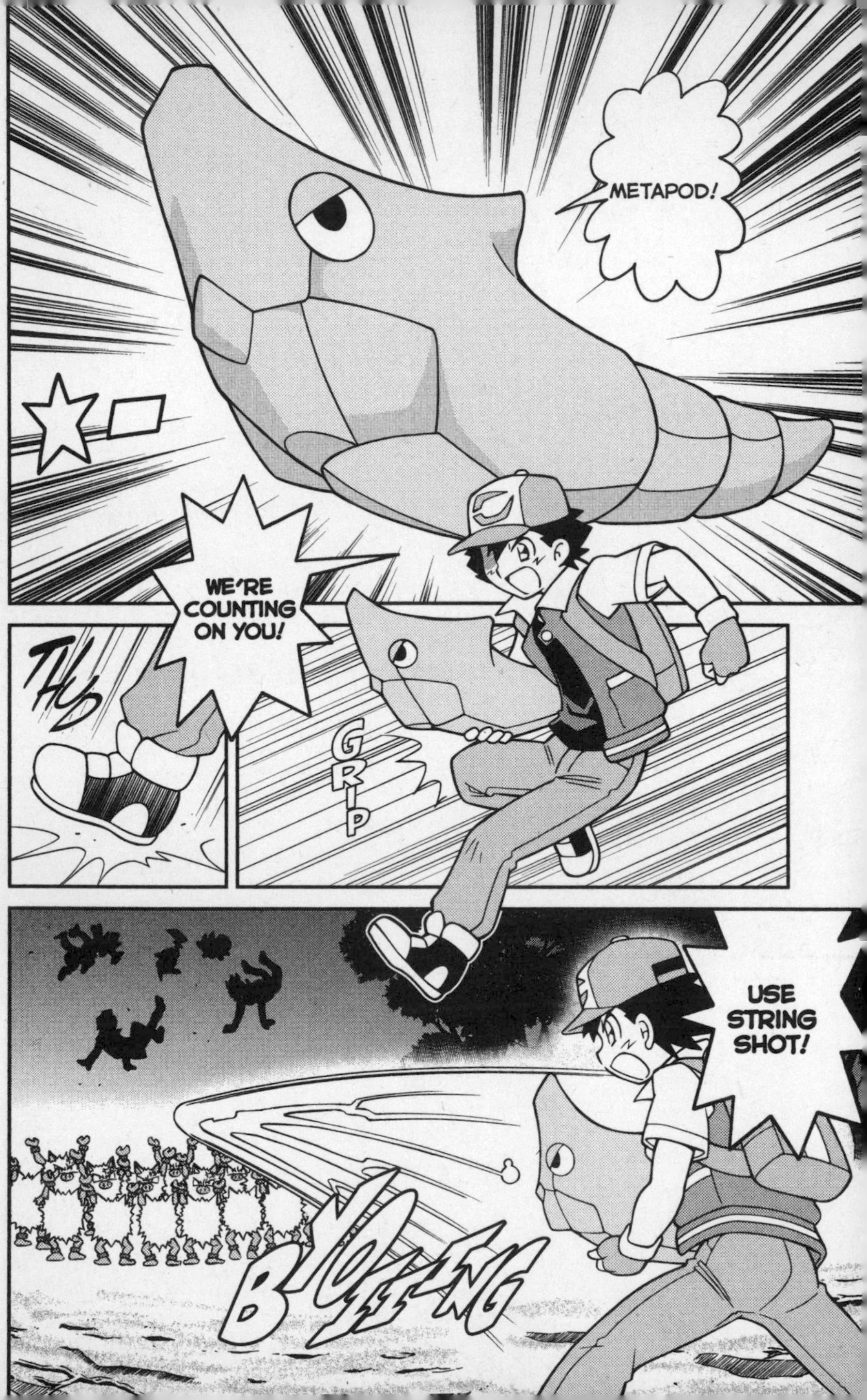
METAPOD!
WE'RE COUNTING ON YOU!
GRIP
USE STRING SHOT!
BOING

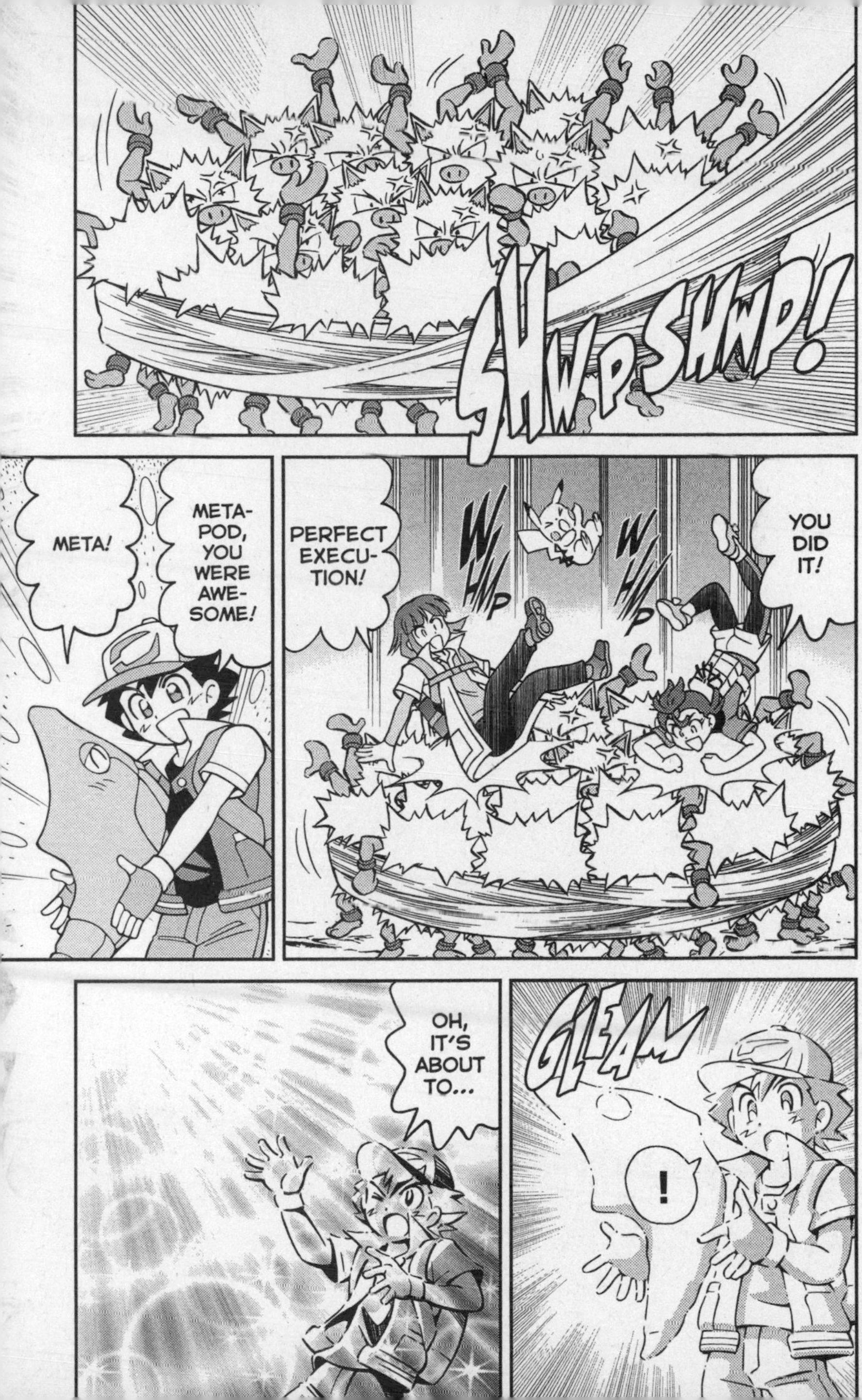
SHWP SHWP!
YOU DID IT!
WHMP
WHMP
PERFECT EXECU-TION!
META-POD, YOU WERE AWE-SOME!
META!
GLEAM
!
OH, IT'S ABOUT TO...

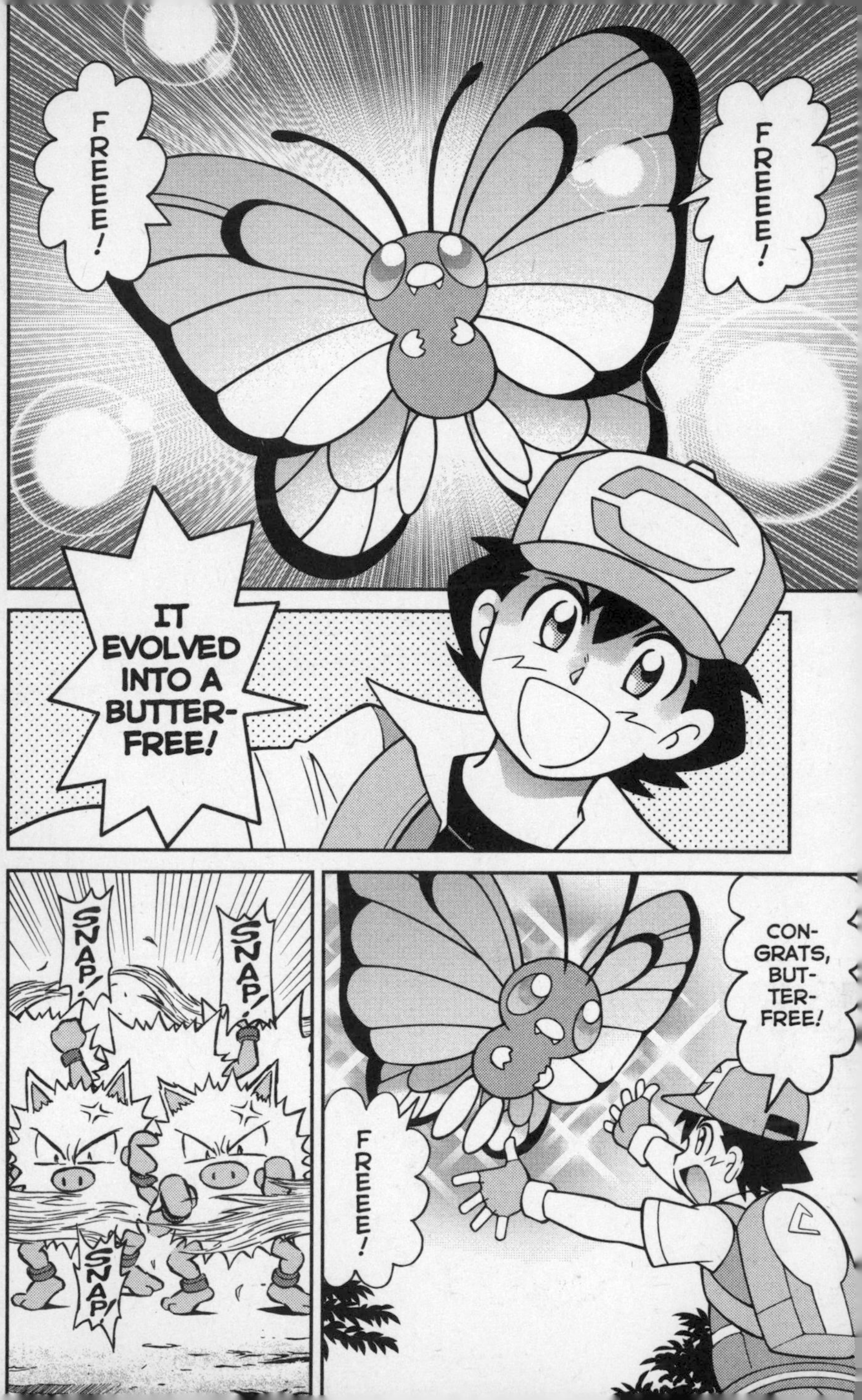
FREEE!
FREEE!
IT EVOLVED INTO A BUTTER-FREE!
CON-GRATS, BUT-TER-FREE!
FREEE!
SNAP!
SNAP!
SNAP!

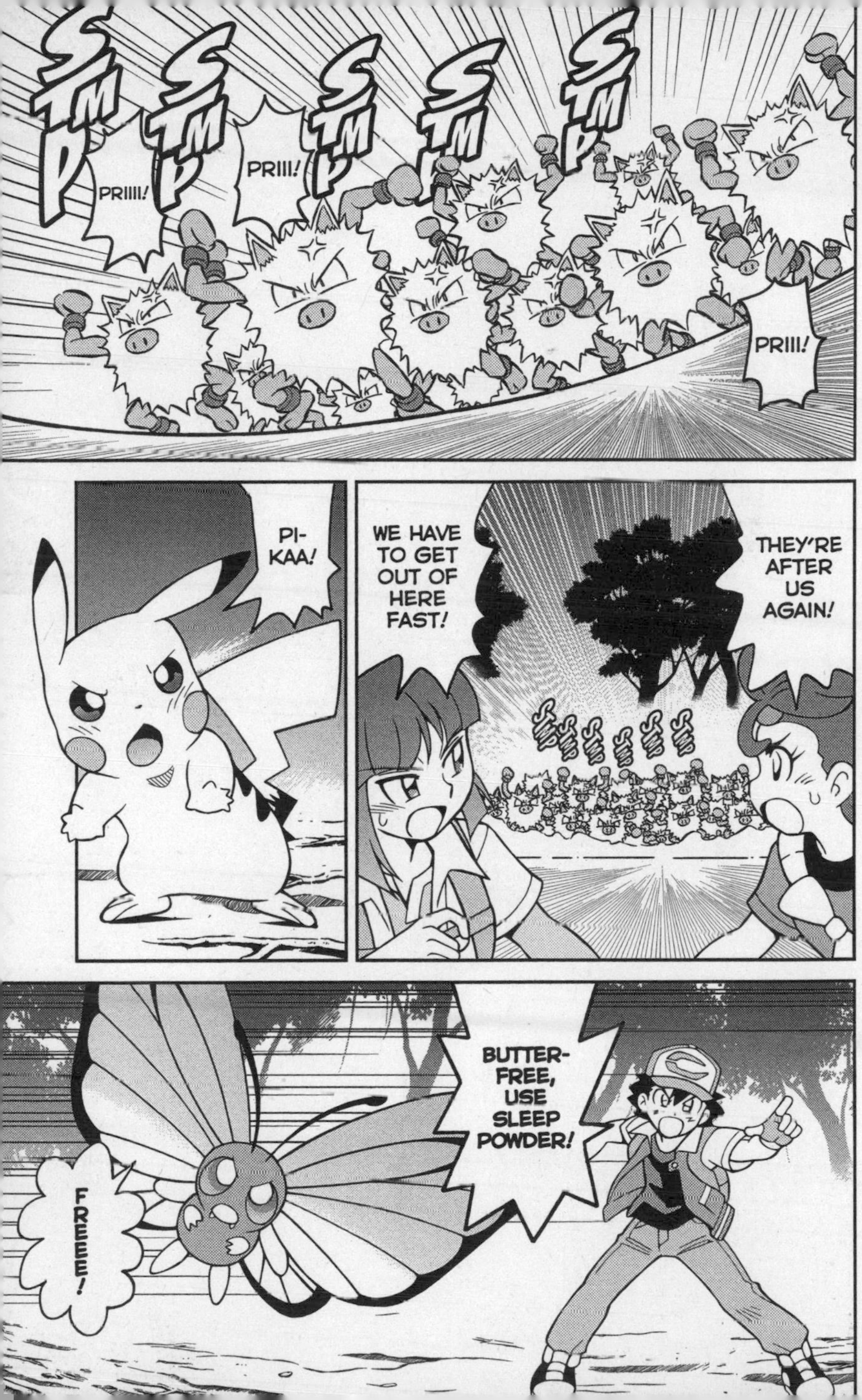
STMP
STMP
STMP
STMP
STMP
PRIII!
PRIII!
PRIIII!
THEY'RE AFTER US AGAIN!
WE HAVE TO GET OUT OF HERE FAST!
PI-KAA!
BUTTER-FREE, USE SLEEP POWDER!
FREEE!

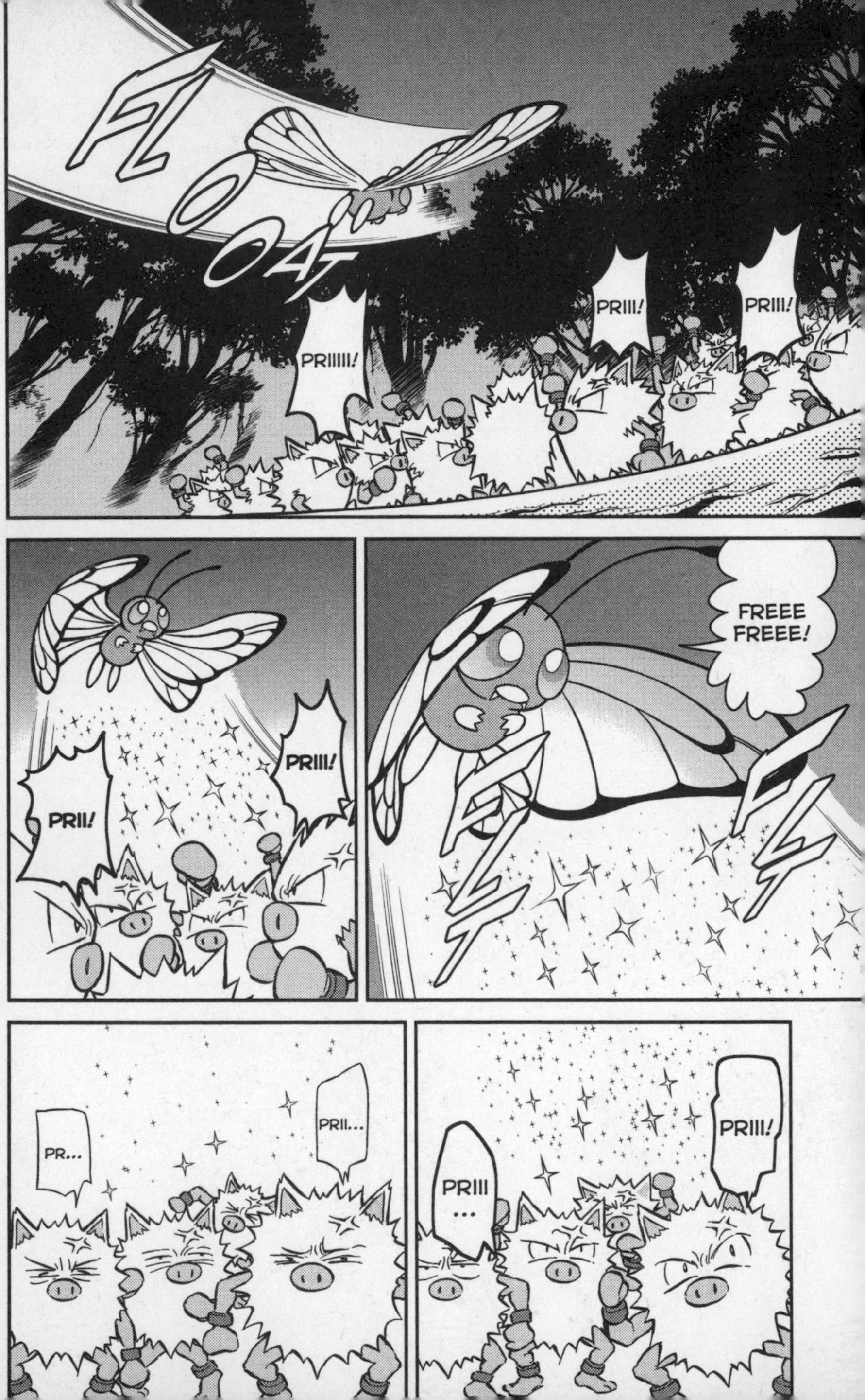
PRIII!
PRIII!
FLOAT
PRIIIII!
FREEE FREEE!
FLY
PRIII!
PRII!
PRIII!
PRIII ...
PRII...
PR...

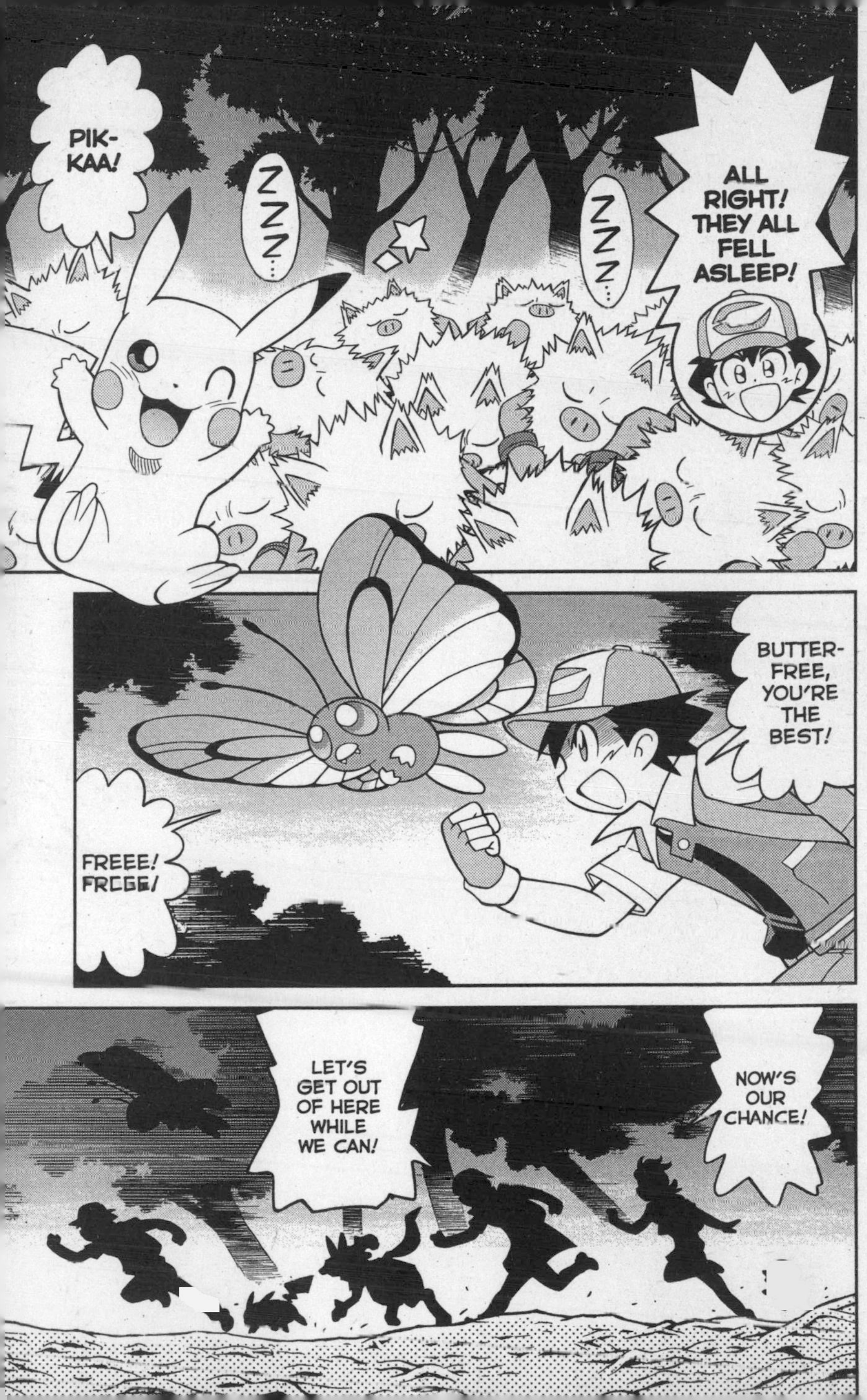
ALL RIGHT! THEY ALL FELL ASLEEP!
ZZZ...
ZZZ...
PIK-KAA!
BUTTER-FREE, YOU'RE THE BEST!
FREEE! FREEE!
NOW'S OUR CHANCE!
LET'S GET OUT OF HERE WHILE WE CAN!

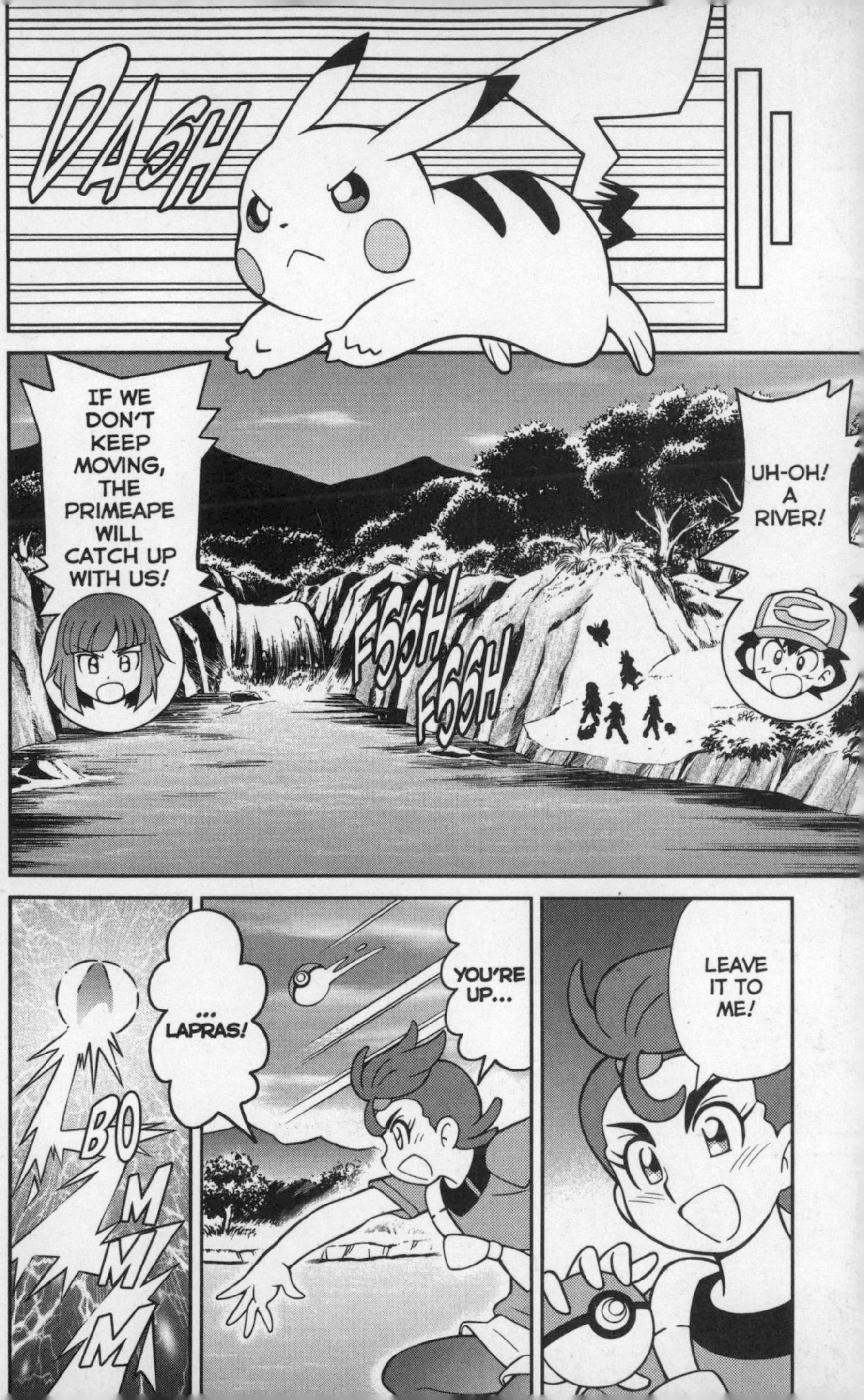
DASH
UH-OH! A RIVER!
IF WE DON'T KEEP MOVING, THE PRIMEAPE WILL CATCH UP WITH US!
FSSH FSSH
LEAVE IT TO ME!
YOU'RE UP...
...LAPRAS!
BOMMMM

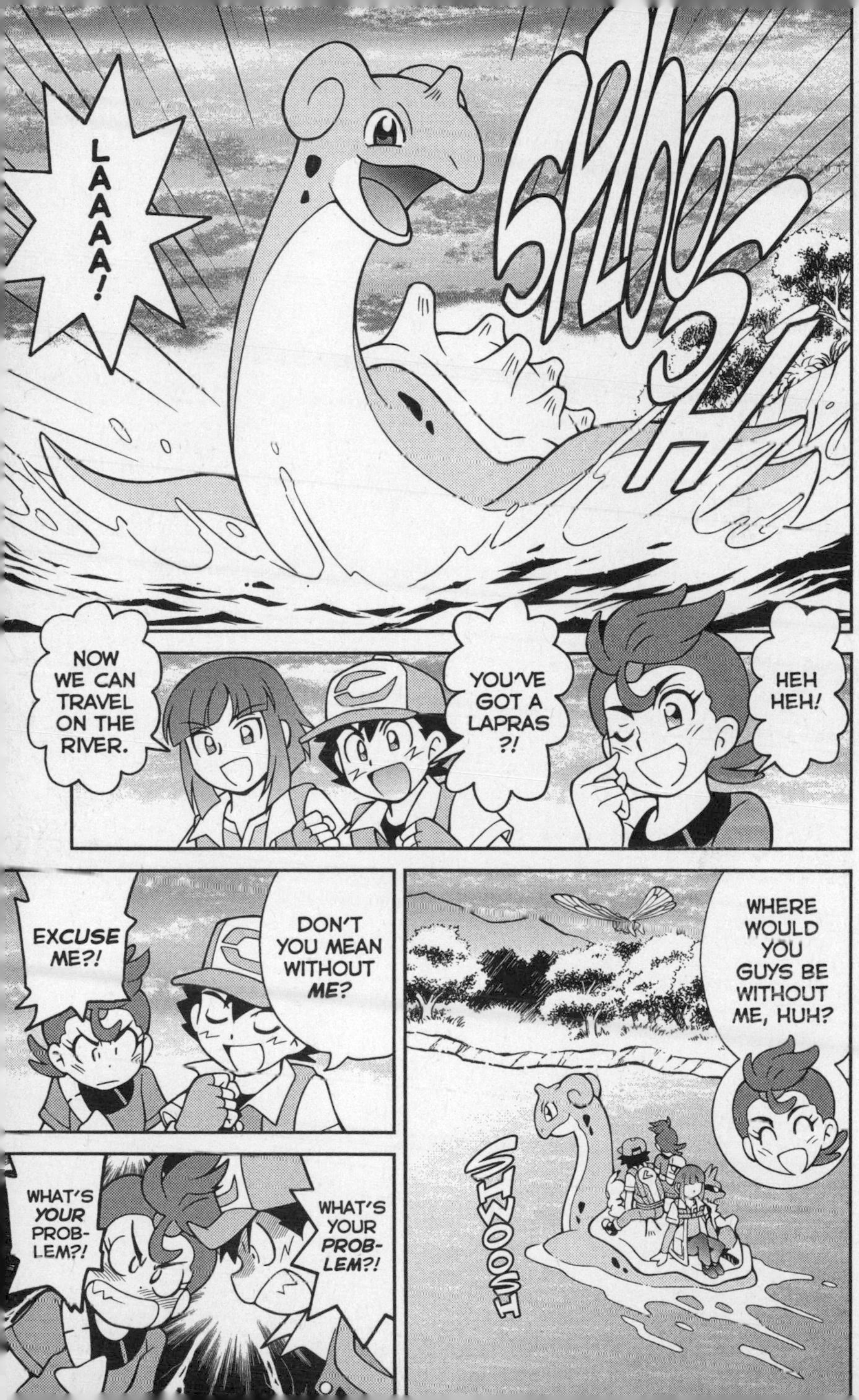
SPLOOOSH
LAAAAA!
HEH HEH!
YOU'VE GOT A LAPRAS?!
NOW WE CAN TRAVEL ON THE RIVER.
WHERE WOULD YOU GUYS BE WITHOUT ME, HUH?
SHWOOSH
DON'T YOU MEAN WITHOUT *ME*?
EXCUSE ME?!
WHAT'S YOUR *PROB-LEM*?!
WHAT'S *YOUR* PROB-LEM?!

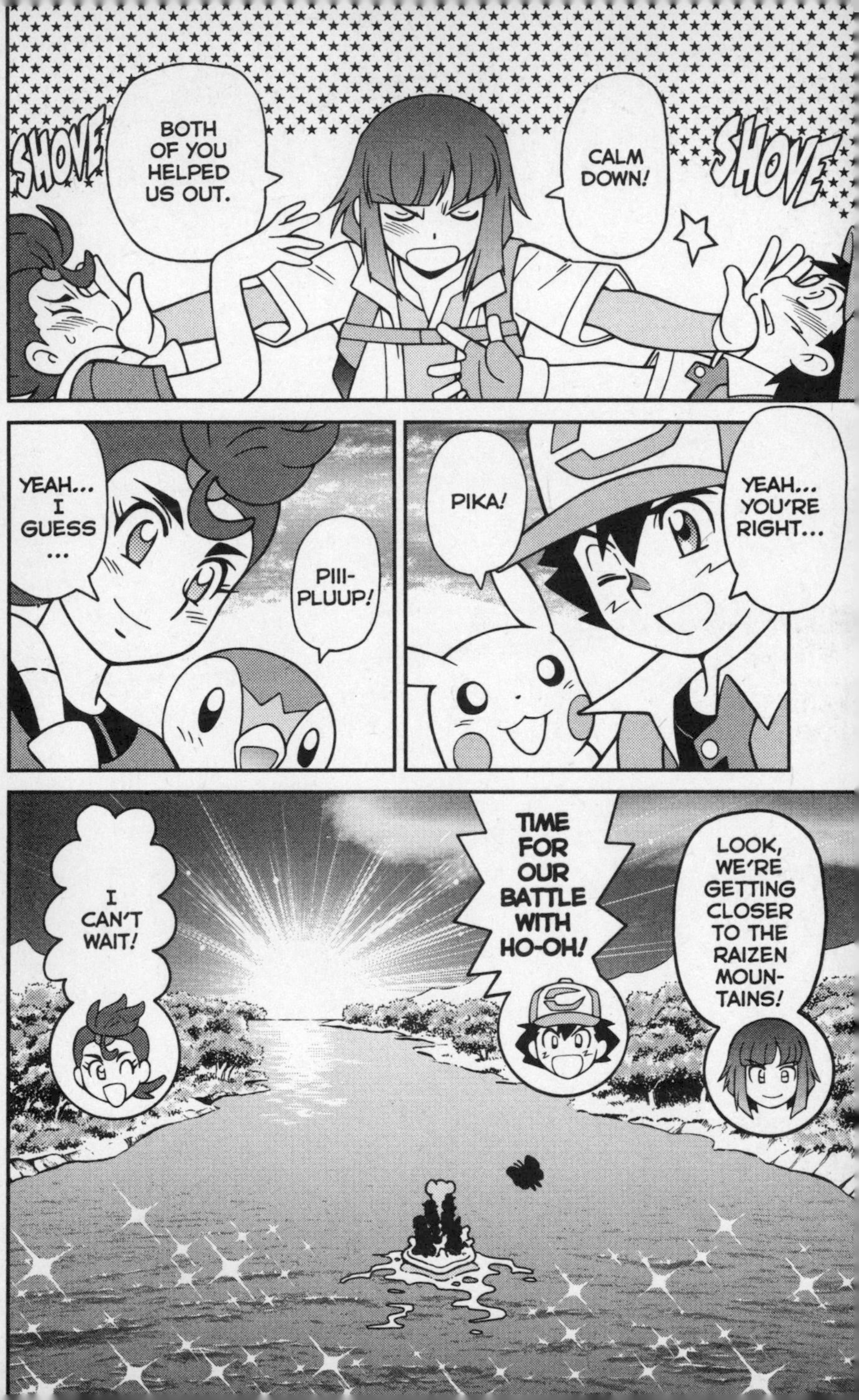
SHOVE
CALM DOWN!
BOTH OF YOU HELPED US OUT.
SHOVE
YEAH... YOU'RE RIGHT...
PIKA!
PIII-PLUUP!
YEAH... I GUESS ...
LOOK, WE'RE GETTING CLOSER TO THE RAIZEN MOUN-TAINS!
TIME FOR OUR BATTLE WITH HO-OH!
I CAN'T WAIT!

CHAPTER 10

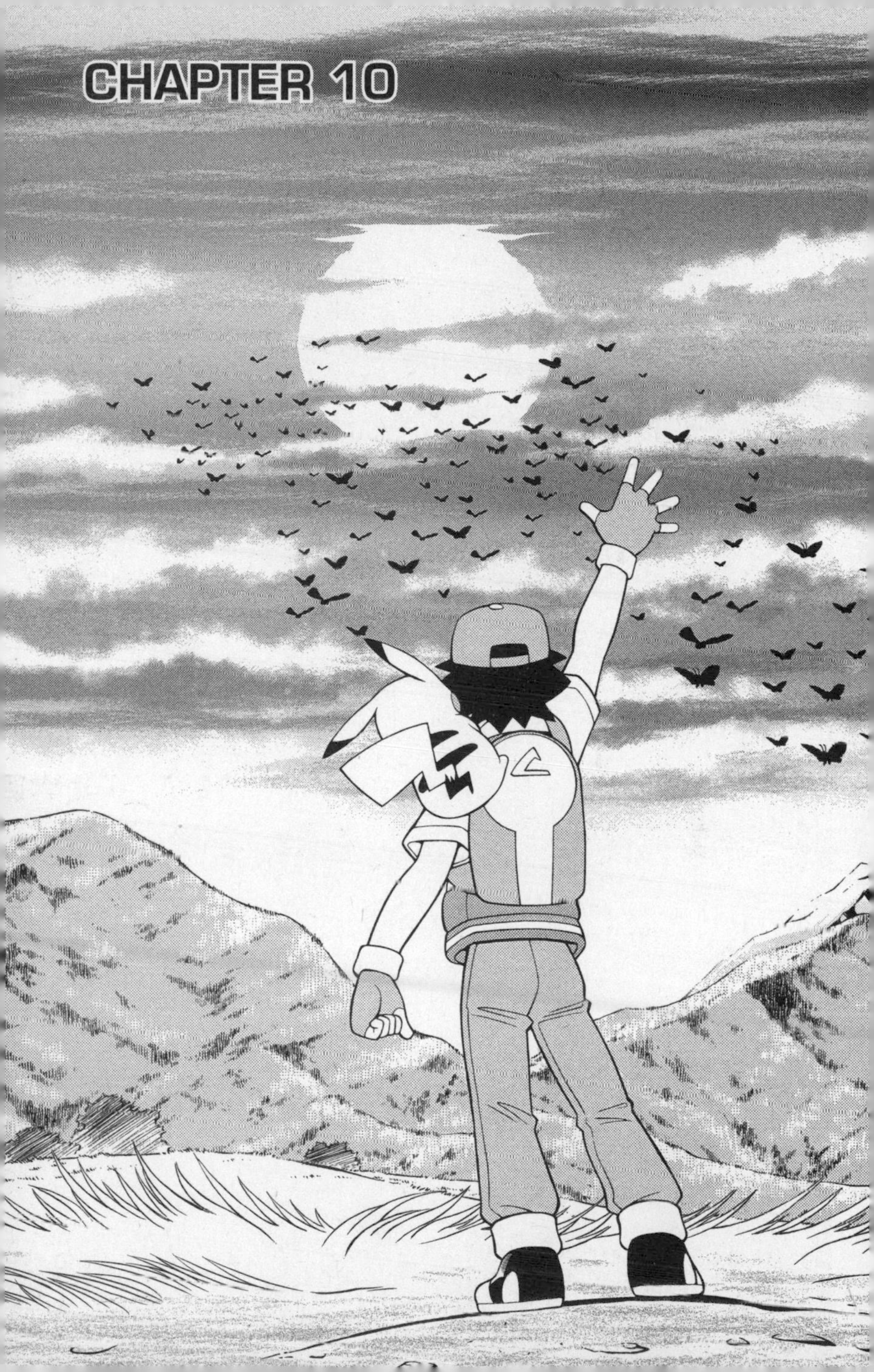

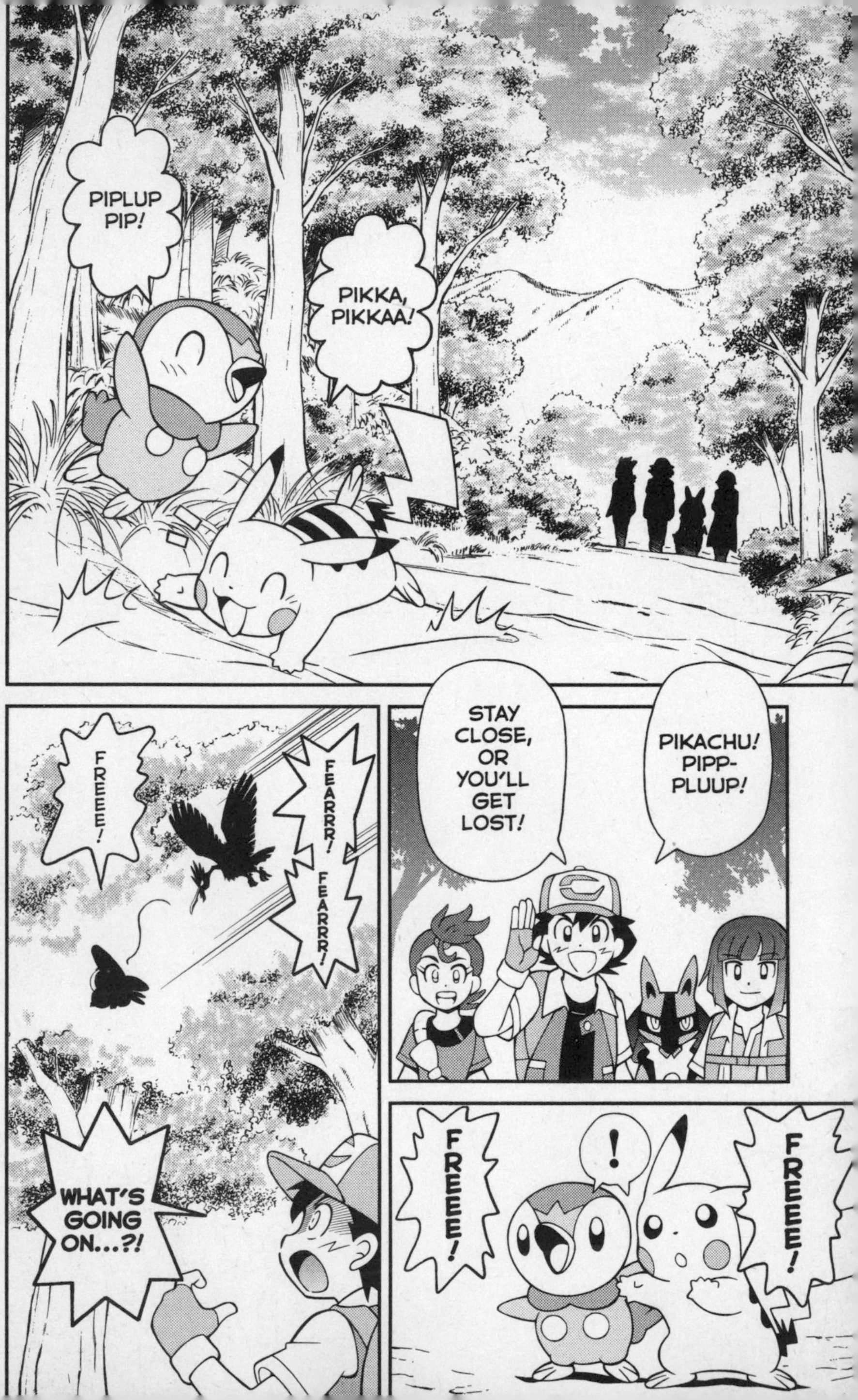
PIKKA, PIKKAA!
PIPLUP PIP!
PIKACHU! PIPP-PLUUP!
STAY CLOSE, OR YOU'LL GET LOST!
FREEEE!
!
FREEE!
FEARRR! FEARRR!
FREEE!
WHAT'S GOING ON...?!

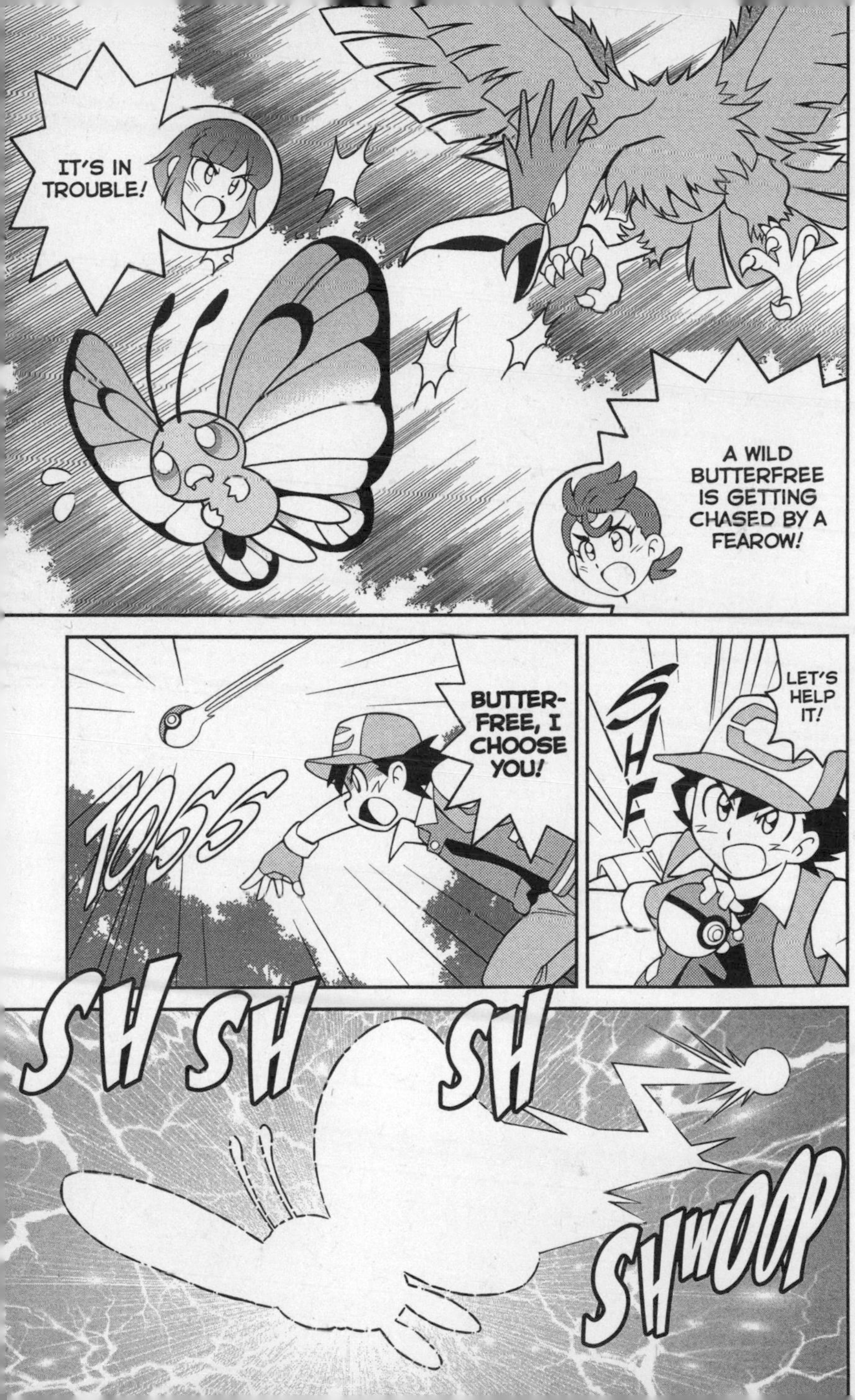
A WILD BUTTERFREE IS GETTING CHASED BY A FEAROW!
IT'S IN TROUBLE!
LET'S HELP IT!
SHF
BUTTER-FREE, I CHOOSE YOU!
TOSS
SH SH SH
SHWOOP

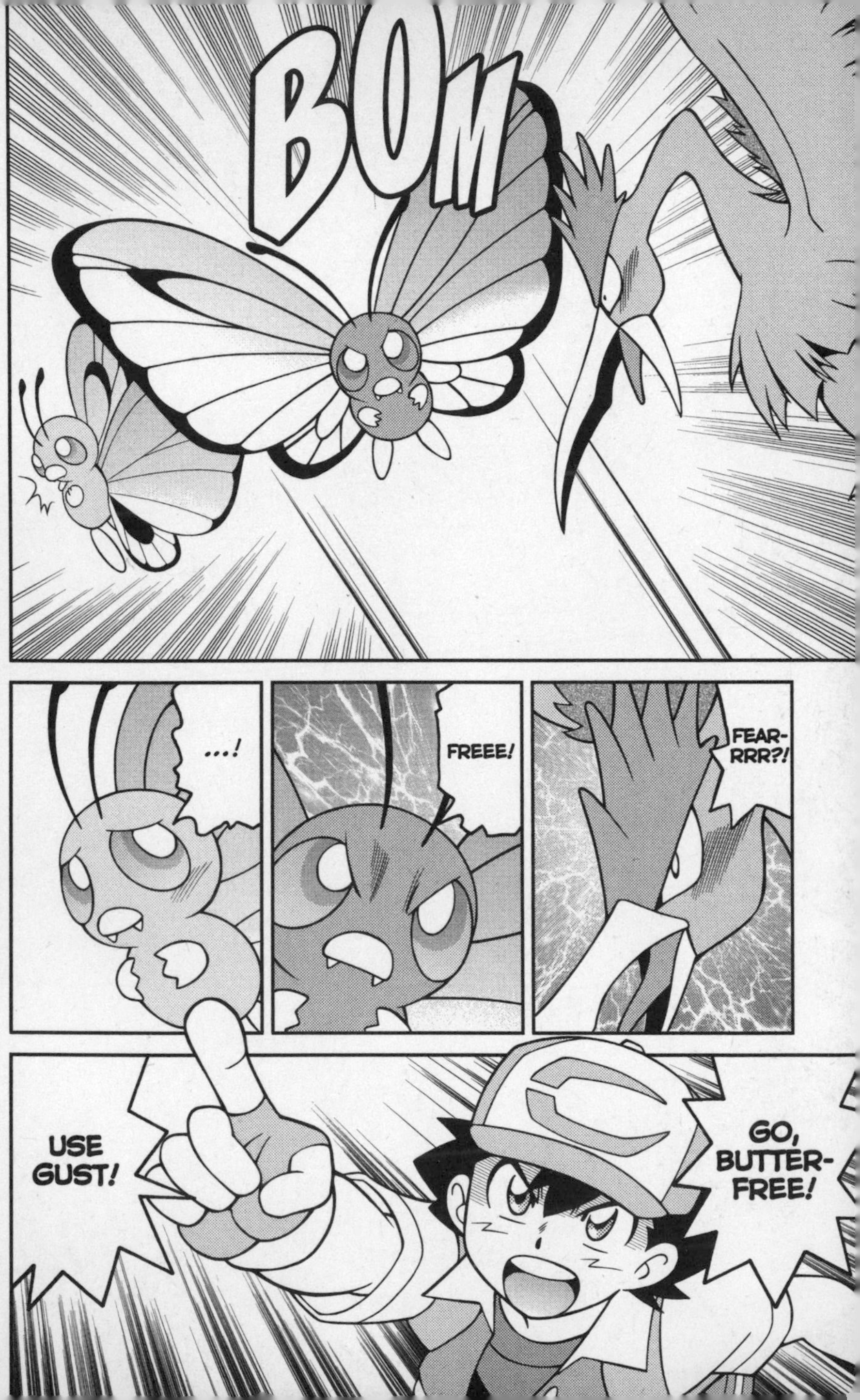
BOM
FEAR-RRR?!
FREEE!
...!
GO, BUTTER-FREE!
USE GUST!

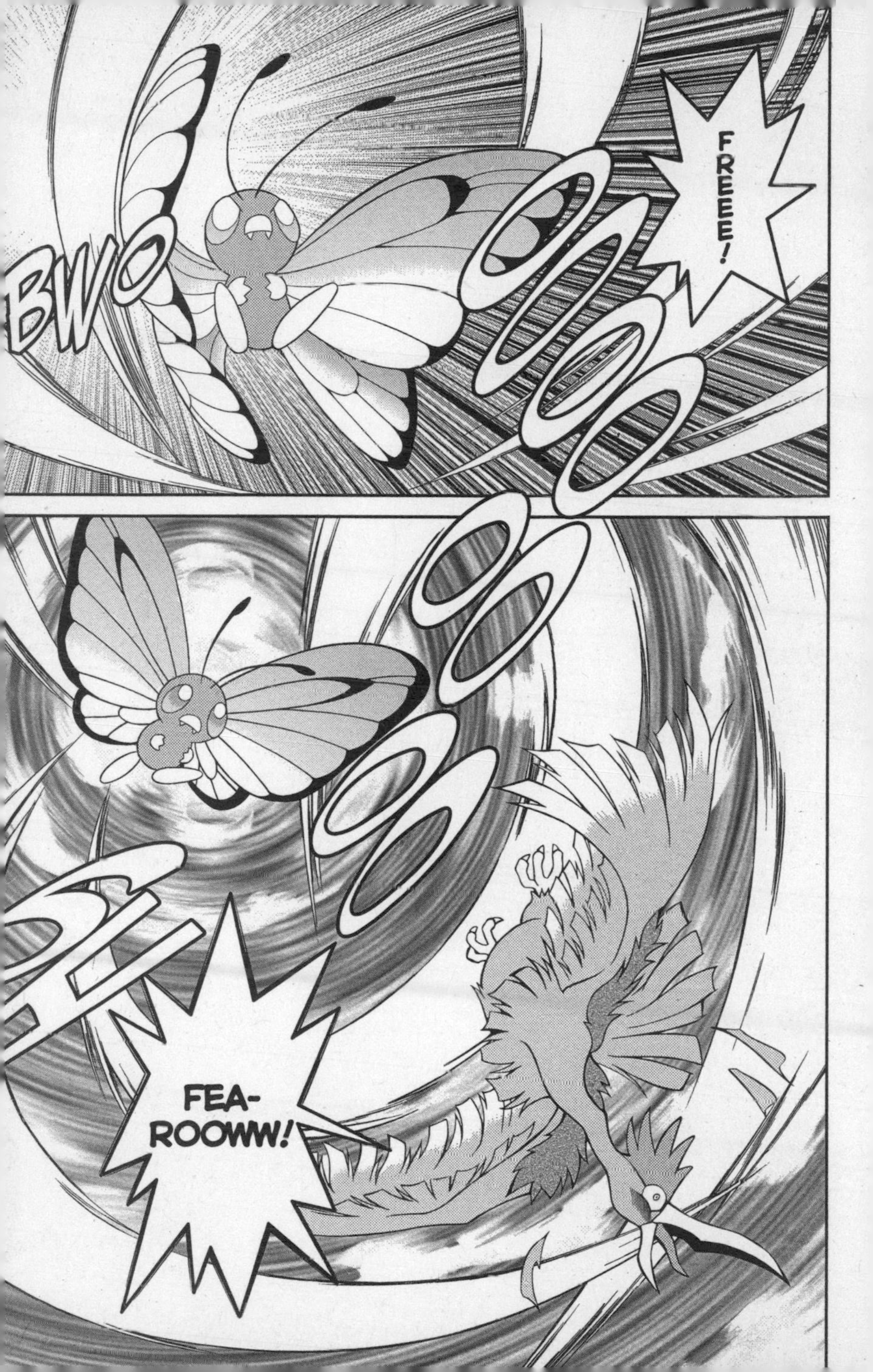
FREEE!
BWO
FEA-
ROOWW!

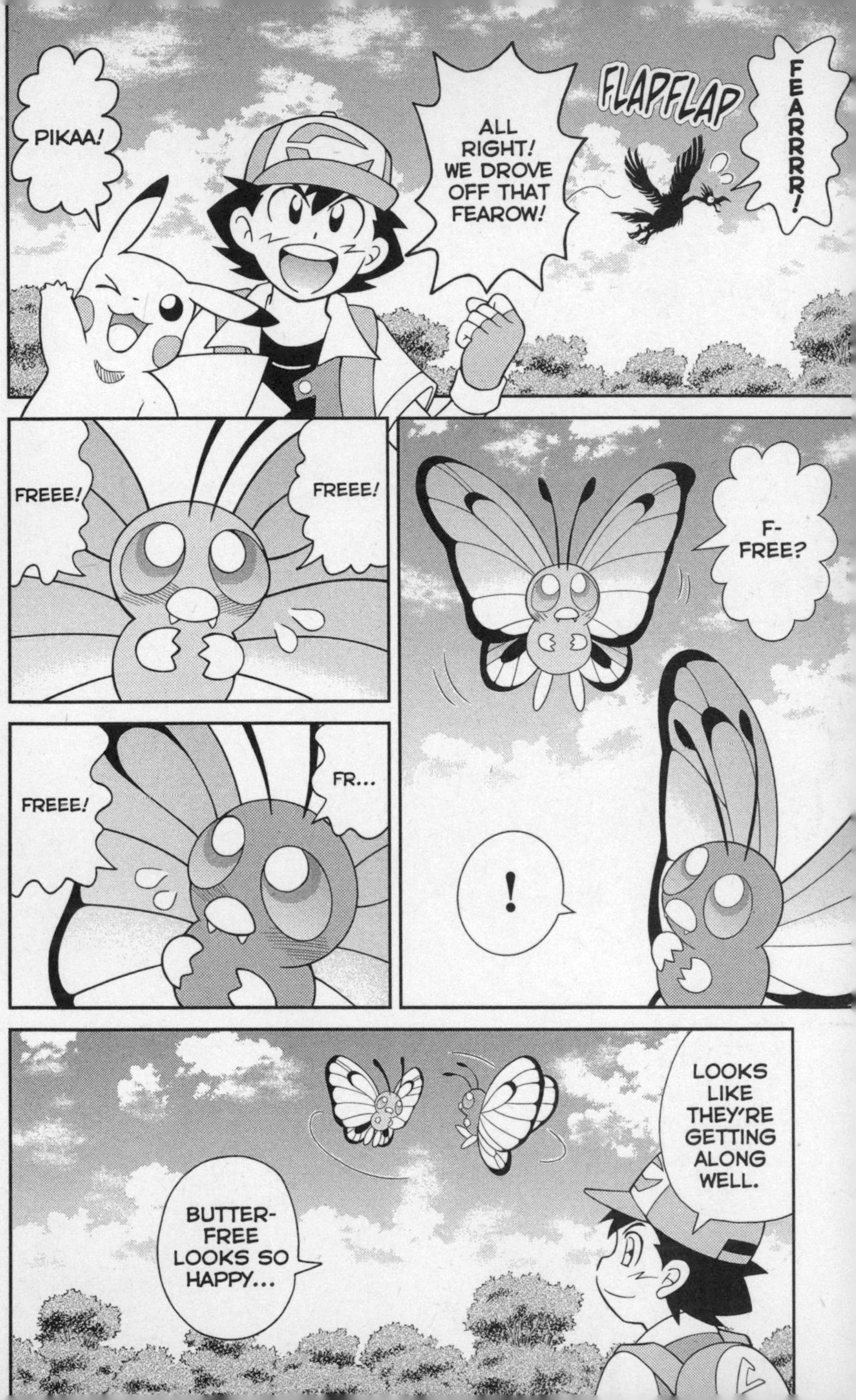
FEARRRR!
FLAPFLAP
ALL RIGHT! WE DROVE OFF THAT FEAROW!
PIKAA!
F-FREE?
!
FREEE!
FREEE!
FR...
FREEE!
LOOKS LIKE THEY'RE GETTING ALONG WELL.
BUTTER-FREE LOOKS SO HAPPY...

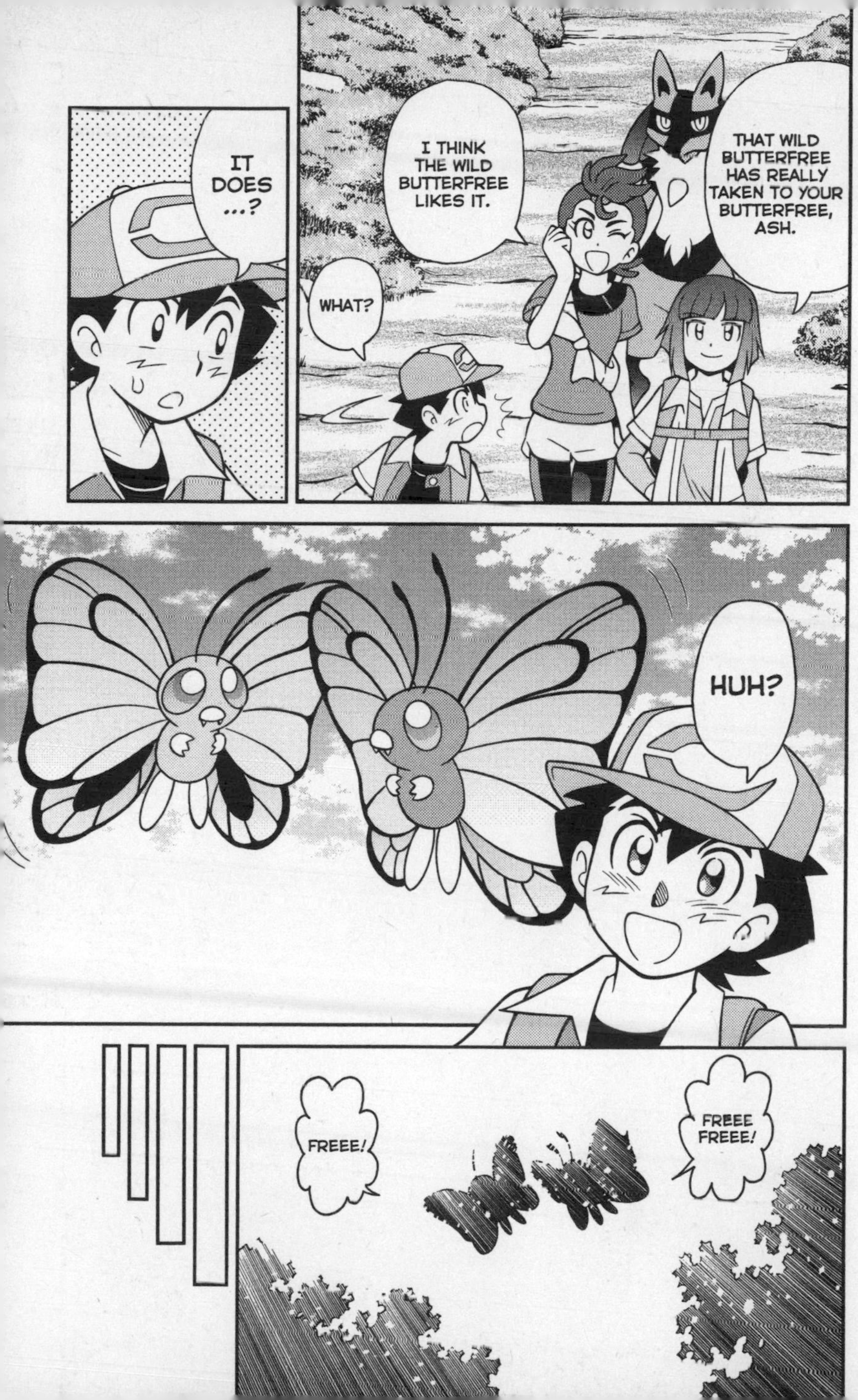
THAT WILD BUTTERFREE HAS REALLY TAKEN TO YOUR BUTTERFREE, ASH.
I THINK THE WILD BUTTERFREE LIKES IT.
WHAT?
IT DOES ...?
HUH?
FREEE FREEE!
FREEE!

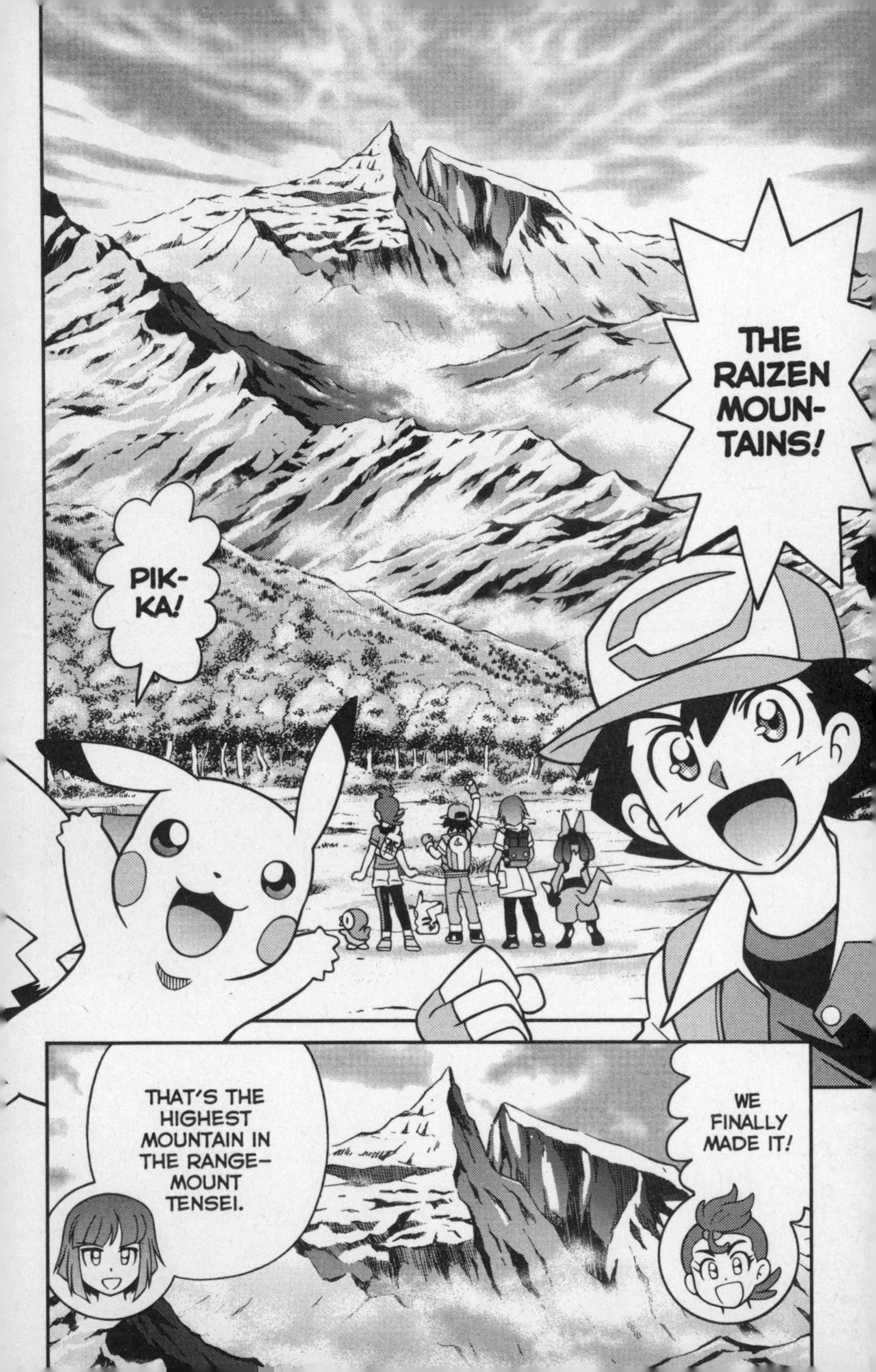
THE RAIZEN MOUN-TAINS!
PIK-KA!
WE FINALLY MADE IT!
THAT'S THE HIGHEST MOUNTAIN IN THE RANGE-MOUNT TENSEI.

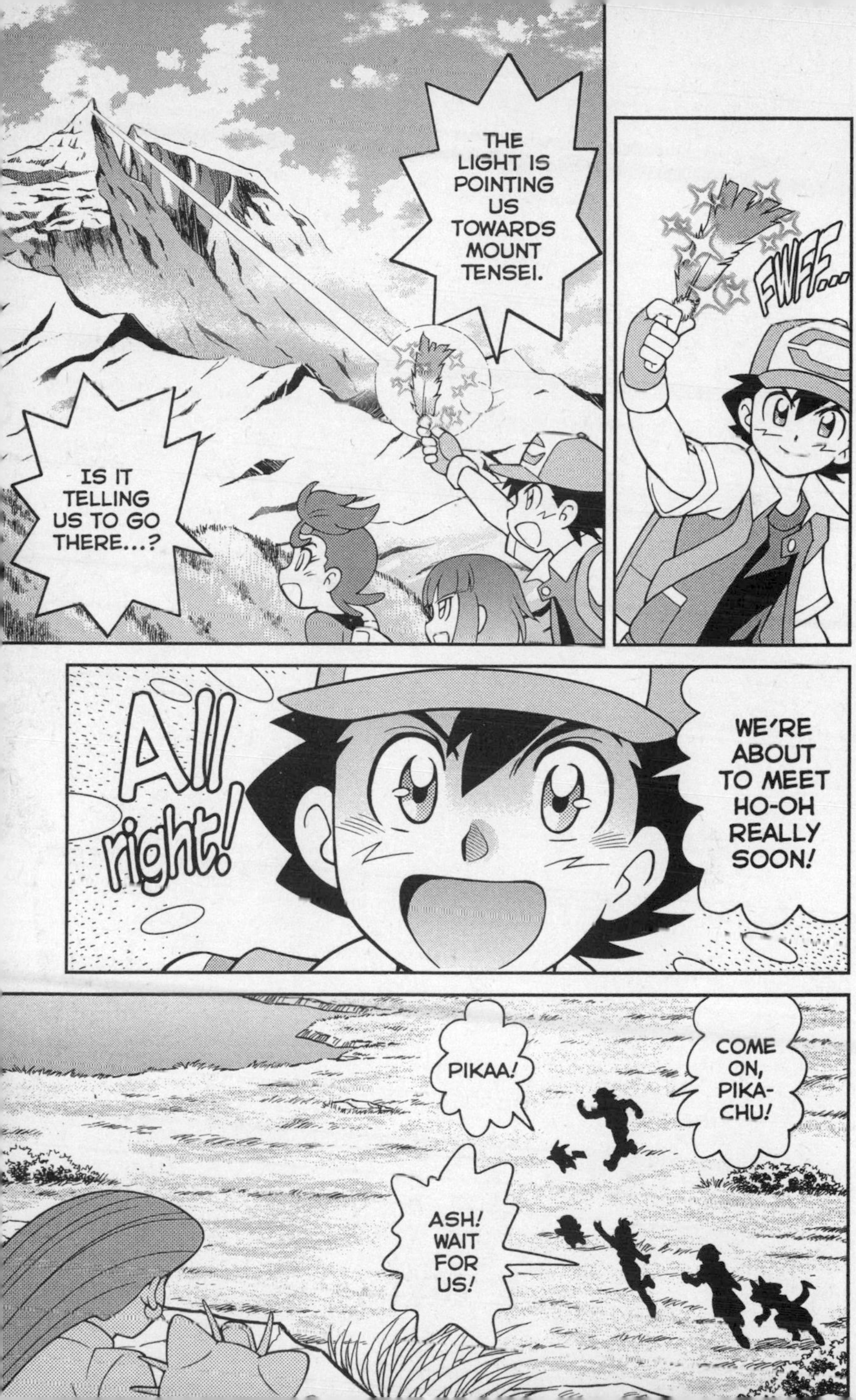
FWFF...
THE LIGHT IS POINTING US TOWARDS MOUNT TENSEI.
IS IT TELLING US TO GO THERE...?
WE'RE ABOUT TO MEET HO-OH REALLY SOON!
All right!
COME ON, PIKA-CHU!
PIKAA!
ASH! WAIT FOR US!

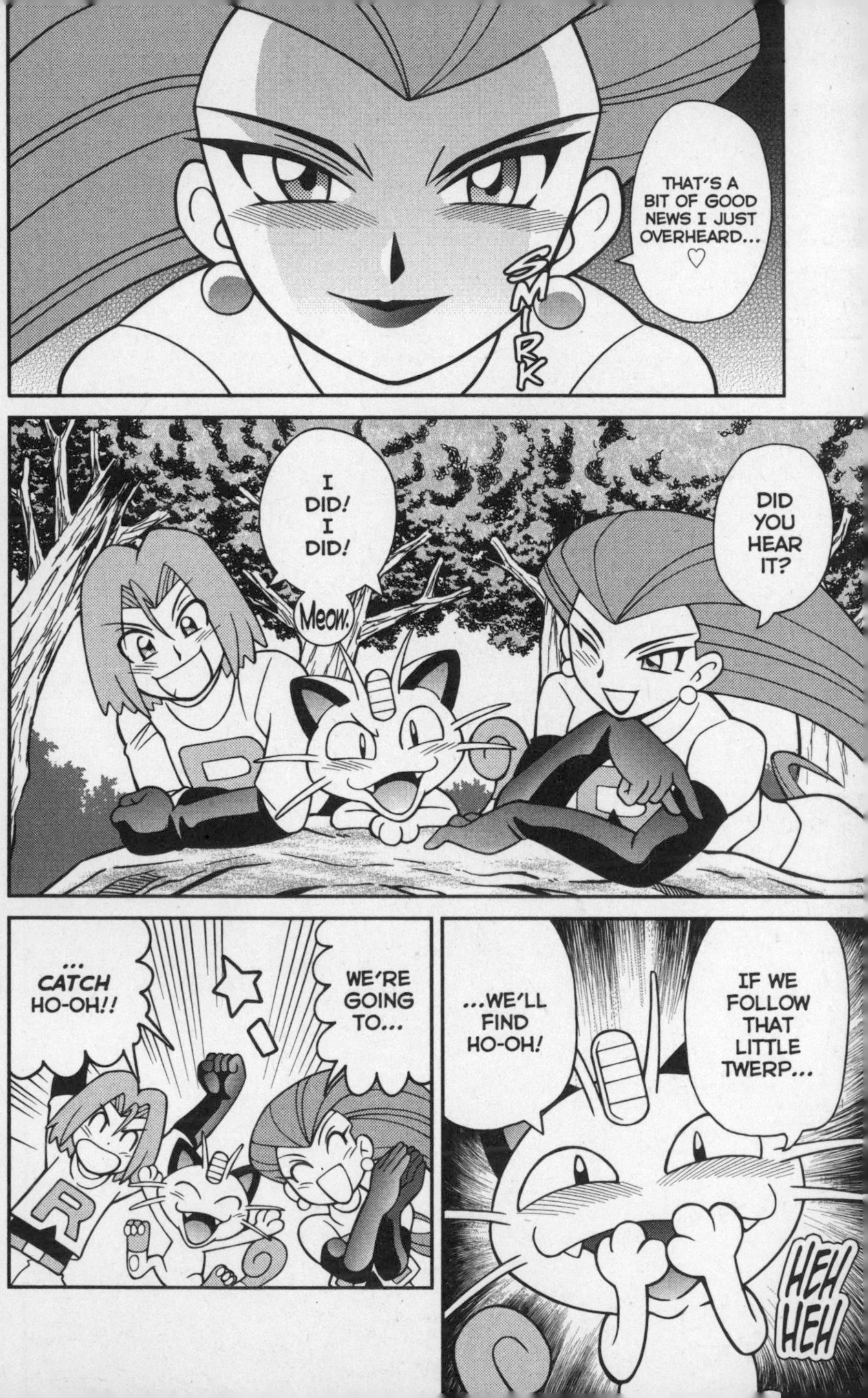
THAT'S A BIT OF GOOD NEWS I JUST OVERHEARD... ♡
SMIRK
DID YOU HEAR IT?
I DID! I DID!
Meow.
IF WE FOLLOW THAT LITTLE TWERP...
...WE'LL FIND HO-OH!
HEH HEH
WE'RE GOING TO...
...CATCH HO-OH!!

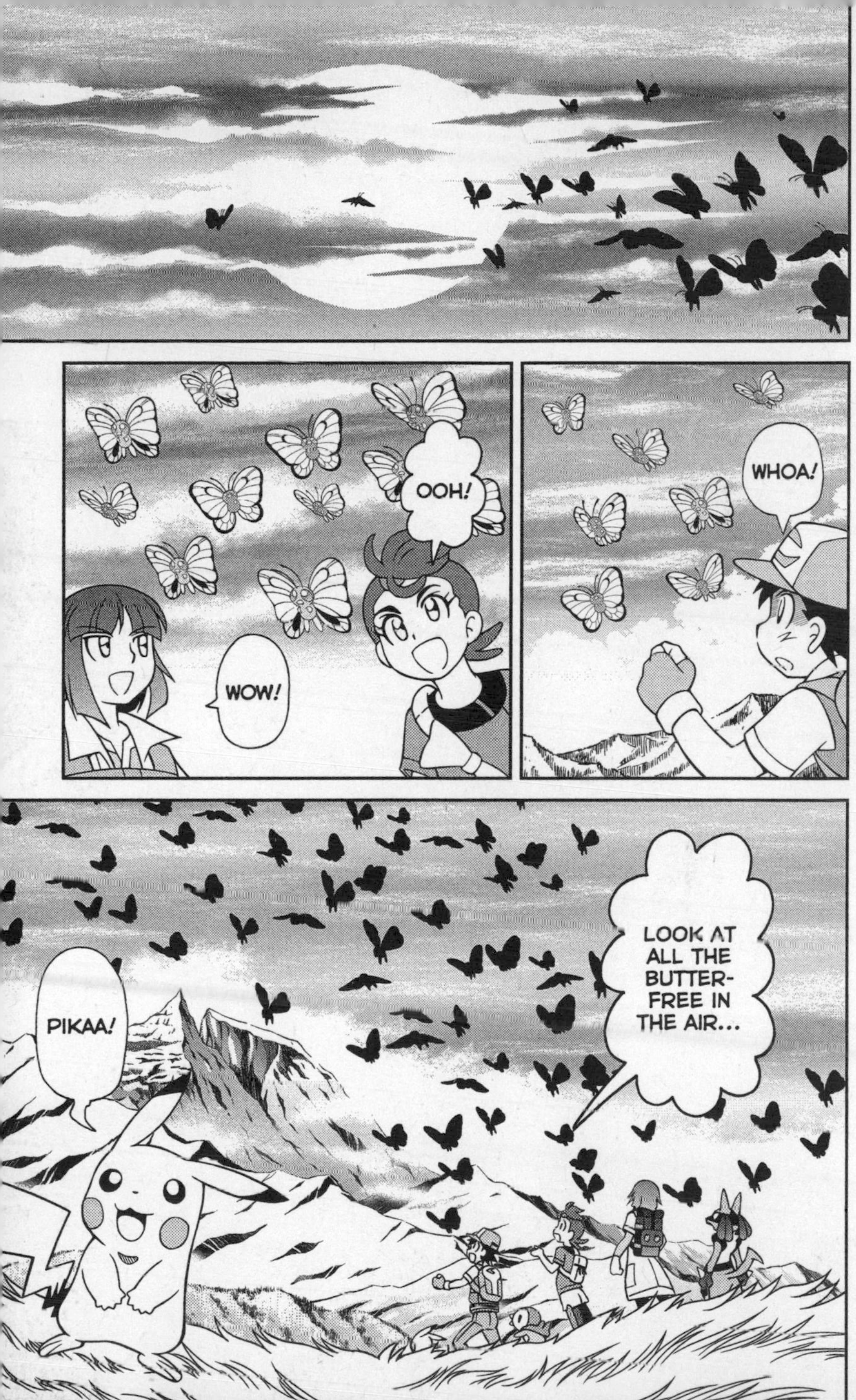
WHOA!
OOH!
WOW!
LOOK AT ALL THE BUTTER-FREE IN THE AIR...
PIKAA!

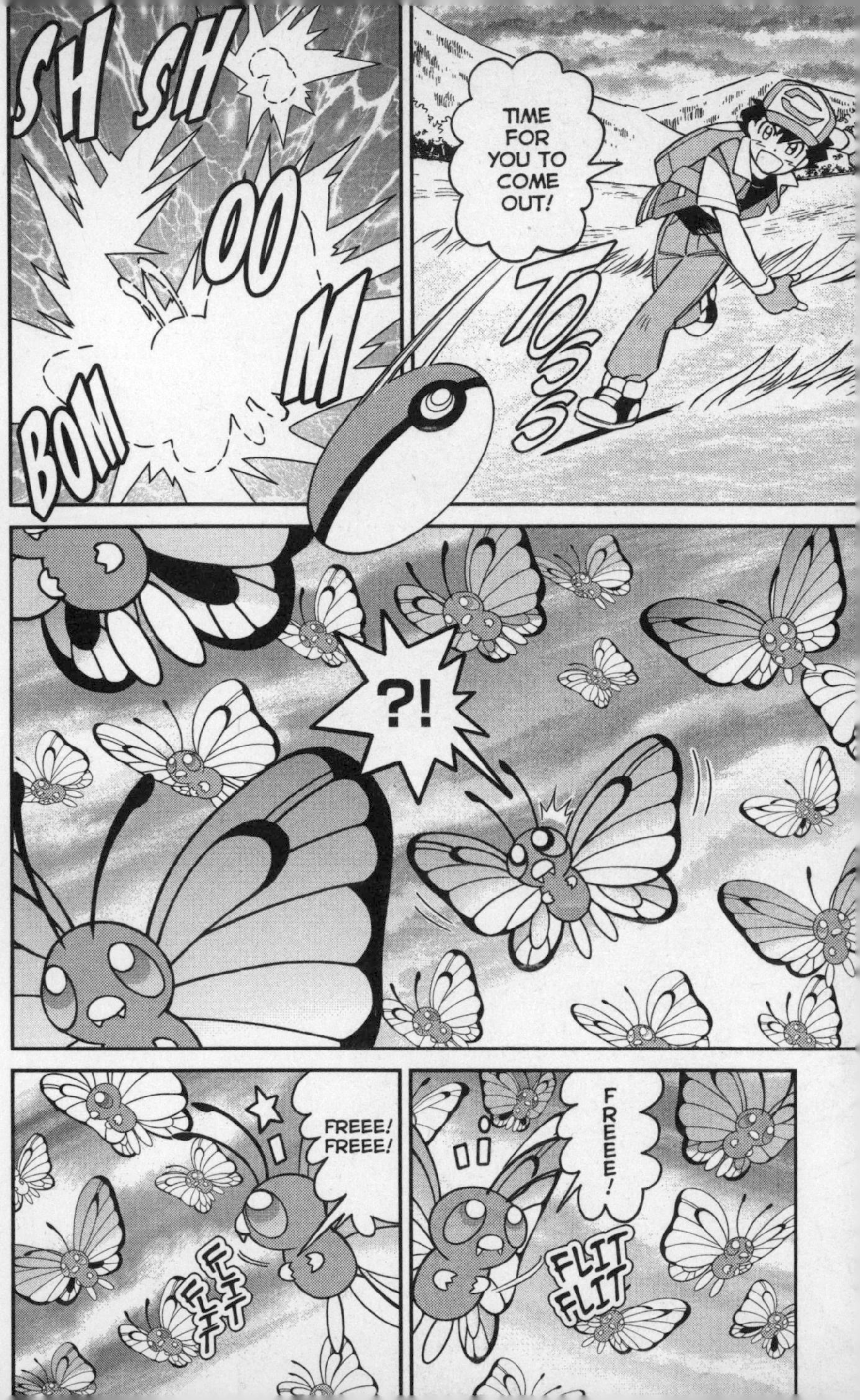
TIME FOR YOU TO COME OUT!
TOSS
SH SH
OO
M
BOM
?!
FREEE!
FLIT FLIT
FREEE! FREEE!
FLIT FLIT

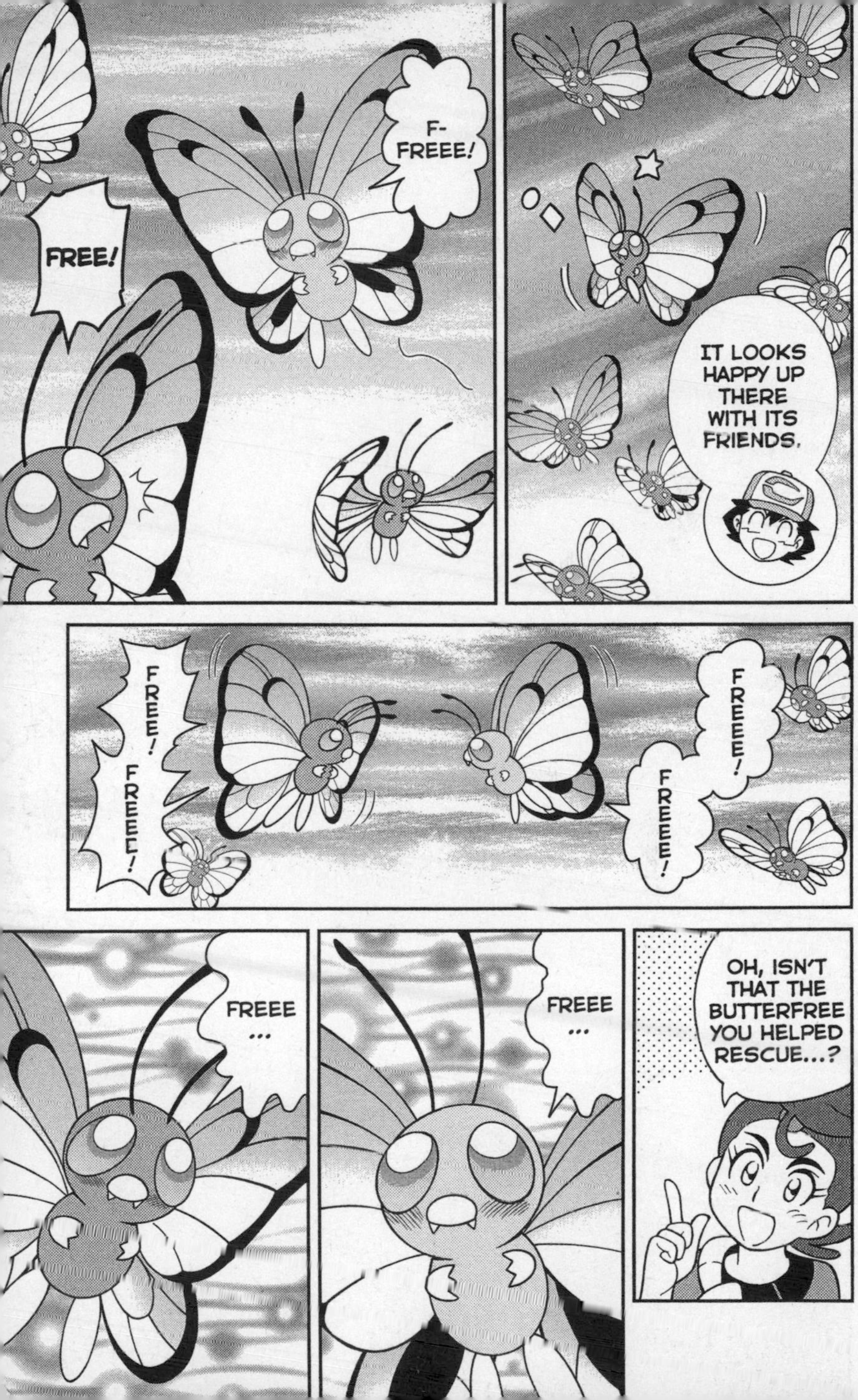
IT LOOKS HAPPY UP THERE WITH ITS FRIENDS.
F- FREEE!
FREE!
FREEE!
FREEE!
FREE! FREEE!
OH, ISN'T THAT THE BUTTERFREE YOU HELPED RESCUE...?
FREEE ...
FREEE ...

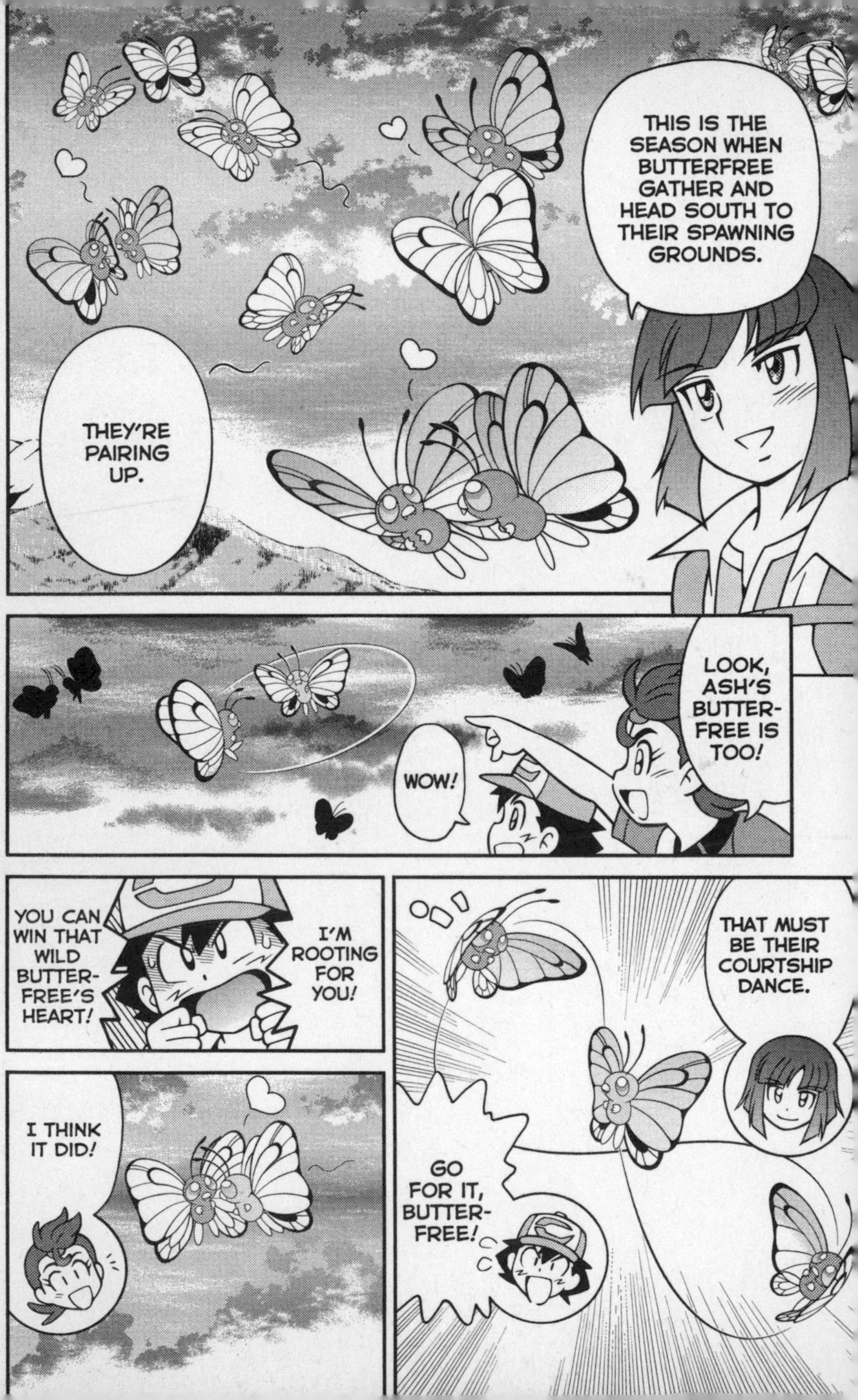
THIS IS THE SEASON WHEN BUTTERFREE GATHER AND HEAD SOUTH TO THEIR SPAWNING GROUNDS.
THEY'RE PAIRING UP.
LOOK, ASH'S BUTTER-FREE IS TOO!
WOW!
THAT MUST BE THEIR COURTSHIP DANCE.
GO FOR IT, BUTTER-FREE!
I'M ROOTING FOR YOU!
YOU CAN WIN THAT WILD BUTTER-FREE'S HEART!
I THINK IT DID!

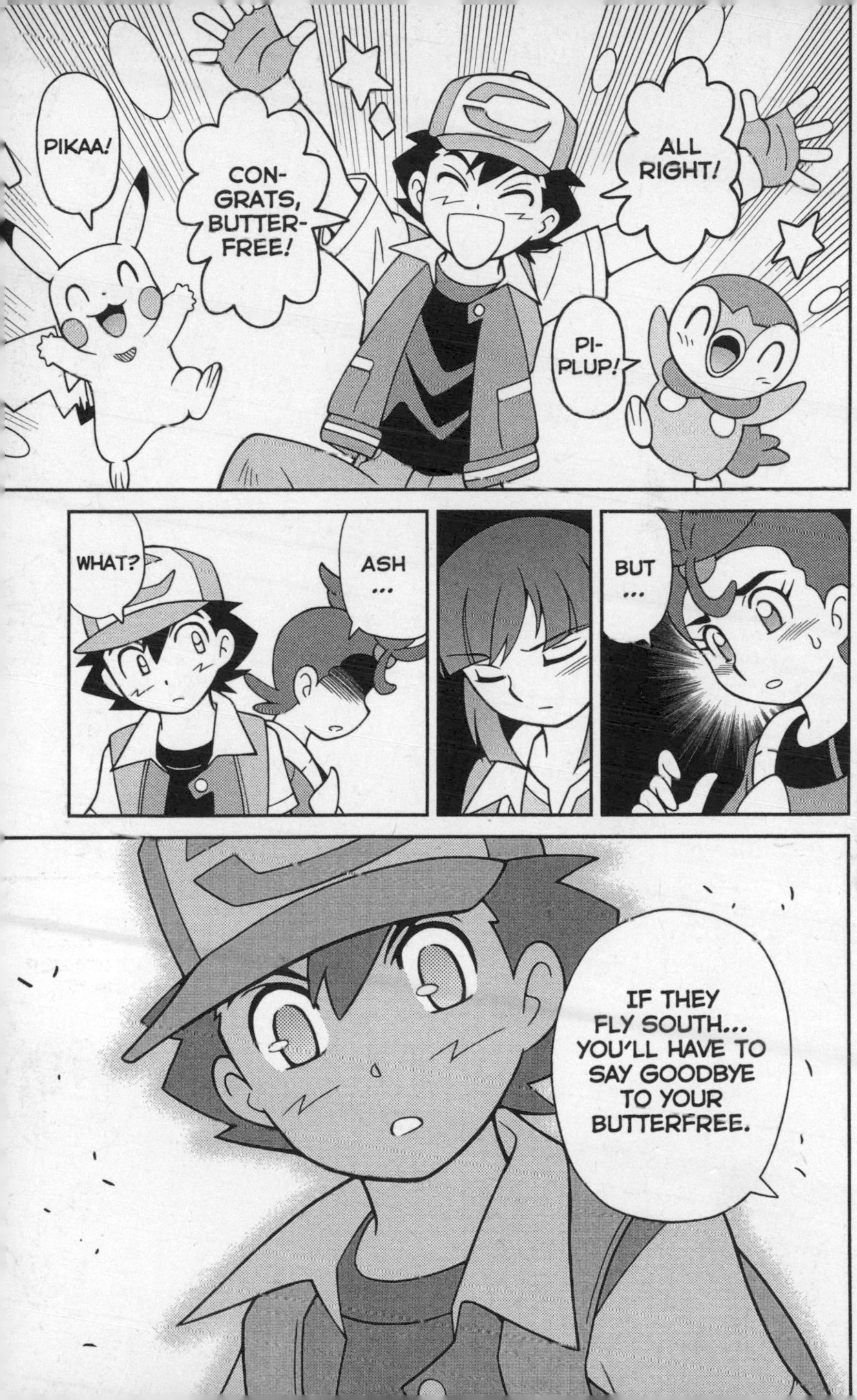
ALL RIGHT!
CONGRATS, BUTTERFREE!
PIKAA!
PI-PLUP!
BUT ...
ASH ...
WHAT?
IF THEY FLY SOUTH... YOU'LL HAVE TO SAY GOODBYE TO YOUR BUTTERFREE.

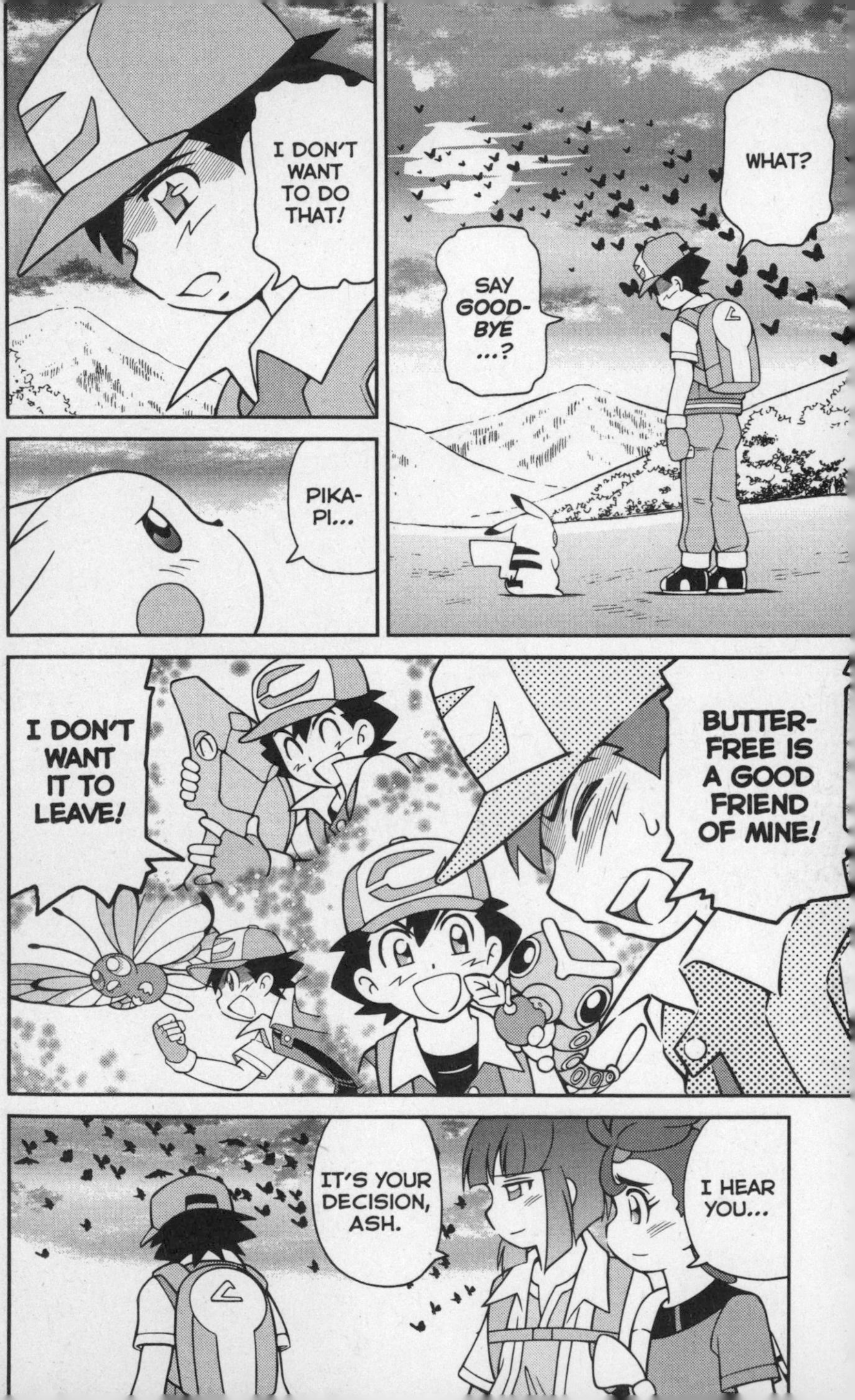
WHAT?
SAY GOOD-BYE...?
I DON'T WANT TO DO THAT!
PIKA-PI...
BUTTERFREE IS A GOOD FRIEND OF MINE!
I DON'T WANT IT TO LEAVE!
I HEAR YOU...
IT'S YOUR DECISION, ASH.

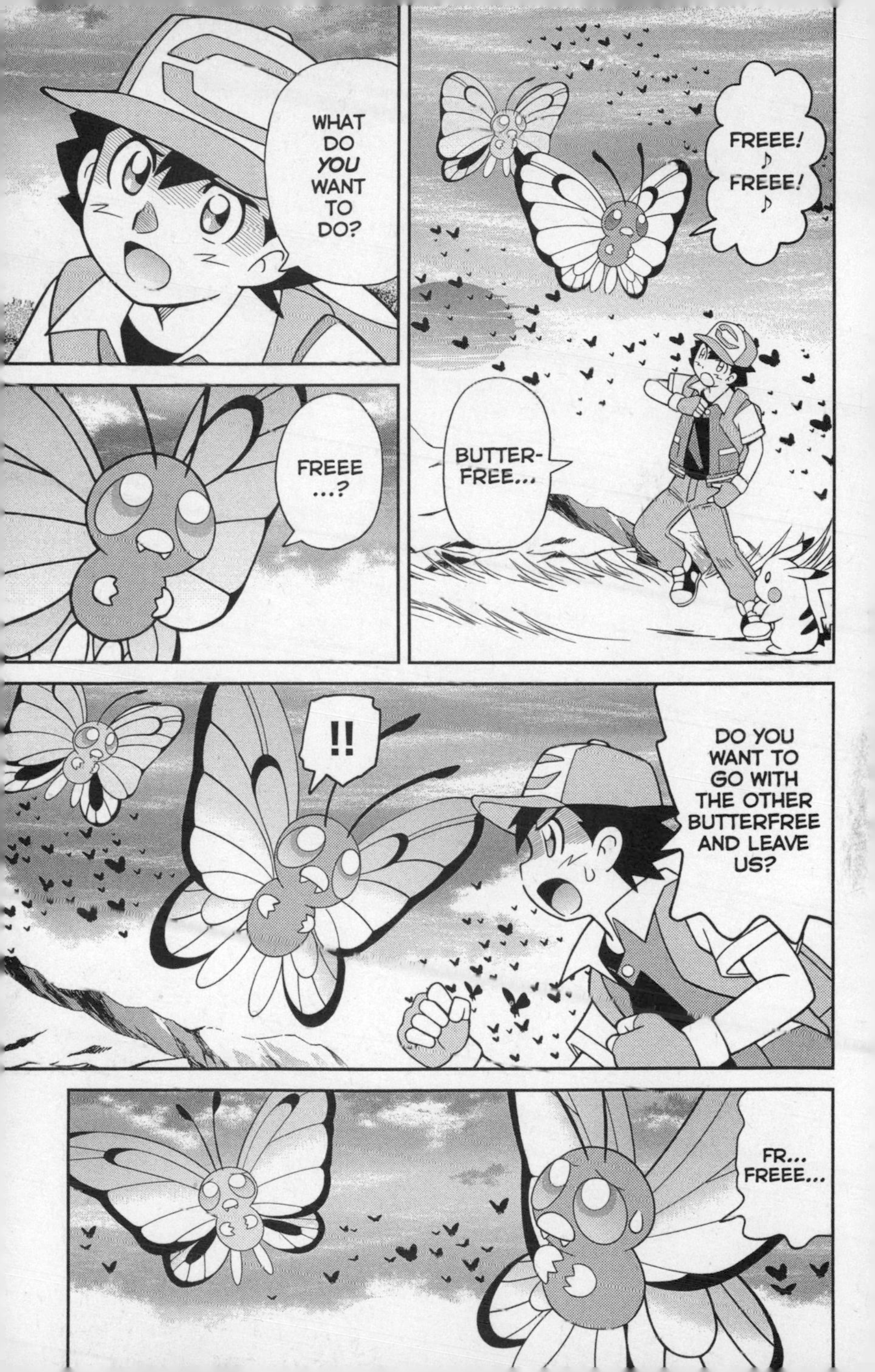
FREEE! ♪ FREEE! ♪
BUTTER-FREE...
WHAT DO *YOU* WANT TO DO?
FREEE ...?
DO YOU WANT TO GO WITH THE OTHER BUTTERFREE AND LEAVE US?
!!
FR... FREEE...

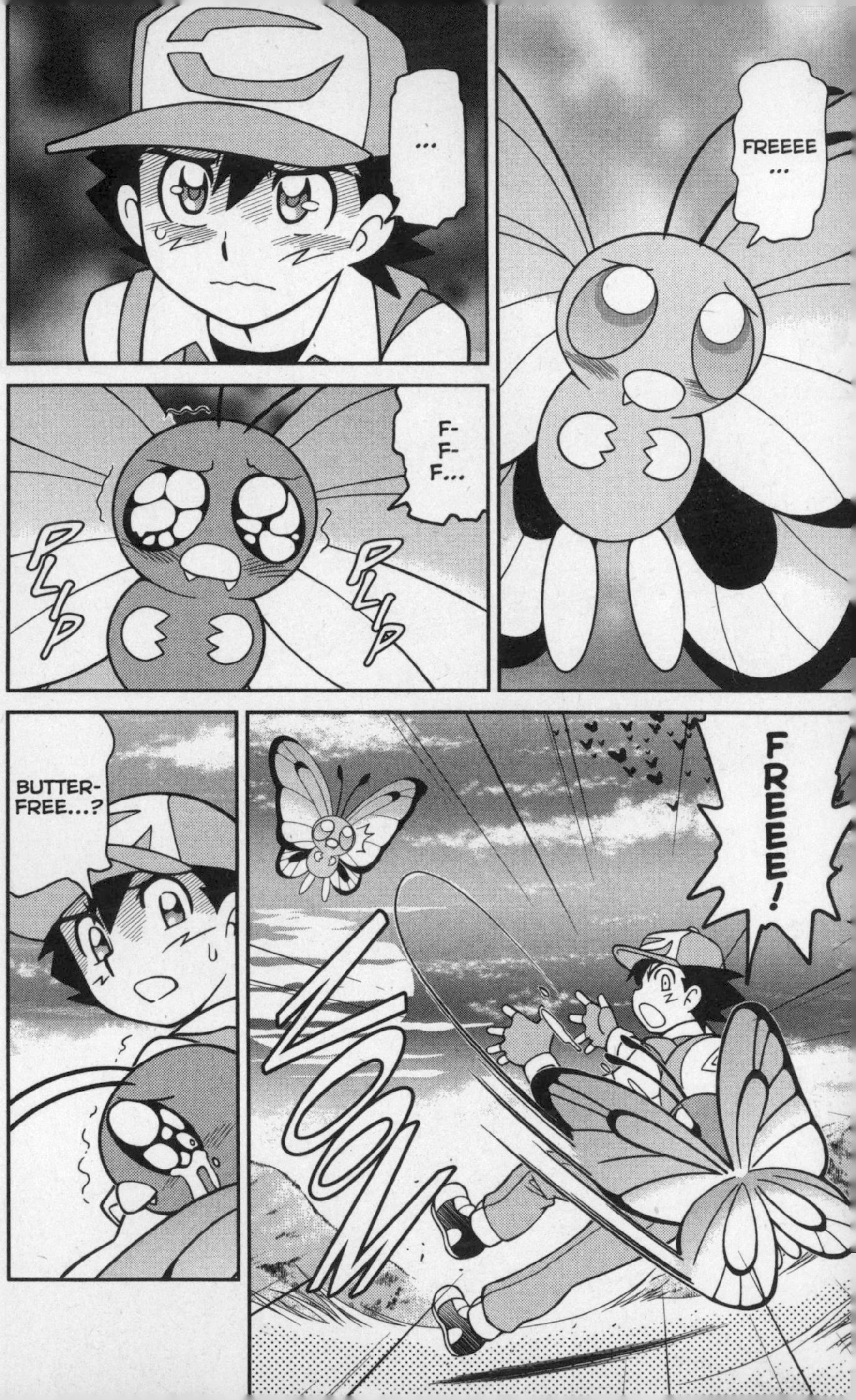
FREEEE ...
...
F- F- F...
PLIP
PLIP
FREEE!
WOOM
BUTTER-FREE...?

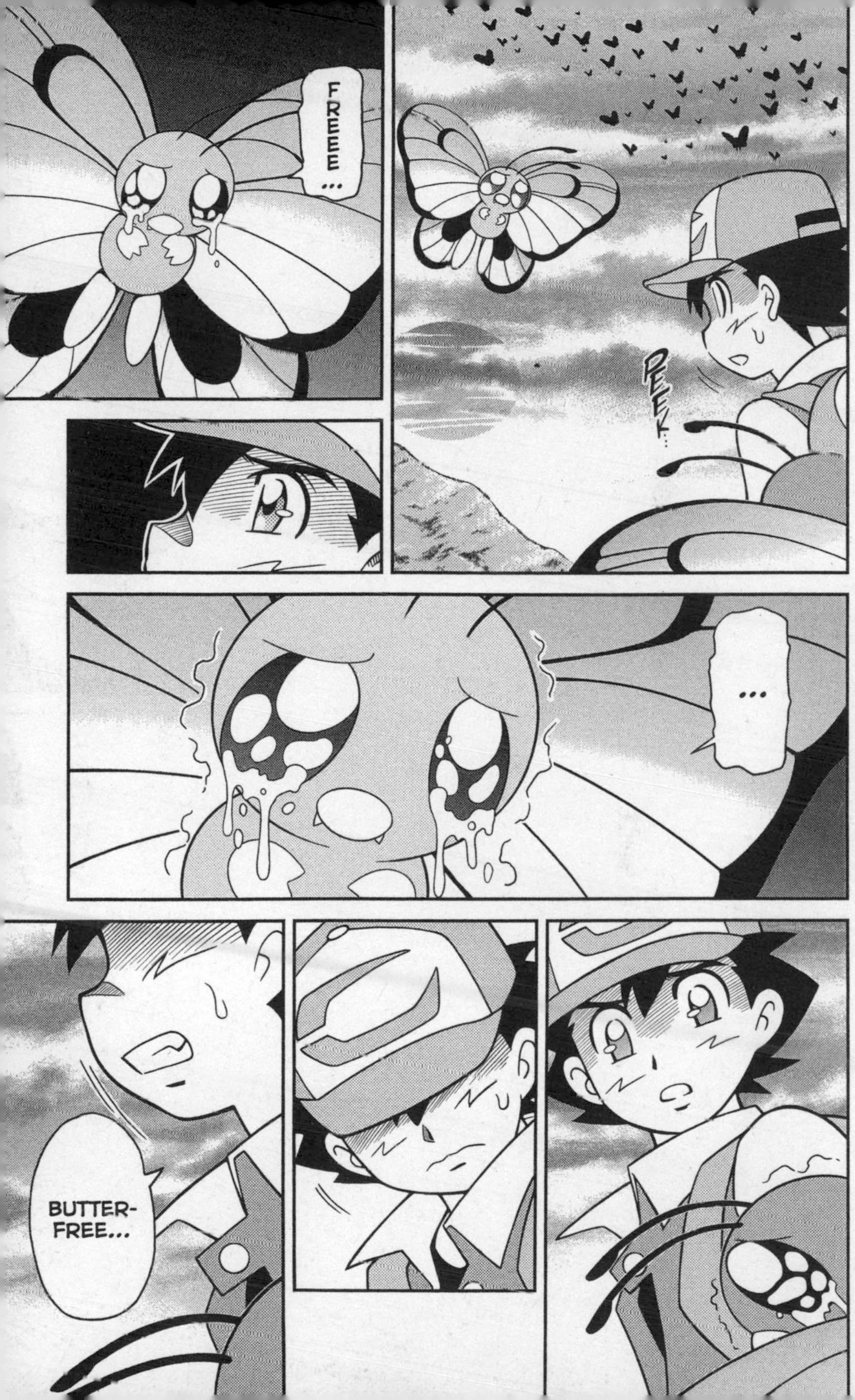
PEEK...
FREEE...
...
BUTTER-FREE...

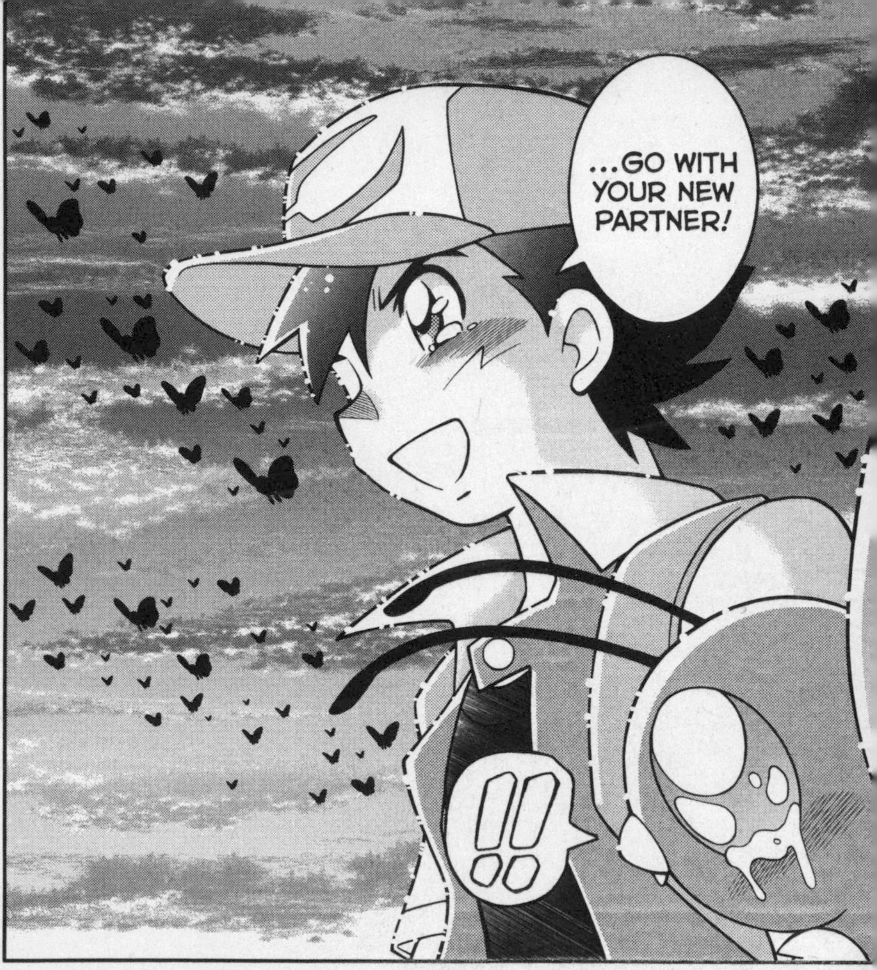
...GO WITH YOUR NEW PARTNER!
!!
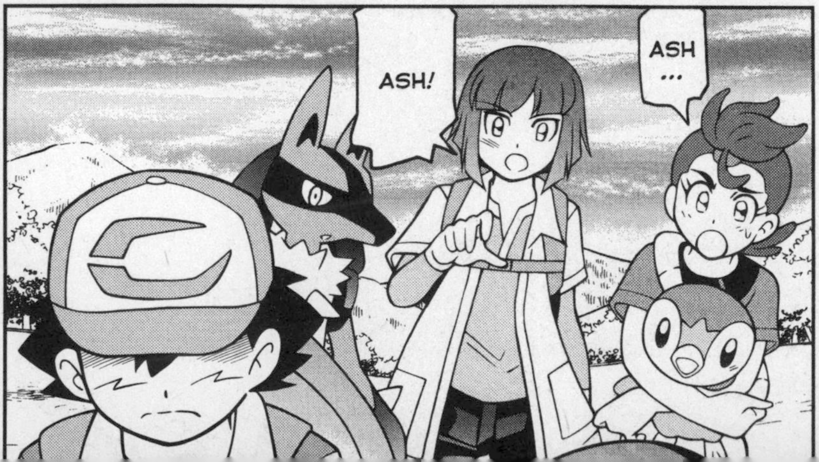
ASH ...
ASH!

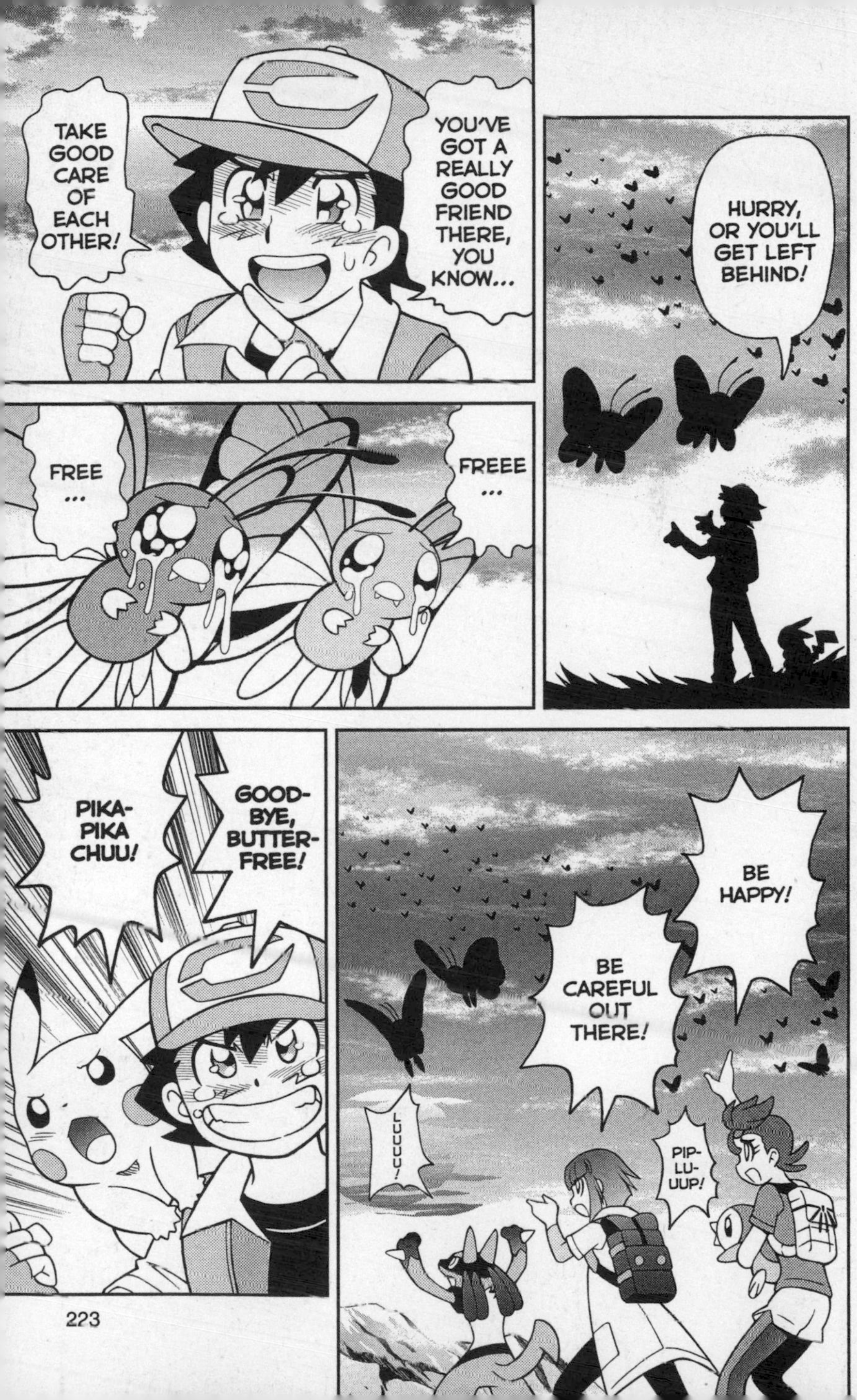
HURRY, OR YOU'LL GET LEFT BEHIND!
YOU'VE GOT A REALLY GOOD FRIEND THERE, YOU KNOW...
TAKE GOOD CARE OF EACH OTHER!
FREEE...
FREE...
BE HAPPY!
BE CAREFUL OUT THERE!
PIP-LUUP!
LUUUU!
GOOD-BYE, BUTTER-FREE!
PIKA-PIKA CHUU!

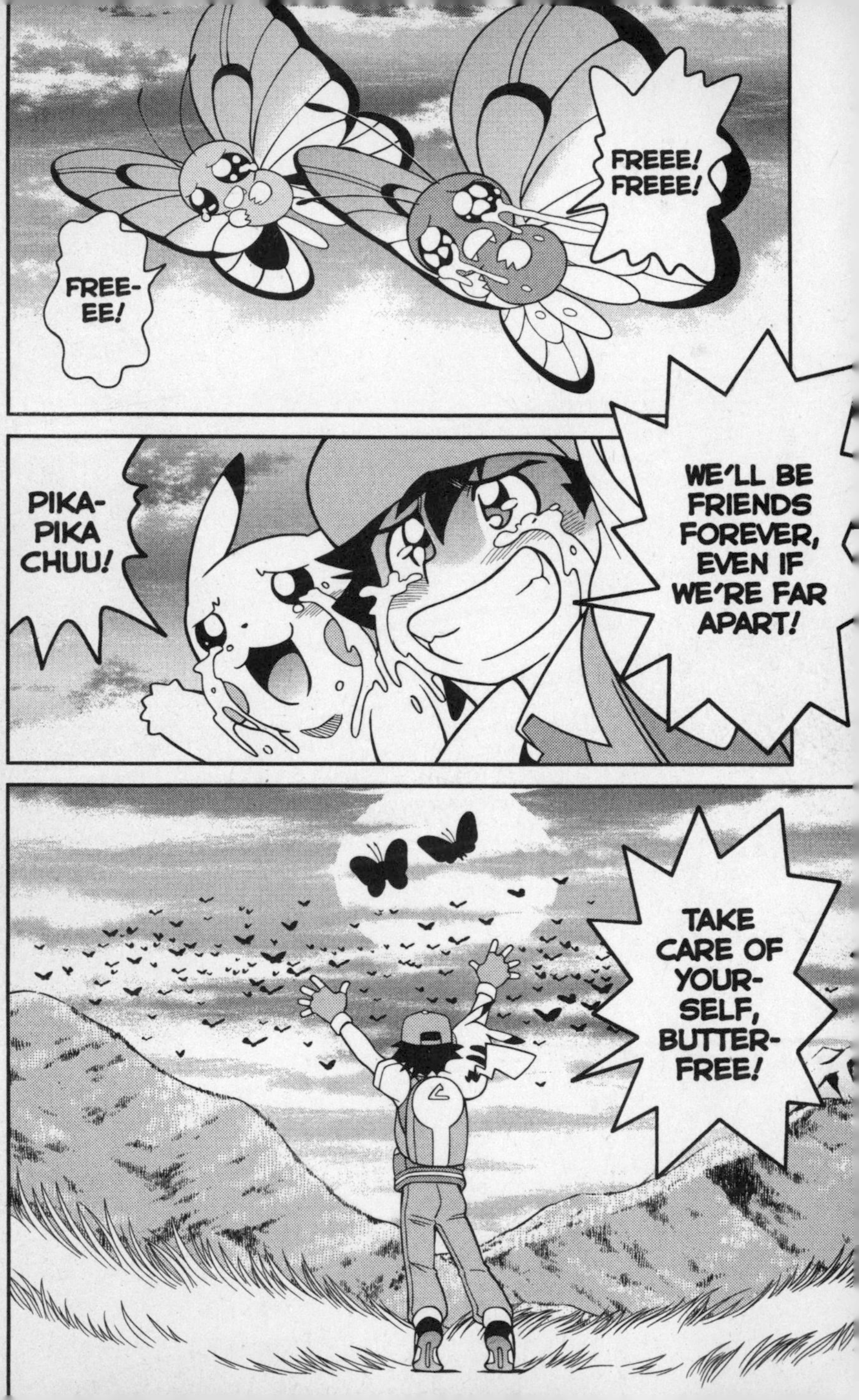
FREEE! FREEE!
FREE-EE!
WE'LL BE FRIENDS FOREVER, EVEN IF WE'RE FAR APART!
PIKA-PIKA CHUU!
TAKE CARE OF YOUR-SELF, BUTTER-FREE!

CHAPTER 11

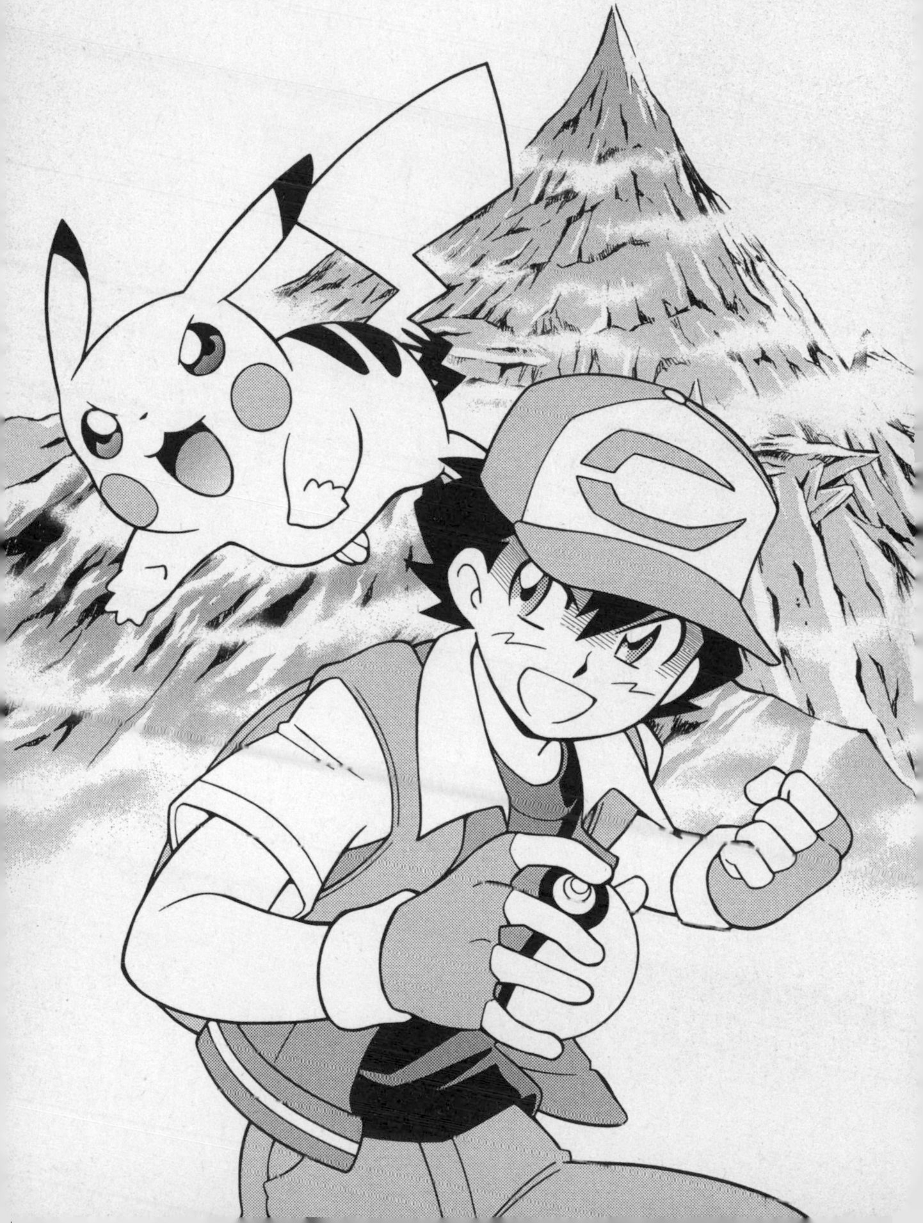

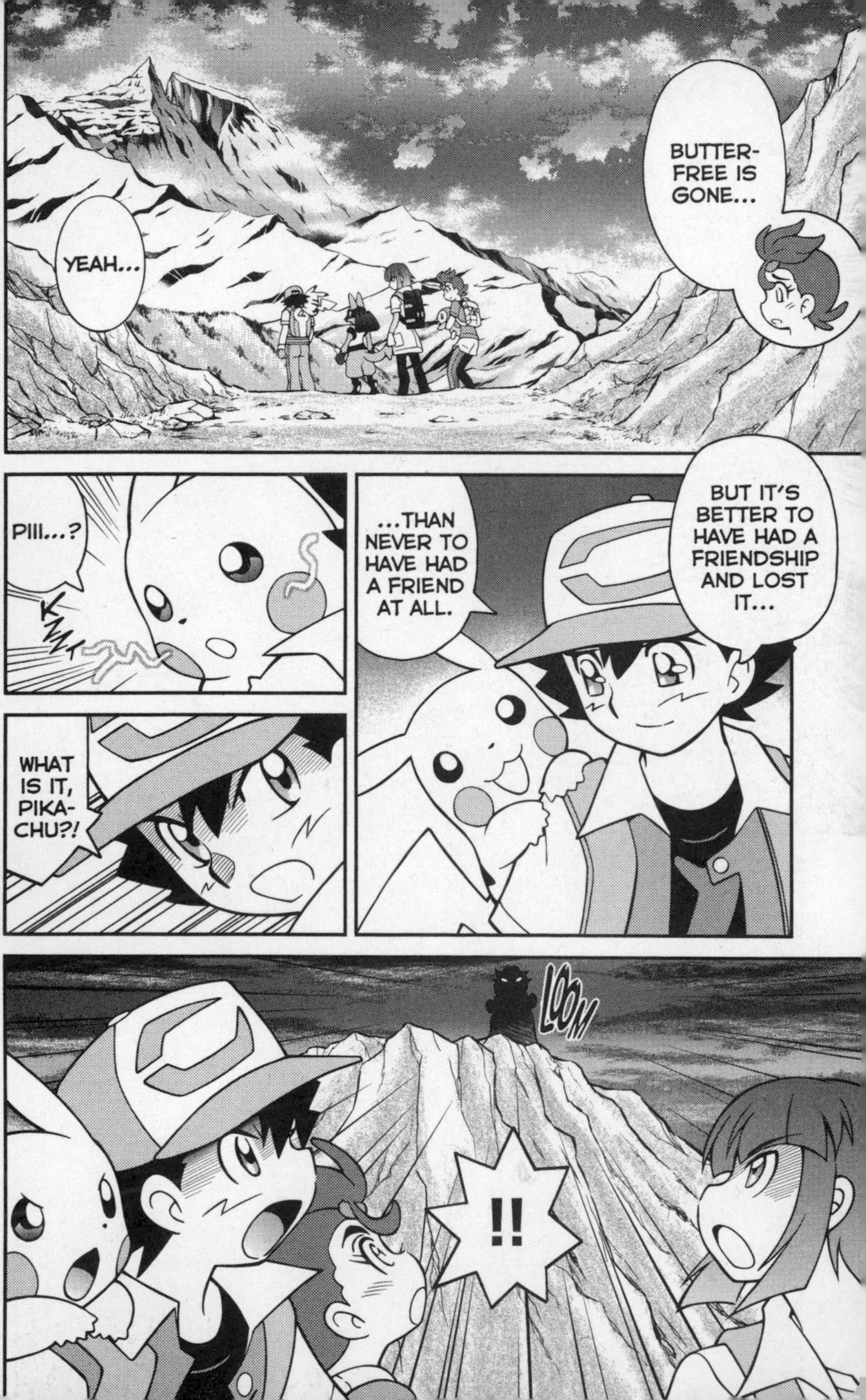
BUTTER-FREE IS GONE...
YEAH...
BUT IT'S BETTER TO HAVE HAD A FRIENDSHIP AND LOST IT...
...THAN NEVER TO HAVE HAD A FRIEND AT ALL.
PIII...?
WHAT IS IT, PIKACHU?!
LOOM
!!

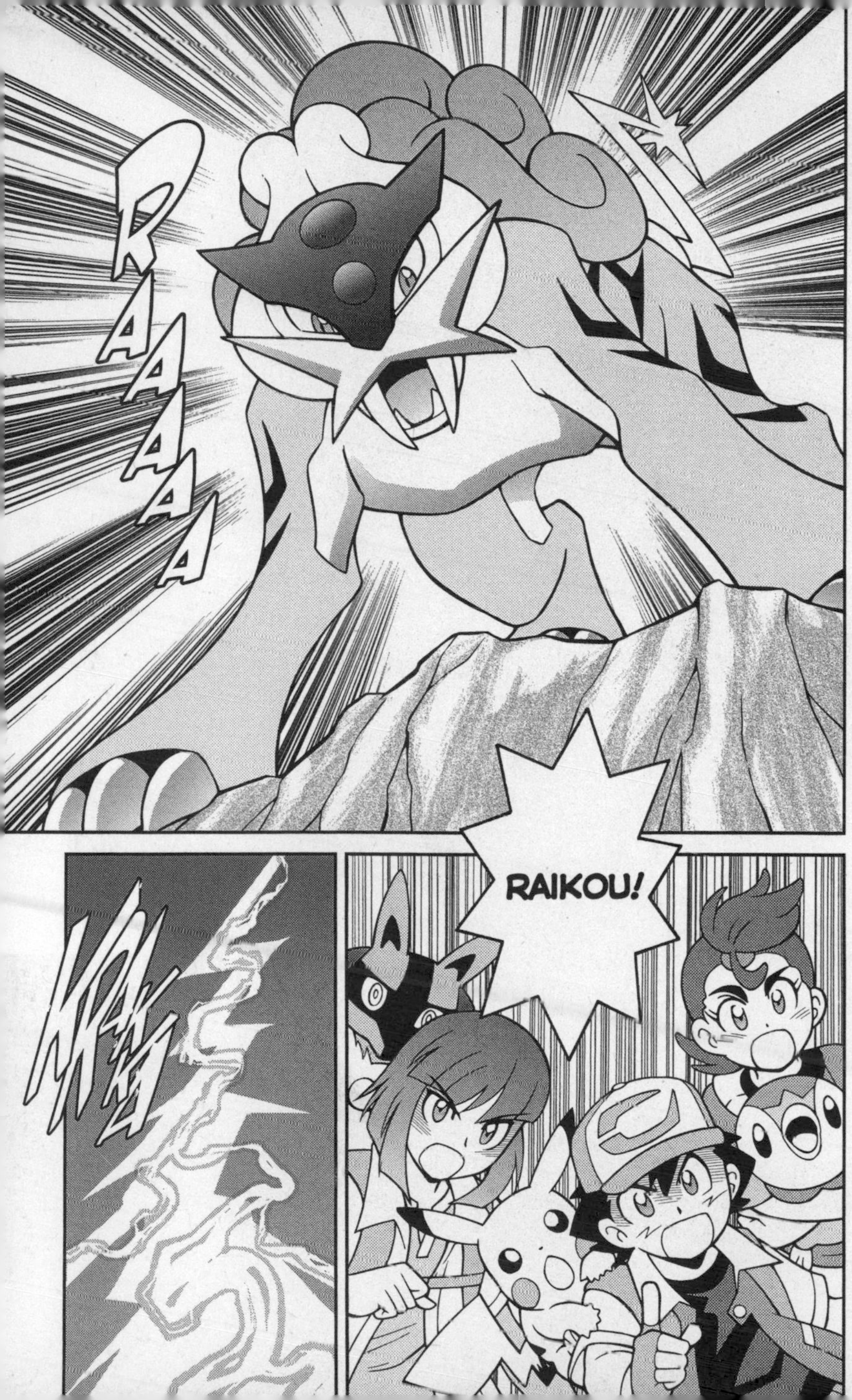
RAAAAAA
RAIKOU!

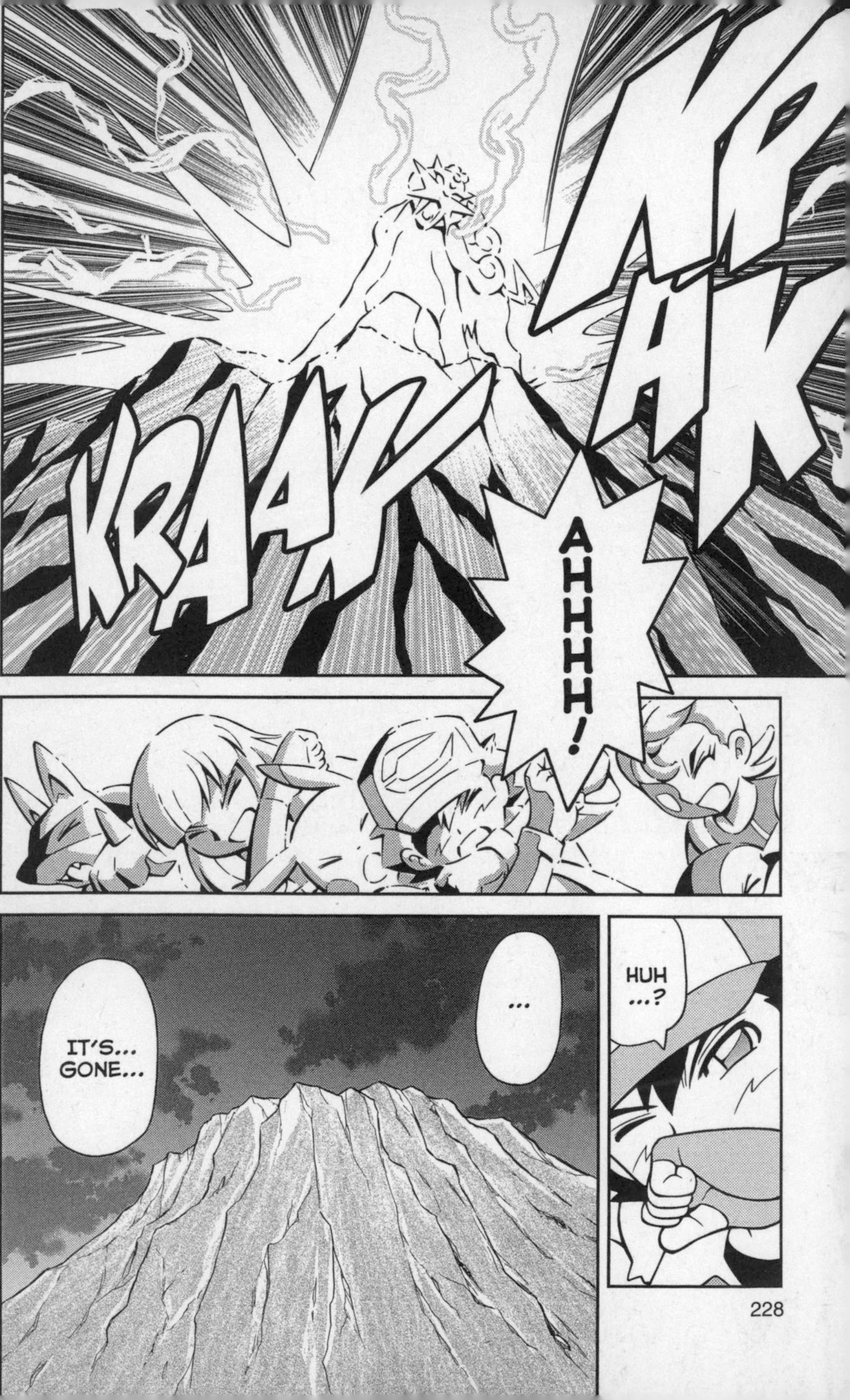
KRAAK
AHHHH!
HUH ...?
...
IT'S... GONE...

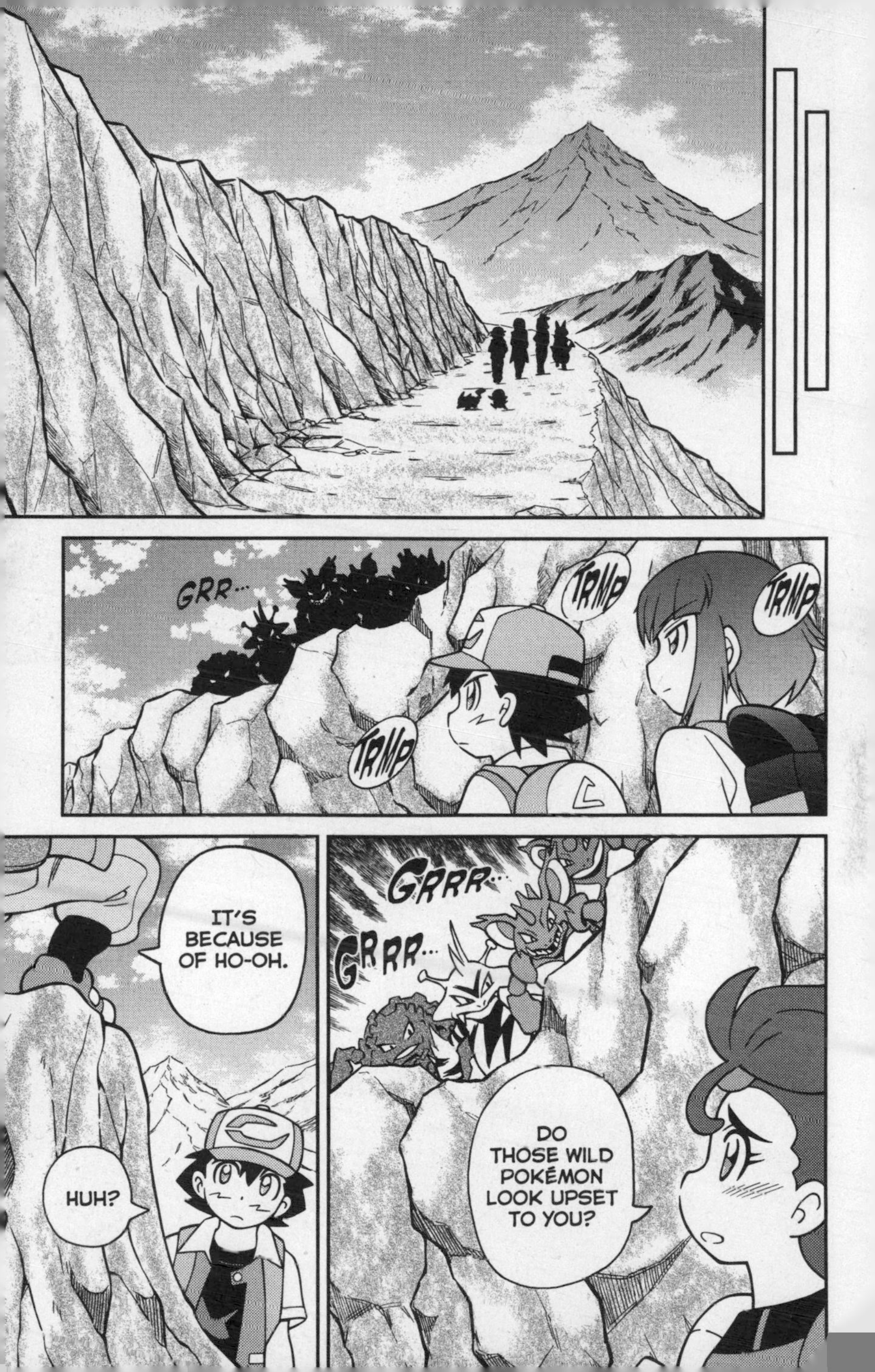
TRMP
TRMP
GRR...
TRMP
GRRR...
GRRR...
DO THOSE WILD POKÉMON LOOK UPSET TO YOU?
IT'S BECAUSE OF HO-OH.
HUH?

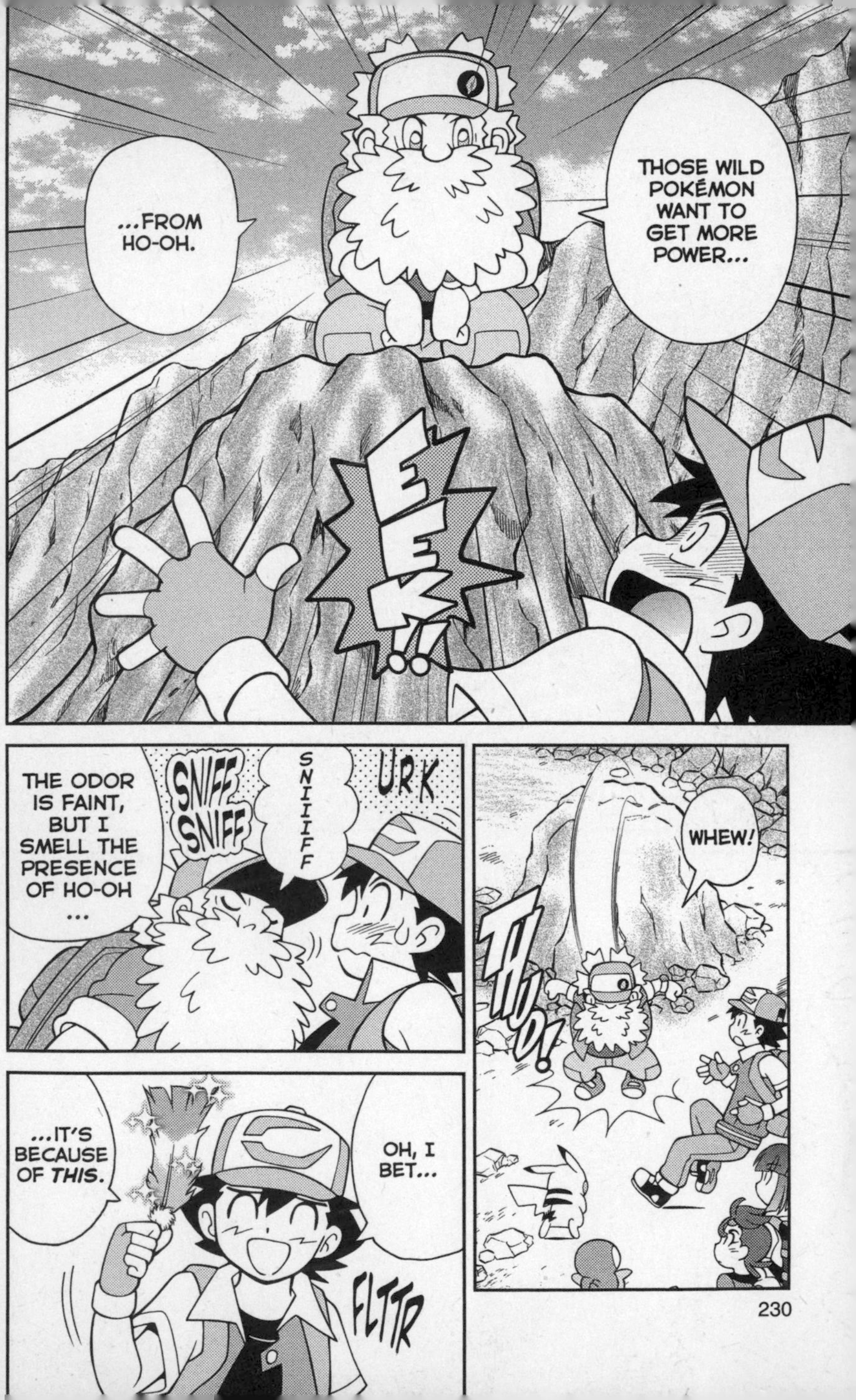
THOSE WILD POKÉMON WANT TO GET MORE POWER...
...FROM HO-OH.
EEK!!
WHEW!
THUD!
URK
SNIIIFF
SNIFF SNIFF
THE ODOR IS FAINT, BUT I SMELL THE PRESENCE OF HO-OH ...
OH, I BET...
...IT'S BECAUSE OF *THIS*.
FLTTR

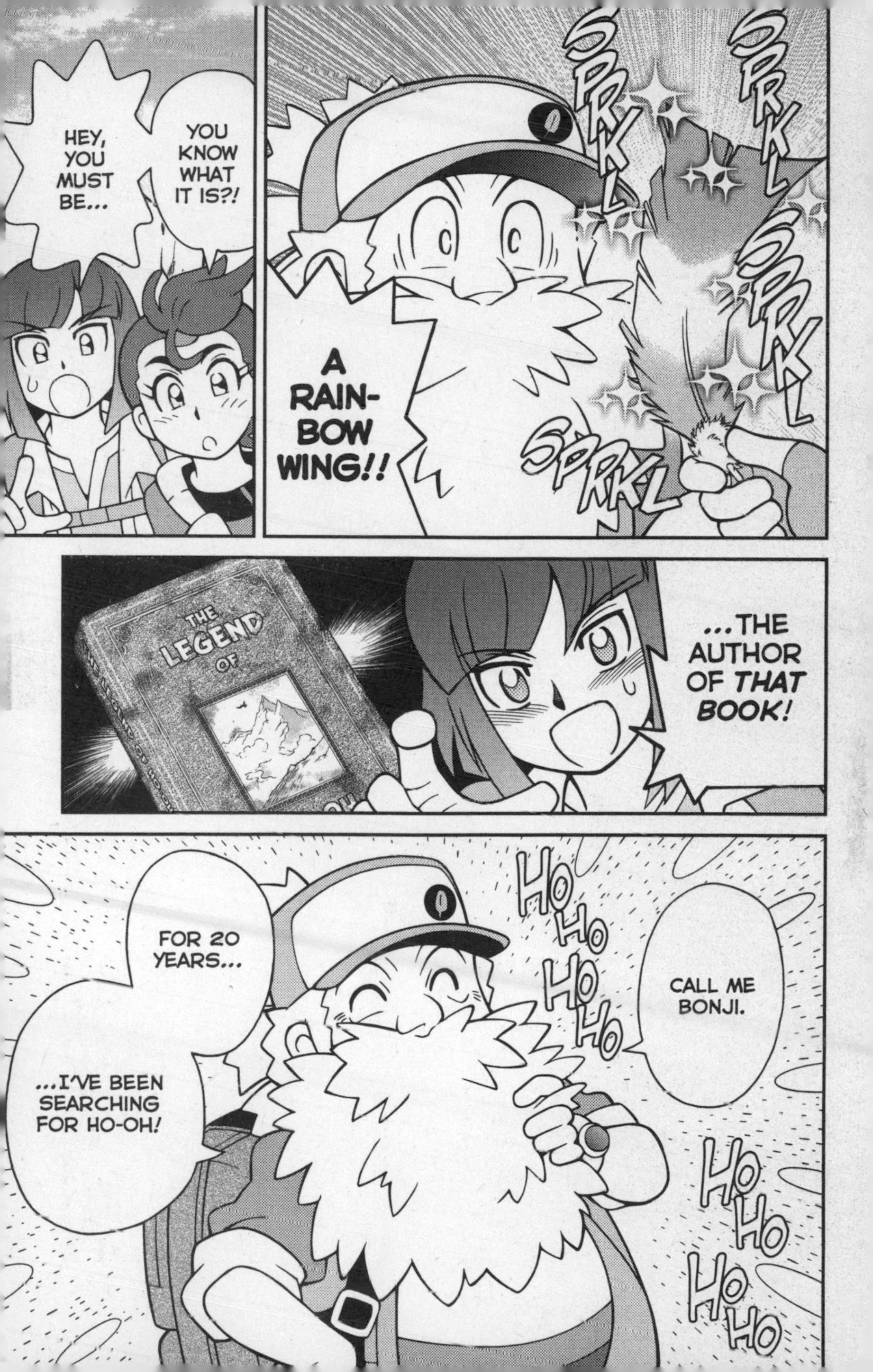
SPRKL
SPRKL
SPRKL
SPRKL
A RAIN-BOW WING!!
YOU KNOW WHAT IT IS?!
HEY, YOU MUST BE...
...THE AUTHOR OF *THAT BOOK!*
THE LEGEND OF
CALL ME BONJI.
HO HO HO HO
HO HO HO HO
FOR 20 YEARS...
...I'VE BEEN SEARCHING FOR HO-OH!

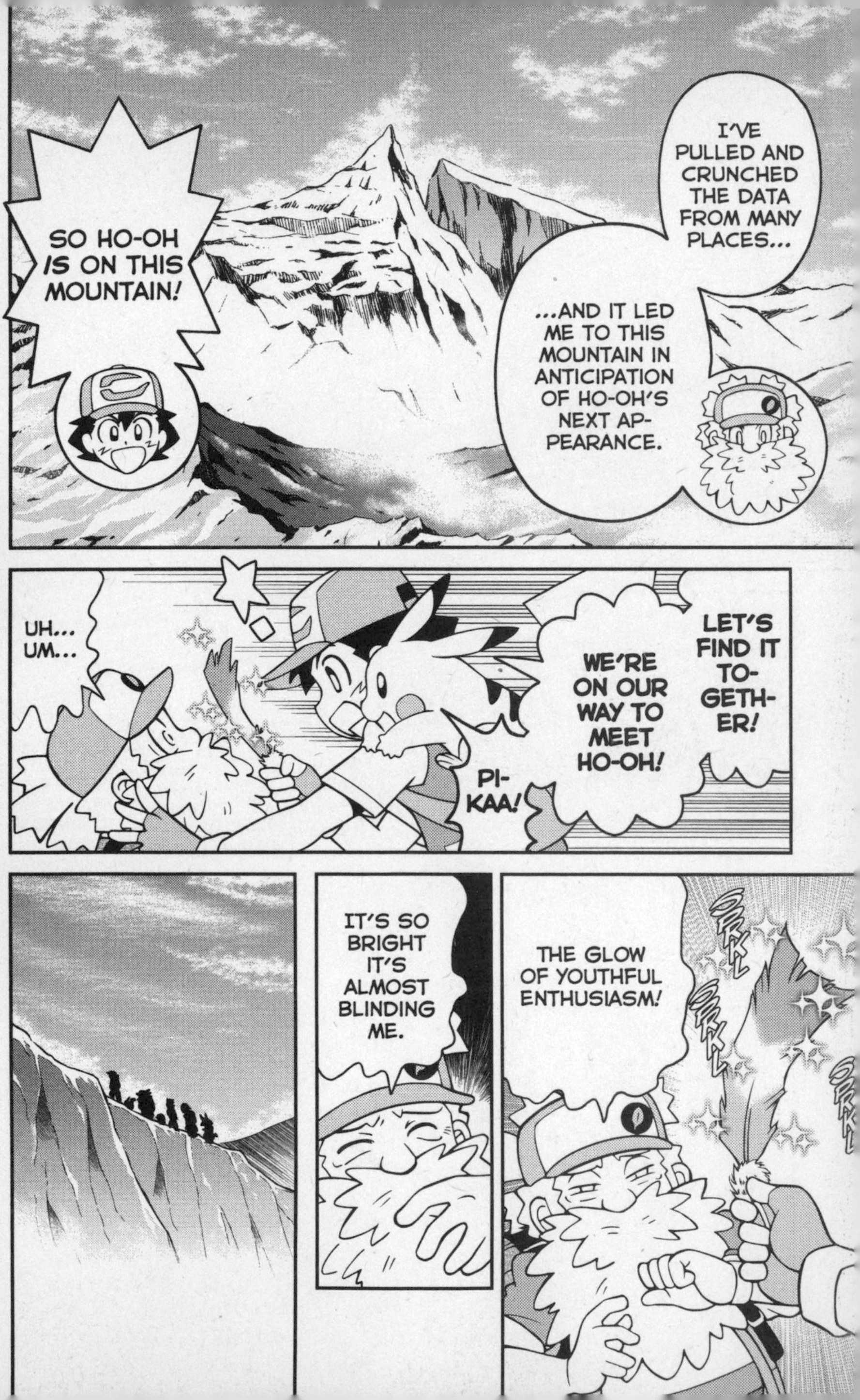
I'VE PULLED AND CRUNCHED THE DATA FROM MANY PLACES...
...AND IT LED ME TO THIS MOUNTAIN IN ANTICIPATION OF HO-OH'S NEXT AP-PEARANCE.
SO HO-OH *IS* ON THIS MOUNTAIN!
LET'S FIND IT TO-GETH-ER!
WE'RE ON OUR WAY TO MEET HO-OH!
PI-KAA!
UH... UM...
SPRKL
SPRKL
THE GLOW OF YOUTHFUL ENTHUSIASM!
IT'S SO BRIGHT IT'S ALMOST BLINDING ME.

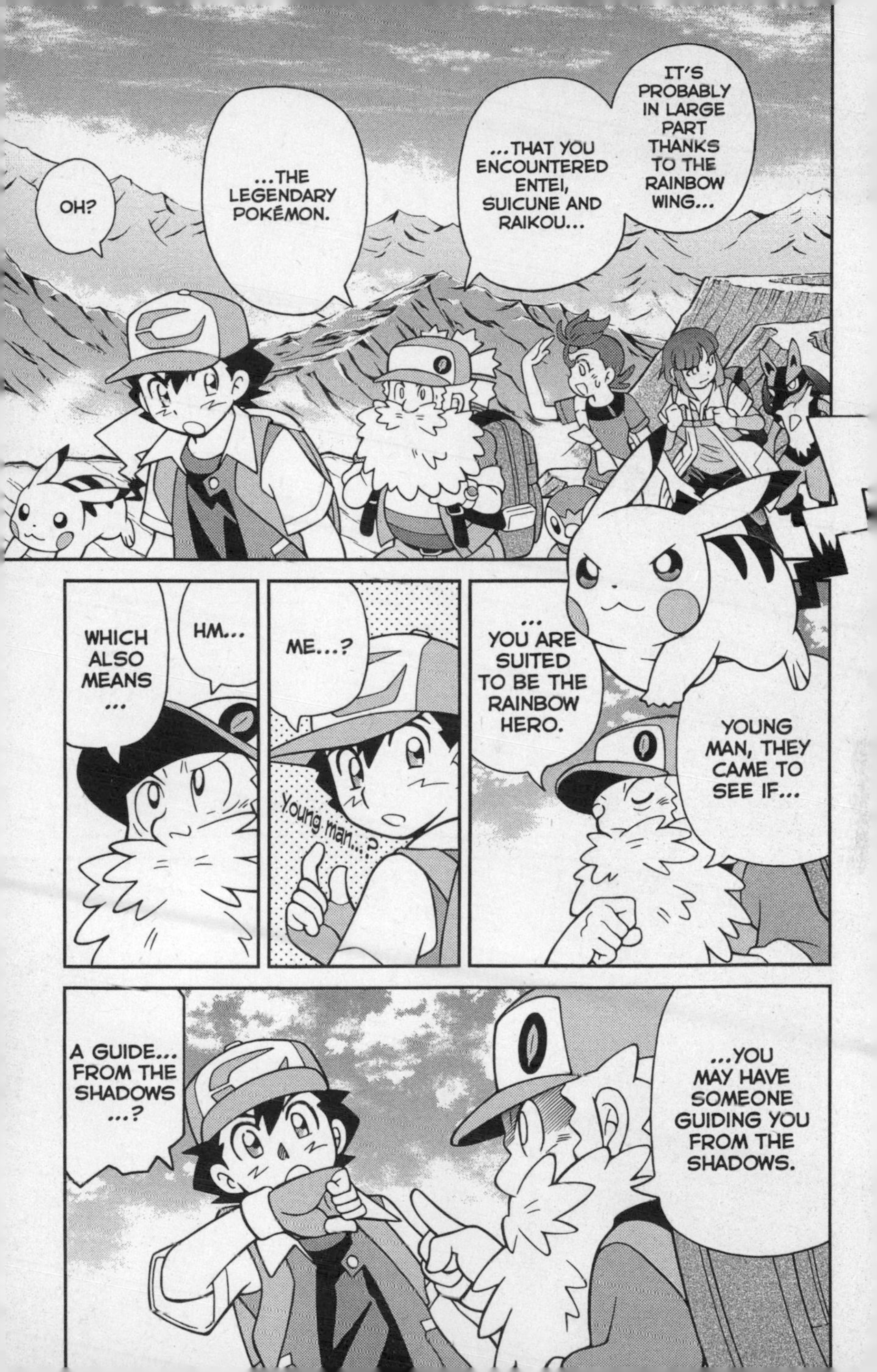
IT'S PROBABLY IN LARGE PART THANKS TO THE RAINBOW WING...
...THAT YOU ENCOUNTERED ENTEI, SUICUNE AND RAIKOU...
...THE LEGENDARY POKÉMON.
OH?
YOUNG MAN, THEY CAME TO SEE IF...
... YOU ARE SUITED TO BE THE RAINBOW HERO.
ME...?
Young man...?
HM...
WHICH ALSO MEANS ...
...YOU MAY HAVE SOMEONE GUIDING YOU FROM THE SHADOWS.
A GUIDE... FROM THE SHADOWS ...?

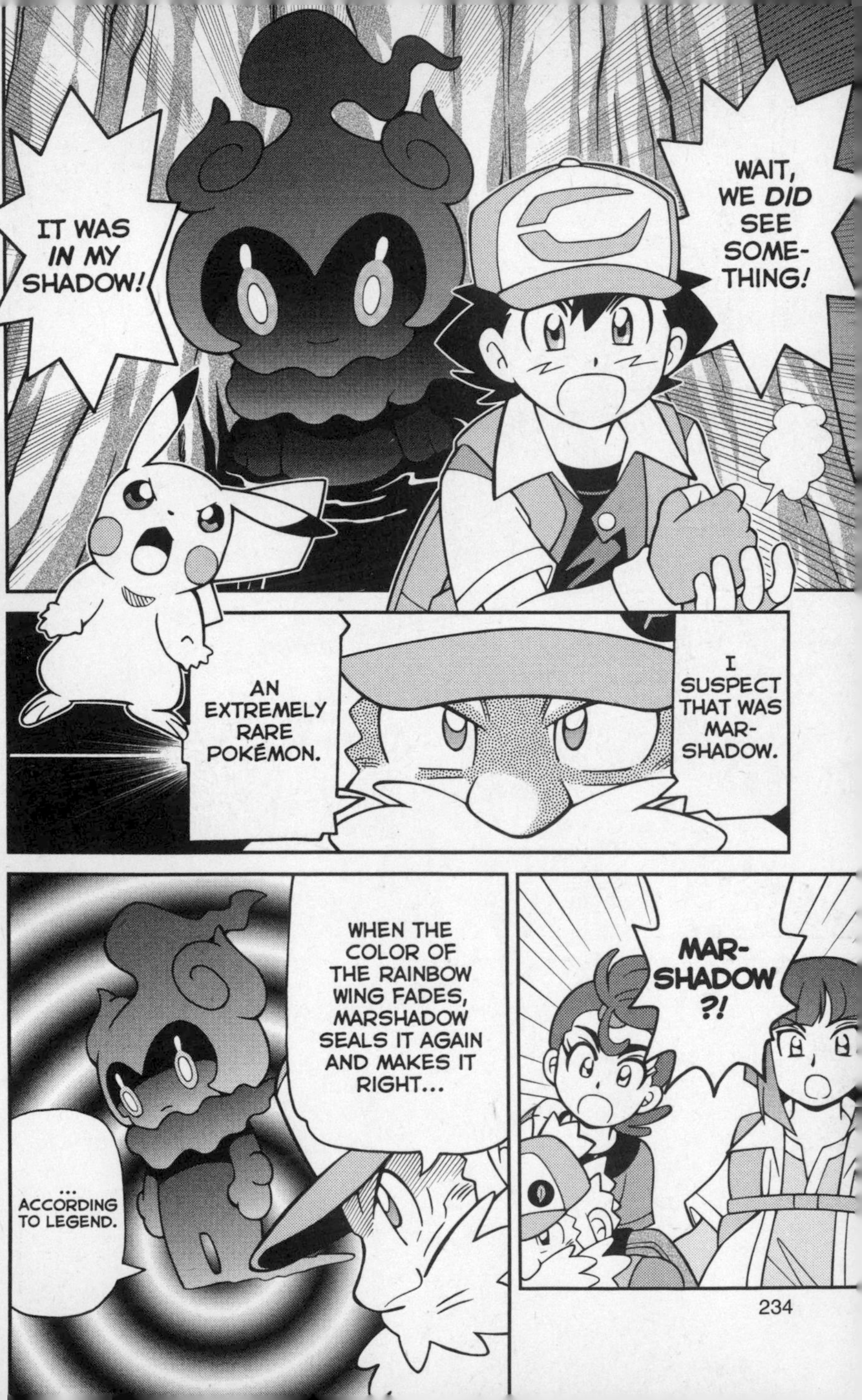
WAIT, WE *DID* SEE SOME-THING!
IT WAS *IN MY* SHADOW!
I SUSPECT THAT WAS MAR-SHADOW.
AN EXTREMELY RARE POKÉMON.
MAR-SHADOW?!
WHEN THE COLOR OF THE RAINBOW WING FADES, MARSHADOW SEALS IT AGAIN AND MAKES IT RIGHT...
...ACCORDING TO LEGEND.

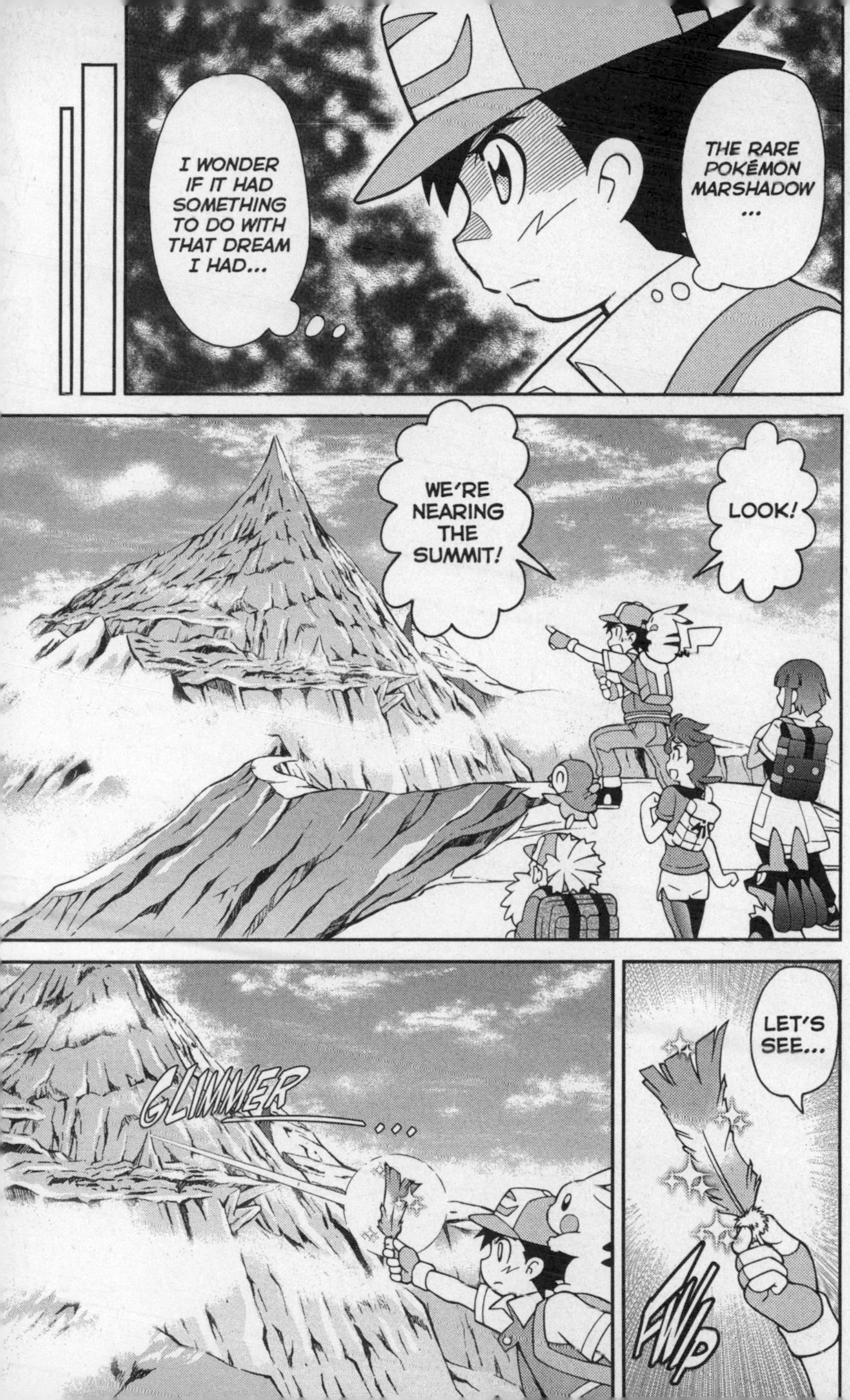
THE RARE POKÉMON MARSHADOW ...
I WONDER IF IT HAD SOMETHING TO DO WITH THAT DREAM I HAD...
LOOK!
WE'RE NEARING THE SUMMIT!
LET'S SEE...
GLIMMER ...

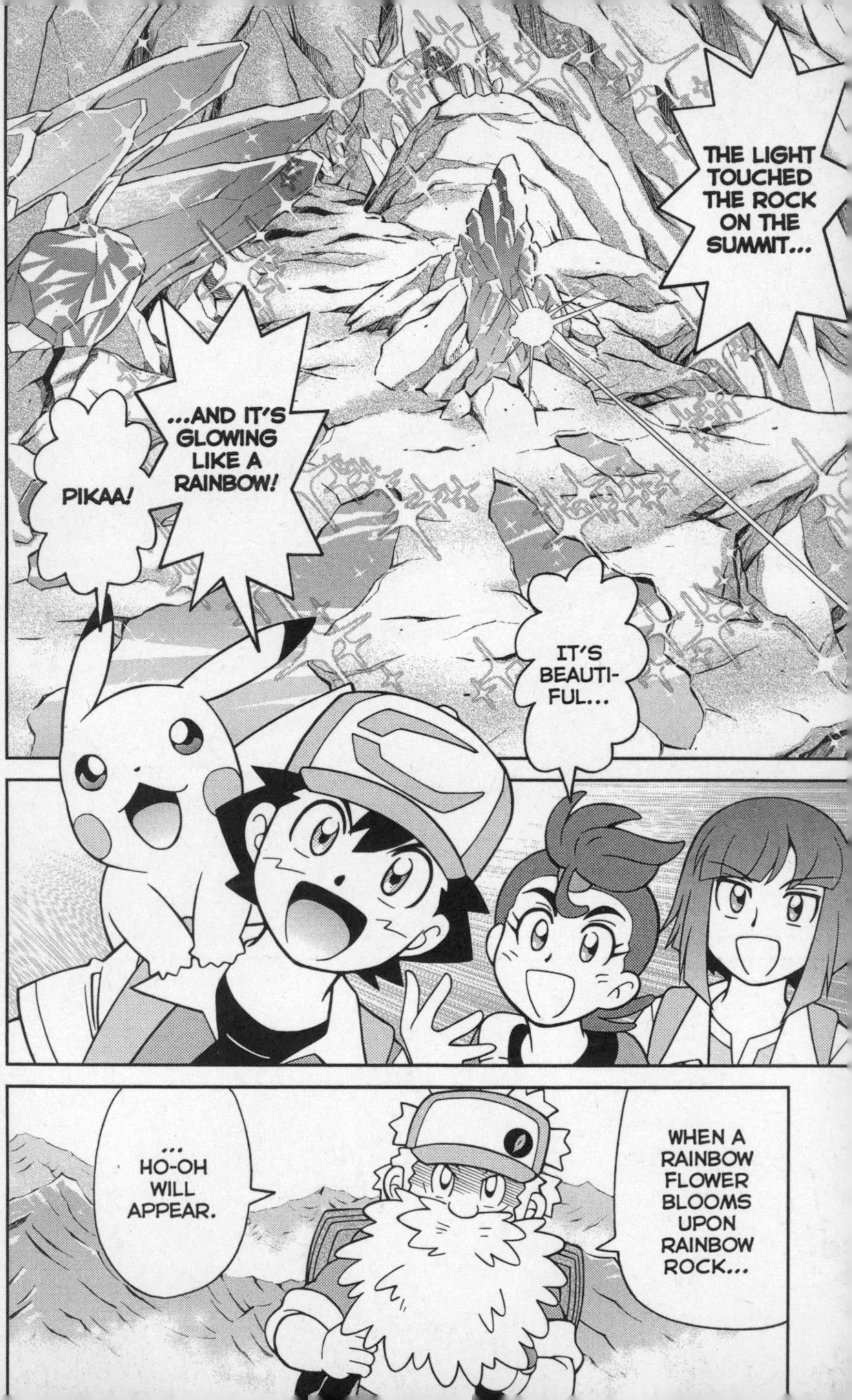
THE LIGHT TOUCHED THE ROCK ON THE SUMMIT...
...AND IT'S GLOWING LIKE A RAINBOW!
PIKAA!
IT'S BEAUTI-FUL...
WHEN A RAINBOW FLOWER BLOOMS UPON RAINBOW ROCK...
... HO-OH WILL APPEAR.

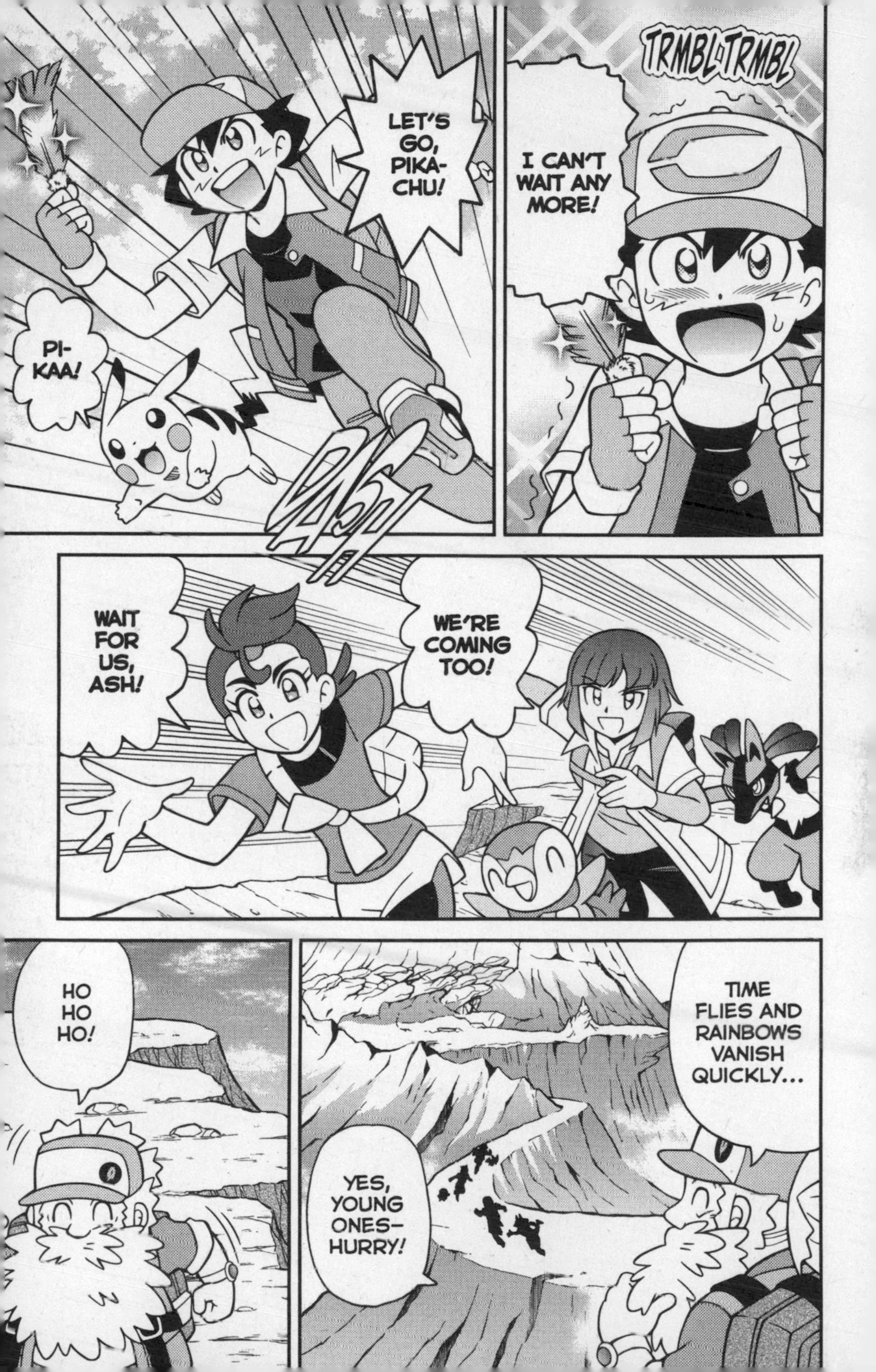
TRMBL TRMBL
I CAN'T WAIT ANY MORE!
LET'S GO, PIKACHU!
PI-KAA!
WE'RE COMING TOO!
WAIT FOR US, ASH!
TIME FLIES AND RAINBOWS VANISH QUICKLY...
YES, YOUNG ONES—HURRY!
HO HO HO!

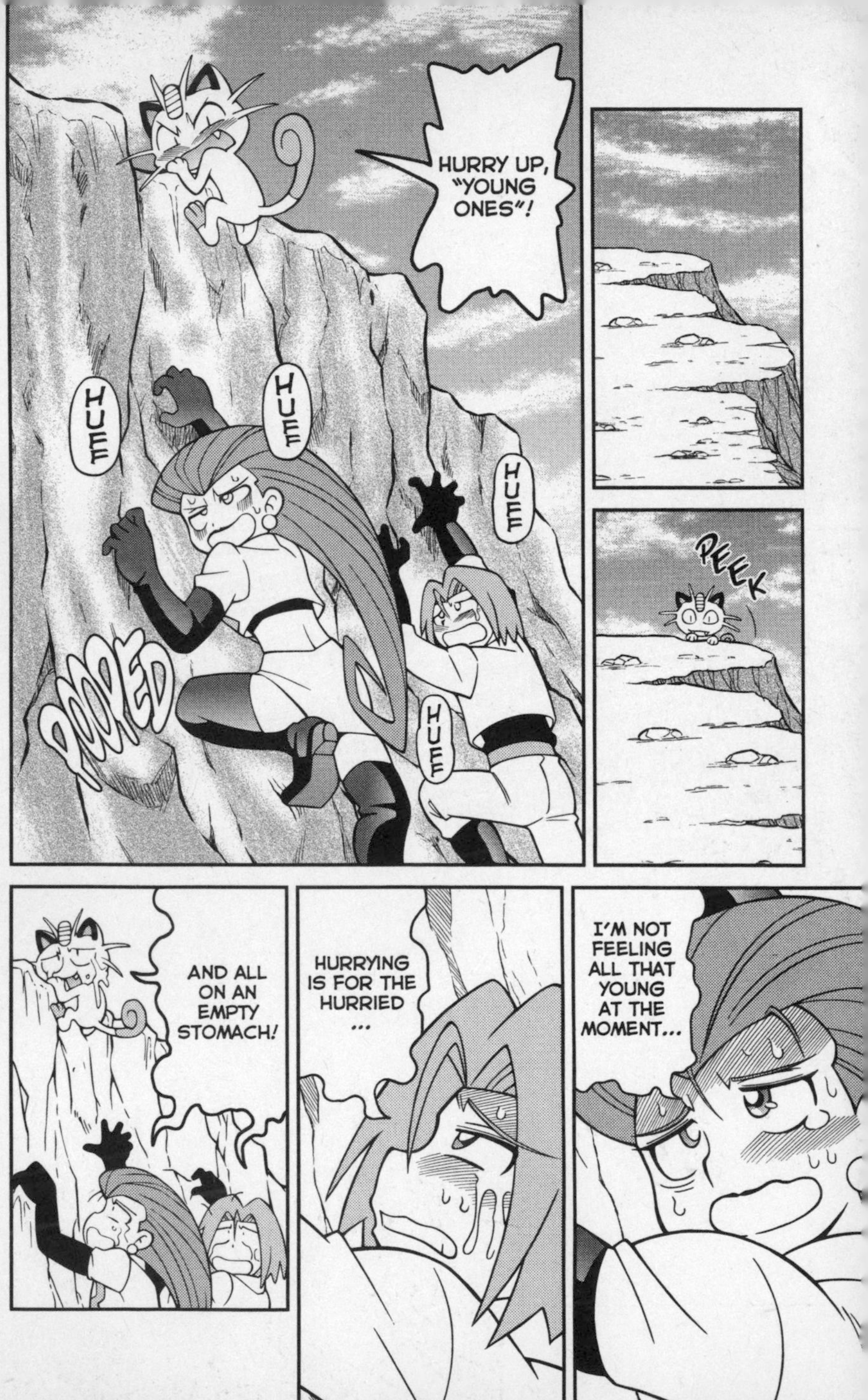
PEEK
HURRY UP, "YOUNG ONES"!
HUFF
HUFF
HUFF
HUFF
POOPED
I'M NOT FEELING ALL THAT YOUNG AT THE MOMENT...
HURRYING IS FOR THE HURRIED...
AND ALL ON AN EMPTY STOMACH!

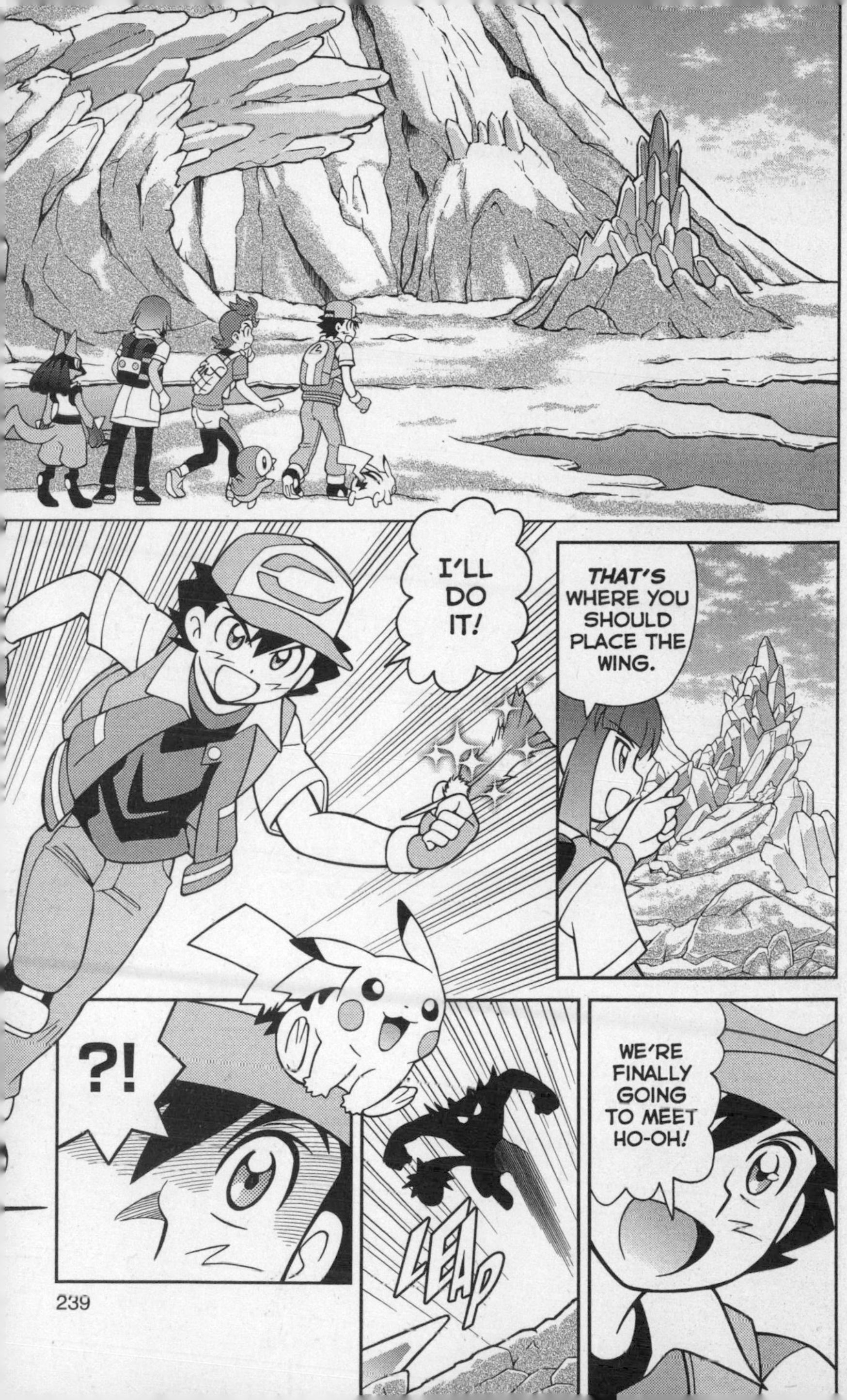

THAT'S WHERE YOU SHOULD PLACE THE WING.
I'LL DO IT!
WE'RE FINALLY GOING TO MEET HO-OH!
LEAP
?!

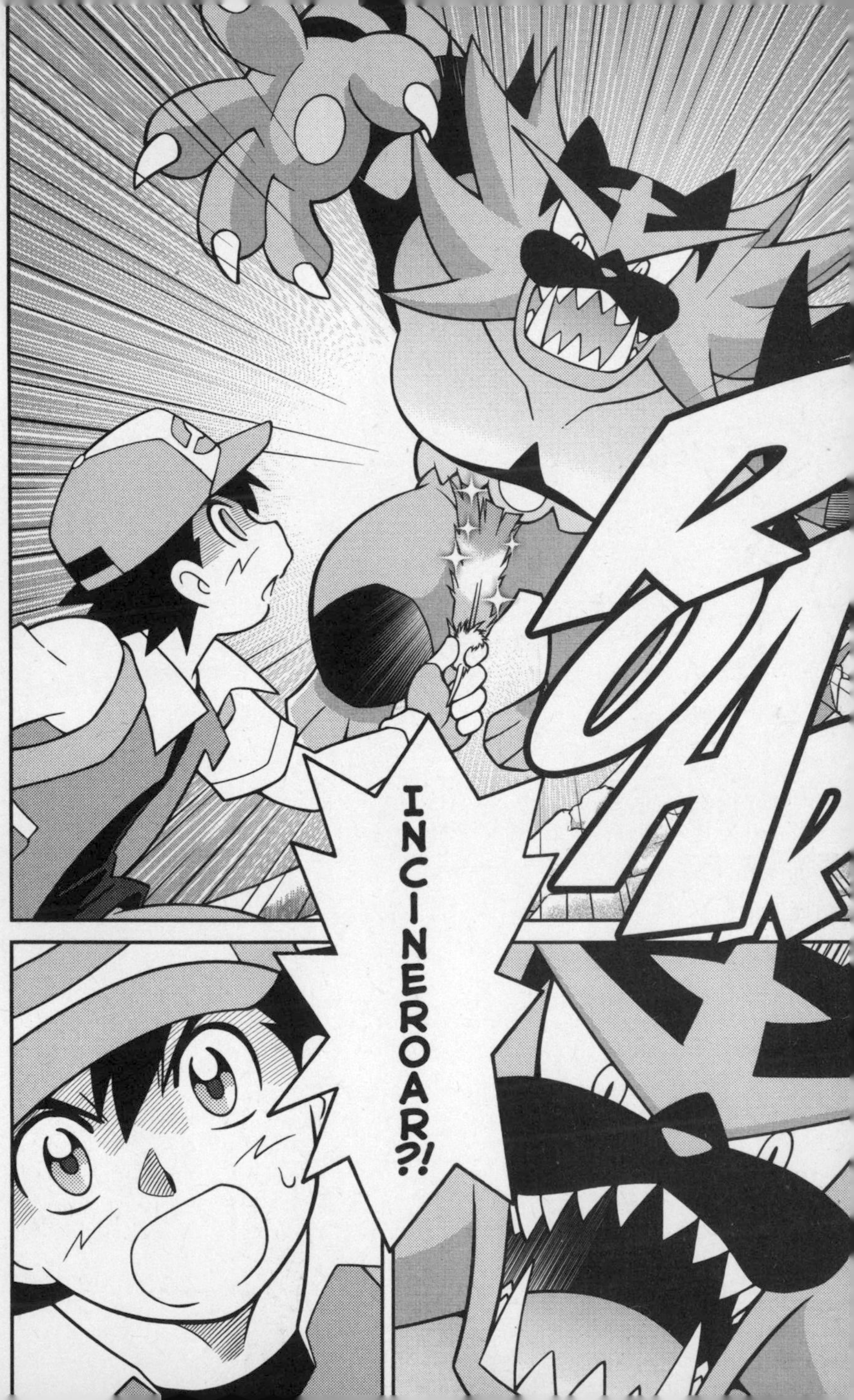
INCINEROAR?!

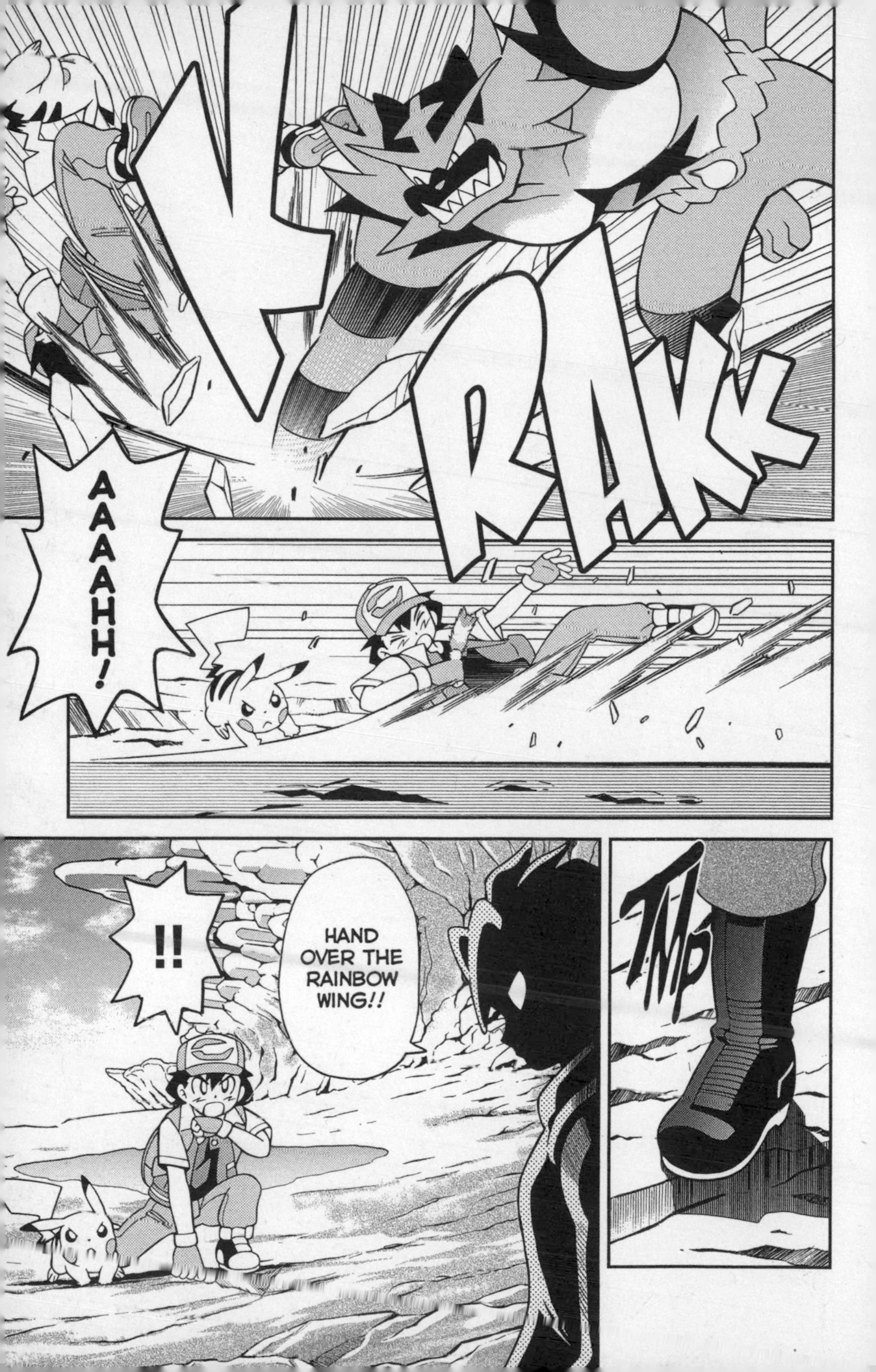
KRAK
AAAAAHH!
TMP
HAND OVER THE RAINBOW WING!!
!!

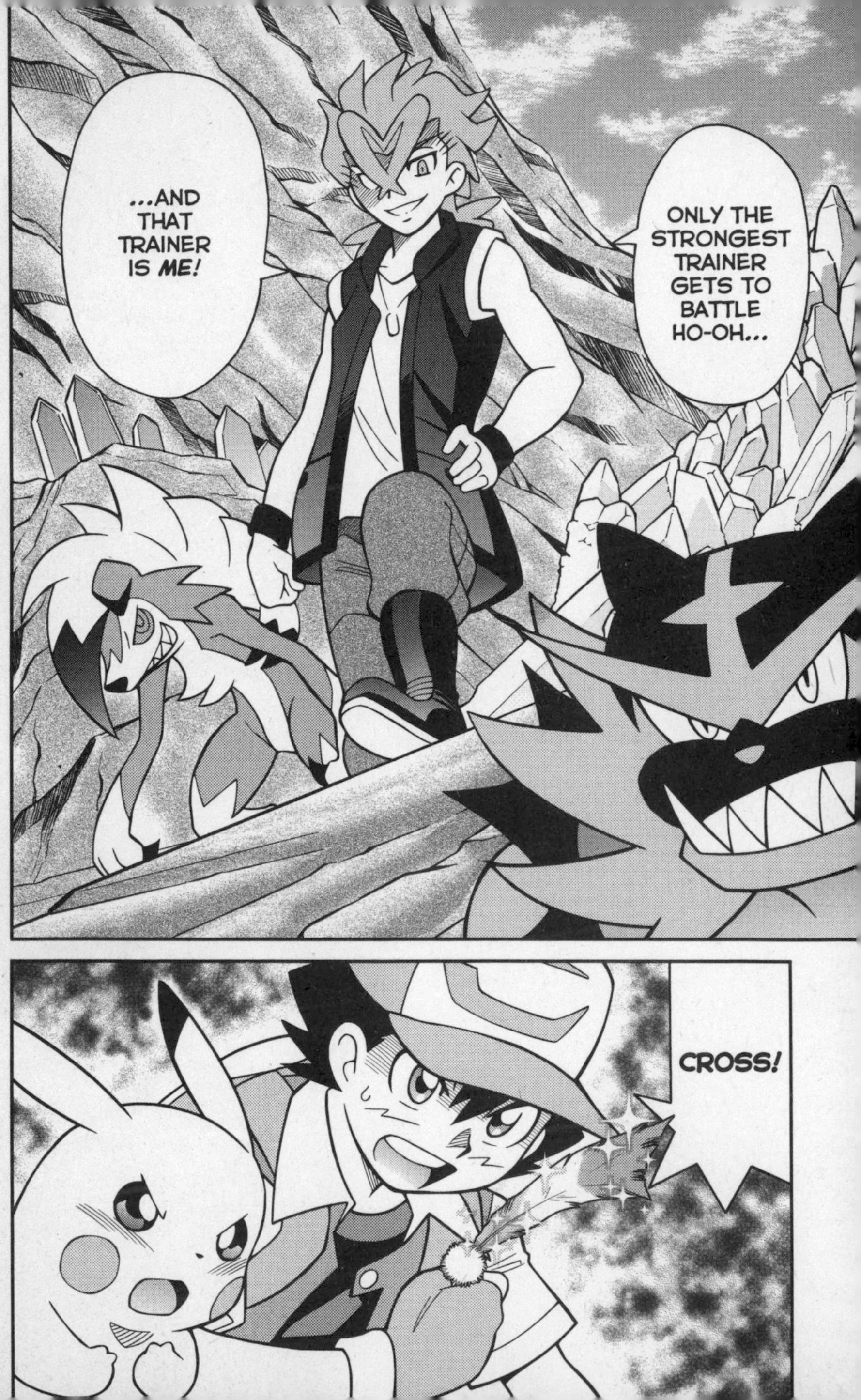
ONLY THE STRONGEST TRAINER GETS TO BATTLE HO-OH...
...AND THAT TRAINER IS *ME*!
CROSS!

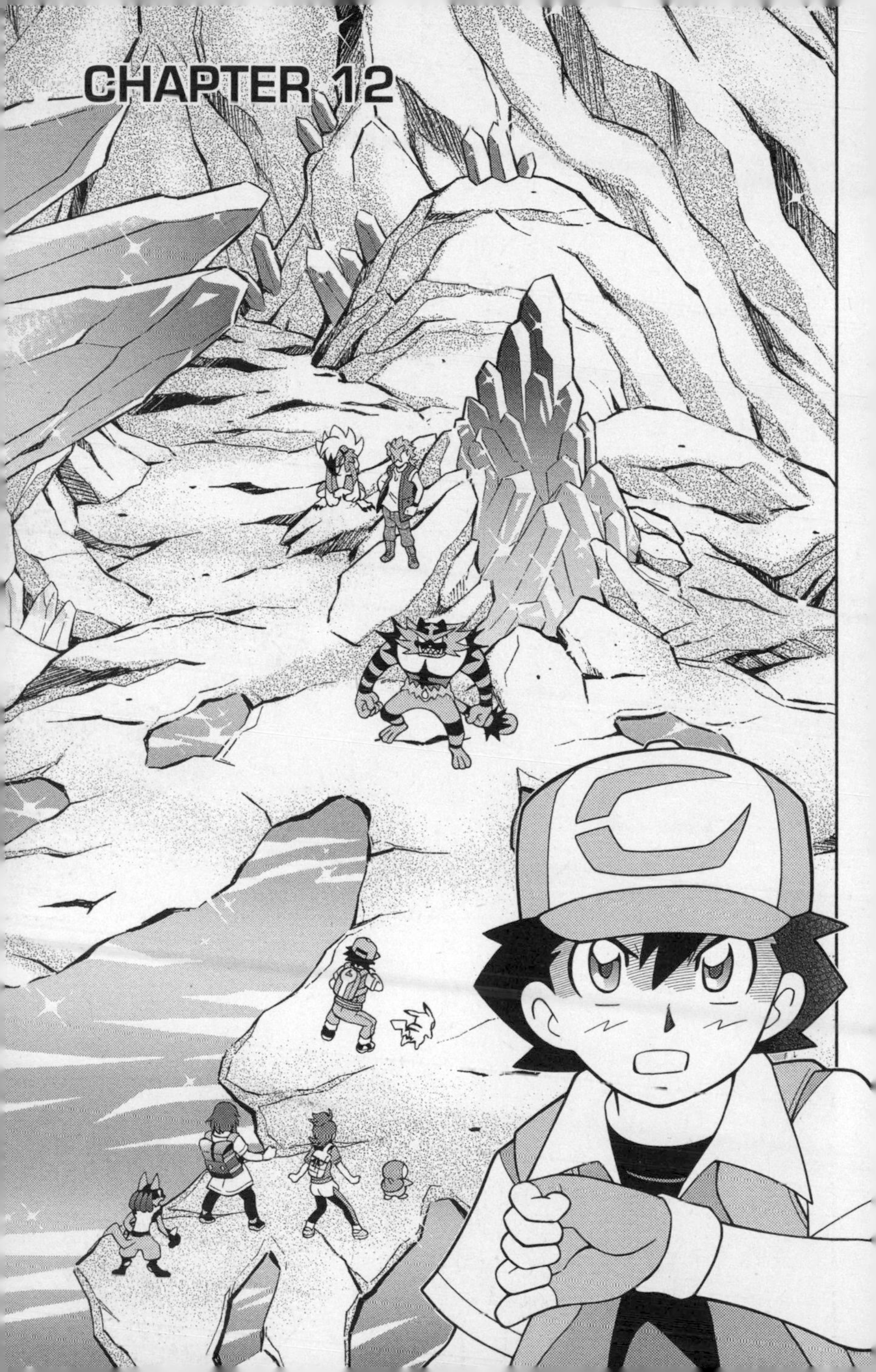
CHAPTER 12

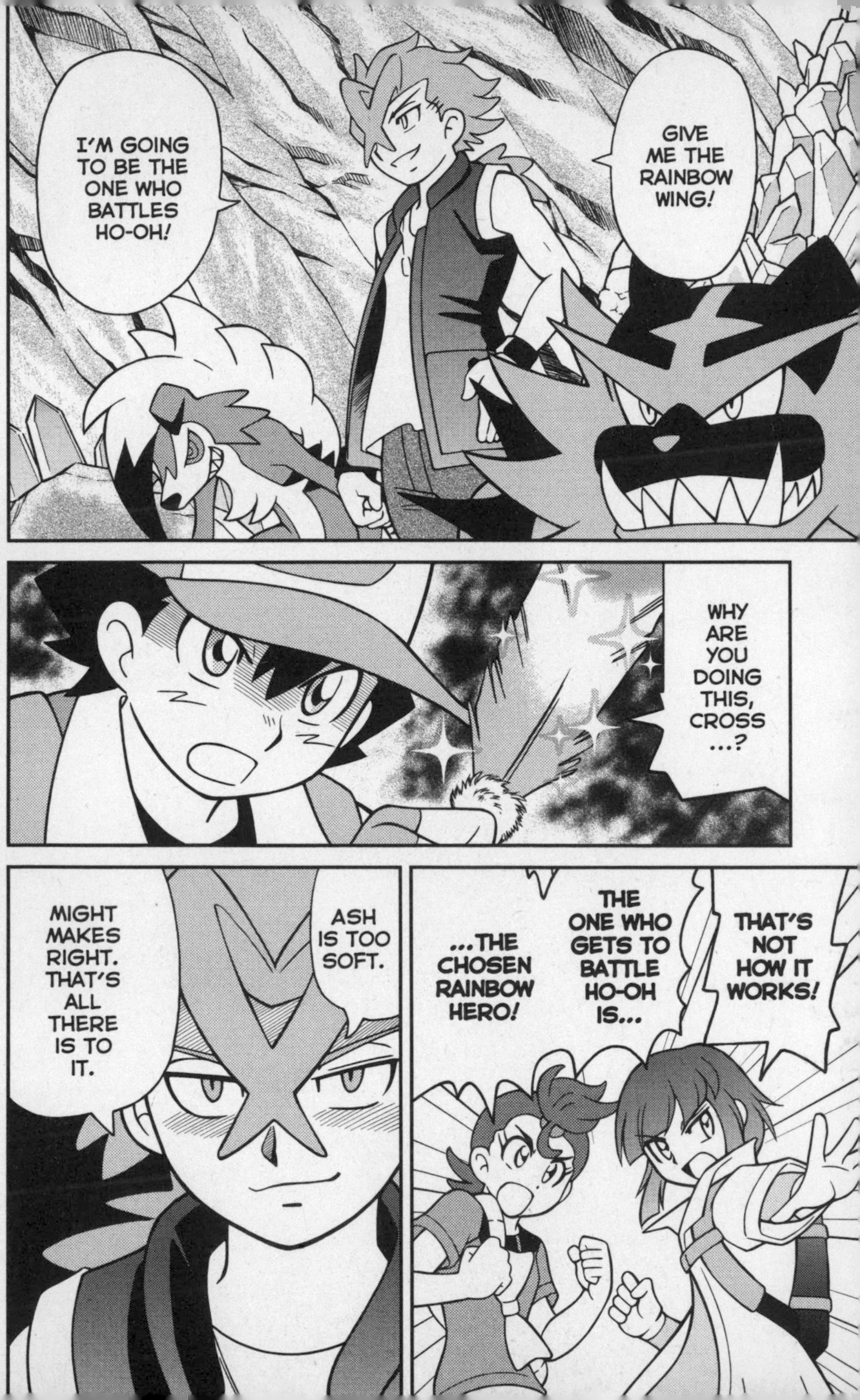
GIVE ME THE RAINBOW WING!
I'M GOING TO BE THE ONE WHO BATTLES HO-OH!
WHY ARE YOU DOING THIS, CROSS ...?
THAT'S NOT HOW IT WORKS!
THE ONE WHO GETS TO BATTLE HO-OH IS...
...THE CHOSEN RAINBOW HERO!
ASH IS TOO SOFT.
MIGHT MAKES RIGHT. THAT'S ALL THERE IS TO IT.

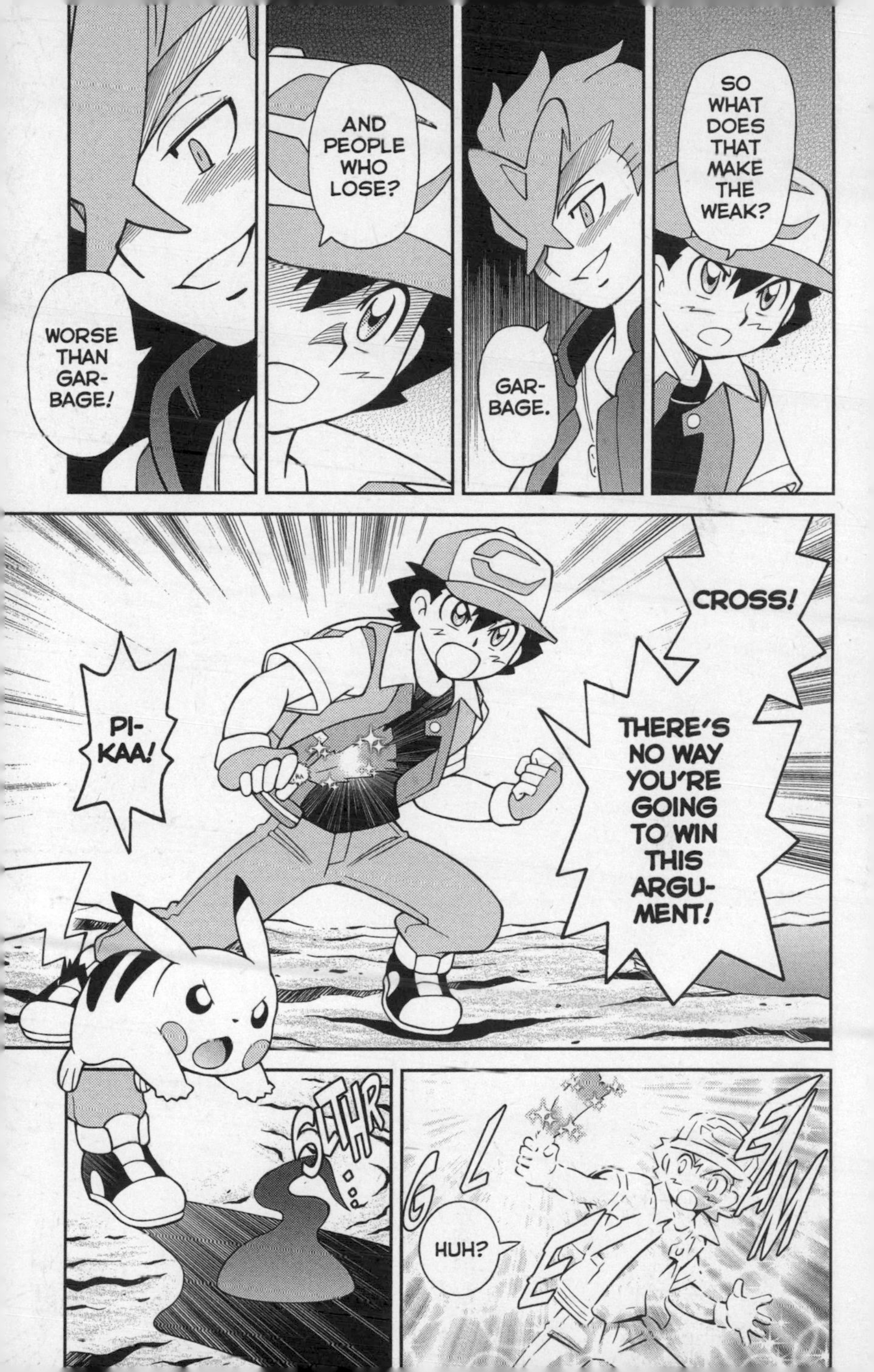
SO WHAT DOES THAT MAKE THE WEAK?
GAR-BAGE.
AND PEOPLE WHO LOSE?
WORSE THAN GAR-BAGE!
CROSS!
THERE'S NO WAY YOU'RE GOING TO WIN THIS ARGU-MENT!
PI-KAA!
HUH?
SLTHR

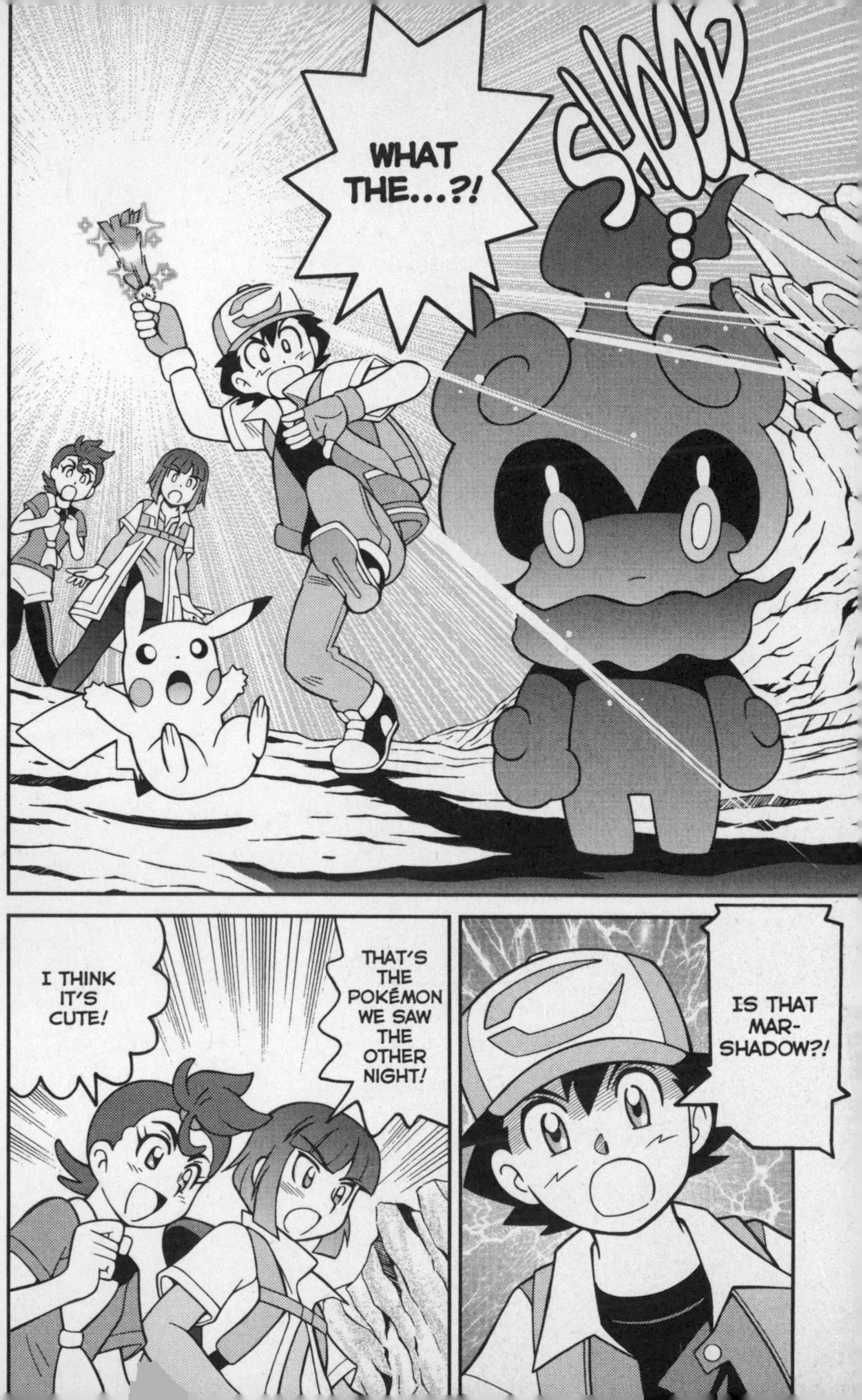
SHOOP
WHAT THE...?!
IS THAT MAR-SHADOW?!
THAT'S THE POKéMON WE SAW THE OTHER NIGHT!
I THINK IT'S CUTE!

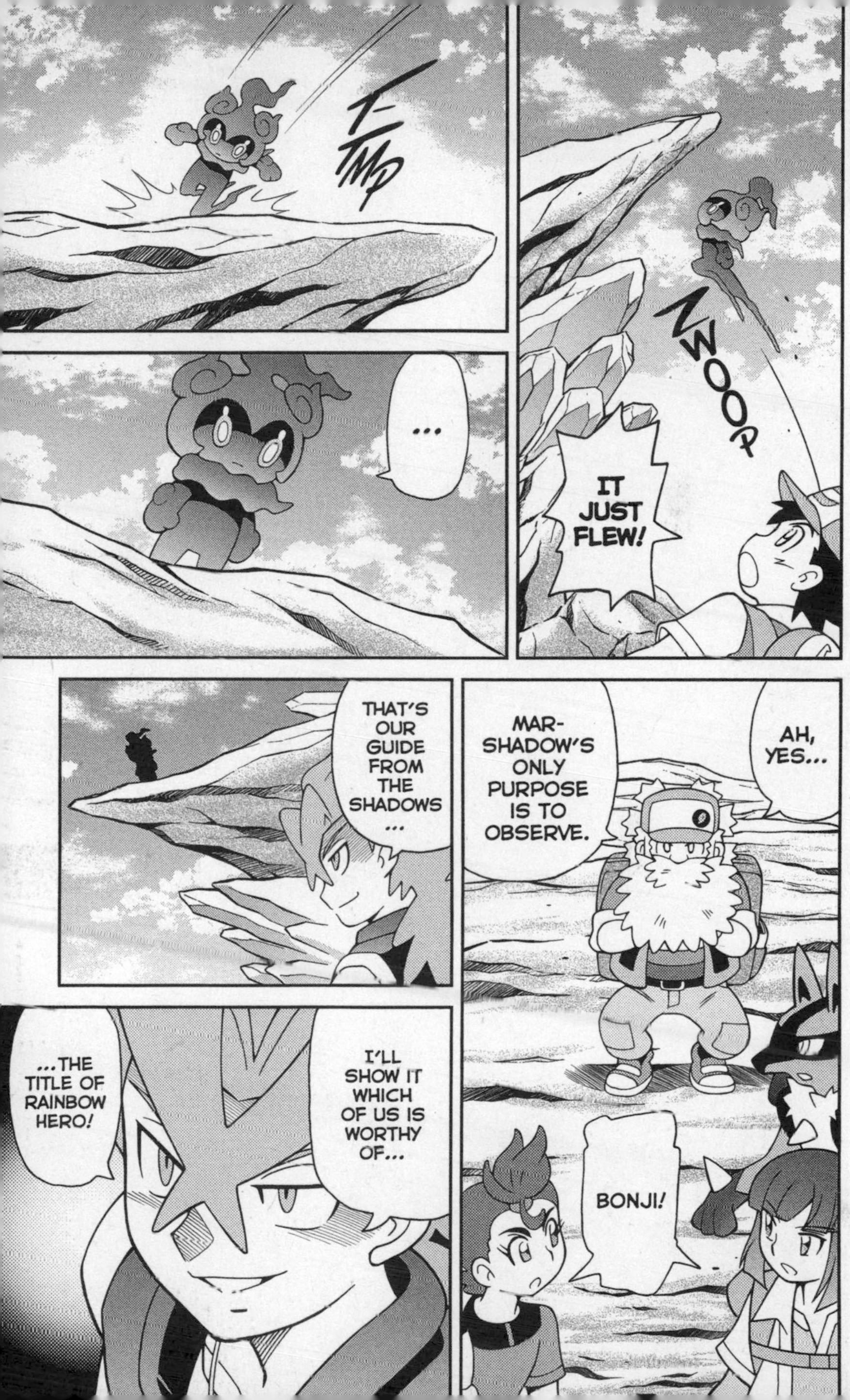
ZWOOOP
IT JUST FLEW!
T-TMP
...
AH, YES...
MAR-SHADOW'S ONLY PURPOSE IS TO OBSERVE.
BONJI!
THAT'S OUR GUIDE FROM THE SHADOWS...
I'LL SHOW IT WHICH OF US IS WORTHY OF...
...THE TITLE OF RAINBOW HERO!

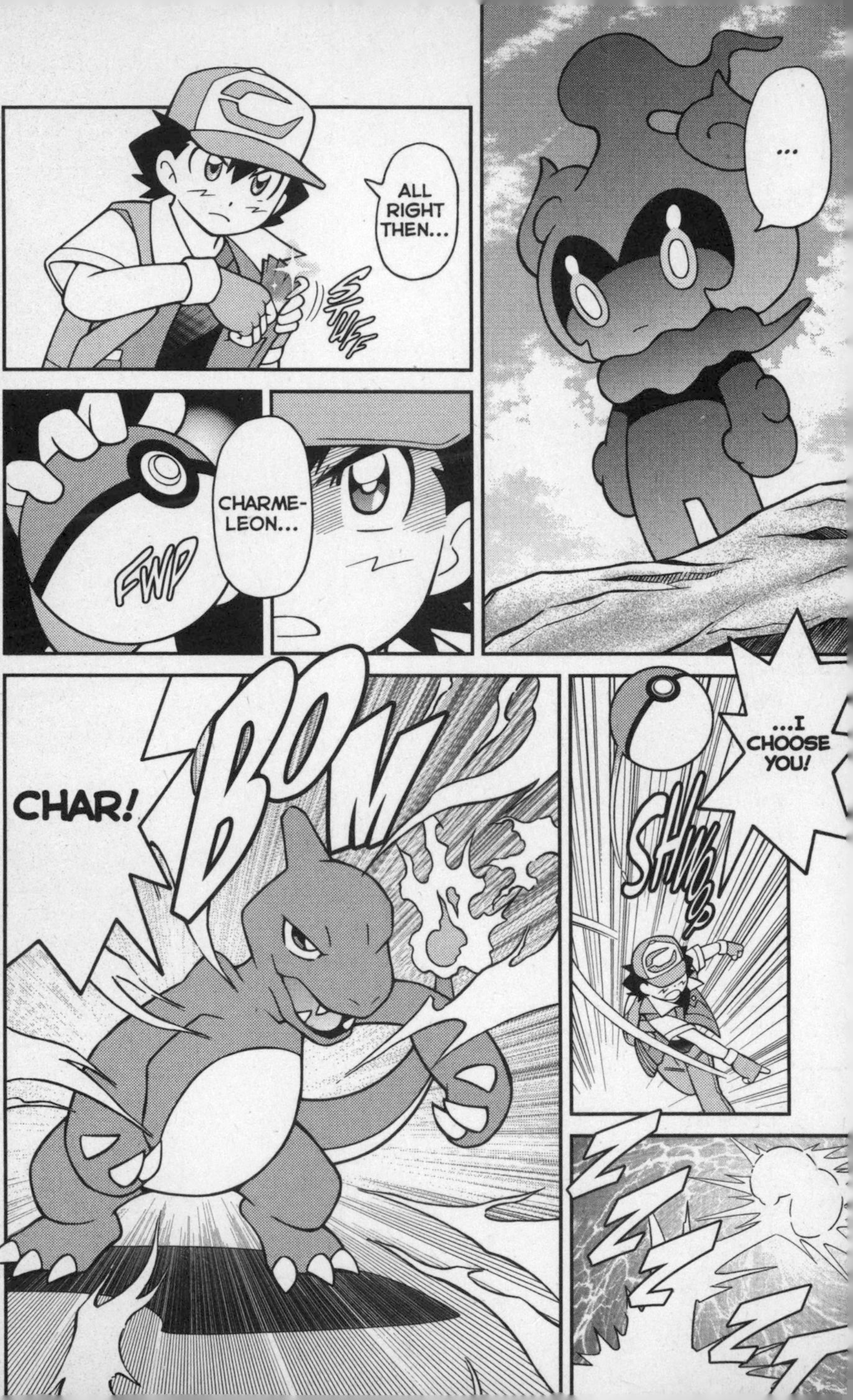
...
ALL RIGHT THEN...
SHUFF
CHARME-LEON...
FWP
...I CHOOSE YOU!
SHUP
BOM
CHAR!

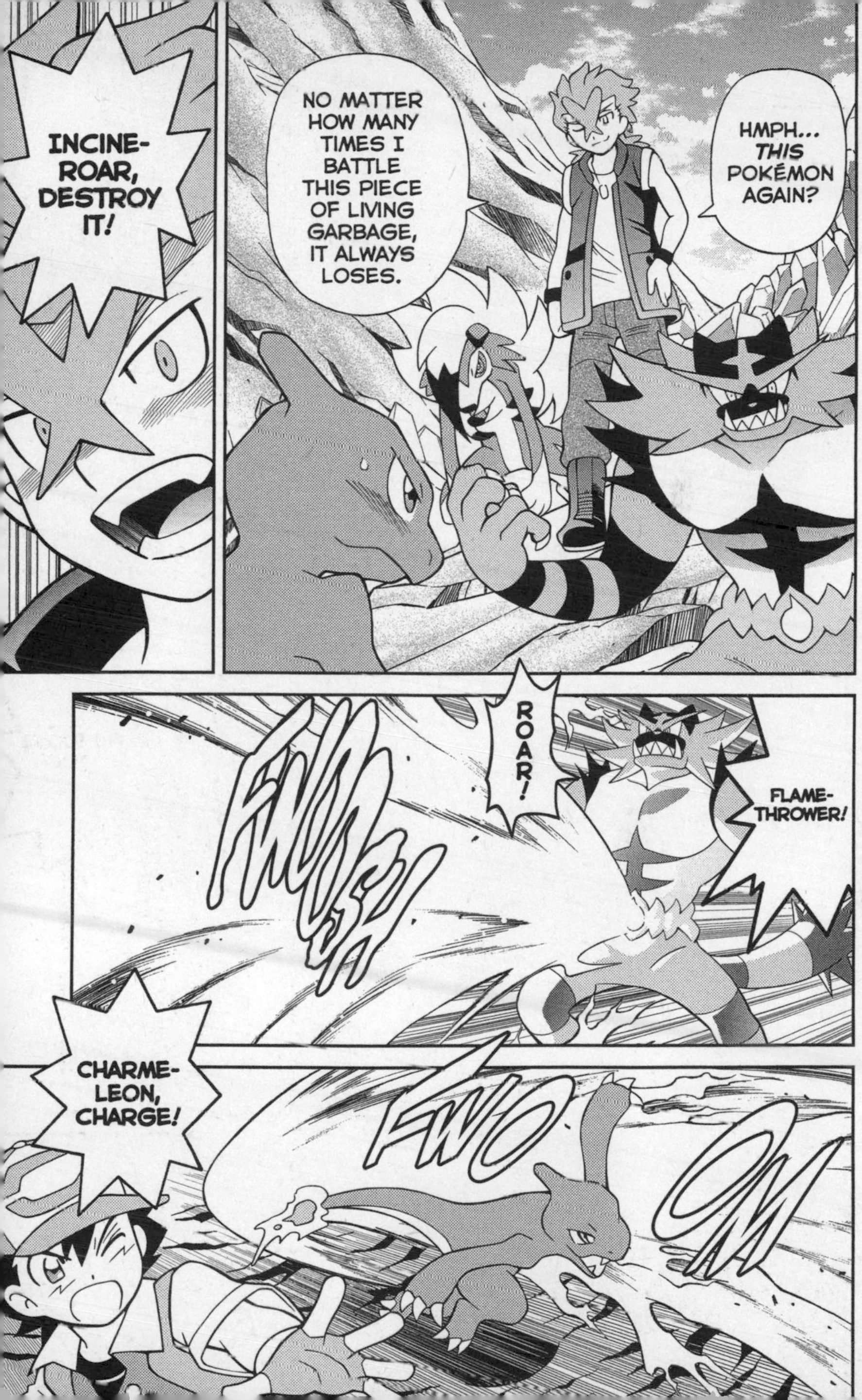
HMPH... *THIS* POKÉMON AGAIN?
NO MATTER HOW MANY TIMES I BATTLE THIS PIECE OF LIVING GARBAGE, IT ALWAYS LOSES.
INCINE-ROAR, DESTROY IT!
FLAME-THROWER!
ROAR!
FWOOSH
CHARME-LEON, CHARGE!
FWOOM

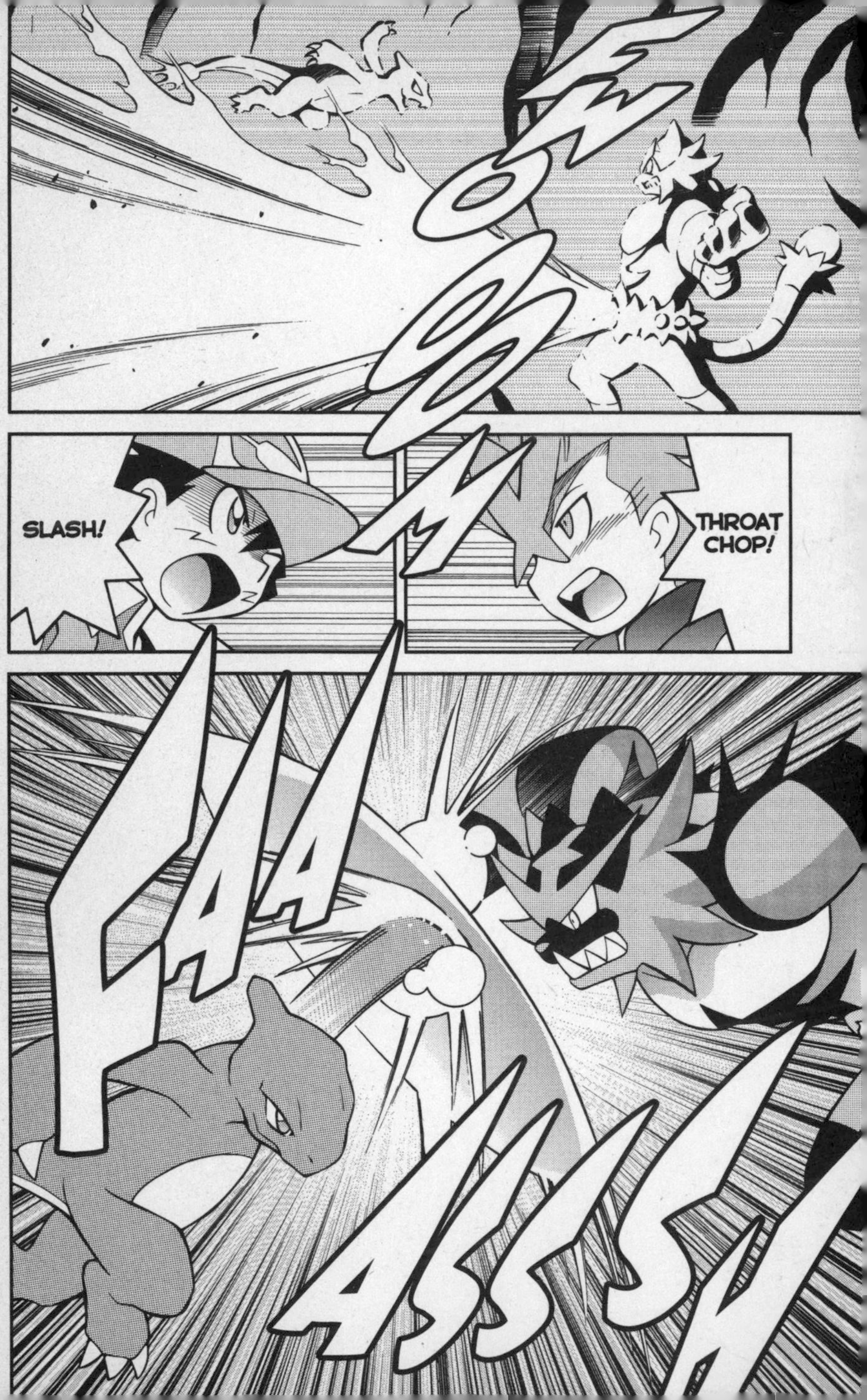
THROAT CHOP!
SLASH!

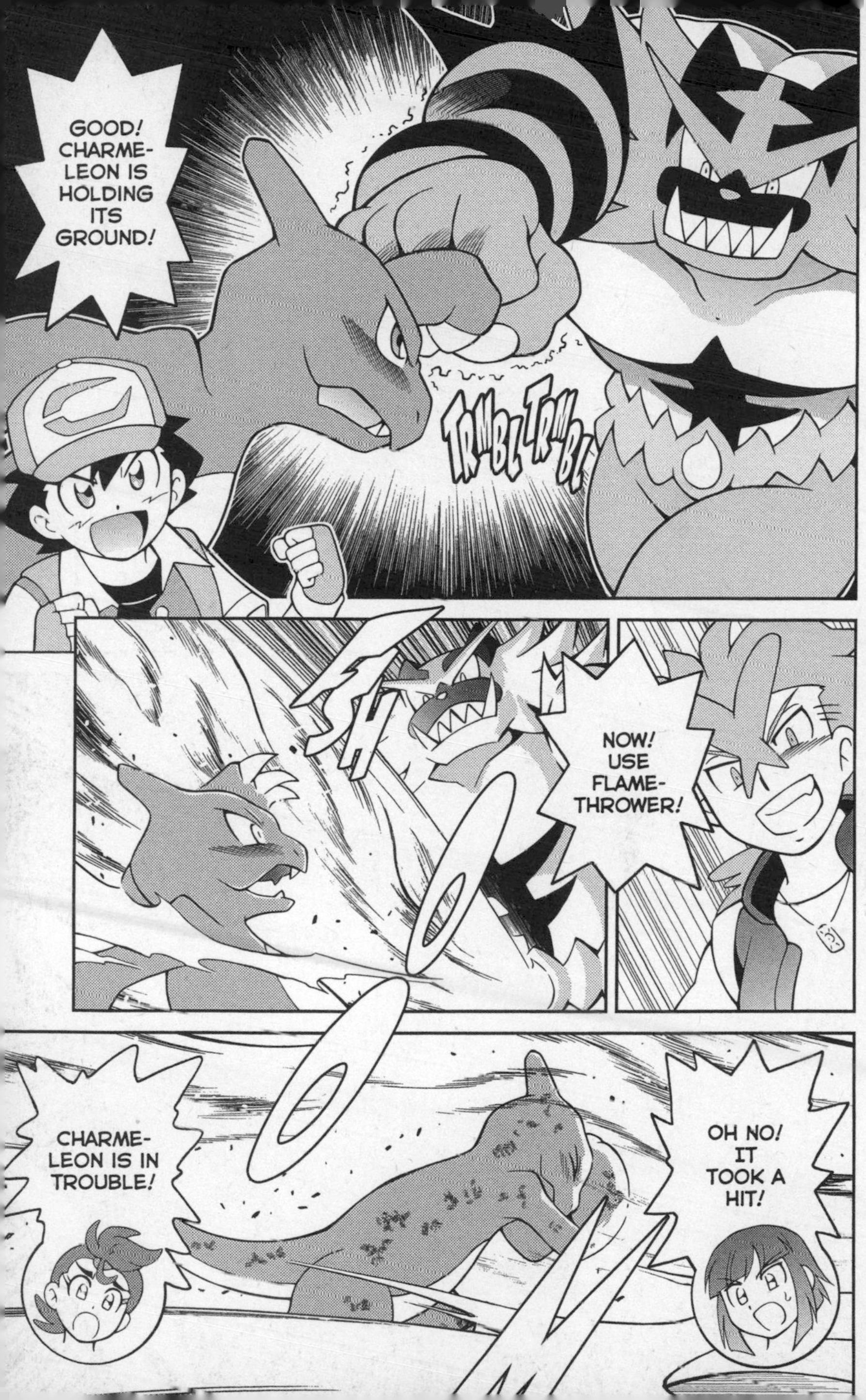
GOOD! CHARME-LEON IS HOLDING ITS GROUND!
TRMBL TRMBL
NOW! USE FLAME-THROWER!
OH NO! IT TOOK A HIT!
CHARME-LEON IS IN TROUBLE!

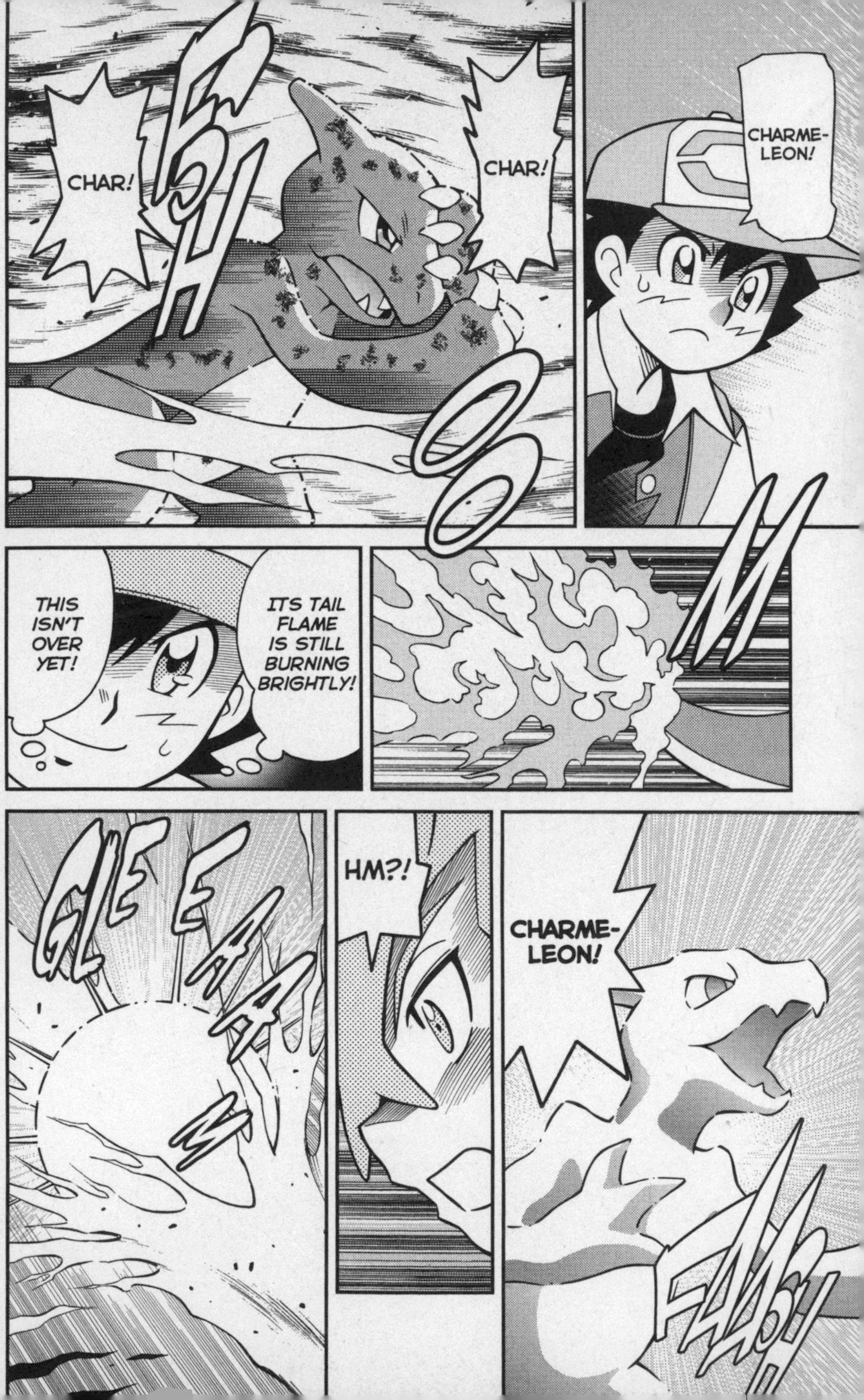
CHARME-LEON!
CHAR!
CHAR!
ITS TAIL FLAME IS STILL BURNING BRIGHTLY!
THIS ISN'T OVER YET!
CHARME-LEON!
HM?!

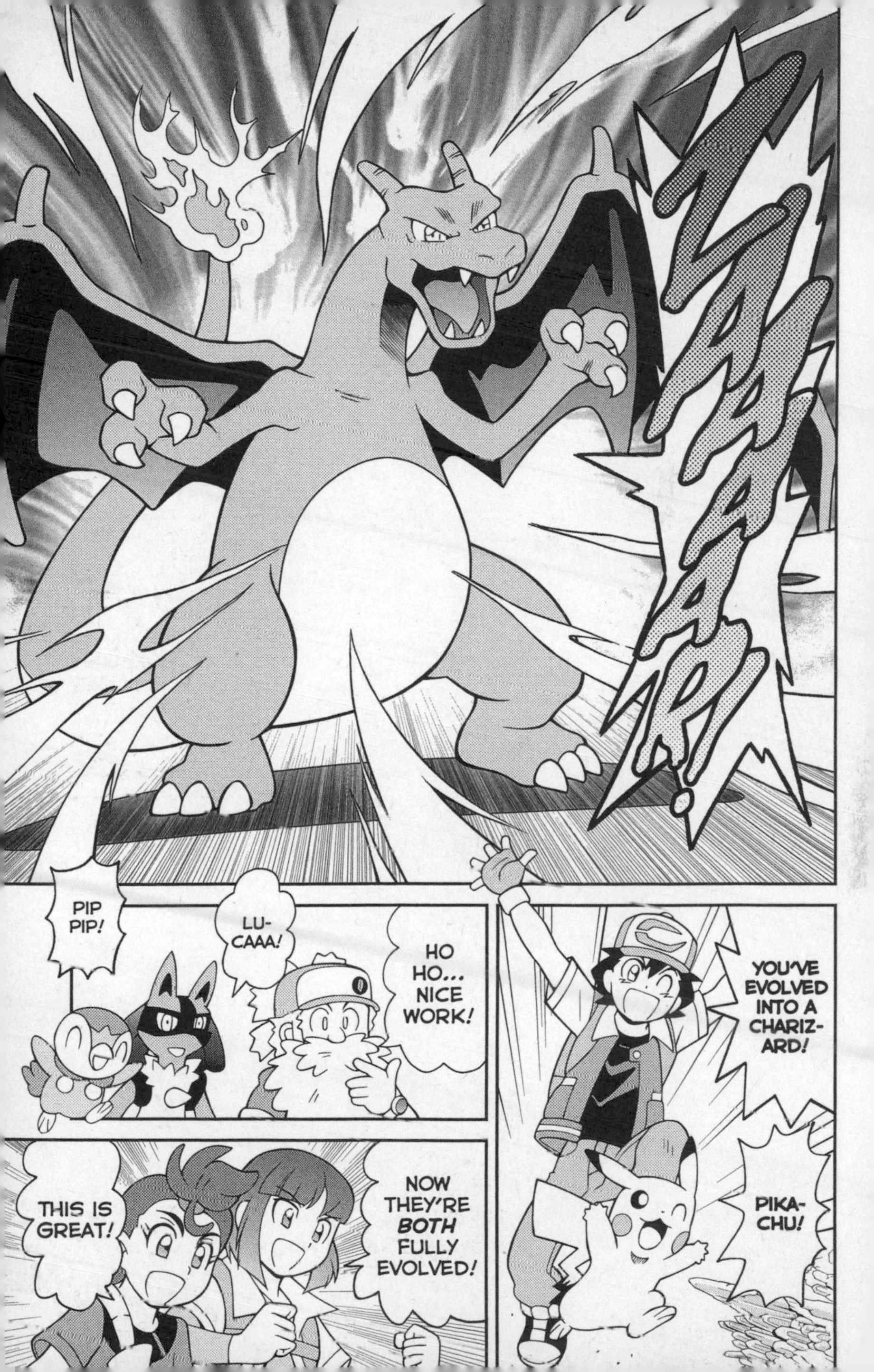
ZAAAAR!
YOU'VE EVOLVED INTO A CHARIZ-ARD!
PIKA-CHU!
HO HO... NICE WORK!
LU-CAAA!
PIP PIP!
NOW THEY'RE *BOTH* FULLY EVOLVED!
THIS IS GREAT!

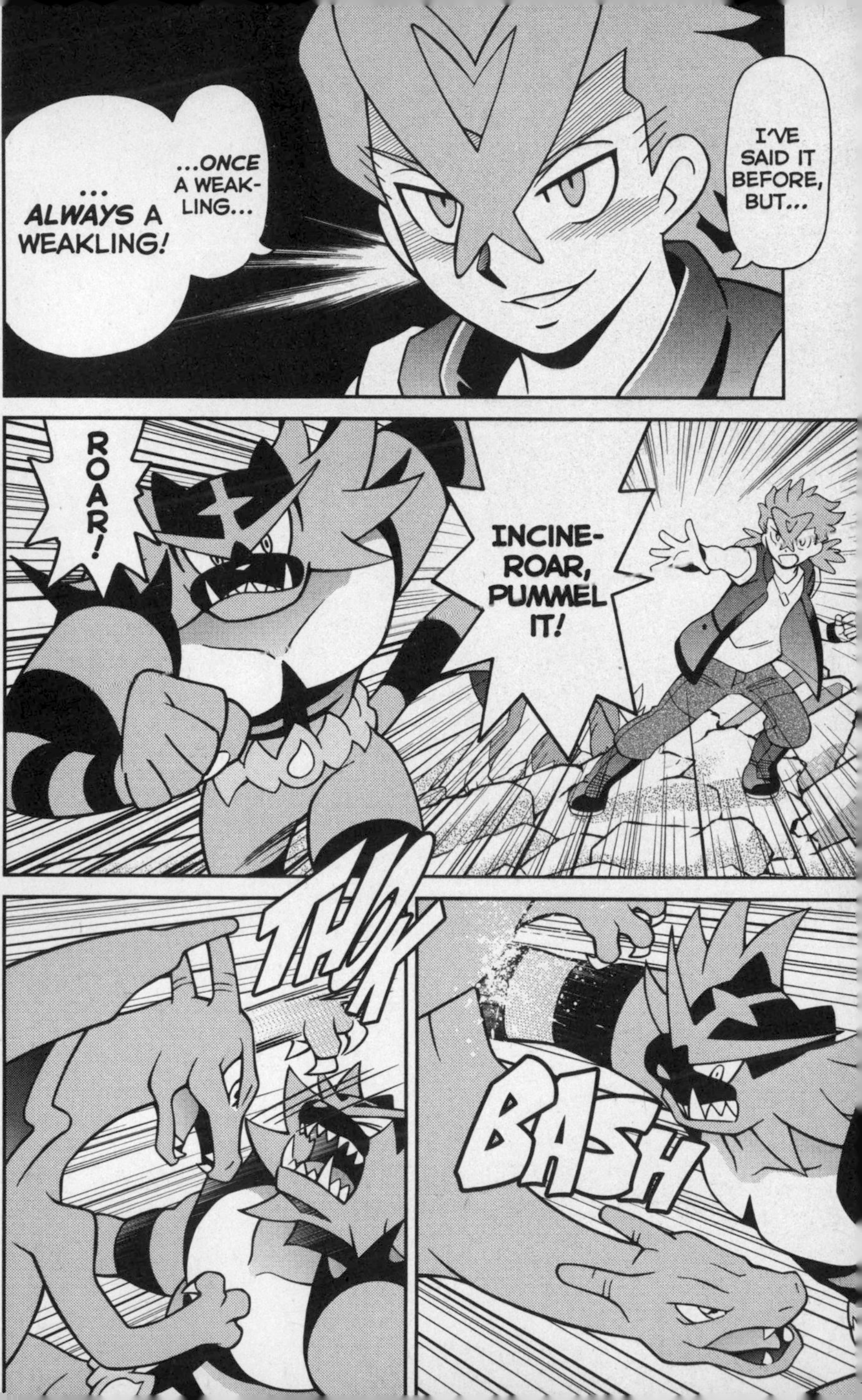
I'VE SAID IT BEFORE, BUT...
...ONCE A WEAK-LING...
... ALWAYS A WEAKLING!
INCINE-ROAR, PUMMEL IT!
ROAR!
BASH
THOK

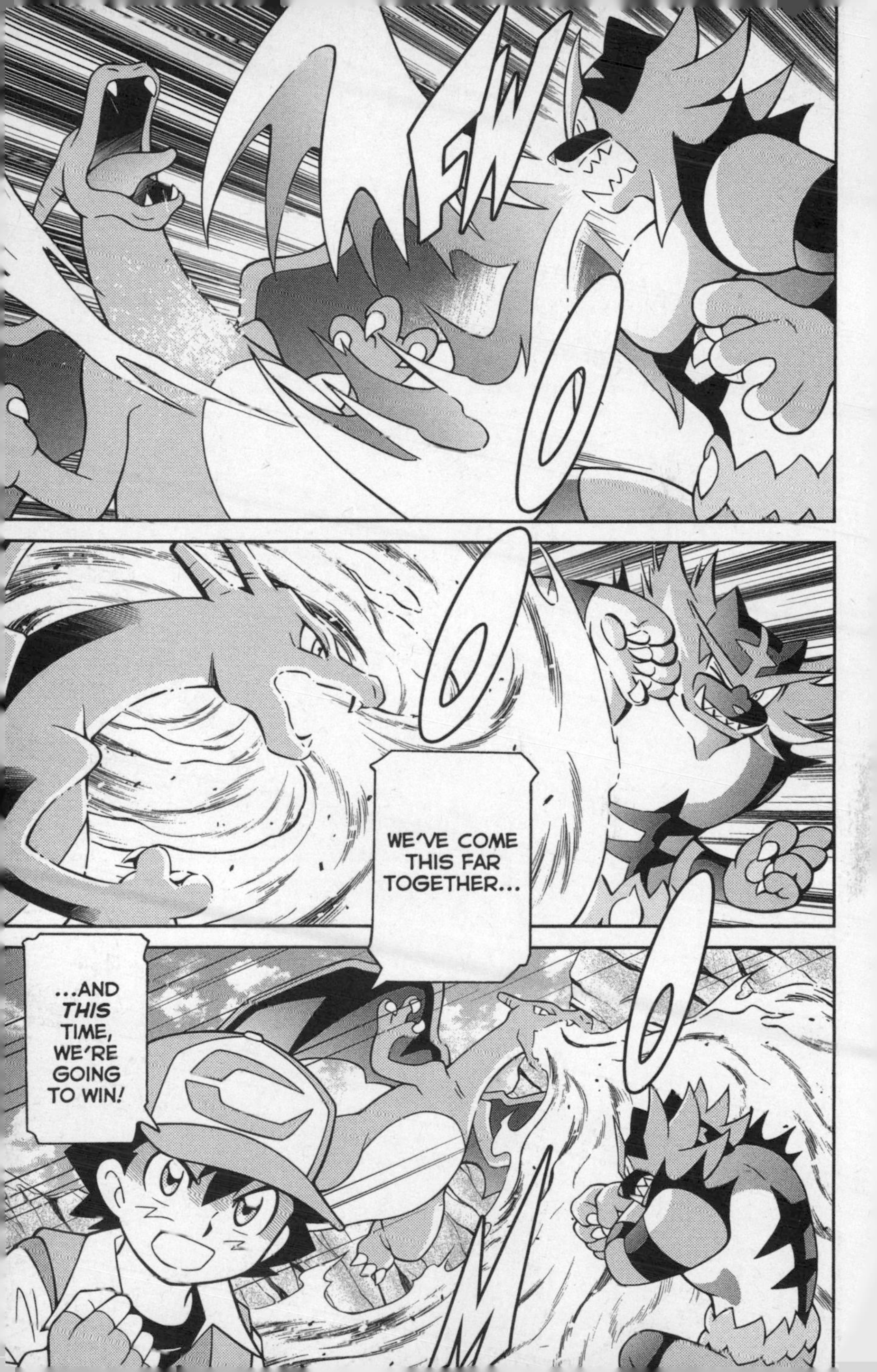
WE'VE COME THIS FAR TOGETHER...
...AND *THIS* TIME, WE'RE GOING TO WIN!

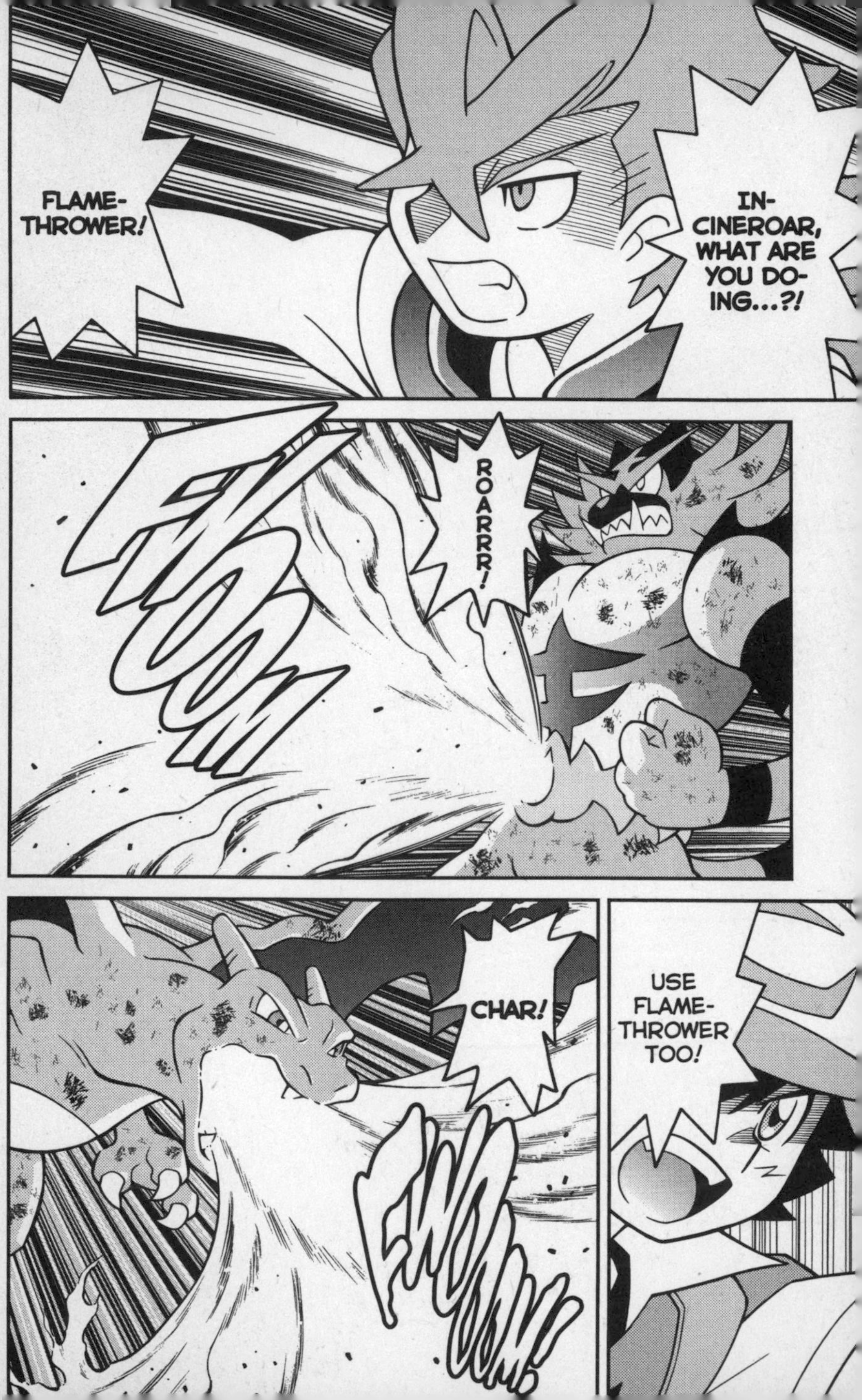
IN-CINEROAR, WHAT ARE YOU DO-ING...?!
FLAME-THROWER!
ROARRR!
FOOM
USE FLAME-THROWER TOO!
CHAR!

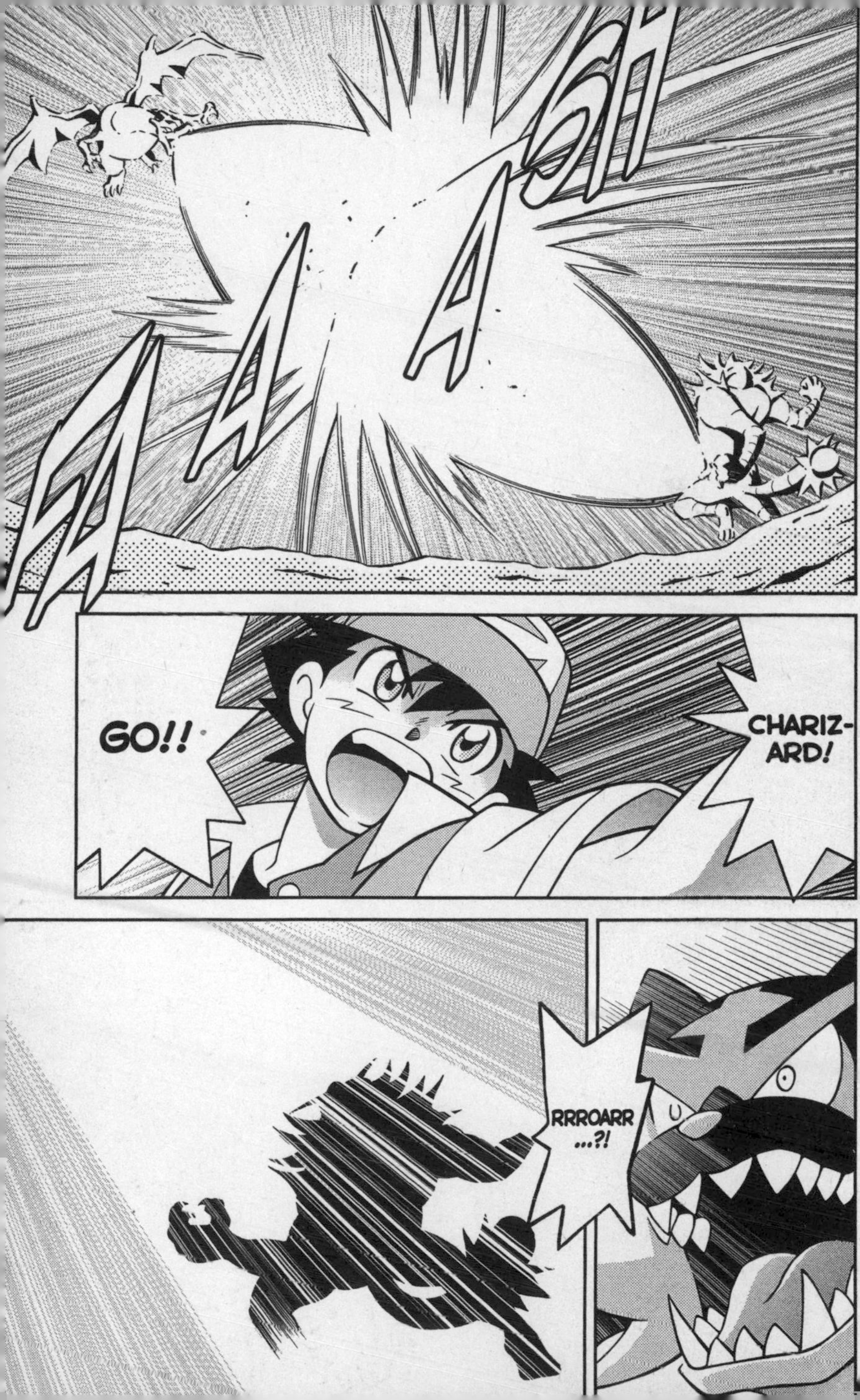
ZAAAAAP
CHARIZ-
ARD!
GO!!
RRROARR
...?!

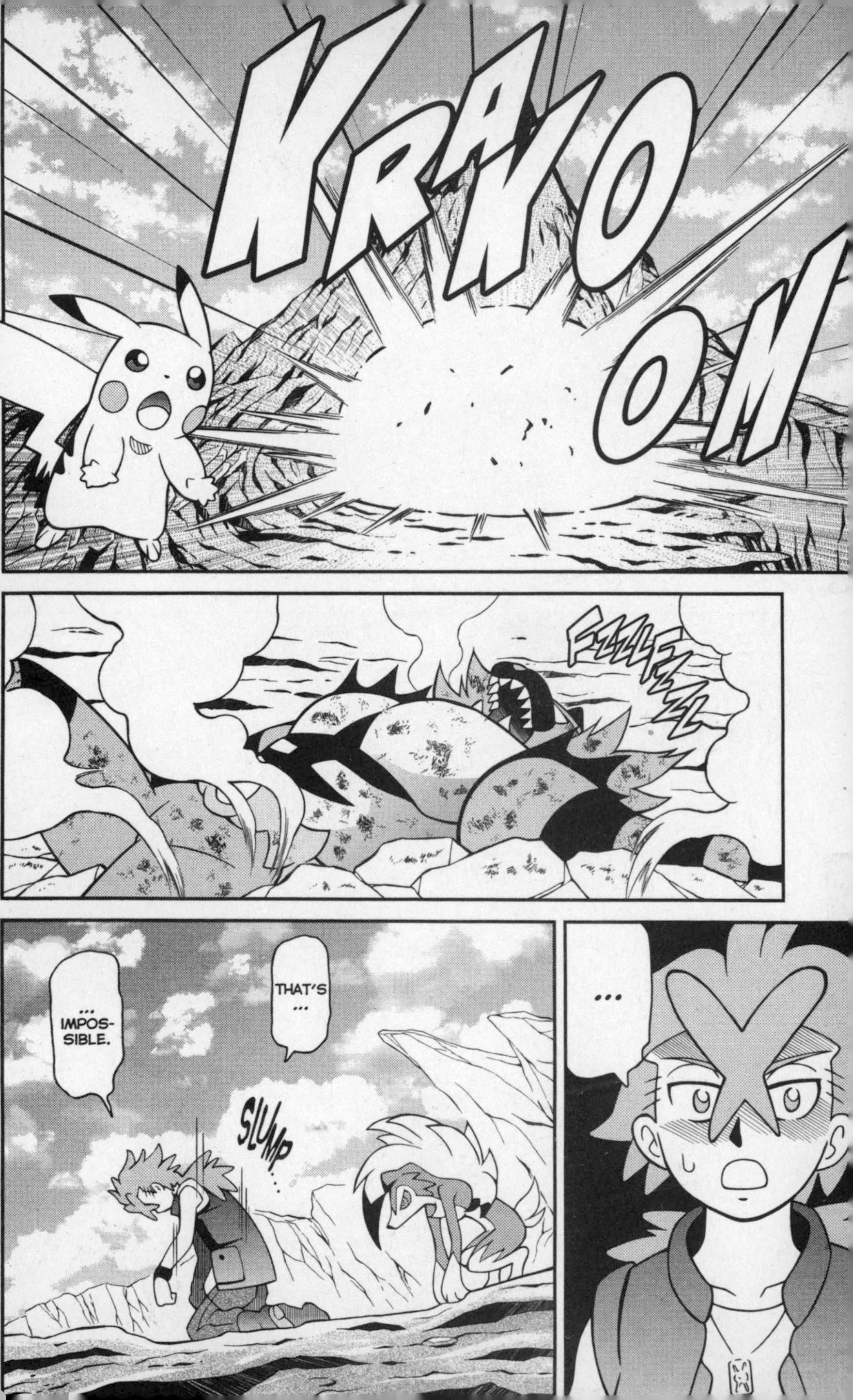
KRAKOOM
FZZZFZZZ
...
THAT'S ...
... IMPOSSIBLE.
SLUMP ...

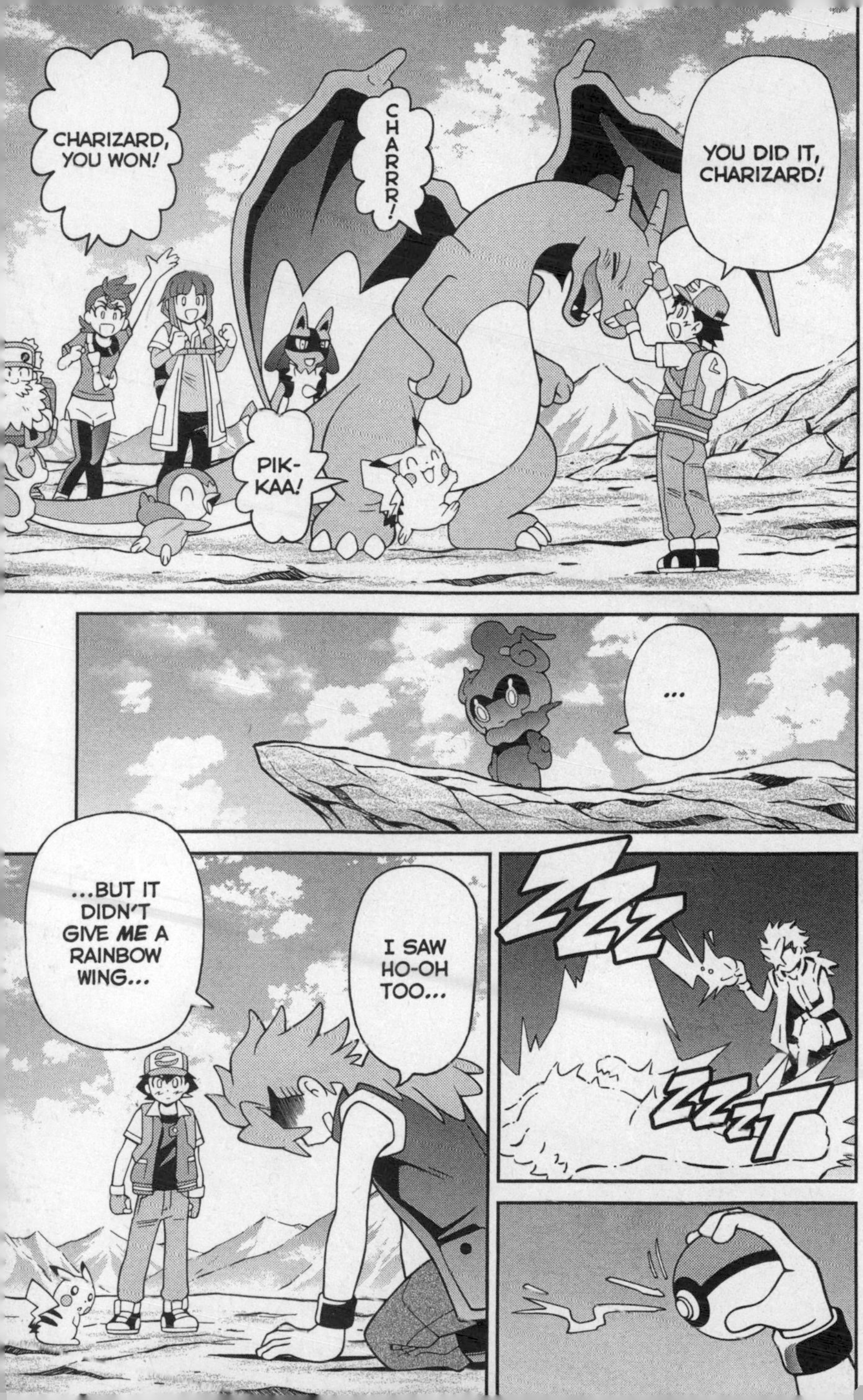
YOU DID IT, CHARIZARD!
CHARRR!
CHARIZARD, YOU WON!
PIK-KAA!
...
ZZZ
ZZZT
I SAW HO-OH TOO...
...BUT IT DIDN'T GIVE *ME* A RAINBOW WING...

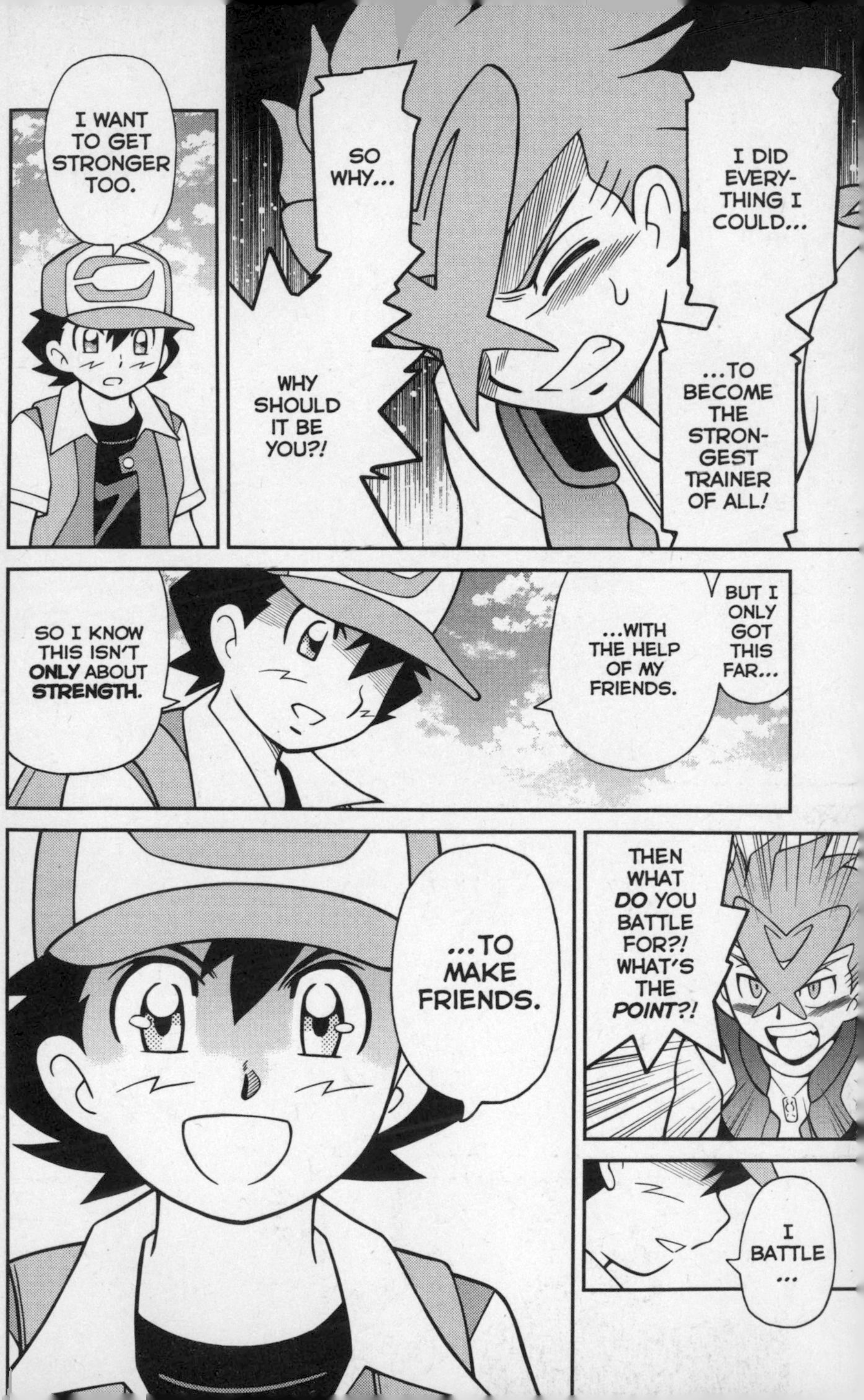
I DID EVERY-THING I COULD...
...TO BECOME THE STRON-GEST TRAINER OF ALL!
SO WHY...
WHY SHOULD IT BE YOU?!
I WANT TO GET STRONGER TOO.
BUT I ONLY GOT THIS FAR...
...WITH THE HELP OF MY FRIENDS.
SO I KNOW THIS ISN'T ONLY ABOUT STRENGTH.
THEN WHAT DO YOU BATTLE FOR?! WHAT'S THE POINT?!
I BATTLE ...
...TO MAKE FRIENDS.

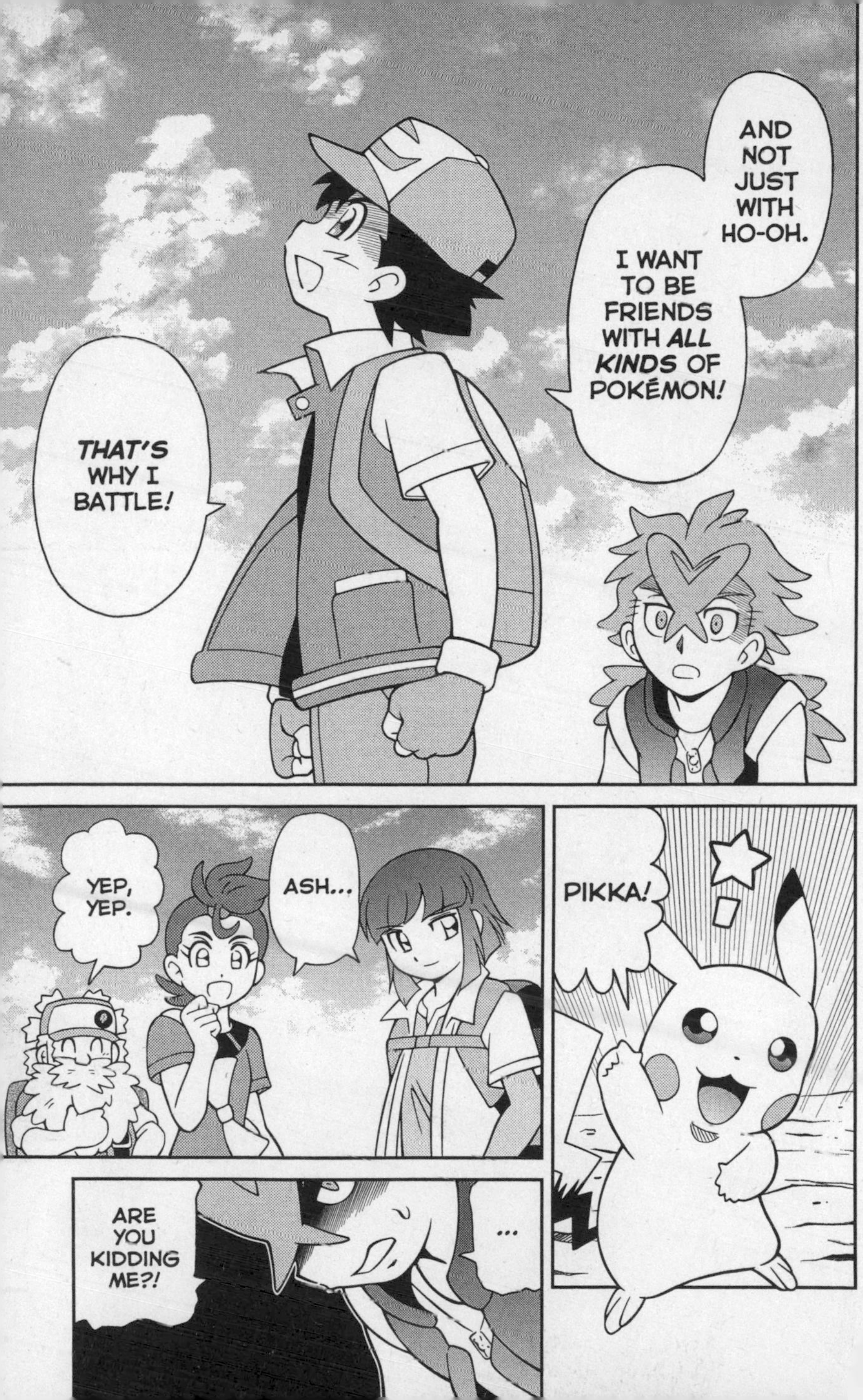
AND NOT JUST WITH HO-OH.
I WANT TO BE FRIENDS WITH *ALL KINDS* OF POKÉMON!
THAT'S WHY I BATTLE!
PIKKA!
ASH...
YEP, YEP.
...
ARE YOU KIDDING ME?!

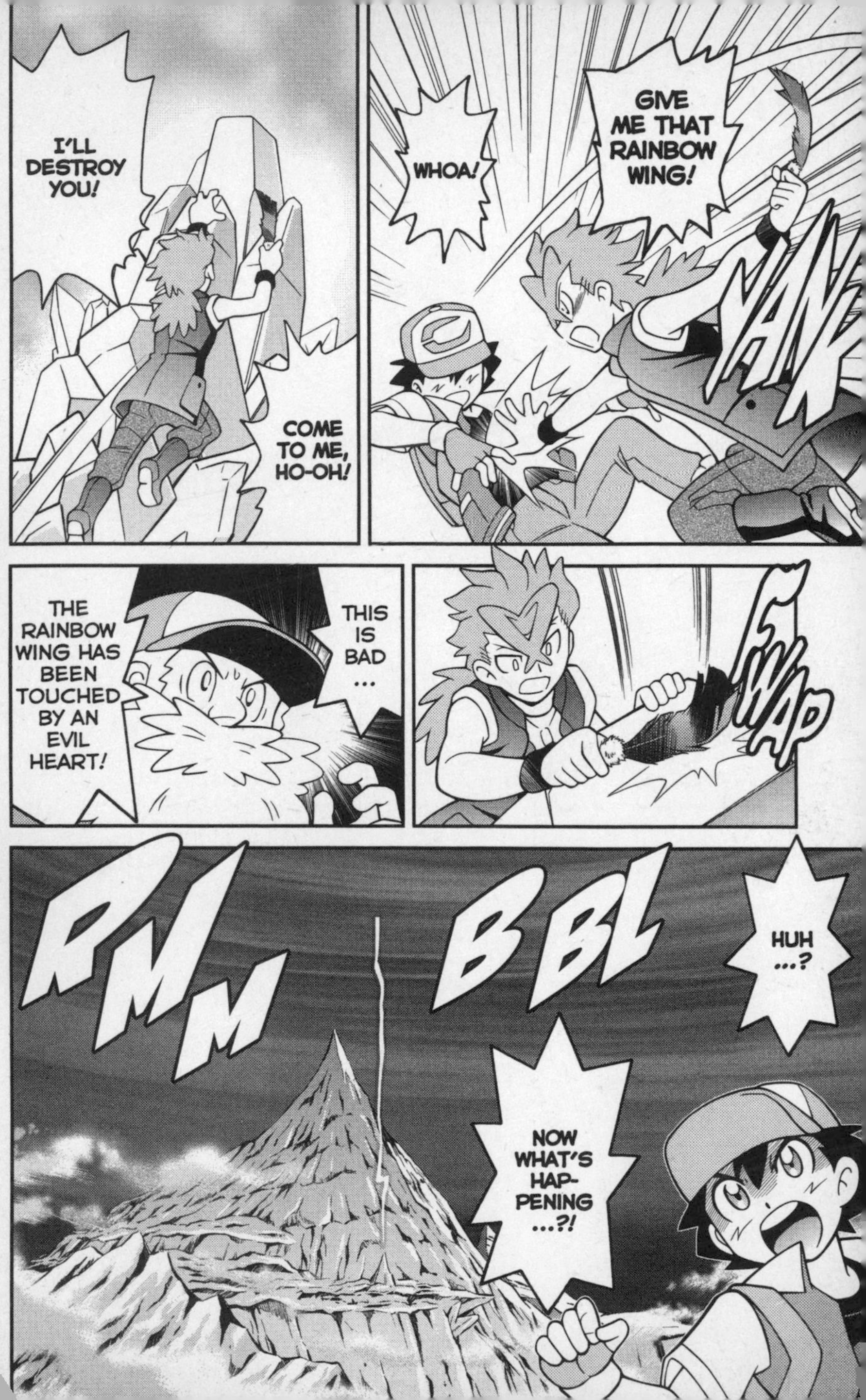
GIVE ME THAT RAINBOW WING!
WHOA!
YANK
I'LL DESTROY YOU!
COME TO ME, HO-OH!
FWAP
THIS IS BAD ...
THE RAINBOW WING HAS BEEN TOUCHED BY AN EVIL HEART!
HUH ...?
RMM BBL
NOW WHAT'S HAP-PENING ...?!

CHAPTER 13

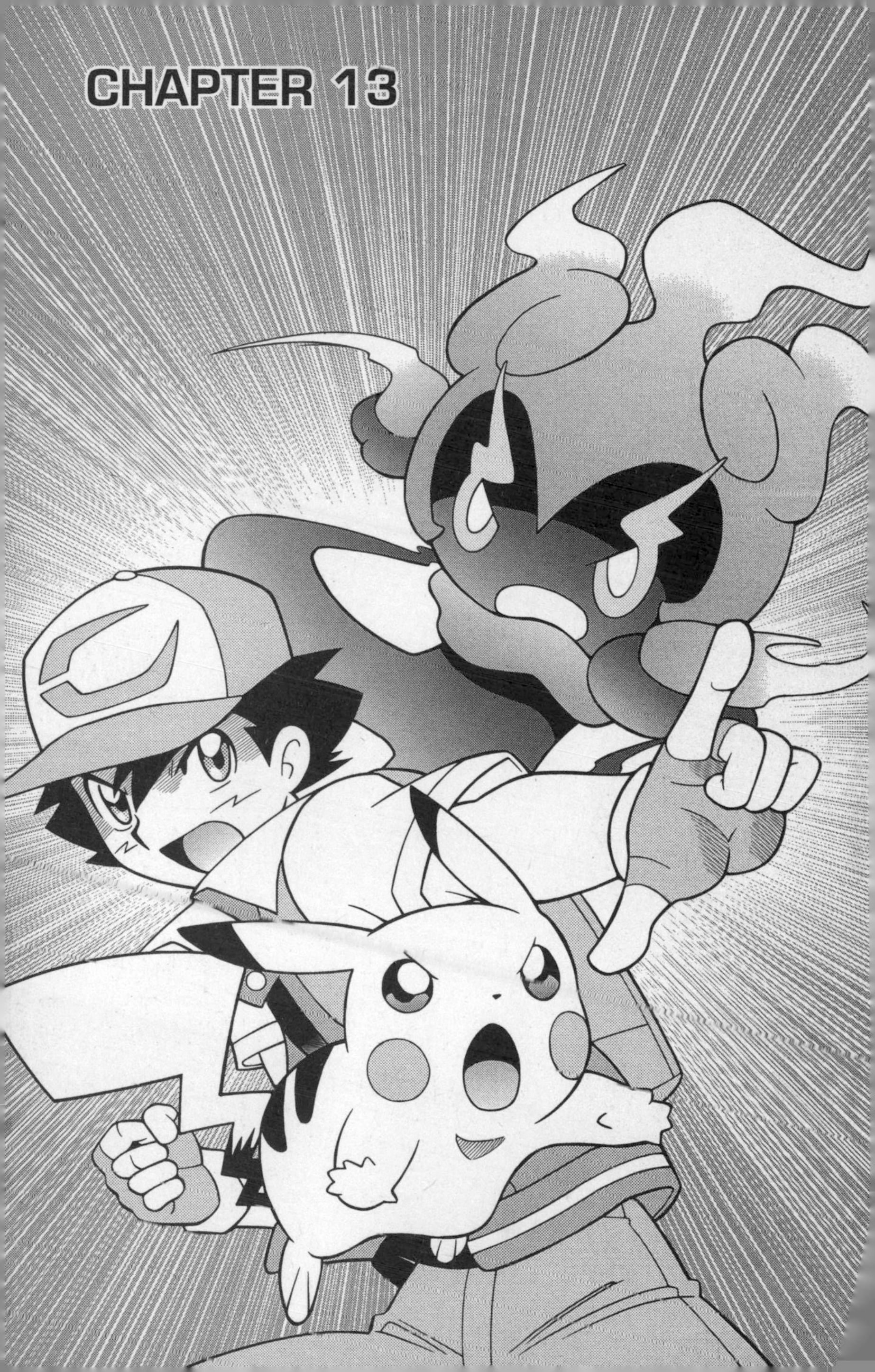

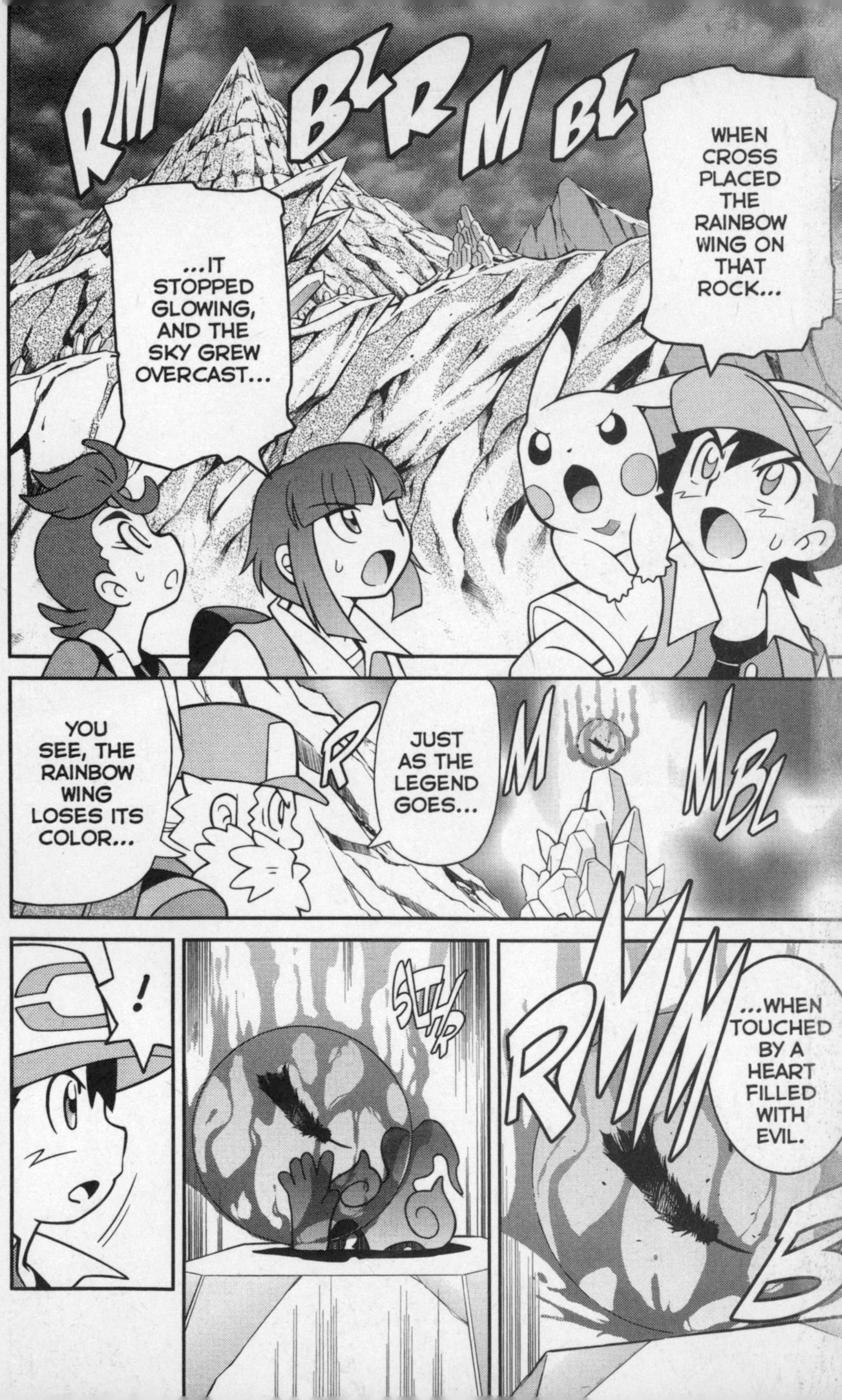
RM
BLR
M
BL
WHEN CROSS PLACED THE RAINBOW WING ON THAT ROCK...
...IT STOPPED GLOWING, AND THE SKY GREW OVERCAST...
M
MBL
JUST AS THE LEGEND GOES...
R
YOU SEE, THE RAINBOW WING LOSES ITS COLOR...
RMM
...WHEN TOUCHED BY A HEART FILLED WITH EVIL.
B
SLTHR
!

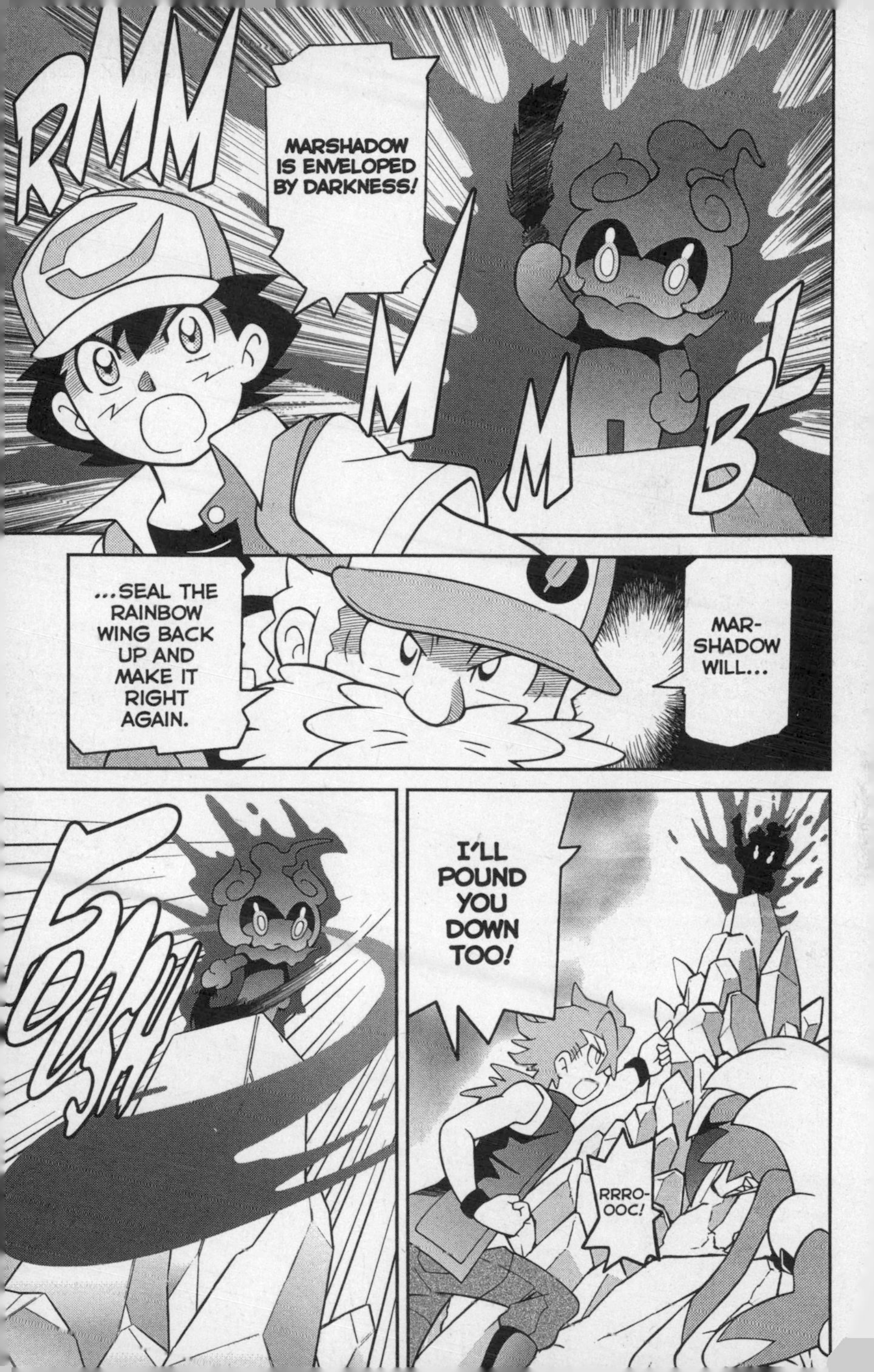
RMMMMMB
MARSHADOW IS ENVELOPED BY DARKNESS!
MAR-SHADOW WILL...
...SEAL THE RAINBOW WING BACK UP AND MAKE IT RIGHT AGAIN.
I'LL POUND YOU DOWN TOO!
RRRO-OOC!

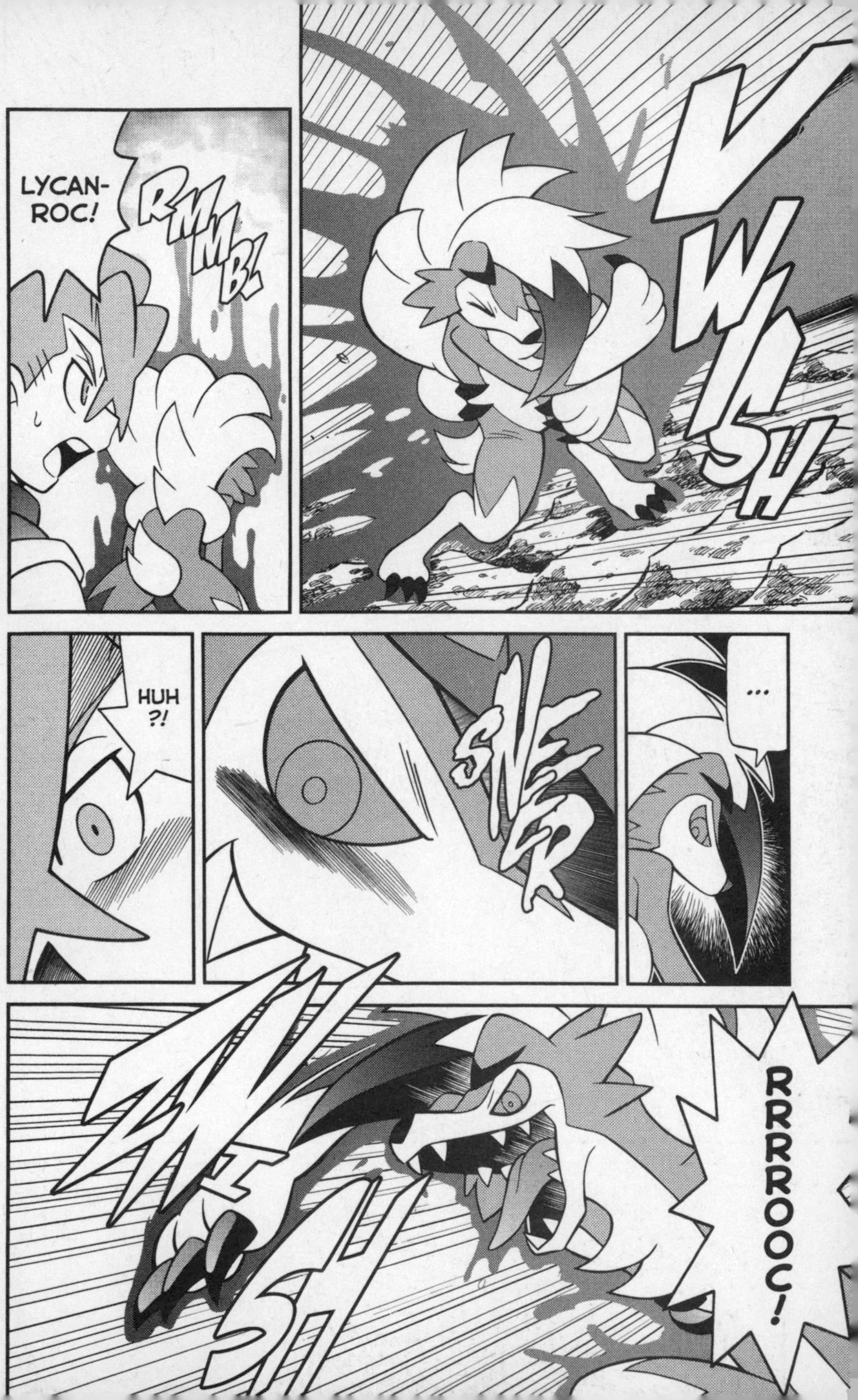
VWISH
LYCAN-ROC!
RMMBL
...
SNER
HUH ?!
RRRROOOC!
WHISH

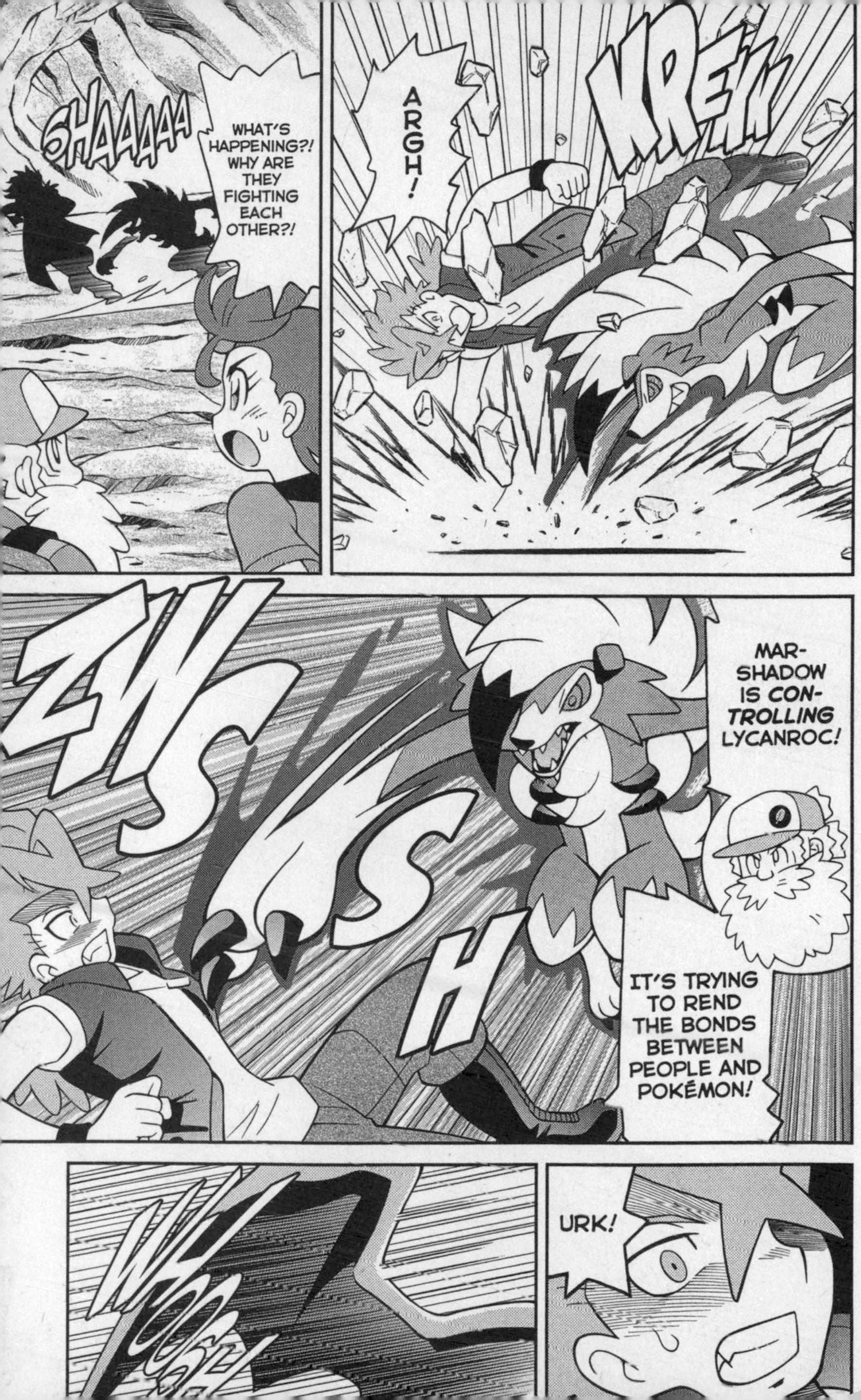
KREAK
ARGH!
SHAAAAA
WHAT'S HAPPENING?! WHY ARE THEY FIGHTING EACH OTHER?!
ZWSSSH
MAR-SHADOW IS *CON-TROLLING* LYCANROC!
IT'S TRYING TO REND THE BONDS BETWEEN PEOPLE AND POKÉMON!
URK!
WHOOSH

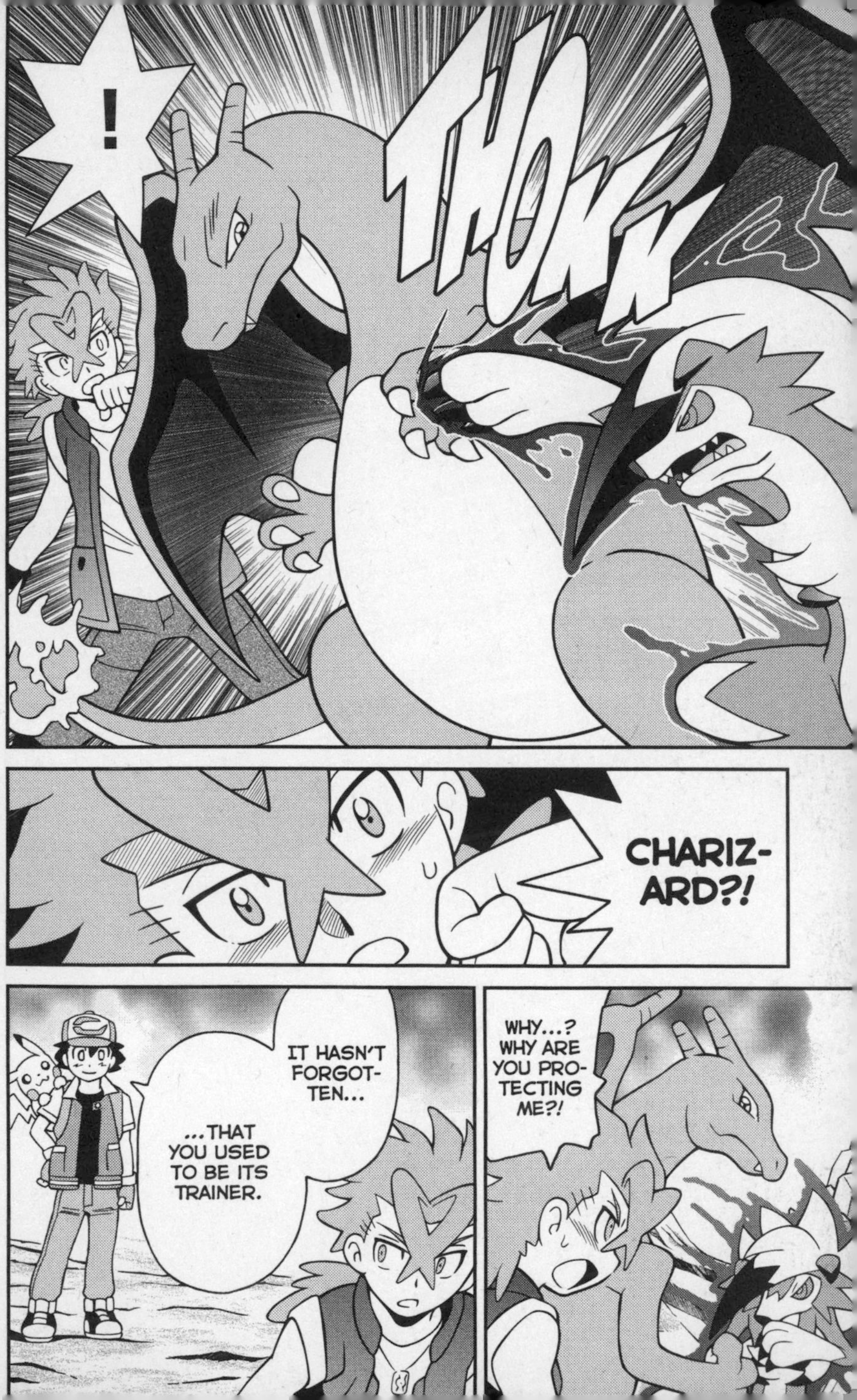
THONK
!
CHARIZ-ARD?!
WHY...? WHY ARE YOU PRO-TECTING ME?!
IT HASN'T FORGOT-TEN...
...THAT YOU USED TO BE ITS TRAINER.

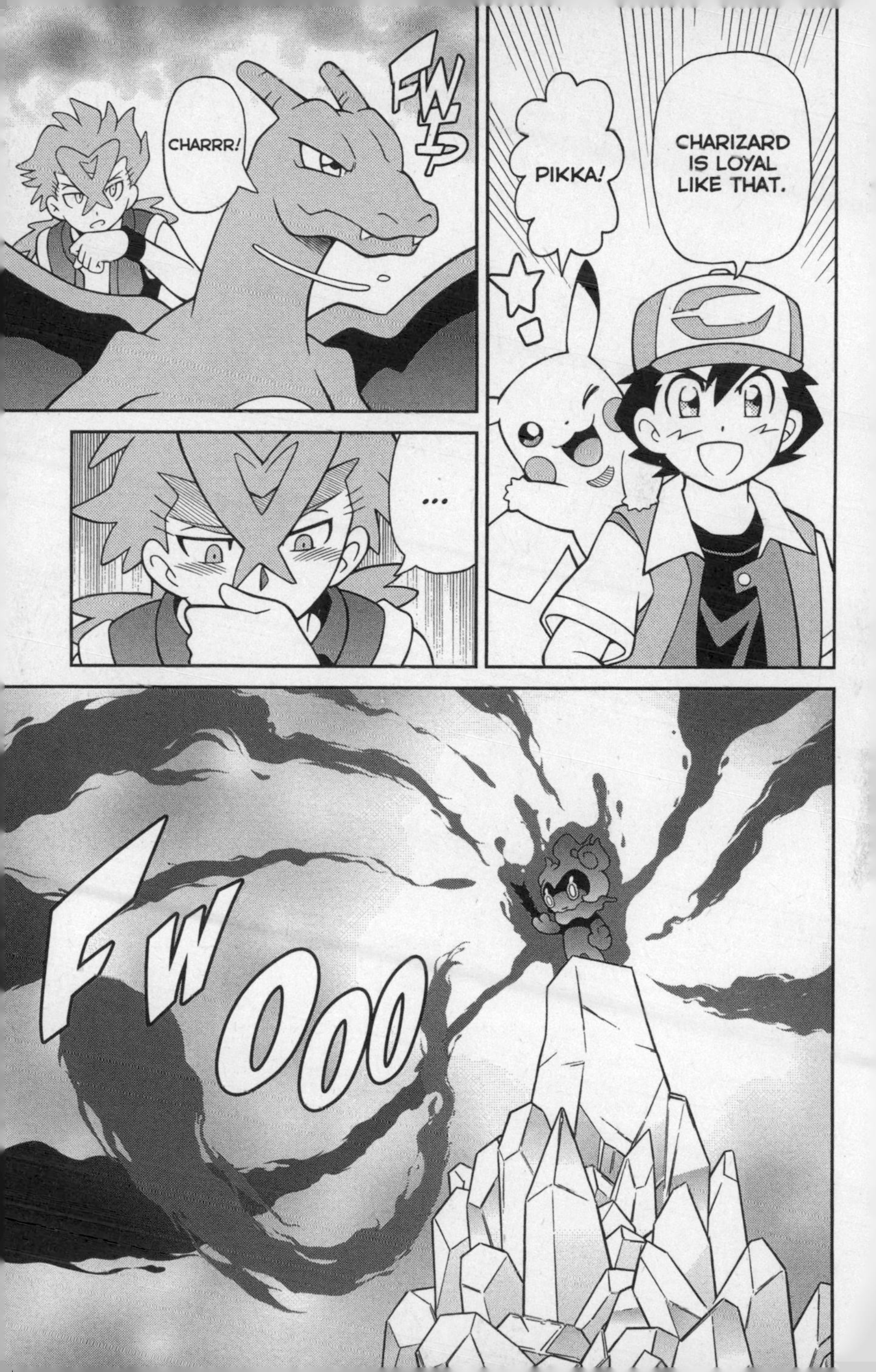
CHARIZARD IS LOYAL LIKE THAT.
PIKKA!
FWIP
CHARRR!
...
FWOOO

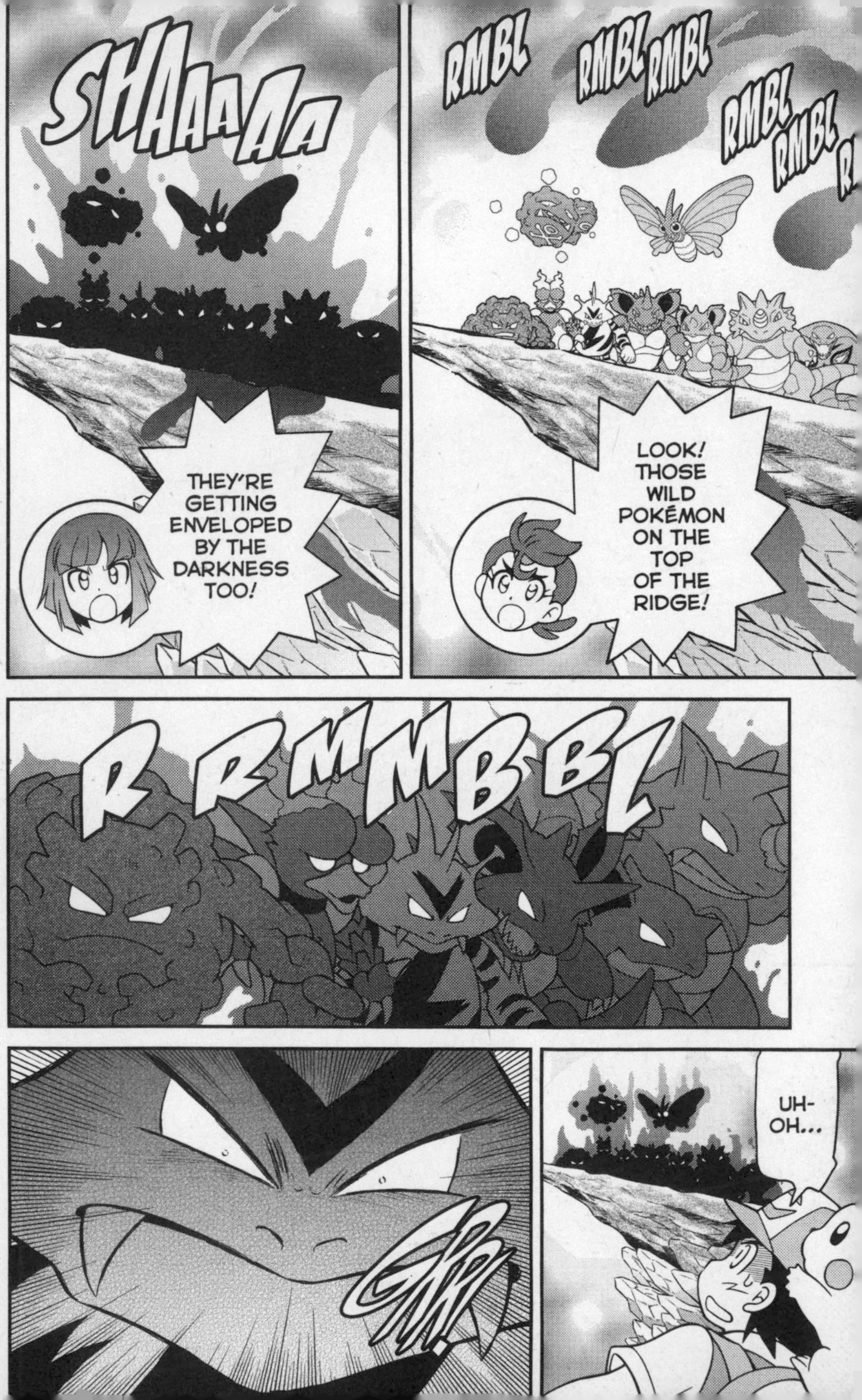
RMBL
RMBL
RMBL
RMBL
RMBL
LOOK! THOSE WILD POKÉMON ON THE TOP OF THE RIDGE!
SHAAAAAA
THEY'RE GETTING ENVELOPED BY THE DARKNESS TOO!
RRMMBBL
UH-OH...

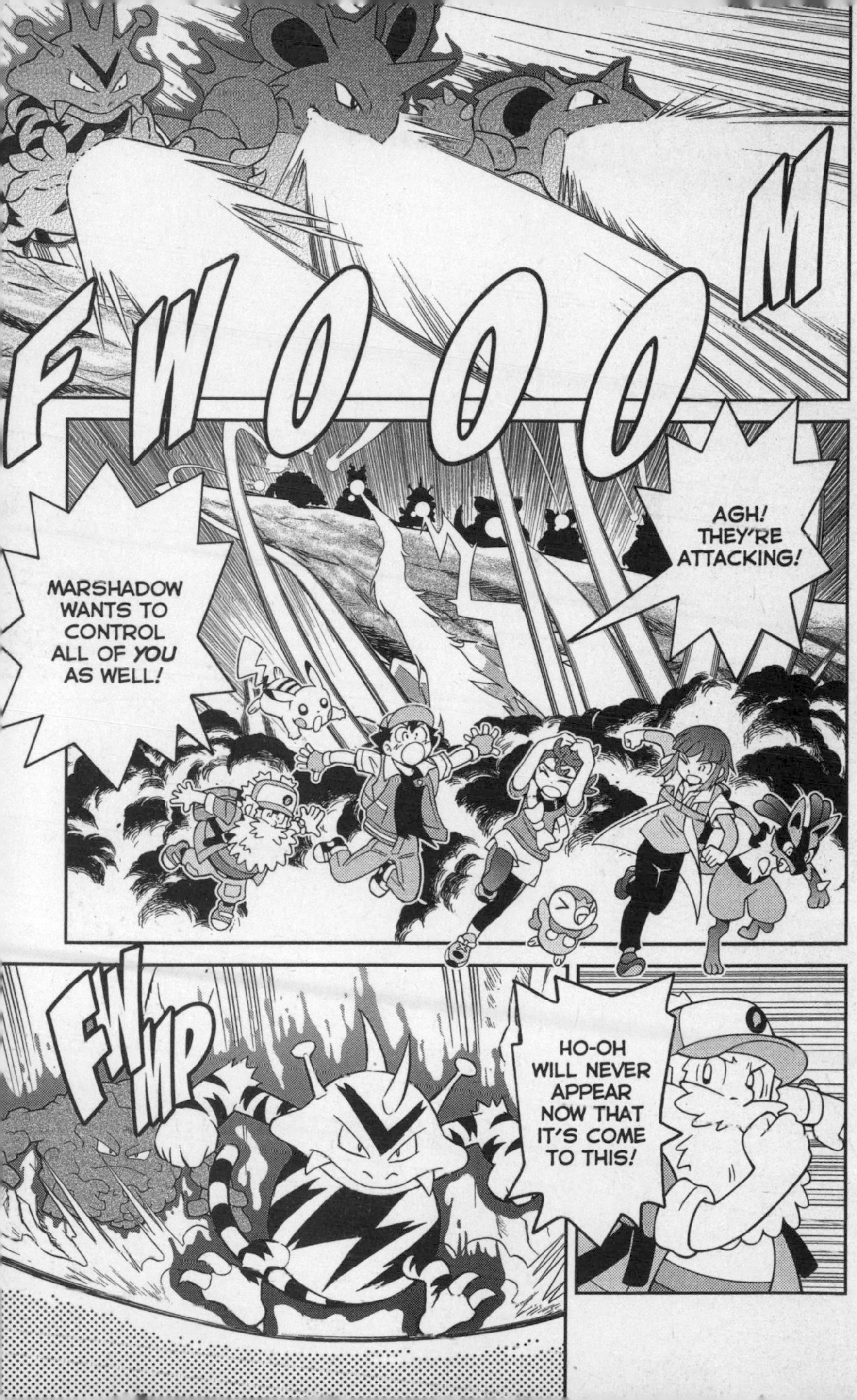
FWOOOM
AGH! THEY'RE ATTACKING!
MARSHADOW WANTS TO CONTROL ALL OF *YOU* AS WELL!
HO-OH WILL NEVER APPEAR NOW THAT IT'S COME TO THIS!
FWMP

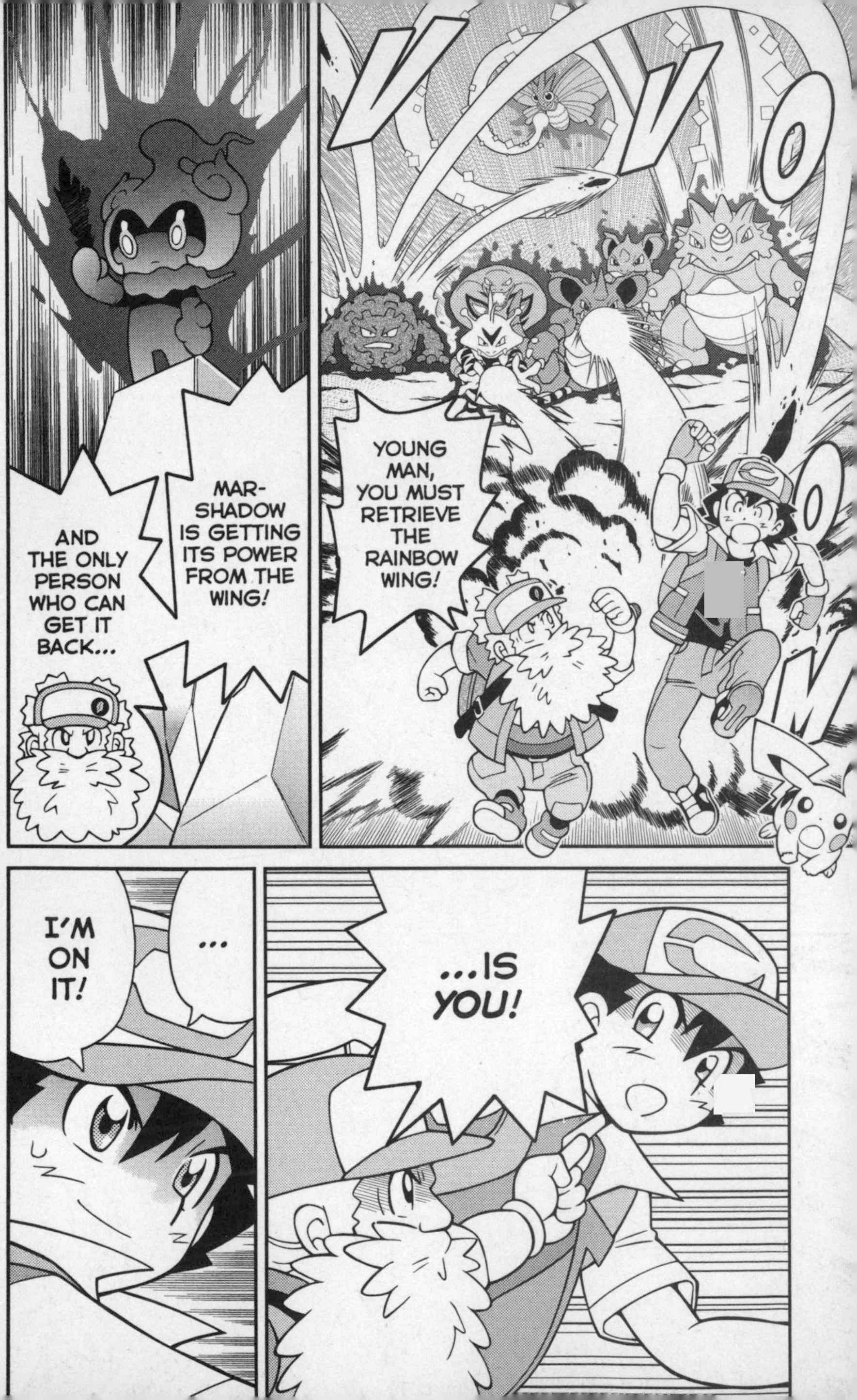
VVOOOM
YOUNG MAN, YOU MUST RETRIEVE THE RAINBOW WING!
MAR-SHADOW IS GETTING ITS POWER FROM THE WING!
AND THE ONLY PERSON WHO CAN GET IT BACK...
...IS YOU!
...
I'M ON IT!

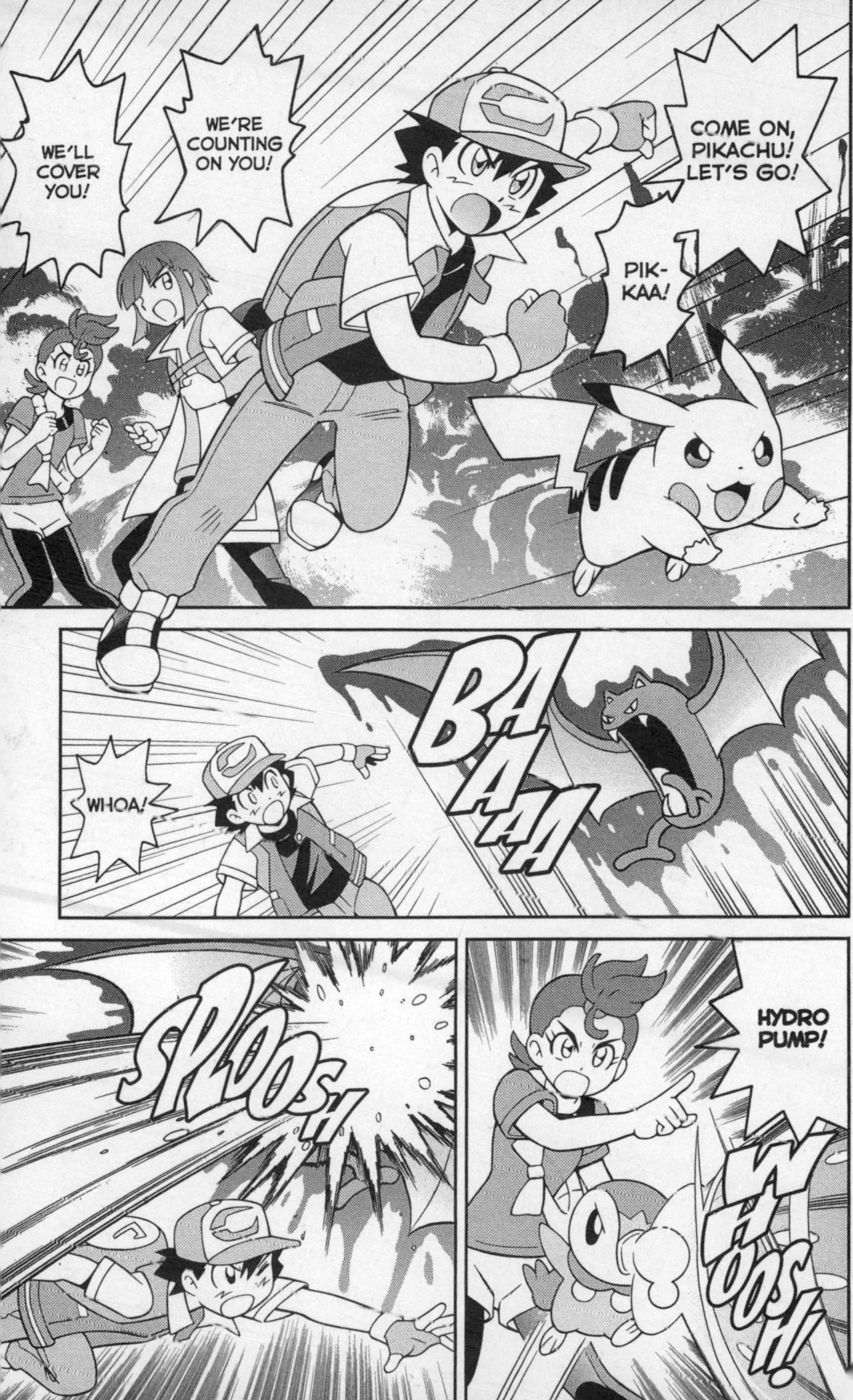
COME ON, PIKACHU! LET'S GO!
PIK-KAA!
WE'RE COUNTING ON YOU!
WE'LL COVER YOU!
BAAAA
WHOA!
HYDRO PUMP!
WHOOSH!
SPLOOSH

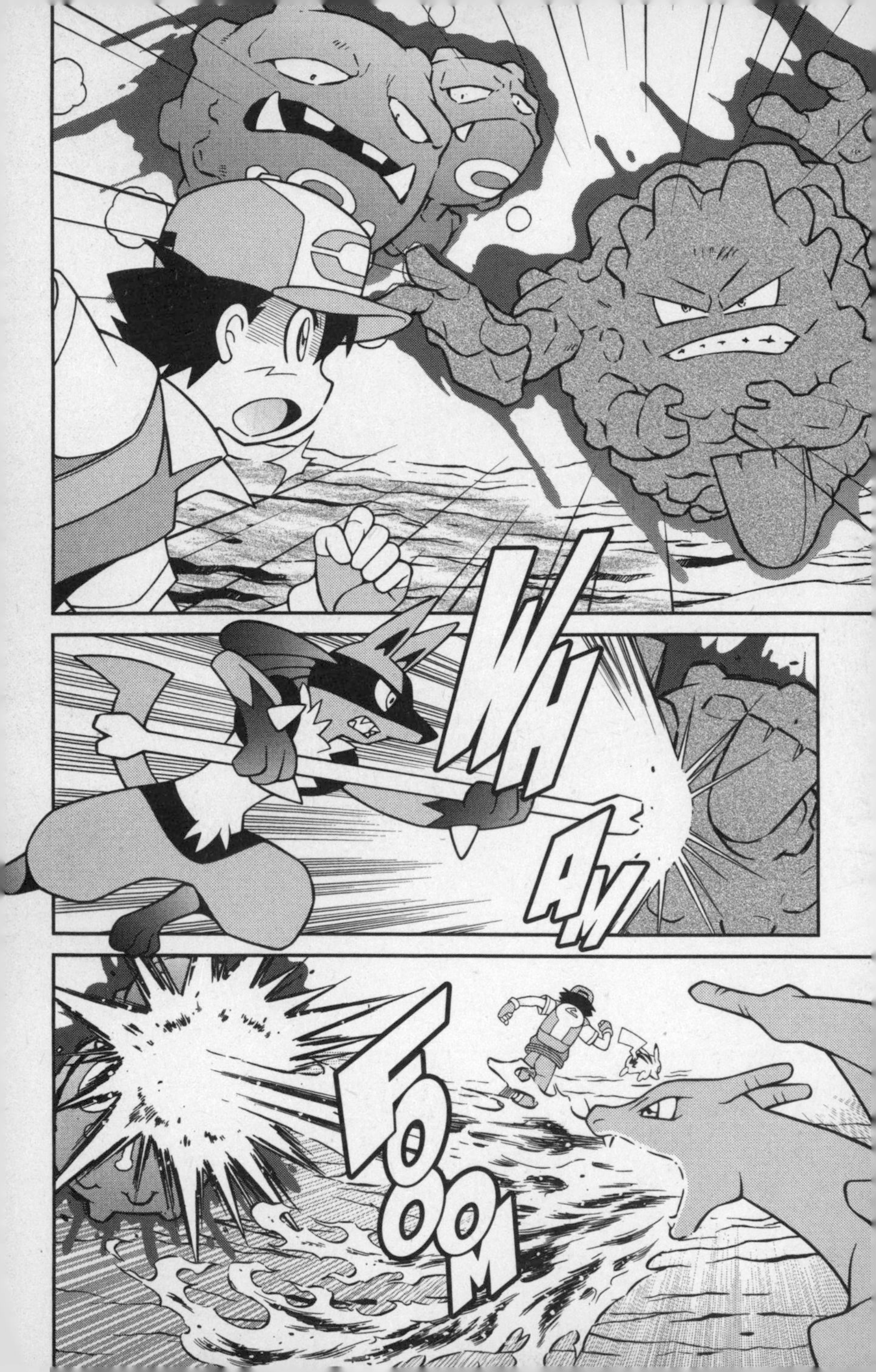
WHAM
FOOOOM

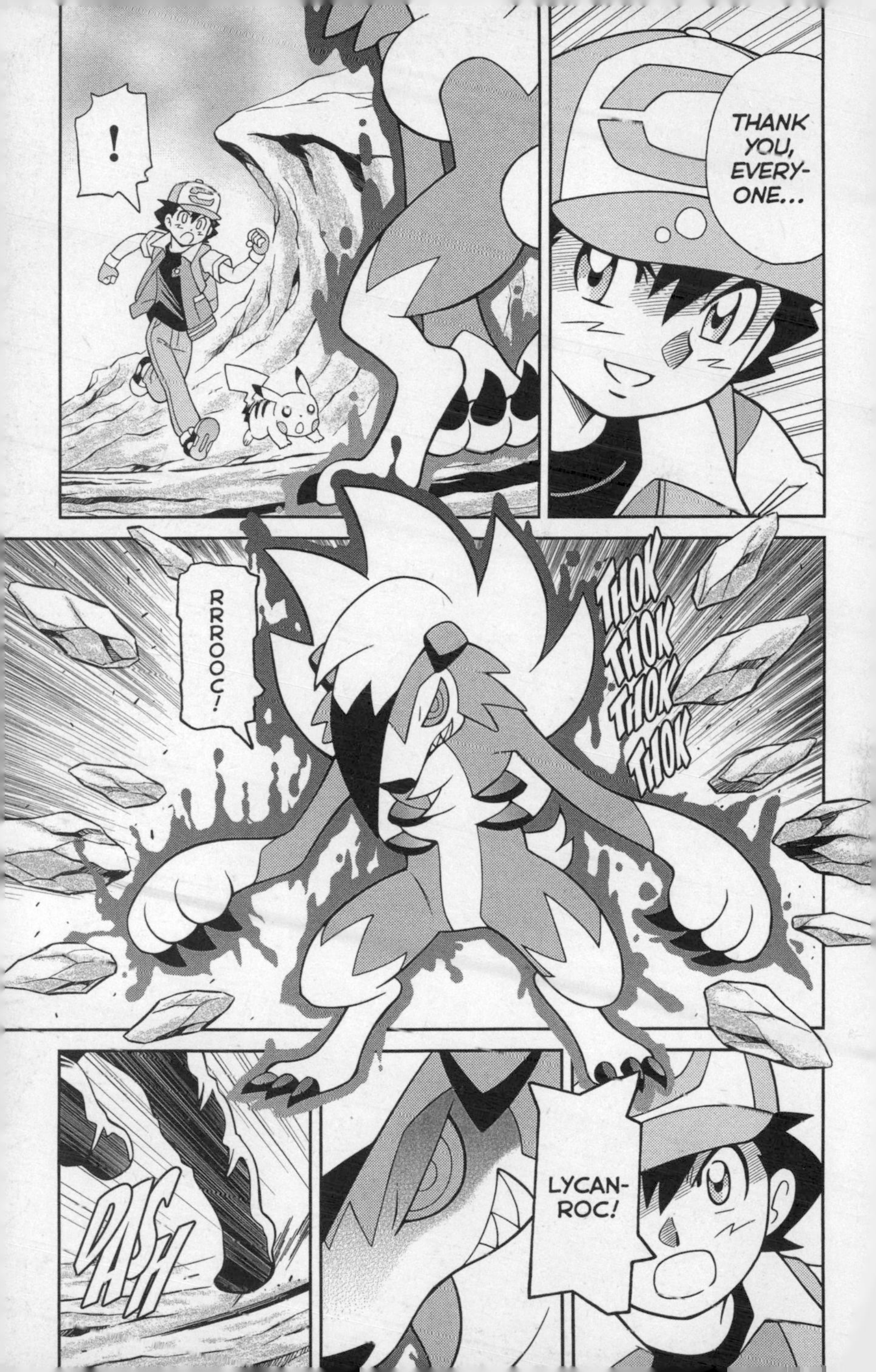
THANK YOU, EVERY-ONE...
!
THOK THOK THOK THOK
RRROOOC!
LYCAN-ROC!
DASH

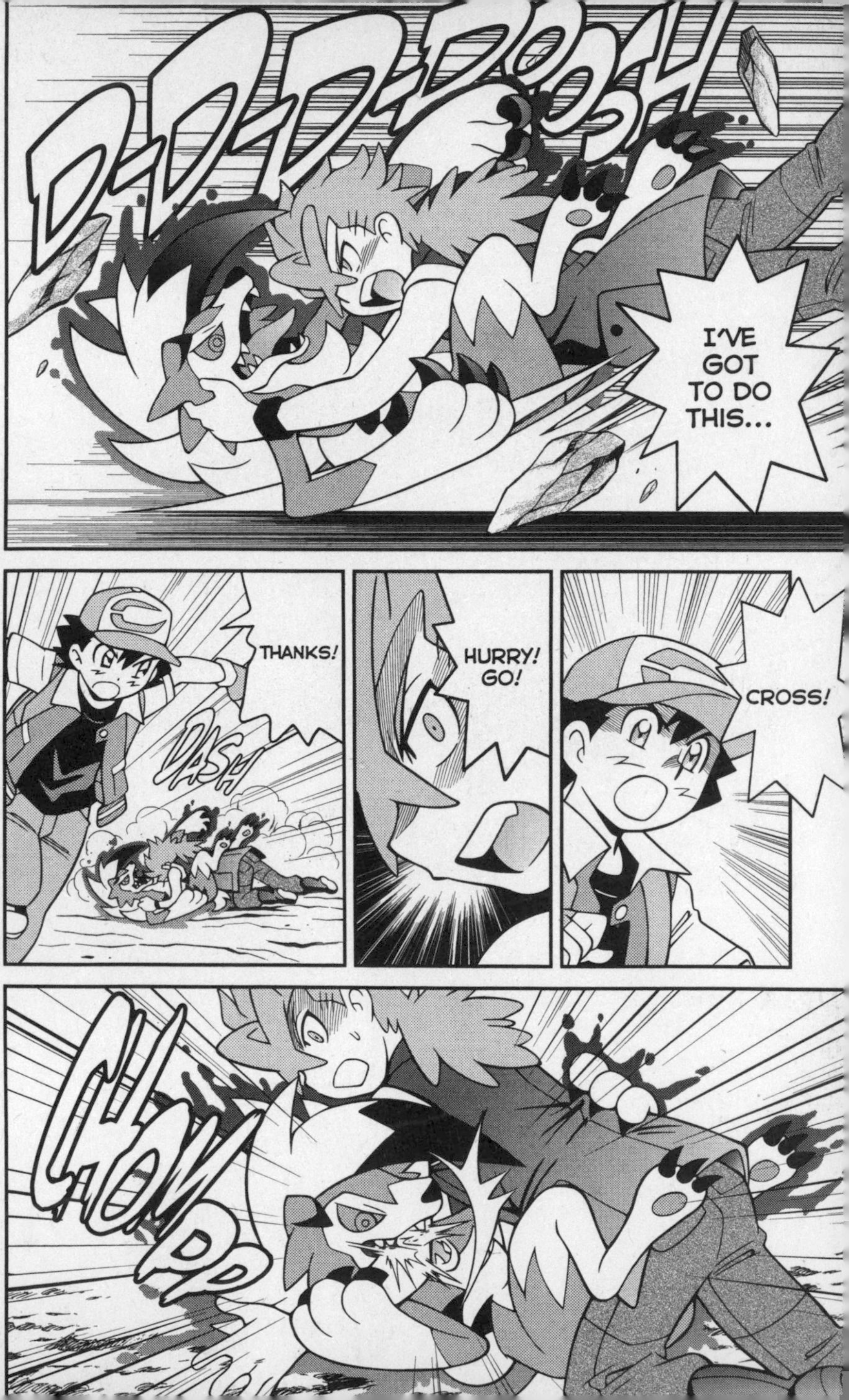
D-D-D-DOOSH
I'VE GOT TO DO THIS...
CROSS!
HURRY! GO!
THANKS!
DASH
CHOMP

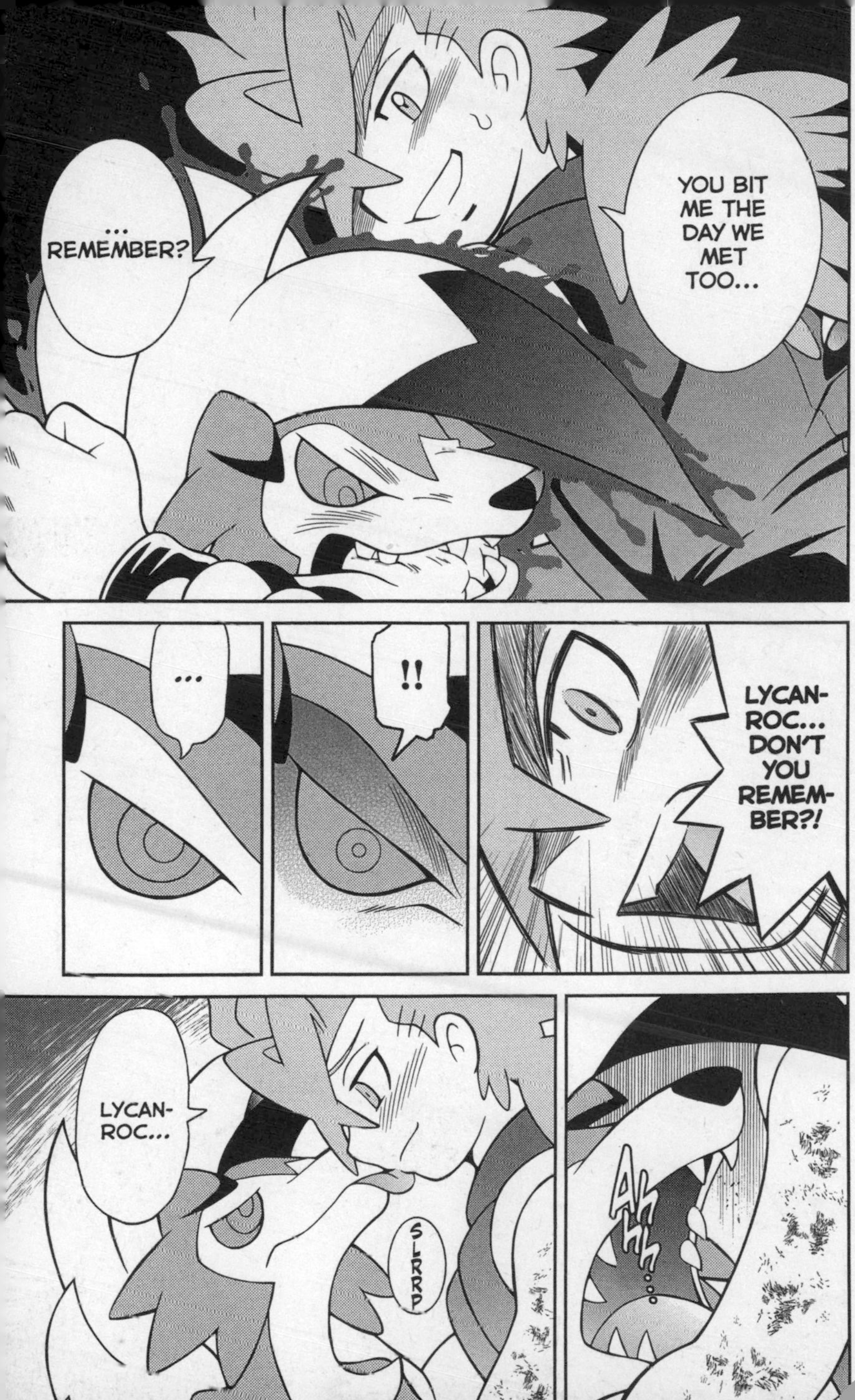
YOU BIT ME THE DAY WE MET TOO...
...REMEMBER?
LYCAN-ROC... DON'T YOU REMEM-BER?!
!!
...
Ahhh...
LYCAN-ROC...
SLRRP

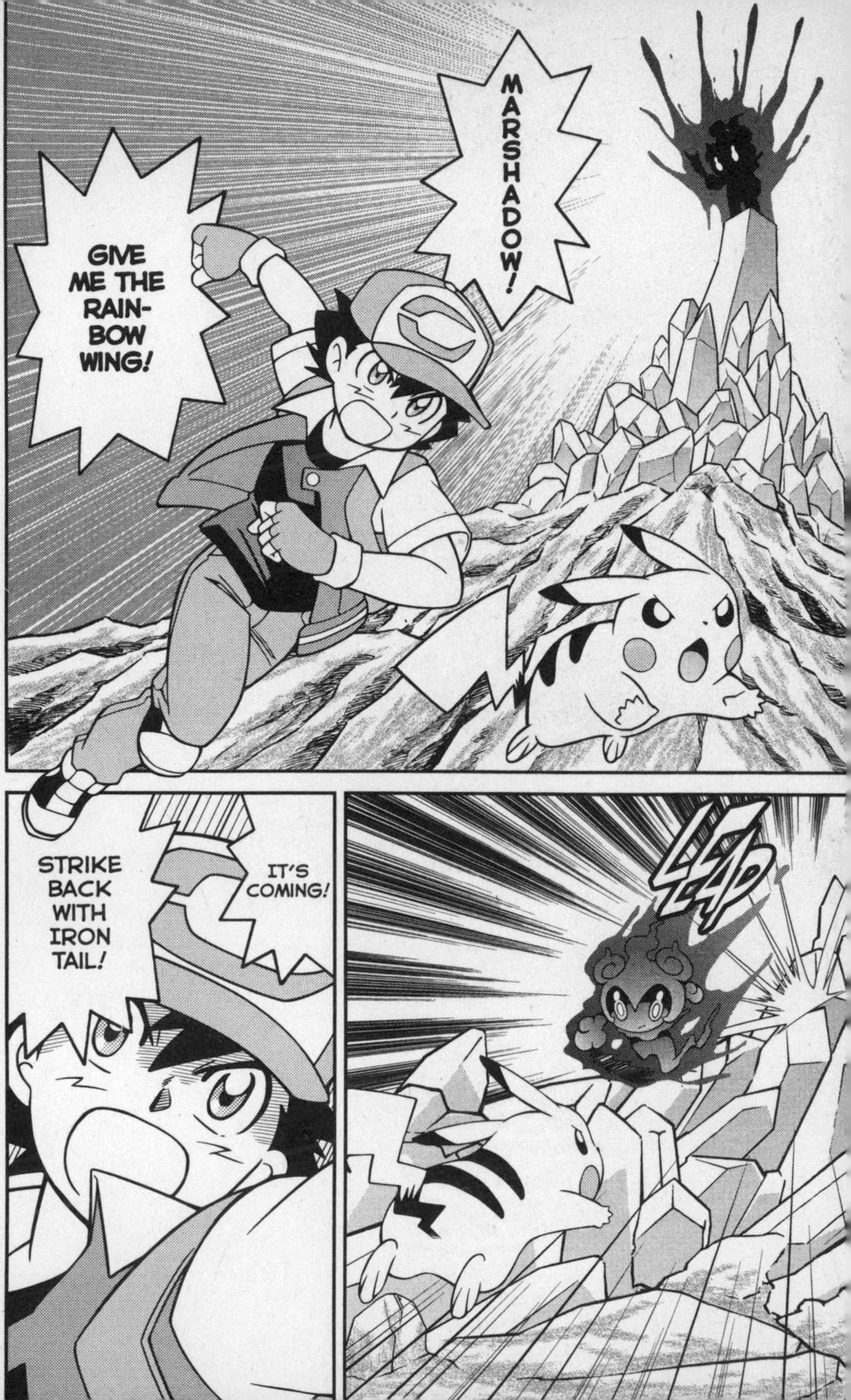
MARSHADOW!
GIVE ME THE RAIN-BOW WING!
LEAP
IT'S COMING!
STRIKE BACK WITH IRON TAIL!

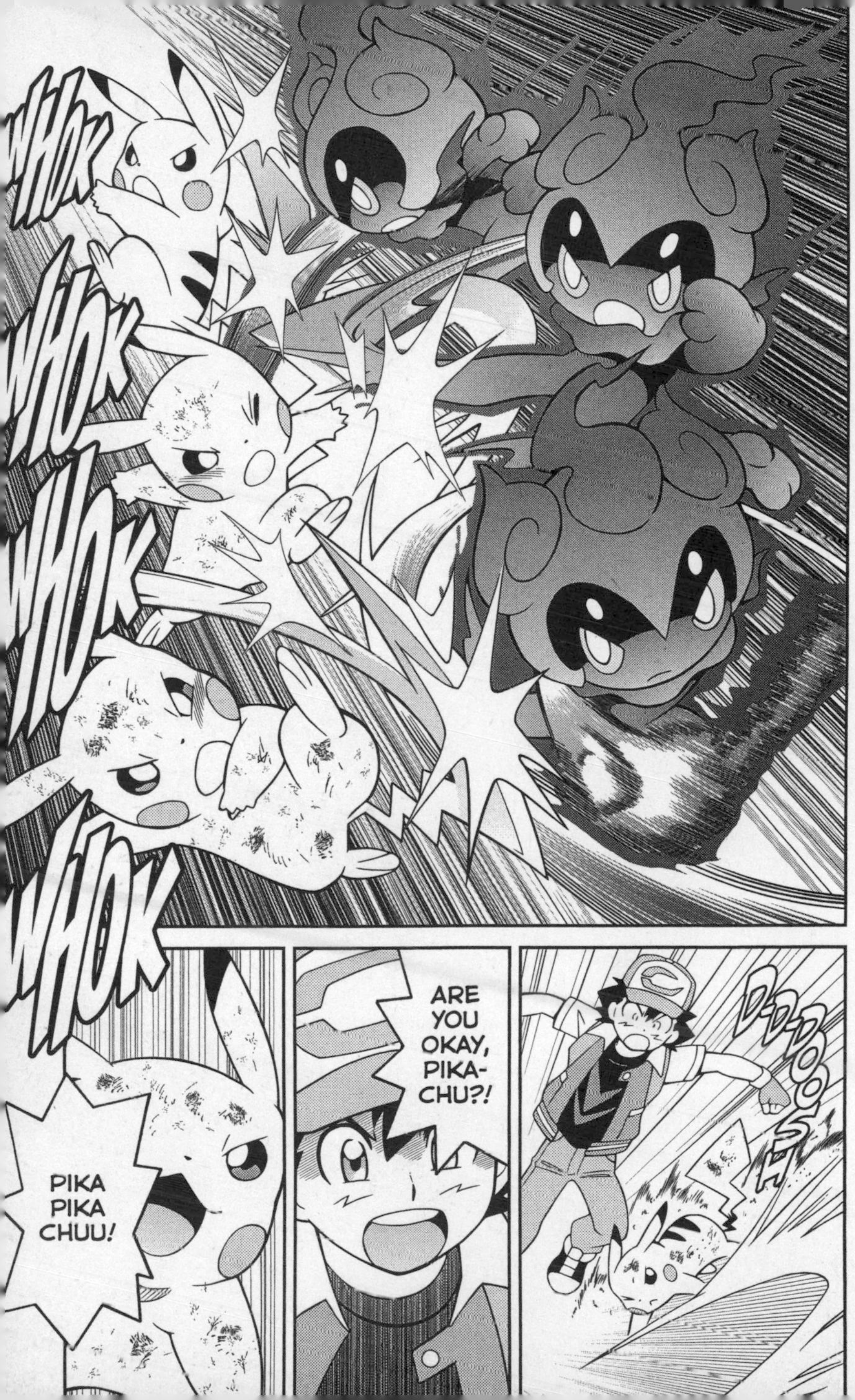
WHOK
WHOK
WHOK
WHOK
D-D-DOOOSH
ARE YOU OKAY, PIKA-CHU?!
PIKA PIKA CHUU!

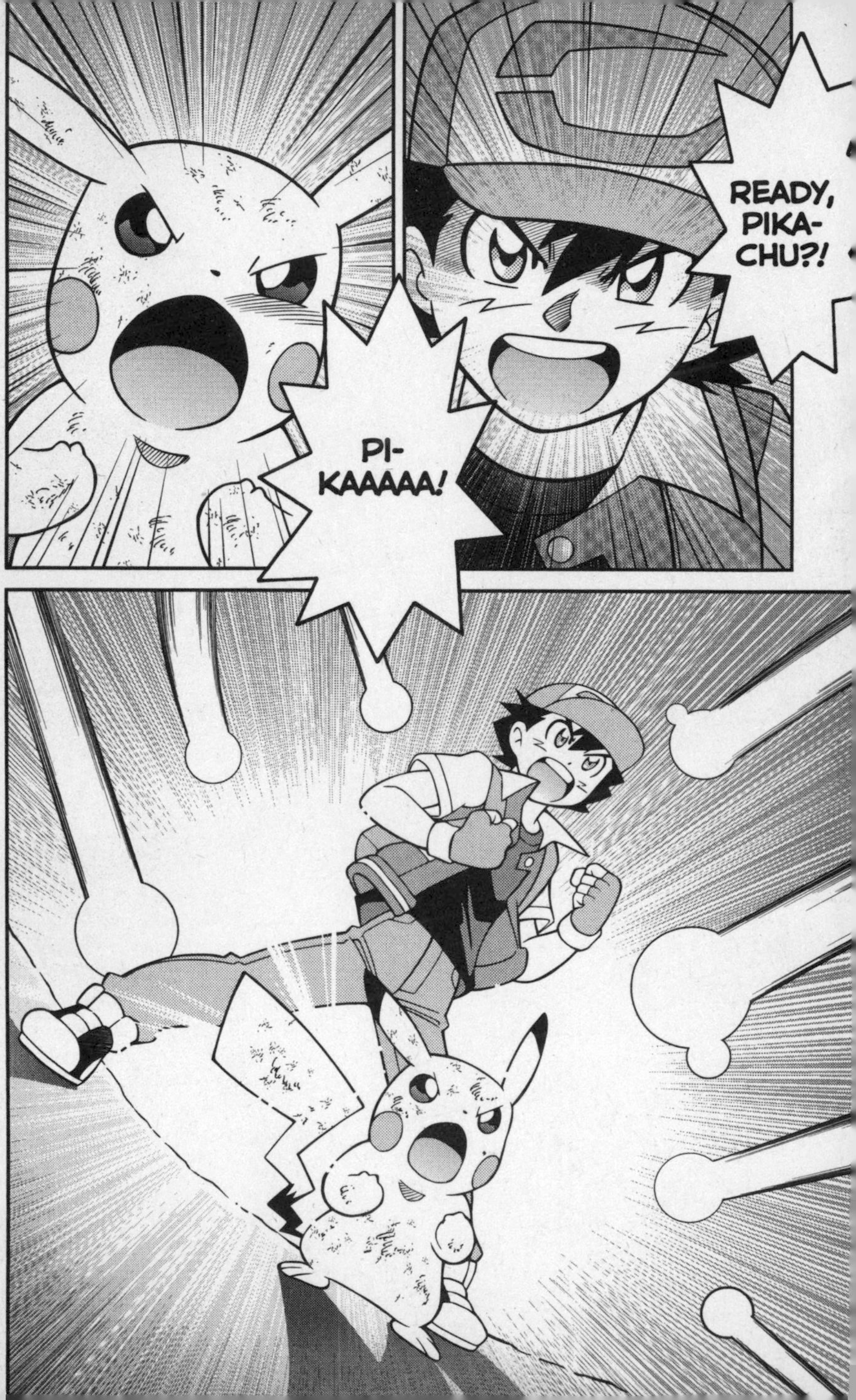
READY, PIKA-CHU?!
PI-KAAAAA!

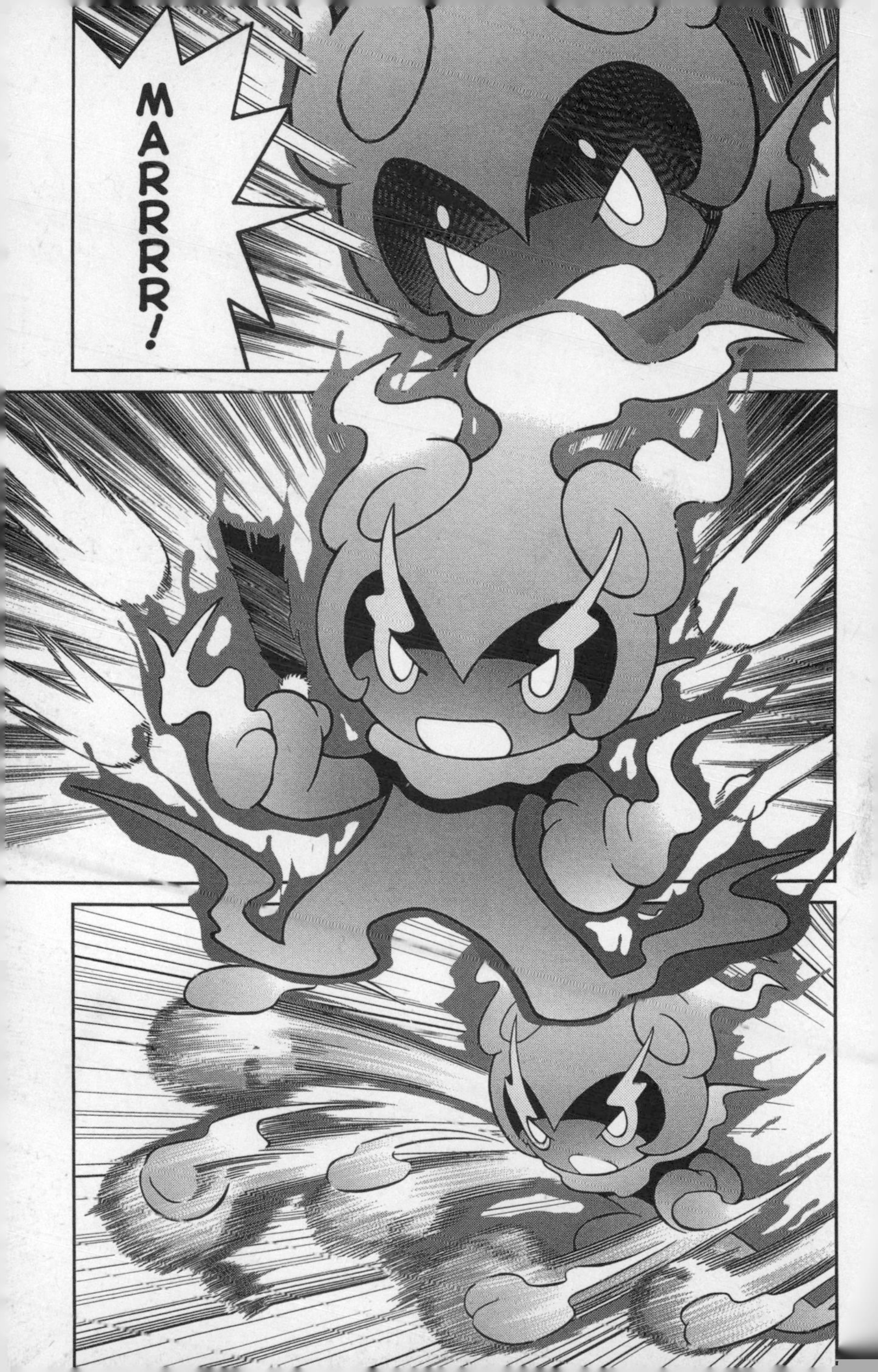
MARRRR!

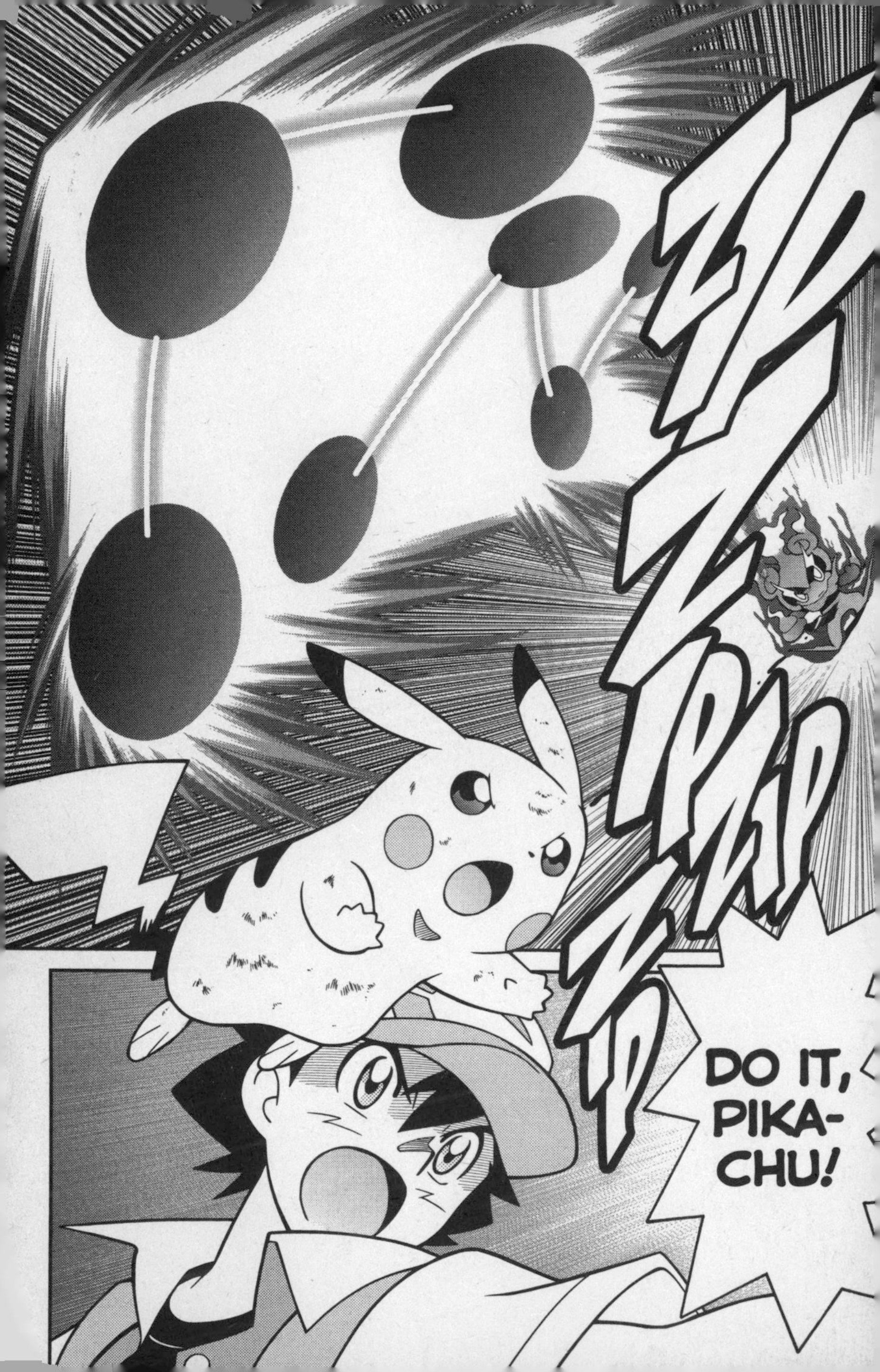
DO IT, PIKA-CHU!

CHAPTER 14

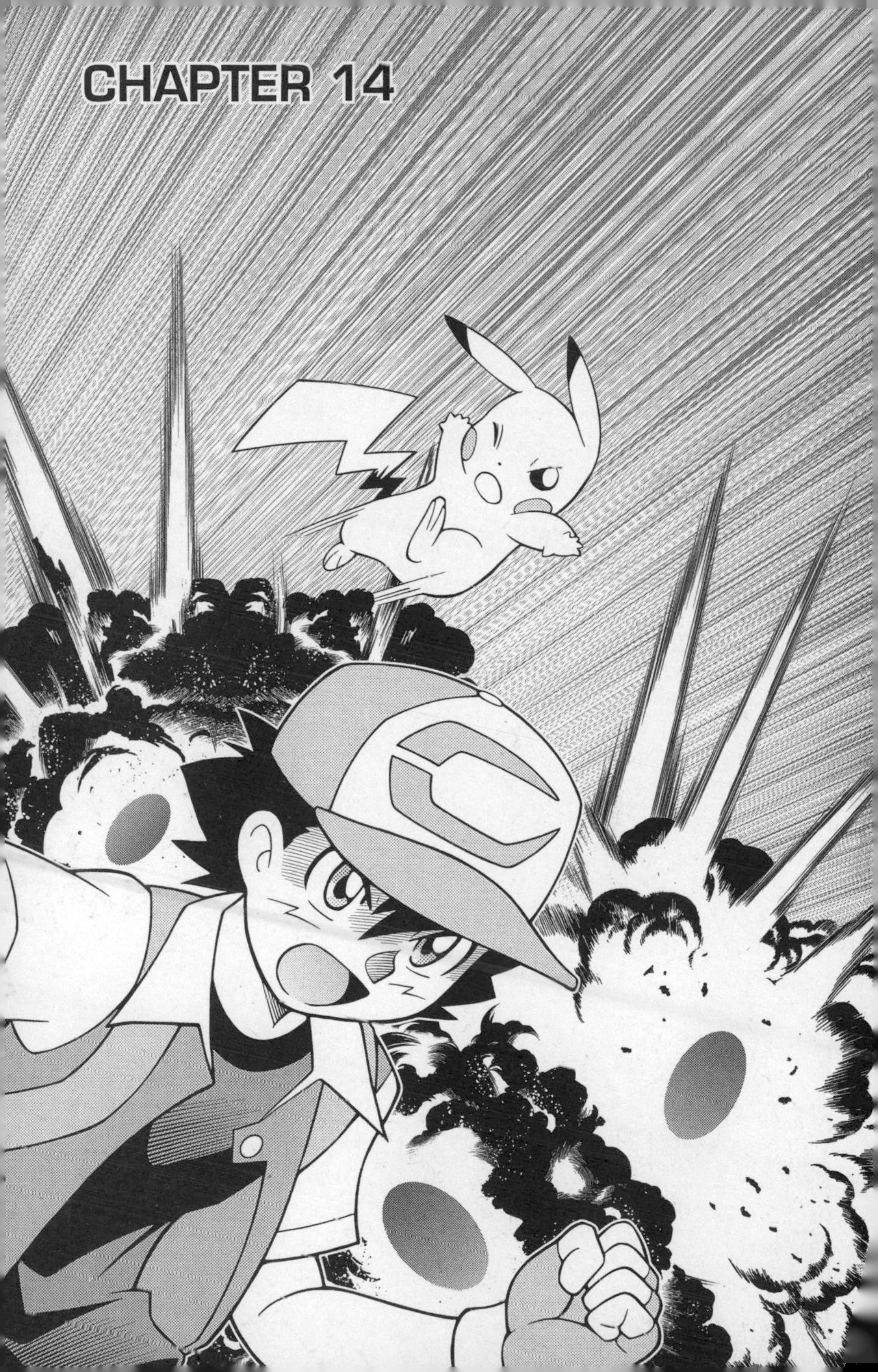

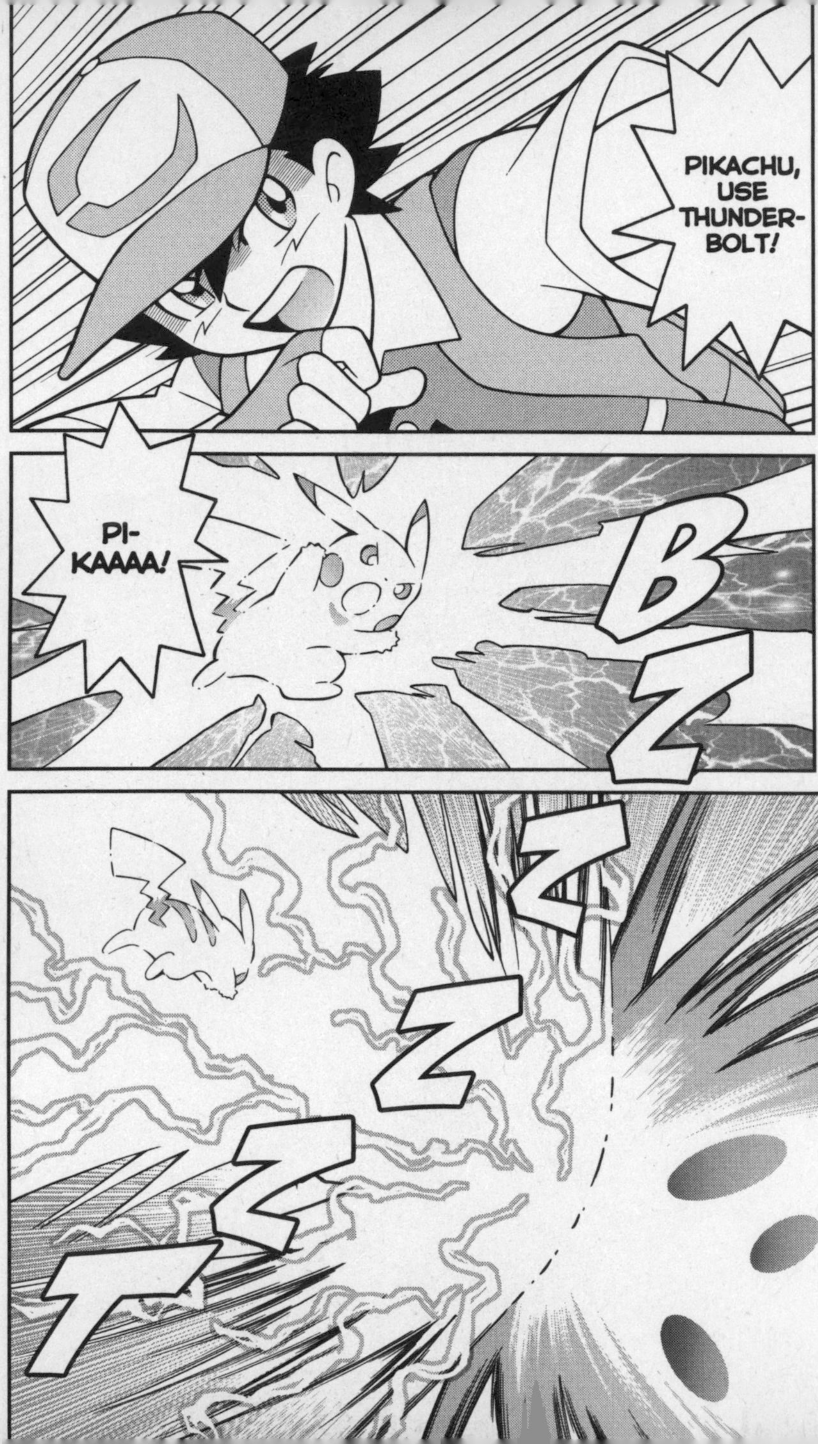
PIKACHU, USE THUNDER-BOLT!
PI-KAAAA!
BZZ
ZZZT

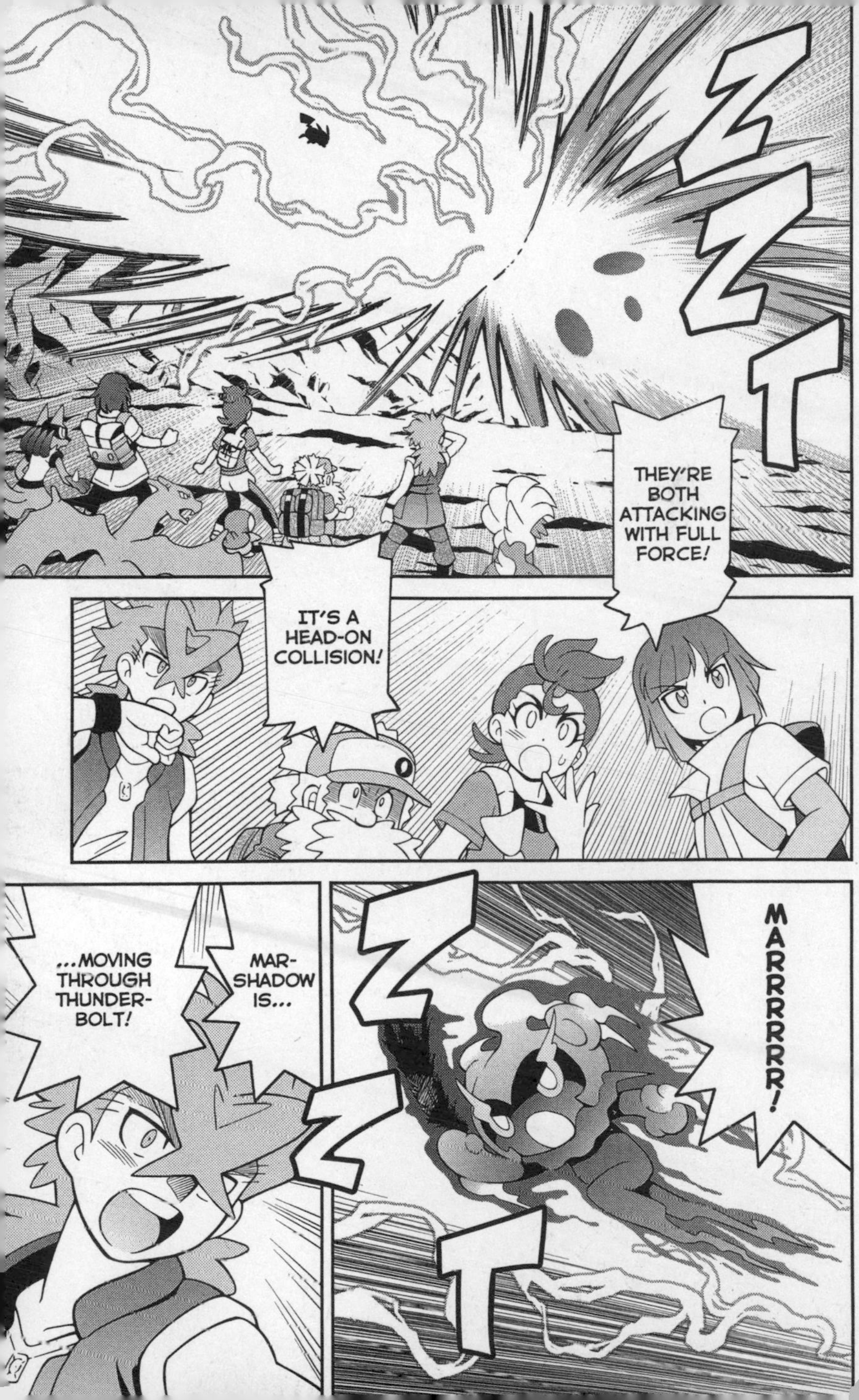
ZZZT
THEY'RE BOTH ATTACKING WITH FULL FORCE!
IT'S A HEAD-ON COLLISION!
ZZZT
MARRRRRR!
MAR-SHADOW IS...
...MOVING THROUGH THUNDER-BOLT!

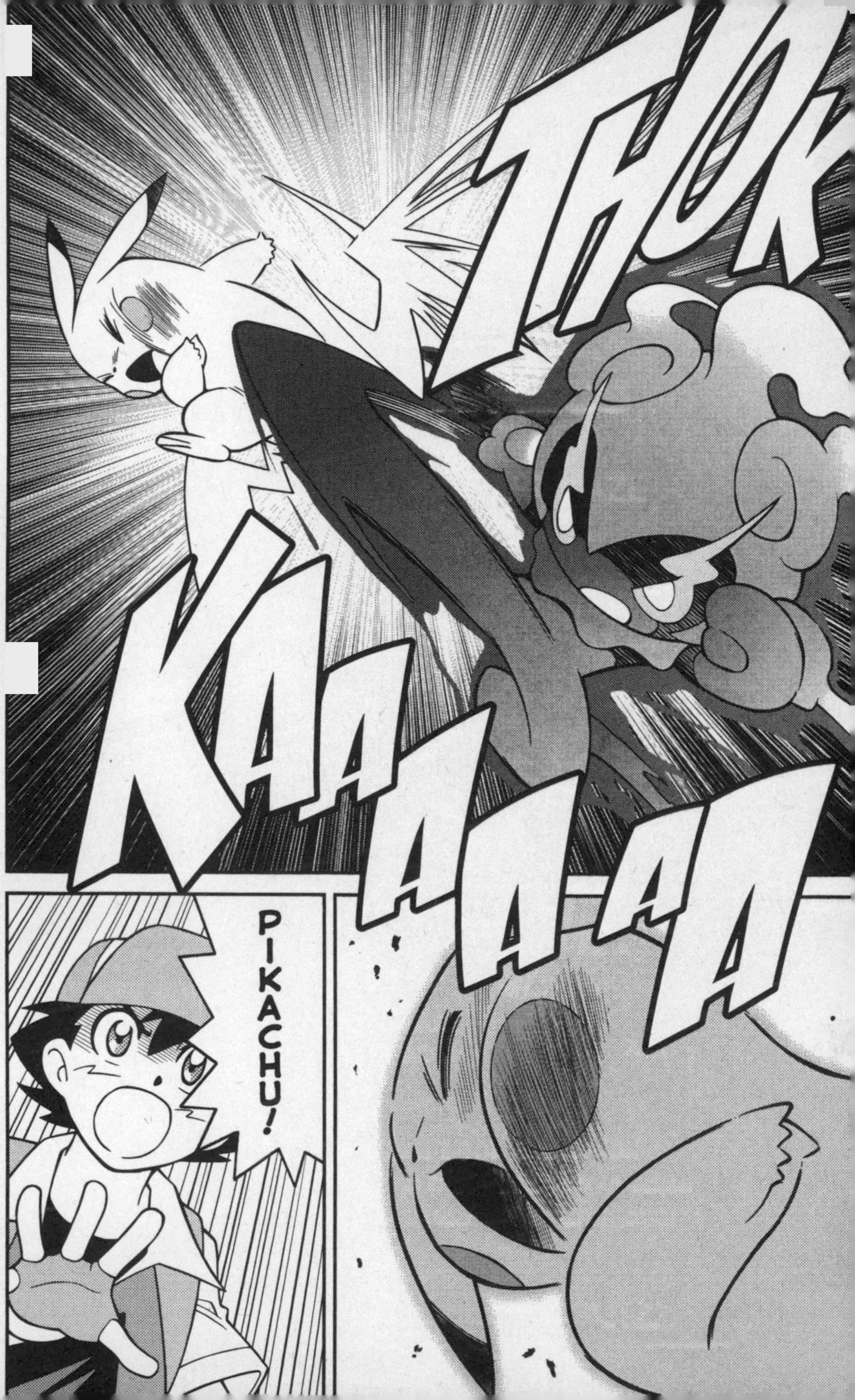
THOK
KAAAAAA
PIKACHU!

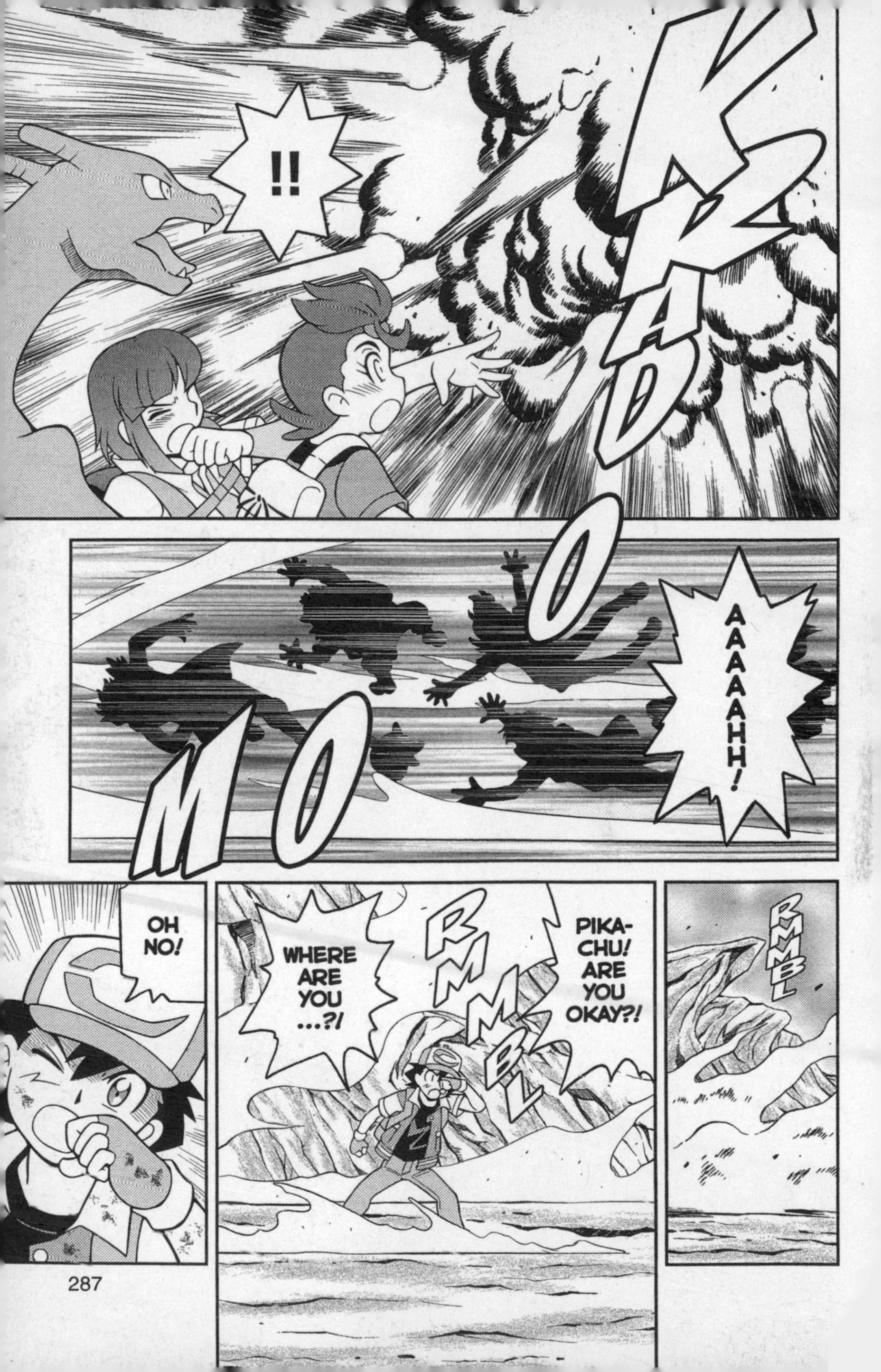
!!
KADOOM
AAAAAAHH!
RMMBL
PIKA-CHU! ARE YOU OKAY?!
RMMBL
WHERE ARE YOU ...?!
OH NO!

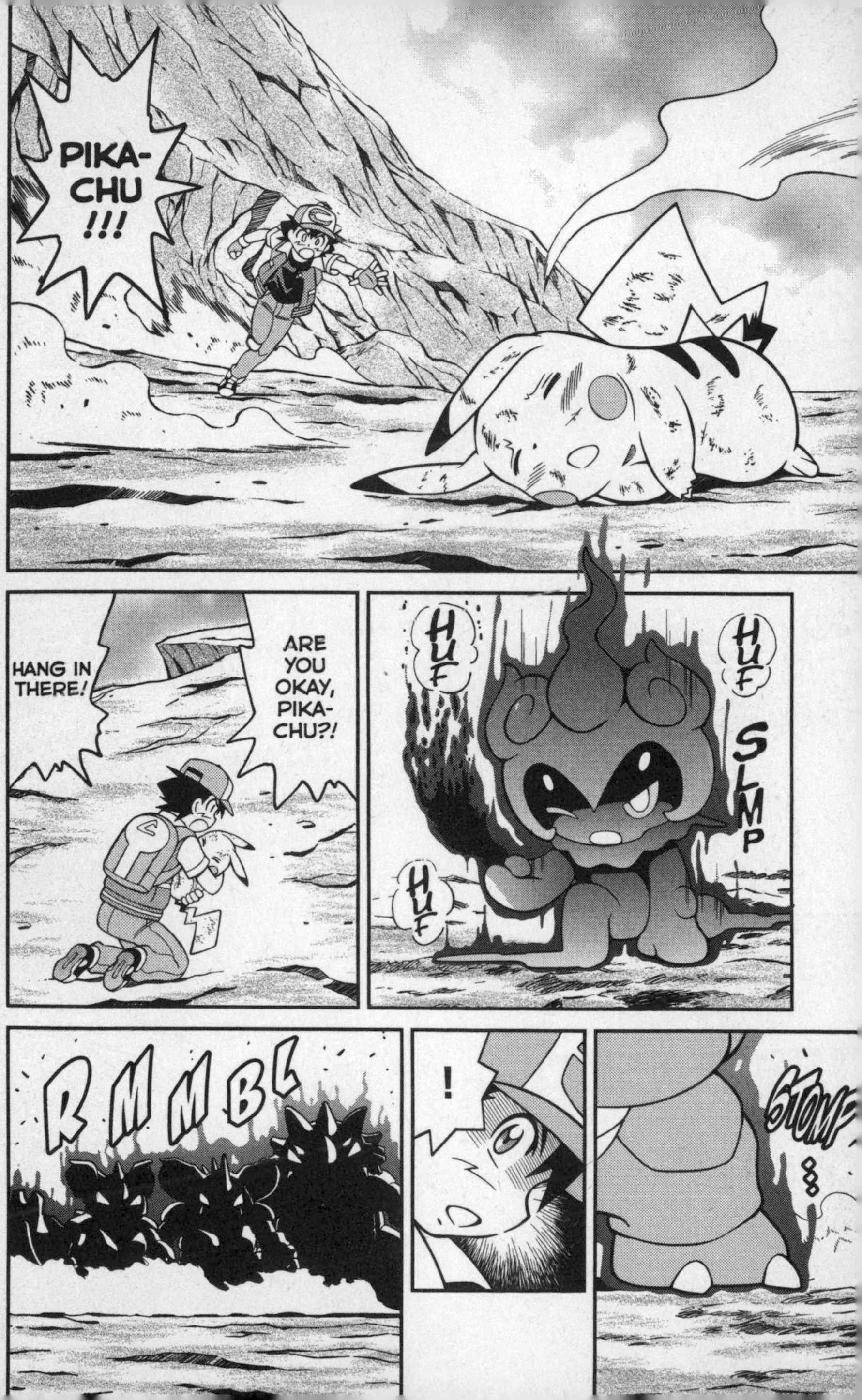
PIKA-CHU!!!
HUF HUF
SLMP
HUF HUF
ARE YOU OKAY, PIKA-CHU?!
HANG IN THERE!
STOMP
!
RMMBL

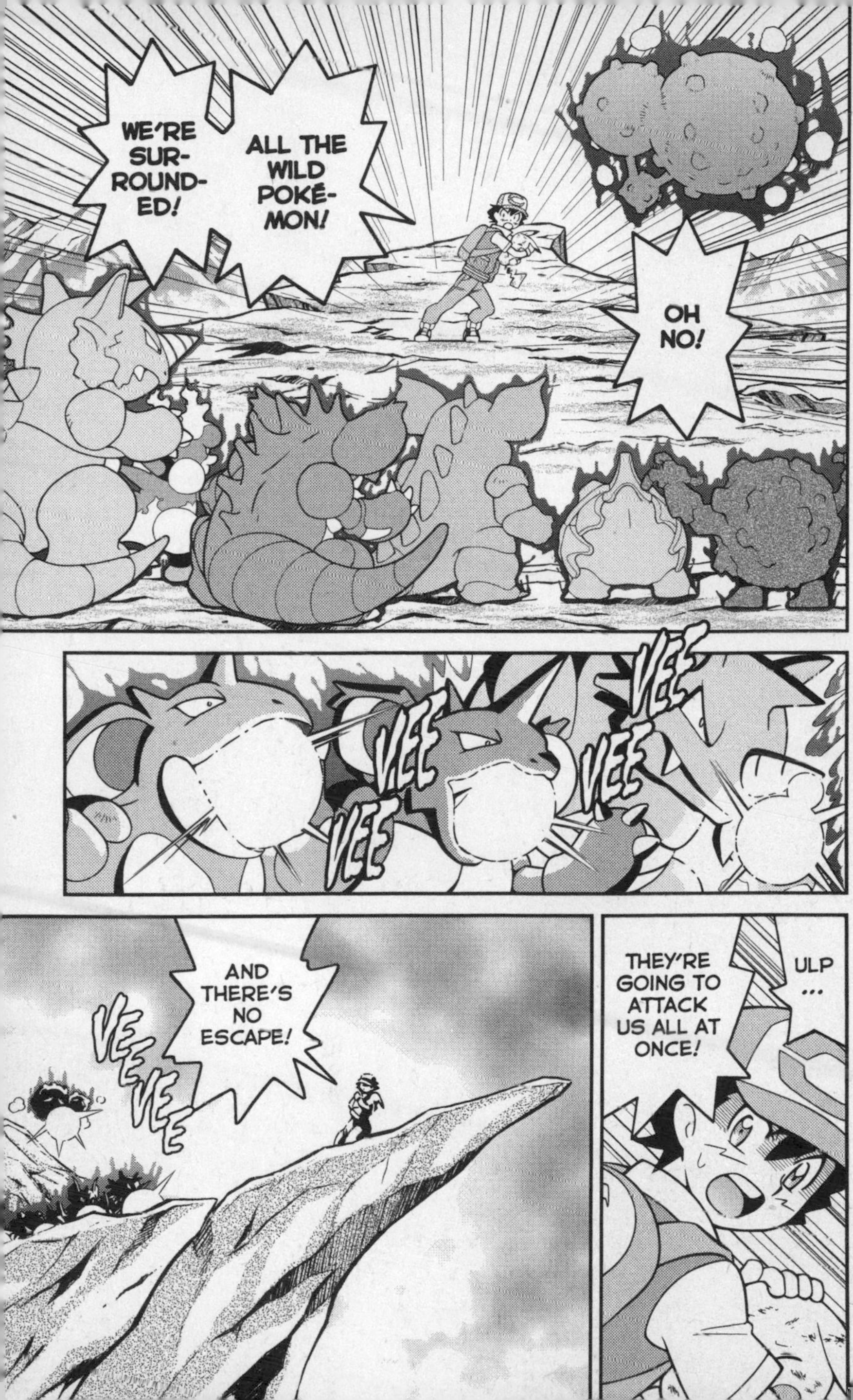
OH NO!
ALL THE WILD POKÉ-MON!
WE'RE SUR-ROUND-ED!
VEE
VEE
VEE
VEE
ULP ...
THEY'RE GOING TO ATTACK US ALL AT ONCE!
AND THERE'S NO ESCAPE!
VEE VEE VEE

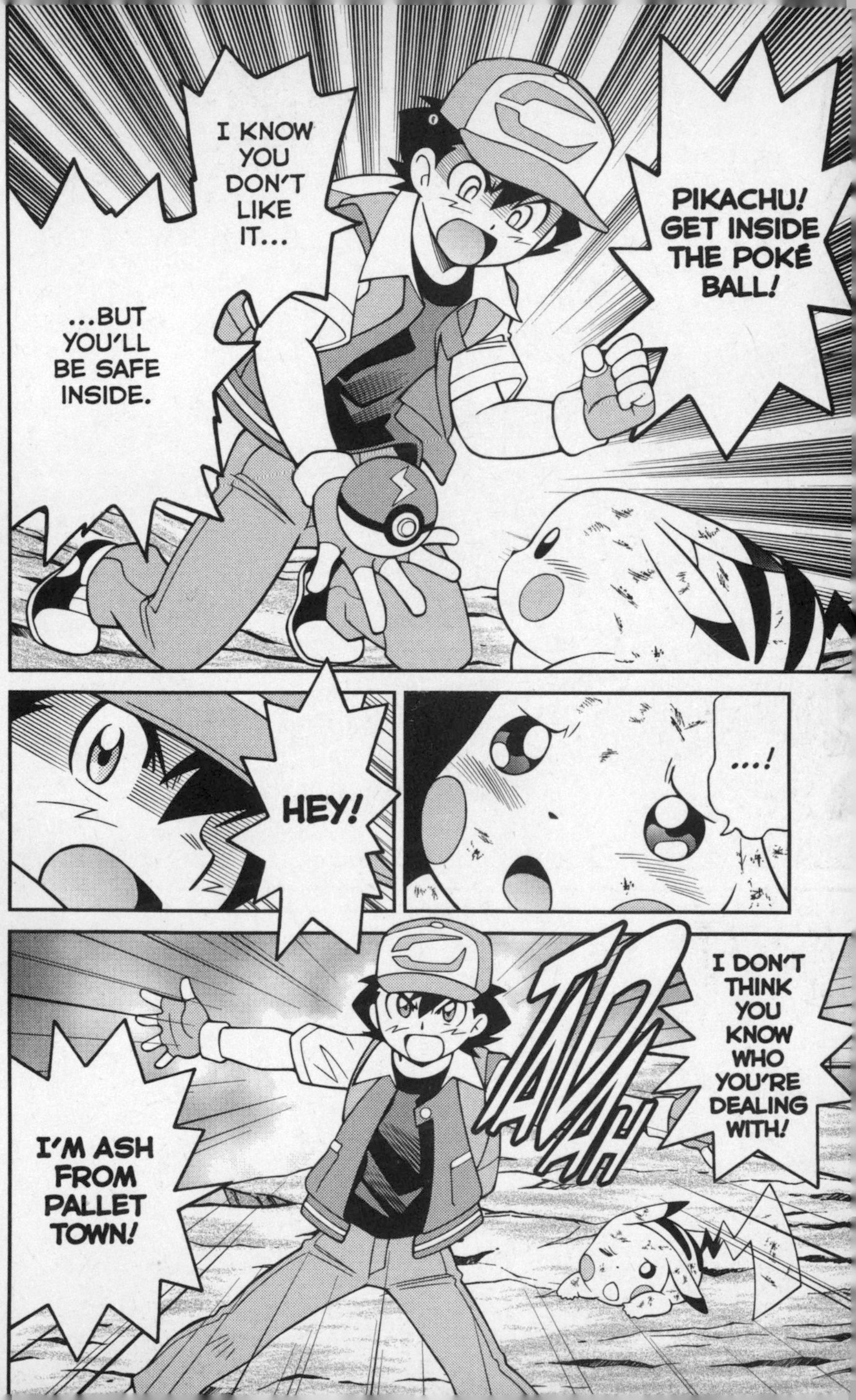
PIKACHU! GET INSIDE THE POKÉ BALL!
I KNOW YOU DON'T LIKE IT...
...BUT YOU'LL BE SAFE INSIDE.
...!
HEY!
I DON'T THINK YOU KNOW WHO YOU'RE DEALING WITH!
I'M ASH FROM PALLET TOWN!

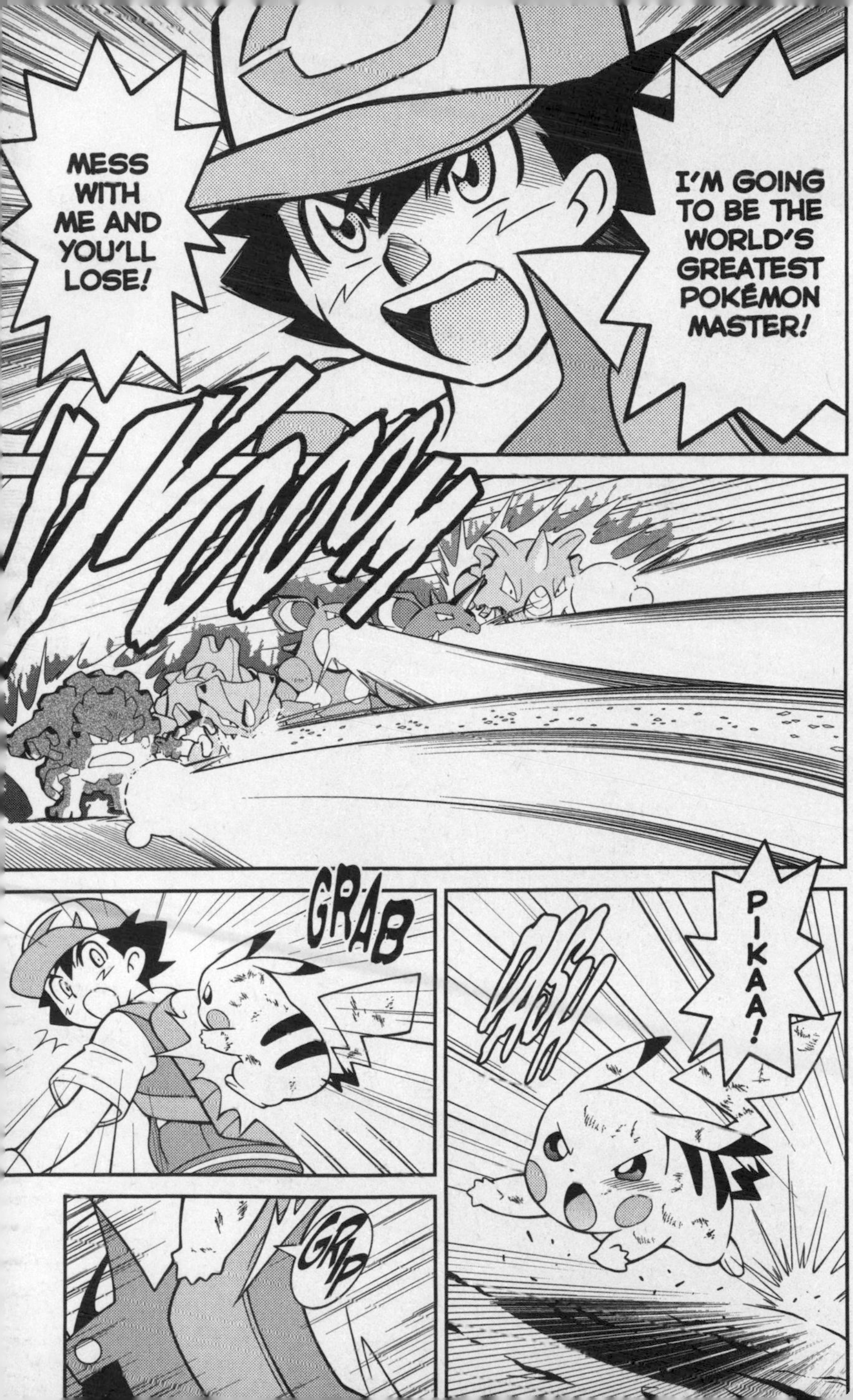
I'M GOING TO BE THE WORLD'S GREATEST POKÉMON MASTER!
MESS WITH ME AND YOU'LL LOSE!
PIKAA!
DASH
GRAB
GRIP

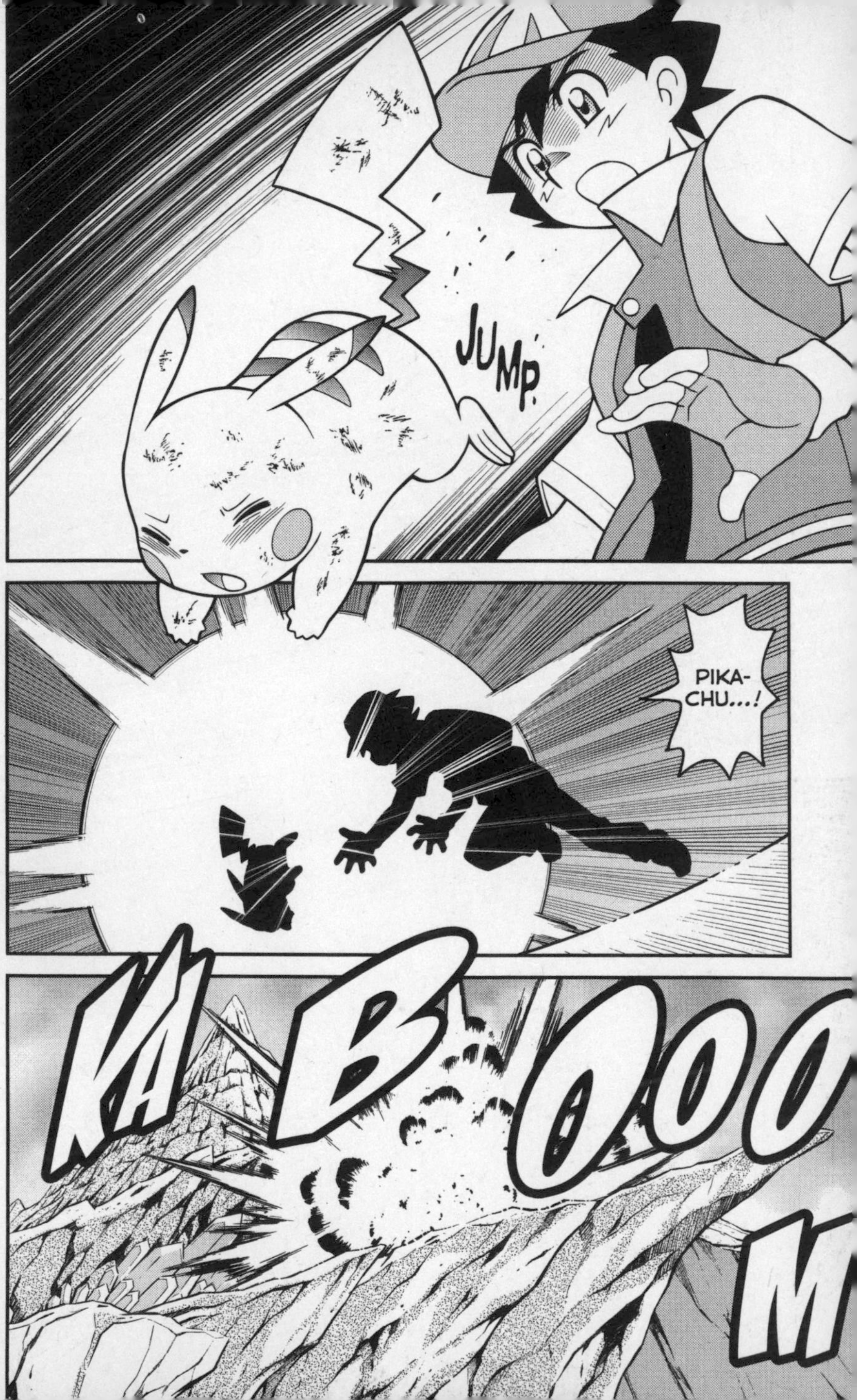
JUMP
PIKA-CHU...!
KABOOOM

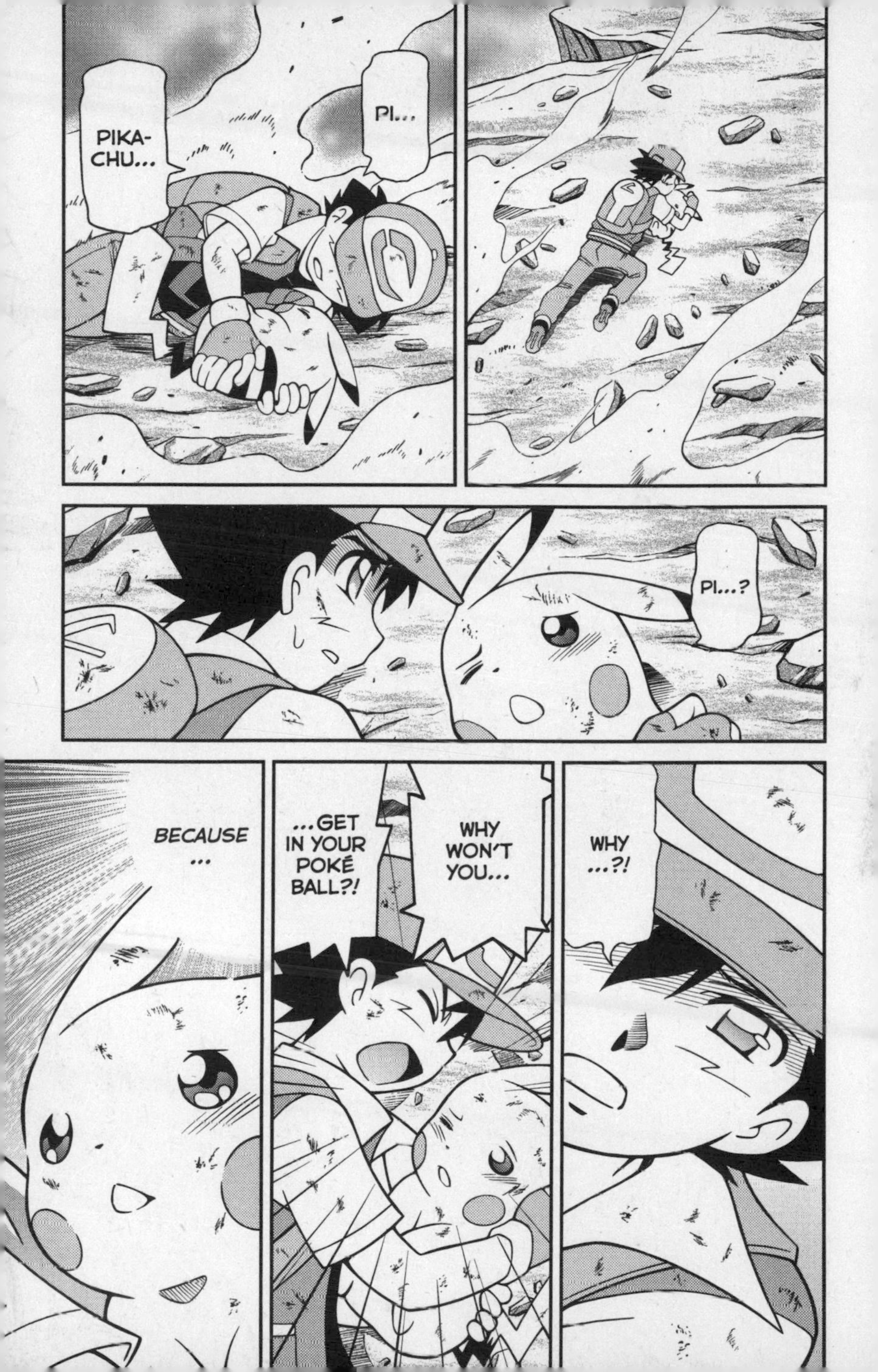
PI...
PIKA-CHU...
PI...?
WHY ...?!
WHY WON'T YOU...
...GET IN YOUR POKÉ BALL?!
BECAUSE ...

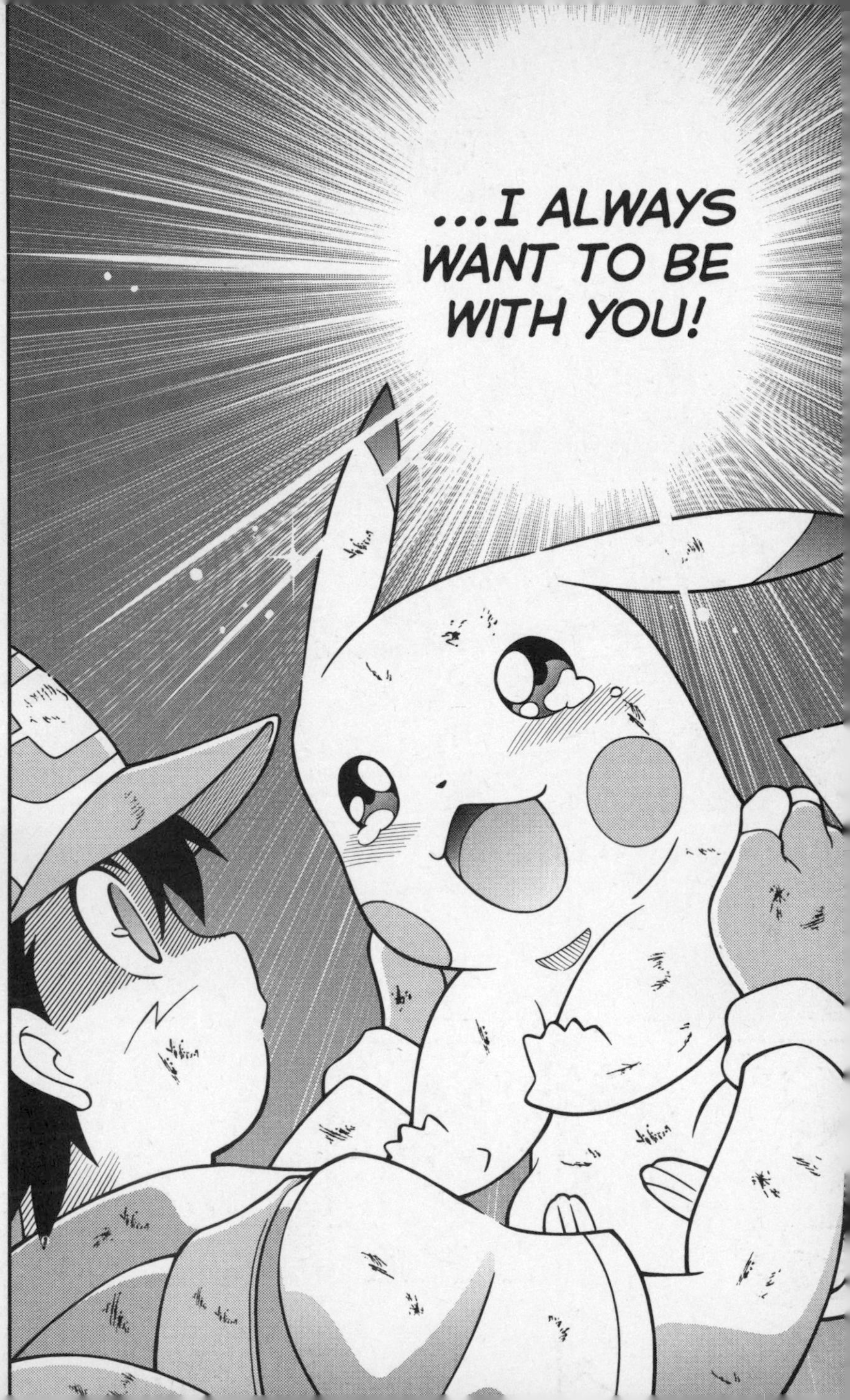
...I ALWAYS WANT TO BE WITH YOU!

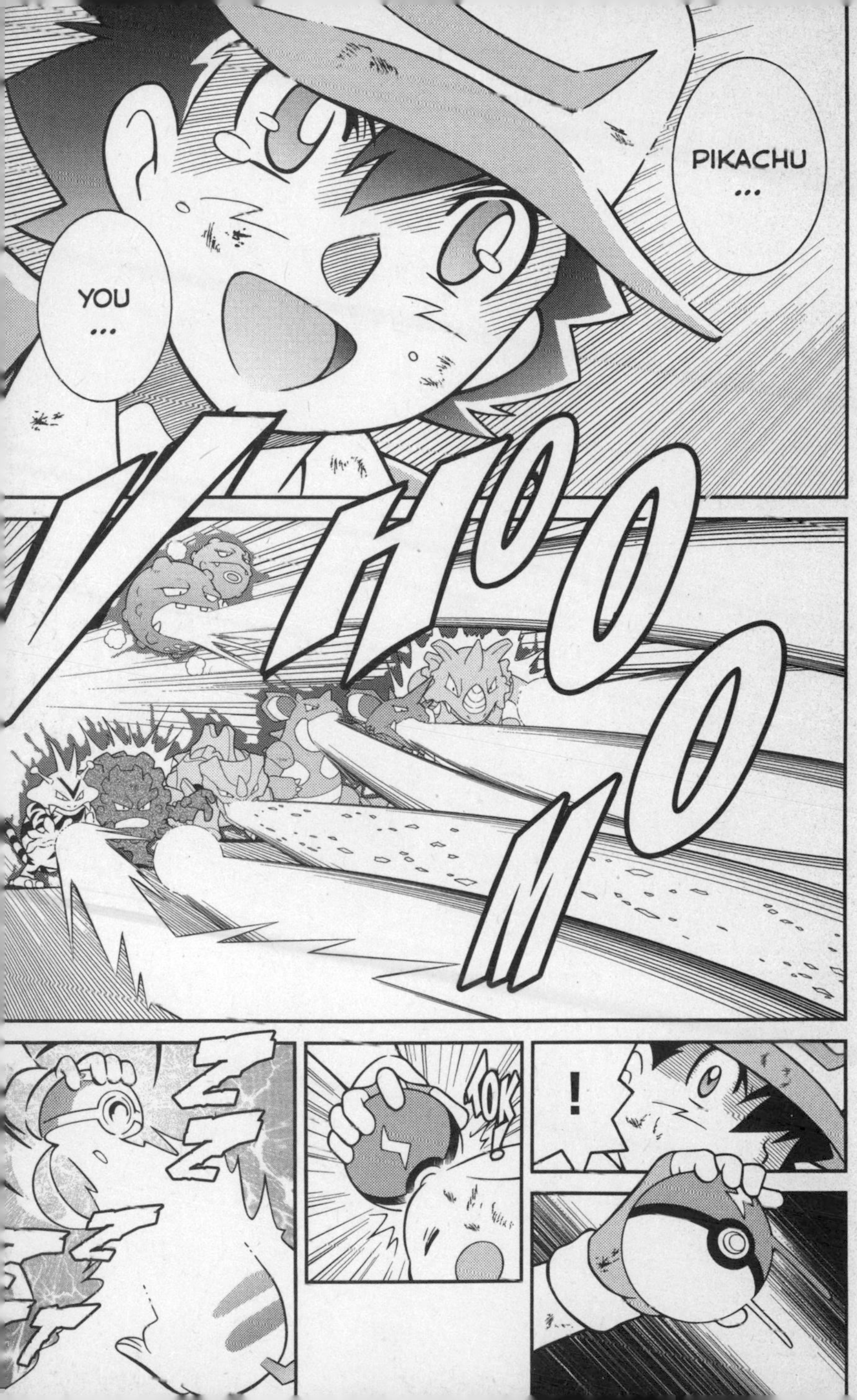
PIKACHU ...
YOU ...
!
TOK!

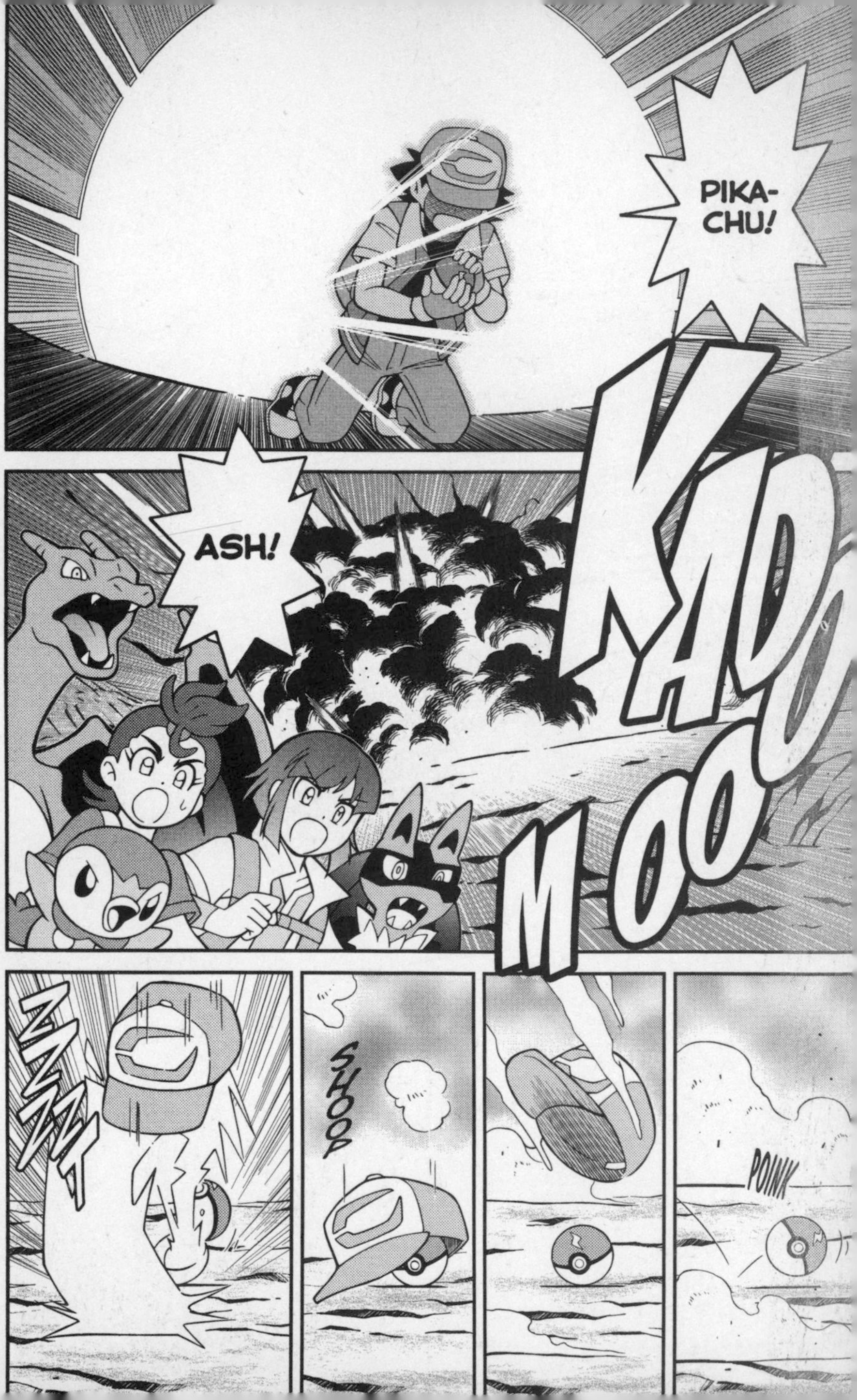
PIKA-
CHU!
ASH!
POINK

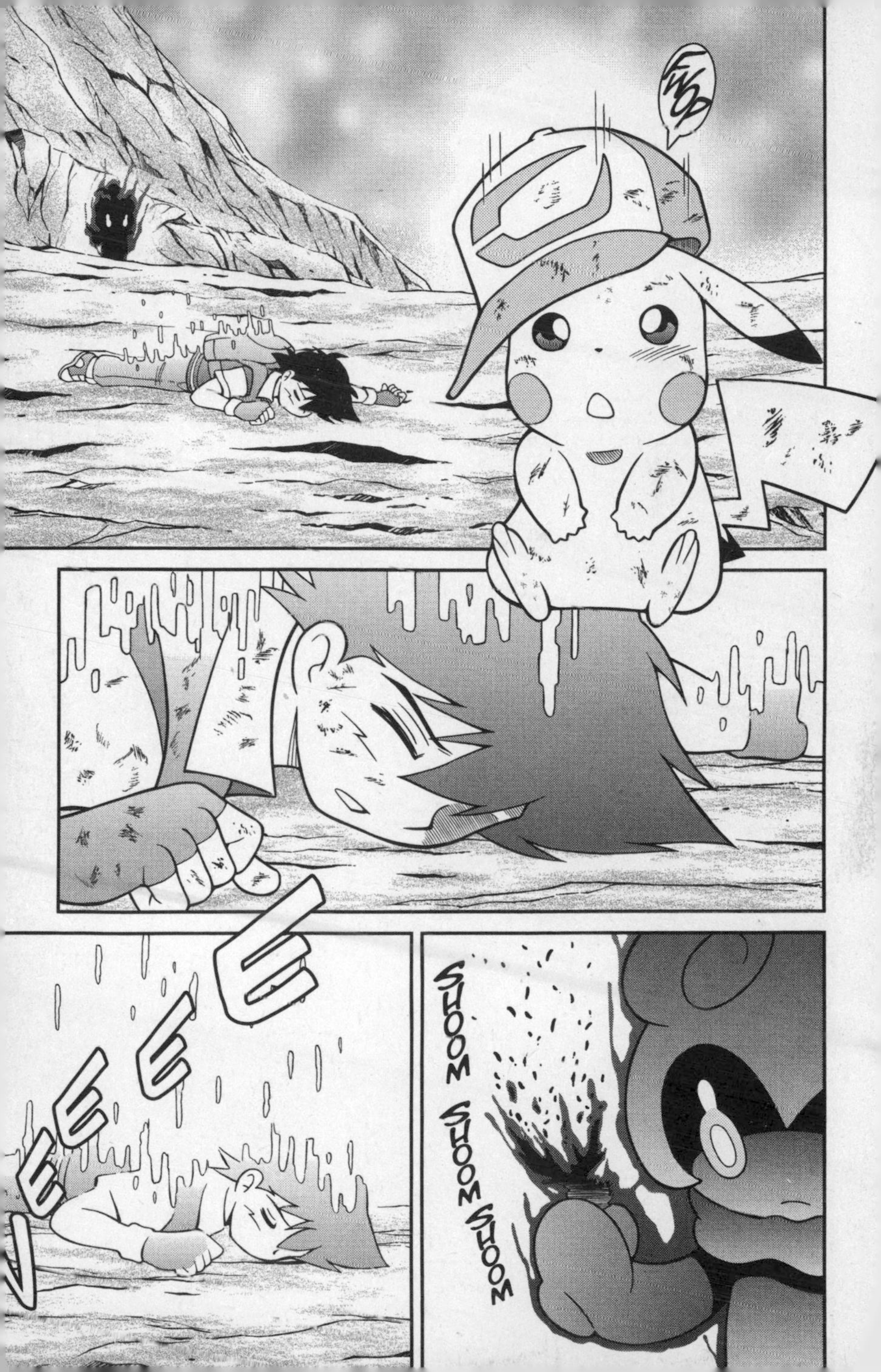
SHOOM SHOOM SHOOM
VEEEE

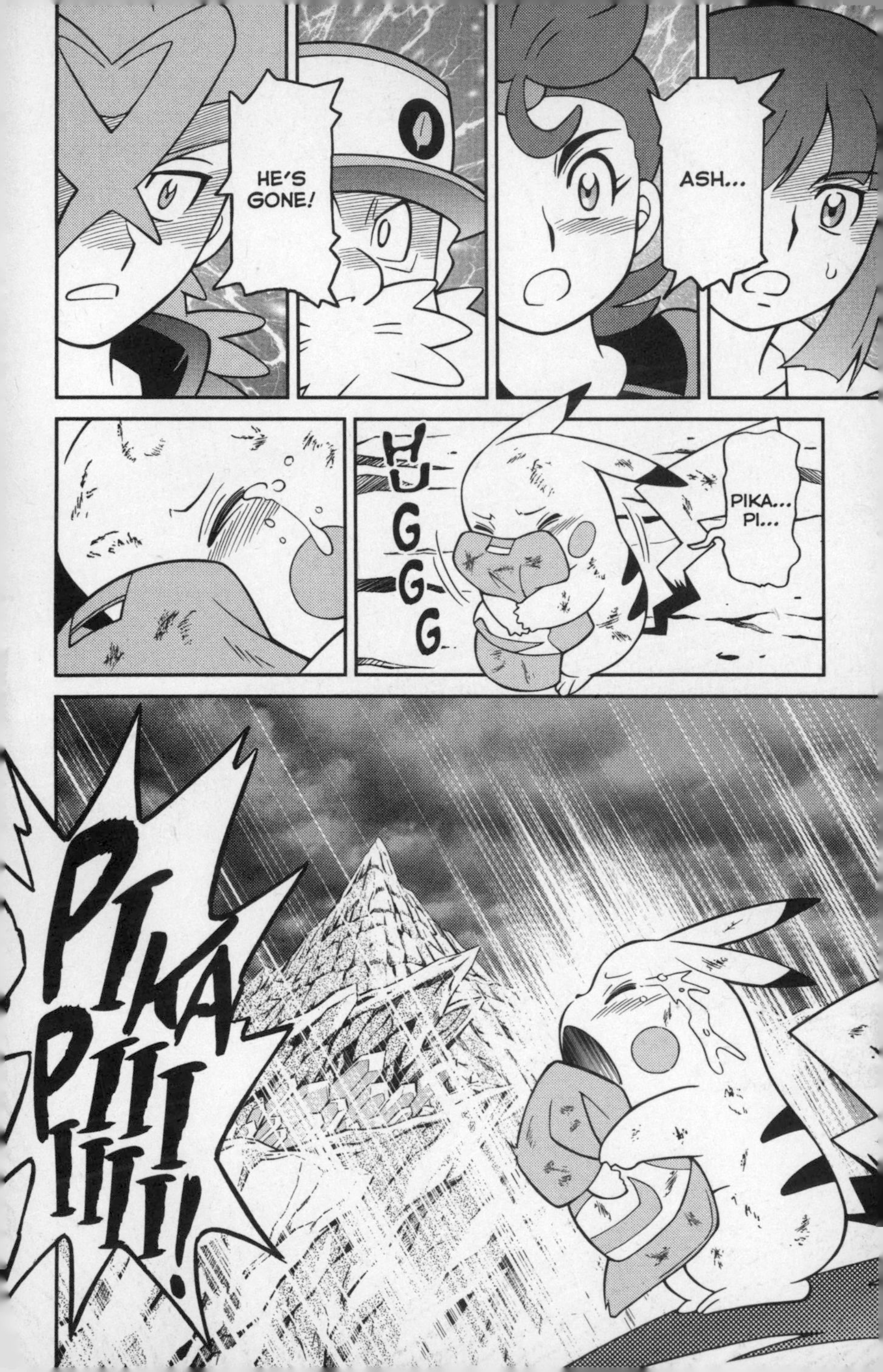
ASH...
HE'S GONE!
PIKA... PI...
HUGGG
PIKA PIIIIIII!

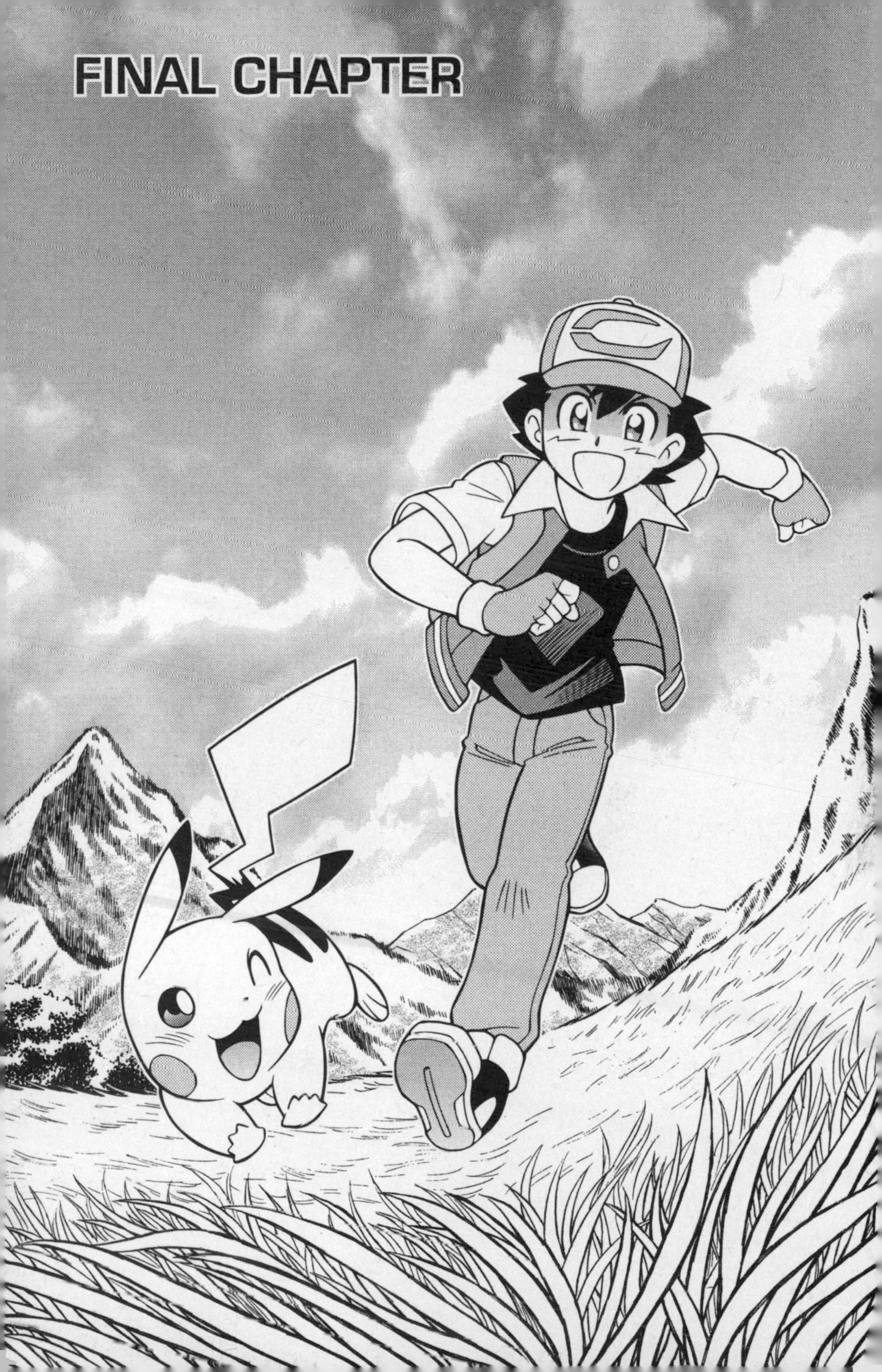
FINAL CHAPTER

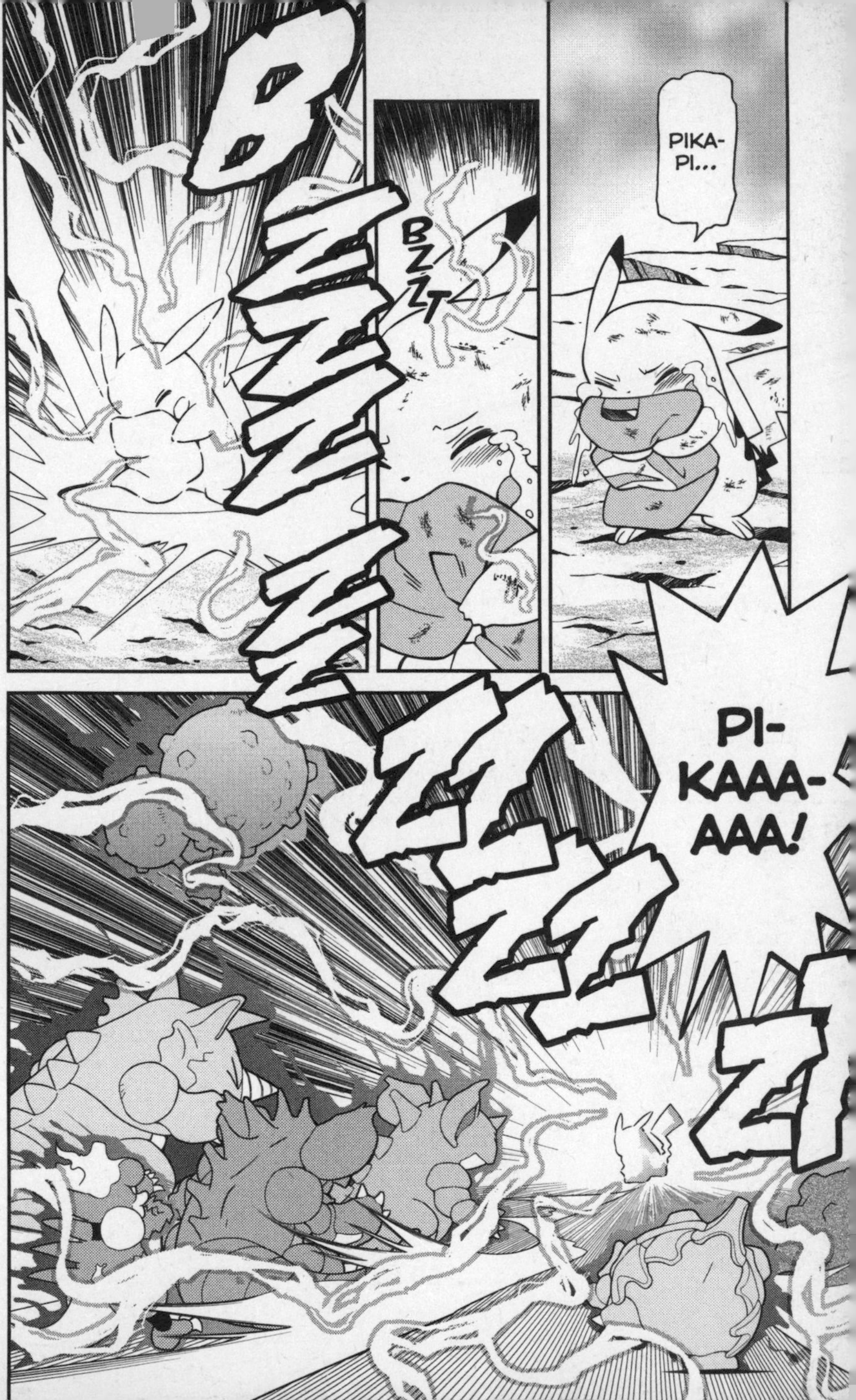
PIKA-
PI...
BZZZT
PI-
KAAAA-
AAA!

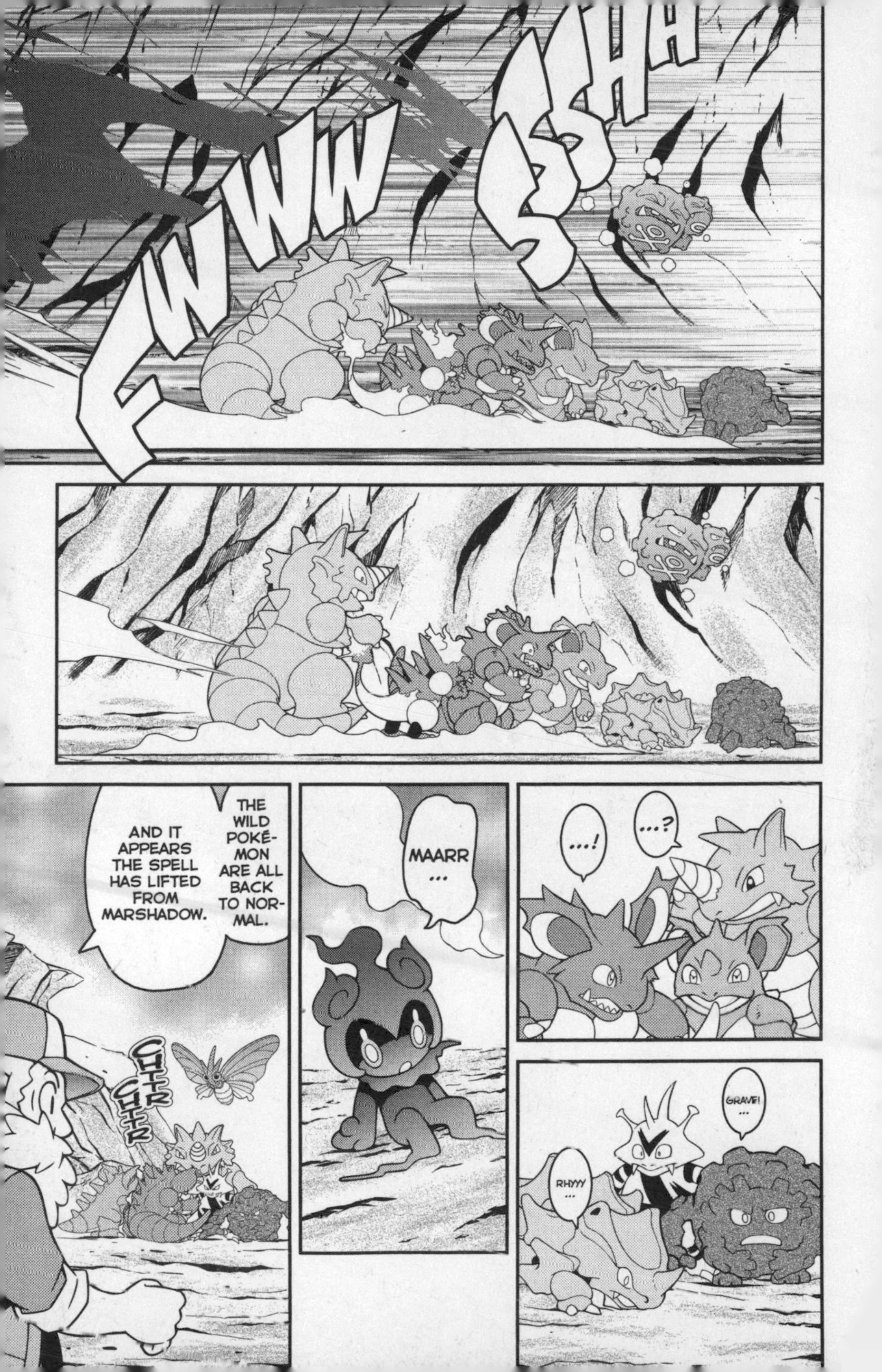
FWWWWSSHA
...?
...!
GRAVE! ...
RHYYY ...
MAARR ...
THE WILD POKÉMON ARE ALL BACK TO NORMAL.
AND IT APPEARS THE SPELL HAS LIFTED FROM MARSHADOW.
CHITTR CHITTR

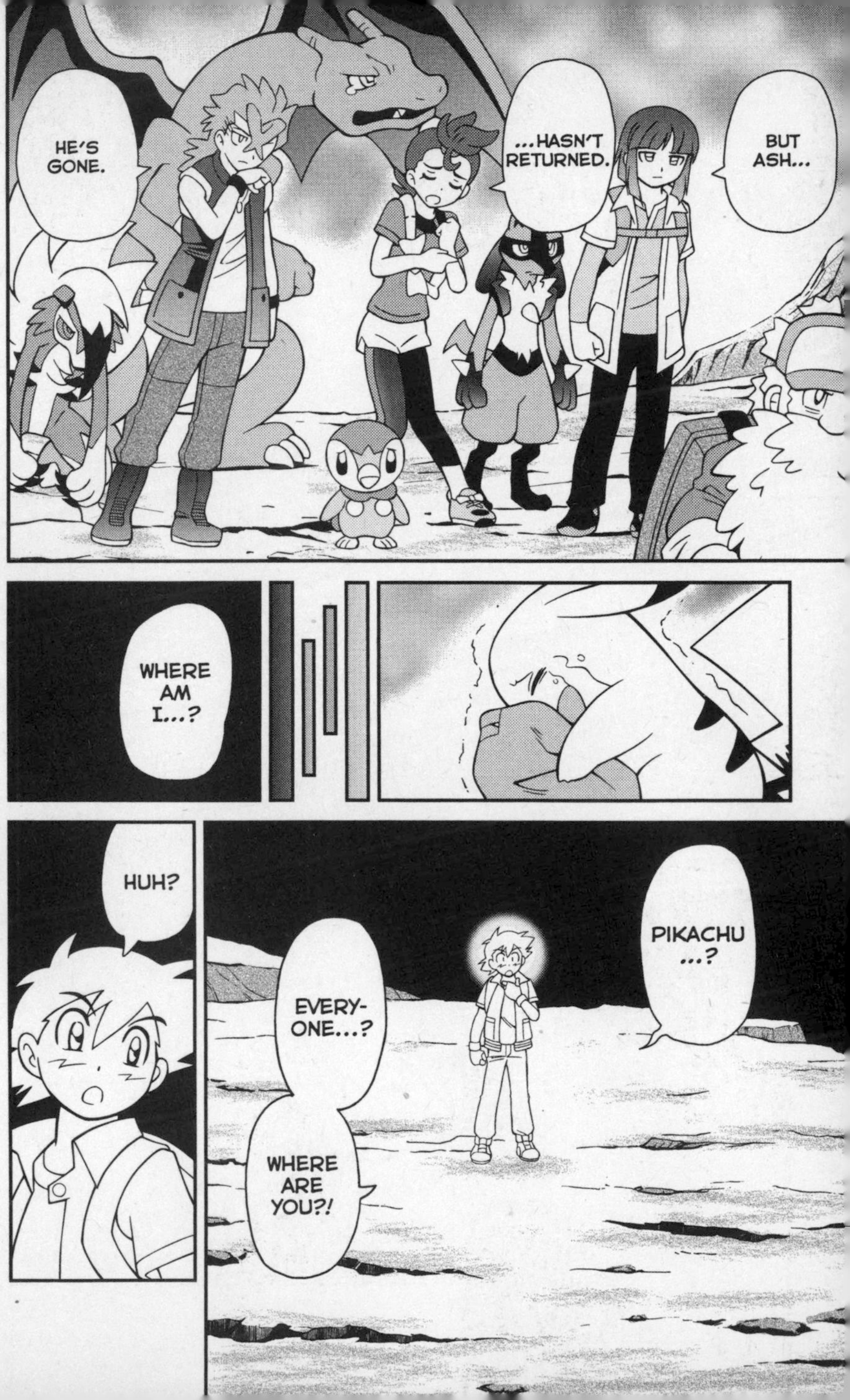
BUT ASH...
...HASN'T RETURNED.
HE'S GONE.
WHERE AM I...?
PIKACHU ...?
EVERY-ONE...?
WHERE ARE YOU?!
HUH?

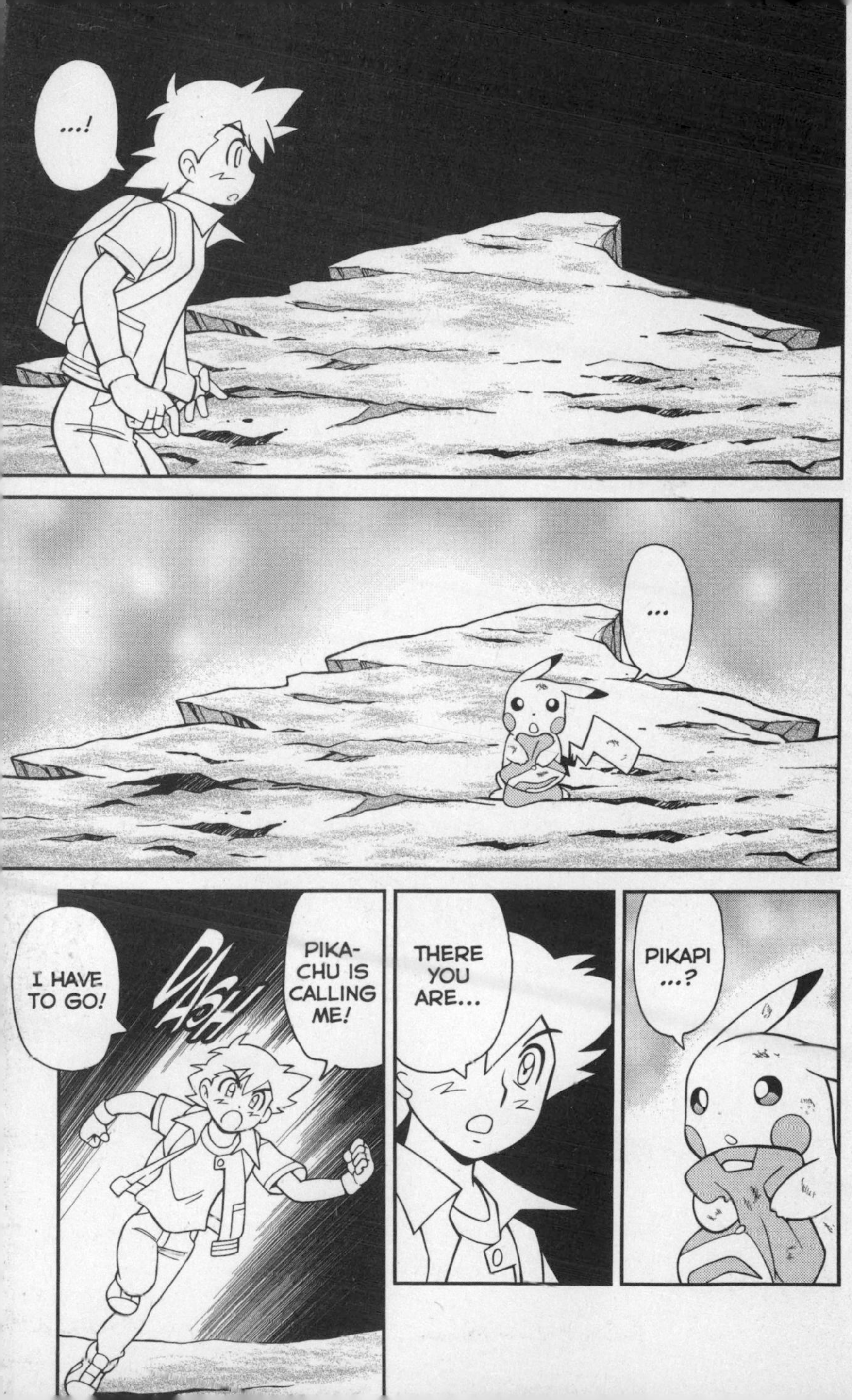
...!
...
PIKAPI ...?
THERE YOU ARE...
PIKA-CHU IS CALLING ME!
DASH
I HAVE TO GO!

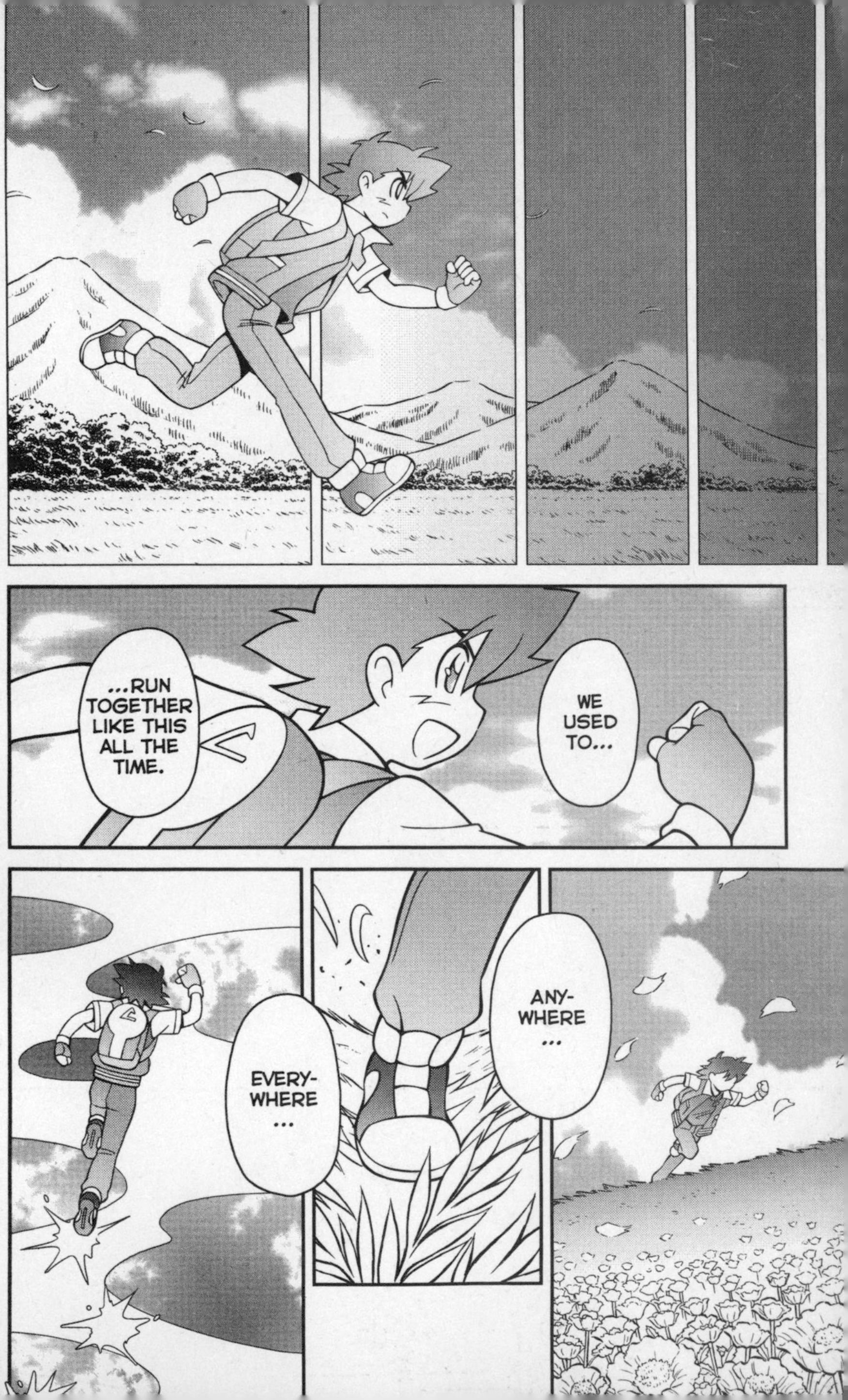
WE USED TO...
...RUN TOGETHER LIKE THIS ALL THE TIME.
ANY-WHERE ...
EVERY-WHERE ...

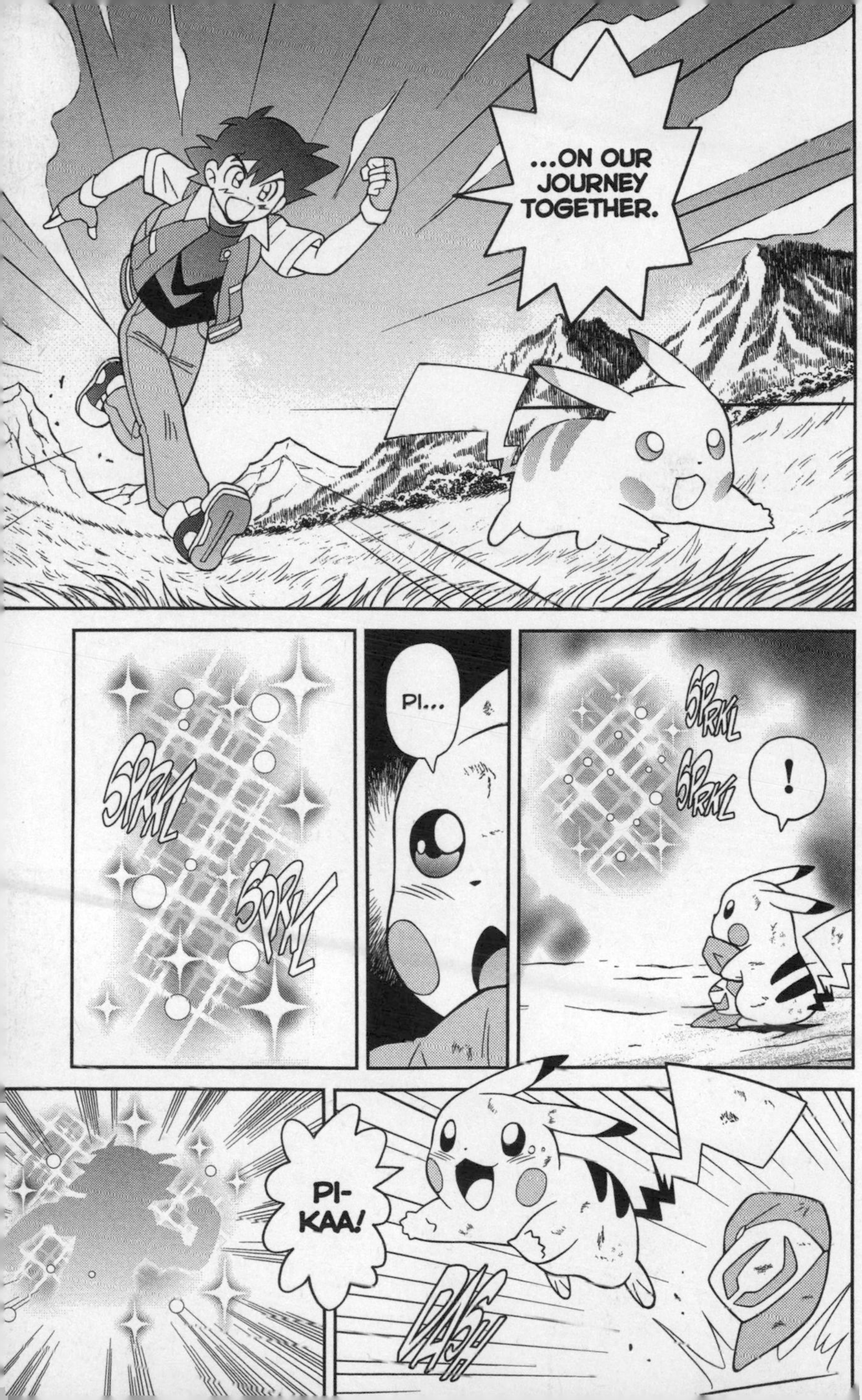
...ON OUR JOURNEY TOGETHER.
SPRKL
SPRKL
!
PI...
SPRKL
SPRKL
PI-KAA!
DASH!

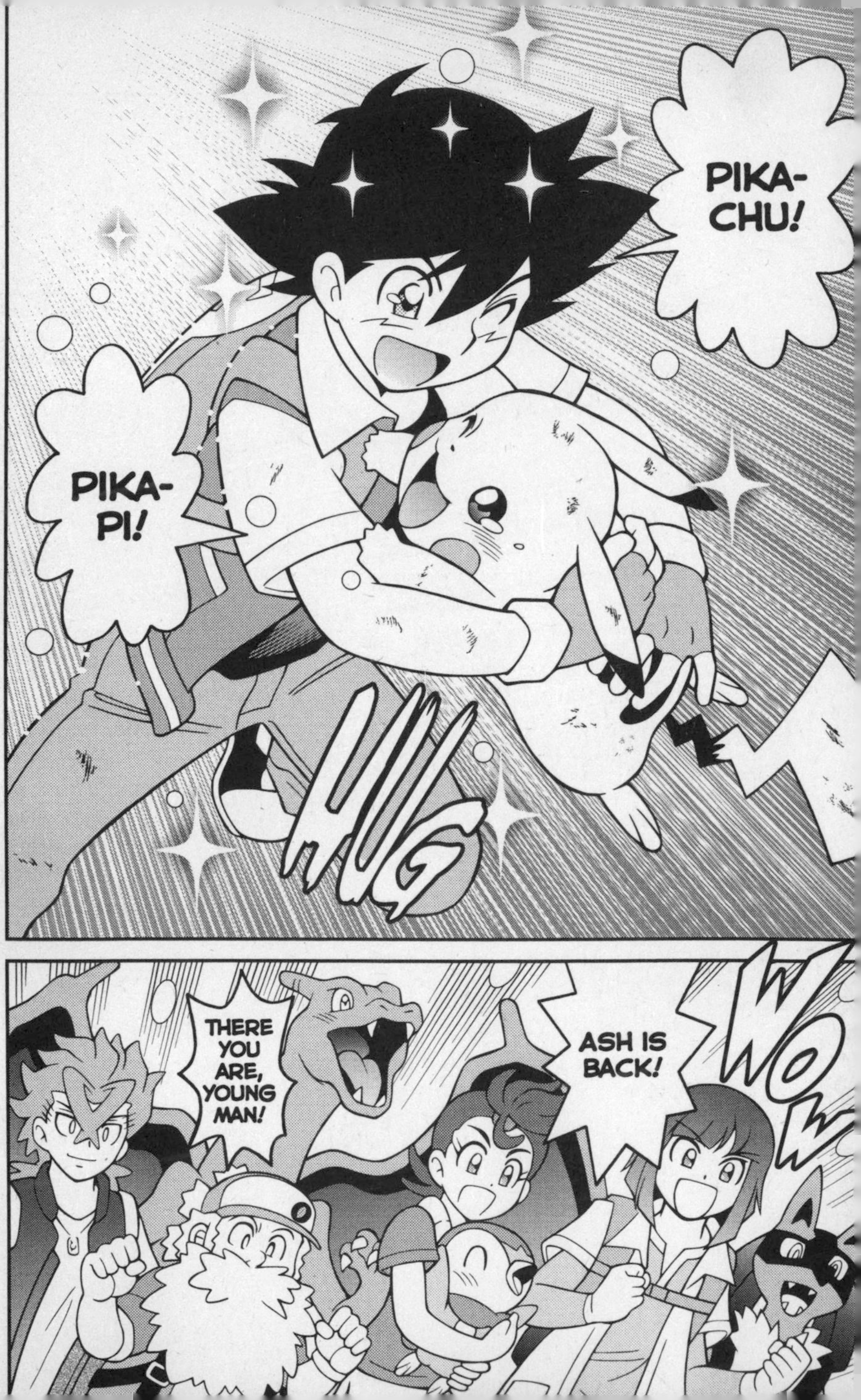
PIKA-CHU!
PIKA-PI!
HUG
WOW
ASH IS BACK!
THERE YOU ARE, YOUNG MAN!

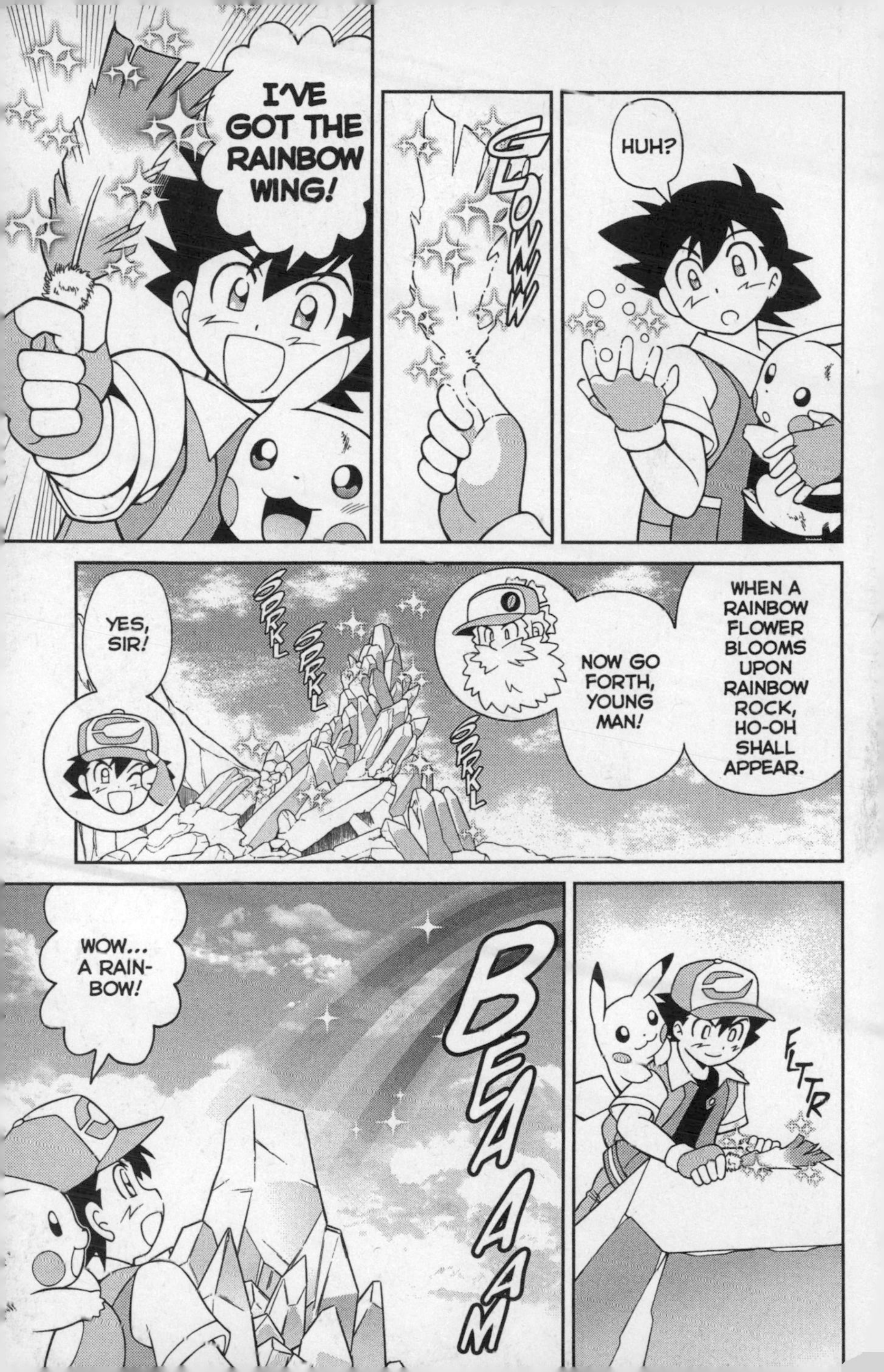
HUH?
GLOWWW
I'VE GOT THE RAINBOW WING!
WHEN A RAINBOW FLOWER BLOOMS UPON RAINBOW ROCK, HO-OH SHALL APPEAR.
NOW GO FORTH, YOUNG MAN!
SPRKL
SPRKL
SPRKL
YES, SIR!
FLTTR
BEAAAM
WOW... A RAIN-BOW!

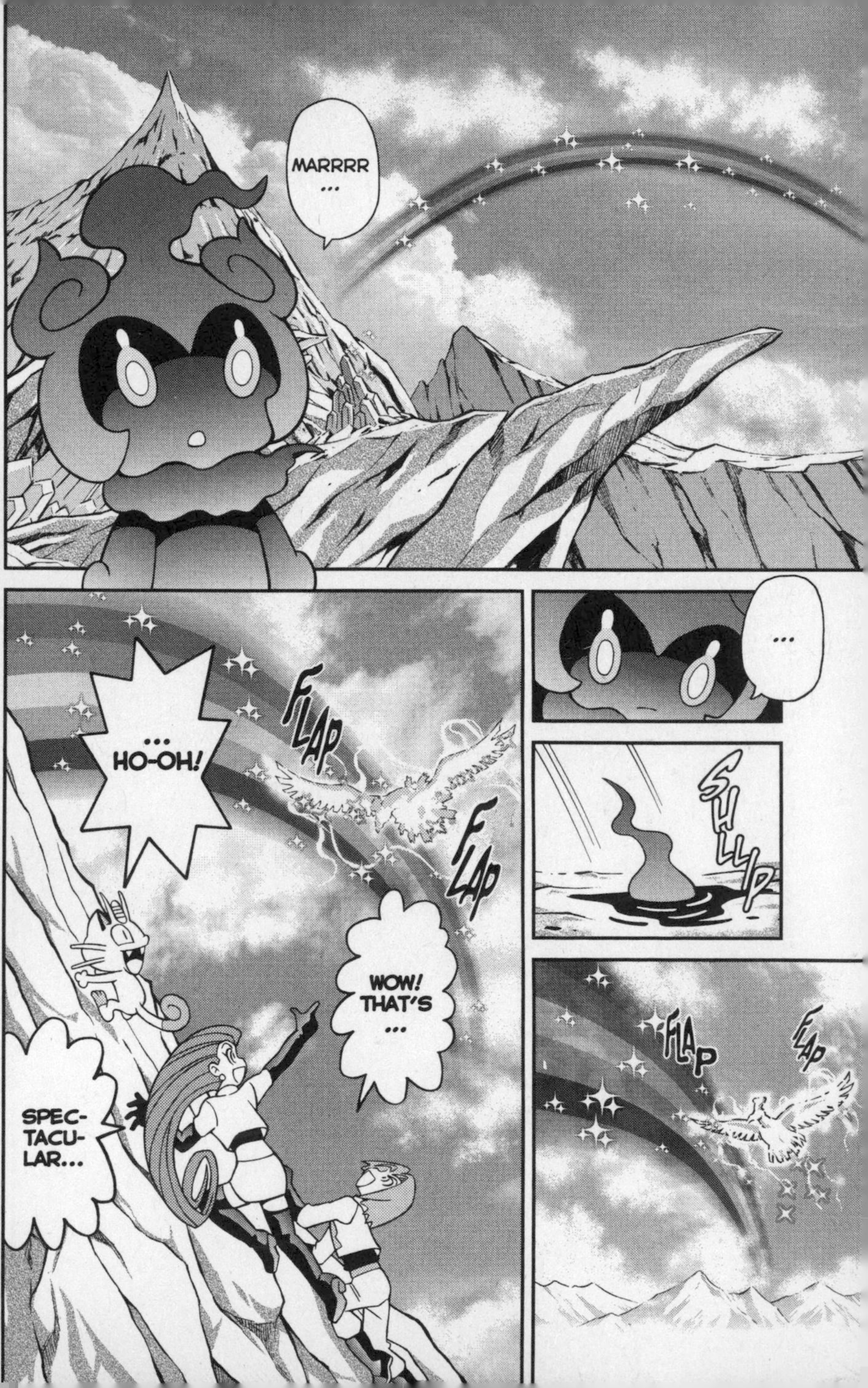
MARRRR ...
...
SHLLP
FLAP
FLAP
FLAP
FLAP
... HO-OH!
WOW! THAT'S ...
SPEC-TACU-LAR...

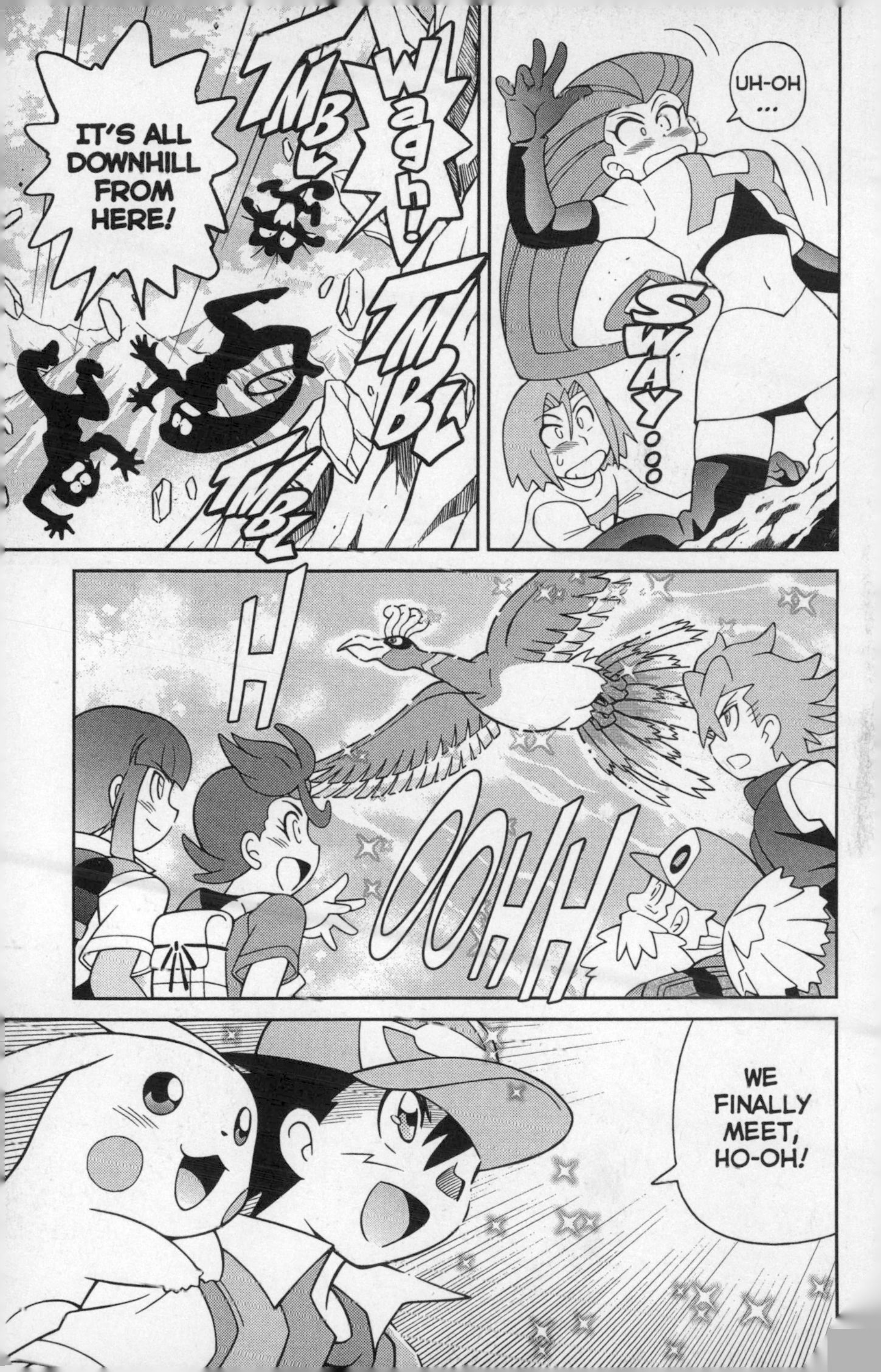
UH-OH ...
SWAY...
Wagh!
TMBL
IT'S ALL DOWNHILL FROM HERE!
TMBL
TMBL
H
OOHH
WE FINALLY MEET, HO-OH!

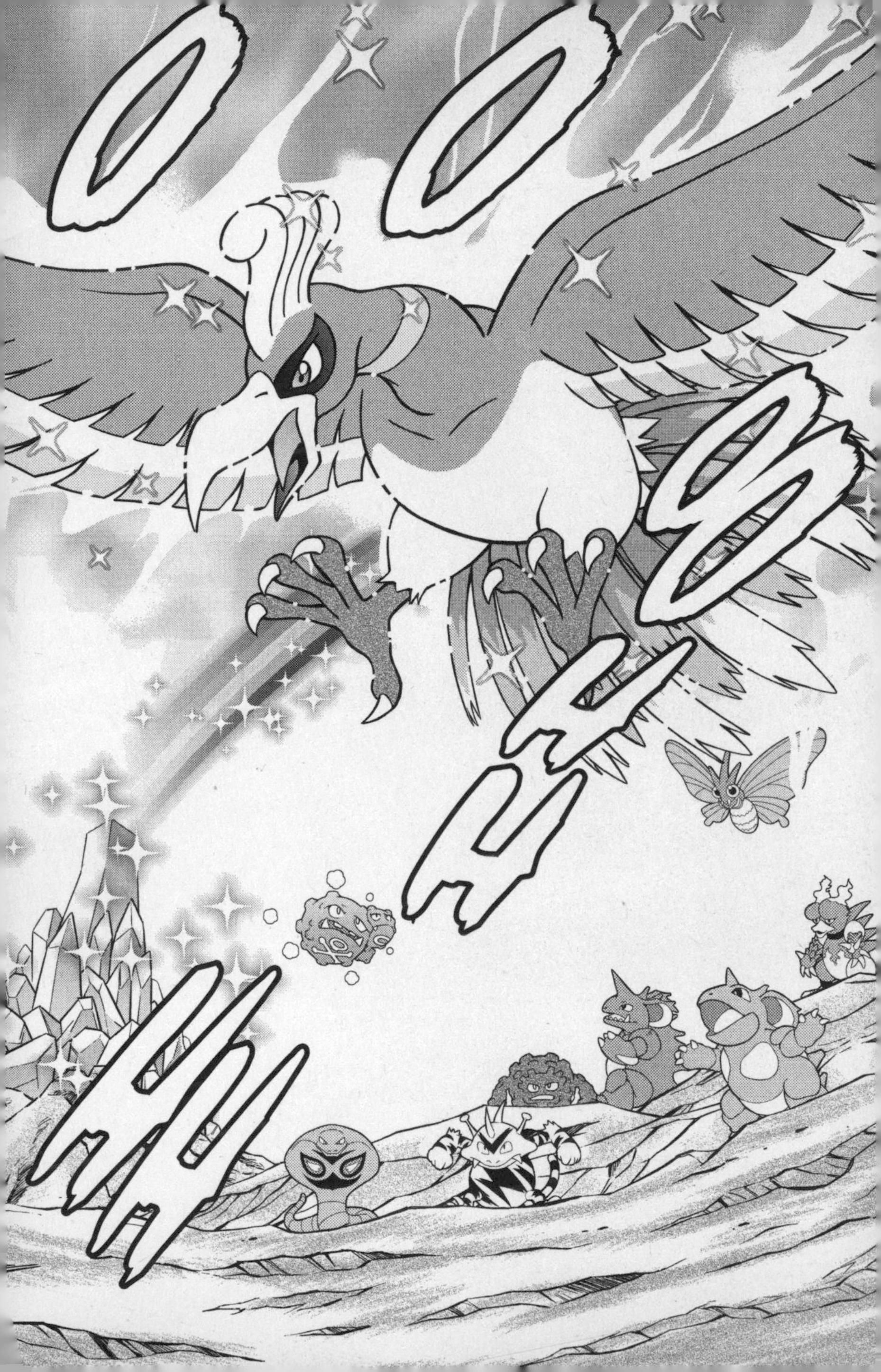

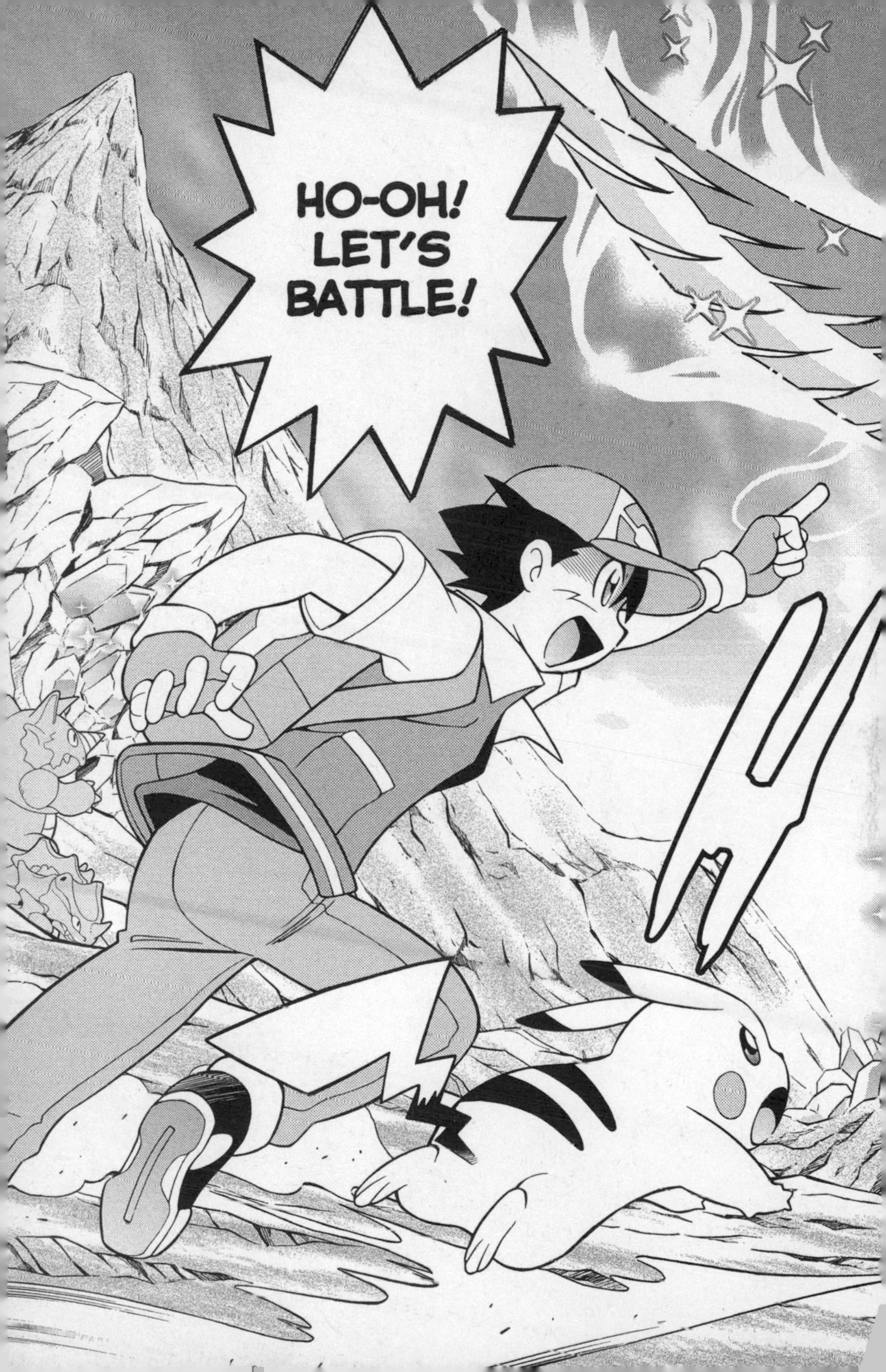
HO-OH! LET'S BATTLE!

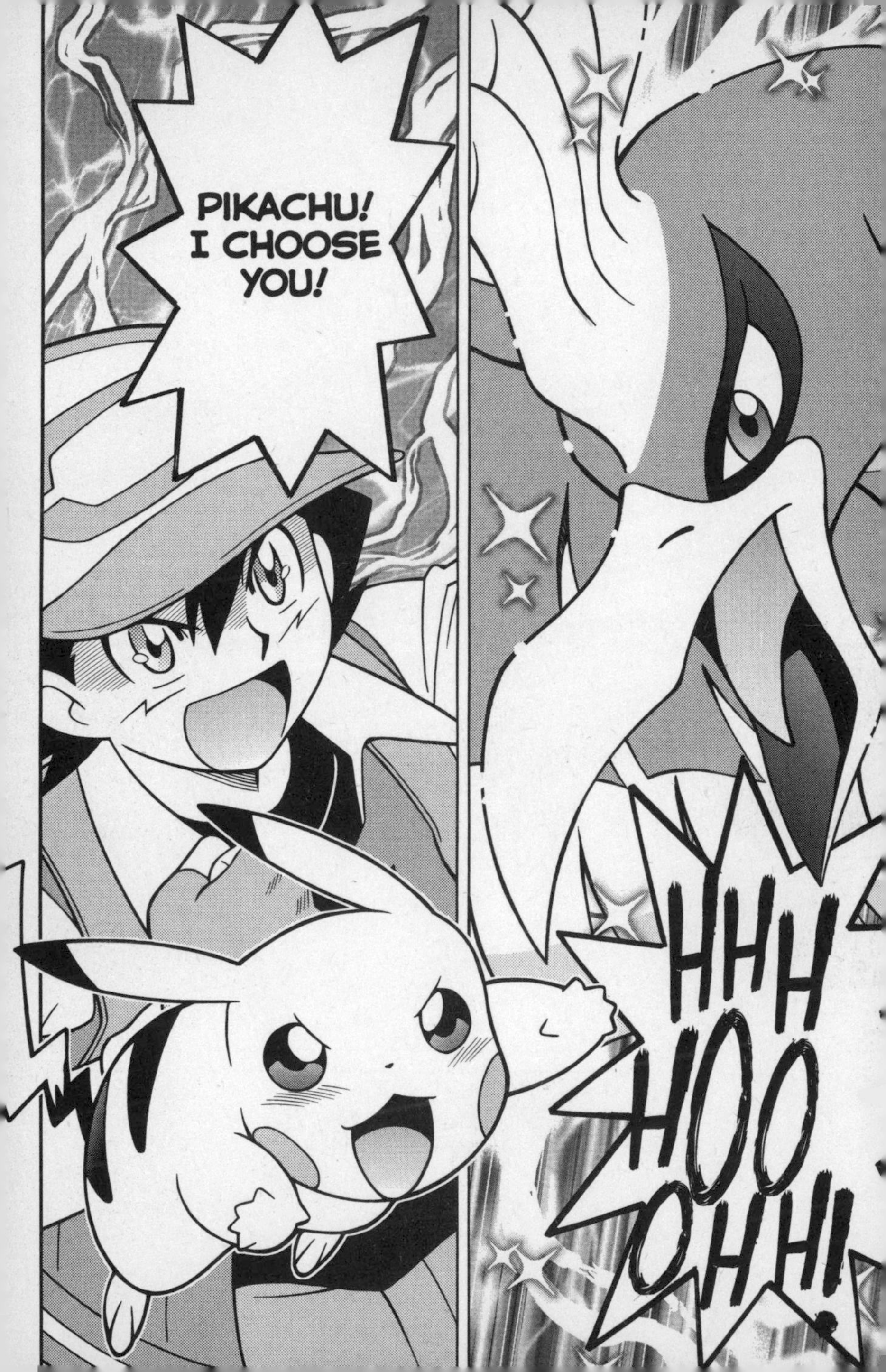
HHH
HOO
OHH!
PIKACHU! I CHOOSE YOU!

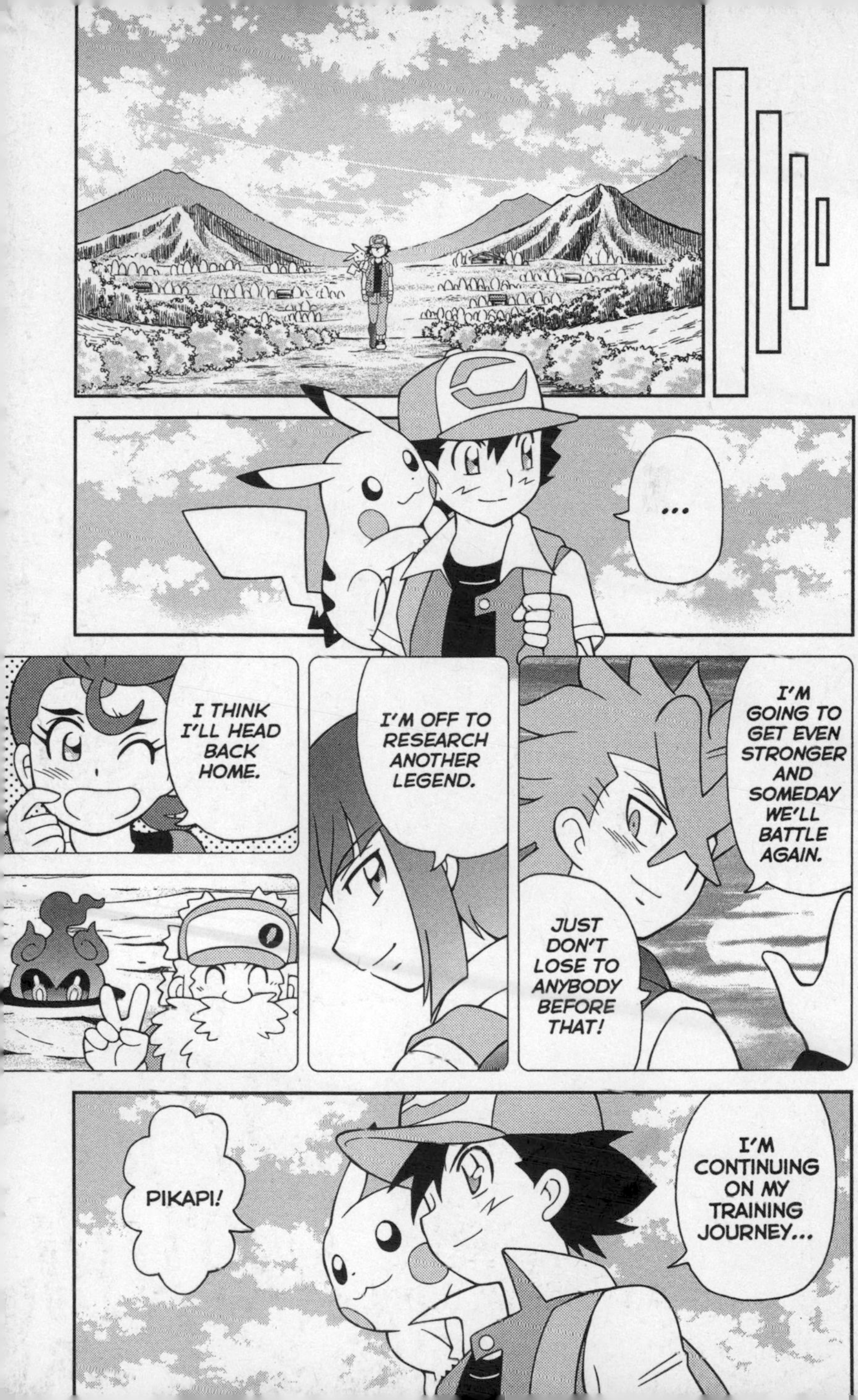
...
I'M GOING TO GET EVEN STRONGER AND SOMEDAY WE'LL BATTLE AGAIN.
JUST DON'T LOSE TO ANYBODY BEFORE THAT!
I'M OFF TO RESEARCH ANOTHER LEGEND.
I THINK I'LL HEAD BACK HOME.
I'M CONTINUING ON MY TRAINING JOURNEY...
PIKAPI!

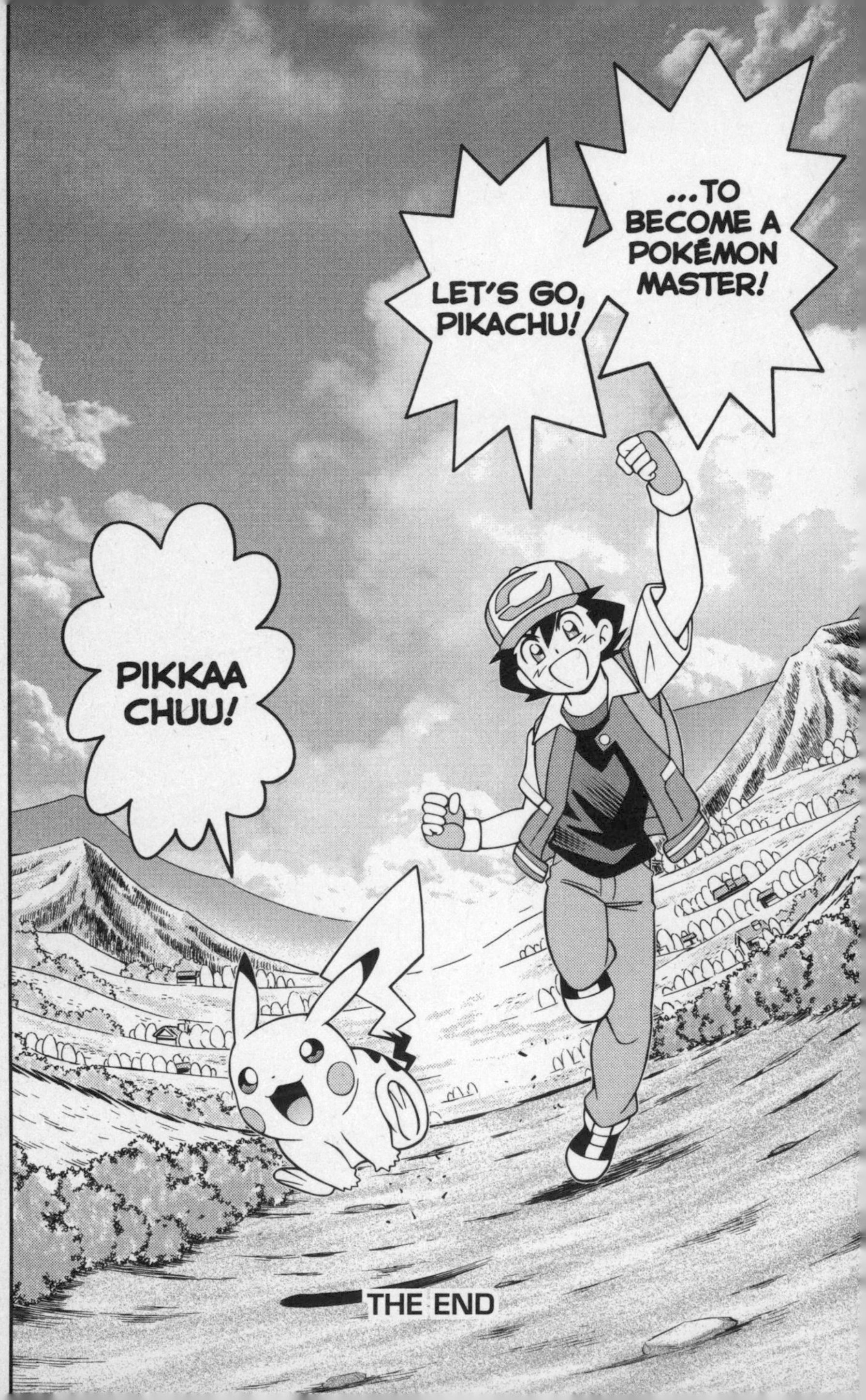
...TO BECOME A POKÉMON MASTER!
LET'S GO, PIKACHU!
PIKKAA CHUU!
THE END

The graphic novel version of *I Choose You!* is now complete. It was a big project, but it went by quickly, and for me, it was a truly enjoyable journey!

I want to thank my readers and everyone else who helped make this manga possible.

We'll see Ash and Pikachu again on television and in movies. And it's my hope that we'll get to see Cross, Verity and Sorrel again too

And with that…here's a bonus illustration of the Team Rocket trio! (Though they didn't appear much this time, the truth is that I wish I could have drawn more of them!)

POKÉMON THE MOVIE

I Choose you!

VIZ MEDIA EDITION
STORY AND ART BY **Ryo Takamisaki**

©2018 Pokémon.
©1998–2017 PIKACHU PROJECT.
©1997–2017 Nintendo, Creatures, GAME FREAK, TV Tokyo, ShoPro, JR Kikaku.
TM, ®, and character names are trademarks of Nintendo.
GEKIJOBAN POCKET MONSTERS KIMI NI KIMETA! Vol. 1, 2 by Ryo TAKAMISAKI
©2017 Ryo TAKAMISAKI
All rights reserved.
Original Japanese edition published by SHOGAKUKAN.
English translation rights in the United States of America, Canada,
the United Kingdom, Ireland, Australia
and New Zealand arranged with SHOGAKUKAN.

Original Cover Design/Plus One

Translation & Adaptation/Emi Louie-Nishikawa
Touch-Up & Lettering/James Gaubatz
Design/John Kim
Editor/Annette Roman

The stories, characters and incidents mentioned
in this publication are entirely fictional.

Printed in the U.S.A.

Published by VIZ Media, LLC
P.O. Box 77010
San Francisco, CA 94107

10 9 8 7 6 5 4 3 2 1
First printing, December 2018

PARENTAL ADVISORY
POKÉMON THE MOVIE:
I CHOOSE YOU! is rated A
and is suitable for readers
of all ages.

POKÉMON

ΩRUBY • αSAPPHIRE
OMEGA • ALPHA

STORY BY
HIDENORI KUSAKA

ART BY
SATOSHI YAMAMOTO

Awesome adventures inspired by the best-selling
Pokémon Omega Ruby and Pokémon Alpha Sapphire
video games that pick up where the *Pokémon Adventures
Ruby & Sapphire* saga left off!

viz media
viz.com

RATED
A
FOR
ALL AGES

POCKET COMICS

STORY & ART BY SANTA HARUKAZE

BLACK & WHITE

LEGENDARY POKÉMON

X•Y

A Pokémon pocket-sized book chock-full of
four-panel gags, Pokémon trivia and fun quizzes
based on the characters you know and love!

www.viz.com